the Leiber chronicles
fifty years of fritz Leiber

the Leiber chronicles
fifty years of fritz Leiber

— Edited By —
MARTIN H. GREENBERG

DARK HARVEST
Arlington Hts., Illinois · 1990

FIRST EDITION

Dark Harvest / P.O. Box 941 / Arlington Heights, IL / 60006

The Publishers would like to express their gratitude to the following people. Thank you: Kathy Jo Camacho, Stan and Phyllis Mikol, Wayne Sommers, Dr. Stan Gurnick PhD, Tony Hodes, Bertha Curl, Kurt Scharrer, Gary Fronk, Linda Solar, the people of the All American Print Center, Dick Spelman, Bob Eggleton, Luis Trevino, Raymond, Teresa and Mark Stadalsky, Tom Pas, Ken and Lynda Fotos, and Ann Cameron Williams.

And, of course, special thanks go to: Martin H. Greenberg and Fritz Leiber.

TABLE OF CONTENTS

Two Sought Adventure

The Jewels in the Forest

It was the Year of the Behemoth, the Month of the Hedgehog, the Day of the Toad. A hot, late summer sun was sinking down toward evening over the somber, fertile land of Lankhmar. Peasants toiling in the endless grain fields paused for a moment and lifted their earth-stained faces and noted that it would soon be time to commence lesser chores. Cattle cropping the stubble began to move in the general direction of home. Sweaty merchants and shopkeepers decided to wait a little longer before enjoying the pleasures of the bath. Thieves and astrologers moved restlessly in their sleep, sensing that the hours of night and work were drawing near.

At the southernmost limit of the land of Lankhmar, a day's ride beyond the village of Soreev, where the grain fields give way to rolling forests of maple and oak, two horsemen cantered leisurely along a narrow, dusty road. They presented a sharp contrast. The larger wore a tunic of unbleached linen, drawn tight at the waist by a very broad leather belt. A fold of linen cloak was looped over his head as a protection against the sun. A long sword with a pomegranate-shaped golden pommel was strapped to his side. Behind his right shoulder, a quiver of arrows jutted up. Half sheathed in a saddle-case was a thick yew bow, unstrung. His great, lean muscles, white skin, copper hair, green eyes, and above all the pleasant yet untamed expression of his massive countenance, all hinted at a land of origin colder, rougher, and more barbarous than that of Lankhmar.

Even, as everything about the larger man suggested the wilderness, so the general appearance of the smaller man—and he was considerably smaller—spoke of the city. His dark face was that of a jester. Bright, black eyes, snub nose, and little lines of irony about the mouth. Hands of a conjurer. Something about the set of his wiry frame betokening exceptional competence in street fights and tavern brawls. He was clad from head to foot in garments of gray silk, soft and curiously loose of weave. His slim sword, cased in gray mouseskin, was slightly curved toward the tip. From his belt hung a sling and a pouch of missiles.

Despite their many dissimilarities, it was obvious that the two men were comrades, that they were united by a bond of subtle mutual understanding, woven of melancholy, humor, and many another strand. The smaller rode a dappled gray mare; the larger, a chestnut gelding.

They were nearing a point where the narrow road came to the end of a rise, made a slight turn, and wound down into the next valley. Green walls of leaves pressed in on either side. The heat was considerable, but not oppressive. It brought to mind thoughts of satyrs and centaurs dozing in hidden glades.

Then the gray mare, slightly in the lead, whinnied. The smaller man tightened his hold on the reins, his black eyes darting quick, alert glances, first to one side of the road and then to the other. There was a faint scraping sound, as of wood on wood.

Without warning the two men ducked down, clinging to the side harness of their horses. Simultaneously came the musical twang of bowstrings, like the prelude of some forest concert, and several arrows buzzed angrily through the spaces that had just been vacated. Then the mare and the gelding were around the turn and galloping like the wind, their hooves striking up great puffs of dust.

From behind came excited shouts and answers as the pursuit got underway. There seemed to have been fully seven or eight men in the ambuscade—squat, sturdy rogues wearing chain-mail shirts and steel caps. Before the mare and the gelding had gone a stone's throw down the road, they were out and after, a black horse in the lead, a black-bearded rider second.

But those pursued were not wasting time. The larger man rose to a stand in his stirrups, whipping the yew bow from its case. With his left hand he bent it against the stirrup, with his right he drew the upper loop of the string into place. Then his left hand slipped down the bow to the grip and his right reached smoothly back over his shoulder for an arrow. Still guiding his horse with his knees, he rose even higher and turned in his saddle and sent an eagle-feathered shaft whirring. Meanwhile his comrade had placed a small leaden ball in his sling, whirled it twice about his head, so that it hummed stridently, and loosed his cast.

Arrow and missile sped and struck together. The one pierced the shoulder of the leading horseman and the other smote the second on his steel cap and tumbled him from his saddle. The pursuit halted abruptly in a tangle of plunging and rearing horses. The men who had caused this confusion pulled up at the next bend in the road and turned back to watch.

"By the hedgehog," said the smaller, grinning wickedly, "but they will think twice before they play at ambuscades again!"

"Blundering fools," said the larger. "Haven't they even learned to shoot from their saddles? I tell you, Gray Mouser, it takes a barbarian to fight his horse properly."

"Except for myself and a few other people," replied the one who bore the feline nickname of Gray Mouser. "But look, Fafhrd, the rogues retreat bearing their wounded, and one gallops far ahead. *Tcha*, but I dinted black beard's pate for him. He hangs over his nag like a bag of meal. If he'd have known who we were, he wouldn't have been so hot on the chase."

There was some truth to this last boast. The names of the Gray Mouser and the Northerner Fafhrd were not unknown in the lands around Lankhmar and in proud Lankhmar, too. Their taste for strange adventure, their mysterious comings and goings, and their odd sense of humor were matters that puzzled almost all men alike.

Abruptly Fafhrd unstrung his bow and turned forward in his saddle.

"This should be the very valley we are seeking," he said. "See, there are the two hills, each with two close-set humps, of which the document speaks. Let's have another look at it, to test my guess."

The Gray Mouser reached into his capacious leather pouch and withdrew a page of thick vellum, ancient and curiously greenish. Three edges were frayed and worn; the fourth showed a clean and recent cut. It was inscribed with the intricate hieroglyphs of Lankhmarian writing, done in the black ink of the squid. But it was not to these that the Mouser turned his attention, but to several faint lines of diminutive red script, written into the margin. These he read.

"Let kings stack their treasure houses ceiling-high, and merchants burst their vaults with hoarded coin, and fools envy them. I have a treasure that out-values theirs. A diamond as big as a man's skull. Twelve rubies each as big as the skull of a cat. Seventeen emeralds each as big as the skull of a mole. And certain rods of crystal and bars of orichalcum. Let overlords swagger jewel-bedecked and queens load themselves with gems, and fools adore them. I have a treasure that will outlast theirs. A treasure house have I built for it in the far southern forest, where the two hills hump double, like sleeping camels, a day's ride beyond the village of Soreev.

"A giant treasure house with a high tower, fit for a king's dwelling—yet no king may dwell there. Immediately below the keystone of the chief dome my treasure lies hid, eternal as the glittering stars. It will outlast me and my name, I, Urgaan of Angarngi. It is my hold on the future. Let fools seek it. They shall win it not. For although my treasure house be empty as air, no deadly creature in rocky lair, no sentinel outside anywhere, no pitfall, poison, trap, or snare, above and below the whole place bare, of demon or devil not a hair, no serpent lethal-fanged yet fair, no skull with mortal eye a-glare, yet have I left a guardian there. Let the wise read this riddle and forbear."

"The man's mind runs to skulls," muttered the Mouser. "He must have been a gravedigger or a necromancer."

"Or an architect," observed Fafhrd thoughtfully, "in those past days when graven images of the skulls of men and animals served to bedeck temples."

"Perhaps," agreed the Mouser. "Surely the writing and ink are old enough. They date at least as far back as the Century of the Wars with the East—five long lifespans."

The Mouser was an accomplished forger, both of handwriting and of objects of art. He knew what he was talking about.

Satisfied that they were near the goal of their quest, the two comrades gazed through a break in the foliage down into the valley. It was shaped like the inside of a pod—shallow, long, and narrow. They were viewing it from one of the narrow ends. The two peculiarly humped hills formed the long sides. The whole of the valley was green with maple and oak, save for a small gap toward the middle. That, thought the Mouser, might mark a peasant's dwelling and the cleared space around it.

Beyond the gap he could make out something dark and squarish rising a little above the treetops. He called his companion's attention to it, but they could not decide whether it was indeed a tower such as the document mentioned, or just a peculiar shadow, or perhaps even the dead, limbless trunk of a gigantic oak. It was too far away.

"Almost sufficient time has passed," said Fafhrd, after a pause, "for one of those rogues to have sneaked up through the forest for another shot at us. Evening draws near."

They spoke to their horses and moved on slowly. They tried to keep their eyes fixed on the thing that looked like a tower, but since they were descending, it almost immediately dropped out of sight below the treetops. There would be no further chance of seeing it until they were quite close at hand.

The Mouser felt a subdued excitement running through his flesh. Soon they would discover if there was a treasure to be had or not. A diamond as big as a man's skull . . . rubies . . . emeralds . . . He found an almost nostalgic delight in prolonging and savoring to the full this last, leisurely stage of their quest. The recent ambuscade served as a necessary spice.

13

He thought of how he had slit the interesting-looking vellum page from the ancient book on architecture that reposed in the library fo the rapacious and overbearing Lord Rannarsh. Of how, half in jest, he had sought out and interrogated several peddlers from the South. Of how he had found one who had recently passed through a village named Soreev. Of how that one had told him of a stone structure in the forest south of Soreev, called by the peasants the House of Angarngi and reputed to be long deserted. The peddler had seen a high tower rising above the trees. The Mouser recalled the man's wizened, cunning face and chuckled. And that brought to mind the greedy, sallow face of Lord Rannarsh, and a new thought occurred to him.

"Fafhrd," he said, "those rogues we just now put to flight—what did you take them for?"

The Northerner grunted humorous contempt.

"Run-of-the-manger ruffians. Waylayers of fat merchants. Pasture bravos. Bumpkin bandits!"

"Still, they were all well armed, and armed alike—as if they were in some rich man's service. And that one who rode far ahead. Mightn't he have been hastening to report to some master?"

"What is your thought?"

The Mouser did not reply for some moments.

"I was thinking," he said, "that Lord Rannarsh is a rich man and a greedy one, who slavers at the thought of jewels. And I was wondering if he ever read those faint lines of red lettering and made a copy of them, and if my theft of the original sharpened his interest."

The Northerner shook his head.

"I doubt it. You are oversubtle. But if he did, and if he seeks to rival us in this treasure quest, he'd best watch each step twice—and choose servitors who can fight on horseback."

They were moving so slowly that the hooves of the mare and the gelding hardly stirred up the dust. They had no fear of danger from the rear. A well-laid ambuscade might surprise them, but not a man or horse in motion. The narrow road wound along in a purposeless fashion. Leaves brushed their faces, and occasionally they had to swing their bodies out of the way of encroaching branches. The ripe scent of the late summer forest was intensified now that they were below the rim of the valley. Mingled with it were whiffs of wild berries and aromatic shrubs. Shadows imperceptibly lengthened.

"Nine chances out of ten," murmured the Mouser dreamily, "the treasure house of Urgaan of Angarngi was looted some hundred years ago, by men whose bodies are already dust."

"It may be so," agreed Fafhrd. "Unlike men, rubies and emeralds do not rest quietly in their graves."

This possibility, which they had discussed several times before, did not disturb them now, or make them impatient. Rather did it impart to their quest the pleasant melancholy of a lost hope. They drank in the rich air and let their horses munch random mouthfuls of leaves. A jay called shrilly from overhead and off in the forest a catbird was chattering, their sharp voices breaking in on the low buzzing and droning of the insects. Night was drawing near. The almost-horizontal rays of the sun gilded the treetops. Then Fafhrd's sharp ears caught the hollow lowing of a cow.

A few more turns brought them into the clearing they had spied. In line with their surmise, it proved to contain a peasant's cottage—a neat little low-eaved house of weathered wood, situated in the midst of an acre of grain. To one side was a bean patch; to the other, a woodpile which almost dwarfed the house. In front of the cottage stood a wiry old man, his skin as brown as his homespun tunic. He had evidently just heard the horses and turned around to look.

"Ho, father," called the Mouser, "it's a good day to be abroad in, and a good home you have here."

The peasant considered these statements and then nodded his head in agreement.

"We are two weary travelers," continued the Mouser.

Again the peasant nodded gravely.

"In return for two silver coins will you give us lodging for the night?"

The peasant rubbed his chin and then held up three fingers.

"Very well, you shall have three silver coins," said the Mouser, slipping from his horse. Fafhrd followed suit.

Only after giving the old man a coin to seal the bargain did the Mouser question casually, "Is there not an old, deserted place near your dwelling called the House of Angarngi?"

The peasant nodded.

"What's it like?"

The peasant shrugged his shoulders.

"Don't you know?"

The peasant shook his head.

"But haven't you ever seen the place?" The Mouser's voice carried a note of amazement he did not bother to conceal.

He was answered by another head-shake.

"But, father, it's only a few minutes' walk from your dwelling, isn't it?"

The peasant nodded tranquilly, as if the whole business were no matter for surprise.

A muscular young man, who had come from behind the cottage to take their horses, offered a suggestion.

"You can see tower from other side the house. I can point her out."

At this the old man proved he was not completely speechless by saying in a dry, expressionless voice: "Go ahead. Look at her all you want."

And he stepped into the cottage. Fafhrd and the Mouser caught a glimpse of a child peering around the door, an old woman stirring a pot, and someone hunched in a big chair before a tiny fire.

The upper part of the tower proved to be barely visible through a break in the trees. The last rays of the sun touched it with deep red. It looked about four or five bowshots distant. And then, even as they watched, the sun dipped under and it became a featureless square of black stone.

"She's an old place," explained the young man vaguely. "I been all around her. Father, he's just never bothered to look."

"You've been inside?" questioned the Mouser.

The young man scratched his head.

"No. She's just an old place. No good for anything."

"There'll be a fairly long twilight," said Fafhrd, his wide green eyes drawn to the tower as if by a lodestone. "Long enough for us to have a closer look."

"I'd show the way," said the young man, "save I got water to fetch."

"No matter," replied Fafhrd. "When's supper?"

"When the first stars show."

They left him holding their horses and walked straight into the woods. Immediately it became much darker, as if twilight were almost over, rather than just begun. The vegetation proved to be somewhat thicker than they had anticipated. There were vines and thorns to be avoided. Irregular, pale patches of sky appeared and disappeared overhead.

The Mouser let Fafhrd lead the way. His mind was occupied with a queer sort of reverie about the peasants. It tickled his fancy to think how they had stolidly lived their toilsome lives, generation after generation, only a few steps from what might be one of the greatest treasure-troves in the world. It seemed incredible. How could people sleep so near jewels and not dream of them? But probably they never dreamed.

So the Gray Mouser was sharply aware of few things during the journey through the woods, save that Fafhrd seemed to be taking a long time—which was strange, since the barbarian was an accomplished woodsman.

Finally a deeper and more solid shadow loomed up through the trees, and in a moment they were standing in the margin of a small, boulder-studded clearing, most of which was occupied by the bulky structure they sought. Abruptly, even before his eyes took in the details of the place, the Mouser's mind was filled with a hundred petty perturbations. Weren't they making a mistake in leaving their horses with those strange peasants? And mightn't those rogues have followed them to the cottage? And wasn't this the Day of the Toad, an unlucky day for entering deserted houses? And shouldn't they have a short spear along, in case they met a leopard? And wasn't that a whippoor-will he heard crying on his left hand, an augury of ill omen?

The treasure house of Urgaan of Angarngi was a peculiar structure. The main feature was a large, shallow dome, resting on walls that formed an octagon. In front, and merging into it, were two lesser domes. Between these gaped a great square door-way. The tower rose asymmetrically from the rear part of the chief dome. The eyes of the Mouser sought hurriedly through the dimming twilight for the cause of the salient peculiarity of the structure, and decided it lay in the utter simplicity. There were no pillars, no outjuting cornices, no friezes, no architectural ornaments of any sort, skull-embellished or otherwise. Save for the doorway and a few tiny windows set in unex-pected places, the House of Angarngi was a compact mass of uniformly dark gray stones most closely joined.

But now Fafhrd was striding up the short flight of terraced steps that led toward the open door, and the Mouser followed him, although he would have liked to spy around a little longer. With every step he took forward he sensed an odd reluctance growing within him. His earlier mood of pleasant expectancy vanished as suddenly as if he'd stepped into quicksand. It seemed to him that the black doorway yawned like a toothless mouth. And then a little shudder went through him, for he saw the mouth had a tooth—a bit of ghostly white that jutted up from the floor. Fafhrd was reaching down toward the object.

"I wonder whose skull this may be?" said the Northerner calmly.

The Mouser regarded the thing, and the scattering of bones and fragments of bone beside it. His feeling of uneasiness was fast growing toward a climax, and he had the unpleasant conviction that, once it did reach a climax, something would happen. What was the answer to Fafhrd's question? What form of death had struck down that earlier intruder? It was very dark inside the treasure house. Didn't the manuscript mention something about a guardian? It was hard to think of a flesh-and-blood guardian per-sisting for three hundred years, but there were things that were immortal or nearly immortal. He could tell that Fafhrd was not in the least affected by any premonitory disquietude, and was quite capable of instituting an immediate search for the treasure. That must be prevented at all costs. He remembered that the Northerner loathed snakes.

16

"This cold, damp stone," replied Fafhrd angrily. "I'm willing to wager there's not a single serpent inside. Urgaan's note said, 'No deadly creature in rocky lair,' and to cap that, 'no serpent lethal-fanged yet fair.'"

"I am not thinking of guardian snakes Urgaan may have left here," the Mouser explained, "but only of serpents that may have wandered in for the night. Just as that skull you hold is not one set there by Urgaan 'with mortal eye a-glare,' but merely the brain-case of some unfortunate wayfarer who chanced to perish here."

"I don't know," Fafhrd said, calmly eyeing the skull.

"Its orbits might glow phosphorescently in absolute dark."

A moment later he was agreeing it would be well to postpone the search until daylight returned, now that the treasure house was located. He carefully replaced the skull.

As they re-entered the woods, the Mouser heard a little inner voice whispering to him, *Just in time. Just in time.* Then the sense of uneasiness departed as suddenly as it had come, and he began to feel somewhat ridiculous. This caused him to sing a bawdy ballad of his own invention, wherein demons and other supernatural agents were ridiculed obscenely. Fafhrd chimed in good-naturedly on the choruses.

It was not as dark as they expected when they reached the cottage. They saw to their horses, found they had been well cared for, and then fell to the savory mess of beans, porridge, and pot herbs that the peasant's wife ladled into oak bowls. Fresh milk to wash it down was provided in quaintly carved oak goblets. The meal was a satisfying one and the interior of the house was neat and clean, despite its stamped earthen floor and low beams, which Fafhrd had to duck.

There turned out to be six in the family, all told. The father, his equally thin and leathery wife, the older son, a young boy, a daughter, and a mumbling grandfather, whom extreme age confined to a chair before the fire. The last two were the most interesting of the lot.

The girl was in the gawkish age of mid-adolescence, but there was a wild, coltish grace in the way she moved her lanky legs and slim arms with their prominent elbows. She was very shy, and gave the impression that at any moment she might dart out the door and into the woods.

In order to amuse her and win her confidence, the Mouser began to perform small feats of legerdemain, plucking copper coins out of the ears of the astonished peasant, and bone needles from the nose of his giggling wife. He turned beans into buttons and back again into beans, swallowed a large fork, made a tiny wooden manikin jig on the palm of his hand, and utterly bewildered the cat by pulling what seemed to be a mouse out of its mouth.

The old folks gaped and grinned. The little boy became frantic with excitement. His sister watched everything with concentrated interest, and even smiled warmly when the Mouser presented her with a square of fine, green linen he had conjured from the air, although she was still too shy to speak.

Then Fafhrd roared sea-chanteys that rocked the roof and sang lusty songs that set the old grandfather gurgling with delight. Meanwhile the Mouser fetched a small wineskin from his saddlebags, concealed it under his cloak, and filled the oak goblets as if by magic. These rapidly fuddled the peasants, who were unused to so potent a beverage, and by the time Fafhrd had finished telling a bloodcurdling tale of the frozen north, they were all nodding, save the girl and the grandfather.

The latter looked up at the merry-making adventurers, his watery eyes filled with a kind of impish, senile glee, and mumbled, "You two be right clever men. Maybe you be beast-dodgers." But before this remark could be elucidated, his eyes had gone vacant again, and in a few moments he was snoring.

Soon all were asleep. Fafhrd and the Mouser keeping their weapons close at hand, but only variegated snores and occasional snaps from the dying embers disturbed the silence of the cottage.

The Day of the Cat dawned clear and cool. The Mouser stretched himself luxuriously and, catlike, flexed his muscles and sucked in the sweet, dewy air. He felt exceptionally cheerful and eager to be up and doing. Was not this *his* day, the day of the Gray Mouser, a day in which luck could not fail him?

His slight movements awakened Fafhrd and together they stole silently from the cottage so as not to disturb the peasants, who were oversleeping with the wine they had taken. They refreshed their faces and hands in the wet grass and visited their horses. Then they munched some bread, washed it down with drafts of cool well water flavored with wine, and made ready to depart.

This time their preparations were well thought out. The Mouser carried a mallet and a stout iron pry-bar, in case they had to attack masonry, and made certain that candles, flint, wedges, chisels, and several other small tools were in his pouch. Fafhrd borrowed a pick from the peasant's implements and tucked a coil of thin, strong rope in his belt. He also took his bow and quiver of arrows.

The forest was delightful at this early hour. Bird cries and chatterings came from overhead, and once they glimpsed a black, squirrel-like animal scampering along a bough. A couple of chipmunks scurried under a bush dotted with red berries. What had been shadow the evening before was now a variety of green-leafed beauty. The two adventurers trod softly.

They had hardly gone more than a bowshot into the woods when they heard a faint rustling behind them. The rustling came rapidly nearer, and suddenly the peasant girl burst into view. She stood breathless and poised, one hand touching a treetrunk, the other pressing some leaves, ready to fly away at the first sudden move. Fafhrd and the Mouser stood as stock-still as if she were a doe or a dryad. Finally she managed to conquer her shyness and speak.

"You go there?" she questioned, indicating the direction of the treasure house with a quick, ducking nod. Her dark eyes were serious.

"Yes, we go there," answered Fafhrd, smiling.

"Don't." This word was accompanied by a rapid headshake.

"But why shouldn't we, girl?" Fafhrd's voice was gentle and sonorous, like an integral part of the forest. It seemed to touch some spring within the girl that enabled her to feel more at ease. She gulped a big breath and began.

"Because I watch it from the edge of the forest, but never go close. Never, never, never. I say to myself there be a magic circle I must not cross. And I say to myself there be a giant inside. Queer and fearsome giant." Her words were coming rapidly now, like an undammed stream. "All gray he be, like the stone of his house. All gray—eyes and hair and fingernails, too. And he be big, bigger than you, twice as big." Here she nodded at Fafhrd. "And with his club he kills, kills, kills. But only if you go close. Every day, almost, I play a game with him. I pretend to be going to cross the magic circle. And he watches from inside the door, where I can't see him, and he thinks I'm going to cross. And I dance through the forest all around the house, and he follows me, peering from the little windows. And I get closer and closer to the circle, closer and closer. But I never cross. And he be very angry and gnash his teeth, like rocks rubbing rocks, so that the house shakes. And I run, run, run away. But you mustn't go inside. Oh, you mustn't."

She paused, as if startled by her own daring. Her eyes were fixed anxiously on Fafhrd. She seemed drawn toward him. The Northerner's reply carried no overtone of patronizing laughter.

"But you've never actually seen the gray giant, have you?"

"Oh, no. He be too cunning. But I say to myself he must be there inside. I know he be inside. And that's the same thing, isn't it? Grandfather knows about him. We used to talk about him, when I was little. Grandfather calls him the beast. But the others laugh at me, so I don't tell."

Here was another astounding peasant-paradox, thought the Mouser with an inward grin. Imagination was such a rare commodity with them that this girl unhesitatingly took it for reality.

"Don't worry about us, girl. We'll be on the watch for your gray giant," he started to say, but he had less success than Fafhrd in keeping his voice completely natural or else the cadence of his words didn't chime so well with the forest setting.

The girl uttered one more warning. "Don't go inside, oh, please," and turned and darted away.

The two adventurers looked at each other and smiled. Somehow the unexpected fairy tale, with its conventional ogre and its charmingly naïve narrator added to the delight of the dewy morning. Without a comment they resumed their soft-stepping progress. And it was well that they went quietly, for when they had gotten within a stone's throw of the clearing, they heard low voices that seemed to be in grumbling argument. Immediately they cached the pick and pry-bar and mallet under a clump of bushes, and stole forward, taking advantage of the natural cover and watching where they planted their feet.

On the edge of the clearing stood half a dozen stocky men in black chain-mail shirts, bows on their backs, shortswords at their sides. They were immediately recognizable as the rogues who had laid the ambuscade. Two of them started for the treasure house, only to be recalled by a comrade. Whereupon the argument apparently started afresh.

"That red-haired one," whispered the Mouser after an unhurried look. "I can swear I've seen him in the stables of Lord Rannarsh. My guess was right. It seems we have a rival."

"Why do they wait, and keep pointing at the house?" whispered Fafhrd. "Is it because some of their comrades are already at work inside?"

The Mouser shook his head. "That cannot be. See those picks and shovels and levers they have rested on the ground? No, they wait for someone—for a leader. Some of them want to examine the house before he arrives. Others counsel against it. And I will bet my head against a bowling ball that the leader is Rannarsh himself. He is much too greedy and suspicious to entrust a treasure quest to any henchmen."

"What's to do?" murmured Fafhrd. "We cannot enter the house unseen, even if it were the wise course, which it isn't. Once in, we'd be trapped."

"I've half a mind to loose my sling at them right now and teach them something about the art of ambuscade," replied the Mouser, slitting his eyes grimly. "Only then the survivors would flee into the house and hold us off until, mayhap, Rannarsh came, and more men with him."

"We might circle part way around the clearing," said Fafhrd, after a moment's pause, "keeping to the woods. Then we can enter the clearing unseen and shelter ourselves behind one of the small domes. In that way we become masters of the doorway, and can prevent their taking cover inside. Thereafter I will address them suddenly and try to frighten them off, you meanwhile staying hid and giving substance to my threats by making enough racket for ten men."

This seemed the handiest plan to both of them, and they managed the first part of it without a hitch. The Mouser crouched behind the small dome, his sword, sling, daggers, and a couple of sticks of wood laid ready for either noise-making or fight. Then Fafhrd strode briskly forward, his bow held carelessly in front of him, an arrow fitted to the string. It was done so casually that it was a few moments before Rannarsh's henchmen noticed him. Then they quickly reached for their own bows and as quickly desisted when they saw that the huge newcomer had the advantage of them. They scowled in irritated perplexity.

"Ho, rogues!" began Fafhrd. "We allow you just as much time as it will take you to make yourselves scarce, and no more. Don't think to resist or come skulking back. My men are scattered through the woods. At a sign from me they will feather you with arrows."

Meanwhile the Mouser had began a low din and was slowly and artistically working it up in volume. Rapidly varying the pitch and intonation of his voice and making it echo first from some part of the building and then from the forest wall, he created the illusion of a squad of bloodthirsty bow-men. Nasty cries of "Shall we let fly?" "You take the redhead," and "Try for the belly shot; it's surest," kept coming now from one point and now another, until it was all Fafhrd could do to refrain from laughing at the woebegone, startled glances the six rogues kept darting around. But his merriment was extinguished when, just as the rogues were starting to slink shamefacedly away, an arrow arched erratically out of the woods, passing a spear's length above his head.

"Curse that branch!" came a deep, guttural voice the Mouser recognized as issuing from the throat of Lord Rannarsh. Immediately after, it began to bark commands.

"At them, you fools! It's all a trick. There are only the two of them. Rush them!"

Fafhrd turned without warning and loosed point-blank at the voice, but did not silence it. Then he dodged back behind the small dome and ran with the Mouser for the woods.

The six rogues, wisely deciding that a charge with drawn swords would be overly heroic, followed suit, unslinging their bows as they went. One of them turned before he had reached sufficient cover, nocking an arrow. It was a mistake. A ball from the Mouser's sling took him low in the forehead, and he toppled forward and was still.

The sound for that hit and fall was the last heard in the clearing for quite a long time, save for the inevitable bird cries, some of which were genuine, and some of which were communications between Fafhrd and the Mouser. The conditions of the death-dealing contest were obvious. Once it had fairly begun, no one dared enter the clearing, since he would become a fatally easy mark; and the Mouser was sure that none of the five remaining rogues had taken shelter in the treasure house. Nor did either side dare withdraw all its men out of sight of the doorway, since that would allow someone to take a commanding position in the top of the tower, providing the tower had a negotiable stair. Therefore it was a case of sneaking about near the edge of the clearing, circling and counter-circling, with a great deal of squatting in a good place and waiting for somebody to come along and be shot.

The Mouser and Fafhrd began by adopting the latter strategy, first moving about twenty paces nearer the point at which the rogues had disappeared. Evidently their patience was a little better than that of their opponents. For after about ten minutes of nerve-racking waiting, during which pointed seed pods had a queer way of looking like arrowheads, Fafhrd got the redhaired henchman full in the throat just as he was bending his bow for a shot at the Mouser. That left four besides Rannarsh himself. Immediately the two adventurers changed their tactics and separated, the Mouser circling rapidly around the treasure house and Fafhrd drawing as far back from the open space as he dared.

Rannarsh's men must have decided on the same plan, for the Mouser almost bumped into a scar-faced rogue as soft-footed as himself. At such close range, bow and sling were both useless—in their normal function. Scarface attempted to jab the barbed arrow he held into the Mouser's eye. The Mouser weaved his body to one side, swung his sling like a whip, and felled the man senseless with a blow from the horn handle. Then he retreated a few paces, thanked the Day of the Cat that there had not been two of them, and took to the trees as being a safer, though slower method of progress. Keeping to the middle heights, he scurried along with the sure-footedness of a rope walker, swinging from branch to branch only when it was necessary, making sure he always had more than one way of retreat open.

He had completed three-quarters of his circuit when he heard the clash of swords a few trees ahead. He increased his speed and was soon looking down on a sweet little combat. Fafhrd, his back to a great oak, had his broadsword out and was holding off two of Rannarsh's henchmen, who were attacking with their shorter weapons. It was a tight spot and the Northerner realized it. He knew that ancient sagas told of heroes who could best four or more men at swordplay. He also knew that such sagas were lies, providing the hero's opponents were reasonably competent.

And Rannarsh's men were veterans. They attacked cautiously but incessantly, keeping their swords well in front of them and never slashing wildly. Their breath whistled through their nostrils, but they were grimly confident, knowing the Northerner dared not lunge strongly at one of them because it would lay him wide open to a thrust by the other. Their game was to get one on each side of him and then attack simultaneously.

Fafhrd's counter was to shift position quickly and attack the nearer one murderously before the other could get back in range. In that way he managed to keep them side by side, where he could hold their blades in check by swift feints and crosswise sweeps. Sweat beaded his face and blood dripped from a scratch on his left thigh. A fearsome grin showed his white teeth, which occasionally parted to let slip a base, primitive insult.

The Mouser took in the situation at a glance, descended rapidly to a lower bough, and poised himself, aiming a dagger at the back of one of Fafhrd's adversaries. He was, however, standing very close to the thick trunk, and around this trunk darted a horny hand tipped with a short sword. The third henchman had also thought it wise to take to the trees. Fortunately for the Mouser, the man was uncertain of his footing and therefore his thrust, although well aimed, came a shade slow. As it was the little gray-clad man only managed to dodge by dropping off.

Thereupon he startled his opponent with a modest acrobatic feat. He did not drop to the ground, knowing that would put everyone at the mercy of the man in the tree. Instead, he grabbed hold of the branch on which he had been standing, swung himself smartly up again, and grappled. Steadying themselves now with one hand, now another, they drove for each other's throats, ramming with knees and elbows whenever they got a chance. At the first onset both dagger and sword were dropped, the latter sticking point-down in the ground directly between the two battling henchmen and startling them so that Fafhrd almost got home an attack.

The Mouser and his man surged and teetered along the branch away from the trunk, inflicting little damage on each other since it was hard to keep balance. Finally they slid off at the same time, but grabbed the branch with their hands. The puffing henchman aimed a vicious kick. The Mouser escaped it by yanking up his body and doubling up his legs. The latter he let fly violently, taking the henchman full in the chest, just where the ribs stop. The unfortunate retainer of Rannarsh fell to the ground, where he had the wind knocked out of him a second time.

At the same moment one of Fafhrd's opponents tried a trick that might have turned out well. When his companion was pressing the Northerner closely, he snatched for the shortsword sticking in the ground, intending to hurl it underhanded as if it were a javelin. But Fafhrd, whose superior endurance was rapidly giving him an advantage in speed, anticipated the movement and simultaneously made a brilliant counterattack against the other man. There were two thrusts, both lightninglike, the first a feint at the belly, the second a slicing stab that sheared through the throat to the spine. Then he whirled around and, with a quick sweep, knocked both weapons out of the hands of the first man, who looked up in bewilderment and promptly collapsed into a sitting position, panting in utter exhaustion, though with enough breath left to cry, "Mercy!"

To cap the situation, the Mouser dropped lightly down, as if out of the sky. Fafhrd automatically started to raise his sword, for a backhand swipe. Then he stared at the Mouser for as long a time as it took the man sitting on the ground to give three tremendous gasps. Then he began to laugh, first uncontrollable snickers and later thundering peals. It was a laughter in which the battle-begotten madness, completely sated anger, and relief at escape from death were equally mingled.

"Oh, by Glaggerk and by Kos!" he roared. "By the Behemoth! Oh, by the Cold Waste and the guts of the Red God! Oh! Oh! Oh!" Again the insane bellowing burst out. "Oh, by the Killer Whale and the Cold Woman and her spawn!" By degrees the laughter died away, choking in his throat. He rubbed his forehead with the palm of his hand and his face became starkly grave. Then he knelt beside the man he had just slain, and straightened his limbs, and closed his eyes, and began to weep in a dignified way that would have seemed ridiculous and hypocritical in anyone but a barbarian.

Meanwhile the Mouser's reactions were nowhere near as primitive. He felt worried, ironic, and slightly sick. He understood Fafhrd's emotions, but knew that he would not feel the full force of his own for some time yet, and by then they would be deadened and somewhat choked. He peered about anxiously, fearful of an anticlimactic attack that would find his companion helpless. He counted over the tally of their opponents. Yes, the six henchmen were all accounted for. But Rannarsh himself, where was Rannarsh? He fumbled in his pouch to make sure he had not lost his good-luck talismans and amulets. His lips moved rapidly as he murmured two or three prayers and cantrips. But all the while he held his sling ready, and his eyes never once ceased their quick shifting.

From the middle of a thick clump of bushes he heard a series of agonized gasps, as the man he had felled from the tree began to regain his wind. The henchman whom Fafhrd had disarmed, his face ashy pale from exhaustion rather than fright, was slowly edging back into the forest. The Mouser watched him carelessly, noting the comical way in which the steel cap had slipped down over his forehead and rested against the bridge of his nose. Meanwhile the gasps of the man in the bushes were taking on a less agonized quality. At almost the same instant, the two rose to their feet and stumbled off into the forest.

The Mouser listened to their blundering retreat. He was sure that there was nothing more to fear from them. *They* wouldn't come back. And then a little smile stole into his face, for he heard the sounds of a third person joining them in their flight. That would be Rannarsh, thought the Mouser, a man cowardly at heart and incapable of carrying on single-handed. It did not occur to him that the third person might be the man he had stunned with his sling handle.

Mostly just to be doing something, he followed them leisurely for a couple of bowshots into the forest. Their trail was impossible to miss, being marked by trampled bushes and thorns bearing tatters of cloth. It led in a beeline away from the clearing. Satisfied, he returned, going out of his way to regain the mallet, pick, and pry-bar.

He found Fafhrd tying a loose bandage around the scratch on his thigh. The Northerner's emotions had run their gamut and he was himself again. The dead man for whom he had been somberly grieving now meant no more to him than food for beetles and birds. Whereas for the Mouser it continued to be a somewhat frightening and sickening object.

"And now do we proceed with our interrupted business?" the Mouser asked.

Fafhrd nodded in a matter-of-fact manner and rose to his feet. Together they entered the rocky clearing. It came to them as a surprise how little time the fight had taken. True, the sun had moved somewhat higher, but the atmosphere was still that of early morning. The dew had not dried yet. The treasure house of Urgaan of Angarngi stood massive, featureless, grotesquely impressive.

"The peasant girl predicted the truth without knowing it," said the Mouser with a smile. "We played her game of 'circle-the-clearing and don't-cross-the-magic-circle,' didn't we?"

The treasure house had no fears for him today. He recalled his perturbations of the previous evening, but was unable to understand them. The very idea of a guardian seemed somewhat ridiculous. There were a hundred other ways of explaining the skeleton inside the doorway.

So this time it was the Mouser who skipped into the treasure house ahead of Fafhrd. The interior was disappointing, being empty of any furnishings and as bare and unornamented as the outside walls. Just a large, low room. To either side square doorways led to the smaller domes, while to the rear a long hallway was dimly apparent, and the beginnings of a stair leading to the upper part of the main dome.

With only a casual glance at the skull and the broken skeleton, the Mouser made his way toward the stair.

"Our document," he said to Fafhrd, who was now beside him, "speaks of the treasure as resting just below the keystone of the chief dome. Therefore we must seek in the room or rooms above."

"True," answered the Northerner, glancing around. "But I wonder, Mouser, just what use this structure served. A man who builds a house solely to hide a treasure is shouting to the world that he *has* a treasure. Do you think it might have been a temple?"

The Mouser suddenly shrank back with a sibilant exclamation. Sprawled a little way up the stair was another skeleton, the major bones hanging together in lifelike fashion. The whole upper half of the skull was smashed to bony shards paler than those of a gray pot. "Our hosts are overly ancient and indecently naked," hissed the Mouser, angry with himself for being startled. Then he darted up the stairs to examine the grisly find. His sharp eyes picked out several objects among the bones. A rusty dagger, a tarnished gold ring that looped a knucklebone, a handful of horn buttons, and a slim, green-eaten copper cylinder. The last awakened his curiosity. He picked it up, dislodging hand-bones in the process, so that they fell apart, rattling dryly. He pried off the cap of the cylinder with his dagger point, and shook out a tightly rolled sheet of ancient parchment. This he gingerly unwound. Fafhrd and he scanned the lines of diminutive red lettering by the light from a small window on the landing above.

> Mine is a secret treasure. Orichalcum have I, and crystal, and blood-red amber. Rubies and emeralds that demons would war for, and a diamond as big as the skull of a man. Yet none have seen them save I. I, Urgaan of Angarngi, scorn the flattery and the envy of fools. A fittingly lonely treasure house have I built for my jewels. There, hidden under the keystone, they may dream unperturbed until earth and sky wear away. A day's ride beyond the village of Soreev, in the valley of the two double-humped hills, lies that house, trebly-domed and single-towered. It is empty. Any fool may enter. Let him. I care not.

"The details differ slightly," murmured the Mouser, "but the phrases have the same ring as in our document."

"The man must have been mad," asserted Fafhrd, scowling. "Or else why should he carefully hide a treasure and then, with equal care, leave directions for finding it?"

"We thought *our* document was a memorandum or an oversight," said the Mouser thoughtfully. "Such a notion can hardly explain *two* documents." Lost in speculation, he turned toward the remaining section of the stair, only to find still another skull grinning at him from a shadowy angle. This time he was not startled, yet he experienced the same feeling that a fly must experience when, enmeshed in a spider's web, it sees the dangling, empty corpses of a dozen of its brothers. He began to speak rapidly.

"Nor can such a notion explain *three* or *four* or mayhap a *dozen* such documents. For how came these other questers here, unless each had found a written message? Urgaan of Angarngi may have been mad, but he sought deliberately to lure men here. One thing is certain: this house conceals—or did conceal—some deadly trap. Some guardian. Some giant beast, say. Or perhaps the very stones distill a poison. Perhaps hidden springs release sword blades which stab out through cracks in the walls and then return."

"That cannot be," answered Fafhrd. "These men were killed by great, bashing blows. The ribs and spine of the first were splintered. The second had his skull cracked open. And that third one there. See! The bones of his lower body are smashed."

The Mouser started to reply. Then his face broke into an unexpected smile. He could see the conclusion to which Fafhrd's arguments were unconsciously leading—and he knew that the conclusion was ridiculous. What thing would kill with great, bashing blows? What thing but the gray giant the peasant girl had told them about? The gray giant twice as tall as a man, with his great stone club—a giant fit only for fairy tales and fantasies.

And Fafhrd returned the Mouser's smile. It seemed to him that they were making a great deal of fuss about nothing. These skeletons were suggestive enough, to be sure, but did they not represent men who had died many, many years ago—centuries ago? What guardian could outlast three centuries? Why, that was a long enough time to weary the patience of a demon! And there were no such things as demons, anyhow. And there was no earthly use in mucking around about ancient fears and horrors that were as dead as dust. The whole matter, thought Fafhrd, boiled down to something very simple. They had come to a deserted house to see if there was a treasure in it.

Agreed upon this point, the two comrades made their way up the remaining section of stair that led to the dimmer regions of the House of Angarngi. Despite their confidence, they moved cautiously and kept sharp watch on the shadows lying ahead. This was wise.

24

Just as they reached the top, a flash of steel spun out of the darkness. It nicked the Mouser in the shoulder as he twisted to one side. There was a metallic clash as it fell to the stone floor. The Mouser, gripped by a sudden spasm of anger and fright, ducked down and dashed rapidly through the door from which the weapon had come, straight at the danger, whatever it was.

"Dagger-tossing in the dark, eh, you slick-bellied worm?" Fafhrd heard the Mouser cry, and then he, too, had plunged through the door.

Lord Rannarsh cowered against the wall, his rich hunting garb dusty and disordered, his black, wavy hair pushed back from his forehead, his cruelly handsome face a sallow mask of hate and extreme terror. For the moment the latter emotion seemed to predominate and, oddly enough, it did not appear to be directed toward the men he had just assailed, but toward something else, something unapparent.

"O gods!" he cried. "Let me go from here. The treasure is yours. Let me out of this place. Else I am doomed. The thing has played at cat and mouse with me. I cannot bear it. I cannot bear it!"

"So now we pipe a different tune, do we?" snarled the Mouser. "First dagger-tossing, then fright and pleas!"

"Filthy coward tricks," added Fafhrd. "Skulking here safe while your henchmen died bravely."

"Safe? Safe, you say? O gods!" Rannarsh almost screamed. Then a subtle change became apparent in his rigid-muscled face. It was not that his terror decreased. If anything, that became greater. But there was added to it, over and above, a consciousness of desperate shame, a realization that he had demeaned himself ineradicably in the eyes of these two ruffians. His lips began to writhe, showing tight-clenched teeth. He extended his left hand in a gesture of supplication.

"Oh, mercy, have mercy," he cried piteously, and his right hand twitched a second dagger from his belt and hurled it underhand at Fafhrd.

The Northerner knocked aside the weapon with a swift blow of his palm, then said deliberately, "He is yours, Mouser. Kill the man."

And now it was cat against cornered rat. Lord Rannarsh whipped a gleaming sword from its gold-worked scabbard and rushed in, cutting, thrusting, stabbing. The Mouser gave ground slightly, his slim blade flickering in a defensive counterattack that was wavering and elusive, yet deadly. He brought Rannarsh's rush to a standstill. His blade moved so quickly that it seemed to weave a net of steel around the man. Then it leaped forward three times in rapid succession. At the first thrust it bent nearly double against a concealed shirt of chain mail. The second thrust pierced the belly. The third transfixed the throat. Lord Rannarsh fell to the floor, spitting and gagging, his fingers clawing at his neck. There he died.

"An evil end," said Fafhrd somberly, "although he had fairer play than he deserved, and handled his sword well. Mouser, I like not this killing, although there was surely more justice to it than the others."

The Mouser, wiping his weapon against his opponent's thigh, understood what Fafhrd meant. He felt no elation at his victory, only a cold, queasy disgust. A moment before he had been raging, but now there was no anger left in him. He pulled open his gray jerkin and inspected the dagger wound in his left shoulder. A little blood was still welling from it and trickling down his arm.

"Lord Rannarsh was no coward," he said slowly. "He killed himself, or at least caused his own death, because we had seen him terrified and herd him cry in fright."

And at these words, without any warning whatsoever, stark terror fell like an icy eclipse upon the hearts of the Gray Mouser and Fafhrd. It was as if Lord Rannarsh had left them a legacy of fear, which passed to them immediately upon his death. And the unmanning thing about it was that they had no premonitory apprehension, no hint of its approach. It did not take root and grow gradually greater. It came all at once, paralyzing, overwhelming. Worse still, there was no discernible cause. One moment they were looking down with something of indifference upon the twisted corpse of Lord Rannarsh. The next moment their legs were weak, their guts were cold, their spines prickling, their teeth clicking, their hearts pounding, their hair lifting at the roots.

Fafhrd felt as if he had walked unsuspecting into the jaws of a gigantic serpent. His barbaric mind was stirred to the deeps. He thought of the grim god Kos brooding alone in the icy silence of the Cold Waste. He thought of the masked powers Fate and Chance, and of the game they play for the blood and brains of men. And he did not will these thoughts. Rather did the freezing fear seem to crystallize them, so that they dropped into his consciousness like snow flakes.

Slowly he regained control over his quaking limbs and twitching muscles. As if in a nightmare, he looked around him slowly, taking in the details of his surroundings. The room they were in was semicircular, forming half of the great dome. Two small windows, high in the curving ceiling, let in light.

An inner voice kept repeating, *Don't make a sudden move. Slowly. Slowly. Above all, don't run. The others did. That was why they died so quickly. Slowly. Slowly.*

He saw the Mouser's face. It reflected his own terror. He wondered how much longer this would last, how much longer he could stand it without running amuck, how much longer he could passively endure this feeling of a great invisible paw reaching out over him, span by span, implacably.

The faint sound of footsteps came from the room below. Regular and unhurried footsteps. Now they were crossing into the rear hallway below. Now they were on the stairs. And now they had reached the landing, and were advancing up the second section of the stairs.

The man who entered the room was tall and frail and old and very gaunt. Scant locks of intensely black hair straggled down over his high-domed forehead. His sunken cheeks showed clearly the outlines of his long jawbone, and waxy skin was pulled tight over his small nose. Fanatical eyes burned in deep, bony sockets. He wore the simple, sleeveless robe of a holy man. A pouch hung from the cord round his waist.

He fixed his eyes upon Fafhrd and the Gray Mouser.

"I greet you, you men of blood," he said in a hollow voice.

Then his gaze fell with displeasure upon the corpse of Rannarsh.

"More blood has been shed. It is not well."

And with the bony forefinger of his left hand he traced in the air a curious triple square, the sign sacred to the Great God.

"Do not speak," his calm, toneless voice continued, "for I know your purposes. You have come to take treasure from this house. Others have sought to do the same. They have failed. You will fail. As for myself, I have no lust for treasure. For forty years I have lived on crusts and water, devoting my spirit to the Great God." Again he traced the curious sign. "The gems and ornaments of this world and the jewels and gauds of the world of demons cannot tempt or corrupt me. My purpose in coming here is to destroy an evil thing.

"I"—and here he touched his chest—"I am Arvlan of Angarngi, the ninth lineal descendent of Urgaan of Angarngi. This I always knew, and sorrowed for, because Urgaan of Angarngi was a man of evil. But not until fifteen days ago, on the Day of the

Spider, did I discover from ancient documents that Urgaan had built this house, and built it to be an eternal trap for the unwise and venturesome. He has left a guardian here, and that guardian has endured.

"Cunning was my accursed ancestor, Urgaan, cunning and evil. The most skillful architect in all Lankhmar was Urgaan, a man wise in the ways of stone and learned in geometrical lore. But he scorned the Great God. He longed for improper powers. He had commerce with demons, and won from them an unnatural treasure. But he had no use for it. For in seeking wealth and knowledge and power, he lost his ability to enjoy any good feeling or pleasure, even simple lust. So he hid his treasure, but hid it in such a way that it would wreak endless evil on the world, even as he felt men and one proud, contemptuous, cruel woman—as heartless as this fane—had wreaked evil upon him. It is my purpose and my right to destroy Urgaan's evil.

"Seek not to dissuade me, lest doom fall upon you. As for me, no harm can befall me. The hand of the Great God is poised above me, ready to ward off any danger that may threaten his faithful servant. His will is my will. Do not speak, men of blood! I go to destroy the treasure of Urgaan of Angarngi."

And with these words, the gaunt holy man walked calmly on, with measured stride, like an apparition, and disappeared through the narrow doorway that led into the forward part of the great dome.

Fafhrd stared after him, his green eyes wide, feeling no desire to follow or to interfere. His terror had not left him, but it was transmuted. He was still aware of a dreadful threat, but it no longer seemed to be directed against him personally.

Meanwhile, a most curious notion had lodged in the mind of the Mouser. He felt that he had just now seen, not a venerable holy man, but a dim reflection of the centuries-dead Urgaan of Angarngi. Surely Urgaan had that same high-domed forehead, that same secret pride, that same air of command. And those locks of youthfully black hair, which contrasted so ill with the aged face also seemed part of a picture looming from the past. A picture dimmed and distorted by time, but retaining something of the power and individuality of the ancient original.

They heard the footsteps of the holy man proceed a little way into the other room. Then for the space of a dozen heartbeats there was complete silence. Then the floor began to tremble slightly under their feet, as if the earth were quaking, or as if a giant were treading near. Then there came a single quavering cry from the next room, cut off in the middle by a single sickening crash that made them lurch. Then, once again, utter silence.

Fafhrd and the Mouser looked at one another in blank amazement—not so much because of what they had just heard but because, almost at the moment of the crash, the pall of terror had lifted from them completely. They jerked out their swords and hurried into the next room.

It was a duplicate of the one they had quitted, save that instead of two small windows, there were three, one of them near the floor. Also, there was but a single door, the one through which they had just entered. All else was closely morticed stone—floor, walls, and hemi-doomed ceiling.

Near the thick center wall, which bisected the dome, lay the body of the holy man. Only "lay" was not the right word. Left shoulder and chest were mashed against the floor. Life was fled. Blood puddled around.

Fafhrd's and the Mouser's eyes searched wildly for a being other than themselves and the dead man and found none—no, not one gnat hovering amongst the dust motes revealed by the narrow shafts of sunlight shooting down through the windows. Their imaginations searched as wildly and as much in vain for a being that could strike such a man-killing blow and vanish through one of the three tiny orifices of the windows. A giant, striking serpent with a granite head . . .

Set in the wall near the dead man was a stone about two feet square, jutting out a little from the rest. On this was boldly engraved, in antique Lankhmarian hieroglyphs: "Here rests the treasure of Urgaan of Angarngi."

The sight of that stone was like a blow in the face to the two adventurers. It roused every ounce of obstinacy and reckless determination in them. What matter that an old man sprawled smashed beside it? They had their swords! What matter they now had proof some grim guardian resided in the treasure house? They could take care of themselves! Run away and leave that stone unmoved, with its insultingly provocative inscription? No, by Kos, and the Behemoth! They'd see themselves in Nehwon's hell first!

Fafhrd ran to fetch the pick and the other large tools, which had been dropped on the stairs when Lord Rannarsh tossed his first dagger. The Mouser looked more closely at the jutting stone. The cracks around it were wide and filled with a dark, tarry mixture. It gave out a slightly hollow sound when he tapped it with his sword hilt. He calculated that the wall was about six feet thick at this point—enough to contain a sizable cavity. He tapped experimentally along the wall in both directions, but the hollow ring quickly ceased. Evidently the cavity was a fairly small one. He noted that the crevices between all the other stones were very fine, showing no evidence of any cementing substance whatsoever. In fact, he couldn't be sure that they weren't false crevices, superficial cuts in the surface of solid rock. But that hardly seemed possible. He heard Fafhrd returning, but continued his examination.

The state of the Mouser's mind was peculiar. A dogged determination to get at the treasure overshadowed other emotions. The inexplicably sudden vanishing of his former terror had left certain parts of his mind benumbed. It was as if he had decided to hold his thoughts in leash until he had seen what the treasure cavity contained. He was content to keep his mind occupied with material details, and yet make no deductions from them.

His calmness gave him a feeling of at least temporary safety. His experiences had vaguely convinced him that the guardian, whatever it was, which had smashed the holy man and played cat and mouse with Rannarsh and themselves, did not strike without first inspiring a premonitory terror in its victims.

Fafhrd felt very much the same way, except that he was even more single-minded in his determination to solve the riddle of the inscribed stone.

They attacked the wide crevices with chisel and mallet. The dark tarry mixture came away fairly easily, first in hard lumps, later in slightly rubbery, gouged strips. After they had cleared it away to the depth of a finger, Fafhrd inserted the pick and managed to move the stone slightly. Thus the Mouser was enabled to gouge a little more deeply on that side. Then Fafhrd subjected the other side of the stone to the leverage of the pick. So the work proceeded, with alternate pryings and gougings.

They concentrated on each detail of the job with unnecessary intensity, mainly to keep their imaginations from being haunted by the image of a man more than two hundred years dead. A man with high-domed forehead, sunken cheeks, nose of a skull —that is, if the dead thing on the floor was a true type of the breed of Angarngi. A man who had somehow won a great treasure, and then hid it away from all eyes, seeking to obtain neither glory nor material profit from it. Who said he scorned the envy of fools, and who yet wrote many provocative notes in diminutive red lettering in order to inform fools of his treasure and make them envious. Who seemed to be reaching out across the dusty centuries, like a spider spinning a web to catch a fly on the other side of the world.

And yet, he was a skillful architect, the holy man had said. Could such an architect build a stone automaton twice as tall as a tall man? A gray stone automaton with a great club? Could he make a hiding place from which it could emerge, deal death, and then return? No, no, such notions were childish, not to be entertained! Stick to the job in hand. First find what lay behind the inscribed stone. Leave thoughts until afterward.

The stone was beginning to give more easily to the pressure of the pick. Soon they would be able to get a good purchase on it and pry it out.

Meanwhile an entirely new sensation was growing in the Mouser—not one of terror at all, but of physical revulsion. The air he breathed seemed thick and sickening. He found himself disliking the texture and consistency of the tarry mixture gouged from the cracks, which somehow he could only liken to wholly imaginary substances, such as the dung of dragons or the solidified vomit of the Behemoth. He avoided touching it with his fingers, and he kicked away the litter of chunks and strips that had gathered around his feet. The sensation of queasy loathing became difficult to endure.

He tried to fight it, but had no more success than if it had been seasickness, which in some ways it resembled. He felt unpleasantly dizzy. His mouth kept filling with saliva. The cold sweat of nausea beaded his forehead. He could tell that Fafhrd was unaffected, and he hesitated to mention the matter; it seemed ridiculously out of place, especially as it was unaccompanied by any fear or fright. Finally the stone itself began to have the same effect on him as the tarry mixture, filling him with a seemingly causeless, but none the less sickening revulsion. Then he could bear it no longer. With a vaguely apologetic nod to Fafhrd, he dropped his chisel and went to the low window for a breath of fresh air.

This did not seem to help matters much. He pushed his head through the window and gulped deeply. His mental processes were overshadowed by the general indifference of extreme nausea, and everything seemed very far away. Therefore when he saw that the peasant girl was standing in the middle of the clearing, it was some time before he began to consider the import of the fact. When he did, part of his sickness left him; or at least he was enabled to overpower it sufficiently to stare at her with gathering interest.

Her face was white, her fists were clenched, her arms held rigid at her sides. Even at the distance he could catch something of the mingled terror and determination with which her eyes were fixed on the great doorway. Toward this doorway she was forcing herself to move, one jerking step after another, as if she had to keep screwing her courage to a higher pitch. Suddenly the Mouser began to feel frightened, not for himself at all, but for the girl. Her terror was obviously intense, and yet she must be doing what she was doing—braving her "queer and fearsome gray giant"—for his sake and Fafhrd's. At all costs, he thought, she must be prevented from coming closer. It was wrong that she be subjected for one moment longer to such a horribly intense terror.

His mind was confused by his abominable nausea, yet he knew what he must do. He hurried toward the stairs with shaky strides, waving Fafhrd another vague gesture. Just as he was going out of the room he chanced to turn up his eyes, and spied something peculiar on the ceiling. What it was he did not fully realize for some moments.

Fafhrd hardly noticed the Mouser's movements, much less his gestures. The block of stone was rapidly yielding to his efforts. He had previously experienced a faint suggestion of the Mouser's nausea, but perhaps because of his greater single-mindedness, it had not become seriously bothersome. And now his attention was wholly concentrated on the stone. Persistent prying had edged it out a palm's breadth from the wall. Seizing it firmly in his two powerful hands, he tugged it from one side to the other, back and forth. The dark, viscous stuff clung to it tenaciously, but with each sidewise jerk it moved forward a little.

The Mouser lurched hastily down the stairs, fighting vertigo. His feet kicked bones and sent them knocking against the walls. What was it he had seen on the ceiling? Somehow, it seemed to mean something. But he must get the girl out of the clearing. She mustn't come any closer to the house. She mustn't enter.

Fafhrd began to feel the weight of the stone, and knew that it was nearly clear. It was damnably heavy—almost a foot thick. Two carefully gauged heaves finished the job. The stone overbalanced. He stepped quickly back. The stone crashed ponderously on the floor. A rainbow glitter came from the cavity that had been revealed. Fafhrd eargerly thrust his head into it.

The Mouser staggered toward the doorway. It was a bloody smear he had seen on the ceiling. And just above the corpse of the holy man. But why should that be? He'd been smashed against the floor, hadn't he? Was it blood splashed up from his lethal clubbing? But then why smeared? No matter. The girl. He must get to the girl. He must. There she was, almost at the doorway. He could see her. He felt the stone floor vibrating slightly beneath his feet. But that was his dizziness, wasn't it?

Fafhrd felt the vibration, too. But any thought he might have had about it was lost in his wonder at what he saw. The cavity was filled to a level just below the surface of the opening, with a heavy metallic liquid that resembled mercury, except that it was night-black. Resting on this liquid was a more astonishing group of gems that Fafhrd had ever dreamed of.

In the center was a titan diamond, cut with a myriad of oddly angled facets. Around it were two irregular circles, the inner formed of twelve rubies, each a decahedron, the outer formed of seventeen emeralds, each an irregular octahedron. Lying between these gems, touching some of them, sometimes connecting them with each other, were thin, fragile-looking bars of crystal, amber, greenish tourmaline, and honey-pale orichalchum. All these objects did not seem to be floating in the metallic liquid so much as resting upon it, their weight pressing down the surface into shallow depressions, some cup-shaped, others trough-like. The rods glowed faintly, while each of the gems glittered with a light that Fafhrd's mind strangely conceived to be refracted starlight.

His gaze shifted to the mercurous heavy fluid, where it bulged up between, and he saw distorted reflections of stars and constellations which he recognized, stars and constellations which would be visible now in the sky overhead, were it not for the concealing brilliance of the sun. An awesome wonder engulfed him. His gaze shifted back to the gems. There was something tremendously meaningful about their complex arrangement, something that seemed to speak of overwhelming truths in an alien symbolism. More, there was a compelling impression of inner movement, or sluggish thought, of inorganic consciousness. It was like what the eyes see when they close at night—not utter blackness, but a shifting, fluid pattern of many-colored points of light. Feeling that he was reaching impiously into the core of a thinking mind, Fafhrd gripped with his right hand for the diamond as big as a man's skull.

The Mouser blundered through the doorway. There could be no mistaking it now. That bloody smear, as if the ceiling had champed down upon the holy man, crushing him against the floor, or as if the floor had struck upward. But there was the girl, her terror-wide eyes fastened upon him, her mouth open for a scream that did not come. He must drag her away, out of the clearing.

But why should he feel that a fearful threat was now directed at himself as well? Why should he feel that something was poised above him, threatening? As he stumbled down the terraced steps, he looked over his shoulder and up. The tower. The tower! It was falling. It was falling toward him. It was dipping at him over the dome. But there were no fractures along its length. It was not breaking. It was not falling. It was bending.

Fafhrd's hand jerked back, clutching the great, strangely faceted jewel, so heavy that he had difficulty in keeping his hold upon it. Immediately the surface of the metallic, star-reflecting fluid was disturbed. It bobbled and shook. Surely the whole house was shaking, too. The other jewels began to dart about erratically, like water insects on the surface of a puddle. The various crystalline and metallic bars began to spin, their tips attracted now to one jewel and now to another, as if the jewels were lodestone and the bars iron needles. The whole surface of the fluid was in a whirling, jerking confusion that suggested a mind gone mad because of loss of its chief part.

For an agonizing instant the Mouser stared up amazement-frozen at the clublike top of the tower, ponderously hurling itself down upon him. Then he ducked and lunged forward at the girl, tackling her, rapidly rolling over and over with her. The tower top struck a sword's length behind them, with a thump that jolted them momentarily off the ground. Then it jerked itself up from the pitlike depression it had made.

Fafhrd tore his gaze away from the incredible, alien beauty of the jewel-confused cavity. His right hand was burning. The diamond was hot. No, it was cold beyond belief. By Kos, the room was changing shape! The ceiling was bulging downward at a point. He made for the door, then stopped dead in his tracks. The door was closing like a stony mouth. He turned and took a few steps over the quaking floor toward the small, low window. It snapped shut, like a sphincter. He tried to drop the diamond. It clung painfully to the inside of his hand. With a snap of his wrist he whipped it away from him. It hit the floor and began to bounce about, glaring like a living star.

The Mouser and the peasant girl rolled toward the edge of the clearing. The tower made two more tremendous bashes at them, but both went yards wide, like the blows of a blind madman. Now they were out of range. The Mouser lay sprawled on his side, watching a stone house that hunched and heaved like a beast, and a tower that bent double as it thumped grave-deep pits into the ground. It crashed into a group of boulders and its top broke off, but the jaggedly fractured end continued to beat the boulders in wanton anger, smashing them into fragments. The Mouser felt a compulsive urge to take out his dagger and stab himself in the heart. A man had to die when he saw something like that.

Fafhrd clung to sanity because he was threatened from a new direction at every minute and because he could say to himself, "I know. I know. The house is a beast, and the jewels are its mind. Now that mind is mad. I know. I know." Walls, ceiling, and floor quaked and heaved, but their movements did not seem to be directed especially at him. Occasional crashes almost deafened him. He staggered over rocky swells, dodging stony advances that were half bulges and half blows, but that lacked the speed and directness of the tower's first smash at the Mouser. The corpse of the holy man was jolted about in grotesque mechanical reanimation.

Only the great diamond seemed aware of Fafhrd. Exhibiting a fretful intelligence, it kept bounding at him viciously, sometimes leaping as high as his head. He involuntarily made for the door as his only hope. It was champing up and down with convulsive regularity. Watching his chance, he dived at it just as it was opening, and writhed through. The diamond followed him, striking at his legs. The carcass of Rannarsh was flung sprawling in his path. He jumped over it, then slid, lurched, stumbled, fell down stairs in earthquake, where dry bones danced. Surely the beast must die, the house must crash and crush him flat. The diamond leaped for his skull, missed, hurtled through the air, and struck a wall. Thereupon it burst into a great puff of iridescent dust.

Immediately the rhythm of the shaking of the house began to increase. Fafhrd raced across the heaving floor, escaped by inches the killing embrace of the great door-way, plunged across the clearing—passing a dozen feet from the spot where the tower was beating boulders into crushed rock—and then leaped over two pits in the ground. His face was rigid and white. His eyes were vacant. He blundered bull-like into two or three trees, and only came to a halt because he knocked himself flat against one of them.

The house had ceased most of its random movements, and the whole of it was shaking like a huge dark jelly. Suddenly its forward part heaved up like a behemoth in death agony. The two smaller domes were jerked ponderously a dozen feet off the ground, as if they were the paws. The tower whipped into convulsive rigidity. The main dome contracted sharply, like a stupendous lung. For a moment it hung there, poised. Then it crashed to the ground in a heap of gigantic stone shards. The earth shook. The forest resounded. Battered atmosphere whipped branches and leaves. Then all was still. Only from the fractures in the stone a tarry, black liquid was slowing oozing, and here and there iridescent puffs of air suggested jewel-dust.

* * *

Along a narrow, dusty road two horsemen were cantering slowly toward the village of Soreev in the southernmost limits of the land of Lankhmar. They presented a some-what battered appearance. The limbs of the larger, who was mounted on a chestnut gelding showed several bruises, and there was a bandage around his thigh and another around the palm of his right hand. The smaller man, the one mounted on a gray mare, seemed to have suffered an equal number of injuries.

"Do you know where we're headed?" said the latter, breaking a long silence. "We're headed for a city. And in that city are endless houses of stone, stone towers without numbers, streets paved with stone, domes, arches, stairs. *Tcha*, if I feel then as I feel now, I'll never go within a bowshot of Lankhmar's walls."

His large companion smiled.

"What now, little man? Don't tell me you're afraid of—earthquakes?"

The Automatic Pistol

Inky Kozacs never let anyone but himself handle his automatic pistol, or even touch it. It was blue-black and hefty and when you just pressed the trigger once, eight .45 caliber slugs came out of it almost on top of each other.

Inky was something of a mechanic, as far as his automatic went. He would break it down and put it together again, and every once in a while carefully rub a file across the inside trigger catch.

Glasses once told him, "You will make that gun into such a hair-trigger that it will go off in your pocket and blast off all your toes. You will only have to think about it and it will start shooting."

Inky smiled at that, I remember. He was a little wiry man with a pale face, from which he couldn't ever shave off the blue-black of his beard, no matter how close he shaved. His hair was black, too. He talked foreign, but I never could figure what country. He got together with Anton Larsen just after prohibition came, in the days when sea-skiffs with converted automobile motors used to play tag with revenue cutters in New York Bay and off the Jersey coast, both omitting to use lights in order to make the game more difficult. Larsen and Inky Kozacs used to get their booze off a steamer and run it in near the Twin Lights in New Jersey.

It was there that Glasses and I started to work for them. Glasses, who looked like a cross between a college professor and an automobile salesman, came from I don't know where in New York City, and I was a local small-town policeman until I determined to lead a less hypocritical life. We used to ride the stuff back toward Newark in a truck.

Inky always rode in with us; Larsen only occasionally. Neither of them used to talk much; Larsen, because he didn't see any sense in talking unless to give a guy orders or a girl a proposition; and Inky, well, I guess because he wasn't any too happy talking American. And there wasn't a ride Inky took with us but he didn't slip out his automatic and sort of pet it and mutter at it under his breath. Once when we were restfully chugging down the highway Glasses asked him, polite but inquiring:

"Just what is it makes you so fond of that gun? After all, there must be thousands identically like it."

"You think so?" says Inky, giving us a quick stare from his little, glinty black eyes and making a speech for once. "Let me tell you, Glasses" (he made the word sound like 'Hlasses'), "nothing is alike in this world. People, guns, bottles of Scotch—nothing. Everything in the world is different. Every man has different fingerprints; and, of all guns made in the same factory as this one, there is not one like mine. I could pick mine out from a hundred. Yes, even if I hadn't filed the trigger catch, I could do that."

We didn't contradict him. It sounded pretty reasonable. He sure loved that gun, all right. He slept with it under his pillow. I don't think it ever got more than three feet away from him as long as he lived.

Once when Larsen was ridng in with us, he remarked sarcastically, "That is a pretty little gun, Inky, but I am getting very tired of hearing you talk to it so much, especially when no one can understand what you are saying. Doesn't it ever talk back to you?"

Inky smiled at him. "My gun only knows eight words," he said, "and they are all alike."

This was such a good crack that we laughed.

"Let's have a look at it," said Larsen reaching out his hand.

But Inky put it back in his pocket and didn't take it out the rest of the trip.

After that Larsen was always kidding Inky about the gun, trying to get his goat. He was a persistent guy with a very peculiar sense of humor, and he kept it up for a long time after it had stopped being funny. Finally he took to acting as if he wanted to buy it, making Inky crazy offers of one to two hundred dollars.

"Two hundred and seventy-five dollars, Inky," he said one evening as we were rattling past Bayport with a load of cognac and Irish whiskey. "That's my last offer, and you'd better take it."

Inky shook his head and made a funny noise that was almost like a snarl. Then, to my great surprise (I almost ran the truck off the pavement) Larsen lost his temper.

"Hand over that damn gun!" he bellowed, grabbing Inky's shoulders and shaking him. I was almost knocked off the seat. Somebody might even have been hurt, if a motorcycle cop hadn't stopped us just at that moment to ask for his hush-money. By the time he was gone, Larsen and Inky were both cooled down to the freezing point, and there was no more fighting. We got our load safely into the warehouse, nobody saying a word.

Afterward, when Glasses and I were having a cup of coffee at a little open-all-night restaurant, I said, "Those two guys are crazy, and I don't like it a bit. Why the devil do they act that way, now that the business is going so swell? I haven't got the brains Larsen has, but you won't ever find me fighting about a gun as if I was a kid."

Glasses only smiled as he poured a precise half-spoonful of sugar into his cup.

"And Inky's as bad as he is," I went on. "I tell you, Glasses, it ain't natural or normal for a man to feel that way about a piece of metal. I can understand him being fond of it and feeling lost without it. I feel the same way about my lucky half-dollar. It's the way he pets it and makes love to it that gets on my nerves. And now Larsen's acting the same way."

Glasses shrugged. "We're all getting a little jittery, although we won't admit it," he said. "Too many hijackers. And so we start getting on each other's nerves and fighting about trifles—such as automatic pistols."

"You may have something there."

Glasses winked at me. "Why, certainly. No Nose," he said, referring to what had once been done to me with a baseball bat. "I even have another explanation of tonight's events."

"What?"

He leaned over and whispered in a mock-mysterious way, "Maybe there's something queer about the gun itself."

I told him in impolite language to go chase himself.

From that night, however, things were changed. Larsen and Inky Kozacs never spoke to each other any more except in the line of business. And there was no more talk, kidding or serious, about the gun. Inky only brought it out when Larsen wasn't along.

Well, the years kept passing and the bootlegging business stayed good except that the hijackers became more numerous and Inky got a couple of chances to show us what a nice noise his automatic made. Then, too, we got into a row with some competitors bossed by an Irishman named Luke Dugan, and had to watch our step very carefully and change our route every other trip.

Still, business was good. I continued to support almost all my relatives, and Glasses put away a few dollars every month for what he called his Persian Cat Fund. Larsen, I believe, spent about everything he got on women and all that goes with them. He was the kind of guy who would take all the pleasures of life without cracking a smile, but who lived for them just the same.

As for Inky Kozacs, we never knew what happened to the money he made. We never heard of him spending much, so we finally figured he must be saving it—probably in bills in a safety deposit box. Maybe he was planning to go back to the Old Country, wherever that was, and be somebody. At any rate he never told us. By the time Congress took our profession away from us, he must have had a whale of a lot of dough. We hadn't had a big racket, but we'd been very careful.

Finally we ran our last load. We'd have had to quit the business pretty soon anyway, because the big syndicates were demanding more protection money each week. There was no chance left for a small independent operator, even if he was as clever as Larsen. So Glasses and I took a couple of months off for vacation before thinking what to do next for his Persian cats and my shiftless relatives. For the time being we stuck together.

Then one morning I read in the paper that Inky Kozacs had been taken for a ride. He'd been found shot dead on a dump heap near Elizabeth, New Jersey.

"I guess Luke Dugan finally got him," said Glasses.

"A nasty break," I said, "especially figuring all that money he hadn't got any fun out of. I am glad that you and I, Glasses, aren't important enough for Dugan to bother about, I hope."

"Yeah. Say, No Nose, does it say if they found Inky's gun on him?"

I said it told the dead man was unarmed and that no weapon was found on the scene.

Glasses remarked that it was queer to think of Inky's gun being in anyone else's pocket. I agreed, and we spent some time wondering whether Inky had had a chance to defend himself.

About two hours later Larsen called and told us to meet him at the hide-out. He said Luke Dugan was gunning for him too.

The hide-out is a three-room frame bungalow with a big corrugated iron garage next to it. The garage was for the truck, and sometimes we would store a load of booze there when we heard that the police were going to make some arrests for the sake of variety. It is near Bayport, about a mile and a half from the cement highway and about a quarter of a mile from the bay and the little inlet in which we used to hide our boat. Stiff, knife-edged sea-grass taller than a man, comes up near to the house on the bay side, which is north, and on the west too. Under the sea-grass the ground is marshy, though in hot weather and when the tides aren't high, it gets dry and caked; here and there creeks of tidewater go through it. Even a little breeze will make the blades of sea-grass scrape each other with a funny dry sound.

To the east are some fields, and beyond them, Bayport. Bayport is a kind of summer resort town and some of the houses are built up on poles because of the tides and storms. It has a little lagoon for the boats of the fishermen who go out after crabs.

To the south of the hide-out is the dirt road leading to the cement highway. The nearest house is about half a mile away.

It was late in the afternoon when Glasses and I got there. We brought groceries for a couple of days, figuring Larsen might want to stay. Then, along about sunset, we heard Larsen's coupe turning in, and I went out to put it in the big empty garage and carry in his suitcase. When I got back Larsen was talking to Glasses. He was a big man and his shoulders were broad both ways, like a wrestler's. His head was almost bald and what was left of his hair was a dirty yellow. His eyes were little and his face wasn't given much to expression. And that was the way it was when he said, "Yeah, Inky got it."

"Luke Dugan's crazy gunmen sure hold a grudge," I observed.

Larsen nodded his head and scowled.

"Inky got it," he repeated, taking up his suitcase and starting for the bedroom. "And I'm planning to stay here for a few days, just in case they're after me too. I want you and Glasses to stay here with me."

Glasses gave me a funny wink and began throwing a meal together. I turned on the lights and pulled down the blinds, taking a worried glance down the road, which was empty. This waiting around in a lonely house for a bunch of gunmen to catch up with you didn't appeal to me. Nor to Glasses either, I guessed. It seemed to me that it would have been a lot more sensible for Larsen to put a couple of thousand miles between him and New York. But, knowing Larsen, I had sense enough not to make any comments.

After canned corned-beef hash and beans and beer, we sat around the table drinking coffee.

Larsen took an automatic out of his pocket and began fooling with it, and right away I saw it was Inky's. For about five minutes nobody said a word. Glasses played with his coffee, pouring in the cream one drop at a time. I wadded a piece of bread into little pellets which kept looking less and less appetizing.

Finally Larsen looked up at us and said, "Too bad Inky didn't have this with him when he was taken for a ride. He gave it to me just before he planned sailing for the Old Country. He didn't want it with him any more, now that the racket's over."

"I'm glad the guy that killed him hasn't got it now," said Glasses quickly. He talked nervously and in his worst college professor style. I could tell he didn't want the silence to settle down again. "It's a funny thing, Inky giving up his gun—but I can understand his feeling; he mentally associated the gun with our racket; when the one was over he didn't care about the other."

Larsen grunted, which meant for Glasses to shut up.

"What's going to happen to Inky's dough?" I asked.

Larsen shrugged his shoulders and went on fooling with the automatic, throwing a shell into the chamber, cocking it, and so forth. It reminded me so much of the way Inky used to handle it that I got fidgetting and began to imagine I heard Luke Dugan's gunmen creeping up through the sea-grass. Finally I got up and started to walk around.

It was then that the accident happened. Larsen, after cocking the gun, was bringing up his thumb to let the hammer down easy, when it slipped out of his hand. As it hit the floor it went off with a flash and a bang, sending a slug gouging the floor too near my foot for comfort.

As soon as I realizd I wasn't hit, I yelled without thinking, "I always told Inky he was putting too much of a hair trigger on his gun! The crazy fool!"

Larsen sat with his pig eyes staring down at the gun where it lay between his feet.

Then he gave a funny little snort, picked it up and put it on the table.

"That gun ought to be thrown away. It's too dangerous to handle. It's bad luck," I said to Larsen—and then wished I hadn't, for he gave me the benefit of a dirty look and some fancy Swedish swearing.

"Shut up, No Nose," he finished, "and don't tell me what I can do and what I can't. I can take care of you, and I can take care of Inky's gun. Right now I'm going to bed."

He shut the bedroom door behind him, leaving it up to me and Glasses to guess that we were supposed to take out our blankets and sleep on the floor.

But we didn't want to go to sleep right away, if only because we were still thinking about Luke Dugan. So we got out a deck of cards and started a game of stud poker, speaking very low. Stud poker is like the ordinary kind, except that four of the five cards are dealt face up and one at a time.

You bet each time a card is dealt, and so considerable money is apt to change hands, even when you're playinng with a ten-cent limit, like we were. It's a pretty good game for taking money away from suckers, and Glasses and I used to play it by the hour when we had nothing better to do. But since we were both equally smart, neither one of us won consistently.

It was very quiet, except for Larsen's snoring and the rustling of the sea-grass and the occasional chink of a dime.

After about an hour, Glasses happened to look down at Inky's automatic lying on the other side of the table, and something about the way his body twisted around sudden made me look too. Right away I felt something was wrong, but I couldn't tell what; it gave me a funny feeling in the back of the neck. Then Glasses put out two thin fingers and turned the gun halfway around, and I realized what had been wrong—or what I thought had been wrong. When Larsen had put the gun down, I thought it had been pointing at the outside door; but when Glasses and I looked at it, it was pointing more in the direction of the bedroom door. When you have the fidgets your memory gets tricky.

A half-hour later we noticed the gun again pointing toward the bedroom door. This time Glasses spun it around quick, and I got the fidgets for fair. Glasses gave a low whistle and got up, and tried putting the gun on different parts of the table and jiggling the table to see if the gun would move.

"I see what happened now," he whispered finally. "When the gun is lying on its side, it sort of balances on its safety catch.

"Now this little table has got a wobble to it and when we are playing cards the wobble is persistent enough to edge the gun slowly around in a circle."

"I don't care about that," I whispered back. "I don't want to be shot in my sleep just because the table has a persistent wobble. I think the rumble of a train two miles away would be enough to set off that crazy hair-trigger. Give me it."

Glasses handed it over and, taking care always to point it at the floor, I unloaded it, put it back on the table, and put the bullets in my coat pocket. Then we tried to go on with our card game.

"My red bullet bets ten cents," I said, referring to my ace of hearts.

"My king raises you ten cents," responded Glasses.

But it was no use. Between Inky's automatic and Luke Dugan I couldn't concentrate on my cards.

"Do you remember, Glasses," I said, "the evening you said there was maybe something queer about Inky's gun?"

"I do a lot of talking, No Nose, and not much of it is worth remembering. We'd better stick to our cards. My pair of sevens bets a nickel."

I followed his advice, but didn't have much luck, and lost five or six dollars. By two o'clock we were both pretty tired and not feeling quite so jittery; so we got the blankets and wrapped up in them and tried to grab a little sleep. I listened to the sea-grass and the tooting of a locomotive about two miles away, and worried some over the possible activities of Luke Dugan, but finally dropped off.

It must have been about sunrise that the clicking noise woke me up. There was a faint, greenish light coming in through the shades. I lay still, not knowing exactly what I was listening for, but so on edge that it didn't occur to me how prickly hot I was from sleeping without sheets, or how itchy my face and hands were from mosquito bites. Then I heard it again, and it sounded like nothing but the sharp click the hammer of a gun makes when it snaps down on an empty chamber. Twice I heard it. It seemed to be coming from the inside of the room. I slid out of my blankets and rustled Glasses awake.

"It's that damned automatic of Inky's," I whispered shakily. "It's trying to shoot itself."

When a person wakes up sudden and before he should, he's apt to feel just like I did and say crazy things without thinking. Glasses looked at me for a moment, then he rubbed his eyes and smiled. I could hardly see the smile in the dim light, but I could feel it in his voice when he said, "No Nose, you are getting positively psychic."

"I tell you I'd swear to it," I insisted. "It was the click of the hammer of a gun."

Glasses yawned. "Next you will be telling me that the gun was Inky's familiar."

"Familiar what?" I asked him, scratching my head and beginning to get mad. There are times when Glasses' college professor stuff gets me down.

"No Nose," he continued, "have you ever heard of witches?"

I was walking around to the windows and glancing out from behind the blinds to make sure there was no one around. I didn't see anyone. For that matter, I didn't really expect to.

"What do you mean?" I said. "Sure I have. Why, I knew a guy, a Pennsylvania Dutchman, and he told me about witches putting what he called hexes on people. He said his uncle had a hex put on him and he died afterward. He was a traveling salesman —the Dutchman that told me, I mean."

Glasses nodded his head, and then went on, sleepy-like, from the floor, "Well, No Nose, the Devil used to give each witch a pet black cat or dog or maybe a toad to follow it around and protect it and revenge injuries. Those little creatures were called familiars—stooges sent out by the Big Boy to watch over his chosen, you might say. The witches used to talk to them in a language no one else could understand. Now this is what I'm getting at. Times change and styles change—and the style in familiars along with them. Inky's gun is black, isn't it? And he used to mutter at it in a language we couldn't understand, didn't he? And—"

"You're crazy," I told him, not wanting to be kidded.

"Why, No Nose," he said, "you were telling me yourself just now that you thought the gun had a life of its own; that it could cock itself and shoot itself without any human assistance. Weren't you?"

"You're crazy," I repeated, feeling like an awful fool and wishing I hadn't waked Glasses up. "See, the gun's here where I left it on the table, and the bullets are still in my pocket."

"Luckily," he said in a stagy voice he tried to make sound like an undertaker's. "Well, now that you've called me early, I shall wander off and avail us of our neighbor's newspaper. Meanwhile you may run my bath."

I waited until I was sure he was gone, because I didn't want him to make a fool of me again. Then I went over and examined the gun. First I looked for the trade mark or the name of the maker. I found a place which had been filed down, where it might have been once, but that was all. Before this I would have sworn I could have told the make, but now I couldn't. Not that in general it didn't look like an ordinary automatic; it was the details—the grip, the trigger guard, the safety catch—that were unfamiliar. I figured it was some foreign make I'd never happened to see before.

After I'd been handling it for about two minutes I began to notice something queer about the feel of the metal. As far as I could see it was just ordinary blued steel, but somehow it was too smooth and slick and made me want to keep stroking the barrel back and forth. I can't explain it any better; the metal just didn't seem *right* to me. Finally I realized the gun was getting on my nerves and making me imagine things; so I put it down on the mantel.

When Glasses got back, the sun was up and he wasn't smiling any more. He shoved a newspaper on my lap and pointed. It was open to page five. I read:

ANTON LARSEN SOUGHT
IN KOZACS KILLING

Police Believe
Ex-Bootlegger
Slain by Pal

I looked up to see Larsen standing in the bedroom door. He was in his pajama trousers and looked yellow and seedy, his eyelids puffed and his pig eyes staring at us.

"Good morning, boss," said Glasses slowly. "We just noticed in the paper that they are trying to do you a dirty trick. They're claiming you, not Dugan, had Inky shot."

Larsen grunted, came over and took the paper, looked at it quickly, grunted again, and went to the sink to splash some cold water on his face.

"So," he said, turning to us, "all the better we are here at the hideout."

That day was the longest and most nervous I've ever gone through. Somehow Larsen didn't seem to be completely waked up. If he'd been a stranger I'd have diagnosed it as a laudanum jag. He sat around in his pajama trousers, so that by noon he still looked as if he'd only that minute rolled out of bed. The worst thing was that he wouldn't talk or tell us anything about his plans. Of course he never did much talking, but this time there was a difference. His funny pig eyes began to give me the jim-jams; no matter how still he sat they were always moving—like a guy having a laudanum nightmare and about to run amuck.

Finally it started to get on Glasses' nerves, which surprised me, for Glasses usually knows how to take things quietly. He began by making little suggestions—that we should get a later paper, that we should call up a certain lawyer in New York, that I should get my cousin Jake to mosey around the police station at Bayport and see if anything was up, and so on. Each time Larsen shut him up quick.

Once I thought he was going to take a crack at Glasses. And Glasses, like a fool, kept on pestering. I could see a blow-up coming, plain as the absence of my nose. I couldn't figure what was making Glasses do it. I guess when the college professor type gets the jim-jams they get them worse than a dummy like me. They've got trained brains which they can't stop from pecking away at ideas, and that's a disadvantage.

As for me, I tried to keep hold of my nerves. I kept saying to myself, "Larsen is O.K. He's just a little on edge. We all are. Why, I've known him ten years. He's O.K." I only half realized I was saying those things because I was beginning to believe that Larsen wasn't O.K.

The blow-up came at about two o'clock. Larsen's eyes opened wide, as if he'd just remembered something, and he jumped up so quick that I started to look around for Luke Dugan's firing squad—or the police. But it wasn't either of those. Larsen had spotted the automatic on the mantel. Right away as he began fingering it, he noticed it was unloaded.

"Who monkeyed with this?" he asked in a very nasty, thick voice. "And why?"

Glasses couldn't keep quiet.

"I thought you might hurt yourself with it," he said.

Larsen walked over to him and slapped him on the side of the face, knocking him down. I took firm hold of the chair I had been sitting on, ready to use it like a club. Glasses twisted on the floor for a moment, until he got control of the pain. Then he looked up, tears beginning to drip out of his left eye where he had been hit. He had sense enough not to say anything, or to smile. Some fools would have smiled in such a situation, thinking it showed courage. It would have showed courage, I admit, but not good sense.

After about twenty seconds Larsen decided not to kick him in the face.

"Well, are you going to keep your mouth shut?" he asked.

Glasses nodded. I let go my grip on the chair.

"Where's the load?" asked Larsen.

I took the bullets out of my pocket and put them on the table, moving deliberately.

Larsen reloaded the gun. It made me sick to see his big hands sliding along the blue-black metal, because I remembered the feel of it.

"Nobody touches this but me, see?" he said.

And with that he walked into the bedroom and closed the door.

All I could think of was, "Glasses was right when he said that Larsen was crazy on the subject of Inky's automatic. And it's just the same as it was with Inky. He has to have the gun close to him. That's what was bothering him all morning, only he didn't know."

Then I kneeled down by Glasses, who was still lying on the floor, propped up on his elbows looking at the bedroom door. The mark of Larsen's hand was brick-red on the side of his face, with a little trickle of blood on the cheekbone, where the skin was broken.

I whispered, very low, just what I thought of Larsen. "Let's beat it first chance and get the police on him," I finished.

Glasses shook his head a little. He kept staring at the door, his left eye blinking spasmodically. Then he shivered, and gave a funny grunt deep down in his throat.

"I can't believe it," he said.

"He killed Inky," I whispered in his ear. "I'm almost sure of it. And he was within an inch of killing you."

"I don't mean that," said Glasses.

"What do you mean then?"

Glasses shook his head, as if he were trying to change the subject of his thoughts. "Something I saw," he said, "or, rather, something I realized."

"The gun?" I questioned. My lips were dry and it was hard for me to say the word.

He gave me a funny look and got up.

"We'd better both be sensible from now on," he said, and then added in a whisper. "We can't do anything now. Maybe we'll get a chance tonight."

After a long while Larsen called to me to heat some water so he could shave. I brought it to him, and by the time I was frying hash he came out and sat down at the table. He was all washed and shaved, and the straggling patches of hair around his bald head were brushed smooth. He was dressed and had his hat on. But in spite of everything he still had that yellow, seedy, laudanum-jag look. We ate our hash and beans and drank our beer, no one talking. It was dark now, and a tiny wind was making the blades of sea-grass whine.

Finally Larsen got up and walked around the table once and said, "Let's have a game of stud poker."

While I was clearing off the dishes he brought out his suitcase and planked it down on the side table. He took Inky's automatic out of his pocket and looked at it a second. Then he laid the automatic in the suitcase, and shut it up and strapped it tight.

"We're leaving after the game," he said.

I wasn't quite sure whether to feel relieved or not.

We played with a ten-cent limit, and right from the start Larsen began to win. It was a queer game, what with me feeling so jittery, and Glasses sitting there with the left side of his face all swollen, squinting through the right lens of his spectacles because the left lens had been cracked when Larsen hit him, and Larsen all dressed up as if he were sitting in a station waiting for a train. The shades were all down and the hanging light bulb, which was shaded with a foolscap of newspaper, threw a bright circle of light on the table, but left the rest of the room too dark to please me.

It was after Larsen had won about five dollars from each of us that I began hearing the noise. At first I couldn't be sure, because it was very low and because of the dry whining of the sea-grass, but right from the first it bothered me.

Larsen turned up a king and raked in another pot.

"You can't lose tonight," observed Glasses, smiling—and winced because the smile hurt his cheek.

Larsen scowled. He didn't seem pleased at his luck, or at Glasses' remark. His pig eyes were moving in the same way that had given us the jim-jams earlier in the day. And I kept thinking, "Maybe he killed Inky Kozacs. Glasses and me are just small fry to him. Maybe he's trying to figure out whether to kill us too. Or maybe he's got a use for us, and he's wondering how much to tell us. If he starts anything I'll shove the table over on him; that is, if I get the chance." He was beginning to look like a stranger to me, although I'd known him for ten years and he'd been my boss and paid me good money.

Then I heard the noise again, a little plainer this time. It was very peculiar and hard to describe—something like the noise a rat would make if it were tied up in a lot of blankets and trying to work its way out. I looked up and saw that the bruise on Glasses' left cheek stood out plainer.

"My black bullet bets ten cents," said Larsen, pushing a dime into the pot.

"I'm with you," I answered, shoving in two nickels. My voice sounded so dry and choked it startled me.

Glasses put in his money and dealt another card to each of us.

Then *I* felt my face going pale, for it seemed to me that the noise was coming from Larsen's suitcase, and I remembered that he had put Inky's automatic into the suitcase with its muzzle pointing *away* from us.

The noise was louder now. Glasses couldn't bear to sit still without saying anything. He pushed back his chair and started to whisper, "I think I hear—"

Then he saw the crazy, murderous look that came into Larsen's eyes, and he had sense enough to finish, "I think I hear the eleven o'clock train."

"Sit still," said Larsen, "very still. It's only ten forty-five. My ace bets another ten cents."

"I'll raise you," I croaked.

I wanted to jump up. I wanted to throw Larsen's suitcase out the door. I wanted to run out myself. Yet I sat tight. We all sat tight. We didn't dare make a move, for if we had, it would have shown that we believed the impossible was happening. And if a man does that he's crazy. I kept rubbing my tongue against my lips, without wetting them.

I stared at the cards, trying to shut out everything else. The hand was all dealt now. I had a jack and some little ones, and I knew my face-down card was a jack. Glasses had a king showing. Larsen's ace of clubs was the highest card on the board.

And still the sound kept coming. Something twisting, straining, heaving. A muffled sound.

"And I raise *you* ten cents," said Glasses loudly. I got the idea he did it just to make a noise, not because he thought his cards were especially good.

I turned to Larsen, trying to pretend I was interested in whether he would raise or stop betting. His eyes had stopped moving and were staring straight ahead at the suitcase. His mouth was twisted in a funny, set way. After a while his lips began to move. His voice was so low I could barely catch the words.

"Ten cents more. *I killed Inky, you know.* What does your jack say, No Nose?"

"It raises you," I said automatically.

His reply came in the same almost inaudible voice. "You haven't a chance of winning, No Nose. *He didn't bring the money with him, like he said he would. But I made him tell me where he hid it in his room. I can't pull the job myself; the cops would recognize me. But you two ought to be able to do it for me. That's why we're going to New York tonight.* I raise you ten cents more."

"I'll see you," I heard myself saying.

The noise stopped, not gradually but all of a sudden. Right away I wanted ten times worse to jump up and do something. But I was stuck to my chair.

Larsen turned up the ace of spades.

"Two aces. *Inky's little gun didn't protect him, you know. He didn't have a chance to use it.* Clubs and spades. Black bullets. I win."

Then it happened.

I don't need to tell you much about what we did afterward. We buried the body in the sea-grass. We cleaned everything up and drove the coupe a couple of miles inland before abandoning it. We carried the gun away with us and took it apart and hammered it out of shape and threw it into the bay part by part. We never found out anything more about Inky's money or tried to. The police never bothered us. We counted ourselves lucky that we had enough sense left to get away safely, after what happened.

For, with smoke and flame squirting through the little round holes, and the whole suitcase jerking and shaking with the recoils, eight slugs drummed out and almost cut Anton Larsen in two.

Smoke Ghost

Miss Millick wondered just what had happened to Mr. Wran. He kept making the strangest remarks when she took dictation. Just this morning he had quickly turned around and asked, "Have you ever seen a ghost, Miss Millick?" And she had tittered nervously and replied, "When I was a girl there was a thing in white that used to come out of the closet in the attic bedroom when I slept there, and moan. Of course it was just my imagination. I was frightened of lots of things." And he had said, "I don't mean that kind of ghost. I mean a ghost from the world today, with the soot of the factories on its face and the pounding of machinery in its soul. The kind that would haunt coal yards and slip around at night through deserted office buildings like this one. A real ghost. Not something out of books." And she hadn't known what to say.

He'd never been like this before. Of course he might be joking, but it didn't sound that way. Vaguely Miss Millick wondered whether he mightn't be seeking some sort of sympathy from her. Of course, Mr. Wran was married and had a little child, but that didn't prevent her from having daydreams. The daydreams were not very exciting, still they helped fill up her mind. But now he was asking her another of those unprecedented questions.

"Have you ever thought what a ghost of our times would look like, Miss Millick? Just picture it. A smoky composite face with the hungry anxiety of the unemployed, the neurotic restlessness of the person without purpose, the jerky tension of the high-pressure metropolitan worker, the uneasy resentment of the striker, the callous opportunism of the scab, the aggressive whine of the panhandler, the inhibited terror of the bombed civilian, and a thousand other twisted emotional patterns. Each one overlying and yet blending with the other, like a pile of semi-transparent masks?"

Miss Millick gave a little self-conscious shiver and said, "That would be terrible. What an awful thing to think of."

She peered furtively across the desk. She remembered having heard that there had been something impressively abnormal about Mr. Wran's childhood, but she couldn't recall what it was. If only she could do something—laugh at his mood or ask him what was really wrong. She shifted the extra pencils in her left hand and mechanically traced over some of the shorthand curlicues in her notebook.

"Yet, that's just what such a ghost or vitalized projection would look like, Miss Millick," he continued, smiling in a tight way. "It would grow out of the real world. It would reflect the tangled, sordid, vicious things. All the loose ends. And it would be very grimy. I don't think it would seem white or wispy, or favor graveyards. It wouldn't moan. But it would mutter unintelligibly, and twitch at your sleeve. Like a sick, surly ape. What would such a thing want from a person, Miss Millick? Sacrifice? Worship? Or just fear? What could you do to stop it from troubling you?"

Miss Millick giggled nervously. There was an expression beyond her powers of definition in Mr. Wran's ordinary, flat-cheeked, thirtyish face, silhouetted against the dusty window. He turned away and stared out into the gray downtown atmosphere that rolled in from the railroad yards and the mills. When he spoke again his voice sounded far away.

"Of course, being immaterial, it couldn't hurt you physically—at first. You'd have to be peculiarly sensitive to see it, or be aware of it at all. But it would begin to influence your actions. Make you do this. Stop you from doing that. Although only a projection, it would gradually get its hooks into the world of things as they are. Might even get control of suitably vacuous minds. Then it could hurt whomever it wanted."

Miss Millick squirmed and read back her shorthand, like the books said you should do when there was a pause. She became aware of the failing light and wished Mr. Wran would ask her to turn on the overhead. She felt scratchy, as if soot were sifting down on to her skin.

"It's a rotten world, Miss Millick," said Mr. Wran, talking at the window. "Fit for another morbid growth of superstition. It's time the ghosts, or whatever you call them, took over and began a rule of fear. They'd be no worse than men."

"But"—Miss Millick's diaphragm jerked, making her titter inanely—"of course, there aren't any such things as ghosts."

Mr. Wran turned around.

"Of course there aren't, Miss Millick," he said in a loud, patronizing voice, as if she had been doing the talking rather than he. "Science and common sense and psychiatry all go to prove it."

She hung her head and might even have blushed if she hadn't felt so all at sea. Her leg muscles twitched, making her stand up, although she hadn't intended to. She aimlessly rubbed her hand along the edge of the desk.

"Why, Mr. Wran, look what I got off your desk," she said, showing him a heavy smudge. There was a note of clumsily playful reproof in her voice. "No wonder the copy I bring you always gets so black. Somebody ought to talk to those scrubwomen. They're skimping on your room."

She wished he would make some normal joking reply. But instead he drew back and his face hardened.

"Well, to get back," he rapped out harshly, and began to dictate.

When she was gone, he jumped up, dabbed his finger experimentally at the smudged part of the desk, frowned worriedly at the almost inky smears. He jerked open a drawer, snatched out a rag, hastily swabbed off the desk, crumpled the rag into a ball and tossed it back. There were three or four other rags in the drawer, each impregnated with soot.

Then he went over to the window and peered out anxiously through the dusk, his eyes searching the panorama of roofs, fixing on each chimney and water tank.

"It's a neurosis. Must be. Compulsions. Hallucinations," he muttered to himself in a tired, distraught voice that would have made Miss Millick gasp. "It's that damned mental abnormality cropping up in a new form. Can't be any other explanation. But it's so damned real. Even the soot. Good thing I'm seeing the psychiatrist. I don't think I could force myself to get on the elevated tonight." His voice trailed off, he rubbed his eyes, and his memory automatically started to grind.

It had all begun on the elevated. There was a particular little sea of roofs he had grown into the habit of glancing at just as the packed car carrying him homeward lurched around a turn. A dingy, melancholy little world of tar-paper, tarred gravel, and smoky brick. Rusty tin chimneys with odd conical hats suggested abandoned listening posts. There was a washed-out advertisement of some ancient patent medicine on the nearest wall. Superficially it was like ten thousand other drab city roofs. But he always saw it around dusk, either in the smoky half-light, or tinged with red by the flat rays of a dirty sunset, or covered by ghostly windblown white sheets of rain-splash, or patched with blackish snow; and it seemed unusually bleak and suggestive; almost beautifully ugly though in no sense picturesque; dreary, but meaningful. Unconsciously it came to symbolize for Catesby Wran certain disagreeable aspects of the frustrated, frightened century in which he lived, the jangled century of hate and heavy industry and total wars. The quick daily glance into the half darkness became an integral part of his life. Oddly, he never saw it in the morning, for it was then his habit to sit on the other side of the car, his head buried in the paper.

One evening toward winter he noticed what seemed to be a shapeless black sack lying on the third roof from the tracks. He did not think about it. It merely registered as an addition to the well-known scene and his memory stored away the impression for further reference. Next evening, however, he decided he had been mistaken in one detail. The object was a roof nearer than he had thought. Its color and texture, and the grimy stains around it, suggested that it was filled with coal dust, which was hardly reasonable. Then, too, the following evening it seemed to have been blown against a rusty ventilator by the wind—which could hardly have happened if it were at all heavy. Perhaps it was filled with leaves. Catesby was surprised to find himself anticipating his next daily glance with a minor note of apprehension. There was something unwholesome in the posture of the thing that stuck in his mind—a bulge in the sacking that suggested a misshaped head peering around the ventilator. And his apprehension was justified, for that evening the thing was on the nearest roof, though on the farther side, looking as if it had just flopped down over the low brick parapet.

Next evening the sack was gone. Catesby was annoyed at the momentary feeling of relief that went through him, because the whole matter seemed too unimportant to warrant feelings of any sort. What difference did it make if his imagination had played tricks on him, and he'd fancied that the object was slowly crawling and hitching itself closer across the roofs? That was the way any normal imagination worked. He deliberately chose to disregard the fact that there were reasons for thinking his imagination was by no means a normal one. As he walked home from the elevated, however, he found himself wondering whether the sack was really gone. He seemed to recall a vague, smudgy trail leading across the gravel to the nearer side of the roof, which was masked by a parapet. For an instant an unpleasant picture formed in his mind—that of an inky, humped creature crouched behind the parapet, waiting.

The next time he felt the familiar grating lurch of the car, he caught himself trying not to look out. That angered him. He turned his head quickly. When he turned it back, his compact face was definitely pale. There had been only time for a fleeting rearward glance at the escaping roof. Had he actually seen in silhouette the upper part of a head of some sort peering over the parapet? Nonsense, he told himself. And even if he had seen something, there were a thousand explanations which did not involve the supernatural or even true hallucination. Tomorrow he would take a good look and clear up the whole matter. If necessary, he would visit the roof personally, though he hardly knew where to find it and disliked in any case the idea of pampering a silly fear.

He did not relish the walk home from the elevated that evening, and visions of the thing disturbed his dreams, and were in an out of his mind all next day at the office. It was then that he first began to relieve his nerves by making jokingly serious remarks

45

about the supernatural to Miss Millick, who seemed properly mystified. It was on the same day, too, that he became aware fo a growing antipathy to grime and soot. Everything he touched seemed gritty, and he found himself mopping and wiping at his desk like an old lady with a morbid fear of germs. He reasoned that there was no real change in his office, and that he'd just now become sensitive to the dirt that had always been there, but there was no denying an increasing nervousness. Long before the car reached the curve, he was straining his eyes though the murky twilight, determined to take in every detail.

Afterward he realized he must have given a muffled cry of some sort, for the man beside him looked at him curiously, and the woman ahead gave him an unfavorable stare. Conscious of his own pallor and uncontrollable trembling, he stared back at them hungrily, trying to regain the feeling of security he had completely lost. They were the usual reassuringly wooden-faced people everyone rides home with on the elevated. But suppose he had pointed out to one of them what he had seen—that sodden, distorted face of sacking and coal dust, that boneless paw which waved back and forth, unmistakably in his direction, as if reminding him of a future appointment—he involuntarily shut his eyes tight. His thoughts were racing ahead to tomorrow evening. He pictured this same windowed oblong of light and packed humanity surging around the curve— then an opaque monstrous form leaping out from the roof in a parabolic swoop—an unmentionable face pressed close against the window, smearing it with wet coal dust —huge paws fumbling sloppily at the glass—

Somehow he managed to turn off his wife's anxious inquiries. Next mornign he reached a decision and made an appointment for that evening with a psychiatrist a friend had told him about. It cost him a considerable effort, for Catesby had a well-grounded distaste for anything dealing with psychological abnormality. Visiting a psychiatrist meant raking up an episode in his past which he had never fully described even to his wife. Once he had made the decision, however, he felt considerably relieved. The psychiatrist, he told himself, would clear everything up. He could almost fancy him saying, "Merely a bad case of nerves. However, you must consult the oculist whose name I'm writing down for you, and you must take two of these pills in water every four hours," and so on. It was almost comforting, and made the coming revelation he would have to make seem less painful.

But as the smoky dusk rolled in, his nervousness had returned and he had let his joking mystification of Miss Millick run away with him until he had realized he wasn't frightening anyone but himself.

He would have to keep his imagination under better control, he told himself, as he continued to peer out restlessly at the massive, murky shapes of the downtown office buildings. Why, he had spent the whole afternoon building up a kind of neo-medieval cosmology of superstition. It wouldn't do. He realized then that he had been standing at the window much longer than he'd thought, for the glass panel in the door was dark and there was no noise coming from the outer office. Miss Millick and the rest must have gone home.

It was then he made the discovery that there would have been no special reason for dreading the swing around the curve that night. It was, as it happened, a horrible discovery. For, on the shadowed roof across the street and four stories below, he saw the thing huddle and roll across the gravel and, after one upward look of recognition, merge into the blackness beneath the water tank.

As he hurriedly collected his things and made for the elevator, fighting the panicky impulse to run, he began to think of hallucination and mild psychosis as very desirable conditions. For better or for worse, he pinned all his hopes on the psychiatrist.

*   *   *

"So you find youself growing nervous and . . . er . . . jumpy, as you put it," said Dr. Trevethick, smiling with dignified geniality. "Do you notice any more definite physical symptoms? Pain? Headache? Indigestion?"

Catesby shook his head and wet his lips. "I'm especially nervous while riding in the elevated," he murmured swiftly.

"I see. We'll discuss that more fully. But I'd like you first to tell me about something you mentioned earlier. You said there was something about your childhood that might predispose you to nervous ailments. As you know, the early years are critical ones in the development of an individual's behavior pattern."

Catesby studied the yellow reflections of frosted globes in the dark surface of the desk. The palm of his left hand aimlessly rubbed the thick nap of the armchair. After a while he raised his head and looked straight into the doctor's small brown eyes.

"From perhaps my third to my ninth year," he began, choosing the words with care, "I was what you might call a sensory prodigy."

The doctor's expression did not change. "Yes?" he inquired politely.

"What I mean is that I was supposed to be able to see through walls, read letters through envelopes and books through their covers, fence and play ping-pong blindfolded, find things that were buried, read thoughts." The words tumbled out.

"And could you?" The doctor's voice was toneless.

"I don't know. I don't suppose so," answered Catesby, long-lost emotions flooding back into his voice. "It's all confused now. I thought I could, but then they were always encouraging me. My mother . . . was . . . well . . . interested in psychic phenomena. I was . . . exhibited. I seem to remember seeing things other people couldn't. As if most opaque objects were transparent. But I was very young. I didn't have any scientific criteria for judgment."

He was reliving it now. The darkened rooms. The earnest assemblages of gawking, prying adults. Himself alone on a little platform, lost in a straight-backed wooden chair. The black silk handkerchief over his eyes. His mother's coaxing, insistent questions. The whispers. The gasps. His own hate of the whole business, mixed with hunger for the adulation of adults. Then the scientists from the university, the experiments, the big test. The reality of those memories engulfed him and momentarily made him forget the reason why he was disclosing them to a stranger.

"Do I understand that your mother tried to make use of you as a medium for communicating with the . . . er . . . other world?"

Catesby nodded eagerly.

"She tried to, but she couldn't. When it came to getting in touch with the dead, I was a complete failure. All I could do—or thought I could do—was see real, existing, three-dimensional objects beyond the vision of normal people. Objects anyone could have seen except for distance, obstruction, or darkness. It was always a disappointment to mother."

He could hear her sweetish, patient voice saying, "Try again, dear, just this once. Katie was your aunt. She loved you. Try to hear what she's saying." And he had answered, "I can see a woman in a blue dress standing on the other side of Dick's house." And she had replied, "Yes, I know, dear. But that's not Katie. Katie's a spirit. Try again. Just this once, dear." The doctor's voice gently jarred him back into the softly gleaming office.

47

"You mentioned scientific criteria for judgment, Mr. Wran. As far as you know, did anyone ever try to apply them to you?"

Catesby's nod was emphatic.

"They did. When I was eight, two young psychologists from the university got interested in me. I guess they did it for a joke at first, and I remember being very determined to show them I amounted to something. Even now I seem to recall how the note of polite superiority and amused sarcasm drained out of their voices. I suppose they decided at first that it was very clever trickery, but somehow they persuaded mother to let them try me out under controlled conditions. There were lots of tests that seemed very businesslike after mother's slipshod little exhibitions. They found I was clairvoyant —or so they thought. I got worked up and on edge. They were going to demonstrate my supernormal sensory powers to the university psychology faculty. For the first time I began to worry about whether I'd come through. Perhaps they kept me going at too hard a pace, I don't know. At any rate, when the test came, I couldn't do a thing. Everything became opaque. I got desperate and made things up out of my imagination. I lied. In the end I failed utterly, and I believe the two young psychologists got into a lot of hot water as a result."

He could hear the brusque, bearded man saying, "You've been taken in by a child, Flaxman, a mere child. I'm greatly disturbed. You've put yourself on the same plane as common charlatans. Gentlemen, I ask you to banish from your minds this whole sorry episode. It must never be referred to." He winced at the recollection of his feeling of guilt. But at the same time he was beginning to feel exhilarated and almost lighthearted. Unburdening his long-repressed memories had altered his whole viewpoint. The episodes on the elevated began to take on what seemed their proper proportions as merely the bizarre workings of overwrought nerves and an overly suggestible mind. The doctor, he anticipated confidently, would disentangle the obscure subconscious causes, whatever they might be. And the whole business would be finished off quickly, just as his childhood experience—which was beginning to seem a little ridiculous now— had been finished off.

"From that day on," he continued, "I never exhibited a trace of my supposed powers. My mother was frantic and tried to sue the university. I had something like a nervous breakdown. Then the divorce was granted, and my father got custody of me. He did his best to make me forget it. We went on long outdoor vacations and did a lot of athletics, associated with normal matter-of-fact people. I went to business college eventually. I'm in advertising now. But," Catesby paused, "now that I'm having nervous symptoms, I've wondered if there mightn't be a connection. It's not a question of whether I was really clairvoyant or not. Very likely my mother taught me a lot of unconscious deceptions, good enough to fool even young psychology instructors. But don't you think it may have some important bearing on my present condition?"

For several moments the doctor regarded him with a professional frown. Then he said quietly, "And is there some . . . er . . . more specific connection between your experiences then and now? Do you by any chance find that you are once again beginning to . . . er . . . see things?"

Catesby swallowed. He had felt an increasing eagerness to unburden himself of his fears, but it was not easy to make a beginning, and the doctor's shrewd question rattled him. He forced himself to concentrate. The thing he thought he had seen on the roof loomed up before his inner eye with unexpected vividness. Yet it did not frighten him. He groped for words.

Then he saw that the doctor was not looking at him but over his shoulder. Color was draining out of the doctor's face and his eyes did not seem so small. Then the doctor sprang to his feet, walked past Catesby, threw up the window and peered into the darkness.

As Catesby rose, the doctor slammed down the window and said in a voice whose smoothness was marred by a slight, persistent gasping, "I hope I haven't alarmed you. I saw the face of . . . er . . . a Negro prowler on the fire escape. I must have frightened him, for he seems to have gotten out of sight in a hurry. Don't give it another thought. Doctors are frequently bothered by *voyeurs* . . . er . . . Peeping Toms."

"A Negro?" asked Catesy, moistening his lips.

The doctor laughed nervously. "I imagine so, though my first odd impression was that it was a white man in blackface. You see, the color didn't seem to have any brown in it. It was dead-black."

Catesby moved toward the window. There were smudges on the glass. "It's quite all right, Mr. Wran." The doctor's voice had acquired a sharp note of impatience, as if he were trying hard to reassume his professional authority. "Let's continue our conversation. I was asking you if you were"—he made a face—"seeing things."

Catesby's whirling thoughts slowed down and locked into place. "No, I'm not seeing anything that other people don't see, too. And I think I'd better go now. I've been keeping you too long." He disregarded the doctor's half-hearted gesture of denial. "I'll phone you about the physical examination. In a way you've already taken a big load off my mind." He smiled woodenly. "Goodnight, Dr. Trevethick."

* * *

Catesby Wran's mental state was a peculiar one. His eyes searched every angular shadow, he glanced sideways down each chasm-like alley and barren basement passageway, and kept stealing looks at the irregular line of the roofs, yet he was hardly conscious of where he was going. He pushed away the thoughts that came into his mind, and kept moving. He became aware of a slight sense of security as he turned into a lighted street where there were people and high buildings and blinking signs. After a while he found himself in the dim lobby of the structure that housed his office. Then he realized why he couldn't go home, why he daren't go home—after what had happened at the office of Dr. Trevethick.

"Hello, Mr. Wran," said the night elevator man, a burly figure in overalls, sliding open the grille-work door to the old-fashioned cage. "I didn't know you were working nights now, too."

Catesby stepped in automatically. "Sudden rush of orders," he murmured inanely. "Some stuff that has to be gotten out."

The cage creaked to a stop at the top floor. "Be working very late, Mr. Wran?"

He nodded vaguely, watched the car slide out of sight, found his keys, swiftly crossed the outer office, and entered his own. His hand went to the light switch, but then the thought occurred to him that the two lighted windows, standing out against the dark bulk of the building, would indicated his whereabouts and serve as a goal toward which something could crawl and climb. He moved his chair so that the back was against the wall and sat down in the semidarkness. He did not remove his overcoat.

For a long time he sat there motionless, listening to his own breathing and the faraway sounds from the streets below: the thin metallic surge of the crosstown streetcar, the farther one of the elevated, faint lonely cries and honkings, indistinct rumblings.

Words he had spoken to Miss Millick in nervous jest came back to him with the bitter taste of truth. He found himself unable to reason critically or connectedly, but by their own volition thoughts rose up into his mind and gyrated slowly and rearranged themselves with the inevitable movement of planets.

Gradually his mental picture of the world was transformed. No longer a world of material atoms and empty space, but a world in which the bodiless existed and moved according to its own obscure laws or unpredictable impulses. The new picture illuminated with dreadful clarity certain general facts which had always bewildered and troubled him and from which he had tried to hide: the inevitability of hate and war, the diabolically timed mischances which wreck the best of human intentions, the walls of willful misunderstanding that divide one man from another, the eternal vitality of cruelty and ignorance and greed. They seemed appropriate now, necessary parts of the picture. And superstition only a kind of wisdom.

Then his thoughts returned to himself and the questin he had asked Miss Millick, "What would such a thing want from a person? Sacrifices? Worship, Or just fear? What could you do to stop it from troubling you?" It had become a practical question.

With an explosive jangle, the phone began to ring. "Cate, I've been trying everywhere to get you," said his wife. "I never thought you'd be at the office. What are you doing? I've been worried."

He said something about work.

"You'll be home right away?" came the faint anxious question. "I'm a little frightened. Ronny just had a scare. It woke him up. He kept pointing to the window saying, 'Black man, black man.' Of course it's something he dreamed. But I'm frightened. You will be home? What's that, dear? Can't you hear me?"

"I will. Right away," he said. Then he was out of the office, buzzing the night bell and peering down the shaft.

*   *   *

He saw it peering up the shaft at him from the deep shadows three floors below, the sacking face pressed against the iron grille-work. It started up the stair at a shockingly swift, shambling gait, vanishing temporarily from sight as it swung into the second corridor below.

Catesby clawed at the door to the office, realized he had not locked it, pushed it in, slammed and locked it behind him, retreated to the other side of the room, cowered between the filing cases and the wall. His teeth were clicking. He heard the groan of the rising cage. A silhouette darkened the frosted glass of the door, blotting out part of the grotesque reverse of the company name. After a little the door opened.

The big-globed overhead light flared on and, standing inside the door, her hand on the switch, was Miss Millick.

"Why, Mr. Wran," she stammered vacuously, "I didn't know you were here. I'd just come in to do some extra typing after the movie. I didn't . . . but the lights weren't on. What were you—"

He stared at her. He wanted to shout in relief, grab hold of her, talk rapidly. He realized he was grinning hysterically.

"Why, Mr. Wran, what's happened to you?" she asked embarrassedly, ending with a stupid titter. "Are you feeling sick? Isn't there something I can do for you?"

He shook his head jerkily and managed to say, "No, I'm just leaving. I was doing some extra work myself."

"But you *look* sick," she insisted, and walked over toward him. He inconsequentially realized she must have stepped in mud, for her high-heeled shoes left neat black prints.

"Yes, I'm sure you must be sick. You're so terribly pale." She sounded like an enthusiastic, incompetent nurse. Her face brightened with a sudden inspiration. "I've got something in my bag, that'll fix you up right away," she said. "It's for indigestion."

She fumbled at her stuffed oblong purse. He noticed that she was absent-mindedly holding it shut with one hand while she tried to open it with the other. Then, under his very eyes, he saw her bend back the thick prongs of metal locking the purse as if they were tinfoil, or as if her fingers had become a pair of steel pliers.

Instantly his memory recited the words he had spoken to Miss Millick that afternoon. "It couldn't hurt you physically—at first . . . gradually get its hooks into the world . . . might even get control of suitably vacuous minds. Then it could hurt whomever it wanted." A sickish, cold feelign grew inside him. He began to edge toward the door.

But Miss Millick hurried ahead of him.

"You don't have to wait, Fred," she called. "Mr. Wran's decided to stay a while longer."

The door to the cage shut with a mechanical rattle. The cage creaked. Then she turned around in the door.

"Why, Mr. Wran," she gurgled reproachfully, "I just couldn't think of letting you go home now. I'm sure you're terribly unwell. Why, you might collapse in the street. You've just got to stay here until you feel different."

The creaking died away. He stood in the center of the office, motionless. His eyes traced the coal-black course of Miss Millick's footprints to where she stood blocking the door. Then a sound that was almost a scream was wrenched out of him, for it seemed to him that the blackness was creeping up her legs under the thin stockings.

"Why, Mr. Wran," she said, "you're acting as if you were crazy. You must lie down for a while. Here, I'll help you off with your coat."

The nauseously idiotic and rasping note was the same; only it had been intensified. As she came toward him he turned and ran through the storeroom, clattered a key desperately at the lock of the second door to the corridor.

"Why, Mr. Wran," he heard her call, "are you having some kind of a fit? You must let me help you."

The door came open and he plunged out into the corridor and up the stairs immediately ahead. It was only when he reached the top that he realized the heavy steel door in front of him led to the roof. He jerked up the catch.

"Why, Mr. Wran, you mustn't run away. I'm coming after you."

Then he was out on the gritty gravel of the roof. The night sky was clouded and murky, with a faint pinkish glow from the neon signs. From the distant mills rose a ghostly spurt of flame. He ran to the edge. The street lights glared dizzily upward. Two men were tiny round blobs of hat and shoulders. He swung around.

The thing was in the doorway. The voice was no longer solicitous but moronically playful, each sentence ending in a titter.

"Why, Mr. Wran, why have you come up here? We're all alone. Just think, I might push you off."

The thing came slowly toward him. He moved backward until his heels touched the low parapet. Without knowing why, or what he was going to do, he dropped to his knees. He dared not to look at the face as it came nearer, a focus for the worst in the world, a gathering point for poisons from everywhere. Then the lucidity of terror took possession of his mind, and words formed on his lips.

"I will obey you. You are my god," he said. "You have supreme power over man and his animals and his machines. You rule this city and all others. I recognize that."

Again the titter, closer. "Why, Mr. Wran, you never talked like this before. Do you mean it?"

"The world is yours to do with as you will, save or tear to pieces," he answered fawningly, the words automatically fitting themselves together in vaguely liturgical patterns. "I recognize that. I will praise, I will sacrifice. In smoke and soot I will worship you for ever."

The voice did not answer. He looked up. There was only Miss Millick, deathly pale and swaying drunkenly. Her eyes were closed. He caught her as she wobbled toward him. His knees gave way under the added weight and they sank down together on the edge of the roof.

After a while she began to twitch. Small noises came from her throat and her eyelids edged open.

"Come on, we'll go downstairs," he murmured jerkily, trying to draw her up. "You're feeling bad."

"I'm terribly dizzy," she whispered. "I must have fainted, I didn't eat enough. And then I'm so nervous lately, about the war and everything, I guess. Why, we're on the roof! Did you bring me up here to get some air? Or did I come up without knowing it? I'm awfully foolish. I used to walk in my sleep, my mother said."

As he helped her down the stairs, she turned and looked at him. "Why, Mr. Wran," she said, faintly, "you've got a big black smudge on your forehead. Here, let me get it off for you." Weakly she rubbed at it with her handkerchief. She started to sway again and he steadied her.

"No, I'll be all right," she said. "Only I feel cold. What happened, Mr. Wran? Did I have some sort of fainting spell?"

He told her it was something like that.

Later, riding home in the empty elevated car, he wondered how long he would be safe from the thing. It was a purely practical problem. He had no way of knowing, but instinct told him he had satisfied the brute for some time. Would it want more when it came again? Time enough to answer that question when it arose. It might be hard, he realized, to keep out of an insane asylum. With Helen and Ronny to protect, as well as himself, he would have to be careful and tight-lipped. He began to speculate as to how many other men and women had seen the thing or things like it.

The elevated slowed and lurched in a familiar fashion. He looked at the roofs near the curve. They seemed very ordinary, as if what made them impressive had gone away for a while.

The Hound

David Lashley huddled the skimpy blankets around him and dully watched the cold light of morning seep through the window and stiffen in his room. He could not recall the exact nature of the terror against which he had fought his way to wakefulness, except that it had been in some way gigantic and had brought back to him the fear-ridden helplessness of childhood. It had lurked near him all night and finally it had crouched over him and thrust down toward his face.

The radiator whined dismally with the first push of steam from the basement, and he shivered in response. He thought that his shivering was an ironically humorous recognition of the fact that his room was never warm except when he was out of it. But there was more to it than that. The penetrating whine had touched something in his mind without being quite able to dislodge it into consciousness. The mounting rumble of city traffic, together with the hoarse panting of a locomotive in the railroad yards, mingled themselves with the nearer sound, intensifying its disturbing tug at hidden fears. For a few moments he lay inert, listening. There was an unpleasant stench too in the room, he noticed, but that was nothing to be surprised at. He had experienced more than once the strange olfactory illusions that are part of the aftermath of flu. Then he heard his mother moving around laboriously in the kitchen, and that stung him into action.

"Have you another cold?" she asked, watching him anxiously as he hurriedly spooned in a boiled egg before its heat should be entirely lost in the chilly plate. "Are you sure?" she persisted. "I heard someone sniffling all night."

"Perhaps Father—" he began. She shook her head. "No, he's all right. His side was giving him a lot of pain yesterday evening, but he slept quietly enough. That's why I thought it must be you, David. I got up twice to see, but"—her voice became a little doleful—"I know you don't like me to come poking into your room at all hours."

"That's not true!" He contradicted. She looked so frail and little and worn, standing there in front of the stove with one of Father's shapeless bathrobes hugged around her, so like a sick sparrow trying to appear chipper, that a futile irritation, an indignation that he couldn't help her more, welled up within him, choking his voice a little. "It's that I don't want you getting up all the time and missing your sleep. You have enough to do taking care of Father all day long. And I've told you a dozen times that you mustn't make breakfast for me. You know the doctor says you need all the rest you can get."

"Oh, *I'm* all right," she answered quickly, "but I was sure you'd caught another cold. All night long I kept hearing it—a sniffling and a snuffling—"

Coffee spilled over into the saucer as David set down the half-raised cup. His mother's words had reawakened the elusive memory, and now that it had come back he did not want to look it in the face.

"It's late, I'll have to rush," he said.

She accompanied him to the door, so accustomed to his hastiness that she saw in it nothing unusual. Her wan voice followed him down the dark apartment stair: "I hope a rat hasn't died in the walls. Did you notice the nasty smell?"

And then he was out of the door and had lost himself and his memories in the early morning rush of the city. Tires singing on asphalt. Cold engines coughing, then starting with a roar. Heels clicking on the sidewalk, hurrying, trotting, converging on street car intersections and elevated stations. Low heels, high heels, heels of stenographers bound downtown, and of war workers headed for the outlying factories. Shouts of newsboys and glimpses of headlines: "AIR BLITZ ON . . . BATTLESHIP SUNK . . . BLACKOUT EXPECTED HERE . . . DRIVEN BACK."

But sitting in the stuffy solemnity of the street car, it was impossible to keep from thinking of it any longer. Besides, the stale medicinal smell of the yellow woodwork immediately brought back the memory of that other smell. David Lashley clenched his hands in his overcoat pockets and asked himself how it was possible for a grown man to be so suddenly overwhelmed by a fear from childhood. Yet in the same instant he knew with acute certainty that this was no childhood fear, this thing that had pursued him up the years, growing ever more vast and menacing, until, like the demon wolf Fenris at Ragnarok, its gaping jaws scraped heaven and earth, seeking to open wider. This thing that had dogged his footsteps, sometimes so far behind that he forget its existence, but now so close that he could feel its cold sick breath on his neck. Werewolves? He had read up on such things at the library, fingering dusty books in uneasy fascination, but what he had read made them seem innocuous and without significance—dead super-stitions—in comparison with this thing that was part and parcel of the great sprawling cities and chaotic peoples of the Twentieth Century, so much a part that he, David Lashley, winced at the endlessly varying howls and growls of traffic and industry—sounds at once animal and mechanical; shrank back with a start from the sight of head-lights at night—those dazzling unwinking eyes; trembled uncontrollably if he heard the scuffling of rats in an alley or caught sight in the evenings of the shadowy forms of lean mongrel dogs looking for food in vacant lots. "Sniffling and snuffling," his mother had said. What better words could you want to describe the inquisitive, persistent pryings of the beast that had crouched outside the bedroom door all night in his dreams and then finally pushed through to plant its dirty paws on his chest. For a moment he saw, superimposed on the yellow ceiling and garish advertising placards of the streetcar, its malformed muzzle . . . the red eyes like thickly scrummed molten metal . . . the jaws slavered with thick black oil . . .

Wildly he looked around at his fellow passengers, seeking to blot out that vision, but it seemed to have slipped down into all of them, infecting them, giving their features an ugly canine cast—the slack, receding jaw of an otherwise pretty blond, the narrow head and wide-set eyes of an unshaven mechanic returning from the night shift. He sought refuge in the open newspaper of the man sitting beside him, studying it intently without regard for the impression of rudeness he was creating. But there was a wolf in the cartoon and he quickly turned away to stare through the dusty pane at the stores sliding by. Gradually the sense of oppressive menace lifted a little. But the cartoon had established another contact in his brain—the memory of a cartoon from the First World War. What the wolf or hound in that earlier cartoon had represented—

war, famine, or the ruthlessness of the enemy—he could not say, but it had haunted his dreams for weeks, crouched in corners, and waited for him at the head of the stairs. Later he had tried to explain to friends the horrors that may lie in the concrete symbolisms and personifications of a cartoon if interpreted naively by a child, but had been unable to get his idea across.

The conductor growled out the name of a downtown street, and once again he lost himself in the crowd, finding relief in the never-ceasing movement, the brushing of shoulders against his own. But as the time-clock emitted its delayed musical bong! and he turned to stick his card in the rack, the girl at the desk looked up and remarked, "Aren't you going to punch in for your dog, too?"

"My dog?"

"Well, it was there just a second ago. Came in right behind you, looking as if it owned you—I mean you owned it." She giggled briefly through her nose. "One of Mrs. Montmorency's mastiffs came to inspect conditions among the working class, I presume."

He continued to stare at her blankly. "A joke," she explained patiently, and returned to her work.

"I've got to get a grip on myself," he found himself muttering tritely as the elevator lowered him noiselessly to the basement.

He kept repeating it as he hurried to the locker room, left his coat and lunch, gave his hair a quick careful brushing, hurried again through the still-empty aisles, and slipped in behind the socks-and-handkerchiefs counter. "It's just nerves. I'm not crazy. But I've got to get a grip on myself."

"Of course you're crazy. Don't you know that talking to yourself and not noticing anybody is the first symptom of insanity?"

Gertrude Rees had stopped on her way over to neckties. Light brown hair, painstakingly waved and ordered, framed a serious not-too-pretty face.

"Sorry," he murmured. "I'm jittery." What else could you say? Even to Gertrude.

She grimaced sympathetically. Her hand slipped across the counter to squeeze his for a moment.

But even as he watched her walk away, his hands automatically setting out the display boxes, the new question was furiously hammering in his brain. What else could you say? What words could you use to explain it? Above all, to whom could you tell it? A dozen names printed themselves in his mind and were as quickly discarded.

One remained. Tom Goodsell. He would tell Tom. Tonight, after the first-aid class.

Shoppers were already filtering into the basement. "He wears size eleven, Madam? Yes, we have some new patterns. These are silk and lisle." But their ever-increasing numbers gave him no sense of security. Crowding the aisles, they became shapes behind which something might hide. He was continually peering past them. A little child who wandered behind the counter and pushed at his knee, gave him a sudden fright.

Lunch came early for him. He arrived at the locker room in time to catch hold of Gertrude Rees as she retreated uncertainly from the dark doorway.

"Dog," she gasped. "Huge one. Gave me an awful start. Talk about jitters! Wonder where he could have come from? Watch out. He looked nasty."

But David, impelled by sudden recklessness born of fear and shock, was already inside and switching on the light.

"No dog in sight," he told her.

"You're crazy. It must be there." Her face, gingerly poked through the doorway, lengthened in surprise. "But I tell you I—Oh, I guess it must have pushed out through the other door."

He did not tell her that the other door was bolted.

"I suppose a customer brought it in," she rattled on nervously. "Some of them can't seem to shop unless they've got a pair of Russian wolfhounds. Though that kind usually keeps out of the bargain basement. I suppose we ought to find it before we eat lunch. It looked dangerous."

But he hardly heard her. He had just noticed that his locker was open and his over-coat dragged down on the floor. The brown paper bag containing his lunch had been torn open and the contents rummaged through, as if an animal had been nosing at it. As he stooped, he saw that there were greasy, black stains on the sandwiches, and a familiar stale stench rose to his nostrils.

That night he found Tom Goodsell in a nervous, expansive mood. The latter had been called up and would start for camp in a week. As they sipped coffee in the empty little restaurant, Tom poured out a flood of talk about old times. David would have been able to listen better, had not the uncertain, shadowy shapes outside the window been continually distracting his attention. Eventually he found an opportunity to turn the conversation down the channels which absorbed his mind.

"The supernatural beings of a modern city?" Tom answered, seeming to find nothing out of the way in the question. "Sure, they'd be different from the ghosts of yesterday. Each culture creates its own ghosts. Look, the Middle Ages build cathedrals, and pretty soon there were little gray shapes gliding around at night to talk with the gargoyles. Same thing ought to happen to us, with our skyscrapers and factories." He spoke eagerly, with all his old poetic flare, as if he'd just been meaning to discuss this very matter. He would talk about anything tonight. "I'll tell you how it works, Dave. We begin by denying all the old haunts and superstitions. Why shouldn't we? They belong to the era of cottage and castle. They can't take root in the new environment. Science goes materialistic, proving that there isn't anything in the universe except tiny bundles of energy. As if, for that matter, a tiny bundle of energy mightn't mean anything.

"But wait, that's just the beginning. We go on inventing and discovering and organizing. We cover the earth with huge structures. We pile them together in great heaps that make old Rome and Alexandria and Babylon seem almost toy-towns by com-parison. The new environment, you see, is forming."

David stared at him with incredulous fascination, profoundly disturbed. This was not at all what he had expected or hoped for—this almost telepathic prying into his most hidden fears. He had wanted to talk about these things—yes—but in a skeptical reassuring way. Instead, Tom sounded almost serious. David started to speak, but Tom held up his finger for silence, aping the gesture of a schoolteacher.

"Meanwhile, what's happening inside each one of us? I'll tell you. All sorts of inhibited emotions are accumulating. Fear is accumulating. Horror is accumulating. A new kind of awe of the mysteries of the universe is accumulating. A psychological environment is forming, along with the physical one. Wait, let me finish. Our culture becomes ripe for infection. From somewhere. It's just like a bacteriologist's culture—I didn't intend the pun—when it gets to the right temperature and consistency for supporting a colony of germs. Similarly, our culture suddenly spawns a horde of demons. And, like germs, they have a peculiar affinity for our culture. They're unique. They fit in. You wouldn't find the same kind any other time or place.

"How would you know when the infection had taken place? Say, you're taking this pretty seriously, aren't you? Well, so am I, maybe. Why, they'd haunt us, terrorize us, try to rule us. Our fears would be their fodder. A parasite-host relationship. Supernatural symbiosis. Some of us—the sensitive ones—would notice them sooner than others. Some of us might see them without knowing what they were. Others might know about them without seeing them. Like me, eh?

"What was that? I didn't catch your remark. Oh, about werewolves. Well, that's a pretty special question, but tonight I'd take a crack at anything. Yes, I think there'd be werewolves among our demons, but they wouldn't be much like the old ones. No nice clean fur, white teeth and shining eyes. Oh, no. Instead you'd get some nasty hound that wouldn't surprise you if you saw it nosing at a garbage pail or crawling out from under a truck. Frighten and terrorize you, yes. But surprise, no. It would fit into the environment. Look as if it belonged in a city and smell the same. Because of the twisted emotions that would be its food, your emotions and mine. A matter of diet."

Tom Goodsell chuckled loudly and lit another cigarette. But David only stared at the scarred counter. He realized he couldn't tell Tom what had happened this morning —or this noon. Of course, Tom would immediately scoff and be skeptical. But that wouldn't get around the fact that Tom had already agreed—agreed in partial jest perhaps, but still agreed. And Tom himself confirmed this, when, in a more serious, friendlier voice, he said:

"Oh, I know I've talked a lot of rot tonight, but still, you know, the way things are, there's something to it. At least, I can't express my feelings any other way."

They shook hands at the corner, and David rode the surging street car home through a city whose every bolt and stone seemed subtly infected, whose every noise carried shuddering overtones. His mother was waiting up for him, and after he had wearily argued with her about getting more rest and seen her off to bed, he lay sleepless himself, all through the night, like a child in a strange house, listening to each tiny noise and watching intently each changing shape taken by the shadows.

That night nothing shouldered through the door or pressed its muzzle against the window pane.

Yet he found that it cost him an effort to go down to the department store next morning, so conscious was he of the thing's presence in the faces and forms, the structures and machines around him. It was as if he were forcing himself into the heart of a monster. Destation of the city grew within him. As yesterday, the crowded aisles seemed only hiding places, and he avoided the locker room. Gertrude Rees remarked sympathetically on his fatigued look, and he took the opportunity to invite her out that evening. Of course, he told himself while they sat watching the movie, she wasn't very close to him. None of the girls had been close to him—a not-very-competent young man tied down to the task of supporting parents whose little reserve of money had long ago dribbled away. He had dated them for a while, talked to them, told them his beliefs and ambitions, and then one by one they had drifted off to marry other men. But that did not change the fact that he needed the wholesomeness Gertrude could give him.

And as they walked home through the chilly night, he found himself talking inconsequentially and laughing at his own jokes. Then, as they turned to one another in the shadowy vestibule and she lifted her lips, he sensed her features altering queerly, lengthening. "A funny sort of light here," he thought as he took her in his arms. But the thin strip of fur on her collar grew matted and oily under his touch, her fingers grew hard and sharp against his back, he felt her teeth pushing out against her lips, and then a sharp, prickling sensation as of icy needles.

Blindly he pushed away from her, then saw—and the sight stopped him dead—that she had not changed at all or that whatever change had been was now gone.

"What's the matter, dear?" he heard her ask startledly. "What's happened? What's that you're mumbling? Changed, you say? What's changed? Infected with it? What do you mean? For heaven's sake, don't talk that way. You've done it to me, you say? Done what?" He felt her hand on his arm, a soft hand now. "No, you're not crazy. Don't think of such things. But you're neurotic and maybe a little batty. For heaven's sake, pull yourself together."

"I don't know what happened to me," he managed to say, in his right voice again. Then, because he had to say something more: "My nerves all jumped, like someone had snapped them."

He expected her to be angry, but she seemed only puzzledly sympathetic, as if she liked him but had become afraid of him, as if she sensed something wrong in him beyond her powers of understanding or repair.

"Do take care of yourself," she said doubtfully. "We're all a little crazy now and then, I guess. My nerves get like wires too. Goodnight."

He watched her disappear up the stair. Then he turned and ran.

At home his mother was waiting up again, close to the hall radiator to catch its dying warmth, the inevitable shapeless bathrobe wrapped about her. Because of a new thought that had come to the forefront of his brain, he avoided her embrace and, after a few brief words, hurried off toward his room. But she followed him down the hall.

"You're not looking at all well, David," she told him anxiously, whispering because Father might be asleep. "Are you sure you're not getting flu again? Don't you think you should see the doctor tomorrow?" Then she went on quickly to another subject, using that nervously apologetic tone with which he was so familiar. "I shouldn't bother you with it, David, but you really must be more careful of the bedclothes. You'd laid something greasy on the coverlet and there were big, black stains."

He was pushing open the bedroom door. Her words halted his hand only for an instant. How could you avoid the thing by going one place rather than another?

"And one more thing," she added, as he switched on the lights. "Will you try to get some cardboard tomorrow to black out the windows? They're out of it at the stores around here and the radio says we should be ready."

"Yes, I will. Goodnight, Mother."

"Oh, and something else," she persisted, lingering uneasily just beyond the door. "That really must be a dead rat in the walls. The smell keeps coming in waves. I spoke to the real-estate agent, but he hasn't done anything about it. I wish you'd speak to him."

"Yes. Goodnight, Mother."

He waited until he heard her door softly close. He lit a cigarette and slumped down on the bed to try and think as clearly as he could about something to which everyday ideas could not be applied.

Question One (and he realized with an ironic twinge that it sounded melodramatic enough for a dime-novel): Was Gertrude Rees what might be called, for want of a better term, a werewolf? Answer: Almost certainly not, in any ordinary sense of the word. What had momentarily come to her had been something he had communicated to her. It had happened because of his presence. And either his own shock had interrupted the transformation or else Gertrude Rees had not proved a suitable vehicle of incarnation for the thing.

Question Two: Might he not communicate the thing to some other person? Answer: Yes. For a moment his thinking paused, as there swept before his mind's eye kaleidoscopic visions of the faces which might, without warning, begin to change in his presence: His mother, his father, Tom Goodsell, the prim-mouthed real estate agent, a customer at the store, a panhandler who would approach him on a rainy night.

Question Three: Was there any escape from the thing? Answer: No. And yet—there was one bare possibility. Escape from the city. The city had bred the thing; might it not be chained to the city? It hardly seemed to be a reasonable possibility; how could a supernatural entity be tied down to one locality? And yet—he stepped quickly to the window and, after a moment's hesitation, jerked it up. Sounds which had been temporarily blotted out by his thinking now poured past him in quadrupled volume, mixing together discordantly like instruments tuning up for some titanic symphony—the racking surge of street car and elevated, the coughing of a locomotive in the yards, the hum of tires on asphalt and the growl of engines, the mumbling of radio voices, the faint mournful note of distant horns. But now they were no longer separate sounds. They all issued from one cavernous throat—a single moan, infinitely penetrating, infinitely menacing. He slammed down the window and put his hands to his ears. He switched out the lights and threw himself on the bed, burying his head in the pillows. Still the sound came through. And it was then he realized that ultimately, whether he wanted it to or not, the thing would drive him from the city. The moment would come when the sound would begin to penetrate too deeply, to reverberate too unendurably in his ears.

The sight of so many faces, trembling on the brink of an almost unimaginable change, would become too much for him. And he would leave whatever he was doing and go away.

That moment came a little after four o'clock next afternoon. He could not say what sensation it was that, adding its straw-weight to the rest, drove him to take the step. Perhaps it was a heaving movement in the rack of dresses two counters away; perhaps it was the snoutlike appearance momentarily taken by a crumpled piece of cloth. Whatever it was, he slipped from behind the counter without a word, leaving a customer to mutter indignantly, and walked up the stairs and out into the street, moving almost like a sleep-walker yet constantly edging from side to side to avoid any direct contact with the crowd engulfing him. Once in the street, he took the first car that came by, never noting its number, and found himself an empty place in the corner of the front platform.

With ominous slowness at first, then with increasing rapidity the heart of the city was left behind. A great gloomy bridge spanning an oily river was passed over, and the frowning cliffs of the buildings grew lower. Warehouses gave way to factories, factories to apartment buildings, apartment buildings to dwellings which were at first small and dirty white, then large and mansion-like but very much decayed, then new and monotonous in their uniformity. Peoples of different economic status and racial affiliation filed in and emptied out as the different strata of the city were passed through. Finally the vacant lots began to come, at first one by one, then in increasing numbers, until the houses were spaced out two or three to a block.

"End of the line," sang out the conductor, and without hesitation David swung down from the platform and walked on in the same direction that the steet car had been going. He did not hurry. He did not lag. He moved as an automaton that had been wound up and set going, and will not stop until it runs down.

The sun was setting smokingly red in the west. He could not see it because of a tree-fringed rise ahead, but its last rays winked at him from the window panes of little houses blocks off to the right and left, as if flaming lights had been lit inside. As he moved they flashed on and off like signals. Two blocks further on the sidewalk ended, and he walked down the center of a muddy lane. After passing a final house, the lane also came to an end, giving way to a narrow dirt path between high weeds. The path led up the rise and through the fringe of trees. Emerging on the other side, he slowed his pace and finally stopped, so bewilderingly fantastic was the scene spread out before him. The sun had set, but high cloud-banks reflected its light, giving a spectral glow to the landscape.

Immediately before him stretched the equivalent of two or three empty blocks, but beyond that began a strange realm that seemed to have been plucked from another climate and another geological system and set down here outside the city. There were strange trees and shrubs, but, most striking of all, great uneven blocks of reddish stone which rose from the earth at unequal intervals and culminated in a massive central eminence fifty or sixty feet high.

As he gazed, the light drained from the landscape, as if a cloak had been flipped over the earth, and in the sudden twilight there rose from somewhere in the region ahead a faint howling, mournful and sinister, but in no way allied to the other howling that had haunted him day and night. Once again he moved forward, but now impulsively toward the source of the new sound.

A small gate in a high wire fence pushed open, giving him access to the realm of rocks. He found himself following a gravel path between thick shrubs and trees. At first it seemed quite dark, in contrast to the open land behind him. And with every step he took, the hollow howling grew closer. Finally the path turned abruptly around a shoulder of rock, and he found himself at the sound's source.

A ditch of rough stone about eight feet wide and of similar depth separated him from a space overgrown with short, brownish vegetation and closely surrounded on the other three sides by precipitous, rocky walls in which were the dark mouths of two or three caves. In the center of the open space were gathered a half dozen white-furred canine figures, their muzzles pointing toward the sky, giving voice to the mournful cry that had drawn him here.

It was only when he felt the low iron fence against his knees and made out the neat little sign reading, ARCTIC WOLVES, that he realized where he must be—in the famous zoological gardens which he had heard about but never visited, where the animals were kept in as nearly natural conditions as was feasible. Looking around, he noted the outlines of two or three low inconspicuous buildings, and some distance away he could see the form of a uniformed guard silhouetted against a patch of dark sky. Evidently he had come in after hours and through an auxiliary gate that should have been locked.

Swinging around again, he stared with casual curiosity at the wolves. The turn of events had the effect of making him feel stupid and bewildered, and for a long time he pondered dully as to why he should find these animals unalarming and even attractive.

Perhaps it was because they were so much a part of the wild, so little of the city. That great brute there, for instance, the biggest of the lot, who had come forward to the edge of the ditch to stare back at him. He seemed an incarnation of primitive strength. His fur so creamy white—well, perhaps not so white; it seemed darker than he had thought at first, streaked with black—or was that due to the fading light? But at least his eyes were clear and clean, shining faintly like jewels in the gathering dark. But no, they weren't clean; their reddish gleam was thickening, scumming over, until they looked more like two tiny peepholes in the walls of a choked furnace. And why hadn't he noticed before that the creature was obviously malformed? And why should the other wolves draw away from it and snarl as if afraid?

60

Then the brute licked its black tongue across its greasy jowls, and from its throat came a faint familiar growl that had in it nothing of the wild, and David Lashley knew that before him crouched the monster of his dreams, finally made flesh and blood.

With a choked scream he turned and fled blindly down the gravel path that led between thick shrubs to the little gate, fled in panic across empty blocks, stumbling over the uneven ground and twice falling. When he reached the fringe of trees he looked back, to see a low, lurching form emerge from the gate. Even at this distance he could tell that the eyes were those of no animal.

It was dark in the trees, and dark in the lane beyond. Ahead the street lamps glowed, and there were lights in the houses. A pang of helpless terror gripped him when he saw there was no street car waiting, until he realized—and the realization was like the onset of insanity—that nothing whatever in the city promised him refuge. This—everything that lay ahead—was the thing's hunting ground. It was driving him in toward its lair for the kill.

Then he ran, ran with the hopeless terror of a victim in the arena, of a rabbit loosed before greyhounds, ran until his sides were walls of pain and his grasping throat seemed aflame, and then still ran. Over mud, dirt and brick, and then onto the endless sidewalks. Past the neat suburban dwellings which in their uniformity seemed like monoliths lining some avenue of Egypt. The streets were almost empty, and those few people he passed stared at him as at a madman.

Brighter lights came into view, a corner with two or three stores. There he paused to look back. For a moment he saw nothing. Then it emerged from the shadows a block behind him, loping unevenly with long strides that carried it forward with a rush, its matted fur shining oilily under a street lamp. With a croaking sob he turned and ran on.

The thing's howling seemed suddenly to increase a thousandfold, becoming a pulsating wail, a screaming ululation that seemed to blanket the whole city with sound. And as that demoniac screeching continued, the lights in the houses began to go out one by one. Then the streetlights vanished in a rush, and an approaching street car was blotted out, and he knew that the sound did not come altogether or directly from the thing. This was the long-predicted blackout.

He ran on with arms outstretched, feeling rather than seeing the intersections as he approached them, misjudging his step at curbs, tripping and falling flat, picking himself up to stagger on half-stunned. His diaphragm contracted to a knot of pain that tied itself tighter and tighter. Breath rasped like a file in his throat. There seemed no light in the whole world, for the clouds had gathered thicker and thicker ever since sunset. No light, except those twin points of dirty red in the blackness behind.

A solid edge of darkness struck him down, inflicting pain on his shoulder and side. He scrambled up. Then a second solid obstacle in his path smashed him full in the face and chest. This time he did not rise. Dazed, tortured by exhaustion, motionless, he waited its approach.

First a padding of footsteps, with the faint scraping of claws on cement. Then a snuffling. Then a sickening stench. Then a glimpse of red eyes. And then the thing was upon him, its weight pinning him down, its jaws thrusting at his throat. Instinctively his head went up, and his forearm was clamped by teeth whose icy sharpness stung through the layers of cloth, while a foul oily fluid splattered his face.

At that moment light flooded them, and he was aware of a malformed muzzle retreating into the blackness, and of weight lifted from him. Then silence and cessation of movement. Nothing, nothing at all—except the light flooding down. As consciousness and sanity teetered in his brain, his eyes found the source of light, a glaring white disk only a few feet away. A flashlight, but nothing visible in the blackness behind it. For what seemed an eternity, there was no change in the situation—himself supine and exposed upon the ground in the unwavering circle of light.

Then a voice from the darkness, the voice of a man paralyzed by supernatural fear. "God, God, God," over and over again. Each word dragged out with prodigious effort.

An unfamiliar sensation stirred in David, a feeling almost of security and relief.

"You—saw it then?" he heard issue from his own dry throat. "The hound? the—wolf?"

"Hound? Wolf?" The voice from behind the flashlight was hideously shaken. "It was nothing like that. It was—" Then the voice broke, became earthly once more. "Good grief, man, we must get you inside."

Sanity

"Come in, Phy, and make yourself comfortable."

The mellow voice—and the suddenly dilating doorway—caught the general secretary of the World playing with a blob of greenish gasoid, squeezing it in his fist and watching it ooze between his fingers in spatulate tendrils that did not dissipate. Slowly, crookedly, he turned his head. World Manager Carrsbury became aware of a gaze that was at once oafish, sly, vacuous. Abruptly the expression was replaced by a nervous smile. The thin man straightened himself, as much as his habitually drooping shoulders would permit, hastily entered, and sat down on the extreme edge of a pneumatically form-fitting chair.

He embarrassedly fumbled the blob of gasoid, looking around for a convenient disposal vent or a crevice in the upholstery. Finding none, he stuffed it hurriedly into his pocket. Then he repressed his fidgetings by clasping his hands resolutely together, and sat with downcast eyes.

"How are you feeling, old man?" Carrsbury asked in a voice that was warm with a benign friendliness.

The general secretary did not look up.

"Anything bothering you, Phy?" Carrsbury continued solicitously. "Do you feel a bit unhappy, or dissatisfied, about your . . .er . . . transfer, now that the moment has arrived?"

Still the general secretary did not respond. Carrsbury leaned forward across the dully silver, semicircular desk and, in his most winning tones, urged, "Come on, old fellow, tell me all about it."

The general secretary did not lift his head, but he rolled up his strange, distant eyes until they were fixed directly on Carrsbury. He shivered a little, his body seemed to contract, and his bloodless hands tightened their interlocking grip.

"I know," he said in a low, effortful voice. "You think I'm insane."

Carrsbury sat back, forcing his brows to assume a baffled frown under the mane of silvery hair.

"Oh, you needn't pretend to be puzzled," Phy continued, swiftly now that he had broken the ice. "You know what that word means as well as I do. Better—even though we both had to do historical research to find out."

"Insane," he repeated dreamily, his gaze wavering. "Significant departure from the norm. Inability to conform to basic conventions underlying all human conduct."

"Nonsense!" said Carrsbury, rallying and putting on his warmest and most compelling smile. "I haven't the slightest idea of what you're talking about. That you're a

63

little tired, a little strained, a little distraught—that's quite understandable, considering the burden you've been carrying, and a little rest will be just the thing to fix you up, a nice long vacation away from all this. But as for your being . . . why, ridiculous!"

"No," said Phy, his gaze pinning Carrsbury. "You think I'm insane. You think all my colleagues in the World Management Service are insane. That's why you're having us replaced with those men you've been training for ten years in your Institute of Political Leadership—ever since, with my help and connivance, you became World manager."

Carrsbury retreated before the finality of the statement. For the first time his smile became a bit uncertain. He started to say something, then hesitated and looked at Phy, as if half hoping he would go on.

But that individual was once again staring rigidly at the floor.

Carrsbury leaned back, thinking. When he spoke it was in a more natural voice, much less consciously soothing and fatherly.

"Well, all right, Phy. But look here, tell me something, honestly. Won't you—and the others—be a lot happier when you've been relieved of all your responsibilities?"

Phy nodded somberly. "Yes," he said, "we will . . . but"—his face became strained —"you see—"

"But—?" Carrsbury prompted.

Phy swallowed hard. He seemed unable to go on. He had gradually slumped toward one side of the chair, and the pressure had caused the green gasoid to ooze from his pocket. His long fingers crept over and kneaded it fretfully.

Carrsbury stood up and came around the desk. His sympathetic frown, from which perplexity had ebbed, was not quite genuine.

"I don't see why I shouldn't tell you all about it now, Phy," he said simply. "In a queer sort of way I owe it all to you. And there isn't any point now in keeping it a secret . . . there isn't any danger—"

"Yes," Phy agreed with a quick bitter smile, "you haven't been in any danger of a *coup d'état* for some years now. If ever we should have revolted, there'd have been"— his gaze shifted to a point in the opposite wall where a faint vertical crease indicated the presence of a doorway—"your secret police."

*   *   *

Carrsbury started. He hadn't thought Phy had known. Disturbingly, there loomed in his mind a phrase *The cunning of the insane*. But only for a moment. Friendly complacency flooded back. He went behind Phy's chair and rested his hands on the sloping shoulders.

"You know, I've always had a special feeling toward you, Phy," he said, "and not only because your whims made it a lot easier for me to become World manager. I've always felt that you were different from the others, that there were times when—" He hesitated.

Phy squirmed a little under the friendly hands. "When I had my moments of sanity?" he finished flatly.

"Like now," said Carrsbury softly, after a nod the other could not see. "I've always felt that sometimes, in a kind of twisted, unrealistic way, you *understood*. And that has meant a lot to me. I've been alone, Phy, dreadfully alone, for ten whole years. No companionship anywhere, not even among the men I've been training in the Institute of Political Leadership—for I've had to play a part with them too, keep them in ignorance of certain facts, for fear they would try to seize power over my head before they were sufficiently prepared. No companionship anywhere, except for my hopes—and for occasional moments with you. Now that it's over and a new regime is beginning for us both, I can tell you that. And I'm glad."

There was a silence. Then—Phy did not look around, but one lean hand crept up and touched Carrsbury's. Carrsbury cleared his throat. Strange, he thought, that there could be even a momentary rapport like this between the sane and the insane. But it was so.

He disengaged his hands, strode rapidly back to his desk, turned.

"I'm a throwback, Phy," he began in a new, unused, eager voice. "A throwback to a time when human mentality was far sounder. Whether my case was due chiefly to heredity, or to certain unusual accidents of environment, or to both, is unimportant. The point is that a person had been born who was in a position to criticize the present state of mankind in the light of the past, to diagnose its condition, and to begin its cure. For a long time I refused to face the facts, but finally my researches—especially those in the literature of the twentieth century—left me no alternative. The mentality of mankind had become—aberrant. Only certain technological advances, which had resulted in making the business of living infinitely easier and simpler, and the fact that war had been ended with the creation of the present world state, were staving off the inevitable breakdown of civilization. But only staving it off—delaying it. The great masses of mankind had become what would once have been called hopelessly neurotic. Their leaders had become . . . you said it first, Phy . . . insane. Incidentally, this latter phenomenon—the drift of psychological aberrants toward leadership—has been noted in all ages."

He paused. Was he mistaken, or was Phy following his words with indications of a greater mental clarity than he had ever noted before, even in the relatively non-violent World secretary? Perhaps—he had often dreamed wistfully of the possibility—there was still a chance of saving Phy. Perhaps, if he just explained to him clearly and calmly—

"In my historical studies," he continued, "I soon came to the conclusion that the crucial period was that of the Final Amnesty, concurrent with the founding of the present world state. We are taught that at that time there were released from confinement millions of political prisoners—and millions of others. Just who were those others? To this question, our present histories gave only vague and platitudinous answers. The semantic difficulties I encountered were exceedingly obstinate. But I kept hammering away. Why, I asked myself, have such words as insanity, lunacy, madness, psychosis, disappeared from our vocabulary—and the concepts behind them from our thought? Why has the subject 'abnormal psychology' disappeared from the curricula of our schools? Of greater significance, why is our modern psychology strikingly similar to the field of abnormal psychology as taught in the twentieth century, and to that field alone? Why are there no longer, as there were in the twentieth century, any institutions for the confinement and care of the psychologically aberrant?"

Phy's head jerked up. He smiled twistedly. "Because," he whispered slyly, "everyone's insane now."

*   *   *

The cunning of the insane. Again that phrase loomed warningly in Carrsbury's mind. But only for a moment. He nodded.

"At first I refused to make that deduction. But gradually I reasoned out the why and wherefore of what had happened. It wasn't only that a highly technological civilization had subjected mankind to a wider and more swiftly-tempoed range of stimulations, conflicting suggestions, mental strains, emotional wrenchings. In the literature of the twentieth century psychiatry there are observations on a kind of psychosis that results from success. An unbalanced individual keeps going so long as he is fighting something, struggling toward a goal. He reaches his goal—and goes to pieces. His repressed confusions come to the surface, he realizes that he doesn't know what he wants at all, his energies hitherto engaged in combatting something outside himself are turned against himself, he is destroyed. Well, when war was finally outlawed, when the whole world became one unified state, when social inequality was abolished . . . you see what I'm driving at?"

Phy nodded slowly. "That," he said in a curious, distant voice, "is a very interesting deduction."

"Having reluctantly accepted my main premise," Carrsbury went on, "everything became clear. The cyclic six-months' fluctuations in world credit—I realized at once that Morganstern of Finance must be a manic-depressive with a six-months' phase, or else a duel personality with one aspect a spendthrift, the other a miser. It turned out to be the former. Why was the Department of Cultural Advancement stagnating? Because Manager Hobart was markedly catatonic. Why the boom in Extraterrestrial Research? Because McElvy was a euphoric."

Phy looked at him wonderingly. "But naturally," he said, spreading his lean hands, from one of which the gasoid dropped like a curl of green smoke.

Carrsbury glanced at him sharply. He replied. "Yes, I know that you and several of the others have a certain warped awareness of the differences between your . . . personalities, though none whatsoever of the basic aberration involved in them all. But to get on. As soon as I realized the situation, my course was marked out. As a sane man, capable of entertaining fixed realistic purposes, and surrounded by individuals of whose inconsistencies and delusions it was easy to make use, I was in a position to attain, with time and tact, any goal at which I might aim. I was already in the Managerial Service. In three years I became World manager. Once there, my range of influence was vastly enhanced. Like the man in Archimedes' epigram, I had a place to stand from which I could move the world. I was able, in various guises and on various pretexts, to promulgate regulations the actual purpose of which was to soothe the great neurotic masses by curtailing upsetting stimulations and introducing a more regimented and orderly program of living. I was able, by humoring my fellow executives and making the fullest use of my greater capacity for work, to keep world affairs staggering along fairly safely—at least stave off the worst. At the same time I was able to begin my Ten Years' Plan—the training, in comparative isolation, first in small numbers, then in larger, as those instructed could in turn become instructors, of a group of prospective leaders carefully selected on the basis of their relative freedom from neurotic tendencies."

"But that—" Phy began rather excitedly, starting up.

"But what?" Carrsbury inquired quickly.

"Nothing," muttered Phy dejectedly, sinking back.

"That about covers it," Carrsbury concluded, his voice suddenly grown a little duller. "Except for one secondary matter. I couldn't afford to let myself go ahead without any protection. Too much depended on me. There was always the risk of being wiped out by some ill-co-ordinated but none the less effective spasm of violence,

66

momentarily uncontrollable by tack, on the part of my fellow executives. So, only because I could see no alternative, I took a dangerous step. I created"—his glance strayed toward the faint crease in the side wall—"my secret police. There is a type of insanity known as paranoia, an exaggerated suspiciousness involving delusions of persecution. By means of the late twentieth century Rand technique of hypnotism, I inculated a number of these unfortunate individuals with the fixed idea that their lives depended on me and that I was threatened from all sides and must be protected at all costs. A distasteful expedient, even though it served its purpose. I shall be glad, very glad to see it discontinued. You can understand, can't you, why I had to take that step?"

He looked questioningly at Phy—and became aware with a shock that that in-dividual was grinning at him vacuously and holding up the gasoid between two fingers.

"I cut a hole in my couch and lot of this stuff came out," Phy explained in a thick naive voice. "Ropes of it got all over my office. I kept tripping." His fingers patted at it deftly, sculpturing it into the form of a hideous transparent green head, which he proceeded to squeeze out of existence. "Queer stuff," he rambled on. "Rarefied liquid. Gas of fixed volume. And all over my office floor, tangled up with the furniture."

*   *   *

Carrsbury leaned back and shut his eyes. His shoulders slumped. He felt suddenly a little weary, a little eager for his day of triumph to be done. He knew he shouldn't be despondent because he had failed with Phy. After all, the main victory was won. Phy was the merest of side issues. He had always known that, except for flashes, Phy was hopeless as the rest. Still—

"You don't need to worry about your office floor, Phy," he said with a listless kindliness. "Never any more. Your successor will have to see about cleaning it up. Already, you know, to all intents and purposes, you have been replaced."

"That's just it!" Carrsbury started at Phy's explosive loudness. The World secretary jumped up and strode toward him, pointing an excited hand. "That's what I came to see you about! That's what I've been trying to tell you! I can't be replaced like that! None of the others can, either! It won't work! You can't do it!"

With a swiftness born of long practice, Carrsbury slipped behind his desk. He forced his features into that expression of calm, smiling benevolence of which he had grown unutterably weary.

"Now, now, Phy," he said brightly, soothingly, "if I can't do it, of course I can't do it. But don't you think you ought to tell me why? Don't you think it would be very nice to sit down and talk it all over and you tell me why?"

Phy halted and hung his head, abashed.

"Yes, I guess it would," he said slowly, abruptly falling back into the low, effortful tones. "I guess I'll have to. I guess there just isn't any other way. I had hoped, though, not to have to tell you everything." The last sentence was half question. He looked up wheedlingly at Carrsbury. The latter shook his head, continuing to smile. Phy went back and sat down.

"Well," he finally began, gloomily kneading the gasoid, "it all began when you first wanted to be World manager. You weren't the usual type, but I thought it would be kind of fun—yes, and kind of helpful." He looked up at Carrsbury. "You've really done the world a lot of good in quite a lot of ways, always remember that," he assured him. "Of course," he added, again focusing the tortured gasoid, "they weren't exactly the ways you thought."

"No?" Carrsbury prompted automatically. *Humor him. Humor him.* The wornout refrain droned in his mind.

Phy sadly shook his head. "Take those regulations you promulgated to soothe people—"

"Yes?"

"—they kind of got changed on the way. For instance, your prohibition, regarding reading tapes, of all exciting literature . . . oh, we tried a little of the soothing stuff you suggested at first. Everyone got a great kick out of it. They laughed and laughed. But afterwards, well, as I said, it kind of got changed—in this case to a prohibition of all *unexciting* literature."

Carrsbury's smile broadened. For a moment the edge of his mind had toyed with a fear, but Phy's last remark had banished it.

"Every day I coast past several reading stands," Carrsbury said gently. "The fiction tapes offered for sale are always in the most chastely and simply colored containers. None of those wild and lurid pictures that one used to see everywhere."

"But did you ever buy one and listen to it? Or project the visual text?" Phy questioned apologetically.

"For ten years I've been a very busy man," Carrsbury answered. "Of course I've read the official reports regarding such matters, and at times glanced through sample resumes of taped fiction."

"Oh, sure, that sort of official stuff," agreed Phy, glancing up at the wall of tape files beyond the desk. "What we did, you see, was to keep the monochrome containers but go back to the old kind of contents. The contrast kind of tickled people. Remember, as I said before, a lot of your regulations have done good. Cut out a lot of unnecessary noise and inefficient foolishness, for one thing."

That sort of official stuff. The phrase lingered unpleasantly in Carrsbury's ears. There was a trace of irrepressible suspicion in his quick over-the-shoulder glance at the tiered tape files.

"Oh, yes," Phy went on, "and that prohibition against yielding to unusual or indecent impulses, with a long listing of specific categories. It went into effect all right, but with a little rider attached: 'unless you really want to.' That seemed absolutely necessary, you know." His fingers worked furiously with the gasoid. "As for the prohibition of various stimulating beverages—well, in this locality they're still served under other names, and an interesting custom has grown up of behaving very soberly while imbibing them. Now when we come to that matter of the eight-hour working day—"

*   *   *

Almost involuntarily, Carrsbury had got up and walked over to the outer wall. With a flip of his hand through an invisible U-shaped beam, he switched on the window. It was as if the outer wall had disappeared. Through its near-perfect transparency, he peered down with fierce curiosity past the sleekly gleaming facades to the terraces and parkways below.

The modest throngs seemed quiet and orderly enough. But then there was a scurry of confusion—a band of people, at this angle all tiny heads with arms and legs, came out from a shop far below and began to pelt another group with what looked like foodstuffs. While, on a side parkway, two small ovoid vehicles, seamless drops of silver because their vision panels were invisible from the outside, butted each other playfully. Someone started to run.

Carrsbury hurriedly switched off the window and turned around. Those were just off-chance occurrences, he told himself angrily. Of no real statistical significance whatever. For ten years mankind had steadily been trending toward sanity despite occasional relapses. He'd seen it with his own eyes, seen the day-to-day progress—at least enough to know. He'd been a fool to let Phy's ramblings effect him—only tired nerves had made that possible.

He glanced at his timepiece.

"Excuse me," he said curtly, striding past Phy's chair, "I'd like to continue this conversation, but I have to get along to the first meeting of the new Central Managerial Staff."

"Oh but you can't!" Instantly Phy was up and dragging at his arm. "You just can't do it, you know! It's impossible!"

The pleading voice rose toward a scream. Impatiently Carrsbury tried to shake loose. The seam in the side wall widened, became a doorway. Instantly both of them stopped struggling.

In the doorway stood a cadaverous giant of a man with a stubby dark weapon in his hand. Straggly black beard shaded into gaunt cheeks. His face was a cruel blend of suspicion and fanatical devotion, the first directed along with the weapon at Phy, the second—and the somnambulistic eyes—at Carrsbury.

"He was threatening you?" the bearded man asked in a harsh voice, moving the weapon suggestively.

For a moment an angry, vindictive light glinted in Carrsbury's eyes. Then it flicked out. What could he have been thinking, he asked himself. This poor lunatic World secretary was no one to hate.

"Not at all, Hartman," he remarked calmly. "We were discussing something and we became excited and allowed our voices to rise. Everything is quite all right."

"Very well," said the bearded man doubtfully, after a pause. Reluctantly he returned his weapon to its holster, but he kept his hand on it and remained standing in the doorway.

"And now," said Carrsbury, disengaging himself, "I must go."

He had stepped on to the corridor slidewalk and had coasted halfway to the elevator before he realized that Phy had followed him and was plucking timidly at his sleeve.

"You can't go off like this," Phy pleaded urgently, with an apprehensive backward glance. Carrsbury noted that Hartman had also followed—an ominous pylon two paces to the rear. "You must give me a chance to explain, to tell you why, just like you asked me."

*   *   *

Humor him. Carrsbury's mind was deadly tired of the drone, but mere weariness prompted him to dance to it a little longer. "You can talk to me in the elevator," he conceded, stepping off the slidewalk. His finger flipped through a U-beam and a serpentine movement of light across the wall traced the elevator's obedient rise.

"You see, it wasn't just that matter of prohibitory regulations," Phy launched out hurriedly. "There were lots of other things that never did work out like your official reports indicated. Departmental budgets for instance. The reports showed, I know, that appropriations for Extraterrestrial Research were being regularly slashed. Actually, in your ten years of office, they increased tenfold. Of course, there was no way for you to know that. You couldn't be all over the world at once and see each separate launching of supra-stratospheric rockets."

The moving light became stationary. A seam dilated. Carrsbury stepped into the elevator. He debated sending Hartman back. Poor babbling Phy was no menace. Still— *the cunning of the insane.* He decided against it, reached out and flipped the control beam at the sector which would bring them to the hundredth and top floor. The door snipped softly shut. The cage became a surging darkness in which floor numerals winked softly. Twenty-one. Twenty-two. Twenty-three.

"And then there was the Military Service. You had it sharply curtailed."

"Of course I did." Sheer weariness stung Carrsbury into talk. "There's only one country in the world. Obviously, the only military requirement is an adequate police force. To say nothing of the risks involved in putting weapons into the hands of the present world population."

"I know," Phy's answer came guiltily from the darkness. "Still, what's happened is that, unknown to you, the Military Service has been increased in size, and recently four rocket squadrons have been added."

Fifty-seven. Fifty-eight. *Humor him.* "Why?"

"Well, you see we've found out that Earth is being reconnoitered. Maybe from Mars. Maybe hostile. Have to be prepared. We didn't tell you . . . well, because we were afraid it might excite you."

The voice trailed off. Carrsbury shut his eyes. How long, he asked himself, how long? He realized with dull surprise that in the last hour people like Phy, endured for ten years, had become unutterably weary to him. For the moment even the thought of the conference over which he would soon be presiding, the conference that was to usher in a sane world, failed to stir him. Reaction to success? To the end of a ten years' tension?

*   *   *

"Do you know how many floors there are in this building?"

Carrsbury was not immediately conscious of the new note in Phy's voice, but he reacted to it.

"One hundred," he replied promptly.

"Then," asked Phy, "just where are we?"

Carrsbury opened his eyes to the darkness. One hundred twenty-seven, blinked the floor numeral. One hundred twenty-eight. One hundred twenty-nine.

Something cold dragged at Carrsbury's stomach, pulled at his brain. He felt as if his mind were being slowly and irresistibly twisted. He thought of hidden dimensions, of unsuspected holes in space. Something remembered from elementary physics danced through his thoughts: If it were possible for an elevator to keep moving upward with uniform acceleration, no one inside an elevator could determine whether the effects they were experiencing were due to acceleration or to gravity—whether the elevator were standing motionless on some planet or shooting up at everincreasing velocity through free space.

One hundred forty-one. One hundred forty-two.

"Or as if you were rising through consciousness into an unsuspected realm of mentality lying above," suggested Phy in his new voice, with its hint of gentle laughter.

One hundred forty-six. One hundred forty-seven. It was slowing now. One hundred forty-nine. One hundred fifty. It had stopped.

This was some trick. The thought was like cold water in Carrsbury's face. Some cunning childish trick of Phy's. An easy thing to hocus the numerals. Carrsbury groped irascibly about in the darkness, encountered the slick surface of a holster, Hartman's gaunt frame.

"Get ready for a surprise," Phy warned from close at his elbow.

As Carrsbury turned and grabbed, bright sunlight drenched him, followed by a griping, heartstopping spasm of vertigo.

He, Hartman, and Phy, along with a few insubstantial bits of furnishings and controls, were standing in the air fifty stories above the hundred-story summit of World Managerial Center.

For a moment he grabbed frantically at nothing. Then he realized they were not falling and his eyes began to trace the hint of walls and ceiling and floor and, immediately below them, the ghost of a shaft.

Phy nodded. "That's all there is to it," he assured Carrsbury casually. "Just another of those charmingly odd modern notions against which you have legislated so persistently—like our incomplete staircases and roads to nowhere. The Buildings and Grounds Committee decided to extend the range of the elevator for sightseeing purposes. The shaft was made air-transparent to avoid spoiling the form of the original building and to improve the view. This was achieved so satisfactorily that an electronic warning system had to be installed for the safety of passing airjets and other craft. Treating the surfaces of the cage like windows was an obvious detail."

He paused and looked quizzically at Carrsbury. "All very simple," he observed, "but don't you find a kind of symbolism in it? For ten years now you've been spending most of your life in that building below. Every day you've used this elevator. But not once have you dreamed in these fifty extra stories. Don't you think that something of the same sort may be true of your observations of other aspects of contemporary social life?"

Carrsbury gaped at him stupidly.

Phy turned to watch the growing speck of an approaching aircraft. "You might look at it too," he remarked to Carrsbury, "for it's going to transport you to a far happier, more restful life."

Carrsbury parted his lips, wet them. "But—" he said, unsteadily. "But—"

Phy smiled. "That's right, I didn't finish my explanation. Well, you might have gone on being World manager all your life, in the isolation of your office and your miles of taped official reports and your occasional confabs with me and the others. Except for your Institute of Political Leadership and your Ten-Year-Plan. That upset things. Of course, we were as much interested in it as we were in you. It had definite possibilities. We hoped it would work out. We would have been glad to retire from office if it had. But, most fortunately, it didn't. And that sort of ended the whole experiment."

He caught the downward direction of Carrsbury's gaze.

"No," he said, "I'm afraid your pupils aren't waiting for you in the conference chamber on the hundredth story. I'm afraid they're still in the Institute." His voice became gently sympathetic. "And I'm afraid that it's become . . . well . . . a somewhat different sort of institute."

*   *   *

71

Carrsbury stood very still, swaying a little. Gradually his thoughts and his will power were emerging from the waking nightmare that had paralyzed them. *The cunning of the insane*—he had neglected that trenchant warning. In the very moment of victory—

No! He had forgotten Hartman! This was the very emergency for which that counterstroke had been prepared.

He glanced sideways at the chief member of his secret police. The black giant, unconcerned by their strange position, was glaring fixedly at Phy as if at some evil magician from whom any malign impossibility could be expected.

Now Hartman became aware of Carrsbury's gaze. He divined his thought.

He drew his dark weapon from its holster, pointed it unwaveringly at Phy.

His black-bearded lips curled. From them came a hissing sound. Then, in a loud voice, he cried, "You're dead, Phy! I disintegrated you."

Phy reached over and took the weapon from his hand.

"That's another respect in which you completely miscalculated the modern temperament," he remarked to Carrsbury, a shade argumentatively. "All of us have certain subjects on which we're a trifle unrealistic. That's only human nature. Hartman's was his suspiciousness—a weakness for ideas involving plots and persecutions. You gave him the worst sort of job—one that catered to and encouraged his weaknesses. In a very short time he became hopelessly unrealistic. Why for years he's never realized that he's been carrying a dummy pistol."

He passed it to Carrsbury for inspection.

"But he added, "give him the proper job and he'd function well enough—say something in creation or exploration. Fitting the man to the job is an art with infinite possibilities. That's why we had Morgenstern in Finance—to keep credit fluctuating in a safe, predictable rhythm. That's why a euphoric is made manager of Extraterrestial Research—to keep it booming. Why a catatonic is given Cultural Advancement—to keep it from tripping on its face in its haste to get ahead."

He turned away. Dully, Carrsbury observed that the aircraft was hovering close to the cage and sidling slowly in.

"But in that case why—" he began stupidly.

"Why were you made World manager?" Phy finished easily. "Isn't that fairly obvious? Haven't I told you several times that you did a lot of good, indirectly? You interested us, don't you see? In fact, you were practically unique. As you know, it's our cardinal principle to let every individual express himself as he wants to. In your case, that involved letting you become World manager. Taken all in all it worked out very well. Everyone had a good time, a number of constructive regulations were promulgated, we learned a lot—oh, we didn't get everything we hoped for, but one never does. Unfortunately, in the end, we were forced to discontinue the experiment."

The aircraft had made contact.

"You understand, of course, why that was necessary?" Phy continued hurriedly, as he urged Carrsbury toward the opening port. "I'm sure you must. It all comes down to a question of sanity. What is sanity—now, in the twentieth century, any time? Adherence to a norm. Conformity to certain basic conventions underlying all human conduct. In our age, departure from the norm has become the norm. Inability to conform has become the standard of conformity. That's quite clear, isn't it? And it enables you to understand, doesn't it, your own case and that of your proteges? Over a long period of years you persisted in adhering to a norm, in conforming to certain basic conventions. You were completely unable to adapt yourself to the society around you. You could only pretend—and your proteges wouldn't have been able to do even that. Despite your many engaging personal characteristics, there was obviously only one course of action open to us."

In the port Carrsbury turned. He had found his voice at last. It was hoarse, ragged. "You mean that all these years you've just been *humoring* me?"

The port was closing. Phy did not answer the question.

As the aircraft edged out, he waved farewell with the blob of green gasoid.

"It'll be very pleasant where you're going," he shouted encouragingly. "Comfortable quarters, adequate facilities for exercise, and a complete library of twentieth century literature to while away your time."

He watched Carrsbury's rigid face, staring whitely from the vision port, until the aircraft had diminished to a speck.

Then he turned away, looked at his hands, noticed the gasoid, tossed it out the open door of the cage, studied its flight for a few moments, then flicked the downbeam.

"I'm glad to see the last of that fellow," he muttered, more to himself than to Hartman, as they plummeted toward the roof. "He was beginning to have a very disturbing influence on me. In fact, I was beginning to fear for my"—his expression became suddenly vacuous—"sanity."

Wanted—An Enemy

The bright stars of Mars made a glittering roof for a fantastic tableau. A being equipped with retinal vision would have seen an Earthman dressed in the familiar coat and trousers of the twentieth century standing on a boulder that put him a few feet above the dusty sand. His face was bony and puritanic. His eyes gleamed wildly from deep sockets. Occasionally his long hair flopped across them. His lips worked vociferously, showing big yellowed teeth, and there was a cloud of blown spittle in front of them, for he was making a speech—in the English language. He so closely resembled an old-style soapbox orator that one looked around for the lamp-post, the dull-faced listeners overflowing the curb, and the strolling cop.

But the puzzling globe of soft radiance surrounding Mr. Whitlow struck highlights from enamel-black shells and jointed legs a little resembling those of an ant under a microscope. Each individual in the crowd consisted of a yard-long oval body lacking a separate head or any sensory or other orifices in its gleaming black surface except for a small mouth that worked like a sliding door and kept opening and closing at regular intervals. To this body were attached eight of the jointed legs, the inner pairs showing highly manipulative end-organs.

These creatures were ranged in a circle around Mr. Whitlow's boulder. Facing him was one who crouched a little apart from the rest, on a smaller boulder. Flanking this one, were two whose faintly silvered shells suggested weathering and, therefore, age.

Beyond them—black desert to a horizon defined only by the blotting out of the star fields.

Low in the heavens gleamed sky-blue Earth, now Mars' evening star, riding close to the meager crescent of Phobos.

To the Martian coleopteroids this scene presented itself in a very different fashion, since they depended on perception rather than any elaborate sensory set-up. Their internal brains were directly conscious of everything within a radius of about fifty yards. For them the blue earthshine was a diffuse photonic cloud just above the threshold of perception, similar to but distinct from the photonic clouds of the starlight and faint moonshine; they could perceive no image of Earth unless they used lenses to create such an image within their perceptive range. They were conscious of the ground beneath them as a sandy hemisphere tunneled through by various wrigglers and the centipedelike burrowers. They were conscious of each other's armored, neatly-compartmented bodies, and each other's thoughts. But chiefly their attention was focused on that squidgy, uninsulated, wasteful jumble of organs that thought of itself as Mr. Whitlow—an astounding moist suppet of life on dry, miserly Mars.

The physiology of the coleopteroids was typical of a depleted-planet economy. Their shells were double; the space between could be evacuated at night to conserve heat, and flooded by day to absorb it. Their lungs were really oxygen accumulators. They inhaled the rarefied atmosphere about one hundred times for every exhalation, the double-valve mouth permitting the building up of high internal pressure. They had one hundred percent utilization of inhaled oxygen, and exhaled pure carbon dioxide freighted with other respiratory excretions. Occasional whiffs of this exceedingly bad breath made Mr. Whitlow wrinkle his flaring nostrils.

Just what permitted Mr. Whitlow to go on functioning, even speechifying, in the chill oxygen dearth was by no means so obvious. It constituted as puzzling a question as the source of the soft glow that bathed him.

Communications between him and his audience was purely telepathic. He was speaking vocally at the request of the coleopteroids, because like most nontelepaths he could best organize and clarify his thoughts while talking. His voice died out abruptly in the thin air. It sounded like a phonograph needle scratching along without amplification, and intensified the eerie ludicrousness of his violent gestures and facial contortions.

* * *

"And so," Whitlow concluded wheezily, brushing the long hair from his forehead, "I come back to my original proposal: Will you attack Earth?"

"And we, Mr. Whitlow," thought the Chief Coleopteroid, "come back to our original question, which you still have not answered: Why should we?"

Mr. Whitlow made a grimace of frayed patience. "As I have told you several times, I cannot make a fuller explanation. But I assure you of my good faith. I will do my best to provide transportation for you, and facilitate the thing in every way. Understand, it need only be a token invasion. After a short time you can retire to Mars with your spoils. Surely you cannot afford to pass up this opportunity."

"Mr. Whitlow," replied the Chief Coleopteroid with a humor as poisonously dry as his planet, "I cannot read your thoughts unless you vocalize them. They are too confused. But I can sense your biases. You are laboring under a serious misconception as to our psychology. Evidently it is customary in your world to think of alien intelligent beings as evil monsters, whose only desire is to ravage, destroy, tyrannize, and inflict unspeakable cruelties on creatures less advanced than themselves. Nothing could be farther from the truth. We are an ancient and unemotional race. We have outgrown the passions and vanities—even the ambitions—of our youth. We undertake no projects except for sound and sufficient reason."

"But if that's the case, surely you can see the practical advantages of my proposal. At little or no risk to yourselves, you will acquire valuable loot."

The Chief Coleopteroid settled back on his boulder, and his thoughts did the same. "Mr. Whitlow, let me remind you that we have never gone to war lightly. During the whole course of our history, our only intelligent enemies have been the molluscoids of the tideless seas of Venus. In the springtide of their culture they came conquesting in their water-filled spaceships, and we fought several long and bitter wars. But eventually they attained racial maturity and a certain dispassionate wisdom, though not equivalent to our own. A perpetual truce was declared, on condition that each party stick to its own planet and attempt no more forays. For ages we have abided by that truce, living in mutual isolation. So you can see, Mr. Whitlow, that we would be anything but inclined to accept such a rash and mysterious proposal as yours."

"May I make a suggestion?" interjected the Senior Coleopteroid on the Chief's right. His thoughts flicked out subtly toward Whitlow. "You seem, Earthling, to possess powers that are perhaps even in excess of our own. Your arrival on Mars without any perceptible means of transport and your ability to endure its rigors without any obvious insulation, are sufficient proofs. From what you tell us, the other inhabitants of your planet possess no such powers. Why don't you attack them by yourself, like the solitary armored poison-worm? Why do you need our aid?"

"My friend," said Mr. Whitlow solemnly, bending forward and fixing his gaze on the silvery-shelled elder, "I abhor war as the foulest evil, and active participation in it as the greatest crime. Nonetheless, I would sacrifice myself as you suggest, could I attain my ends that way. Unfortunately I cannot. It would not have the psychological effect I desire. Moreover"—he paused embarrassedly—"I might as well confess that I am not wholly master of my powers. I don't understand them. The workings of an inscrutable providence have put into my hands a device that is probably the handiwork of creatures vastly more intelligent than any in this solar system, perhaps even this cosmos. It enables me to cross space and time. It protects me from danger. It provides me with warmth and illumination. It concentrates your Martian atmosphere in a sphere around me, so that I can breathe normally. But as for using it in any larger way—I'd be mortally afraid of its getting out of control. My one small experiment was disastrous. I wouldn't dare."

The Senior Coleopteroid shot a guarded aside to the Chief. "Shall I try to hypnotize his disordered mind and get this device from him?"

"Do so."

"Very well, though I'm afraid the device will protect his mind as well as his body. Still, it's worth the chance."

*　　*　　*

"Mr. Whitlow," thought the Chief abruptly, "it is time we got down to cases. Every word you say makes your proposal sound more irrational, and your own motives more unintelligible. If you expect us to take any serious interest, you must give us a clear answer to one question: Why do you want us to attack Earth?"

Whitlow twisted. "But that's the one question I don't want to answer."

"Well, put it this way then," continued the Chief patiently. "What personal advantage do you expect to gain from our attack?"

Whitlow drew himself up and tucked in his necktie. "None! None whatsoever! I seek nothing for myself!"

"Do you want to rule Earth?" the Chief persisted.

"No! No! I detest all tyranny."

"Revenge, then? Has Earth hurt you and are you trying to hurt it back?"

"Absolutely not! I would never stoop to such barbaric behavior. I hate no one. The desire to see anyone injured is furthest from my thoughts."

"Come, come, Mr. Whitlow! You've just begged us to attack Earth. How can you square that with your sentiments?"

Whitlow gnawed his lip baffledly.

The Chief slipped in a quick question to the Senior Coleopteroid. "What progress?"

"None whatsoever. His mind is extraordinarily difficult to grasp. And as I anticipated, there is a shield."

Whitlow rocked uneasily on his shoulder, his eyes fixed on the star-edged horizon.

"I'll tell you this much," he said. "It's solely because I love Earth and mankind so much that I want you to attack her."

"You choose a strange way of showing your affection," the Chief observed.

"Yes," continued Whitlow, warming a bit, his eyes still lost. "I want you to do it in order to end war."

"This gets more and more mysterious. Start war to stop it? That is a paradox which demands explanation. Take care, Mr. Whitlow, or I will fall into your error of looking on alien beings as evil and demented monsters."

Whitlow lowered his gaze until it was fixed on the Chief. He sighed windily. "I guess I'd better tell you," he muttered. "You'd have probably found out in the end. Though it would have been simpler the other way—"

He pushed back the rebellious hair and massaged his forehead, a little wearily. When he spoke again it was in a less oratorical style.

"I am a pacifist. My life is dedicated to the task of preventing war. I love my fellow men. But they are steeped in error and sin. They are victims of their baser passions. Instead of marching on, hand in hand, trustingly, toward the glorious fulfillment of all their dreams, they insist on engaging in constant conflict, in vile war."

"Perhaps there is a reason for that," suggested the Chief mildly. "Some inequalities that require leveling or—"

"Please," said the pacifist reprovingly. "These wars have grown increasingly more violent and terrible. I, and others, have sought to reason with the majority, but it vain. They persist in their delusions. I have racked my brain to find a solution. I have considered every conceivable remedy. Since I came into the possession of . . . er . . . the device, I have sought throughout the cosmos and even in other time-streams, for the secret of preventing war. With no success. Such intelligent races as I encountered were either engaged in war, which rules them out, or had never known war—these were very obliging but obviously could volunteer no helpful information—or else had outgrown war by the painful and horrible process of fighting until there was nothing more to fight about."

"As we have," the Chief thought, in an undertone.

The pacifist spread his hands, palms toward the stars. "So, once more, I was thrown on my own resources. I studied mankind from every angle. Gradually I became convinced that its worst trait—and the one more responsible for war—was its overgrown sense of self-importance. On my planet man is the lord of creation. All the other animals are merely one among many—no species is pre-eminent. The flesh-eaters have their flesh-eating rivals. Each browser or grazer competes with other types for the grass and herbage. Even the fish in the seas and the myriad parasites that swarm in bloodstreams are divided into species of roughly equal ability and competence. This makes for humility and a sense of perspective. No species is inclined to fight among itself when it realizes that by so doing it will merely clear the way for other species to take over. Man alone has no serious rivals. As a result, he has developed delusions of grandeur—and of persecution and hate. Lacking the restraint that rivalry would provide, he fouls his planetary nest with constant civil war.

"I mulled this idea for some time. I thought wistfully of how different mankind's development might have been had he been compelled to share his planet with some equally intelligent species, say a mechanically-minded sea dweller. I considered, how, when great natural catastrophes occur, such as fires and floods and earthquakes and plagues, men temporarily quit squabbling and work hand in hand—rich and poor, friend and enemy alike. Unfortunately such cooperation only lasts until man once more asserts his mastery over his environment. It does not provide a constant sobering threat. And then . . . I had an inspiration."

*　　*　　*

Mr. Whitlow's gaze swept the black-shelled forms—a jumble of satiny crescent highlights ringing the sphere of light enveloping him. Similarly his mind swept their cryptically armored thoughts.

"I remembered an incident from my childhood. A radio broadcast—we make use of high velocity vibrations to transmit sound—had given an impishly realistic fictional report of an invasion of Earth by beings from Mars, beings of that evil and destructive nature which, as you say, we tend to attribute to alien life. Many believed the report. There were brief scares and panics. It occurred to me how, at the first breath of an actual invasion of that sort, warring peoples would forget their differences and join staunchly together to meet the invader. They would realize that the things they were fighting about were really trifling matters, phantoms of moodiness and fear. Their sense of perspective would be restored. They would see that the all-important fact was that they were men alike, facing a common enemy, and they would rise magnificently to the challenge. Ah my friends, when that vision occurred to me, of warring mankind at one stroke united, and united forever, I stood trembling and speechless. I—"

Even on Mars, emotion choked him.

"Very interesting," thought the Senior Coleopteroid blandly, "but wouldn't the method you propose be a contradiction of that higher morality to which I can perceive you subscribe?"

The pacifist bowed his head. "My friend, you are quite right—in the large and ultimate sense. And let me assure you"—the fire crept back into his hoarse voice—"that when that day comes, when the question of interplanetary relations arises, I will be in the vanguard of the interspeciests, demanding full equality for coleopteroid and man alike. But"—his feverish eyes peered up again through the hair that had once more fallen across his forehead—"that is a matter for the future. The immediate question is: How to stop war on Earth. As I said before, your invasion need only be a token one, and of course the more bloodless, the better. It would only take one taste of an outside menace, one convincing proof that he has equals and even superiors in the cosmos, to restore man's normalcy of outlook, to weld him into a mutually-protective brotherhood, to establish peace forever!"

He threw his hands wide and his head back. His hair flipped into its proper place, but his tie popped out again.

"Mr. Whitlow," thought the Chief, with a cold sardonic merriment, "if you have any notion that we are going to invade another planet for the sake of improving the psychology of its inhabitants, disabuse yourself of it at once. Earthlings mean nothing to us. Their rise is such a recent matter that we hardly had taken note of it until you called it to our attention. Let them go on warring, if they want to. Let them kill themselves off. It is no concern of ours."

Whitlow blinked. "Why—" he started angrily. Then he caught himself. "But I wasn't asking you to do it for humanitarian reasons. I pointed out that there would be loot—"

"I very much doubt if your Earthlings have anything that would tempt us."

Whitlow almost backed off his boulder. He started to splutter something, but again abruptly changed his tack. There was a flicker of shrewdness in his expression. "Is it possible you're holding back because you're afraid the Venusian molluscoids will attack you if you violate the perpetual truce by making a foray against another planet?"

"By no means," thought the Chief harshly, revealing for the first time a certain haughtiness and racial pride bred of dry eons of tradition. "As I told you before, the molluscoids are a distinctly inferior race. Mere waterlings. We have seen nothing of them for ages. For all we know they've died out. Certainly we wouldn't be bound by any outworn agreements with them, if there were a sound and profitable reason for breaking them. And we are in no sense—no sense whatever—afraid of them."

Whitlow's thoughts fumbled confusedly, his spatulate-fingered hands making unconsciously appropriate gestures. Driven back to his former argument, he faltered lamely. "But surely then there must be some loot that would make it worth your while to invade Earth. After all, Earth is a planet rich in oxygen and water and minerals and life forms, whereas Mars has to contend with a dearth of all these things."

"Precisely," thought the Chief. "And we have developed a style of life that fits in perfectly with that dearth. By harvesting the interplanetary dust in the neighborhood of Mars, and by a judicious use of transmutation and other techniques, we are assured of a sufficient supply of all necessary raw materials. Earth's bloated abundance would be an embarrassment to us, upsetting our system. An increased oxygen supply would force us to learn a new rhythm of breathing to avoid oxygen-drowning, beside making any invasion of Earth uncomfortable and dangerous. Similar hazards might attend an oversupply of other elements and compounds. And as for Earth's obnoxiously teeming life forms, none of them would be any use to us on Mars—except for the unlucky chance of one of them finding harborage in our bodies and starting an epidemic."

Whitlow winced. Whether he knew it or not, his planetary vanity had been touched. "But you're overlooking the most important things," he argued, "the products of man's industry and ingenuity. He has changed the face of his planet much more fully than you have yours. He has covered it with roads. He does not huddle savagely in the open as you do. He has built vast cities. He has constructed all manner of vehicles. Surely among such a wealth of things you would find many to covet."

"Most unlikely," retorted the Chief. "I cannot see envisaged in your mind any that would awaken even our passing interest. We are adapted to our environment. We have no need of garments and housing and all the other artificialities which your ill-adjusted Earthlings require. Our mastery of our planet is greater than yours, but we do not advertise it so obtrusively. From your picture I can see that your Earthlings are given to a worship of bigness and a crude type of exhibitionism."

"But then there are our machines," Whitlow insisted, seething inwardly, plucking at his collar. "Machines of tremendous complexity, for every purpose. Machines that would be as useful to another species as to us."

"Yes, I can imagine them," commented the Chief cuttingly. "Huge, clumsy, jumbles of wheels and levers, wires and grids. In any case, ours are better."

He shot a swift question to the Senior. "Is his anger making his mind amy more vulnerable?"

"Not yet."

Whitlow made one last effort, with great difficulty holding his indignation in check. "Besides all that, there's our art. Cultural treasures of incalculable value. The work of a species more richly creative than your own. Books, music, paintings, sculpture. Surely—"

"Mr. Whitlow, you are becoming ridiculous," said the Chief. "Art is meaningless apart from its cultural environment. What interest could we be expected to take in the fumbling self-expression of an immature species? Moreover, none of the art forms you mention would be adapted to our style of perception, save sculpture—and in that field our efforts are incomparably superior, since we have a direct consciousness of solidity. Your mind is only a shadow-mind, limited to flimsy two-dimensional patterns."

Whitlow drew himself up and folded his arms across his chest. "Very well!" he grated out. "I see I cannot persuade you. But"—he shook his finger at the Chief—"let me tell you something! You're contemptuous of man. You call him crude and childish. You pour scorn on his industry, his science, his art. You refuse to help him in his need. You think you can afford to disregard him. All right. Go ahead. That's my advice to you. Go ahead—and see what happens!" A vindictive light grew in his eyes. "I know my fellow man. From years of study I know him. War has made him a tyrant and exploiter. He has enslaved the beasts of field and forest. He has enslaved his own kind, when he could, and when he couldn't he has bound them with the subtler chains of economic necessity and the awe of prestige. He's wrong-headed, brutal, a tool of his baser impulses—and also he's clever, doggedly persistent, driven by a boundless ambition! He already has atomic power and rocket transport. In a few decades he'll have spaceships and subatomic weapons. Go ahead and wait! Constant warfare will cause him to develop those weapons to undreamed of heights of efficient destructiveness. Wait for that too! Wait until he arrives on Mars in force. Wait until he makes your acquaintance and realizes what marvelous workers you'd be with your armored adaptability to all sorts of environments. Wait until he picks a quarrel with you and defeats you and enslaves you and ships you off, packed in evil-smelling hulls, to labor in Earth's mines and on her ocean bottoms, in her stratosphere and on the planetoids that man will be desirous of exploiting. Yes, go ahead and wait!"

*   *   *

Whitlow broke off, his chest heaving. For a moment he was conscious only of his vicious satisfaction at having told off these exasperating beetle-creatures. Then he looked around.

The coleopteroids had drawn in. The forms of the foremost were defined with a hatefully spiderish distinctness, almost invading his sphere of light. Similarly their thoughts had drawn in, to form a menacing wall blacker than the encircling Martian night. Gone were the supercilious amusement and dispassionate withdrawal that had so irked him. Incredulously he realized that he had somehow broken through their armor and touched them on a vulnerable spot.

He caught one rapid thought, from the Senior to the Chief: "And if the rest of them are anything like this one, they'll behave just as he says. It is an added confirmation."

He looked slowly around, his hair-curtained forehead bent forward, searching for a clue to the coleopteroids' sudden change in attitude. His baffled gaze ended on the Chief.

"We've changed our minds, Mr. Whitlow," the Chief volunteered grimly. "I told you at the beginning that we never hesitate about undertaking projects when given a sound and sufficient reason. What your silly arguments about humanitarianism and loot failed to provide, your recent outburst has furnished us. It is as you say. The Earthlings will eventually attack us, and with some hope of success, if we wait. So, logically we must take preventive action, the sooner the better. We will reconnoiter Earth, and if conditions there are as you assert, we will invade her."

From the depths of a confused despondency Whitlow was in an instant catapulted to the heights of feverish joy. His fanatical face beamed. His lanky frame seemed to expand. His hair flipped back.

"Marvelous!" he chortled, and then rattled on excitedly, "Of course, I'll do everything I can to help. I'll provide transport—"

"That will not be necessary," the Chief interrupted flatly. "We have no more trust in your larger powers than you have yourself. We have our own spaceships, quite adequate to any undertaking. We do not make an ostentatious display of them, any more than we make a display of the other mechanical aspects of our culture. We do not use them, as your Earthlings would, to go purposely skittering about. Nevertheless, we have them, stored away in the event of need."

But not even this contemptuous rebuff could spoil Whitlow's exultation. His face was radiant. Halfformed tears made him blink his hectic eyes. His Adam's apple bobbed chokingly.

"Ah, my friends . . . my good, good friends! If only I could express to you . . . what this moment means to me! If I could only tell you how happy I am when I envisage the greater moment that is coming! When men will look up from their trenches and foxholes, from their bombers and fighters, from their observation posts and headquarters, from their factories and homes, to see this new menace in the skies. When all their petty differences of opinion will drop away from them like a soiled and tattered garment. When they will cut the barbed-wire entanglements of an illusory hate, and join together, hand in hand, true brothers at last, to meet the common foe. When, in the accomplishment of a common task, they will at last achieve perfect and enduring peace!"

He paused for breath. His glazed eyes were lovingly fixed on the blue star of Earth, now just topping the horizon.

"Yes," faintly came the Chief's dry thought. "To one of your emotional temperament, it will probably be a very satisfying and touching scene—for a little while."

Whitlow glanced down blankly. It was as if the Chief's last thought had lightly scratched him—a feathery flick from a huge poisoned claw. He did not understand it, but he was conscious of upwelling fear.

"What—" he faltered. "What . . . do you mean?"

"I mean," thought the Chief, "that in our invasion of Earth it probably won't be necessary for us to use the divide-and-rule tactics that would normally be indicated in such a case—you know, joining with one faction on Earth to help defeat the other— warring beings never care who their allies are—and then fomenting further disunities, and so on. No, with our superiority in armament, we can probably do a straight cleanup job and avoid bothersome machinations. So you'll probably have that glimpse of Earthlings united that you set so much store by."

Whitlow stared at him from a face white with dawning horror. He licked his lips. "What did you mean by—'for a little while'?" he whispered huskily. "What did you mean by 'glimpse'?"

"Surely that should be obvious to you, Mr. Whitlow," replied the Chief with offensive good humor. "You don't for one minute suppose we'd made some footling little invasion and, after overawing the Earthlings, retire? That would be the one way to absolutely assure their eventual counterinvasion of Mars. Indeed, it would probably hasten it—and they'd come as already hostile destroyers intent on wiping out a menace. No, Mr. Whitlow, when we invade Earth, it will be to protect ourselves from a potential future danger. Our purpose will be total and complete extermination, accomplished as swiftly and efficiently as possible. Our present military superiority makes our success certain."

Whitlow goggled at the Chief blankly, like a dirty and somewhat yellowed plaster statue of himself. He opened his mouth—and shut it without saying anything.

"You never believed, did you, Mr. Whitlow," continued the Chief kindly, "that we'd ever do anything for your sake? Or for anyone's—except us coleopteroids?"

Whitlow stared at the horrible, black, eight-legged eggs crowding ever closer—living embodiments of the poisonous blackness of their planet.

All he could think to mumble was: "But . . . but I thought you said . . . it was a misconception to think of alien beings as evil monsters intent only on ravaging . . . and destroying—"

"Perhaps I did, Mr. Whitlow. Perhaps I did," was the Chief's only reply.

In that instant Mr. Whitlow realized what an alien being really was.

As in a suffocating nightmare, he watched the coleopteroids edge closer. He heard the Chief's contemptuously unguarded aside to the Senior, "Haven't you got hold of his mind yet?" and the Senior's "No," and the Chief's swift order to the others.

Black eggs invaded his lightsphere, cruel armored claws opening to grab—those were Mr. Whitlow's last impression of Mars.

*   *   *

Instants later—for the device provided him with instantaneous transportation across any spatial expanse—Mr. Whitlow found himself inside a bubble that miraculously maintained normal atmospheric pressure deep under the tideless Venusian seas. The reverse of a fish in a tank, he peered out at the gently waving luminescent vegetation and the huge mud-girt buildings it half masked. Gleaming ships and tentacled creatures darted about.

The Chief Molluscoid regarded the trespasser on his private gardens with a haughty disfavor that even surprise could not shake.

"What are you?" he thought coldly.

"I . . . I've come to inform you of a threatened breach in an agelong truce."

Five eyes on longish stalks regarded him with a coldness equal to that of the repeated thought: "But what are you?"

A sudden surge of woeful honesty compelled Mr. Whitlow to reply, "I suppose . . . I suppose you'd call me a warmonger."

Alice and the Allergy

There was a knocking. The doctor put down his pen. Then he heard his wife hurrying down the stairs. He resumed his history of old Mrs. Easton's latest blood-clot.

The knocking was repeated. He reminded himself to get after Engstrand to fix the bell.

After a pause long enough for him to write a sentence and a half, there came a third and louder burst of knocking. He frowned and got up.

It was dark in the hall. Alice was standing on the third step from the bottom, making no move to answer the door. As he went past her he shot her an inquiring glance. He noted that her eyelids looked slightly puffy, as if she were having another attack—an impression which the hoarseness of her voice a moment later confirmed.

"*He* knocked that way," was what she whispered. She sounded frightened. He looked back at her with an expression of greater puzzlement—which almost immediately, however, changed to comprehension. He gave her a sympathetic, semi-professional nod, as if to say, "I understand now. Glad you mentioned it. We'll talk about it later." Then he opened the door.

It was Renshaw from the Allergy Lab. "Got the new kit for you, Howard," he remarked in an amiable Southern drawl. "Finished making it up this afternoon and thought I'd bring it around myself."

"A million thanks. Come on in."

Alice had retreated a few steps farther up the stairs. Renshaw did not appear to notice her in the gloom. He was talkative as he followed Howard into his office.

"An interestin' case turned up. Very unusual. A doctor we supply lost a patient by broncho-spasm. Nurse mistakenly injected the shot into a vein. In ten seconds he was strangling. Edema of the glottis developed. Injected aninophylline and epinephrine—no dice. Tried to get a bronchoscope down his windpipe to give him air, but couldn't manage. Finally did a tracheotomy, but by that time it was too late."

"You always have to be damned careful," Howard remarked.

"Right," Renshaw agreed cheerfully. He set the kit on the desk and stepped back. "Well, if we don't identify the substance responsible for your wife's allergy this time, it won't be for lack of imagination. I added some notions of my own to your suggestions."

"Good."

"You know, she's well on her way to becoming the toughest case I ever made kits for. We've tested all the ordinary substances, and most of the extraordinary."

Howard nodded, his gaze following the dark woodwork toward the hall door.

"Look," he said, "do many doctors tell you about allergy patients showing fits of acute depression during attacks, a tendency to rake up unpleasant memories—especially old fears?"

"Depression seems to be a pretty common symptom," said Renshaw cautiously. "Let's see, how long is it she's been bothered?"

"About two years—ever since six months after our marriage." Howard smiled. "That arouses certain obvious suspicions, but you know how exhaustively we've tested myself, my clothes, my professional equipment."

"I should say so," Renshaw assured him. For a moment the men were silent. Then, "She suffers from depression and fear?"

Howard nodded.

"Fear of anything in particular?"

But Howard did not answer that question.

*   *   *

About ten minutes later, as the outside door closed on the man from the Allergy Lab, Alice came slowly down the stairs.

The puffiness around her eyes was more marked, emphasizing her paleness. Her eyes were still fixed on the door.

"You know Renshaw, of course," her husband said.

"Of course, dear," she answered huskily, with a little laugh. "It was just the knocking. It made me remember *him*."

"That so?" Howard inquired cheerily. "I don't think you've ever told me that detail. I'd always assumed—"

"No," she said, "the bell to Auntie's house was out of order that afternoon. So it was his knocking that drew me through the dark hallway and made me open the door, so that I saw his white avid face and long strong hands—with the dusty couch just behind me, where . . . and my hand on the curtain sash, with which he—"

"Don't think about it." Howard reached up and caught hold of her cold hand. "That chap's been dead for two years now. He'll strangle no more women."

"Are you sure?" she asked.

"Of course. Look, dear, Renshaw's brought a new kit. We'll make the scratch tests right away."

She followed him obediently into the examination room across the hall from the office. He rejected the forearm she offered him—it still showed faint evidences of the last test. As he swabbed off the other, he studied her face.

"Another little siege, eh? Well, we'll ease that with a mild ephedrine spray."

"Oh it's nothing," she said. "I wouldn't mind it at all if it weren't for those stupid moods that go with it."

"I know," he said, blocking out the test areas.

"I always have that idiotic feeling," she continued hesitantly, "that *he's* trying to get at me."

Ignoring her remark, he picked up the needle. They were both silent as he worked with practiced speed and care. Finally he sat back, remarking with considerably more confidence than he felt, "There! I bet you this time we've nailed the elusive little demon who likes to choke you!"—and looked up at the face of the slim, desirable, but sometimes maddeningly irrational person he had made his wife.

"I wonder if you've considered it from my point of view," he said, smiling. "I know it was a horrible experience, just about the worst a woman can undergo. But if it hadn't happened, I'd never have been called in to take care of you—and we'd never have got married."

"That's true," she said, putting her hand on his.

"It was completely understandable that you should have spells of fear afterwards," he continued. "Anyone would. Though I do think your background made a difference. After all, your aunt kept you so shut away from people—men especially. Told you they were all sadistic, evil-minded brutes. You know, sometimes when I think of that woman deliberately trying to infect you with all her rotten fears, I find myself on the verge of forgetting that she was no more responsible for her actions than any other mis-educated neurotic."

She smiled at him gratefully.

"At any rate," he went on, "it was perfectly natural that you should be frightened, especially when you learned that he was a murderer with a record, who had killed other woman and had even, in two cases where he'd been interrupted, made daring efforts to come back and complete the job. Knowing that about him, it was plain realism on your part to be scared—at least intelligently apprehensive—as long as he was on the loose. Even after we were married."

"But then, when you got incontrovertible proof—" He fished in his pocket. "Of course, he didn't formally pay the law's penalty, but he's just as dead as if he had." He smoothed out a worn old newspaper clipping. "You can't have forgotten this," he said gently, and began to read:

MYSTERY STRANGLER
UNMASKED BY DEATH

Lansing, Dec. 22. (Universal Press)—A mysterious boarder who died two days ago at a Kinsey Street rooming house has been conclusively identified as the uncaught rapist and strangler who in recent years terrified three Midwestern cities. Police Lieutenant Jim Galeto, interviewed by reporters in the death room at 1555 Kinsey Street . . .

She covered the clipping with her hand. "Please."

"Sorry," he said, "but an idea had occurred to me—one that would explain your continuing fear. I don't think you've ever hinted at it, but are you really completely satisfied that this was the man? Or is there a part of your mind that still doubts, that believes the police mistaken, that pictures the killer still at large? I know you identified the photographs, but sometimes, Alice, I think it was a mistake that you didn't go to Lansing like they wanted you to and see with your own eyes—"

"I wouldn't want to go near that city, ever." Her lips had thinned.

"But when your peace of mind was at stake . . ."

"No, Howard," she said. "And besides, you're absolutely wrong. From the first moment I never had the slightest doubt that *he* was the man who died—"

"But in that case—"

"And furthermore, it was only then, when my allergy started, that I really began to be afraid of him."

"But surely, Alice—" Calm substituted for anger in his manner. "Oh, I know you can't believe any of that occult rot your aunt was always falling for."

"No, I don't," she said. "It's something very different."

"What?"

But that question was not answered. Alice was looking down at the inside of her arm. He followed her gaze to where a white welt was rapidly filling one of the squares.

"What's it mean?" she asked nervously.

"Mean?" he almost yelled. "Why, you dope, it means we've licked the thing at last! It means we've found the substance that causes your allergy. I'll call Renshaw right away and have him make up the shots."

*   *   *

He picked up one of the vials, frowned, checked it against the area. "That's odd," he said. "HOUSEHOLD DUST. We've tried that a half dozen times. But then, of course, it's always different . . ."

"Howard," she said, "I don't like it. I'm frightened."

He looked at her lovingly. "The little dope," he said to her softly. "She's about to be cured—and she's frightened." And he hugged her. She was cold in his arms.

But by the time they sat down to dinner, things were more like normal. The puffiness had gone out of her eyelids and he was briskly smiling.

"Got hold of Renshaw. He was very 'interested.' HOUSEHOLD DUST was one of his ideas. He's going down to the Lab tonight and will have the shots over early tomorrow. The sooner we start, the better. I also took the opportunity to phone Engstrand. He'll try to get over to fix the bell, this evening. Heard from Mrs. Easton's nurse too. Things aren't so well there. I'm pretty sure there'll be bad news by tomorrow morning at latest. I may have to rush over any minute. I hope it doesn't happen tonight, though."

It didn't and they spent a quiet evening—not even Engstrand showed up—which could have been very pleasant had Alice been a bit less preoccupied.

But about three o'clock he was shaken out of sleep by her trembling. She was holding him tight.

"*He's* coming." Her whisper was whistling, laryngitic.

"What?" He sat up, half pulling her with him. "I'd better give you another eph—"

"Sh! What's that? Listen."

He rubbed his face. "Look, Alice," after a moment, he said, "I'll go downstairs and make sure there's nothing there."

"No, don't!" she clung to him. For a minute or two they huddled there without speaking. Gradually his ears became attuned to the night sounds—the drone and mumble of the city, the house's faint, closer creakings. Something had happened to the street lamp and incongruous unmixed moonlight streamed through the window beyond the foot of the bed.

He was about to say something, when she let go of him and said, in a more normal voice, "There. It's gone."

She slipped out of bed, went to the window, opened it wider, and stood there, breathing deeply.

"You'll get cold, come back to bed," he told her.

"In a while."

The moonlight was in key with her flimsy nightgown. He got up, rummaged around for her quilted bathrobe and, in draping it around her, tried an embrace. She didn't respond.

He got back in bed and watched her. She had found a chair-arm and was looking out the window. The bathrobe had fallen back from her shoulders. He felt wide awake, his mind crawlingly active.

"You know, Alice," he said, "there may be a psychoanalytic angle to your fear."

"Yes?" She did not turn her head.

"Maybe, in a sense, your libido is still tied to the past. Unconsciously, you may still have that distorted conception of sex your aunt drilled into you, something sadistic and murderous. And it's possible your unconscious mind had tied your allergy in with it—you said it was a dusty couch. See what I'm getting at?"

She still looked out the window.

"It's an ugly idea and of course your conscious mind wouldn't entertain it for a moment, but your aunt's influence set the stage and, when all's said and done, *he* was your first experience of men. Maybe in some small way, your libido is still linked to . . . him."

She didn't say anything.

*   *   *

Rather late next morning he awoke feeling sluggish and irritable. He got out of the room quietly, leaving her still asleep, breathing easily. As he was getting a second cup of coffee, a jarringly loud knocking summoned him to the door. It was a messenger with the shots from the Allergy Lab. On his way to the examination room he phoned Engstrand again, heard him promise he'd be over in a half hour sure, cut short a long-winded explanation as to what had tied up the electrician last night.

He started to phone Mrs. Easton's place, decided against it.

He heard Alice in the kitchen.

In the examination room he set some water to boil in the sterilizing pan, got out instruments. He opened the package from the Allergy Lab, frowned at the inscription HOUSEHOLD DUST, set down the container, walked over to the window, came back and frowned again, went to his office and dialed the Lab.

"Renshaw?"

"Uh huh. Get the shots?"

"Yes, many thanks. But I was just wondering . . . you know, it's rather odd we should hit it with household dust after so many misses."

"Not so odd, when you consider . . ."

"Yes, but I was wondering exactly where the stuff came from."

"Just a minute."

He shifted around in his swivel chair. In the kitchen Alice was humming a tune.

"Say, Howard, look, I'm awfully sorry, but Johnson seems to have gone off with the records. I'm afraid I won't be able to get hold of them 'till afternoon."

"Oh, that's all right. Just curiosity. You don't have to bother."

"No, I'll let you know. Well, I suppose you'll be making the first injection this morning?"

"Right away. You know we're both grateful to you for having hit on the substance responsible."

"No credit due me. Just a . . ." Renshaw chuckled ". . . shot in the dark."

Some twenty minutes later, when Alice came into the examination room, Howard was struck, to a degree that quite startled him, with how pretty and desirable she looked. She had put on a white dress and her smiling face showed no signs of last night's attack. For a moment he had the impulse to take her in his arms, but then he remembered last night and decided against it.

As he prepared to make the injection, she eyed the hypodermics, bronchoscope, and scalpels laid out on the sterile towel.

"What are those for?" she asked lightly.

"Just routine stuff, never use them."

"You know," she said laughingly, "I was an awful ninny last night. Maybe you're right about my libido. At any rate, I've put *him* out of my life forever. He can't ever get at me again. From now on, you're the only one."

*   *   *

He grinned, very happily. Then his eyes grew serious and observant as he made the injection, first withdrawing the needle repeatedly to make sure there were no signs of venous blood. He watched her closely.

The phone jangled.

"Damn," he said. "That'll be Mrs. Easton's nurse. Come along with me."

*   *   *

He hurried through the swinging door. She started after him.

But it wasn't Mrs. Easton's nurse. It was Renshaw.

"Found the records. Johnson didn't have them after all. Just misplaced. And there *is* something out of the way. That dust didn't come from there at all. It came from . . ."

There came a knocking. He strained to hear what Renshaw was saying.

"What?" He whipped out a pencil. "Say that again. Don't mind the noise. It's just our electrician coming to fix the bell. What was that city?"

The knocking was repeated.

"Yes, I've got that. And the exact address of the place the dust came from?"

There came a third and louder burst of knocking, which grew to a violent tattoo.

Finishing his scribbling, he hung up with a bare "Thanks," to Renshaw, and hurried to the door just as the knocking died.

There was no one there.

Then he realized. He hardly dared push open the door to the examination room, yet no one could have gone more quickly.

Alice's agonizing arched, suffocated body was lying on the rug. Her heels, which just reached the hardwood flooring, made a final, weak knock-knock. Her throat was swollen like a toad's.

Before he made another movement he could not stop himself from glaring around, window and door, as if for an escaping intruder.

As he snatched for his instruments, knowing for an absolute certainty that it would be too late, a slip of paper floated down from his hand.

On it was scribbled, "Lansing. 1555 Kinsey Street."

90

The Girl with the Hungry Eyes

All right, I'll tell you why the Girl gives me the creeps. Why I can't stand to go down and see the mob slavering up at her on the tower, with that pop bottle or pack of cigarettes or whatever it is beside her. Why I hate to look at magazines any more because I know she'll turn up somewhere in a brassière or a bubble bath. Why I don't like to think of millions of Americans drinking in that poisonous half-smile. It's quite a story—more story than you're expecting.

No, I haven't suddenly developed any long-haired indignation at the evils of advertising and the national glamor-girl complex. That'd be a laugh for a man in my racket, wouldn't it? Though I think you'll agree there's something a little perverted about trying to capitalize on sex that way. But it's okay with me. And I know we've had the Face and the Body and the Look and what not else, so why shouldn't someone come along who sums it all up so completely, that we have to call her the Girl and blazon her on all the billboards from Times Square to Telegraph Hill?

But the Girl isn't like any of the others. She's unnatural. She's morbid. She's unholy.

Oh, these are modern times, you say, and the sort of thing I'm hinting at went out with witchcraft. But you see I'm not altogether sure myself what I'm hinting at, beyond a certain point. There are vampires and vampires, and not all of them suck blood.

And there were the murders, if they were murders. Besides, let me ask you this. Why, when America is obsessed with the Girl, don't we find out more about her? Why doesn't she rate a *Time* cover with a droll biography inside? Why hasn't there been a feature in *Life* or *The Post*? A profile in the *New Yorker*? Why hasn't *Charm* or *Mademoiselle* done her career saga? Not ready for it? Nuts!

Why haven't the movies snapped her up? Why hasn't she been on "Information, Please"? Why don't we see her kissing candidates at political rallies? Why isn't she chosen queen of some sort of junk or other at a convention?

Why don't we read about her tastes and hobbies, her views of the Russian situation? Why haven't the columnists interviewed her in a kimono on the top floor of the tallest hotel in Manhattan and told us who her boy friends are?

Finally—and this is the real killer—why hasn't she ever been drawn or painted?

Oh, no she hasn't. If you knew anything about commercial art you'd know that. Every blessed one of those pictures was worked up from a photograph. Expertly? Of course. They've got the top artists on it. But that's how it's done.

And now I'll tell you the why of all that. It's because from the top to the bottom of the whole world of advertising, news and business, there isn't a solitary soul who knows where the Girl came from, where she lives, what she does, who she is, even what her name is.

You heard me. What's more, not a single solitary soul ever sees her—except one poor damned photographer, who's making more money off her than he ever hoped to in his life and who's scared and miserable as hell every minute of the day.

No, I haven't the faintest idea who he is or where he has his studio. But I know there has to be such a man and I'm morally certain he feels just like I said.

Yes, I might be able to find her, if I tried. I'm not sure though—by now she probably has other safeguards. Besides, I don't want to.

Oh, I'm off my rocker, am I? That sort of thing can't happen in the Era of the Atom? People can't keep out of sight that way, not even Garbo?

Well I happen to know they can, because last year I was that poor damned photographer I was telling you about. Yes, last year, when the Girl made her first poisonous splash right here in this big little city of ours.

Yes, I know you weren't here last year and you don't know about it. Even the Girl had to start small. But if you hunted through the files of the local newspapers, you'd find some ads, and I might be able to locate you some of the old displays—I think Lovelybelt is still using one of them. I used to have a mountain of photos myself, until I burned them.

Yes, I made my cut off her. Nothing like what that other photographer must be making, but enough so it still bought this whiskey. She was funny about money. I'll tell you about that.

But first picture me then. I had a fourth-floor studio in that rathole the Hauser Building, not far from Ardleigh Park.

I'd been working at the Marsh-Mason studios until I'd gotten my bellyful of it and decided to start in for myself. The Hauser Building was awful—I'll never forget how the stairs creaked—but it was cheap and there was a skylight.

Business was lousy. I kept making the rounds of all the advertisers and agencies, and some of them didn't object to me too much personally, but my stuff never clicked. I was pretty near broke. I was behind on my rent. Hell, I didn't even have enough money to have a girl.

It was one of those dark, gray afternoons. The building was very quiet—I'd just finished developing some pix I was doing on speculation for Lovelybelt Girdles and Budford's Pool and Playground. My model had left. A Miss Leon. She was a civics teacher at one of the high schools and modeled for me on the side, just lately on speculation, too. After one look at the prints, I decided that Miss Leon probably wasn't just what Lovelybelt was looking for—or my photography either. I was about to call it a day.

And then the street door slammed four storys down and there were steps on the stairs and she came in.

She was wearing a cheap, shiny black dress. Black pumps. No stockings. And except that she had a gray cloth coat over one of them, those skinny arms of hers were bare. Her arms are pretty skinny, you know, or can't you see things like that any more?

And then the thin neck, the slightly gaunt, almost prim face, the tumbling mass of dark hair, and looking out from under it the hungriest eyes in the world.

That's the real reason she's plastered all over the country today, you know—those eyes. Nothing vulgar, but just the same they're looking at you with a hunger that's all sex and something more than sex. That's what everybody's been looking for since the

Year One—something a little more than sex.

Well, boys, there I was, alone with the Girl, in an office that was getting shadowy, in a nearly empty building. A situation that a million male Americans have undoubtedly pictured to themselves with various lush details. How was I feeling? Scared.

I know sex can be frightening. That cold heart-thumping when you're alone with a girl and feel you're going to touch her. But if it was sex this time, it was overlaid with something else.

At least I wasn't thinking about sex.

I remember that I took a backward step and that my hand jerked so that the photos I was looking at sailed to the floor.

There was the faintest dizzy feeling like something was being drawn out of me. Just a little bit.

That was all. Then she opened her mouth and everything was back to normal for a while.

"I see you're a photographer, mister," she said. "Could you use a model?"

Her voice wasn't very cultivated.

"I doubt it," I told her, picking up the pix. You see, I wasn't impressed. The commercial possibilities of her eyes hadn't registered on me yet, by a long shot. "What have you done?"

Well, she gave me a vague sort of story and I began to check her knowledge of model agencies and studios and rates and what not and pretty soon I said to her, "Look here, you never modeled for a photographer in your life. You just walked in here cold."

Well, she admitted that was more or less so.

All along through our talk I got the idea she was feeling her way, like someone in a strange place. Not that she was uncertain of herself, or of me, but just of the general situation.

"And you think anyone can model?" I asked her pityingly.

"Sure," she said.

"Look," I said, "a photographer can waste a dozen negatives trying to get one halfway human photo of an average woman. How many do you think he'd have to waste before he got a real catchy, glamourous photo of her?"

"I think I could do it," she said.

Well, I should have kicked her out right then. Maybe I admired the cool way she stuck to her dumb little guns. Maybe I was touched by her underfed look. More likely I was feeling mean on account of the way my pictures had been snubbed by everybody and I wanted to take it out on her by showing her up.

"Okay, I'm going to put you on the spot," I told her. "I'm going to try a couple of shots of you. Understand it's strictly on spec. If somebody should ever want to use a photo of you, which is about one chance in two million, I'll pay you regular rates for your time. Not otherwise."

She gave me a smile. The first. "That's swell by me," she said.

Well, I took three or four shots, close-ups of her face since I didn't fancy her cheap dress, and at least she stood up to my sarcasm. Then I remembered I still had the Lovelybelt stuff and I guess the meanness was still working in me because I handed her a girdle and told her to go behind the screen and get into it and she did, without getting flustered as I'd expected, and since we'd gone that far, I figured we might as well shoot the beach scene to round it out, and that was that.

All this time I wasn't feeling anything particular one way or the other, except every once in a while I'd get one of those faint dizzy flashes and wonder if there was something wrong with my stomach or if I could have been a bit careless with my chemicals.

93

Still, you know, I think the uneasiness was in me all the while.

I tossed her a card and pencil. "Write your name and address and phone," I told her and made for the darkroom.

A little later she walked out. I didn't call any good-bys. I was irked because she hadn't fussed around or seemed anxious about her poses, or even thanked me, except for that one smile.

I finished developing the negatives, made some prints, glanced at them, decided they weren't a great deal worse than Miss Leon. On an impulse I slipped them in with the pictures I was going to take on the rounds next morning.

By now I'd worked long enough, so I was a bit fagged and nervous, but I didn't dare waste enough money on liquor to help that. I wasn't very hungry. I think I went to a cheap movie.

I didn't think of the Girl at all, except maybe to wonder faintly why in my present womanless state I hadn't made a pass at her. She had seemed to belong to a—well, distinctly more approachable social strata than Miss Leon. But then, of course, there were all sorts of arguable reasons for my not doing that.

Next morning I made the rounds. My first step was Munsch's Brewery. They were looking for a "Munsch Girl." Papa Munsch had a sort of affection for me, though he razzed my photography. He had a good natural judgment about that, too. Fifty years ago he might have been one of the shoe-string boys who made Hollywood.

Right now he was out in the plant pursuing his favorite occupation. He put down the beaded schooner, smacked his lips, gabbled something technical to someone about hops, wiped his fat hands on the big apron he was wearing, and grabbed my thin stack of pictures.

He was about halfway through, making noises with his tongue and teeth, when he came to her. I kicked myself for even having stuck her in.

"That's her," he said. "The photography's not so hot, but that's the girl."

It was all decided. I wonder now why Papa Munsch sensed what the Girl had right away, while I didn't. I think it was because I saw her first in the flesh, if that's the right word.

At the time I just felt faint.

"Who is she?" he said.

"One of my new models." I tried to make it casual.

"Bring her out tomorrow morning," he told me. "And your stuff. We'll photograph her here."

"Here, don't look so sick," he added. "Have some beer."

Well, I went away telling myself it was just a fluke, so that she'd probably blow it tomorrow with her inexperience, and so on.

Just the same, when I reverently laid my next stack of pictures on Mr. Fitch, of Lovelybelt's, rose-colored blotter, I had hers on top.

Mr. Fitch went through the motins of being an art critic. He leaned over backwards, squinted his eyes, waved his long fingers, and said, "Hmm. What do you think, Miss Willow? Here, in this light, of course, the photograph doesn't show the bias cut. And perhaps we should use the Lovelybelt Imp instead of the Angel. Still, the girl . . . Come over here, Binns." More finger-waving. "I want a married man's reaction."

He couldn't hide the fact that he was hooked.

Exactly the same thing happened at Budford's Pool and Playground, except that Da Costa didn't need a married man's say-so.

"Hot stuff," he said, sucking his lips. "Oh boy, you photographers!"

I hot-footed it back to the office and grabbed up the card I'd given her to put down her name and address.

It was blank.

I don't mind telling you that the next five days were about the worst I ever went through, in an ordinary way. When next morning rolled around and I still hadn't got hold of her, I had to start stalling.

"She's sick," I told Papa Munsch over the phone.

"She's at a hospital?" he asked me.

"Nothing that serious," I told him.

"Get her out here then. What's a little headache?"

"Sorry, I can't."

Papa Munsch got suspicious. "You really got this girl?"

"Of course I have."

"Well, I don't know. I'd think it was some New York model, except I recognized your lousy photography."

I laughed.

"Well, look, you get her here tomorrow morning, you hear?"

"I'll try."

"Try nothing. You get her out here."

He didn't know half of what I tried. I went around to all the model and employment agencies. I did some slick detective work at the photographic and art studios. I used up some of my last dimes putting advertisements in all three papers. I looked at high school yearbooks and at employee photos in local house organs. I went to restaurants and drugstores, looking at waitresses, and to dime stores and department stores, looking at clerks. I watched the crowds coming out of movie theaters. I roamed the streets.

Evenings, I spent quite a bit of time along Pick-Up Row. Somehow that seemed the right place.

The fifth afternoon I knew I was licked. Papa Munsch's deadline—he'd given me several, but this was it—was due to run out at six o'clock. Mr. Fitch had already canceled.

I was at the studio window, looking out at Ardleigh Park.

She walked in.

I'd gone over this moment so often in my mind that I had no trouble putting on my act. Even the faint dizzy feeling didn't throw me off.

"Hello," I said, hardly looking at her.

"Hello," she said.

"Not discouraged yet?"

"No." It didn't sound uneasy or defiant. It was just a statement.

I snapped a look at my watch, got up and said curtly, "Look here, I'm going to give you a chance. There's a client of mine looking for a girl of your general type. If you do a real good job you might break into the modeling business.

"We can see him this afternoon if we hurry," I said. I picked up my stuff. "Come on. And next time if you expect favors, don't forget to leave your phone number."

"Uh, uh," she said, not moving.

"What do you mean?" I said.

"I'm not going out to see any client of yours."

"The hell you aren't," I said. "You little nut, I'm giving you a break."

She shook her head slowly. "You're not fooling me, baby, you're not fooling me at all. They want me." And she gave me the second smile.

95

At the time I thought she must have seen my newspaper ad. Now I'm not so sure.

"And now I'll tell you how we're going to work," she went on. "You aren't going to have my name or address or phone number. Nobody is. And we're going to do all the pictures right here. Just you and me."

You can imagine the roar I raised at that. I was everything—angry, sarcastic, patiently explanatory, off my nut, threatening, pleading.

I would have slapped her face off, except it was photographic capital.

In the end all I could do was phone Papa Munsch and tell him her conditions. I knew I didn't have a chance, but I had to take it.

He gave me a really angry bawling out, said "no" several times and hung up.

It didn't worry her. "We'll start shooting at ten o'clock tomorrow," she said.

It was just like her, using that corny line from the movie magazines.

About midnight Papa Munsch called me up.

"I don't know what insane asylum you're renting this girl from," he said, "but I'll take her. Come round tomorrow morning and I'll try to get it through your head just how I want the pictures. And I'm glad I got you out of bed!"

After that it was a breeze. Even Mr. Fitch reconsidered and after taking two days to tell me it was quite impossible, he accepted the conditions too.

Of course you're all under the spell of the Girl, so you can't understand how much self-sacrifice it represented on Mr. Fitch's part when he agreed to forego supervising the photography of my model in the Lovelybelt Imp or Vixen or whatever it was we finally used.

Next morning she turned up on time according to her schedule, and we went to work. I'll say one thing for her, she never got tired and she never kicked at the way I fussed over shots. I got along okay, except I still had that feeling of something being shoved away gently. Maybe you've felt it just a little, looking at her picture.

When we finished I found out there were still more rules. It was about the middle of the afternoon. I started with her to get a sandwich and coffee.

"Uh, uh," she said. "I'm going down alone. And look, baby, if you ever try to follow me, if you ever so much as stick your head out of that window when I go, you can hire yourself another model."

You can imagine how all this crazy stuff strained my temper—and my imagination. I remember opening the window after she was gone—I waited a few minutes first—and standing there getting some fresh air and trying to figure out what could be behind it, whether she was hiding from the police, or was somebody's ruined daughter, or maybe had got the idea it was smart to be temperamental, or more likely Papa Munsch was right and she was partly nuts.

But I had my pictures to finish up.

Looking back it's amazing to think how fast her magic began to take hold of the city after that. Remembering what came after, I'm frightened of what's happening to the whole country—and maybe the world. Yesterday I read something in *Time* about the Girl's picture turning up on billboards in Egypt.

The rest of my story will help show you why I'm frightened in that big, general way. But I have a theory, too, that helps explain, though it's one of those things that's beyond that "certain point." It's about the Girl. I'll give it to you in a few words.

You know how modern advertising gets everybody's mind set in the same direction, wanting the same things, imagining the same things. And you know the psychologists aren't so skeptical of telepathy as they used to be.

Add up the two ideas. Suppose the identical desires of millions of people focused on one telepathic person. Say a girl. Shaped her in their image.

Imagine her knowing the hiddenmost hungers of millions of men. Imagine her seeing deeper into those hungers than the people that had them, seeing the hatred and the wish for death behind the lust. Imagine her shaping herself in that complete image, keeping herself as aloof as marble. Yet imagine the hunger she might feel in answer to their hunger.

But that's getting a long way from the facts of my story. And some of those facts are darn solid. Like money. We made money.

That was the funny thing I was going to tell you. I was afraid the Girl was going to hold me up. She really had be over a barrel, you know.

But she didn't ask for anything but the regular rates. Later on I insisted on pushing more money at her, a whole lot. But she always took it with that same contemptuous look, as if she were going to toss it down the first drain when she got outside.

Maybe she did.

At any rate, I had money. For the first time in months I had money enough to get drunk, buy new clothes, take taxicabs. I could make a play for any girl I wanted to. I only had to pick.

And so of course I had to go and pick . . .

But first let me tell you about Papa Munsch.

Papa Munsch wasn't the first of the boys to try to meet my model but I think he was the first to really go soft on her. I could watch the change in his eyes as he looked at her pictures. They began to get sentimental, reverent. Mama Munsch had been dead for two years.

He was smart about the way he planned it. He got me to drop some information which told him when she came to work, and then one morning he came pounding up the stairs a few minutes before.

"I've got to see her, Dave," he told me.

I argued with him, I kidded him, I explained he didn't know just how serious she was about her crazy ideas. I even pointed out he was cutting both our throats. I even amazed myself by bawling him out.

He didn't take any of it in his usual way. He just kept repeating, "But, Dave, I've got to see her."

The street door slammed.

"That's her," I said, lowering my voice. "You've got to get out."

He wouldn't, so I shoved him in the darkroom. "And keep quiet," I whispered. "I'll tell her I can't work today."

I knew he'd try to look at her and probably come bustling in, but there wasn't anything else I could do.

The footsteps came to the fourth floor. But she never showed at the door. I got uneasy.

"Get that bum out of there!" she yelled suddenly from beyond the door. Not very loud, but in her commonest voice.

"I'm going up to the next landing," she said. "And if that fat-bellied bum doesn't march straight down to the street, he'll never get another picture of me except spitting in his lousy beer."

Papa Munsch came out of the darkroom. He was white. He didn't look at me as he went out. He never looked at her pictures in front of me again.

That was Papa Munsch. Now it's me I'm telling about. I talked around the subject with her, I hinted, eventually I made my pass.

She lifted my hand off her as if it were a damp rag.

"No, baby," she said. "This is working time."

"But afterwards . . ." I pressed.

"The rules still hold." And I got what I think was the fifth smile.

It's hard to believe, but she never budged an inch from that crazy line. I mustn't make a pass at her in the office, because our work was very important and she loved it and there mustn't be any distractions. And I couldn't see her anywhere else, because if I tried to, I'd never snap another picture of her—and all this with more money coming in all the time and me never so stupid as to think my photography had anything to do with it.

Of course I wouldn't have been human if I hadn't made more passes. But they always got the wet-rag treatment and there weren't any more smiles.

I changed. I went sort of crazy and light-headed—only sometimes I felt my head was going to burst. And I started to talk to her all the time. About myself.

It was like being in a constant delirium that never interfered with business. I didn't pay any attention to the dizzy feeling. It seemed natural.

I'd walk around and for a moment the reflector would look like a sheet of white-hot steel, or the shadows would seem like armies of moths, or the camera would be a big black coal car. But the next instant they'd come all right again.

I think sometimes I was scared to death of her. She'd seem the strangest, most horrible person in the world. But other times . . .

And I talked. It didn't matter what I was doing—lighting her, posing her, fussing with props, snapping my pictures—or where she was—on the platform, behind the screen, relaxing with a magazine—I kept up a steady gab.

I told her everything I knew about myself. I told her about my first girl. I told her about my brother Bob's bicycle. I told her about running away on a freight, and the licking pa gave me when I came home. I told her about shipping to South America and the blue sky at night. I told her about Betty. I told her about my mother dying of cancer. I told her about being beaten up in a fight in an alley behind a bar. I told her about Mildred. I told her about the first picture I ever sold. I told her how Chicago looked from a sailboat. I told her about the longest drunk I was ever on. I told her about Marsh-Mason. I told her about Gwen. I told her about how I met Papa Munsch. I told her about hunting her. I told her about how I felt now.

She never paid the slightest attention to what I said. I couldn't even tell if she heard me.

It was when we were getting our first nibble from national advertisers that I decided to follow her when she went home.

Wait, I can place it better than that. Something you'll remember from the out-of-town papers—those maybe murders I mentioned. I think there were six.

I say "maybe" because the police could never be sure they weren't heart attacks. But there's bound to be suspicion when attacks happen to people whose hearts have been okay, and always at night when they're alone and away from home and there's a question of what they were doing.

The six deaths created one of those "mystery poisoner" scares. And afterwards there was a feeling that they hadn't really stopped, but were being continued in a less suspicious way.

That's one of the things that scares me now.

But at that time my only feeling was relief that I'd decided to follow her.

I made her work until dark one afternoon. I didn't need any excuses, we were snowed under with orders. I waited until the street door slammed, then I ran down. I was wearing rubber-soled shoes. I'd slipped on a dark coat she'd never seen me in, and a dark hat.

I stood in the doorway until I spotted her. She was walking by Ardleigh Park towards the heart of town. It was one of those warm fall nights. I followed her on the other side of the street. My idea for tonight was just to find out where she lived. That would give me a hold on her.

She stopped in front of a display window, of Everley's department store, standing back from the flow. She stood there looking in.

I remembered we'd done a big photograph of her for Everley's, to make a flat model for a lingerie display. That was what she was looking at.

At the time it seemed all right to me that she should adore herself, if that was what she was doing.

When people passed she'd turn away a little or drift back further into the shadows.

Then a man came by alone. I couldn't see his face very well, but he looked middle-aged. He stopped and stood looking in the window.

She came out of the shadows and stepped up beside him.

How would you boys feel if you were looking at a poster of the Girl and suddenly she was there beside you, her arm linked with yours?

This fellow's reaction showed plain as day. A crazy dream had come to life for him.

They talked for a moment. Then he waved a taxi to the curb. They got in and drove off.

I got drunk that night. It was almost as if she'd known I was following her and had picked that way to hurt me. Maybe she had. Maybe this was the finish.

But the next morning she turned up at the usual time and I was back in the delirium, only now with some new angles added.

That night when I followed her she picked a spot under a streetlamp, opposite one of the Munsch Girl billboards.

Now it frightens me to think of her lurking that way.

After about twenty minutes a convertible slowed down going past her, backed up, swung into the curb.

I was closer this time. I got a good look at the fellow's face. He was a little younger, about my age.

Next morning the same face looked up at me from the front page of the paper. The convertible had been found parked on a sidestreet. He had been in it. As in the other maybe-murders, the cause of death was uncertain.

All kinds of thoughts were spinning in my head that day, but there were only two things I knew for sure. That I'd got the first real offer from a national advertiser, and that I was going to take the Girl's arm and walk down the stairs with her when we quit work.

She didn't seem surprised. "You know what you're doing?" she said.

"I know."

She smiled. "I was wondering when you'd get around to it."

I began to feel good. I was kissing everything good-by, but I had my arm around hers.

It was another of those warm fall evenings. We cut across into Ardleigh Park. It was dark there, but all around the sky was a sallow pink from the advertising signs.

We walked for a long time in the park. She didn't say anything and she didn't look at me, but I could see her lips twitching and after a while her hand tightened on my arm.

We stopped. We'd been walking across the grass. She dropped down and pulled me after her. She put her hands on my shoulders. I was looking down at her face. It was the faintest sallow pink from the glow in the sky. The hungry eyes were dark smudges.

I was fumbling with her blouse. She took my hand away, not like she had in the studio. "I don't want that," she said.

*　　*　　*

First I'll tell you what I did afterwards. Then I'll tell you why I did it. Then I'll tell you what she said.

What I did was run away. I don't remember all of that because I was dizzy, and the pink sky was swinging against the dark trees. But after a while I staggered into the lights of the street. The next day I closed up the studio. The telephone was ringing when I locked the door and there were unopened letters on the floor. I never saw the Girl again in the flesh, if that's the right word.

I did it because I didn't want to die. I didn't want the life drawn out of me. There are vampires and vampires, and the ones that suck blood aren't the worst. If it hadn't been for the warning of those dizzy flashes, and Papa Munsch and the face in the morning paper, I'd have gone the way the others did. But I realized what I was up against while there was still time to tear myself away. I realized that wherever she came from, whatever shaped her, she's the quintessence of the horror behind the bright billboard. She's the smile that tricks you into throwing away your money and your life. She's the eyes that lead you on and on, and then show you death. She's the creature you give everything for and never really get. She's the being that takes everything you've got and gives nothing in return. When you yearn towards her face on the billboards, remember that. She's the lure. She's the bait. She's the Girl.

And this is what she said, "I want you. I want your high spots. I want everything that's made you happy and everything that's hurt you bad. I want your first girl. I want that shiny bicycle. I want that licking. I want that pinhole camera. I want Betty's legs. I want the blue sky filled with stars. I want your mother's death. I want your blood on the cobblestones. I want Mildred's mouth. I want the first picture you sold. I want the lights of Chicago. I want the gin. I want Gwen's hands. I want your wanting me. I want your life. Feed me, baby, feed me."

The Man Who Never Grew Young

Maot is becoming restless. Often toward evening she trudges to where the black earth meets the yellow sand and stands looking across the desert until the wind starts.

But I sit with my back to the reed screen and watch the Nile.

It isn't just that she's growing young. She is wearying of the fields. She leaves their tilling to me and lavishes her attention on the flock. Every day she takes the sheep and goats farther to pasture.

I have seen it coming for a long time. For generations the fields have been growing scantier and less diligently irrigated. There seems to be more rain. The houses have become simpler—mere walled tents. And every year some family gathers its flocks and wanders off west.

Why should I cling so tenaciously to these poor relics of civilization—I, who have seen king Cheops' men take down the Great Pyramid block by block and return it to the hills?

I often wonder why I never grow young. It is still as much a mystery to me as to the brown farmers who kneel in awe when I walk past.

I envy those who grow young. I yearn for the sloughing of wisdom and responsibility, the plunge into a period of lovemaking and breathless excitement, the carefree years before the end.

But I remain a bearded man of thirty-odd, wearing the goatskin as I once wore the doublet or the toga, always on the brink of that plunge yet never making it.

It seems to me that I have always been this way. Why, I cannot even remember my own disinterment, and everyone remembers that.

Maot is subtle. She does not ask for what she wants, but when she comes home at evening she sits far back from the fire and murmurs disturbing fragments of song and rubs her eyelids with green pigment to make herself desirable to me and tries in every way to infect me with her restlessness. She tempts me from the hot work at midday and points out how hardy our sheep and goat are becoming.

There are no young men among us any more. All of them start for the desert with the approach of youth, or before. Even toothless, scrawny patriarchs uncurl from their grave-holes, and hardly pausing to refresh themselves with the food and drink dug up with them, collect their flocks and wives and hobble off into the west.

I remember the first disinterment I witnessed. It was in a country of smoke and machines and constant news. But what I am about to relate occurred in a backwater where there were still small farms and narrow roads and simple ways.

There were two old women named Flora and Helen. It could not have been more than a few years since their own disinterments, but those I cannot remember. I think I was some sort of nephew, but I cannot be sure.

They began to visit an old grave in the cemetery a half mile outside town. I remember the little bouquets of flowers they would bring back with them. Their prim, placid faces became troubled. I could see that grief was entering their lives.

The years passed. Their visits to the cemetery became more frequent. Accompanying them once, I noted that the worn inscription on the headstone was growing clearer and sharper, just as was happening to their own features. "John, loving husband of Flora . . ."

Often Flora would sob through half the night, and Helen went about with a set look on her face. Relatives came and spoke comforting words, but these seemed only to intensify their grief.

Finally the headstone grew brand-new and the grass became tender green shoots which disappeared into the raw brown earth. As if these were the signs their obscure instincts had been awaiting, Flora and Helen mastered their grief and visited the minister and the mortician and the doctor and made certain arrangements.

On a cold autumn day, when the brown curled leaves were whirling up into the trees, the procession set out—the empty hearse, the dark silent automobiles. At the cemetery we found a couple of men with shovels turning away unobstrusively from the newly opened grave. Then, while Flora and Helen wept bitterly and the minister spoke solemn words, a long narrow box was lifted from the grave and carried to the hearse.

At home the lid of the box was unscrewed and slid back, and we saw John, a waxen old man with a long life before him.

Next day, in obedience to what seemed an age-old ritual, they took him from the box, and the mortician undressed him and drew a pungent liquid from his veins and injected the red blood. Then they took him and laid him in bed. After a few hours of stoney-eyed waiting, the blood began to work. He stirred and his first breath rattled in his throat. Flora sat down on the bed and strained him to her in a fearful embrace.

But he was very sick and in need of rest, so the doctor waved her from the room. I remember the look on her face as she closed the door.

I should have been happy too, but I seem to recall that I felt there was something unwholesome about the whole episode. Perhaps our first experiences of the great crisis of life always affect us in some such fashion.

*   *   *

I love Maot. The hundreds I have loved before her in my wanderings down the world do not take away from the sincerity of my affection. I did not enter her life, or theirs, as lovers ordinarily do—from the grave or in the passion of some terrible quarrel. I am always the drifter.

Maot knows there is something strange about me. But she does not let that interfere with her efforts to make me do the thing she wants.

I love Maot and eventually I will accede to her desire. But first I will linger a while by the Nile and the mighty pageantry conjured up by its passage.

My first memories are always the most difficult and I struggle the hardest to interpret them. I have the feeling that if I could get back a little beyond them, a terrifying understanding would come to me. But I never seem able to make the necessary effort.

They begin without antecedent in cloud and turmoil, darkness and fear. I am a citizen of a great country far away, beardless and wearing ugly confining clothing, but no different in age and appearance from today. The country is a hundred times bigger than Egypt, yet it is only one of many. All the peoples of the world are known to each other, and the world is round, not flat, and it floats in an endless immensity dotted with islands of suns, not confined under a star-speckled bowl.

Machines are everywhere, and news goes round the world like a shout, and desires are many. There are undreamed-of abundance, unrivaled opportunities. Yet men are not happy. They live in fear. The fear, if I recall rightly, is of a war that will engulf and perhaps destroy us all. It overhangs us like the dark.

The weapons they have ready for that war are terrible. Great engines that sail pilotless, not through the water but the air, halfway around the world to destroy some enemy city. Others that dart up beyond the air itself, to come in attacking from the stars. Poisoned clouds. Deadly motes of luminous dust.

But worst of all are the weapons that are only rumored.

For months that seem eternities we wait on the brink of that war. We know that the mistakes have been made, the irrevocable steps taken, the last chances lost. We only await the event.

It would seem that there must have been some special reason for the extremity of our hopelessness and horror. As if there had been previous worldwide wars and we had struggled back from each desperately promising ourselves that it would be the last. But of any such, I can remember nothing. I and the world might well have been created under the shadow of that catastrophe, in a universal disinterment.

The months wear on. Then, miraculously, unbelievably, the war begins to recede. The tension relaxes. The clouds lift. There is great activity, conferences and plans. Hopes for lasting peace ride high.

This does not last. In sudden holocaust, there arises an oppressor named Hitler. Odd, how that name should come back to me after these millennia. His armies fan out across the globe.

But their success is short-lived. They are driven back, and Hitler trails off into oblivion. In the end he is an obscure agitator, almost forgotten.

Another peace then, but neither does it last. Another war, less fierce than the preceding, and it too trails off into a quieter era.

And so on.

I sometimes think (I must hold on to this) that time once flowed in the opposite direction, and that, in revulsion from the ultimate war, it turned back upon itself and began to retrace its former course. That our present lives are only a return and an unwinding. A great retreat.

In that case time may turn again. We may have another chance to scale the barrier. But no . . .

The thought has vanished in the rippling Nile.

Another family is leaving the valley today. All morning they have toiled up the sandy gorge. And now, returning perhaps for a last glimpse, to the verge of the yellow cliffs, they are outlined against the morning sky—upright specks for men, flat specks for animals.

Maot watches beside me. But she makes no comment. She is sure of me.

The cliff is bare again. Soon they will have forgotten the Nile and its disturbing ghosts of memories.

All our life is a forgetting and a closing in. As the child is absorbed by its mother, so great thoughts are swallowed up in the mind of genius. At first they are everywhere. They environ us like the air. Then there is a narrowing in. Not all men know them. Then there comes one great man, and he takes them to himself, and they are a secret. There only remains the disturbing conviction that something worthy has vanished.

I have seen Shakespeare unwrite the great plays. I have watched Socrates unthink the great thoughts. I have heard Jesus unsay the great words.

There is an inscription in stone, and it seems eternal. Coming back centuries later I find it the same, only a little less worn, and I think that it, at least, may endure. But some day a scribe comes and laboriously fills in the grooves until there is only blank stone.

Then only he knows what was written there. And as he grows young, that knowledge dies forever.

It is the same in all we do. Our houses grow new and we dismantle them and stow the materials inconspicuously away, in mine and quarry, forest and field. Our clothes grow new and we put them off. And we grow new and forget and blindly see a mother.

* * *

All the people are gone now. Only I and Maot linger.

I had not realized it would come so soon. Now that we are near the end, Nature seems to hurry.

I suppose that there are other stragglers here and there along the Nile, but I like to think that we are the last to see the vanishing fields, the last to look upon the river with some knowledge of what it once symbolized, before oblivion closes in.

Ours is a world in which lost causes conquer. After the second war of which I spoke, there was a long period of peace in my native country across the sea. There were among us at that time a primitive people called Indians, neglected and imposed upon and forced to live apart in unwanted areas. We gave no thought to these people. We would have laughed at anyone who told us they had power to hurt us.

But from somewhere a spark of rebellion appeared among them. They formed bands, armed themselves with bows and inferior guns, took the warpath against us.

We fought them in little unimportant wars that were never quite conclusive. They persisted, always returning to the fight, laying ambushes for our men and wagons, harrying us continually, eventually making sizable inroads.

Yet we still considered them of such trifling importance that we found time to engage in a civil war among ourselves.

The issue of this war was sad. A dusky portion of our citizenry were enslaved and made to toil for us in house and field.

The Indians grew formidable. Step by step they drove us back across the wide midwestern rivers and plains, through the wooded mountains to eastward.

On the eastern coast we held for a while, chiefly by leaguing with a transoceanic island nation, to whom we surrendered our independence.

There was an enheartening occurrence. The enslaved Negroes were gathered together and crowded in ships and taken to the southern shores of this continent, and there liberated or given into the hands of warlike tribes who eventually released them.

But the pressure of the Indians, sporadically aided by foreign allies, increased. City by city, town by town, settlement by settlement, we pulled up our stakes and took ship ourselves across the sea. Toward the end the Indians became strangely pacific, so that the last boatloads seemed to flee not so much in physical fear as in supernatural terror of the green silent forests that had swallowed up their homes.

To the south the Aztecs took up their glass knives and flint-edged swords and drove out the . . . I think they were called Spaniards.

In another century the whole western continent was forgotten, save for dim, haunting recollections.

Growing tyranny and ignorance, a constant contraction of frontiers, rebellions of the downtrodden, who in turn became oppressors—these constituted the next epoch of history.

Once I thought the tide had turned. A strong and orderly people, the Romans, arose and put most of the diminished world under their sway.

But this stability proved transitory. Once again the governed rose against the governors. The Romans were driven back—from England, from Egypt, from Gaul, from Asia, from Greece. Rising from barren fields came Carthage to contest successfully Rome's preeminence. The Romans took refuge in Rome, became unimportant, dwindled, were lost in a maze of migrations.

Their energizing thoughts flamed up for one glorious century in Athens, then ceased to carry weight.

After that, the decline continued at a steady pace. Never again was I deceived into thinking the trend had changed.

Except this one last time.

Because she was stony and sun-drenched and dry, full of temples and tombs, given to custom and calm, I thought Egypt would endure. The passage of almost changeless centuries encouraged me in this belief. I thought that if we had not reached the turning point, we had at least come to rest.

But the rains have come, the temples and tombs fill the scars in the cliffs, and the custom and calm have given way to the restless urges of the nomad.

If there is a turning point, it will not come until man is one with the beasts.

And Egypt must vanish like the rest.

* * *

Tomorrow Maot and I set out. Our flock is gathered. Our tent is rolled.

Maot is afire with youth. She is very loving.

It will be strange in the desert. All too soon we will exchange our last and sweetest kiss and she will prattle to me childishly and I will look after her until we find her mother.

Or perhaps some day I will abandon her in the desert, and her mother will find her. And I will go on.

Coming Attraction

The coupe with the fishhooks welded to the fender shouldered up over the curb like the nose of a nightmare. The girl in its path stood frozen, her face probably stiff with fright under her mask. For once my reflexes weren't shy. I took a fast step toward her, grabbed her elbow, yanked her back. Her black skirt swirled out.

The big coupe shot by, its turbine humming. I glimpsed three faces. Something ripped. I felt the hot exhaust on my ankles as the big coupe swerved back into the street. A thick cloud like a black flower blossomed from its jouncing rear end, while from the fishhooks flew a black shimmering rag.

"Did they get you?" I asked the girl.

She had twisted around to look where the side of her skirt was torn away. She was wearing nylon tights.

"The hooks didn't touch me," she said shakily. "I guess I'm lucky."

I heard voices around us:

"They're a menace. They ought to be arrested."

Sirens screamed at a rising pitch as two motor-police, their rocket-assist jets full on, came whizzing toward us after the coupe. But the black flower had become an inky fog obscuring the whole street. The motor-police switched from rocket assists to rocket brakes and swerved to a stop near the smoke cloud.

"Are you English?" the girl asked me. "You have an English accent."

Her voice came shudderingly from behind the sleek black satin mask. I fancied her teeth must be chattering. Eyes that were perhaps blue searched my face from behind the black gauze covering the eyeholes of the mask. I told her she'd guessed right. She stood close to me. "Will you come to my place tonight?" she asked rapidly. "I can't thank you now. And there's something else you can help me about."

My arm, still lightly circling her waist, felt her body trembling. I was answering the plea in that as much as in her voice when I said, "Certainly." She gave me an address south of Inferno, an apartment number and a time. She asked me my name and I told her.

"Hey, you!"

I turned obediently to the policeman's shout. He shooed away the small clucking crowd of masked women and barefaced men. Coughing from the smoke that the black coupe had thrown out, he asked for my papers. I handed him the essential ones.

He looked at them and then at me. "British Barter? How long will you be in New York?"

Suppressing the urge to say, "For as short a time as possible," I told him I'd be here for a week or so.

"May need you as a witness," he explained. "Those kids can't use smoke on us. When they do that, we pull them in."

He seemed to think the smoke was the bad thing. "They tried to kill the lady," I pointed out.

He shook his head wisely. "They always pretend they're going to, but actually they just want to snag skirts. I've picked up rippers with as many as fifty skirt-snags tacked up in their rooms. Of course, sometimes they come a little too close."

I explained that if I hadn't yanked her out of the way, she'd have been hit by more than hooks. But he interrupted, "If she'd thought it was a real murder attempt, she'd have stayed here."

I looked around. It was true. She was gone.

"She was fearfully frightened," I told him.

"Who wouldn't be? Those kids would have scared old Stalin himself."

"I mean frightened of more than 'kids.' They didn't look like 'kids.'"

"What did they look like?"

I tried without much success to describe the three faces. A vague impression of viciousness and effeminacy doesn't mean much.

"Well, I could be wrong," he said finally. "Do you know the girl? Where she lives?"

"No," I half lied.

The other policeman hung up his radiophone and ambled toward us, kicking at the tendrils of dissipating smoke. The black cloud no longer hid the dingy facades with their five-year-old radiation flashburns, and I could begin to make out the distant stump of the Empire State Building, thrusting up out of Inferno like a mangled finger.

"They haven't been picked up so far," the approaching policeman grumbled. "Left smoke for five blocks, from what Ryan says."

The first policeman shook his head. "That's bad," he observed solemnly.

I was feeling a bit uneasy and ashamed. An Englishman shouldn't lie, at least not on impulse.

"They sound like nasty customers," the first policeman continued in the same grim tone. "We'll need witnesses. Looks as if you may have to stay in New York longer than you expect."

I got the point. I said, "I forgot to show you all my papers," and handed him a few others, making sure there was a five dollar bill in among them.

*　　*　　*

When he handed them back a bit later, his voice was no longer ominous. My feelings of guilt vanished. To cement our relationship, I chatted with the two of them about their job.

"I suppose the masks give you some trouble," I observed. "Over in England we've been reading about your new crop of masked female bandits."

"Those things get exaggerated," the first policeman assured me. "It's the men masking as women that really mix us up. But, brother, when we nab them, we jump on them with both feet."

"And you get so you can spot women almost as well as if they had naked faces," the second policeman volunteered. "You know, hands and all that."

"Especially all that," the first agreed with a chuckle. "Say, is it true that some girls don't mask over in England?"

"A number of them have picked up the fashion," I told him. "Only a few, though—the ones who always adopt the latest style, however extreme."

"They're usually masked in the British newscasts."

"I imagine it's arranged that way out of deference to American taste," I confessed. "Actually, not very many do mask."

The second policeman considered that. "Girls going down the street bare from the neck up." It was not clear whether he viewed the prospect with relish or moral distaste. Likely both.

"A few members keep trying to persuade Parliament to enact a law forbidding all masking," I continued, talking perhaps a bit too much.

The second policeman shook his head. "What an idea. You know, masks are a pretty good thing, brother. Couple of years more and I'm going to make my wife wear hers around the house."

The first policeman shrugged. "If women were to stop wearing masks, in six weeks you wouldn't know the difference. You get used to anything, if enough people do or don't do it."

I agreed, rather regretfully, and left them. I turned north on Broadway (old Tenth Avenue, I believe) and walked rapidly until I was beyond Inferno. Passing such an area of undecontaminated radioactivity always makes a person queasy. I thanked God there weren't any such in England, as yet.

The street was almost empty, though I was accosted by a couple of beggars with faces tunnelled by H-bomb scars, whether real or of makeup putty, I couldn't tell. A fat woman held out a baby with webbed fingers and toes. I told myself it would have been deformed anyway and that she was only capitalizing on our fear of bomb-induced mutations. Still, I gave her a seven-and-a-half-cent piece. Her mask made me feel I was paying tribute to an African fetish.

"May all your children be blessed with one head and two eyes, sir."

"Thanks," I said, shuddering, and hurried past her.

*   *   *

". . . There's only trash behind the mask, so turn your head, stick to your task: Stay away, stay away—from—the—girls!"

This last was the end of an anti-sex song being sung by some religionists half a block from the circle-and-cross insignia of a femalist temple. They reminded me only faintly of our small tribe of British monastics. Above their heads was a jumble of billboards advertising predigested foods, wrestling instruction, radio handles and the like.

I stared at the hysterical slogans with disagreeable fascination. Since the female face and form have been banned on American signs, the very letters of the advertiser's alphabet have begun to crawl with sex—the fat-bellied, big-breasted capital B, the lascivious double O. However, I reminded myself, it is chiefly the mask that so strangely accents sex in America.

A British anthropologist has pointed out, that, while it took more than 5,000 years to shift the chief point of sexual interest from the hips to the breasts, the next transition to the face has taken less than 50 years. Comparing the American style with Moslem tradition is not valid; Moslem women are compelled to wear veils, the purpose of which is to make a husband's property private, while American women have only the compulsion of fashion and use masks to create mystery.

Theory aside, the actual origins of the trend are to be found in the anti-radiation clothing of World War III, which led to masked wrestling, now a fantastically popular sport, and that in turn led to the current female fashion. Only a wild style at first, masks quickly became as necessary as brassières and lipsticks had been earlier in the century.

I finally realized that I was not speculating about masks in general, but about what lay behind one in particular. That's the devil of the things; you're never sure whether a girl is heightening loveliness or hiding ugliness. I pictured a cool, pretty face in which fear showed only in widened eyes. Then I remembered her blonde hair, rich against the blackness of the satin mask. She'd told me to come at the twenty-second hour—10 P.M.

*   *   *

I climbed to my apartment near the British Consulate; the elevator shaft had been shoved out of plumb by an old blast, a nuisance in these tall New York buildings. Before it occurred to me that I would be going out again, I automatically tore a tab from the film strip under my shirt. I developed it just to be sure. It showed that the total radiation I'd taken that day was still within the safety limit. I'm not phobic about it, as so many people are these days, but there's no point in taking chances.

I flopped down on the day bed and stared at the silent speaker and the dark screen of the video set. As always, they made me think, somewhat bitterly, of the two great nations of the world. Mutilated by each other, yet still strong, they were crippled giants poisoning the planet with their respective dreams of an impossible equality and an impossible success.

I fretfully switched on the speaker. By luck the newscaster was talking excitedly of the prospects of a bumper wheat crop, sown by planes across a dust bowl moistened by seeded rains. I listened carefully to the rest of the program (it was remarkably clear of Russian telejamming) but there was no further news of interest to me. And, of course, no mention of the Moon, though everyone knows that America and Russia are racing to develop their primary bases into fortresses capable of mutual assault and the launching of alphabet-bombs toward Earth. I myself knew perfectly well that the British electronic equipment I was helping trade for American wheat was destined for use in spaceships.

I switched off the newscast. It was growing dark and once again I pictured a tender, frightened face behind a mask. I hadn't had a date since England. It's exceedingly difficult to become acquainted with a girl in America, where as little as a smile, often, can set one of them yelping for the police—to say nothing of the increasingly puritanical morality and the roving gangs that keep most women indoors after dark. And naturally, the masks which are definitely not, as the Soviets claim, a last invention of capitalist degeneracy, but a sign of great psychological insecurity. The Russians have no masks, but they have their own signs of stress.

I went to the window and impatiently watched the darkness gather. I was getting very restless. After a while a ghostly violet cloud appeared to the south. My hair rose. Then I laughed. I had momentarily fancied it a radiation from the crater of the Hell-bomb, though I should instantly have known it was only the radio-induced glow in the sky over the amusement and residential area south of Inferno.

Promptly at twenty-two hours I stood before the door of my unknown girl-friend's apartment. The electronic say-who-please said just that. I answered clearly, "Wysten Turner," wondering if she'd given my name to the mechanism. She evidently had, for the door opened. I walked into a small empty living-room, my heart pounding a bit.

110

The room was expensively furnished with the latest pneumatic hassocks and sprawlers. There were some midgie books on the table. The one I picked up was the standard hard-boiled detective story in which two female murderers go gunning for each other.

The television was on. The masked girl in green was crooning a love song. Her right hand held something that blurred off into the foreground. I saw the set had a handie, which we haven't in England as yet, and curiously thrust my hand into the handie orifice beside the screen. Contrary to my expectations, it was not like slipping into a pulsing rubber glove, but rather as if the girl on the screen actually held my hand.

A door opened behind me. I jerked out my hand with as guilty a reaction as if I'd been caught peering through a keyhole.

She stood in the bedroom doorway. I think she was trembling. She was wearing a grey fur coat, white speckled, and a grey velvet evening mask, with shirred grey lace around the eyes and mouth. Her fingernails twinkled like silver.

It hadn't occurred to me that she'd expect us to go out.

"I should have told you," she said softly. Her mask veered nervously toward the books and the screen and the room's dark corners. "But I can't possibly talk to you here."

I said doubtfully, "There's a place near the Consulate . . ."

"I know where we can be together and talk," she said rapidly. "If you don't mind."

As we entered the elevator I said, "I'm afraid I dismissed the cab."

*   *   *

But the cab driver hadn't gone for some reason of his own. He jumped out and smirkingly held the front door open for us. I told him we preferred to sit in back. He sulkily opened the rear door, slammed it after us, jumped in front and slammed the door behind him.

My companion leaned forward. "Heaven," she said.

The driver switched on the turbine and televisor.

"Why did you ask if I were a British subject?" I said, to start the conversation.

She leaned away from me, tilting her mask close to the window. "See the Moon," she said in a quick, dreamy voice.

"But why, really?" I pressed, conscious of an irritation that had nothing to do with her.

"It's edging up into the purple of the sky."

"And what's your name?"

"The purple makes it look yellower."

Just then I became aware of the source of my irritation. It lay in the square of writhing light in the front of the cab beside the driver.

I don't object to ordinary wrestling matches, though they bore me, but I simply detest watching a man wrestle a woman. The fact that the bouts are generally "on the level," with the man greatly outclassed in weight and reach and the masked females young and personable, only makes them seem worse to me.

"Please turn off the screen," I requested the driver.

He shook his head without looking around. "Uh-uh, man," he said. "They've been grooming that babe for weeks for this bout with Little Zirk."

Infuriated, I reached forward, but my companion caught my arm. "Please," she whispered frightenedly, shaking her head.

I settled back, frustrated. She was closer to me now, but silent and for a few moments I watched the heaves and contortions of the powerful masked girl and her wiry masked opponent on the screen. His frantic scrambling at her reminded me of a male spider.

I jerked around, facing my companion. "Why did those three men want to kill you?" I asked sharply.

The eyeholes of her mask faced the screen. "Because they're jealous of me," she whispered.

"Why are they jealous?"

She still didn't look at me. "Because of him."

"Who?"

She didn't answer.

I put my arm around her shoulders. "Are you afraid to tell me?" I asked. "What *is* the matter?"

She still didn't look my way. She smelled nice.

"See here," I said laughingly, changing my tactics, "you really should tell me something about yourself, I don't even know what you look like."

I half playfully lifted my hand to the band of her neck. She gave it an astonishingly swift slap. I pulled it away in sudden pain. There were four tiny indentations on the back. From one of them a tiny bead of blood welled out as I watched. I looked at her fingernails and saw they were actually delicate and pointed metal caps.

"I'm dreadfully sorry," I heard her say, "but you frightened me. I thought for a moment you were going to . . ."

At last she turned to me. Her coat had fallen open. Her evening dress was Cretan Revival, a bodice of lace beneath and supporting the breasts without covering them.

"Don't be angry," she said, putting her arms around my neck. "You were wonderful this afternoon."

The soft grey velvet of her mask, moulding itself to her cheek, pressed mine. Through the mask's lace the wet warm tip of her tongue touched my chin.

"I'm not angry," I said. "Just puzzled and anxious to help."

The cab stopped. To either side were black windows bordered by spears of broken glass. The sickly purple light showed a few ragged figures slowly moving toward us.

The driver muttered, "It's the turbine, man. We're grounded." He sat there hunched and motionless. "Wish it had happened somewhere else."

My companion whispered, "Five dollars is the usual amount."

She looked out so shudderingly at the congregating figures that I suppressed my indignation and did as she suggested. The driver took the bill without a word. As he started up, he put his hand out the window and I heard a few coins clink on the pavement.

My companion came back into my arms, but her mask faced the television screen, where the tall girl had just pinned the convulsively kicking Little Zirk.

"I'm so frightened," she breathed.

*　　*　　*

Heaven turned out to be an equally ruinous neighborhood, but it had a club with an awning and a huge doorman uniformed like a spaceman, but in gaudy colors. In my sensuous daze I rather liked it all. We stepped out of the cab just as a drunken old

112

woman came down the sidewalk, her mask awry. A couple ahead of us turned their heads from the half revealed face, as if from an ugly body at the beach. As we followed them in I heard the doorman say, "Get along, grandma, and cover yourself."

Inside, everything was dimness and blue glows. She had said we could talk here, but I didn't see how. Besides the inevitable chorus of sneezes and coughs (they say America is fifty per cent allergic these days), there was a band going full blast in the latest robop style, in which an electronic composing machine selects an arbitrary sequence of tones into which the musicians weave their raucous little individualities.

Most of the people were in booths. The band was behind the bar. On a small platform beside them, a girl was dancing, stripped to her mask. The little cluster of men at the shadowy far end of the bar weren't looking at her.

We inspected the menu in gold script on the wall and pushed the buttons for breast of chicken, fried shrimps and two scotches. Moments later, the serving bell tinkled. I opened the gleaming panel and took out our drinks.

The cluster of men at the bar filed off toward the door, but first they stared around the room. My companion had just thrown back her coat. Their look lingered on our booth. I noticed that there were three of them.

The band chased off the dancing girl with growls. I handed my companion a straw and we sipped our drinks.

"You wanted me to help you about something," I said. "Incidentally, I think you're lovely."

She nodded quick thanks, looked around, leaned forward. "Would it be hard for me to get to England?"

"No," I replied, a bit taken aback. "Provided you have an American passport."

"Are they difficult to get?"

"Rather," I said, surprised at her lack of information. "Your country doesn't like its nationals to travel, though it isn't quite as stringent as Russia."

"Could the British Consulate help me get a passport?"

"It's hardly their . . ."

"Could you?"

I realized we were being inspected. A man and two girls had paused opposite our table. The girls were tall and wolfish-looking, with spangled masks. The man stood between them like a fox on its hind legs.

My companion didn't glance at them, but she sat back. I noticed that one of the girls had a big yellow bruise on her forearm. After a moment they walked to a booth in the deep shadows.

"Know them?" I asked. She didn't reply. I finished my drink. "I'm not sure you'd like England," I said. "The austerity's altogether different from your American brand of misery."

She leaned forward again. "But I must get away," she whispered.

"Why?" I was getting impatient.

"Because I'm so frightened."

There were chimes. I opened the panel and handed her the fried shrimps. The sauce on my breast of chicken was a delicious steaming compound of almonds, soy and ginger. But something must have been wrong with the radionic oven that had thawed and heated it, for at the first bite I crunched a kernel of ice in the meat. These delicate mechanisms need constant repair and there aren't enough mechanics.

I put down my fork. "What are you really scared of?" I asked her.

For once her mask didn't waver away from my face. As I waited I could feel the fears gathering without her naming them, tiny dark shapes swarming through the curved night outside, converging on the radioactive pest spot of New York, dipping into the margins of the purple. I felt a sudden rush of sympathy, a desire to protect the girl opposite me. The warm feeling added itself to the infatuation engendered in the cab.

"Everything," she said finally.

I nodded and touched her hand.

"I'm afraid of the Moon," she began, her voice going dreamy and brittle as it had in the cab. "You can't look at it and not think of guided bombs."

"It's the same Moon over England," I reminded her.

"But it's not England's Moon any more. It's ours and Russia's. You're not responsible.

"Oh, and then," she said with a tilt of her mask, "I'm afraid of the cars and the gangs and the loneliness and Inferno. I'm afraid of the lust that undresses your face. And—" her voice hushed—"I'm afraid of the wrestlers."

* * *

"Yes?" I prompted softly after a moment.

Her mask came forward. "Do you know something about the wrestlers?" she asked rapidly. "The ones that wrestle women, I mean. They often lose, you know. And then they have to have a girl to take their frustration out on. A girl who's soft and weak and terribly frightened. They need that, to keep them men. Other men don't want them to have a girl. Other men want them just to fight women and be heroes. But they must have a girl. It's horrible for her."

I squeezed her fingers tighter, as if courage could be transmitted—granting I had any. "I think I can get you to England," I said.

Shadows crawled onto the table and stayed there. I looked up at the three men who had been at the end of the bar. They were the men I had seen in the big coupe. They wore black sweaters and close-fitting black trousers. Their faces were as expressionless as dopers. Two of them stood about me. The other loomed over the girl.

"Drift off, man," I was told. I heard the other inform the girl: "We'll wrestle a fall, sister. What shall it be? Judo, slapsie or kill-who-can?"

I stood up. There are times when and Englishman simply must be maltreated. But just them the foxlike man came gliding in like the star of a ballet. The reaction of the other three startled me. They were acutely embarrassed.

He smiled at them thinly. "You won't win my favour by tricks like this," he said.

"Don't get the wrong idea, Zirk," one of them pleaded.

"I will if it's right," he said. "She told me what you tried to do this afternoon. That won't endear you to me, either. Drift."

They backed off awkwardly. "Let's get out of here," one of them said loudly, as they turned. "I know a place where they fight naked with knives."

Little Zirk laughed musically and slipped into the seat beside my companion. She shrank from him, just a little. I pushed my feet back, leaned forward.

"Who's your friend, baby?" he asked, not looking at her.

She passed the question to me with a little gesture. I told him.

"British," he observed. "She's been asking you about getting out of the country? About passports?" He smiled pleasantly. "She likes to start running away. Don't you, baby?" His small hand began to stroke her wrist, the fingers bent a little, the tendons ridged, as if he were about to grab and twist.

"Look here," I said sharply. "I have to be grateful to you for ordering off those bullies, but—"

"Think nothing of it," he told me. "They're no harm except when they're behind steering wheels. A well-trained fourteen-year-old girl could cripple any one of them. Why even Theda here, if she went in for that sort of thing . . ." He turned to her, shifting his hand from her wrist to her hair. He stroked it, letting the strands slip slowly through his fingers. "You know I lost tonight, baby, don't you?" he said softly.

I stood up. "Come along," I said to her. "Let's leave."

She just sat there, I couldn't even tell if she was trembling. I tried to read a message in her eyes through the mask.

"I'll take you away," I said to her. "I can do it. I really will."

He smiled at me. "She'd like to go with you," he said. "Wouldn't you, baby?"

"Will you or won't you?" I said to her. She still just sat there.

He slowly knotted his fingers in her hair.

"Listen, you little vermin," I snapped at him. "Take your hands off her."

He came up from the seat like a snake. I'm no fighter. I just know that the more scared I am, the harder and straighter I hit. This time I was lucky. But as he crumpled back, I felt a slap and four stabs of pain in my cheek. I clapped my hand to it. I could feel the four gashes made by her dagger finger caps, and the warm blood oozing out from them.

She didn't look at me. She was bending over Little Zirk and cuddling her mask to his cheek and crooning: "There, there, don't feel bad, you'll be able to hurt me afterward."

There were sounds around us, but they didn't come close. I leaned forward and ripped the mask from her face.

I really don't know why I should have expected her face to be anything else. It was very pale, of course, and there weren't any cosmetics. I suppose there's no point in wearing any under a mask. The eyebrows were untidy and the lips chapped. But as for the general expression, as for the feelings crawling and wriggling across it—

Have you ever lifted a rock from damp soil? Have you ever watched the slimy white grubs?

I looked down at her, she up at me. "Yes, you're so frightened, aren't you?" I said sarcastically. "You dread this little nightly drama, don't you? You're scared to death."

And I walked right out into the purple night, still holding my hand to my bleeding cheek. No one stopped me, not even the girl wrestlers. I wished I could tear a tab from under my shirt, and test it then and there, and find I'd taken too much radiation, and so be able to ask to cross the Hudson and go down New Jersey, past the lingering radiance of the Narrows Bomb, and so on to Sandy Hook to wait for the rusty ship that would take me back over the seas to England.

A Pail of Air

Pa had sent me out to get an extra pail of air. I'd just about scooped it full and most of the warmth had leaked from my fingers when I saw the thing.

You know, at first I thought it was a young lady. Yes, a beautiful young lady's face all glowing in the dark and looking at me from the fifth floor of the opposite apartment, which hereabouts is the floor just above the white blanket of frozen air four storeys thick. I'd never seen a live young lady before, except in the old magazines—Sis is just a kid and Ma is pretty sick and miserable—and it gave me such a start that I dropped the pail. Who wouldn't, knowing everyone on Earth was dead except Pa and Ma and Sis and you?

Even at that, I don't suppose I should have been surprised. We all see things now and then. Ma sees some pretty bad ones, to judge from the way she bugs her eyes at nothing and just screams and screams and huddles back against the blankets hanging around the Nest. Pa says it is natural we should react like that sometimes.

When I'd recovered the pail and could look again at the opposite apartment, I got an idea of what Ma might be feeling at those times, for I saw it wasn't a young lady at all but simply a light—a tiny light that moved steathily from window to window, just as if one of the cruel little stars had come down out of the airless sky to investigate why the Earth had gone away from the Sun, and maybe to hunt down something to torment or terrify, now that the Earth didn't have the Sun's protection.

I tell you, the thought of it gave me the creeps. I just stood here shaking, and almost froze my feet and did frost my helmet so solid on the inside that I couldn't have seen the light even if it had come out of one of the windows to get me. Then I had the wit to go back inside.

Pretty soon I was feeling my familiar way through the thirty or so blankets and rugs and rubbery sheets Pa has got hung and braced around to slow down the escape of air from the Nest, and I wasn't quite so scared. I began to hear the tick-ticking of the clocks in the Nest and knew I was getting back into air, because there's no sound outside in the vacuum, of course. But my mind was still crawly and uneasy as I pushed through the last blankets—Pa's got them faced with aluminum foil to hold in the heat—and came into the Nest.

*   *   *

Let me tell you about the Nest. It's low and snug, just room for the four of us and our things. The floor is covered with thick woolly rugs. Three of the sides are blankets,

117

and the blankets roofing it touch Pa's head. He tells me it's inside a much bigger room, but I've never seen the real walls or ceiling.

Against one of the blanket-walls is a big set of shelves, with tools and books and other stuff, and on top of it a whole row of clocks. Pa's very fussy about keeping them wound. He says we must never forget time, and without a sun or moon, that would be easy to do.

The fourth wall has blankets all over except around the fireplace, in which there is a fire that must never go out. It keeps us from freezing and does a lot more besides. One of us must always watch it. Some of the clocks are alarm and we can use them to remind us. In the early days there was only Ma to take turns with Pa—I think of that when she gets difficult—but now there's me to help, and Sis too.

It's Pa who is the chief guardian of the fire, though. I always think of him that way: a tall man sitting crosslegged, frowning anxiously at the fire, his lined face golden in its light, and every so often carefully placing on it a piece of coal from the big heap beside it. Pa tells me there used to be guardians of the fire sometimes in the very old days— vestals, he calls them—although there was unfrozen air all around then and a sun too and you didn't really need a fire.

He was sitting just that way now, though he got up quick to take the pail from me and bawl me out for loitering—he'd spotted my frozen helmet right off. That roused Ma and she joined in picking on me. She's always trying to get the load off her feelings, Pa explains. He shut her up pretty fast. Sis let off a couple of silly squeals too.

Pa handled the pail of air in a twist cloth. Now that it was inside the Nest, you could really feel its coldness. It just seemed to suck the heat out of everything. Even the flames cringed away from it as Pa put it down close by the fire.

Yet it's that glimmery blue-white stuff in the pail that keeps us alive. It slowly melts and vanishes and refreshes the Nest and feeds the fire. The blankets keep it from escaping too fast. Pa's like to seal the whole place, but he can't—building's too earth-quake-twisted, and besides he has to leave the chimney open for smoke. But the chimney has special things Pa calls baffles up inside it, to keep the air from getting out too quick that way. Sometimes Pa, making a joke, says it baffles him they keep on working, or work at all.

Pa says air is tiny molecules that fly away like a flash if there isn't something to stop them. We have to watch sharp not to let the air run low. Pa always keeps a big reserve supply of it in buckets behind the first blankets, along with extra coal and cans of food and bottles of vitamins and other things, such as pails of snow to melt for water. We have to go way down to the bottom floor for that stuff, which is a mean trip, and get it through a door to outside.

You see, when the Earth got cold, all the water in the air froze first and made a blanket ten feet thick or so everywhere, and then down on top of that dropped the crystals of frozen air, making another mostly white blanket sixty or seventy feet thick maybe.

Of course, all the parts of the air didn't freeze and snow down at the same time.

First to drop out was the carbon dioxide—when you're shovelling for water, you have to make sure you don't go too high and get any of that stuff mixed in, for it would put you to sleep, maybe for good, and make the fire go out. Next there's the nitrogen, which doesn't count one way or the other, though it's the biggest part of the blanket. On top of that and easy to get at, which is lucky for us, there's the oxygen that keeps us alive. It's pale blue, which helps you tell it from the nitrogen. It has to be colder for oxygen to freeze solid than nitrogen. That's why the oxygen snowed down last.

Pa says we live better than kings ever did, breathing pure oxygen, but we're used to it and don't notice.

Finally, at the very top, there's a slick of liquid helium, which is funny stuff.

All of these gases are in neat separate layers. Like a pussy caffay, Pa laughingly says, whatever that is.

*   *   *

I was busting to tell them all about what I'd seen, and so as soon as I'd ducked out of my helmet and while I was still climbing out of my suit, I cut loose. Right away Ma got nervous and began making eyes at the entry-slit in the blankets and wringing her hands together—the hand where she'd lost three fingers from frostbite inside the good one, as usual. I could tell that Pa was annoyed at me scaring her and wanted to explain it all away quickly, yet I knew he knew I wasn't fooling.

"And you watched this light for some time, son?" he asked when I finished.

I hadn't said anything about first thinking it was a young lady's face. Somehow that part embarrassed me.

"Long enough for it to pass five windows and go to the next floor."

"And it didn't look like stray electricity or crawling liquid or starlight focused by a growing crystal, or anything like that?"

He wasn't just making up those ideas. Odd things happen in a world that's about as cold as can be, and just when you think matter would be frozen dead, it takes on a strange new life. A slimy stuff comes crawling toward the Nest, just like an animal snuffing for heat—that's the liquid helium. And once, when I was little, a bolt of lightning—not even Pa could figure where it came from—hit the nearby steeple and crawled up and down it for weeks, until the glow finally died.

"Not like anything I ever saw," I told him.

He stood for a moment frowning. Then, "I'll go out with you, and you show it to me," he said.

Ma raised a howl at the idea of being left alone, and Sis joined in, too, but Pa quieted them. We started climbing into our outside clothes—mine had been warming by the fire. Pa made them. They have triple-pane plastic headpieces that were once big double-duty transparent food cans, but they keep heat and air in and can replace the air for a little while, long enough for our trips for water and coal and food and so on.

Ma started moaning again, "I've always known there was something outside there, waiting to get us. I've felt it for years—something that's part of the cold and hates all warmth and wants to destroy the Nest. It's been watching us all this time, and now it's coming after us. It'll get you and then come for me. Don't go, Harry!"

Pa had everything on but his helmet. He knelt by the fireplace and reached in and shook the long metal rod that goes up the chimney and knocks off the ice that keeps trying to clog it. Once a week he goes up on the roof to check if it's working all right. That's our worst trip and Pa won't let me make it alone.

"Sis," Pa said quietly, "come watch the fire. Keep an eye on the air, too. If it gets low or doesn't seem to be boiling fast enough, fetch another bucket from behind the blanket. But mind your hands. Use the cloth to pick up the bucket."

Sis quit helping Ma be frightened and came over and did as she was told. Ma quieted down pretty suddenly, though her eyes were still kind of wild as she watched

Pa fix on his helmet tight and pick up a pail and the two of us go out.

Pa led the way and I took hold of his belt. It's a funny thing, I'm not afraid to go by myself, but when Pa's along I always want to hold on to him. Habit, I guess, and then there's no denying that this time I was a bit scared.

You see, it's this way. We know that everything is dead out there. Pa heard the last radio voices fade away years ago, and had seen some of the last folks die who weren't as lucky or well-protected as us. So we knew that if there was something groping around out there, it couldn't be anything human or friendly.

Besides that, there's a feeling that comes with it always being night, *cold* night. Pa says there used to be some of that feeling even in the old days, but then every morning the Sun would come and chase it away. I have to take his word for that, not ever remembering the Sun as being anything more than a big star. You see, I hadn't been born when the dark star snatched us away from the Sun, and by now it's dragged us out beyond the orbit of the planet Pluto, Pa says, and taking us farther out all the time.

We can see the dark star as it crosses the sky because it blots out stars, and especially when it's outlined by the Milky Way. It's pretty big, for we're closer to it than the planet Mercury was to the Sun, Pa says, but we don't care to look at it much and Pa won't set his clocks by it.

I found myself wondering whether there mightn't be something on the dark star that wanted us, and if that was why it had captured the Earth. Just then we came to the end of the corridor and I followed Pa out on the balcony.

I don't know what the city looked like in the old days, but now its's beautiful. The starlight lets you see it pretty well—there's quite a bit of light in those steady points speckling the blackness above. (Pa says the stars used to twinkle once, but that was because there was air.) We are on a hill and the shimmery plain drops away from us and then flattens out, cut up into neat squares by the troughs that used to be streets. I sometimes make my mashed potatoes look like it, before I pour on the gravy.

Some taller buildings push up out of the feathery plain, topped by rounded caps of air crystals, like the fur hood Ma wears, only whiter. On those buildings you can see the darker squares of windows, underlined by white dashes of air crystals. Some of them are on a slant, for many of the buildings are pretty badly twisted by the quakes and all the rest that happened when the dark star captured the Earth.

Here and there a few icicles hang, water icicles from the first days of the cold, other icicles of frozen air that melted on the roofs and dropped and froze again. Sometimes one of those icicles will catch the light of a star and send it to you so brightly you think the star has swooped into the city. That was one of the things Pa had been thinking of when I told him about the light, but I had thought of it myself first and known it wasn't so.

He touched his helmet to mine so we could talk easier and he asked me to point out the windows to him. But there wasn't any light moving around inside them now, or anywhere else. To my surprise, Pa didn't bawl me out and tell me I'd been seeing things. He looked all around quite a while after filling his pail, and just as we were going inside he whipped around without warning, as if to take some peeping thing off guard.

I could feel it, too. The old peace was gone. There was something lurking out there, watching, waiting, getting ready.

Inside, he said to me, touching helmets, "If you see something like that again, son, don't tell the others. Your Ma's sort of nervous these days and we owe her all the feeling of safety we can give her. Once—it was when your sister was born—I was ready to give up and die, but your Mother kept me trying. Another time she kept the fire going a whole week all by herself when I was sick. Nursed me and took care of two of you, too.

"You know that game we sometimes play, sitting in a square in the Nest, tossing a ball around? Courage is like a ball, son. A person can hold it only so long, and then he's got to toss it to someone else. When it's tossed your way, you've got to catch it and hold it tight—and hope there'll be someone else to toss it to when you get tired of being brave."

His talking to me that way made me feel grown-up and good. But it didn't wipe away the thing outside from the back of my mind—or the fact that Pa took it seriously.

*   *   *

It's hard to hide your feelings about such a thing. When we got back in the Nest and took off our outside clothes, Pa laughed about it all and told them it was nothing and kidded me for having such an imagination, but his words fell flat. He didn't convince Ma and Sis any more than he did me. It looked for a minute like we were all fumbling the courage-ball. Something had to be done, and almost before I knew what I was going to say, I heard myself asking Pa to tell us about the old days, and how it all happened.

He sometimes doesn't mind telling that story, and Sis and I sure like to listen to it, and he got my idea. So we were all settled around the fire in a wink, and Ma pushed up some cans to thaw for supper, and Pa began. Before he did, though, I noticed him casually get a hammer from the shelf and lay it down beside him.

It was the same old story as always—I think I could recite the main thread of it in my sleep—though Pa always puts in a new detail or two and keeps improving it in spots.

He told us how the Earth had been swinging around the Sun ever so steady and warm, and the people on it fixing to make money and wars and have a good time and get power and treat each other right or wrong, when without warning there comes charging out of space this dead star, this burned out sun, and upsets everything.

You know, I find it hard to believe in the way those people felt, any more than I can believe in the swarming number of them. Imagine people getting ready for the horrible sort of war they were cooking up. Wanting it even, or at least wishing it were over so as to end their nervousness. As if all folks didn't have to hang together and pool every bit of warmth just to keep alive. And how can they have hoped to end danger, any more than we can hope to end the cold?

Sometimes I think Pa exaggerates and makes things out too black. He's cross with us once in a while and was probably cross with all those folks. Still, some of the things I read in the old magazines sound pretty wild. He may be right.

*   *   *

The dark star, as Pa went on telling it, rushed in pretty fast and there wasn't much time to get ready. At the beginning they tried to keep it a secret from most people, but then the truth came out, what with the earthquakes and floods—imagine, oceans of *unfrozen* water!—and people seeing stars blotted out by something on a clear night. First off they thought it would hit the Sun, and then they thought it would hit the Earth. There was even the start of a rush to get to a place called China, because people thought the star would hit on the other side. Not that that would have helped them, they were just crazy with fear. But then they found it wasn't going to hit either side, but was going to come very close to the Earth.

Most of the other planets were on the other side of the Sun and didn't get involved. The Sun and the newcomer fought over the Earth for a little while—pulling it this way and that, in a twisty curve, like two dogs growling over a bone, Pa described it this time—and then the newcomer won and carried us off. The Sun got a consolation prize, though. At the last minute he managed to hold on to the Moon.

That was the time of the monster earthquakes and floods, twenty times worse than anything before. It was also the time of the Big Swoop, as Pa calls it, when the Earth speeded up, going into a close orbit around the dark star.

I've asked Pa, wasn't the Earth yanked then, just as he has done to me sometimes, grabbing me by the collar to do it, when I've been sitting too far from the fire. But Pa says no, gravity doesn't work that way. It was like a yank, but nobody felt it. I guess it was like being yanked in a dream.

You see, the dark star was going through space faster than the Sun, and in the opposite direction, and it had to speed up the world a lot in order to take it away.

The Big Swoop didn't last long. It was over as soon as the Earth was settled down in its new orbit around the dark star. But the earthquakes and floods were terrible while it lasted, twenty times worse than anything before. Pa says that all sorts of cliffs and buildings toppled, oceans slopped over, swamps and sandy deserts gave great sliding surges that buried nearby lands. Earth's blanket of air, still up in the sky then, was stretched out and got so thin in spots that people keeled over and fainted—though of course, at the same time, they were getting knocked down by the earthquakes that went with the Big Swoop and maybe their bones broke or skulls cracked.

We've often asked Pa how people acted during that time, whether they were scared or brave or crazy or stunned, or all four, but he's sort of leery of the subject, and he was again tonight. He says he was mostly too busy to notice.

You see, Pa and some scientist friends of his had figured out part of what was going to happen—they'd known we'd get captured and our air would freeze—and they'd been working like mad to fix up a place with airtight walls and doors, and insulation against the cold, and big supplies of food and fuel and water and bottled air. But the place got smashed in the last earthquakes and all Pa's friends were killed then and in the Big Swoop. So he had to start over and throw the Nest together quick without any advantages, just using any stuff he could lay his hands on.

I guess he's telling pretty much the truth when he says he didn't have any time to keep an eye on how other folks behaved, either then or in the Big Freeze that followed—followed very quick, you know, both because the dark star was pulling us away very fast and because Earth's rotation had been slowed by the tug-of-war and the tides, so that the nights were longer.

Still, I've got an idea of some of the things that happened from the frozen folk I've seen, a few of them in other rooms in our building, others clustered around the furnaces in the basements where we go for coal.

In one of the rooms, an old man sits stiff in a chair with an arm and a leg in splints. In another, a man and woman are huddled together in a bed with heaps of covers over them. You can just see their heads peeking out, close together. And in another a beautiful young lady is sitting with a pile of wraps huddled around her, looking hopefully toward the door, as if waiting for someone who never came back with warmth and food. They're all still and stiff as statues, of course, but just like life.

Pa showed them to me once in quick winks of his flashlight, when he still had a fair supply of batteries and could afford to waste a little light. They scared me pretty bad and made my heart pound, especially the young lady.

*　　*　　*

Now, with Pa telling his story for the umpteenth time to take our minds off another scare, I got to thinking of the frozen folk again. All of a sudden I got an idea that scared me worse than anything yet. You see, I'd just remembered the face I'd thought I'd seen in the window. I'd forgotten about that on account of trying to hide it from the others.

What, I asked myself, if the frozen folk were coming to life? What if they were like the liquid helium that got a new lease on life and started crawling toward the heat just when you thought its molecules ought to freeze solid for ever? Or like the electricity that moves endlessly when it's just about as cold as that? What if the ever-growing cold, with the temperature creeping down the last few degrees to the last zero, had mysteriously wakened the frozen folk to life—not warm-blooded life, but something icy and horrible?

That was a worse idea than the one about something coming down from the dark star to get us.

Or maybe, I thought, both ideas might be true. Something coming down from the dark star and making the frozen folk move, using them to do its work. That would fit with both things I'd seen—the beautiful young lady and the moving, starlight light.

The frozen folk with minds from the dark star behind their unwinking eyes, creeping, crawling, snuffing their way, following the heat to the Nest, maybe wanting the heat, but more likely hating it and wanting to chill it for ever, snuff out our fire.

I tell you, that thought gave me a very bad turn and I wanted very badly to tell the others my fears, but I remembered what Pa had said and clenched my teeth and didn't speak.

We were all sitting very still. Even the fire was burning silently. There was just the sound of Pa's voice and the clocks.

And then, from beyond the blankets, I thought I heard a tiny noise. My skin tightened all over me.

Pa was telling about the early years in the Nest and had come to the place where he philosophizes.

"So I asked myself then," he said, "what's the use of dragging it out for a few years? Why prolong a doomed existence of hard work and cold and loneliness? The human race is done. The Earth is done. Why not give up, I asked myself—and all of a sudden I got the answer."

Again I heard the noise, louder this time, a kind of uncertain, shuffling tread, coming closer. I couldn't breathe.

"Life's always been a business of working hard and fighting the cold," Pa was saying. "The Earth's always been a lonely place, millions of miles from the next planet. And no matter how long the human race might have lived, the end would have come some night. Those things don't matter. What matters is that life is good. It has a lovely texture, like some thick fur or the petals of flowers—you've never seen those, but you know our ice-flowers—or like the texture of flames, never twice the same. It makes everything else worth while. And that's as true for the last man as the first."

And still the steps kept shuffling closer. It seemed to me that the inmost blanket trembled and bulged a little. Just as if they were burned into my imagination, I kept seeing those peering, frozen eyes.

123

"So right then and there," Pa went on, and now I could tell that he heard the steps, too, and was talking loud so we maybe wouldn't hear them, "right then and there I told myself, that I was going on as if we had all eternity ahead of us. I'd have children and teach them all I could. I'd get them to read books. I'd plan for the future, try to enlarge and seal the Nest. I'd do what I could to keep everything beautiful and growing. I'd keep alive my feeling of wonder even at the cold and the dark and the distant stars."

But then the blanket actually did move and lift. And there was a bright light somewhere behind it. Pa's voice stopped and his eyes turned to the widening slit and his hand went out until it touched and gripped the handle of the hammer beside him.

In through the blanket stepped the beautiful young lady. She stood there looking at us in the strangest way, and she carried something bright and unwinking in her hand. And two other faces peered over her shoulders—men's faces, white and staring.

Well, my heart couldn't have been stopped for more than four or five beats before I realized she was wearing a suit and helmet like Pa's homemade ones, only fancier, and that the men were, too—and that the frozen folk certainly wouldn't be wearing those. Also, I noticed that the bright thing in her hand was just a kind of flashlight.

Sinking down very softly, Ma fainted.

The silence kept on while I swallowed hard a couple of times, and after that there was all sorts of jabbering and commotion.

They were simply people, you see. We hadn't been the only ones to survive; we'd just thought so, for natural enough reasons. These three people had survived, and quite a few others with them. And when we found out *how* they'd survived, Pa let out the biggest whoop of joy.

They were from Los Alamos and they were getting their heat and power from atomic energy. Just using the uranium and plutonium intended for bombs, they had enough to go on for thousands of years. They had a regular little airtight city, with airlocks and all. They even generated electric light and grew plants and animals by it. (At this Pa let out a second whoop, waking Ma from her faint.)

But if we were flabbergasted at them, they were double flabbergasted at us.

One of the men kept saying, "But it's impossible, I tell you. You can't maintain an air supply without hermetic sealing. It's simply impossible."

That was after he had got his helmet off and was using our air. Meanwhile, the young lady kept looking around at us as if we were saints, and telling us we'd done something amazing, and suddenly she broke down and cried.

They'd been scouting around for survivors, but they never expected to find any in a place like this. They had rocket ships at Los Alamos and plenty of chemical fuel. As for liquid oxygen, all you had to do was go out and shovel the air blanket at the top level. So after they'd got things going smoothly at Los Alamos, which had taken years, they'd decided to make some trips to likely places where there might be other survivors. No good trying longdistance radio signals, of course, since there was no atmosphere, no ionosphere, to carry them around the curve of the Earth. That was why all the radio signals had died out.

Well, they'd found other colonies at Argonne and Brookhaven and way around the world at Harwell and Tanna Tuva. And now they'd been giving our city a look, not really expecting to find anything. But they had an instrument that noticed the faintest heat waves and it had told them there was something warm down here, so they'd landed to investigate. Of course we hadn't heard them land, since there was no air to carry the sound, and they'd had to investigate around quite a while before finding us. Their instruments had given them a wrong steer and they'd wasted some time in the building across the street.

*   *   *

By now, all five adults were talking like sixty. Pa was demonstrating to the men how he worked the fire and got rid of the ice in the chimney and all that. Ma had perked up wonderfully and was showing the young lady her cooking and sewing stuff, and even asking about how the women dressed at Los Alamos. The strangers marvelled at everything and praised it to the skies. I could tell from the way they wrinkled their noses that they found the Nest a bit smelly, but they never mentioned that at all and just asked bushels of questions.

In fact, there was so much talking and excitement that Pa forgot about things, and it wasn't until they were all getting groggy that he looked and found the air had all boiled away in the pail. He got another bucket of air quick from behind the blankets. Of course that started them all laughing and jabbering again. The newcomers even got a little drunk. They weren't used to so much oxygen.

Funny thing, though—I didn't do much talking at all and Sis hung on to Ma all the time and hid her face when anybody looked at her. I felt pretty uncomfortable and disturbed myself, even about the young lady. Glimpsing her outside there, I'd had all sorts of mushy thoughts, but now I was just embarrassed and scared of her, even though she tried to be nice as anything to me.

I sort of wished they'd all quit crowding the Nest and let us be alone and get our feelings straightened out.

And when the newcomers began to talk about our all going to Los Alamos, as if that were taken for granted, I could see that something of the same feeling struck Pa and Ma, too. Pa got very silent all of a sudden and Ma kept telling the young lady, "But I wouldn't know how to act there and I haven't any clothes."

The strangers were puzzled like anything at first, but then they got the idea. As Pa kept saying, "It just doesn't seem right to let this fire go out."

*   *   *

Well, the strangers are gone, but they're coming back. It hasn't been decided yet just what will happen. Maybe the Nest will be kept up as what one of the strangers called a "survival school." Or maybe we will join the pioneers who are going to try to establish a new colony at the uranium mines at Great Slave Lake or in the Congo.

Of course, now that the strangers are gone, I've been thinking a lot about Los Alamos and those other tremendous colonies. I have a hankering to see them for myself.

You ask me, Pa wants to see them, too. He's been getting pretty thoughtful, watching Ma and Sis perk up.

"It's different, now that we know others are alive," he explains to me. "Your mother doesn't feel so hopeless any more. Neither do I, for that matter, not having to carry the whole responsibility for keeping the human race going, so to speak. It scares a person."

I looked around at the blanket walls and the fire and the pails of air boiling away and Ma and Sis sleeping in the warmth and the flickering light.

"It's not going to be easy to leave the Nest," I said, wanting to cry, kind of. "It's so small and there's just the four of us. I get scared at the idea of big places and a lot of strangers."

125

He nodded and put another piece of coal on the fire. Then he looked at the little pile and grinned suddenly and put a couple of handfuls on, just as if it was one of our birthdays or Christmas.

"You'll quickly get over that feeling, son," he said. "The trouble with the world was that it kept getting smaller and smaller, till it ended with just the Nest. Now it'll be good to start building up to a real huge world again, the way it was in the beginning."

I guess he's right. You think the beautiful young lady will wait for me till I grow up? I asked her that and she smiled to thank me and then she told me she's got a daughter almost my age and that there are lots of children at the atomic places. Imagine that.

Poor Superman

The first angry rays of the sun—which, startlingly enough, still rose in the east at twenty-four-hour intervals—pierced the lacy tops of Atlantic combers and touched thousands of sleeping Americans with unconscious fear, because of their unpleasant similarity to the rays from World War III's atomic bombs.

They turned to blood the witch circle of rusty steel skeletons around Inferno in Manhattan. Without comment, they pointed a cosmic finger at the tarnished brass plaque commemorating the martyrdom of the three physicists after the dropping of the Hell Bomb. They tenderly touched the rosy skin and strawberry bruises on the naked shoulders of a girl sleeping off a drunk on the furry and radiantly heated floor of a nearby roof garden. They struck green magic from the glassy blot that was Old Washington. Twelve hours before, they had revealed things as eerily beautiful, and more ravaged, in Asia and Russia. They pinked the white walls of the colonial dwelling of Morton Opperly near the Institute for Advanced Studies; upstairs they slanted impartially across the Pharaohlike and open-eyed face of the elderly physicist and the ugly, sleep-surly one of young Willard Farquar in the next room. And in nearby New Washington they made of the spire of the Thinkers' Foundation a blue and optimistic glory that outshone White House, Jr.

It was America approaching the end of the twentieth century. America of juke-box burlesque and your local radiation hospital. America of the mask fad for women and Mystic Christianity. America of the off-the-bosom dress and the New Blue Laws. America of the Endless War and the loyalty detector. America of marvelous Maizie and the monthly rocket to Mars. America of the Thinkers and (a few remembered) the institute. "Knock on titanium," "Whadya do for blackouts?" "Please, lover, don't think when I'm around" America, as combat-shocked and crippled as the rest of the bomb-shattered planet.

Not one impudent photon of the sunlight penetrated the triple-paned, polarizing windows of Jorj Helmuth's bedroom in the Thinkers' Foundation, yet the clock in his brain awakened him to the minute, or almost. Switching off the Educational Sandman in the midst of the phrase, ". . . applying tensor calculus to the nucleus," he took a deep, even breath and cast his mind to the limits of the world and his knowledge. It was a somewhat shadowy vision, but, he noted with impartial approval, definitely less shadowy than yesterday morning.

Employing a rapid mental scanning technique, he next cleared his memory chains of false associations, including those acquired while asleep. These chores completed, he held his finger on a bedside button, which rotated the polarizing windowpanes until the room slowly filled with a muted daylight. Then, still flat on his back, he turned his head until he could look at the remarkably beautiful blond girl asleep beside him.

Remembering last night, he felt a pang of exasperation, which he instantly quelled by taking his mind to a higher and dispassionate level from which he could look down on the girl and even himself as quaint, clumsy animals. Still, he grumbled silently, Caddy might have had enough consideration to clear out before he awoke. He wondered if he shouldn't have used his hypnotic control on the girl to smooth their relationship last night, and for a moment the word that would send her into deep trance trembled on the tip of his tongue. But no, that special power of his over her was reserved for far more important purposes.

Pumping dynamic tension into his twenty-year-old muscles and confidence into his sixty-year-old mind, the forty-year-old Thinker rose from bed. No covers had to be thrown off; nuclear central heating made them unnecessary. He stepped into his clothing—the severe tunic, tights, and sockassins of the modern businessman. Next he glanced at the message tape beside his phone, washing down with ginger ale a vita-amino-enzyme tablet, and walked to the window. There, gazing along the rows of newly planted mutant oaks lining Decontamination Avenue, his smooth face broke into a smile.

It had come to him, the next big move in the intricate game making up his life—and mankind's. Come to him during sleep, as so many of his best decisions did, because he regularly employed the timesaving technique of somno-thought, which could function at the same time as somno-learning.

He set his who?-where? robot for "Rocket Physicist" and "Genius Class." While it worked, he dictated to his steno-robot the following brief message:

Dear Fellow Scientist:
   A project is contemplated that will have a crucial bearing on man's future in deep space. Ample non-military government funds are available. There was a time when professional men scoffed at the Thinkers. Then there was a time when the Thinkers perforce neglected the professional men. Now both times are past. May they never return! I would like to consult you this afternoon, three o'clock sharp, Thinkers' Foundation I.

                                                                    Jorj Helmuth

Meanwhile the who?-where? had tossed out a dozen cards. He glanced through them, hesitated at the name "Willard Farquar," looked at the sleeping girl, then quickly tossed them all into the addresso-robot and plugged in the steno-robot.

The buzz light blinked green and he switched the phone to audio.

"The President is waiting to see Maizie, sir," a clear feminine voice announced. "He has the general staff with him."

"Martian peace to him," Jorj Helmuth said. "Tell him I'll be down in a few minutes."

*   *   *

Huge as a primitive nuclear reactor, the great electronic brain loomed above the knot of hush-voiced men. It almost filled a two-story room in the Thinkers' Foundation. Its front was an orderly expanse of controls, indicators, telltales, and terminals, the upper ones reached by a chair on a boom.

Although, as far as anyone knew, it could sense only the information and questions fed into it on a tape, the human visitors could not resist the impulse to talk in whispers and glance uneasily at the great cryptic cube. After all, it had lately taken to moving some of its own controls—the permissible ones—and could doubtless improvise a hearing apparatus if it wanted to.

For this was the thinking machine beside which the Marks and Eniacs and Maniacs and Maddidas and Minervas and Mimirs were less than morons. This was the machine with a million times as many synapses as the human brain, the machine that remembered by cutting delicate notches in the rims of molecules (instead of kindergarten paper punching or the Coney Island shimmying of columns of mercury). This was the machine that had given instructions on building the last three quarters of itself. This was the goal, perhaps, toward which fallible human reasoning and biased human judgment and feeble human ambition had evolved.

This was the machine that really thought—a million-plus!

This was the machine that the timid cyberneticists and stuffy professional scientists had said could not be built. Yet this was the machine that the Thinkers, with characteristic Yankee push, *had* built. And nicknamed, with characteristic Yankee irreverence and girl-fondness, "Maizie."

Gazing up at it, the President of the United States felt a chord plucked within him that hadn't been sounded for decades, the dark and shivery organ chord of his Baptist childhood. Here, in a strange sense, although his reason rejected it, he felt he stood face to face with the living God: infinitely stern with the sternness of reality, yet infinitely just. No tiniest error or willful misstep could ever escape the scrutiny of this vast mentality. He shivered.

The grizzled general—there was also one who was gray—was thinking that this was a very odd link in the chain of command. Some shadowy and usually well-controlled memories from World War II faintly stirred his ire. Here he was giving orders to a being immeasurably more intelligent than himself. And always orders of the "Tell me how to kill that man" rather than the "Kill that man" sort. The distinction bothered him obscurely. It relieved him to know that Maizie had built-in controls which made her always the servant of humanity, or of humanity's right-minded leaders—even the Thinkers weren't certain which.

The gray general was thinking uneasily, and, like the President, at a more turbid level, of the resemblance between Papal infallibility and the dictates of the machine. Suddenly his bony wrists began to tremble. He asked himself: Was this the Second Coming? Mightn't an incarnation be in metal rather than flesh?

The austere Secretary of State was remembering what he'd taken such pains to make everyone forget: his youthful flirtation at Lake Success with Buddhism. Sitting before his guru, his teacher, feeling the Occidental's awe at the wisdom of the East, or its pretense, he had felt a little like this.

The burly Secretary of Space, who had come up through United Rockets, was thanking his stars that at any rate the professional scientists weren't responsible for this job. Like the grizzled general, he'd always felt suspicious of men who kept telling you how to do things, rather than doing them themselves. In World War III he'd had his fill of the professional physicists, with their eternal taint of a misty sort of radicalism and free-thinking. The Thinkers were better—more disciplined, more human. They'd called their brain machine Maizie, which helped take the curse off her. Somewhat.

The President's secretary, a paunchy veteran of party caucuses, was also glad that it was the Thinkers who had created the machine, though he trembled at the power that it gave them over the Administration. Still, you could do business with the Thinkers. And nobody (not even the Thinkers) could do business (that sort of business) with Maizie!

Before that great square face with its thousands of tiny metal features only Jorj Helmuth seemed at ease, busily entering on the tape the complex Questions of the Day that the high officials had handed him: logistics for the Endless War in Pakistan, optimum size for next year's sugar-corn crop, current thought trends in average Soviet minds—profound questions, yet many of them phrased with surprising simplicity. For figures, technical jargon, and layman's language were alike to Maizie; there was no need to translate into mathematical shorthand, as with the lesser brain machines.

The click of the taper went on until the Secretary of State had twice nervously fired a cigarette with his ultrasonic lighter and twice quickly put it away. No one spoke.

Jorj looked up at the Secretary of Space. "Section Five, Question Four—whom would that come from?"

The burly man frowned. "That would be the physics boys, Opperly's group. Is anything wrong?"

Jorj did not answer. A bit later he quit taping and began to adjust controls, going up on the boom chair to reach some of them. Eventually he came down and touched a few more, then stood waiting.

From the great cube came a profound, steady purring. Involuntarily the six officials backed off a bit. Somehow it was impossible for a man to get used to the sound of Maizie starting to think.

Jorj turned, smiling. "And now, gentlemen, while we wait for Maizie to cerebrate, there should be just enough time for us to watch the take-off of the Mars rocket."

He switched on a giant television screen. The others made a quarter turn, and there before them glowed the rich ochers and blues of a New Mexico sunrise and, in the middle distance, a silvery spindle.

Like the generals, the Secretary of Space suppressed a scowl. Here was something that ought to be spang in the center of his official territory, and the Thinkers had locked him completely out of it. That rocket there—just an ordinary Earth satellite vehicle commandeered from the Army, but equipped by the Thinkers with Maizie-designed nuclear motors capable of the Mars journey and more. The first spaceship—and the Secretary of Space was not in on it!

Still, he told himself, Maizie had decreed it that way. And when he remembered what the Thinkers had done for him in rescuing him from breakdown with their mental science, in rescuing the whole Administration from collapse, he realized he had to be satisfied. And that was without taking into consideration the amazing additional mental discoveries that the Thinkers were bringing down from Mars.

"Lord!" the President said to Jorj, as if voicing the Secretary's feeling. "I wish you people could bring a couple of those wise little devils back with you this trip. Be a good thing for the country."

Jorj looked at him a bit coldly. "It's quite unthinkable," he said. "The telepathic abilities of the Martians make them extremely sensitive. The conflicts of ordinary Earth minds would impinge on them psychotically, even fatally. As you know, the Thinkers were able to contact them only because of our degree of learned mental poise and errorless memory chains. So for the present it must be our task alone to glean from the Martians their astounding mental skills. Of course, some day in the future, when we have discovered how to armor the minds of the Martians—"

"Sure, I know," the President said hastily. "Shouldn't have mentioned it, Jorj."

130

Conversation ceased. They waited with growing tension for the great violet flames to bloom from the base of the silvery shaft.

Meanwhile the question tape, like a New Year's streamer tossed out a high window into the night, sped on its dark way along spinning rollers. Curling with an intricate aimlessness curiously like that of such a streamer, it tantalized the silvery fingers of a thousand relays, saucily evaded the glances of ten thousand electric eyes, impishly darted down a narrow black alleyway of memory banks, and, reaching the center of the cube, suddenly emerged into a small room where a suave fat man in shorts sat drinking beer.

He flipped the tape over to him with practiced finger, eyeing it as a stockbroker might have studied a ticker tape. He read the first question, closed his eyes and frowned for five seconds. Then with the staccato self-confidence of a hack writer, he began to tape out the answer.

For many minutes the only sounds were the rustle of the paper ribbon and the click of the taper, except for the seconds the fat man took to close his eyes, or to drink beer. Once, too, he lifted a phone, asked a concise question, waited half a minute, listened to an answer, then went back to the grind.

Until he came to Section Five, Question Four. That time he did his thinking with his eyes open.

The question was: "Does Maizie stand for Maelzel?"

He sat for a while slowly scratching his thigh. His loose, persuasive lips tightened, without closing, into the shape of a snarl.

Suddenly he began to tape again.

"Maizie does not stand for Maelzel. Maizie stands for amazing, humorously given the form of a girl's name. Section Six, Answer One: The mid-term election viewcasts should be spaced as follows . . ."

But his lips didn't lose the shape of a snarl.

*   *   *

Five hundred miles above the ionosphere, the Mars rocket cut off its fuel and slumped gratefully into an orbit that would carry it effortlessly around the world at that altitude. The pilot unstrapped himself and stretched, but he didn't look out the viewport at the dried-mud disk that was Earth, cloaked in its haze of blue sky. He knew he had two maddening months ahead of him in which to do little more than that. Instead, he unstrapped Sappho.

Used to free fall from two previous experiences, and loving it, the fluffy little cat was soon bounding about the cabin in curves and gyrations that would have made her the envy of all back-alley and parlor felines on the planet below. A miracle cat in the dream world of free fall. For a long time she played with a string that the man would toss out lazily. Sometimes she caught the string on the fly, sometimes she swam for it frantically.

After a while the man grew bored with the game. He unlocked a drawer and began to study the details of the wisdom he would discover on Mars this trip—priceless spiritual insights that would be balm to a war-battered mankind.

The cat carefully selected a spot three feet off the floor, curled up on the air, and went to sleep.

*   *   *

Jorj Helmuth snipped the emerging answer tape into sections and handed each to the appropriate man. Most of them carefully tucked theirs away with little more than a glance, but the Secretary of Space puzzled over his.

"Who the devil would Maelzel be?" he asked.

A remote look came into the eyes of the Secretary of Space. "Edgar Allan Poe," he said frowningly, with eyes half closed.

The grizzled general snapped his fingers. "Sure! Maelzel's chess player. Read it when I was a kid. About an automaton that played chess. Poe proved it had a man inside it."

The Secretary of Space frowned. "Now what's the point in a fool question like that?"

"You said it came from Opperly's group?" Jorj asked sharply.

The Secretary of Space nodded. The others looked at the two men puzzledly.

"Who would that be?" Jorj pressed. "The group, I mean."

The Secretary of Space shrugged. "Oh, the usual little bunch over at the Institute. Hindeman, Gregory, Opperly himself. Oh yes, and young Farquar."

"Sounds like Opperly's getting senile," Jorj commented coldly. "I'd investigate."

The Secretary of Space nodded. He suddenly looked tough. "I will. Right away."

*　　*　　*

Sunlight striking through french windows spotlighted a ballet of dust motes untroubled by air-conditioning. Morton Opperly's living room was well kept but worn and quite behind the times. Instead of reading tapes there were books; instead of steno-robots, pen and ink; while in place of a four-by-six TV screen, a Picasso hung on the wall. Only Opperly knew that the painting was still faintly radioactive, that it had been riskily so when he'd smuggled it out of his bomb-singed apartment in New York City.

The two physicists fronted each other across a coffee table. The face of the elder was cadaverous, large-eyed, and tender—fined down by a long life of abstract thought. That of the younger was forceful, sensuous, bulky as his body, and exceptionally ugly. He looked rather like a bear.

Opperly was saying, "So when he asked who was responsible for the Maelzel question, I said I didn't remember." He smiled. "They still allow me my absent-mindedness, since it nourishes their contempt. Almost my sole remaining privilege." The smile faded. "Why do you keep on teasing the zoo animals, Willard?" he asked without rancor. "I've maintained many times that we shouldn't truckle to them by yielding to their demand that we ask Maizie questions. You and the rest have overruled me. But then to use those questions to convey veiled insults isn't reasonable. Apparently the Secretary of Space was bothered enough about this last one to pay me a 'copter call within twenty minutes of this morning's meeting at the foundation. Why do you do it, Willard?"

The features of the other convulsed unpleasantly. "Because the Thinkers are charlatans who must be exposed," he rapped out. "We know their Maizie is no more than a tea-leaf-reading fake. We've traced their Mars rockets and found they go nowhere. We know their Martian mental science is bunk."

"But we've already exposed the Thinkers very thoroughly," Opperly interposed quietly. "You know the good it did."

Farquar hunched his Japanese-wrestler shoulders. "Then it's got to be done until it takes."

132

Opperly studied the bowl of lilies-of-the-valley by the coffeepot. "I think you just want to tease the animals, for some personal reason of which you probably aren't aware."

Farquar scowled. "We're the ones in the cages."

Opperly continued his inspection of the flowers' bells. "All the more reason not to poke sticks through the bars at the lions and tigers strolling outside. No, Willard, I'm not counseling appeasement. But consider the age in which we live. It wants magicians." His voice grew especially tranquil. "A scientist tells people the truth. When times are good—that is, when the truth offers no threat—people don't mind. But when times are very, very bad—" A shadow darkened his eyes. "Well, we all know what happened to—" And he mentioned three names that had been household words in the middle of the century. They were the names on the brass plaque dedicated to the three martyred physicists.

He went on, "A magician, on the other hand, tells people what they wish were true—that perpetual motion works, that cancer can be cured by colored lights, that a psychosis is no worse than a head cold, that they'll live forever. In good times magicians are laughed at. They're a luxury of the spoiled wealthy few. But in bad times people sell their souls for magic cures and buy perpetual-motion machines to power their war rockets."

Farquar clenched his fist. "All the more reason to keep chipping away at the Thinkers. Are we supposed to beg off from a job because it's difficult and dangerous?"

Opperly shook his head. "We're to keep clear of the infection of violence. In my day, Willard, I was one of the Frightened Men. Later I was one of the Angry Men and then one of the Minds of Despair. Now I'm convinced that all my posturings were futile."

"Exactly!" Farquar agreed harshly. "You postured. You didn't act. If you men who discovered atomic energy had only formed a secret league, if you'd only had the foresight and the guts to use your tremendous bargaining position to demand the power to shape mankind's future—"

"By the time you were born, Willard," Opperly interrupted dreamily, "Hitler was merely a name in the history books. We scientists weren't the stuff out of which cloak-and-dagger men are made. Can you imagine Oppenheimer wearing a mask or Einstein sneaking into the Old White House with a bomb in his brief case?" He smiled. "Besides, that's not the way power is seized. New ideas aren't useful to the man bargaining for power—his weapons are established facts, or lies."

"Just the same, it would have been a good thing if you'd had a little violence in you."

"No," Opperly said.

"I've got violence in me," Farquar announced, shoving himself to his feet.

Opperly looked up from the flowers. "I think you have," he agreed.

"But what are we to do?" Farquar demanded. "Surrender the world to charlatans without a struggle?"

Opperly mused for a while. "I don't know what the world needs now. Everyone knows Newton as the great scientist. Few remember that he spent half his life muddling with alchemy, looking for the philosopher's stone. That was the pebble by the seashore he really wanted to find."

"Now you are justifying the Thinkers!"

"No, I leave that to history."

"And history consists of the actions of men," Farquar concluded. "I intend to act. The Thinkers are vulnerable, their power fantastically precarious. What's it based on?

A few lucky guesses. Faithhealing. Some science hocus-pocus, on the level of those juke-box burlesque acts between strips. Dubious mental comfort given to a few nerve-torn neurotics in the Inner Cabinet—and their wives. The fact that the Thinkers' clever stage-managing won the President a doubtful election. The erroneous belief that the Soviets pulled out of Iraq and Iran because of the Thinkers' Mind Bomb threat. A brain machine that's just a cover for Jan Tregarron's guesswork. Oh yes, and that hogwash of 'Martian Wisdom.' All of it mere bluff! A few pushes at the right times and points are all that are needed—and the Thinkers know it! I'll bet they're terrified already, and will be more so when they find that we're gunning for them. Eventually they'll be making overtures to us, turning to us for help. You wait and see."

"I am thinking again of Hitler," Opperly interposed quietly. "On his first half-dozen big steps, he had nothing but bluff. His generals were against him. They knew they were in a cardboard fort. Yet he won every battle, until the last. Moreover," he pressed on, cutting Farquar short, "the power of the Thinkers isn't based on what they've got, but on what the world hasn't got—peace, honor, a good conscience—"

The front-door knocker clanked. Farquar answered it. A skinny old man with a radiation scar twisting across his temple handed him a tiny cylinder. "Radiogram for you, Willard." He grinned across the hall at Opperly. "When are you going to get a phone put in, Mr. Opperly?"

The physicist waved to him. "Next year, perhaps, Mr. Berry."

The old man snorted with good-humored incredulity and trudged off.

"What did I tell you about the Thinkers making overtures?" Farquar chortled suddenly. "It's come sooner than I expected. Look at this."

He held out the radiogram, but the older man didn't take it. Instead he asked, "Who's it from? Tregarron?"

"No, from Helmuth. There's a lot of sugar corn about man's future in deep space, but the real reason is clear. They know that they're going to have to produce an actual nuclear rocket pretty soon, and for that they'll need our help."

"An invitation?"

Farquar nodded. "For this afternoon." He noticed Opperly's anxious though distant frown. "What's the matter?" he asked. "Are you bothered about my going? Are you thinking it might be a trap—that after the Maelzel question they may figure I'm better rubbed out?"

The older man shook his head. "I'm not afraid for your life, Willard. That's yours to risk as you choose. No, I'm worried about other things they might do to you."

"What do you mean?" Farquar asked.

Opperly looked at him with a gentle appraisal. "You're a strong and vital man, Willard, with a strong man's prides and desires." His voice trailed off for a bit. Then, "Excuse me, Willard, but wasn't there a girl once? A Miss Arkady—"

Farquar's ungainly figure froze. He nodded, curtly, face averted.

"And didn't she go off with a Thinker?"

"If girls find me ugly, that's their business," Farquar said harshly, still not looking at Opperly. "What's that got to do with this invitation?"

Opperly didn't answer the question. His eyes got more distant. Finally he said, "In my day we had it a lot easier. A scientist was an academician, cushioned by tradition."

Willard snorted. "Science had already entered the era of the police inspectors, with laboratory directors and political appointees stifling enterprise."

"Perhaps," Opperly agreed. "Still, the scientist lived the safe, restricted, highly respectable life of a university man. He wasn't exposed to the temptations of the world."

Farquar turned on him. "Are you implying that the Thinkers will somehow be able to buy me off?"

"Not exactly."

"You think I'll be persuaded to change my aims?" Farquar demanded angrily.

Opperly shrugged his helplessness. "No, I don't think you'll change your aims."

Clouds encroaching from the west blotted the parallelogram of sunlight between the two men.

*   *   *

As the slideway whisked him gently along the corridor toward his apartment Jorj Helmuth was thinking of his spaceship. For a moment the silver-winged vision crowded everything else out of his mind.

Just think, a spaceship with sails! He smiled a bit, marveling at the paradox.

Direct atomic power. Direct utilization of the force of the flying neutrons. No more ridiculous business of using a reactor to drive a steam engine, or boil off something for a jet exhaust—processes that were as primitive and wasteful as burning gunpowder to keep yourself warm.

Chemical jets would carry his spaceship above the atmosphere. Then would come the thrilling order, "Set sail for Mars!" The vast umbrella would unfold and open out around the stern, its rear or earthward side a gleaming expanse of radioactive ribbon perhaps only an atom thick and backed with a material that would reflect neutrons. Atoms in the ribbon would split, blasting neutrons astern at fantastic velocities. Reaction would send the spaceship hurtling forward.

In airless space, the expanse of sails would naturally not retard the ship. More radioactive ribbon, manufactured as needed in the ship itself, would feed out onto the sail as that already there became exhausted.

A spaceship with direct nuclear drive—and he, a Thinker, had conceived it completely except for the technical details! Having strengthened his mind by hard years of somno-learning, mind-casting, memory-straightening, and sensory training, he had assured himself of the executive power to control the technicians and direct their specialized abilities. Together they would build the true Mars rocket.

But that would only be a beginning. They would build the true Mind Bomb. They would build the true Selective Microbe Slayer. They would discover the true laws of ESP and the inner life. They would even—his imagination hesitated a moment, then strode boldly forward—build the true Maizie!

And then—then the Thinkers would be on even terms with the scientists. Rather, they'd be far ahead. No more deception.

He was so exalted by this thought that he almost let the slideway carry him past his door. He stepped inside and called, "Caddy!" He waited a moment, then walked through the apartment, but she wasn't there.

Confound the girl! he couldn't help thinking. This morning, when she should have made herself scarce, she'd sprawled about sleeping. Now, when he felt like seeing her, when her presence would have added a pleasant final touch to his glowing mood, she chose to be absent. He really should use his hypnotic control on her, he decided, and again there sprang into his mind the word—a pet form of her name—that would send her into obedient trance.

No, he told himself again, that was to be reserved for some moment of crisis or desperate danger, when he would need someone to strike suddenly and unquestioningly for himself and mankind. Caddy was merely a willful and rather silly girl, incapable at present of understanding the tremendous tensions under which he operated. When he had time for it, he would train her up to be a fitting companion without hypnosis.

Yet the fact of her absence had a subtly disquieting effect. It shook his perfect self-confidence just a fraction. He asked himself if he'd been wise in summoning the rocket physicists without consulting Tregarron.

But this mood, too, he conquered quickly. Tregarron wasn't his boss, but just the Thinkers' most clever salesman, an expert in the mumbo-jumbo so necessary for social control in this chaotic era. He himself, Jorj Helmuth, was the real leader in theoretics and over-all strategy, the mind behind the mind behind Maizie.

He stretched himself on the bed, almost instantly achieved maximum relaxation, turned on the somno-learner, and began the two-hour rest he knew would be desirable before the big conference.

*   *   *

Jan Tregarron had supplemented his shorts with pink coveralls, but he was still drinking beer. He emptied his glass and lifted it a lazy inch. The beautiful girl beside him refilled it without a word and went on stroking his forehead.

"Caddy," he said reflectively, without looking at her, "there's a little job I want you to do. You're the only one with the proper background. The point is: it will take you away from Jorj for some time."

"I'd welcome it," she said with decision. "I'm getting pretty sick of watching his push-ups and all his other mind and muscle stunts. And that damn somno-learner of his keeps me awake."

Tregarron smiled. "I'm afraid Thinkers make pretty sad sweethearts."

"Not all of them," she told him, returning his smile tenderly.

He chuckled. "It's about one of those rocket physicists in the list you brought me. A fellow named Willard Farquar."

Caddy didn't say anything, but she stopped stroking his forehead.

"What's the matter?" he asked. "You knew him once, didn't you?"

"Yes," she replied and then added, with surprising feeling. "The big, ugly ape!"

"Well, he's an ape whose services we happen to need. I want you to be our contact girl with him."

She took her hands away from his forehead. "Look, Jan," she said, "I wouldn't like this job."

"I thought he was very sweet on you once."

"Yes, as he never grew tired of trying to demonstrate to me. The clumsy, overgrown, bumbling baby! The man's disgusting, Jan. His approach to a woman is a child wanting candy and enraged because Mama won't produce it on the instant. I don't mind Jorj—he's just a pipsqueak and it amuses me to see how he frustrates himself. But Willard is—"

"—a bit frightening?" Tregarron finished for her.

"No!"

"Of course you're not afraid," Tregarron purred. "You're our beautiful, clever Caddy, who can do anything she wants with any man, and without whose—"

"Look, Jan, this is different—" she began agitatedly.

"—and without whose services we'd have got exactly nowhere. Clever, subtle Caddy, whose most charming attainment in the everappreciative eyes of Papa Jan is her ability to handle every man in the neatest way imaginable and without a trace of real feeling. Kitty Kaddy, who—"

"Very well," she said with a sigh. "I'll do it."

"Of course you will," Jan said, drawing her hands back to his forehead. "And you'll begin right away by getting into your nicest sugar-and-cream war clothes. You and I are going to be the welcoming committee when that ape arrives this afternoon."

"But what about Jorj? He'll want to see Willard."

"That'll be taken care of," Jan assured her.

"And what about the other dozen rocket physicists Jorj asked to come?"

"Don't worry about them."

*   *   *

The President looked inquiringly at his secretary across his littered desk in his home study at White House, Jr. "So Opperly didn't have any idea how that odd question about Maizie turned up in Section Five?"

His secretary settled his paunch and shook his head. "Or claimed not to. Perhaps he's just the absent-minded prof, perhaps, something else. The old feud of the physicists against the Thinkers may be getting hot again. There'll be further investigation."

The President nodded. He obviously had something uncomfortable on his mind. He said uneasily, "Do you think there's any possibility of it being true?"

"What?" asked the the secretary guardedly.

"That peculiar hint about Maizie."

The secretary said nothing.

"Mind you, I don't think there is," the President went on hurriedly, his face assuming a sorrowful scowl. "I owe a lot to the Thinkers, both as a private person and as a public figure. Lord, a man has to lean on *something* these days. But just supposing it were true"—he hesitated, as before uttering blasphemy—"that there was a man inside Maizie, what could we do?"

The secretary said stolidly, "The Thinkers won our last election. They chased the Commies out of Iran. We brought them into the Inner Cabinet. We've showered them with public funds." He paused. "We couldn't do a damn thing."

The President nodded with equal conviction, and, not very happily, summed up: "So if anyone should go up against the Thinkers—and I'm afraid I wouldn't want to see that happen, whatever's true—it would have to be a scientist."

*   *   *

Willard Farquar felt his weight change the steps under his feet into an escalator. He cursed under his breath, but let them carry him, a defiant hulk, up to the tall and mystic blue portals, which silently parted when he was five meters away. The escalator changed to a slideway and carried him into a softly gleaming, high-domed room rather like the antechamber of a temple.

"Martian peace to you, Willard Farquar," an invisible voice intoned. "You have entered the Thinkers' Foundation. Please remain on the slideway."

"I want to see Jorj Helmuth," Wilalrd growled loudly.

"The slideway carried him into the mouth of a corridor and paused. A dark opening dilated on the wall. "May we take your hat and coat!" a voice asked politely. After a moment the request was repeated, with the addition of, "Just pass them through."

Willard scowled, then fought his way out of his shapeless coat and passed it and his hat through in a lump. Instantly the opening contracted, imprisoning his wrists, and he felt his hands being washed on the other side of the wall.

He gave a great jerk which failed to free his hands from the snugly padded gyves. "Do not be alarmed," the voice advised him. "It is only an esthetic measure. As your hands are laved, invisible radiations are slaughtering all the germs in your body, while more delicate emanations are producing a benign rearrangement of your emotions."

The rather amateurish curses Willard was gritting between his teeth became more sulphurous. His sensations told him that a towel of some sort was being applied to his hands. He wondered if he would be subjected to a face-washing and even greater indignities. Then, just before his wrists were released, he felt—for a moment only, but unmistakably—the soft touch of a girl's hand.

That touch, like the mysterious sweet chink of a bell in darkness, brought him a sudden feeling of excitement, wonder.

Yet the feeling was as fleeting as that caused by a lurid advertisement, for as the slideway began to move again, carrying him past a series for depth pictures and inscriptions celebrating the Thinkers' achievements, his mood of bitter exasperation returned doubled. This place, he told himself, was a plague spot of the disease of magic in an enfeebled and easily infected world. He reminded himself that he was not without resources—the Thinkers must fear or need him, whether because of the Maelzel question or the necessity of producing a nuclear power spaceship. He felt his determination to smash them reaffirmed.

The slideway, having twice turned into an escalator, veered toward an opalescent door, which opened as silently as the one below. The slideway stopped at the threshold. Momentum carried him a couple of steps into the room. He stopped and looked around.

The place was a sybarite's modernistic dream. Sponge carpeting thick as a mattress and topped with down. Hassocks and couches that looked butter-soft. A domed ceiling of deep glossy blue mimicking the night sky, with the constellations tooled in silver. A wall of niches crammed with statuettes of languorous men, women, beasts. A self-service bar with a score of golden spigots. A depth TV screen simulating a great crystal ball. Here and there barbaric studs of hammered gold that might have been push buttons. A low table set for three with exquisite ware of crystal and gold. An ever-changing scent of resins and flowers.

A smiling fat man clad in pearl gray sports clothes came through one of the curtained archways. Willard recognized Jan Tregarron from his pictures, but did not at once offer to speak to him. Instead he let his gaze wander with an ostentatious contempt around the crammed walls, take in the bar and the set table with its many wineglasses, and finally return to his host.

"And where," he asked with harsh irony, "are the dancing girls?"

The fat man's eyebrows rose. "In there," he said innocently, indicating the second archway. The curtains parted.

"Oh, I *am* sorry," the fat man apologized. "There seems to be only one on duty. I hope that isn't too much at variance with your tastes."

She stood in the archway, demure and lovely in an off-the-bosom frock of pale skylon edged in mutated mink. She was smiling the first smile that Willard had ever had from her lips.

"Mr. Willard Farquar," the fat man murmured, "Miss Arkady Simms."

*   *   *

Jorj Helmuth turned from the conference table with its dozen empty chairs to the two mousily pretty secretaries.

"No word from the door yet, Master," one of them ventured to say.

Jorj twisted in his chair, though hardly uncomfortably, since it was a beautiful pneumatic job. His nervousness at having to face the twelve rocket physicists—a feeling which, he had to admit, had been unexpectedly great—was giving way to impatience.

"What's Willard Farquar's phone?" he asked sharply.

One of the secretaries ran through a clutch of desk tapes, then spent some seconds whispering into her throat-mike and listening to answers from the soft-speaker.

"He lives with Morton Opperly, who doesn't have one," she finally told Jorj in scandalized tones.

"Let me see the list," Jorj said. "Then, after a bit, "Try Dr. Welcome's place."

This time there were results. Within a quarter of a minute he was handed a phone which he hung expertly on his shoulder.

"This is Dr. Asa Welcome," a reedy voice told him.

"This is Helmuth of the Thinkers' Foundation," Jorj said icily. "Did you get my communication?"

The reedy voice became anxious and placating. "Why yes, Mr. Helmuth, I did. Very glad to get it too. Sounded most interesting. Very eager to come. But—"

"Yes?"

"Well, I was just about to hop in my 'copter—my son's 'copter—when the other note came."

"What other note?"

"Why, the note calling the meeting off."

"I sent no other note!"

The other voice became acutely embarrassed. "But I considered it to be from you—or just about the same thing. I really think I had the right to assume that."

"How was it signed?" Jorj rapped.

"Mr. Jan Tregarron."

Jorj broke the connection. He didn't move until a low sound shattered his abstraction and he realized that one of the girls was whispering a call to the door. He handed back the phone and dismissed them. They went in a rustle of jackets and skirtlets, hesitating at the doorway but not quite daring to look back.

He sat motionless a minute longer. Then his hand crept fretfully onto the table and pushed a button. The room darkened and a long section of wall became transparent, revealing a dozen silvery models of spaceships, beautifully executed. He quickly touched another; the models faded and the opposite wall bloomed with an animated cartoon that portrayed with charming humor and detail the designing and construction of a neutron-drive spaceship. A third button, and a depth picture of deep star-speckled space opened behind the cartoon, showing a section of Earth's surface and in the far distance the tiny ruddy globe of Mars. Slowly a tiny rocket rose from the section of Earth and spread its silvery sails.

He switched off the pictures, keeping the room dark. By a faint table light he dejectedly examined his organizational charts for the neutron-drive project, the long list of books he had boned up on by somno-learning, the concealed table of physical constants and all sorts of other crucial details about rocket physics—a cleverly condensed encyclopedic "pony" to help out his memory on technical points that might have arisen in his discussion with the experts.

He switched out all the lights and slumped forward, blinking his eyes and trying to swallow the lump in his throat. In the dark his memory went seeping back, back, to the day when his math teacher had told him, very superciliously, that the marvelous fantasies he loved to read and hoarded by his bed weren't real science at all, but just a kind of lurid pretense. He had so wanted to be a scientist, and the teacher's contempt had cast a damper on his ambition.

And now that the conference was canceled, would he ever know that it wouldn't have turned out the same way today? That his somno-learning hadn't taken? That his "pony" wasn't good enough? That his ability to handle people extended only to credulous farmer Presidents and mousy girls in skirtlets? Only the test of meeting the experts would have answered those questions.

Tregarron was the one to blame! Tregarron with his sly tyrannical ways, Tregarron with his fear of losing the future to me who really understood theoretics and could handle experts. Tregarron, so used to working by deception that he couldn't see when it became a fault and a crime. Tregarron, who must now be shown the light—or, failing that, against whom certain steps must be taken.

For perhaps half an hour Jorj sat very still, thinking. Then he turned to the phone and, after some delay, got his party.

"What is it now, Jorj?" Caddy asked impatiently. "Please don't bother me with any of your moods, because I'm tired and my nerves are on edge."

He took a breath. When steps may have to be taken, he thought, one must hold an agent in readiness. "Caddums," he intoned hypnotically, vibrantly. "Caddums—"

The voice at the other end had instantly changed, become submissive, sleepy, suppliant.

"Yes, Master?"

Morton Opperly looked up from the sheet of neatly penned equations at Willard Farquar, who had somehow acquired a measure of poise. He neither lumbered restlessly nor grimaced. He removed his coat with a certain dignity and stood solidly before his mentor. He smiled. Granting that he was a bear, one might guess he had just been fed.

"You see?" he said. "They didn't hurt me."

"They didn't hurt you?" Opperly asked softly.

Willard slowly shook his head. His smile broadened.

Opperly put down his pen, folded his hands. "And you're as determined as ever to expose and smash the Thinkers?"

"Of course!" The menacing growl came back into the bear's voice, except that it was touched with a certain pleased luxuriousness. "Only from now on I won't be teasing the zoo animals, and I won't embarrass you by asking any more Maelzel questions. I have reached the objective at which those tactics were aimed. After this I shall bore from within."

"Bore from within," Opperly repeated, frowning. "Now where have I heard that phrase before?" His brow cleared. "Oh yes," he said listlessly. "Do I understand that you are becoming a Thinker, Willard?"

The other gave him a faintly pitying smile, stretched himself on the couch and gazed at the ceiling. All his movements were deliberate, easy.

"Certainly. That's the only realistic way to smash them. Rise high in their councils. Out-trick all their trickeries. Organize a fifth column. Then *strike!*"

"The end justifying the means, of course," Opperly said.

"Of course. As surely as the desire to stand up justifies your disturbing the air over your head. All action in this world is nothing but means."

Opperly nodded abstractedly. "I wonder if anyone else ever became a Thinker for those same reasons. I wonder if being a Thinker doesn't simply mean that you've decided you have to use lies and tricks as your chief method."

Willard shrugged. "Could be." There was no longer any doubt about the pitying quality of his smile.

Opperly stood up, squaring together his papers. "So you'll be working with Helmuth?"

"Not Helmuth. Tregarron." The bear's smile became cruel. "I'm afraid that Helmuth's career as a Thinker is going to have quite a setback."

"Helmuth," Opperly mused. "Morgenschein once told me a bit about him. A man of some idealism, despite his affiliations. Best of a bad lot. Incidentally, is he the one with whom—"

"—Miss Arkady Simms ran off?" Willard finished without any embarrassment. "Yes, that was Helmuth. But that's all going to be changed now."

Opperly nodded. "Good-by, Willard," he said.

Willard quickly heaved himself up on an elbow. Opperly looked at him for about five seconds, then, without a word, walked out of the room.

*   *   *

The only obvious furnishings in Jan Tregarron's office were a flat-topped desk and a few chairs. Tregarron sat behind the desk, the top of which was completely bare. He looked almost bored, except that his little eyes were smiling. Jorj Helmuth sat across the desk from him, a few feet back, erect and grim faces, while Caddy, shadowy in the muted light, stood against the wall behind Tregarron. She still wore the fur-trimmed skylon frock she'd put on that afternoon. She took no part in the conversation, seemed almost unaware of it.

"So you just went ahead and canceled the conference without consulting me?" Jorj was saying.

"You called it without consulting me." Tregarron playfully wagged a finger. "Shouldn't do that sort of thing, Jorj."

"But I tell you, I was completely prepared. I was absolutely sure of my ground."

"I know, I know," Tregarron said lightly. "But it's not the right time for it. I'm the best judge of that."

"When will be the right time?"

"Tregarron shrugged. "Look here, Jorj," he said, "every man should stick to his trade, to his forte. Technology isn't ours."

Jorj's lips thinned. "But you know as well as I do that we are going to have to have a nuclear spaceship and actually go to Mars someday."

Tregarron lifted his eyebrows. "Are we?"

"Yes! Just as we're going to have to build a real Maizie. All the things we've done until now have been emergency measures."

141

"Really?"

Jorj stared at him. "Look here, Jan," he said, gripping his knees with his hands, "you and I are going to have to talk things through."

"Are you quite sure of that?" Jan's voice was very cool. "I have a feeling that it might be best if you said nothing and accepted things as they are."

"No!"

"Very well." Tregarron settled himself in his chair.

"I helped you organize the Thinkers," Jorj said, and waited. "At least, I was your first partner."

Tregarron barely nodded.

"Our basic idea was that the time had come to apply science to the life of man on a large scale, to live rationally and realistically. The only things holding the world back from this all-important step were the ignorance, superstition, and inertia of the average man, and the stuffiness and lack of enterprise of the academic scientists.

"Yet we knew that in their deepest hearts the average man and the professionals were both on our side. They wanted the new world visualized by science. They wanted the simplifications and conveniences, the glorious adventures of the human mind and body. They wanted the trips to Mars and into the depts of the human psyche, they wanted the robots and the thinking machines. All they lacked was the nerve to take the first big step—and that was what we supplied.

"It was no time for half measures, for slow and sober plodding. The world was racked by wars and neurosis, in danger of falling into the foulest hands. What was needed was a tremendous and thrilling appeal to the human imagination, an earth-shaking affirmation of the power of science for good.

"But the men who provided that appeal and affirmation couldn't afford to be cautious. They wouldn't check and double check. They couldn't wait for the grudging and jealous approval of the professionals. They had to use stunts, tricks, fakes—*anything to get over the big point*. Once that had been done, once mankind was headed down the new road, it would be easy enough to give the average man the necessary degree of insight to heal the breach with the professionals, to make good in actuality what had been made good only in pretense.

"Have I stated our position fairly?"

Tregarron's eyes were hooded. "You're the one who's telling it."

"On those general assumptions we established our hold on susceptible leaders and the mob," Jorj went on. "We built Maizie and the Mars rocket and the Mind Bomb. We discovered the wisdom of the Martians. We *sold* the people on the science that the professionals had been too high-toned to advertise or bring into the market place.

"But now that we've succeeded, now that we've made the big point, now that Maizie and Mars and science do rule the average human imagination, the time has come to take the second big step, to let accomplishment catch up with imagination, to implement fantasy with fact.

"Do you suppose I'd ever have gone into this with you if it hadn't been for the thought of that second big step? Why, I'd have felt dirty and cheap, a mere charlatan—except for the sure conviction that someday everything would be set right. I've devoted my whole life to that conviction, Jan. I've studied and disciplined myself, using every scientific measn at my disposal, so that I wouldn't be found lacking when the day came to heal the breach between the Thinkers and the professionals. I've trained myself to be the perfect man for the job.

"Jan, the day's come and I'm the man. I know you've been concentrating on other aspects of our work; you haven't had time to keep up with my side of it. But I'm sure that as soon as you see how carefully I've prepared myself, how completely practical the neutron-drive rocket project is, you'll beg me to go ahead!"

Tregarron smiled at the ceiling for a moment. "Your general idea isn't so bad, Jorj, but your time scale is out of whack and your judgment is a joke. Oh yes. Every revolutionary wants to see the big change take place in his lifetime, Tch! It's as if he were watching evolutionary vaudeville and wanted the Ape-to-Man Act over in twenty minutes.

"Time for the second big step? Jorj, the average man's exactly what he was ten years ago, except that he's got a new god. More than ever he thinks of Mars as a Hollywood paradise, with wise men and yummy princesses. Maizie is Mama magnified a million times. As for professional scientists, they're more jealous and stuffy than ever. All they'd like to do is turn the clock back to a genteel dream world of quiet quadrangles and caps and gowns, where every commoneer bows to the passing scholar.

"Maybe in ten thousand years we'll be ready for the second big step. Maybe. Meanwhile, as should be, the clever will rule the stupid for their own good. The realists will rule the dreamers. Those with free hands will rule those who have deliberately handcuffed themselves with taboos.

"Secondly, your judgment. Did you actually think you could have bossed those professionals, kept your mental footing in the intellectual melee? You, a nuclear physicist? A rocket scientist? Why, it's—Take it easy now, boy, and listen to me. They'd have torn you to piecs in twenty minutes and glad of the chance! You baffle me, Jorj. You know that Maizie and the Mars rocket and all that are fakes, yet you believe in your somno-learning and consciousness-expansion and optimism-pumping like the veriest yokel. I wouldn't be surprised to hear you'd taken up ESP and hypnotism. I think you should take stock of yourself and get a new slant. It's overdue."

He leaned back. Jorj's face had become a mask. His eyes did not flicker from Tregarron's, yet there was a subtle change in his expression. Behind Tregarron, Caddy swayed as if in a sudden gust of intangible wind and took a silent step forward from the wall.

"That's your honest opinion?" Jorj asked very quietly.

"It's more than that," Tregarron told him, just as unmelodramatically. "It's orders."

Jorj stood up purposefully. "Very well," he said. "In that case I have to tell you that—"

Casually, but with no waste motion, Tregarron slipped an ultrasonic pistol from under the desk and laid it on the empty top.

"No," he said, "let me tell you something. I was afraid this would happen and I made preparations. If you've studied your Nazi, Fascist, and Soviet history, you know what happens to old revolutionaries who don't move with the times. But I'm not going to be too harsh. I have a couple of boys waiting outside. They'll take you by 'copter to the field, then by jet to New Mex. Bright and early tomorrow morning, Jorj, you're leaving on a trip to Mars."

Jorj hardly reacted to the words. Caddy was two steps nearer Tregarron.

"I decided Mars would be the best place for you," the fat man continued. "The robot controls will be arranged so that your 'visit' to Mars lasts two years. Perhaps in that time you will have learned wisdom, such as realizing that the big liar must never fall for his own big lie.

"Meanwhile, there will have to be a replacement for you. I have in mind a person who may prove peculiarly worthy to occupy your position, with all its perquisites. A person who seems to understand that force and desire are the motive powers of life, and that anyone who believes the big lie proves himself strictly a jerk."

Caddy was standing behind Tregarron now, her half-closed, sleepy eyes fixed on Jorj's.

"His name is Willard Farquar. You see, I too believe in cooperating with the scientists, Jorj, but by subversion rather than conference. My idea is to offer the hand of friendship to a selected few of them—the hand of friendship with a nice big bribe in it." He smiled. "You were a good man, Jorj, for the early days, when we needed a publicist with catchy ideas about Mind Bombs, ray guns, plastic helmets, fancy sweaters, space brassières, and all that other corn. Now we can afford a soldier sort of person."

Jorj moistened his lips.

"We'll have a neat explanation of what's happened to you. Callers will be informed that you've gone on an extended visit to imbibe the wisdom of the Martians."

Jorj whispered, "Caddums."

Caddy leaned forward. Her arms snaked down Tregarron's, as if to imprison his wrists. But instead she reached out and took the ultrasonic pistol and put it in Tregarron's right hand. Then she looked up at Jorj with eyes that were very bright.

She said very sweetly and sympathetically, "Poor Superman."

Yesterday House

I

The narrow cove was quiet as the face of an expectant child, yet so near the ruffled Atlantic that the last push of wind carried the *Annie O.* its full length. The man in gray flannels and sweatshirt let the sail come crumpling down and hurried past its white folds at a gait made comically awkward by his cramped muscles. Slowly the rocky ledge came nearer. Slowly the blue V inscribed on the cove's surface by the sloop's prow died. Sloop and ledge kissed so gently that he hardly had to reach out his hand.

He scrambled ashore, dipping a sneaker in the icy water, and threw the line around a boulder. Unkinking himself, he looked back through the cove's high and rocky mouth at the gray-green scattering of islands and the faint dark line that was the coast of Maine. He almost laughed in satisfaction at having disregarded vague warnings and done the thing every man yearns to do once in his lifetime—gone to the farthest island out.

He must have looked longer than he realized, because by the time he dropped his gaze the cove was again as glassy as if the *Annie O.* had always been there. And the splotches made by his sneaker on the rock had faded in the hot sun. There was something very unusual about the quietness of this place. As if time, elsewhere hurrying frantically, paused here to rest. As if all changes were erased on this one bit of earth.

The man's lean, melancholy face crinkled into a grin at the banal fancy. He turned his back on his new friend, the little green sloop, without one thought for his nets and specimen bottles, and set out to explore. The ground rose steeply at first and the oaks were close, but after a little way things went downhill and the leaves thinned and he came out on more rocks—and realized that he hadn't quite gone to the farthest one out.

Joined to this island by a rocky spine, which at the present low tide would have been dry but for the spray, was another green, high island that the first had masked from him all the while he had been sailing. He felt a thrill of discovery, just as he'd wondered back in the woods whether his might not be the first human feet to kick through the underbrush. After all, there were thousands of these islands.

Then he was dropping down the rocks, his lanky limbs now moving smoothly enough.

To the landward side of the spine, the water was fairly still. It even began with another deep cove, in which he glimpsed the spiny spheres of sea urchins. But from seaward the waves chopped in, sprinkling his trousers to the knees and making him wince pleasurably at the thought of what vast wings of spray and towers of solid water must crash up from here in a storm.

He crossed the rocks at a trot, ran up a short grassy slope, raced through a fringe of trees—and came straight up against an eight-foot fence of heavy mesh topped with barbed wire and backed at a short distance with high, heavy shrubbery.

Without pausing for surprise—in fact, in his holiday mood, using surprise as a goad—he jumped for the branch of an oak whose trunk touched the fence, scorning the easier lower branch on the other side of the tree. Then he drew himself up, worked his way to some higher branches that crossed the fence, and dropped down inside.

Suddenly cautious, he gently parted the shrubbery and, before the first surprise could really sink in, had another.

A closely mown lawn dotted with more shrubbery ran up to a snug white Cape Cod cottage. The single strand of a radio aerial stretched the length of the roof. Parked on a neat gravel driveway that crossed just in front of the cottage was a short, square-lined touring car that he recognized from remembered pictures as an ancient Essex. The whole scene had about it the same odd quietness as the cove.

Then, with the air of a clockwork toy coming to live, the white door opened and an elderly woman came out, dressed in a long, lace-edged dress and wide, lacy hat. She climbed into the driver's seat of the Essex, sitting there very stiff and tall. The motor began to chug bravely, gravel skittered, and the car rolled off between the trees.

The door of the house opened again and a slim girl emerged. She wore a white silk dress that fell straight from square neckline to hip-height waistline, making the skirt seem very short. Her dark hair was bound with a white bandeau so that it curved close to her cheeks. A dark necklace dangled against the white of the dress. A newspaper was tucked under her arm.

She crossed the driveway and tossed the paper down on a rattan table between three rattan chairs and stood watching a squirrel zigzag across the lawn.

The man stepped through the wall of shrubbery, called, "Hello!" and walked toward her.

She whirled around and stared at him as still as if her heart had stopped beating. Then she darted behind the table and waited for him there. Granting the surprise of his appearance, her alarm seemed not so much excessive as eerie. As if, the man thought, he were not an ordinary stranger, but a visitor from another planet.

Approaching closer, he saw that she was trembling and that her breath was coming in rapid, irregular gasps. Yet the slim, sweet, patrician face that stared into his had an underlying expression of expectancy that reminded him of the cove. She couldn't have been more than eighteen.

He stopped short of the table. Before he could speak, she stammered out, "Are you he?"

"What do you mean?" he asked, smiling puzzledly.

"The one who sends me the little boxes."

"I was out sailing and I happened to land in the far cove. I didn't dream that anyone lived on this island, or even came here."

"No one ever does come here," she replied. Her manner had changed, becoming at once more wary and less agitated, though still eerily curious.

"It startled me tremendously to find this place," he blundered on. "Especially the road and the car. Why, this island can't be more than a quarter of a mile wide."

"The road goes down to the wharf," she explained, "and up to the top of the island, where my aunts have a treehouse."

He tore his mind away from the picture of a woman dressed like Queen Mary clambering up a tree. "Was that your aunt I saw driving off?"

"One of them. The other's taken the motorboat in for supplies." She looked at him doubtfully. "I'm not sure they'll like it if they find someone here."

"There are just the three of you?" he cut in quickly, looking down the empty road that vanished among the oaks.

She nodded.

"I suppose you go in to the mainland with your aunts quite often?"

She shook her head.

"It must get pretty dull for you."

"Not very," she said, smiling. "My aunts bring me the papers and other things. Even movies. We've got a projector. My favorite stars are Antonio Morino and Alice Terry. I like her better even than Clara Bow."

He looked at her hard for a moment. "I suppose you read a lot?"

She nodded. "Fitzgerald's my favorite author." She started around the table, hesitated, suddenly grew shy. "Would you like some lemonade?"

He'd noticed the dewed silver pitcher, but only now realized his thirst. Yet when she handed him a glass, he held it untasted and said awkwardly, "I haven't introduced myself. I'm Jack Barr."

She stared at his outstretched right hand, slowly extended her own toward it, shook it up and down exactly once, then quickly dropped it.

He chuckled and gulped some lemonade. "I'm a biology student. Been working at Wood's Hole the first part of the summer. But now I'm here to do research in marine ecology—that's sort of sea-life patterns—of the inshore islands. Under the direction of Professor Kesserich. You know about him, of course?"

She shook her head.

"Probably the greatest living biologist," he was proud to inform her. "Human physiology as well. Tremendous geneticist. In a class with Carlson and Jacques Loeb. Martin Kesserich—he lives over there at town. I'm staying with him. You ought to have heard of him." He grinned. "Matter of fact, I'd never have met you if it hadn't been for Mrs. Kesserich."

The girl looked puzzled.

Jack explained. "The old boy's been off to Europe on some conferences, won't be back for a couple days more. But I was to get started anyhow. When I went out this morning Mrs. Kesserich—she's a drab sort of person—said to me. 'Don't try to sail to the farther islands.' So, of course, I had to. By the way, you still haven't told me your name."

"Mary Alice Pope," she said, speaking slowly and with an odd wonder, as if she were saying it for the first time.

"You're pretty shy, aren't you?"

"How would I know?"

The question stopped Jack. He couldn't think of anything to say to this strangely attractive girl dressed almost like a "flapper."

"Will you sit down?" she asked him gravely.

The rattan chair sighed under his weight. He made another effort to talk. "I'll bet you'll be glad when summer's over."

"Why?"

"So you'll be able to go back to the mainland."

"But I never go to the mainland."

"You mean you stay out here all winter?" he asked incredulously, his mind filled with a vision of snow and frozen spray and great gray waves.

"Oh, yes. We get all our supplied on hand before winter. My aunts are very capable. They don't always were long lace dresses. And now I help them."

"But that's impossible!" he said with sudden sympathetic anger. "You can't be shut off this way from people your own age!"

"You've the first one I ever met." She hesitated. "I never saw a boy or a man before, except in movies."

"You're joking!"

"No, it's true."

"But why are they doing it to you?" he demanded, leaning forward. "Why are they inflicting this loneliness on you, Mary?"

She seemed to have gained poise from his loss of it. "I don't know why. I'm to find out soon. But actually I'm not lonely. May I tell you a secret?" She touched his hand, this time with only the faintest trembling. "Every night the loneliness gathers in around me—you're right about that. But then every morning new life comes to me in a little box."

"What's that?" he said sharply.

"Sometimes there's a poem in the box, sometimes a book, or pictures, or flowers, or a ring, but always a note. Next to the notes I like the poems best. My favorite is the one by Matthew Arnold that ends,

> **Ah, love, let us be true**
> **To one another! for the world, which seems**
> **To lie before us like a land of dreams,**
> **So various, so beautiful, so new,**
> **Hath really neither joy, nor love, nor light,**
> **Nor certitude—"**

"Wait a minute," he interrupted. "Who sends you these boxes?"

"I don't know."

"But how are the notes signed?"

"They're wonderful notes," she said. "So wise, so gay, so tender, you'd imagine them being written by John Barrymore or Lindbergh."

"Yes, but how are they signed?"

She hesitated. "Never anything but 'Your Lover.'"

"And so when you first saw me, you thought—" He began, then stopped because she was blushing.

"How long have you been getting them?"

"Ever since I can remember. I have two closets of the boxes. The new ones are either by my bed when I wake or at my place at breakfast."

"But how does this—person get these boxes to you out here? Does he give them to your aunts and do they put them there?"

"I'm not sure."

"But how can they get them in winter?"

"I don't know."

"Look here," he said, pouring himself more lemonade, "how long is it since you've been to the mainland?"

"Almost eighteen years. My aunts tell me I was born there in the middle of the war."

148

"What war?" he asked startledly, spilling some lemonade.

"The World War, of course. What's the matter?"

Jack Barr was staring down at the spilled lemonade and feeling a kind of terror he'd never experienced in his waking life. Nothing around him had changed. He could still feel the same hot sun on his shoulders, the same icy glass in his hand, scent the same lemon-acid odor in his nostrils. He could still hear the faint *chop-chop* of the waves.

And yet everything had changed, gone dark and dizzy as a landscape glimpsed just before a faint. All the little false notes had come to a sudden focus. For the lemonade had spilled on the headline of the newspaper the girl had tossed down, and the headline read:

HITLER IN NEW DEFIANCE

Under the big black banner of that head swam smaller ones:

FOES OF MACHADO RIOT IN HAVANA
BIG NRA PARADE PLANNED
BALBO SPEAKS IN NEW YORK

Suddenly he felt a surge of relief. He had noticed that the paper was yellow and brittle-edged.

"Why are you so interested in old newspapers?" he asked.

"I wouldn't call day-before-yesterday's paper old," the girl objecte, pointing at the deadline: July 20, 1933.

"You're trying to joke," Jack told her.

"No, I'm not."

"But it's 1953."

"Now it's you who are joking."

"But the paper's yellow."

"The paper's always yellow."

He laughed uneasily. "Well, if you actually think it's 1933, perhaps you're to be envied," he said, with a sardonic humor he didn't quite feel. "Then you can't know anything about the Second World War, or television, or the V-2s, or bikini bathing suits, or the atomic bomb, or—"

"Stop!" She had sprung up and retreated around her chair, white-faced. "I don't like what you're saying."

"But—"

"No, please! Jokes that may be quite harmless on the mainland sound different here."

"I'm really not joking," he said after a moment.

She grew quite frantic at that. "I can show you all last week's papers! I can show you magazines and other things. I can prove it!"

She started toward the house. He followed. He felt his heart begin to pound.

At the white door she paused, looking worriedly down the road. Jack thought he could hear the faint *chug* of a motorboat. She pushed open the door and he followed her inside. The small windowed room was dark after the sunlight. Jack got an impression of solid old furniture, a fireplace with brass andirons.

"Flash!" croaked a gritty voice. "After their disastrous break day before yesterday, stocks are recovering. Leading issues . . ."

Jack realized that he had started and had involuntarily put his arm around the girl's shoulders. At the same time he noticed that the voice was coming from the curved brown trumpet of an old-fashioned radio loudspeaker.

The girl didn't pull away from him. He turned toward her. Although her gray eyes were on him, her attention had gone elsewhere.

"I can hear the car. They're coming back. They won't like it that you're here."

"All right, they won't like it."

Her agitation grew. "No, you must go."

"I'll come back tomorrow," he heard himself saying.

"Flash! It looks as if the World Economic Conference may soon adjourn, mouthing jeers at old Uncle Sam who is generally referred to as Uncle Shylock."

Jack felt a numbness on his neck. The room seemed to be darkening, the girl growing stranger still.

"You must go before they see you."

"Flash! Wiley Post has just completed his solo circuit of the globe, after a record-breaking flight of seven days, eighteen hours and forty-five minutes. Asked how he felt after the energy-draining feat, Post quipped . . ."

He was halfway across the lawn before he realized the terror into which the grating radio voice had thrown him.

He leaped for the branch overhanging the fence, vaulted up with the risky help of a foot on the barbed top. A surprised squirrel, lacking time to make its escape up the trunk, sprang to the ground ahead of him. With terrible suddenness, two steel-jawed semicircles clanked together just over the squirrel's head. Jack landed with one foot to either side of the sprung trap, while the squirrel darted off with a squeak.

Jack plunged down the slope to the rocky spine and ran across it, spray from the rising waves spattering him to the waist. Panting now, he stumbled up into the oaks and undergrowth of the first island, fought his way through it, finally reached the silent cove. He loosed the line of the *Annie O.*, dragged it as near to the cove's mouth as he could, plunged knee-deep in freezing water to give it a final shove, scrambled aboard, snatched up the boathook and punched at the rocks.

As soon as the *Annie O.* was nosing out of the cove into the cross waves, he yanked up the sail. The freshening wind filled it and sent the sloop heeling over, with inches of white water over the lee rail, and plunging ahead.

For a long while, Jack was satisfied to think of nothing but the wind and the waves and the sail and speed and danger, to have all his attention taken up balancing one against the other, so that he wouldn't have to ask himself what year it was and whether time was an illusion, and wonder about flappers and hidden traps.

When he finally looked back at the island, he was amazed to see how tiny it had grown, as distant as the mainland.

Then he saw a gray motorboat astern. He watched it as it slowly overtook him. It was built like a lifeboat, with a sturdy low cabin in the bow and wheel amidship. Whoever was at the wheel had long gray hair that whipped in the wind. The longer he looked, the surer he was that it was a woman wearing a lace dress. Something that stuck up inches over the cabin flashed darkly beside her. Only when she lifted it to the roof of the cabin did it occur to him that it might be a rifle.

But just then the motorboat swung around in a turn that sent waves drenching over it, and headed back toward the island. He watched if for a minute in wonder, then his attention was jolted by an angry hail.

Three fishing smacks, also headed toward town, were about to cross his bow. He came around into the wind and waited with shaking sail, watching a man in a lumpy sweater shake a fist at him. Then he turned and gratefully followed the dark, wide, fanlike sterns and age-yellowed sails.

II

The exterior of Martin Kesserich's home—a weathered white cube with narrow, sharp-paned windows, topped by a cupola—was nothing like its lavish interior.

In much the same way, Mrs. Kesserich clashed with the darkly gleaming furniture, Persian rugs and bronze vases around her. Her shapeless black form, poised awkwardly on the edge of a huge sofa, made Jack think of a cow that had strayed into the drawing room. He wondered again how a man like Kesserich had come to marry such a creature.

Yet when she lifted up her little eyes from the shadows, he had the uneasy feeling that she knew a great deal about him. The eyes were still those of a domestic animal, but of a wise one that has been watching the house a long, long while from the barnyard.

He asked abruptly, "Do you know anything of a girl around here named Mary Alice Pope?"

The silence lasted so long that he began to think she'd gone into some bovine trance. Then, without a word, she got up and went over to a tall cabinet. Feeling on a ledge behind it for a key, she opened a panel, opened a cardboard box inside it, took something from the box and handed him a photograph. He held it up to the failing light and sucked in his breath with surprise.

It was a picture of the girl he'd met that afternoon. Same flat-bosomed dress—flowered rather than white—no bandeau, same beads. Same proud, demure expression, perhaps a bit happier.

"That is Mary Alice Pope," Mrs. Kesserich said in a strangely flat voice. "She was Martin's fiancee. She was killed in a railway accident in 1933."

The small sound of the cabinet door closing brought Jack back to reality. He realized that he no longer had the photograph. Against the gloom by the cabinet, Mrs. Kesserich's white face looked at him with what seemed a malicious eagerness.

"Sit down," she said, "and I'll tell you about it."

Without a thought as to why she hadn't asked him a single question—he was much too dazed for that—he obeyed. Mrs. Kesserich resumed her position on the edge of the sofa.

"You must understand, Mr. Barr, that Mary Alice Pope was the one love of Martin's life. He is a man of very deep and strong feelings, yet as you probably know, anything but kindly or demonstrative. Even when he first came here from Hungary with his older sisters Hani and Hilda, there was a cloak of loneliness about him—or rather about the three of them.

"Hani and Hilda were athletic outdoor women, yet fiercely proud—I don't imagine they ever spoke to anyone in America except as to a servant—and with a seething distaste for all men except Martin. They showered all their devotion on him. So of course, though Martin didn't realize it, they were consumed with jealousy when he fell in love with Mary Alice Pope. They'd thought that since he'd reached forty without marrying, he was safe.

"Mary Alice came from a purebred, or as a biologist would say, inbred British stock. She was very young, but very sweet, and up to a point very wise. She sensed Hani and Hilda's feelings right away and did everything she could to win them over. For instance, though she was afraid of horses, she took up horseback riding, because that was Hani and Hilda's favorite pastime. Naturally, Martin knew nothing of her fear, and naturally his sisters knew about it from the first. But—and here is where Mary's wisdom fell short—her brave gesture did not pacify them; it only increased their hatred.

"Except for his research, Martin was blind to everything but his love. It was a beautiful and yet frightening passion, an insane cherishing as narrow and intense as his sisters' hatred."

With a start, Jack remembered that it was Mrs. Kesserich telling him all this.

She went on, "Martin's love directed his every move. He was building a home for himself and Mary, and in his mind he was building a wonderful future for them as well—not vaguely, if you know Martin, but year by year, month by month. This winter, he'd plan, they would visit Buenos Aires, next summer they would sail down the inland passage and he would teach Mary Hungarian for their trip to Buda-Pesth the year after, where he would occupy a chair at the university for a few months . . . and so on. Finally the time for their marriage drew near. Martin had been away. His research was keeping him very busy—"

Jack broke in with, "Wasn't that about the time he did his definitive work on growth and fertilization?"

Mrs. Kesserich nodded with solemn appreciation in the gathering darkness. "But now he was coming home, his work done. It was early evening, very chilly, but Hani and Hilda felt they had to ride down to the station to meet their brother. And although she dreaded it, Mary rode with them, for she knew how delighted he would be at her cantering to the puffing train and his running up to lift her down from the saddle to welcome him home.

"Of course there was Martin's luggage to be considered, so the station wagon had to be sent down for that." She looked defiantly at Jack. "I drove the station wagon. I was Martin's laboratory assistant."

She paused. "It was almost dark, but there was still a white cold line of sky to the west. Hani and Hilda, with Mary between them, were waiting on their horses at the top of the hill that led down to the station. The train had whistled and its headlight was graying the gravel of the crossing.

"Suddenly Mary's horse squealed and plunged down the hill. Hani and Hilda followed—to try to catch her, they said—but they didn't manage that, only kept her horse from veering off. Mary never screamed, but as her horse reared on the tracks, I saw her face in the headlight's glare.

"Martin must have guessed, or at least feared what had happened, for he was out of the train and running along the track before it stopped. In fact, he was the first to kneel down beside Mary—I mean, what had been Mary—and was holding her all bloody and shattered in his arms."

A door slammed. There were steps in the hall. Mrs. Kesserich stiffened and was silent. Jack turned.

The blur of a face in the doorway to the hall—a seemingly young, sensitive, suavely handsome face with aristocratic jaw. Then there was a click and the lights flared up and Jack saw the close-cropped gray hair and the lines around the eyes and nostrils, while the sensitive mouth grew sardonic. Yet the handsomeness stayed, and somehow the youth, too, or at least a tremendous inner vibrancy.

"Hello, Barr," Martin Kesserich said, ignoring his wife.

The great biologist had come home.

III

"Oh, yes, and Jamieson had a feeble paper on what he called individualization in marine worms. Barr, have you ever thought much about the larger aspects of the problem of individuality?"

Jack jumped slightly. He had let his thoughts wander very far.

"Not especially, sir," he mumbled.

The house was still. A few minutes after the professor's arrival. Mrs. Kesserich had gone off with an anxious glance at Jack. He knew why and wished he could reassure her that he would not mention their conversation to the professor.

Kesserich had spent perhaps a half hour briefing him on the more important papers delivered at the conferences. Then, almost as if it were a teacher's trick to show up a pupil's inattention, he had suddenly posed this question about individuality.

"You know what I mean, of course," Kesserich pressed. "The factors that make you you, and me me."

"Heredity and environment," Jack parroted like a freshman.

Kesserich nodded. "Suppose—this is just speculation—that we could control heredity and environment. Then we could recreate the same individual at will."

Jack felt a shiver go through him. "To get exactly the same pattern of hereditary traits. That'd be far beyond us."

"What about identical twins?" Kesserich pointed out. "And then there's pathenogenesis to be considered. One might produce a duplicate of the mother without the intervention of the male." Although his voice had grown more idly speculative, Kesserich seemed to Jack to be smiling secretly. "There are many examples in the lower animal forms, to say nothing of the technique by which Loeb caused a sea urchin to reproduce with no more stimulus than a salt solution."

Jack felt the hair rising on his neck. "Even then you wouldn't get exactly the same pattern of hereditary traits."

"Not if the parent were of very pure stock? Not if there were some special technique for selecting ova that would reproduce all the mother's traits?"

"But environment would change things," Jack objected. "The duplicate would be bound to develop differently."

"Is environment so important? Newman tells about a pair of identical twins separated from birth, unaware of each other's existence. They met by accident when they were twenty-one. Each was a telephone repairman. Each had a wife the same age. Each had a baby son. And each had a fox terrier called 'Trixie.' That's without trying to make environments similar. But suppose you did try. Suppose you saw to it that each of them had exactly the same experiences at the same times . . ."

For a moment it seemed to Jack that the room was dimming and wavering, becoming a dark pool in which the only motionless thing was Kesserich's sphinxlike face.

"Well, we've escaped quite far enough from Jamieson's marine worms," the biologist said, all brisk again. He said it as if Jack were the one who had led the conversation down wild and unprofitable channels. "Let's get on to your project. I want to talk it over now, because I won't have any time for it tomorrow."

Jack looked at him blankly.

"Tomorrow I must attend to a very important matter," the biologist explained.

IV

Morning sunlight brightened the colors of the wax flowers under glass on the high bureau that always seemed to emit the faint odor of old hair combings. Jack pulled back the diamond-patterned quilt and blinked the sleep from his eyes. He expected his mind to be busy wondering about Kesserich and his wife—things said and half said last night —but found instead that his thoughts swung instantly to Mary Alice Pope, as if to a farthest island in a world of people.

Downstairs, the house was empty. After a long look at the cabinet—he felt behind it, but the key was gone—he hurried down to the waterfront. He stopped only for a bowl of chowder and, as an afterthought, to buy half a dozen newspapers.

The sea was bright, the brisk wind just right for the *Annie O*. There was eagerness in the way it smacked the sail and in the creak of the mast. And when he reached the cove, it was no longer still, but nervous with faint ripples, as if time had finally begun to stir.

After the same struggle with the underbrush, he came out on the rocky spine and passed the cove of the sea urchins. The spiny creatures struck an uncomfortable chord in his memory.

This time he climbed the second island cautiously, scraping the innocent-seeming ground ahead of him intently with a boathook he'd brought along for the purpose. He was only a few yards from the fence when he saw Mary Alice Pope standing behind it.

He hadn't realized that his heart would begin to pound or that, at the same time, a shiver of almost supernatural dread would go through him.

The girl eyes him with an uneasy hostility and immediately began to speak in a hushed, hurried voice. "You must go away at once and never come back. You're a wicked man, but I don't want you to be hurt. I've been watching for you all morning."

He tossed the newspapers over the fence. "You don't have to read them now," he told her. "Just look at the datelines and a few of the headlines."

When she finally lifted her eyes to his again, she was trembling. She tried unsuccessfully to speak.

"Listen to me," he said. "You've been the victim of a scheme to make you believe you were born around 1916 instead of 1933, and that it's 1933 now instead of 1953. I'm not sure why it's been done, though I think I know who you really are."

"But," the girl faltered, "my aunts tell me it's 1933."

"They would."

"And there are the papers . . . the magazines . . . the radio."

"The papers are old ones. The radio's faked—some sort of recording. I could show you if I could get at it."

"*These* papers might be faked," she said, pointing to where she'd let them drop on the ground.

"They're new," he said. "Only old papers get yellow."

"But why would they do it to me? *Why?*"

"Come with me to the mainland, Mary. That'll set you straight quicker than anything."

"I couldn't," she said, drawing back. "He's coming tonight."

"He?"

"The man who sends me the boxes . . . and my life."

Jack shivered. When he spoke, his voice was rough and quick. "A life that's completely a lie, that's cut you off from the world. Come with me, Mary."

She looked up at him wonderingly. For perhaps ten seconds the silence held and the spell of her eerie sweetness deepened.

"I love you, Mary," Jack said softly.

She took a step back.

"Really, Mary, I do."

She shook her head. "I don't know what's true. Go away."

"Mary," he pleaded, "read the papers I've given you. Think things through. I'll wait for you here."

"You can't. My aunts would find you."

"Then I'll go away and come back. About sunset. Will you give me an answer?"

She looked at him. Suddenly she whirled around. He, too, heard the *chuff* of the Essex. "They'll find us," she said. "And if they find you, I don't know what they'll do. Quick, run!" And she darted off herself, only to turn back to scramble for the papers.

"But will you give me an answer?" he pressed.

She looked frantically up from the papers. "I don't know. You mustn't risk coming back."

"I will, no matter what you say."

"I can't promise. Please go."

"Just one question," he begged. "What are your aunts' names?"

"Hani and Hilda," she told him, and then she was gone. The hedge shook where she'd darted through.

Jack hesitated, then started for the cove. He thought for a moment of staying on the island, but decided against it. He could probably conceal himself successfully, but whoever found his boat would have him at a disadvantage. Besides, there were things he must try to find out on the mainland.

As he entered the oaks, his spine tightened for a moment, as if someone were watching him. He hurried to the rippling cove, wasted no time getting the *Annie O.* - underway. With the wind still in the west, he knew it would be a hard sail. He'd need half a dozen tacks to reach the mainland.

When he was about a quarter of a mile out from the cove, there was a sharp *smack* beside him. He jerked around, heard a distant *crack* and saw a foot-long splinter of fresh wood dangling from the edge of the sloop's cockpit, about a foot from his head.

He felt his skin tighten. He was the bull's-eye of a great watery target. All the air between him and the island was tainted with menace.

Water splashed a yard from the side. There was another distant *crack*. He lay on his back in the cockpit, steering by the said, taking advantage of what little cover there was.

There were several more *cracks*. After the second, there was a hole in the sail.

Finally Jack looked back. The island was more than a mile astern. He anxiously

155

scanned the sea ahead for craft. There were none. Then he settled down to nurse more speed from the sloop and wait for the motorboat.

But it didn't come out to follow him.

V

Same as yesterday, Mrs. Kesserich was sitting on the edge of the couch in the living room, yet from the first Jack was aware of a great change. Something had filled the domestic animal with grief and fury.

"Where's Dr. Kesserich?" he asked.

"Not here!"

"Mrs. Kesserich," he said, dropping down beside her, "you were telling me something yesterday when we were interrupted."

She looked at him. "You *have* found the girl?" she almost shouted.

"Yes," Jack was surprised into answering.

A look of slyness came into Mrs. Kesserich's bovine face. "Then I'll tell you everything. I can now."

"When Martin found Mary dying, he didn't go to pieces. You know how controlled he can be when he chooses. He lifted Mary's body as if the crowd and the railway men weren't there, and carried it to the station wagon. Hani and Hilda were sitting on their horses nearby. He gave them one look. It was as if he had said, 'Murderers!'

"He told me to drive home as fast as I dared, but when I got there, he stayed sitting by Mary in the back. I knew he must have given up what hope he had for her life, or else she was dead already. I looked at him. In the domelight, his face had the most deadly and proud expression I've ever seen on a man. I worshiped him, you know, though he had never shown me one ounce of feeling. So I was completely unprepared for the naked appeal in his voice.

"Yet all he said at first was, 'Will you do something for me?' I told him, 'Surely,' and as we carried Mary in, he told me the rest. He wanted me to be the mother of Mary's child."

Jack stared at her blankly.

Mrs. Kesserich nodded. "He wanted to remove an ovum from Mary's body and nurture it in mine, so that Mary, in a way, could live on."

"But that's impossible!" Jack objected. "The technique is being tried on cattle, I know, so that a prize heifer can have several calves a year, all nurtured in 'scrub heifers,' as they're called. But no one's ever dreamed of trying it on human beings!"

Mrs. Kesserich looked at him contemptuously. "Martin had mastered the technique twenty years ago. He was willing to take the chance. And so was I—partly because he fired my scientific imagination and reverence, but mostly because he said he would marry me. He barred the doors. We worked swiftly. As far as anyone was concerned, Martin, in a wild fit of grief, had locked himself up for several hours to mourn over the body of his fiancée.

"Within a month we were married, and I finally gave birth to the child."

Jack shook his head. "You gave birth to your own child."

She smiled bitterly. "No, it was Mary's. Martin did not keep his whole bargain with me—I was nothing more than his 'scrub wife' in every way."

"You *think* you gave birth to Mary's child."

Mrs. Kesserich turned on Jack in anger. "I've been wounded by him, day in and day out, for years, but I've never failed to recognize his genius. Besides, you've seen the girl, haven't you?"

Jack had to nod. What confounded him most was that, granting the near-impossible physiological feat Mrs. Kesserich had described, the girl should look so much like the mother. Mother and daughters don't look that much alike; only identical twins did. With a thrill of fear, he remembered Kesserich's casual words: ". . . parthenogenesis . . . pure stock . . . special techniques . . ."

"Very well," he forced himself to say, "granting that the child was Mary's and Martin's—"

"No! Mary's alone!"

Jack suppressed a shudder. He continued quickly, "What became of the child?"

Mrs. Kesserich lowered her head. "The day it was born, it was taken away from me. After that, I never saw Hilda and Hani, either."

"You mean," Jack asked, "that Martin sent them away to bring up the child?"

Mrs. Kesserich turned away. "Yes."

Jack asked incredulously, "He trusted the child with the two people he suspected of having caused the mother's death?"

"Once when I was his assistant," Mrs. Kesserich said softly, "I carelessly broke some laboratory glassware. He kept me up all night building a new setup, though I'm rather poor at working with glass and usually get burned. Bringing up the child was his sisters' punishment."

"And they went to that house on the farthest island? I suppose it was the house he'd been building for Mary and himself."

"Yes."

"And they were to bring up the child as his daughter?"

Mrs. Kesserich started up, but when she spoke it was as if she had to force out each word. "As his wife—as soon as she was grown."

"How can you know that?" Jack asked shakily.

The rising wind rattled the windowpane.

"Because today—eighteen years after—Martin broke all of his promise to me. He told me he was leaving me."

VI

White waves shooting up like dancing ghosts in the moon-sketched, spray-swept dark were Jack's first beacon of the island and brought a sense of physical danger, breaking the trancelike yet frantic mood he had felt ever since he had spoken with Mrs. Kesserich.

Coming around farther into the wind, he scudded past the end of the island into the choppy sea on the landward side. A little later he let down the reefed sail in the cove of the sea urchins, where the water was barely moving, although the air was shaken by the pounding of the surf on the spine between the two islands.

After making fast, he paused a moment for a scrap of cloud to pass the moon. The thought of the spiny creatures in the black fathoms under the *Annie O.* sent an odd quiver of terror through him.

The moon came out and he started across the glistening rocks of the spine. But he had forgotten the rising tide. Midway, a wave clamped around his ankles, tried to carry him off, almost made him drop the heavy object he was carrying. Sprawling and drenched, he clung to the rough rock until the surge was past.

Making it finally up to the fence, he snipped a wide gate with the wire-cutters.

The windows of the house were alight. Hardly aware of the shivering, he crossed the lawn, slipping from one clump of shrubbery to another, until he reached one just across the drive from the doorway. At that moment he heard the approaching *chuff* of the Essex, the door of the cottage opened, and Mary Alice Pope stepped out, closely followed by Hani or Hilda.

Jack shrank close to the shrubbery. Mary looked pale and blank-faced, as if she had retreated within herself. He was acutely conscious of the inadequacy of his screen as the ghostly headlights of the Essex began to probe through the leaves.

But then he sensed that something more was about to happen than just the car arriving. It was a change in the expression of the face behind Mary that gave him the cue—a widening and sideways flickering of the cold eyes, the puckered lips thinning into a cruel smile.

The Essex shifted into second and, without any warning, accelerated. Simultaneously, the woman behind Mary gave her a violent shove. But at almost exactly the same instant, Jack ran. He caught Mary as she sprawled toward the gravel, and lunged ahead without checking. The Essex bore down upon them, a square-snouted, roaring monster. It swerved viciously, missed them by inches, threw up gravel in a skid, and rocked to a stop, stalled.

The first, incredulous voice that broke the pulsing silence, Jack recognized as Martin Kesserich's. It came from the car, which was slewed around so that it almost faced Jack and Mary.

"Hani, you tried to kill her! You and Hilda tried to kill her again!"

The woman slumped over the wheel slowly lifted her head. In the indistinct light, she looked the twin of the woman behind Jack and Mary.

"Did you really think we wouldn't?" she asked in a voice that spat with passion. "Did you actually believe that Hilda and I would serve this eighteen years' penance just to watch you go off with her?" She began to laugh wildly. "You never understood your sisters at all!"

Suddenly she broke off and stiffly stepped down from the car. Lifting her skirts a little, she strode past Jack and Mary.

Martin Kesserich followed her. In passing, he said, "Thanks, Barr." It occurred to Jack that Kesserich made no more question of his appearance on the island than of his presence in the laboratory. Like Mrs. Kesserich, the great biologist took him for granted.

Kesserich stopped a few feet short of Hani and Hilda. Without shrinking from him, the sisters drew closer together. They looked like two gaunt hawks.

"But you waited eighteen years," he said. "You could have killed her at any time, yet you chose to throw away so much of your lives just to have this moment."

"How do you know we didn't like waiting eighteen years?" Hani answered him.

"Why shouldn't we want to make as strong an impression on you as anyone? And as for throwing our lives away, that was your doing. Oh, Martin, you'll never know anything about how your sisters feel!"

He raised his hands baffledly. "Even assuming that you hate me"—at the word "hate" both Hani and Hilda laughed softly—"and that you were prepared to strike at both my love and my work, still, that you should have waited . . ."

Hani and Hilda said nothing.

Kesserich shrugged. "Very well," he said in a voice that had lost all its tension. "You've wasted a third of a lifetime looking forward to an irrational revenge. And you've failed. That should be sufficient punishment."

Very slowly, he turned around and for the first time looked at Mary. His face was clearly revealed by the twin beams from the stalled car.

Jack grew cold. He fought against accepting the feelings of wonder, of poignant triumph, of love, of renewed youth he saw entering the face in the headlights. But most of all he fought against the sense that Martin Kesserich was successfully drawing them all back into the past, to 1933 and another accident. There was a distant hoot and Jack shook. For a moment he had thought it a railway whistle and not a ship's horn.

The biologist said tenderly, "Come, Mary."

Jack's trembling arm tightened a trifle on Mary's waist. He could feel *her* trembling.

"Come, Mary," Kesserich repeated.

Still she didn't reply.

Jack wet his lips. "Mary isn't going with you, Professor," he said.

"Quiet, Barr," Kesserich ordered absently. "Mary, it is necessary that you and I leave the island at once. Please come."

"But Mary isn't coming," Jack repeated.

Kesserich looked at him for the first time. "I'm grateful to you for the unusual sense of loyalty—or whatever motive it may have been—that led you to follow me out here tonight. And of course I'm profoundly grateful to you for saving Mary's life. But I must ask you not to interfere further in a matter which you can't possibly understand."

He turned to Mary. "I know how shocked and frightened you must feel. Living two lives and then having to face two deaths—it must be more terrible than anyone can realize. I expected this meeting to take place under very different circumstances. I wanted to explain everything to you very naturally and gently, like the messages I've sent you every day of your second life. Unfortunately, that can't be.

"You and I must leave the island right now."

Mary stared at him, then turned wonderingly toward Jack, who felt his heart begin to pound warmly.

"You still don't understand what I'm trying to tell you, Professor," he said, boldly now. "Mary is not going with you. You've deceived her all her life. You've taken a fantastic amount of pains to bring her up under the delusion that she is Mary Alice Pope, who died in—"

"She *is* Mary Alice Pope," Kesserich thundered at him. He advanced toward them swiftly. "Mary, darling, you're confused, but you must realized who you are and who I am and the relationship between us."

"Keep away," Jack warned, swinging Mary half behind him. "Mary doesn't love you. She can't marry you, at any rate. How could she, when you're her father?"

"Barr!"

"Keep off!" Jack shot out the flat of his hand and Kesserich went staggering backward. "I've talked with your wife—your wife on the mainland. She told me the whole thing."

Kesserich seemed about to rush forward again, then controlled himself. "You've got everything wrong. You hardly deserve to be told, but under the circumstances I have no choice. Mary is not my daughter. To be precise, she has no father at all. Do you remember the work that Jacques Loeb did with sea urchins?"

Jack frowned angrily. "You mean what we were talking about last night?"

"Exactly. Loeb was able to cause the egg of a sea urchin to develop normally without union with a male germ cell. I have done the same thing with a human being. This girl is Mary Alice Pope. She has exactly the same heredity. She has had exactly the same life, so far as it could be reconstructed. She's heard and read the same things at exactly the same times. There have been the old newspapers, the books, even the old recorded radio programs. Hani and Hilda have had their daily instructions, to the letter. She's retraced the same time-trail."

"Rot!" Jack interrupted. "I don't for a moment believe what you say about her birth. She's Mary's daughter—or the daughter of your wife on the mainland. And as for retracing the same time-trail, that's senile self-delusion. Mary Alice Pope had a normal life. This girl has been brought up in cruel imprisonment by two insane, vindictive old women. In your own frustrated desire, you've pretended to yourself that you've recreated the girl you lost. You haven't. You couldn't. Nobody could—the great Martin Kesserich or anyone else!"

Kesserich, his features working, shifted his point of attack. "Who are you, Mary?"

"Don't answer him," Jack said. "He's trying to confuse you."

"Who are you?" Kesserich insisted.

"Mary Alice Pope," she said rapidly in a breathy whisper before Jack could speak again.

"And when were you born?" Kesserich pressed on.

"You've been tricked all your life about that," Jack warned.

But already the girl was saying, "In nineteen hundred and sixteen."

"And who am I then?" Kesserich demanded eagerly. "Who am I?"

The girl swayed. She brushed her head with her hand.

"It's so strange," she said, with a dreamy, almost laughing throb in her voice that turned Jack's heart cold. "I'm sure I've never seen you before in my life, and yet it's as if I'd known you forever. As is you were closer to me than—"

"Stop it!" Jack shouted at Kesserich. "Mary loves me. She loves me because I've shown her the lie her life has been, and because she's coming away with me now. Aren't you, Mary?"

He swung her around so that her blank face was inches from his own. "It's me you love, isn't it, Mary?"

She blinked doubtfully.

At that moment Kesserich charged at them, went sprawling as Jack's fist shot out. Jack swept up Mary and ran with her across the lawn. Behind him he heard an agonized cry—Kesserich's—and cruel, mounting laughter from Hani and Hilda.

Once through the ragged doorway in the fence, he made his way more slowly, gasping. Out of the shelter of the trees, the wind tore at them and the ocean roared. Moonlight glistened, now on the spine of black wet rocks, now on the foaming surf.

Jack realized that the girl in his arms was speaking rapidly, disjointedly, but he couldn't quite make out the sense of the words and then they were lost in the crash of the surf. She struggled, but he told himself that it was only because she was afraid of the menacing waters.

He pushed recklessly into the breaking surf, raced gasping across the middle of the spine as the rocks uncovered, sprang to the higher ones as the next wave crashed behind, showering them with spray. His chest burning with exertion, he carried the girl the remaining yards to where the *Annie O.* was tossing. A sudden great gust of wind almost did what the waves had failed to do, but he kept his footing and lowered the girl into the boat, then jumped in after.

She stared at him wildly. "What's that?"

He, too, had caught the faint shout. Looking back along the spine just as the moon came clear again, he saw white spray rise and fall—and then the figure of Kesserich stumbling through it.

"Mary, wait for me!"

The figure was halfway across when it lurched, started forward again, then was jerked back as if something had caught its ankle. Out of the darkness, the next wave sent a line of white at it neck-high, crashed.

Jack hesitated, but another great gust of wind tore at the half-raised sail, and it was all he could do to keep the sloop from capsizing and head her into the wind again.

Mary was tugging at his shoulder. "You must help him," she was saying. "He's caught in the rocks."

He heard a voice crying, screaming crazily above the surf:

> "Ah, love, let us be true
> To one another! for the world—"

The sloop rocked. Jack had it finally headed into the wind. He looked around for Mary.

She had jumped out and was hurrying back, scrambling across the rocks toward the dark, struggling figure that even as he watched was once more engulfed in the surf.

Letting go the lines, Jack sprany toward the stern of the sloop.

But just then another giant blow came, struck the sail like a great fist of air, and sent the boom slashing at the back of his head.

His last recollection was being toppled out onto the rocks and wondering how he could cling to them while unconscious.

VII

The little cove was once again as quiet as time's heart. Once again the *Annie O.* was a sloop embedded in a mirror. Once again the rocks were warm underfoot.

Jack Barr lifted his fiercely aching head and looked at the distant line of the mainland, as tiny and yet as clear as something viewed through the wrong end of a telescope. He was very tired. Searching the island, in his present shaky condition, had taken all the strength out of him.

He looked at the peacefully rippling sea outside the cove and thought of what a churning pot it had been during the storm. He thought wonderingly of his rescue—a man wedged unconscious between two rock teeth, kept somehow from being washed away by the merest chance.

He thought of Mrs. Kesserich sitting alone in her house, scanning the newspapers that had nothing to tell.

He thought of the empty island behind him and the vanished motorboat.

He wondered if the sea had pulled down Martin Kesserich and Mary Alice Pope. He wondered if only Hani and Hilda had sailed away.

He winced, remembering what he had done to Martin and Mary by his blundering infatuation. In his way, he told himself, he had been as bad as the two old women.

He thought of death, and of time, and of love that defies them.

He stepped limpingly into the *Annie O.* to set sail—and realized that philosophy is only for the unhappy.

Mary was asleep in the stern.

The Moon is Green

"Effie! What the devil are you up to?"

Her husband's voice, chopping through her mood of terrified rapture, made her heart jump like a startled cat, yet by some miracle of feminine self-control her body did not show a tremor.

Dear God, she thought, *he mustn't see it. It's so beautiful, and he always kills beauty.*

"I'm just looking at the Moon," she said listlessly. "It's green."

Mustn't, mustn't see it. And now, with luck, he wouldn't. For the face, as if it also heard and sensed the menace in the voice, was moving back from the window's glow into the outside dark, but slowly, reluctantly, and still faunlike, pleading, cajoling, tempting, and incredibly beautiful.

"Close the shutters at once, you little fool, and come away from the window!"

"Green as a beer bottle," she went on dreamily, "green as emeralds, green as leaves with sunshine striking through them and green grass to lie on." She couldn't help saying those last words. They were her token to the face, even though it couldn't hear.

"Effie!"

She knew what the last tone meant. Wearily she swung shut the ponderous lead inner shutters and drove home the heavy bolts. That hurt her fingers; it always did, but he mustn't know that.

"You know that those shutters are not to be touched! Not for five more years at least!"

"I only wanted to look at the Moon," she said, turning around, and then it was all gone—the face, the night, the Moon, the magic—and she was back in the grubby, stale little hole, facing an angry, stale little man. It was then that the eternal thud of the air-conditioning fans and the crackle of the electrostatic precipitators that sieved out the dust reached her consciousness again like the bite of a dentist's drill.

"Only wanted to look at the Moon!" he mimicked her in falsetto. "Only wanted to die like a little fool and make me that much more ashamed of you!" Then his voice went gruff and professional. "Here, count yourself."

She silently took the Geiger counter he held at arm's length, waited until it settled down to a steady ticking slower than a clock—due only to cosmic rays and indicating nothing dangerous—and then began to comb her body with the instrument. First her head and shoulders, then out along her arms and back along their under side. There was something oddly voluptuous about her movements, although her features were gray and sagging.

163

The ticking did not change its tempo until she came to her waist. Then it suddenly spurted, clicking faster and faster. Her husband gave an excited grunt, took a quick step forward, froze. She goggled for a moment in fear, then grinned foolishly, dug in the pocket of her grimy apron and guiltily pulled out a wristwatch.

He grabbed it as it dangled from her fingers, saw that it had a radium dial, heaved it up as if to smash it on the floor, but instead put it carefully on the table.

"You imbecile, you incredible imbecile," he softly changed to himself through clenched teeth, with eyes half closed.

She shrugged faintly, put the Geiger counter on the table, and stood there slumped.

He waited until the chanting had soothed his anger before speaking again. He said quietly, "I do suppose you still realize the sort of world you're living in?"

*   *   *

She nodded slowly, staring at nothingness. Oh, she realized all right, realized only too well. It was the world that hadn't realized. The world that had gone on stockpiling hydrogen bombs. The world that had put those bombs in cobalt shells, although it had promised it wouldn't, because the cobalt made them much more terrible and cost no more. The world that had started throwing those bombs, always telling itself that it hadn't thrown enough of them yet to make the air really dangerous with the deadly radioactive dust that came from the cobalt. Thrown them and kept on throwing until the danger point, where air and ground become fatal to all human life, was approached.

Then, for about a month, the two enemy groups had hesitated. And then each, unknown to the other, had decided it could risk one last gigantic and decisive attack without exceeding the danger point. It had been planned to strip off the cobalt cases, but someone forgot and then there wasn't time. Besides, the military scientists of each group were confident that the lands of the other had got the most dust. The two attacks came within an hour of each other.

After that, the Fury. The Fury of doomed men who think only of taking with them as many as possible of the enemy, and in this case—they hoped—all. The Fury of suicides who know they have botched up life for good. The Fury of cocksure men who realized they have been outsmarted by fate, the enemy, and themselves, and know that they will never be able to improvise a defense when arraigned before the high court of history—and whose unadmitted hope is that there will be no high court of history left to arraign them. More cobalt bombs were dropped during the Fury than in all the preceding years of the war.

After the Fury, the Terror. Men and women with death sifting into their bones through their nostrils and skin, fighting for bare survival under a dust-hazed sky that played fantastic tricks with the light of Sun and Moon, like the dust from Krakatoa that drifted around the world for years. Cities, countryside, and air were alike poisoned, alive with deadly radiation.

The only realistic chance for continued existence was to retire, for the five or ten years the radiation would remain deadly, to some well-sealed and radiation-shielded place that must also be copiously supplied with food, water, power, and a means of air-conditioning.

Such places were prepared by the far-seeing, seized by the stronger, defended by them in turn against the desperate hordes of the dying . . . until there were no more of those.

After that, only the waiting, the enduring. A mole's existence, without beauty or tenderness, but with fear and guilt as constant companions. Never to see the sun, to walk among the trees—or even know if there were still trees.

Oh, yes, she realized what the world was like.

*   *   *

"You understand, too, I suppose, that we were allowed to reclaim this ground-level apartment only because the Committee believed us to be responsible people, and because I've been making a damn good showing lately?"

"Yes, Hank."

"I thought you were eager for privacy. You want to go back to the basement tenements?"

God, no! Anything rather than that fetid huddling, that shameless communal sprawl. And yet, was this so much better? The nearness to the surface was meaningless; it only tantalized. And the privacy magnified Hank.

She shook her head dutifully and said, "No, Hank."

"Then why aren't you careful? I've told you a million times, Effie, that glass is no protection against the dust that's outside that window. The lead shutter must never be touched! If you make one single slip like that and it gets around, the Committee will send us back to the lower levels without blinking an eye. And they'll think twice before trusting me with any important jobs."

"I'm sorry, Hank."

"Sorry? What's the good of being sorry? The only thing that counts is never to make a slip! Why the devil do you do such things, Effie? What drives you to it?"

She swallowed. "It's just that it's so dreadful being cooped up like this," she said hesitatingly, "shut away from the sky and the sun. I'm just hungry for a little beauty."

"And do you suppose I'm not?" he demanded. "Don't you suppose I want to get outside, too, and be carefree and have a good time? But I'm not so damn selfish about it. I want my children to enjoy the sun, and my children's children. Don't you see that that's the all-important thing and that we have to behave like mature adults and make sacrifices for it?"

"Yes, Hank."

He surveyed her slumped figure, her lined and listless face. "You're a fine one to talk about hunger for beauty," he told her. Then his voice grew softer, more deliberate. "You haven't forgotten, have you, Effie, that until last month the Committee was so concerned about your sterility? That they were about to enter my name on the list of those waiting to be allotted a free woman? Very high on the list, too!"

She could nod even at that one, but not while looking at him. She turned away. She knew very well that the Committee was justified in worrying about the birth rate. When the community finally moved back to the surface again, each additional healthy young person would be an asset, not only in the struggle for bare survival, but in the resumed war against Communism which some of the Committee members still counted on.

It was natural that they should view a sterile woman with disfavor, and not only because of the waste of her husband's germplasm, but because sterility might indicate that she had suffered more than the average from radiation. In that case, if she did bear children later on, they would be more apt to carry a defective heredity, producing an undue number of monsters and freaks in future generations, and so contaminating the race.

Of course she understood it. She could hardly remember the time when she didn't. Years ago? Centuries? There wasn't much difference in a place where time was endless.

*   *   *

His lecture finished, her husband smiled and grew almost cheerful.

"Now that you're going to have a child, that's all in the background again. Do you know, Effie, that when I first came in, I had some very good news for you? I'm to become a member of the Junior Committee and the announcement will be made at the banquet tonight." He cut short her mumbled congratulations. "So brighten yourself up and put on your best dress. I want the other Juniors to see what a handsome wife the new member has got." He paused. "Well, get a move on!"

She spoke with difficulty, still not looking at him. "I'm terribly sorry, Hank, but you'll have to go alone. I'm not well."

He straightened up with an indignant jerk. "There you go again! First that infantile, inexcusable business of the shutters, and now this! No feeling for my reputation at all. Don't be ridiculous, Effie. You're coming!"

"Terribly sorry," she repeated blindly, "but I really can't. I'd just be sick. I wouldn't make you proud of me at all."

"Of course you won't," he retorted sharply. "As it is, I have to spend half my energy running around making excuses for you—why you're so odd, why you always seem to be ailing, why you're always stupid and snobbish and say the wrong thing. But tonight's really important, Effie. It will cause a lot of bad comment if the new member's wife isn't present. You know how just a hint of sickness starts the old radiation-disease rumor going. You've *got* to come, Effie."

She shook her head helplessly.

"Oh, for heaven's sake, come on!" he shouted, advancing on her. "This is just a silly mood. As soon as you get going, you'll snap out of it. There's nothing really wrong with you at all."

He put his hand on her shoulder to touch her around, and at his touch her face suddenly grew so desperate and gray that for a moment he was alarmed in spite of himself.

"Really?" he asked, almost with a note of concern.

She nodded miserably.

"Hmm!" He stepped back and strode about irresolutely. "Well, of course, if that's the way it is . . ." He checked himself and a sad smile crossed his face. "So you don't care enough about your old husband's success to make one supreme effort in spite of feeling bad?"

Again the helpless headshake. "I just can't go out tonight, under any circumstances." And her gaze stole toward the lead shutters.

He was about to say something when he caught the direction of her gaze. His eyebrows jumped. For seconds he stared at her incredulously, as if some completely new and almost unbelievable possibility had popped into his mind. The look of incredulity slowly faded, to be replaced by a harder, more calculating expression. But when he spoke again, his voice was shockingly bright and kind.

"Well, it can't be helped, naturally, and I certainly wouldn't want you to go if you weren't able to enjoy it. So you hop right into bed and get a good rest. I'll run over to the men's dorm to freshen up. No, really, I don't want you to have to make any effort at all. Incidentally, Jim Barnes isn't going to be able to come to the banquet either—touch of the old 'flu, he tells me, of all things."

He watched her closely as he mentioned the other man's name, but she didn't react noticebly. In fact, she hardly seemed to be hearing his chatter.

"I got a bit sharp with you, I'm afraid, Effie," he continued contritely. "I'm sorry about that. I was excited about my new job and I guess that was why things upset me. Made me feel let down when I found you weren't feeling as good as I was. Selfish of me. Now you get into bed right away and get well. Don't worry about me a bit. I know you'd come if you possibly could. And I know you'll be thinking about me. Well, I must be off now."

He started toward her, as if to embrace her, then seemed to think better of it. He turned back at the doorway and said, emphasizing the words, "You'll be completely alone for the next four hours." He waited for her nod, then bounced out.

She stood still until his footsteps died away. Then she straightened up, walked over to where he'd put down the wristwatch, picked it up and smashed it hard on the floor. The crystal shattered, the case flew apart, and something went *zing!*

She stood there breathing heavily. Slowly her sagged features lifted, formed themselves into the beginning of a smile. She stole another look at the shutters. The smile became more definite. She felt her hair, wet her fingers and ran them along her hairline and back over her ears. After wiping her hands on her apron, she took it off. She straightened her dress, lifted her head with a little flourish, and stepped smartly toward the window.

Then her face went miserable again and her steps slowed.

No, it couldn't be, and it won't be, she told herself. It had been just an illusion, a silly romantic dream that she had somehow projected out of her beauty-starved mind and given a moment's false reality. There couldn't be anything alive outside. There hadn't been for two whole years.

And if there conceivably were, it would be something altogether horrible. She remembered some of the pariahs—hairless, witless creatures, with radiation welts crawling over their bodies like worms, who had come begging for succor during the last months of the Terror—and been shot down. How they must have hated the people in refuges!

But even as she was thinking these things, her fingers were caressing the bolts, gingerly drawing them, and she was opening the shutters gently, apprehensively.

No, there couldn't be anything outside, she assured herself wryly, peering out into the green night. Even her fears had been groundless.

But the face came floating up toward the window. She started back in terror, then checked herself.

For the face wasn't horrible at all, only very thin, with full lips and large eyes and a thin proud nose like the jutting beak of a bird. And no radiation welts or scars marred the skin, olive in the tempered moonlight. It looked, in fact, just as it had when she had seen it the first time.

For a long moment the face started deep, deep into her brain. Then the full lips smiled and a half-clenched, thin-fingered hand materialized itself from the green darkness and rapped twice on the grimy pane.

Her heart pounding, she furiously worked the little crank that opened the window. It came unstuck from the frame with a tiny explosion of dust and a *zing* like that of the watch, only louder. A moment later it swung open wide and a puff of incredibly fresh air caressed her face and the inside of her nostrils, stinging her eyes with unanticipated tears.

The man outside balanced on the sill, crouching like a faun, head high, one elbow on knee. He was dressed in scarred, snug trousers and an old sweater.

"Is it tears I get for a welcome?" he mocked her gently in a musical voice. "Or are those only to greet God's own breath, the air?"

He swung down inside and now she could see he was tall. Turning, he snapped his fingers and called, "Come, puss."

A black cat with a twisted stump of a tail and feet like small boxing gloves and ears almost as big as rabbits' hopped clumsily in view. He lifted it down, gave it a pat. Then, nodding familiarly to Effie, he unstrapped a little pack from his back and laid it on the table.

She couldn't move. She even found it hard to breathe.

"The window," she finally managed to get out.

He looked at her inquiringly, caught the direction of her stabbing finger. Moving without haste, he went over and closed it carelessly.

"The shutters, too," she told him, but he ignored that, looking around.

"It's a snug enough place you and your man have," he commented. "Or is it that this is a free-love town or a harem spot, or just a military post?" He checked her before she could answe. "But let's not be talking about such things now. Soon enough I'll be scared to death for both of us. Best enjoy the kick of meeting, which is always good for twenty minutes at the least." He smiled at her rather shyly. "Have you food? Good, then bring it."

She set cold meat and some precious canned bread before him and had water heating for coffee. Before he fell to, she shredded a chunk of meat and put it on the floor for the cat, which left off its sniffing inspection of the walls and ran up eagerly mewing. Then the man began to eat, chewing each mouthful slowly and appreciatively.

From across the table Effie watched him, drinking in his every deft movement, his every cryptic quirk of expression. She attended to making the coffee, but that took only a moment. Finally she could contain herself no longer.

"What's it like up there?" she asked breathlessly. "Outside, I mean."

He looked at her oddly for quite a space. Finally, he said flatly, "Oh, it's a wonderland for sure, more amazing than you tombed folk could ever imagine. A veritable fairyland." And he quickly went on eating.

"No, but really," she pressed.

Noting her eagerness, he smiled and his eyes filled with playful tenderness. "I mean it, on my oath," he assured her. "You think the bombs and the dust made only death and ugliness. That was true at first. But then, just as the doctors foretold, they changed the life in the seeds and loins that were brave enough to stay. Wonders bloomed and walked." He broke off suddenly and asked, "Do any of you ever venture outside?"

"A few of the men are allowed to," she told him, "for short trips in special protective suits, to hunt for canned food and fuel and batteries and things like that."

"Aye, and those blind-souled slugs would never see anything but what they're looking for," he said, nodding bitterly. "They'd never see the garden where a dozen buds blossom where one did before, and the flowers have petals a yard across, with stingless bees big as sparrows gently supping their nectar. Housecats grown spotted and huge as leopards (not little runts like Joe Louis here) stalk through those gardens. But they're gentle beasts, no more harmful than the rainbow-scaled snakes that glide around their paws, for the dust burned all the murder out of them, as it burned itself out.

"I've even made up a little poem about that. It starts, 'Fire can hurt me, or water, or the weight of Earth. But the dust is my friend.' Oh, yes, and then the robins like cockatoos and squirrels like a princess's ermine! All under a treasure chest of Sun and Moon and stars that the dust's magic powder changes from ruby to emerald and sapphire and amethyst and back again. Oh, and then the new children—"

"You're telling the truth?" she interrupted him, her eyes brimming with tears. "You're not making it up?"

"I am not," he assured her solemnly. "And if you could catch a glimpse of one of the new children, you'd never doubt me again. They have long limbs as brown as this coffee would be if it had lots of fresh cream in it, and smiling delicate faces and the whitish teeth and the finest hair. They're so nimble that I—a sprightly man and somewhat enlivened by the dust—feel like a cripple beside them. And their thoughts dance like flames and make me feel a very imbecile.

"Of course, they have seven fingers on each hand and eight toes on each foot, but they're the more beautiful for that. They have large pointed ears that the Sun shines through. They play in the garden, all day long, slipping among the great leaves and blooms, but they're so swift that you can hardly see them, unless one chooses to stand still and look at you. For that matter, you have to look a bit hard for all these things I'm telling you."

"But it is true?" she pleaded.

"Every word of it," he said, looking straight into her eyes. He put down his knife and fork. "What's your name?" he asked softly. "Mine's Patrick."

"Effie," she told him.

He shook his head. "That can't be," he said. Then his face brightened. "Euphemia," he exclaimed. "That's what Effie is short for. Your name is Euphemia." As he said that, looking at her, she suddenly felt beautiful. He got up and came around the table and stretched out his hand toward her.

"Euphemia—" he began.

"Yes?" she answered huskily, shrinking from him a little, but looking up sideways, and very flushed.

"Don't either of you move," Hank said.

The voice was flat and nasal because Hank was wearing a nose respirator that was just long enough to suggest an elephant's trunk. In his right hand was a large blue-black automatic pistol.

They turned their faces to him. Patrick's was abruptly alert, shifty. But Effie's was still smiling tenderly, as if Hank could not break the spell of the magic garden and should be pitied for not knowing about it.

"You little—" Hank began with an almost gleeful fury, calling her several shameful names. He spoke in short phrases, closing tight his unmasked mouth between them while he sucked in breath through the respirator. His voice rose in a crescendo. "And not with a man of the community, but a pariah! A *pariah!*"

"I hardly know what you're thinking, man, but you're quite wrong," Patrick took the opportunity to put in hurriedly, conciliatingly. "I just happened to be coming by hungry tonight, a lonely tramp, and knocked at the window. Your wife was a bit foolish and let kindheartedness get the better of prudence—"

"Don't think you've pulled the wool over my eyes, Effie," Hank went on with a screechy laugh, disregarding the other man completely. "Don't think I don't know why you're suddenly going to have a child after four long years."

169

At that moment the cat came nosing up to his feet. Patrick watched him nervously, shifting his weight forward a little, but Hank only kicked the animal aside without taking his eyes off them.

"Even that business of carrying the wristwatch in your pocket instead of on your arm," he went on with a channeled hysteria. "A neat bit of camouflage, Effie. Very neat. And telling me it was my child, when all the while you've been seeing him for months!"

"Man, you're mad; I've not touched her!" Patrick denied hotly though still calculatingly, and risked a step forward, stopping when the gun instantly swung his way.

"Pretending you were going to give me a healthy child," Hank raved on, "when all the while you knew it would be—either in body or germ plasm—a thing like *that!*"

He waved his gun at the malformed cat, which had leaped to the top of the table and was eating the remains of Patrick's food, though its watchful green eyes were fixed on Hank.

"I should shoot him down!" Hank yelled, between sobbing, chest-racking inhalations through the mask. "I should kill him this instant for the contaminated pariah he is!"

All this while Effie had not ceased to smile compassionately. Now she stood up without haste and went to Patrick's side. Disregarding his warning, apprehensive glance, she put her arm lightly around him and faced her husband.

"Then you'd be killing the bringer of the best news we've ever had," she said, and her voice was like a flood of some warm sweet liquor in that musty, hate-charged room. "Oh, Hank, forget your silly, wrong jealousy and listen to me. Patrick here has something wonderful to tell us."

Hank stared at her. For once he screamed no reply. It was obvious that he was seeing for the first time how beautiful she had become, and that the realization jolted him terribly.

"What do you mean?" he finally asked unevenly, almost fearfully.

"I mean that we no longer need to fear the dust," she said, and now her smile was radiant. "It never really did hurt people the way the doctors said it would. Remember how it was with me, Hank, the exposure I had and recovered from, although the doctors said I wouldn't at first—and without even losing my hair? Hank, those who were brave enough to stay outside, and who weren't killed by terror and suggestion and panic—they adapted to the dust. They changed, but they changed for the better. Everything—"

"Effie, he told you lies!" Hank interrupted, but still in that same agitated, broken voice, cowed by her beauty.

"Everything that grew or moved was purified," she went on ringingly. "You men going outside have never seen it, because you've never had eyes for it. You've been blinded to beauty, to life itself. And now all the power in the dust has gone and faded, anyway, burned itself out. That's true, isn't it?"

She smiled at Patrick for confirmation. His face was strangely veiled, as if he were calculating obscure changes. He might have given a little nod; at any rate, Effie assumed that he did, for she turned back to her husband.

"You see, Hank? We can all go out now. We need never fear the dust again. Patrick is a living proof of that," she continued triumphantly, standing straighter, holding him a little tighter. "Look at him. Not a scar or a sign, and he's been out in the dust for years. How could he be this way, if the dust hurt the brave? Oh, believe me, Hank! Believe what you see. Test it if you want. Test Patrick here."

"Effie, you're all mixed up. You don't know—" Hank faltered, but without conviction of any sort.

"Just test him," Effie repeated with utter confidence, ignoring—not even noticing—Patrick's warning nudge.

"All right," Hank mumbled. He looked at the stranger dully. "Can you count?" he asked.

Patrick's face was a complete enigma. Then he suddenly spoke, and his voice was like a fencer's foil—light, bright, alert, constantly playing, yet utterly on guard.

"Can I count? Do you take me for a complete simpleton, man? Of course I can count!"

"Then count yourself," Hank said, barely indicating the table.

"Count myself, should I?" the other retorted with a quick facetious laugh. "Is this a kindergarten? But if you want me to, I'm willing." His voice was rapid. "I've two arms, and two legs, that's four. And ten fingers and ten toes—you'll take my word for them?—that's twenty-four. A head, twenty-five. And two eyes and a nose and a mouth—"

"With this, I mean," Hank said heavily, advanced to the table, picked up the Geiger counter, switched it on, and handed it across the table to the other man.

But while it was still an arm's length from Patrick, the clicks began to mount furiously, until they were like the chatter of a pigmy machine gun. Abruptly the clicks slowed, but that was only the counter shifting to a new scaling circuit, in which each click stood for 512 of the old ones.

With those horrid, rattling little volleys, fear cascaded into the room and filled it, smashing like so much colored glass all the bright barriers of words Effie had raised against it. For no dreams can stand against the Geiger counter, the Twentieth Century's mouthpiece of ultimate truth. It was as if the dust and all the terrors of the dust had incarnated themselves in one dread invading shape that said in words stronger than audible speech, "Those were illusions, whistles in the dark. This is reality, the dreary, pitiless reality of the Burrowing Years."

Hank scuttled back to the wall. Through chattering teeth he babbled, ". . . enough radioactives . . . kill a thousand men . . . freak . . . a freak . . ." In his agitation he forgot for a moment to inhale through the respirator.

Even Effie—taken off guard, all the fears that had been drilled into her twanging like piano wires—shrank from the skeletal seeming shape beside her, held herself to it only by desperation.

Patrick did it for her. He disengaged her arm and stepped briskly away. Then he whirled on them, smiling sardonically, and started to speak, but instead looked with distaste at the chattering Geiger counter he held between fingers and thumb.

"Have we listened to this racket long enough?" he asked.

Without waiting for an answer, he put down the instrument on the table. The cat hurried over to it curiously and the clicks began again to mount in a minor cresendo. Effie lunged for it frantically, switched it off, darted back.

"That's right," Patrick said with another chilling smile. "You do well to cringe, for I'm death itself. Even in death I could kill you, like a snake." And with that his voice took on the tones of a circus barker. "Yes, I'm a freak, as the gentleman so wisely said. That's what one doctor who dared talk with me for a minute told me before he kicked me out. He couldn't tell me why, but somehow the dust doesn't kill me. Because I'm a freak, you see, just like the men who ate nails and walked on fire and ate arsenic and stuck themselves through with pins. Step right up, ladies and gentlemen—only not too close!—and examine the man the dust can't harm. Rappaccini's child, brought up to date; his embrace, death!

"And now," he said, breathing heavily, "I'll get out and leave you in your damned lead cave."

He started toward the window. Hank's gun followed him shakingly.

"Wait!" Effie called in an agonized voice. He obeyed. She continued falteringly, "When we were together earlier, you didn't act as if . . ."

"When we were together earlier, I wanted what I wanted," he snarled at her. "You don't suppose I'm a bloody saint, do you?"

"And all the beautiful things you told me?"

"That," he said cruelly, "is just a line I've found that women fall for. They're all so bored and so starved for beauty—as *they* generally put it."

"Even the garden?" Her question was barely audible through the sobs that threatened to suffocate her.

He looked at her and perhaps his expression softened just a little.

"What's outside," he said flatly, "is just a little worse than either of you can imagine." He tapped his temple. "The garden's all here."

"You've killed it," she wept. "You've killed it in me. You've both killed everything that's beautiful. But you're worse," she screamed at Patrick, "because he only killed beauty once, but you brought it to life just so you could kill it again. Oh, I can't stand it! I won't stand it!" And she began to scream.

Patrick started toward her, but she broke off and whirled away from him to the window, her eyes crazy.

"You've been lying to us," she cried. "The garden's there. I know it is. But you don't want to share it with anyone."

"No, no, Euphemia," Patrick protested anxiously. "It's hell out there, believe me. I wouldn't lie to you about it."

"Wouldn't lie to me!" she mocked. "Are you afraid, too?"

With a sudden pull, she jerked open the window and stood before the blank green-tinged oblong of darkness that seemed to press into the room like a menacing, heavy, wind-urged curtain.

At that Hank cried out a shocked, pleading "Effie!"

She ignored him. "I can't be cooped up here any longer," she said. "And I won't, now that I know. I'm going to the garden."

Both men sprang at her, but they were too late. She leaped lightly to the sill, and by the time they had flung themselves against it, her footsteps were already hurrying off into the darkness.

"Effie, come back! Come back!" Hank shouted after her desperately, no longer thinking to cringe from the man beside him, or how the gun was pointed. "I love you, Effie. Come back!"

Patrick added his voice. "Come back, Euphemia. You'll be safe if you come back right away. Come back to your home."

No answer to that at all.

They both strained their eyes through the greenish murk. they could barely make out a shadowy figure about half a block down the near-black canyon of the dismal, dust-blown street, into which the greenish moonlight hardly reached. It seemed to them that the figure was scooping something up from the pavement and letting it sift down along its arms and over its bosom.

"Go out and get her, man," Patrick urged the other. "For if I go out for her, I warn you I won't bring her back. She said something about having stood the dust better than most, and that's enough for me."

But Hank, chained by his painfully learned habits and by something else, could not move.

172

And then a ghostly voice came whispering down the street, chanting, "Fire can hurt me, or water, or the weight of the Earth. But the dust is my friend."

Patrick spared the other man one more look. Then, without a word, he vaulted up and ran off.

Hank stood there. After perhaps a half minute he remembered to close his mouth when he inhaled. Finally he was sure the street was empty. As he started to close the window, there was a little *mew*.

He picked up the cat and gently put it outside. Then he did close the window, and the shutters, and bolted them, and took up the Geiger counter, and mechanically began to count himself.

A Bad Day For Sales

The big bright doors parted with a *whoosh* and Robie glided suavely onto Times Square. The crowd that had been watching the fifty-foot tall clothing-ad girl get dressed, or reading the latest news about the Hot Truce scrawl itself in yard-high script, hurried to look.

Robie was still a novelty. Robie was fun. For a little while yet he could steal the show.

But the attention did not make Robie proud. He had no more vanity than the pink plastic giantess, and she did not even flicker her blue mechanical eyes.

Robie radared the crowd, found that it surrounded him solidly, and stopped. With a calculated mysteriousness, he said nothing.

"Say, ma, he doesn't look like a robot at all. He looks sort of like a turtle."

Which was not completely inaccurate. The lower part of Robie's body was a metal hemisphere hemmed with sponge rubber and not quite touching the sidewalk. The upper was a metal box with black holes in it. The box could swivel and duck.

A chromium-bright hoopskirt with a turret on top.

"Reminds me too much of the Little Joe Baratanks," a veteran of the Persian War muttered, and rapidly rolled himself away on wheels rather like Robie's.

His departure made it easier for some of those who knew about Robie to open a path in the crowd. Robie headed straight for the gap. The crowd whooped.

Robie glided very slowly down the path, deftly jogging aside whenever he got too close to ankles in skylon or sockassins. The rubber buffer on his hoopskirt was merely an added safeguard.

The boy who had called Robie a turtle jumped in the middle of the path and stood his ground, grinning foxily.

Robie stopped two feet short of him. The turret ducked. The crowd got quiet.

"Hello, youngster," Robie said in a voice that was smooth as that of a TV star, and was in fact a recording of one.

The boy stopped smiling. "Hello," he whispered.

"How old are you?" Robie asked.

"Nine. No, eight."

"That's nice," Robie observed. A metal arm shot down from his neck, stopped just short of the boy. The boy jerked back.

"For you," Robie said gently.

The boy gingerly took the red polly-lop from the neatly-fashioned blunt metal claws. A gray-haired woman whose son was a paraplegic hurried on.

After a suitable pause Robie continued, "And how about a nice refreshing drink of Poppy Pop to go with your polly-lop?" The boy lifted his eyes but didn't stop licking the candy. Robie wiggled his claws ever so slightly. "Just give me a quarter and within five seconds—"

A little girl wriggled out of the forest of legs. "Give me a polly-lop too, Robie," she demanded.

"Rita, come back here," a woman in the third rank of the crowd called angrily.

Robie scanned the newcomer gravely. His reference silhouettes were not good enough to let him distinguish the sex of children, so he merely repeated, "Hello, youngster."

"Rita!"

"Give me a polly-lop!"

Disregarding both remarks, for a good salesman is single-minded and does not waste bait, Robie said winningly, "I'll bet you read *Junior Space Killers.* Now I have here—"

"Uh-hhh, I'm a girl. *He* got a polly-lop."

At the word "girl" Robie broke off. Rather ponderously he said, "Then—" After another pause he continued, "I'll bet you read *Gee-Gee Jones, Space Stripper.* Now I have here the latest issue of that thrilling comic, not yet in the stationary vending machines. Just give me fifty cents and within five—"

"Please let me through. I'm her mother."

A young woman in the front rank drawled over her powder-sprayed shoulder. "I'll get her for you," and slithered out on six-inch platforms. "Run away, children," she said nonchalantly and lifting her arms behind her head, pirouetted slowly before Robie to show how much she did for her bolero half-jacket and her form-fitting slacks that melted into skylon just above the knees. The little girl glared at her. She ended the pirouette in profile.

At this age-level Robie's reference silhouettes permitted him to distinguish sex, though with occasional amusing and embarrassing miscalls. He whistled admiringly. The crowd cheered.

Someone remarked critically to his friend. "It would go better if he was built more like a real robot. You know, like a man."

The friend shook his head. "This way it's subtler."

No one in the crowd was watching the newscript overhead as it scribbled, "Ice Pack for Hot Truce? Vanadin hints Russ may yield on Pakistan."

Robie was saying, ". . . in the savage new glamor-tint we have christened Mars Blood, complete with spray applicator and fit-all fingerstalls that mask each finger completely except for the nail. Just give me five dollars—uncrumpled bills may be fed into the revolving rollers you see beside my arm—and within five seconds,—"

"No thanks, Robie," the young woman yawned.

"Remember," Robie persisted, "for three more weeks seductivising Mars Blood will be unobtainable from any other robot or human vendor."

"No thanks."

Robie scanned the crowd resourcefully. "Is there any gentleman here . . ." he began just as a woman elbowed her way through the front rank.

"I told you come back!" she snarled at the little girl.

"But I didn't get my polly-lop!"

". . . who would care to . . ."

"Rita!"

"Robie cheated. Ow!"

Meanwhile the young woman in the half-bolero had scanned the nearby gentlemen on her own. Deciding that there was less than a fifty per cent chance of any of them accepting the proposition Robie seemed about to make, she took advantage of the scuffle to slither gracefully back into the ranks. Once again the path was clear before Robie.

He paused, however, for a brief recapitulation of the more magical properties of Mars Blood, including a telling phrase about "the passionate claws of a Martian sunrise."

But no one bought. It wasn't quite time yet. Soon enough silver coins would be clinking, bills going through the rollers faster than laundry, and five hundred people struggling for the privilege of having their money taken away from them by America's only genuine mobile salesrobot.

But how was too soon. There were still some tricks that Robie did free, and one certainly should enjoy those before starting the more expensive fun.

So Robie moved on until he reached the curb. The variation in level was instantly sensed by his under-scanners. He stopped. His head began to swivel. The crowd watched in eager silence. This was Robie's best trick.

Robie's head stopped swiveling. His scanners had found the traffic light. It was green. Robie edged forward. But then it turned red. Robie stopped again, still on the curb. The crowd softly *ahhed* its delight.

Oh, it was wonderful to be alive and watching Robie on such a wonderful day. Alive and amused in the fresh, weather-controlled air between the lines of bright sky-scrapers with their winking windows and under a sky so blue you could almost call it dark.

(But way, way up, where the crowd could not see, the sky was darker still. Purple-dark, with stars showing. And in that purple-dark, a silver-green something, the color of a bud, plunged downward at better than three miles a second. The silver-green was a paint that foiled radar.)

Robie was saying, "While we wait for the light there's time for you youngsters to enjoy a nice refreshing Poppy Pop. Or for you adults—only those over five feet are eligible to buy—to enjoy an exciting Poppy Pop fizz. Just give me a quarter or—I'm licensed to dispense intoxicating liquors—in the case of adults one dollar and a quarter and within five seconds . . ."

But that was not cutting it quite fine enough. Just three seconds later the silver-green bud bloomed above Manhattan into a globular orange flower. The skyscrapers grew brighter and brighter still, the brightness of the inside of the sun. The windows winked white fire.

The crowd around Robie bloomed too. Their clothes puffed into petals of flame. Their heads of hair were torches.

The orange flower grew, stem and blossom. The blast came. The winking windows shattered tier by tier, became black holes. The walls bent, rocked, cracked. A stony dandruff dribbled from their cornices. The flaming flowers on the sidewalk were all leveled at once. Robie was shoved ten feet. His metal hoopskirt dimpled, regained its shape.

The blast ended. The orange flower, grown vast, vanished overhead on its huge, magic beanstalk. It grew dark and very still. The cornice-dandruff pattered down. A few small fragments rebounded from the metal hoopskirt.

Robie made some small, uncertain movements, as if feeling for broken bones. He was hunting for the traffic light, but it no longer shone, red or green.

He slowly scanned a full circle. There was nothing anywhere to interest his reference silhouettes. Yet whenever he tried to move, his under-scanners warned him of low obstructions. It was very puzzling.

The silence was disturbed by moans and a crackling sound, faint at first as the scampering of rats.

A seared man, his charred clothes fuming where the blast had blown out the fire, rose from the curb. Robie scanned him.

"Good day, sir," Robie said. "Would you care for a smoke? A truly cool smoke? Now I have here a yet-unmarketed brand . . ."

But the customer had run away, screaming, and Robie never ran after customers, though he could follow them at a medium brisk roll. He worked his way along the curb where the man had sprawled, carefully keeping his distance from the low obstructions, some of which writhed now and then, forcing him to jog. Shortly he reached a fire hydrant. He scanned it. His electronic vision, though it still worked, had been somewhat blurred by the blast.

"Hello, youngster," Robie said. Then, after a long pause, "Cat got your tongue? Well, I've got a little present for you. A nice, lovely polly-lop." His metal arm snaked down.

"Take it, youngster," he said after another pause. "It's for you. Don't be afraid."

His attention was distracted by other customers, who began to rise up oddly here and there, twisting forms that confused his reference silhouettes and would not stay to be scanned properly. One cried, "Water," but no quarter clinked in Robie's claws when he caught the word and suggested, "How about a nice refreshing drink of Poppy Pop?"

The rat-crackling of the flames had become a jungle muttering. The blind windows began to wink fire again.

A little girl marched up, stepping neatly over arms and legs she did not look at. A white dress and the once taller bodies around her had shielded her from the brilliance and the blast. Her eyes were fixed on Robie. In them was the same imperious confidence, though none of the delight, with which she had watched him earlier.

"Help me, Robie," she said. "I want my mother."

"Hello, youngster," Robie said. "What would you like? Comics? Candy?"

"Where is she, Robie? Take me to her."

"Balloons? Would you like to watch me blow up a balloon?"

The little girl began to cry. The sound triggered off another of Robie's novelty circuits.

"Is something wrong?" he asked. "Are you in trouble? Are you lost?"

"Yes, Robie. Take me to my mother."

"Stay right here," Robie said reassuringly, "and don't be frightened. I will call a policeman." He whistled shrilly, twice.

Time passed. Robie whistled again. The windows flared and roared. The little girl begged, "Take me away, Robie," and jumped onto a little step in his hoopskirt.

"Give me a dime," Robie said. The little girl found one in her pocket and put it in his claws.

"Your weight," Robie said, "is fifty-four and one-half pounds, exactly."

"Have you seen my daughter, have you seen her?" a woman was crying somewhere. "I left her watching that thing while I stepped inside—Rita!"

"Robie helped me," the little girl was telling her moments later. "He knew I was lost. He even called a policeman, but he didn't come. He weighed me too. Didn't you, Robie?"

But Robie had gone off to peddle Poppy Pop to the members of a rescue squad which had just come around the corner, more robot-like than he in their fireproof clothing.

The Night He Cried

I glanced down my neck secretly at the two snowy hillocks, ruby peaked, that were pushing out my blouse tautly without the aid of a brassière. I decided they'd more than do. So I turned away scornfully as his vast top-down convertible cruised past my street lamp. I struck my hip and a big match against the fluted column, and lit a cigarette. I was Lili Marlene to a T—or rather to a V-neckline. (I must tell you that my command of earth-idiom and allusion is remarkable, but if you'd had my training you wouldn't wonder.)

The convertible slowed down and backed up. I smiled. I'd been certain that my magnificently formed milk glands would turn the trick. I puffed on my cigarette languorously.

"Hi, Babe!"

Right from the first I'd known it was the man I was supposed to contact. Handsome hatchet face. Six or seven feet tall. Quite a creature. Male, as they say.

I hopped into his car, vaulting over the low door before he opened it. We zoomed off through New York's purple, smelly twilight.

"What's your name, Big Male?" I asked him.

Scorning to answer, he stripped me with his eyes. But I had confidence in my milk glands. Lord knows, I'd been hours perfecting them.

"Slickie Millane, isn't it?" I prompted recklessly.

"That's possible," he conceded, poker-faced.

"Well then, what are we waiting for?" I asked him, nudging him with the leftermost of my beautifully conical milk glands.

"Look here, Babe," he told me, just a bit coldly, "I'm the one who dispenses sex and justice in this area."

I snuggled submissively under his encircling right arm, still nudging him now and again with my left milk gland. The convertible sped. The skyscrapers shrank, exfoliated, became countryside. The convertible stopped.

As the hand of his encircling arm began to explore my prize possessions, I drew away a bit, not frustratingly, and informed him, "Slickie dear, I am from Galaxy Center . . ."

"What's that—a magazine publisher?" he demanded hotly, being somewhat inflamed by my cool milk glands.

". . . and we are interested in how sex and justice are dispensed in all areas," I went on, disregarding his interruption and his somewhat juvenile fondlings. "To be bold, we suspect that you may be somewhat misled about this business of sex."

Vertical, centimeter-deep furrows creased his brow. His head poised above mine like a hawk's. "What are you talking about, Babe?" he demanded with suspicious rage, even snatching his hands away.

"Briefly, Slickie," I said, "you do not seem to feel that sex is for the production of progeny or for the mutual solace of two creatures. You seem to think—"

His rage exploded into action. He grabbed a great big gun out of the glove compartment. I sprang to my two transmuted nether tentacles—most handsome gams if I, the artist, do say so. He jabbed the muzzle of the gun into my midriff.

'That's exactly what I mean, Slickie," I managed to say before my beautiful midriff, which I'd been at such pains to perfect, erupted into smoke and ghastly red splatter. I did a backward flipflop out of the car and lay still—a most fetching corpse with a rucked-up skirt. As the convertible snorted off triumphantly, I snagged hold of the rear bumper, briefly changing my hand back to a tentacle for better gripping. Before the pavement had abraded more than a few grams of my substance, I pulled myself up onto the bumper, where I preceeded to reconstitute my vanished midriff with material from the air, the rest of my body, and the paint on the trunk case. On this occasion the work went rapidly, with no artistic gropings, since I had the curves memorized from the first time I'd worked them out. Then I touched up my abrasions, stripped myself, whipped myself up a snazzy silver lamé evening frock out of chromium from the bumper, and put in time creating costume jewelry out of the tail light and the rest of the chrome.

The car stopped at a bar and Slickie slid out. For a moment his proud profile was silhouetted against the smoky glow. Then he was inside. I threw away the costume jewelry and climbed over the folded top and popped down on the leather-upholstered seat, scarcely a kilogram lighter than when I'd first sat there.

The minutes dragged. To pass them, I mentally reviewed the thousand-and-some basic types of mutual affection on the million-plus planets, not forgetting the one and only basic type of love.

There was a burst of juke-box jazz. Footsteps tracked from the bar toward the convertible. I leaned back comfortably with my silver-filmed milk glands dramatically highlighted.

"Hi, Slickie," I called, making my voice sweet and soft to cushion the shock.

Nevertheless it was a considerable one. For all of ten seconds he stood there, canted forward a little, like a wooden Indian that's just been nudged from behind and is about to topple.

Then with a naive ingenuity that rather touched me, he asked huskily, "Hey, have you got a twin sister?"

"Could be," I said with a shrug that jogged my milk glands deliciously.

"Well, what are you doing in my car?"

"Waiting for you," I told him simply.

He considered that as he slowly and carefully walked around the car and got behind the wheel, never taking his eyes off me. I nudged him in my usual manner. He jerked away.

"What are you up to?" he inquired suspiciously.

"Why are you surprised, Slickie?" I counted innocently. "I've heard this sort of thing happens to you all the time."

"What sort of thing?"

"Girls turning up in your car, your bar, your bedroom—everywhere."

"Where'd you hear it?"

"I read it in your Spike Mallet books."

"Oh," he said, somewhat mollified. But then his suspicion came back. "But what are you really up to?" he demanded.

"Slickie," I assured him with complete sincerity, bugging my beautiful eyes, "I just love you."

This statement awakened in him an irritation so great that it overrode his uneasiness about me, for he cuffed me in the face—so suddenly that I almost forgot and changed it back to my top tentacle.

"I made the advances around here, Babe," he asserted harshly.

Completely under control again, I welled a tiny trickle of blood out of the left-hand corner of my gorgeous mouth. "Anything you say, Slickie, dear," I assented submissively and cuddled up against him in a prim, girlish way to which he could hardly take exception.

But I must have bothered or at least puzzled him, for he drove slowly, his dark-eaved eyes following an invisible tennis ball that bounded between me and the street ahead. Abruptly the eaves lifted and he smiled.

"Look, I just got an idea for a story," he said. "There's this girl from Galaxy Center—" and he whipped around to watch my reactions, but I didn't blink.

He continued, "I mean, she's sort of from the center of the galaxy, where everything's radioactive. Now there's this guy that's got her up in his attic." His face grew deeply thoughtful. "She's the most beautiful girl in the universe and he loves her like crazy, but she's all streaming with hard radiations and it'll kill him if he touches her."

"Yes, Slickie—and then?" I prompted after the car had dreamed its way for several blocks between high buildings.

He looked at me sharply. "That's all. Don't you get it?"

"Yes, Slickie," I assured him soothingly. My statement seemed to satisfy him, but he was still edgy.

He stopped the car in front of an apartment hotel that thrust toward the stars with a dark presumptuousness. He got out on the street side and walked around the rear end and suddenly stopped. I followed him. He was studying the gray bumper and the patch of raw sheet metal off which I'd used the paint. He looked around at me where I stood sprayed with silver lamé in the revealing lamp light.

"Wipe your chin," he said critically.

"Why not kiss the blood off it, Slickie?" I replied with an ingenuousness I hoped would take the curse off the suggestion.

"Aw nuts," he said nervously and stalked into the foyer so swiftly he might have been trying to get away from me. However, he made no move to stop me when I followed him into the tiny place and the even tinier elevator. In the latter cubicle I maneuvered so as to give him a series of breathtaking scenic views of the Grand Tetons that rose behind the plunging silver horizon of my neckline, and he unfroze considerably. By the time he opened the door of his apartment he had got so positively cordial that he urged me across the threshold with a casual spank.

It was just as I had visualized it—the tiger skins, the gun racks, the fireplace, the open bedroom door, the bar just beside it, the adventures of Spike Mallet in handsomely tooled leather bindings, the vast divan covered with zebra skin . . .

On the last was stretched a beautiful ice-faced blonde in a filmy negligee.

This was a complication for which I wasn't prepared. I stood rooted by the door while Slickie walked swiftly past me.

The blonde slithered to her feet. There was murder in her glacial eyes. "You two-timing rat!" she grated. Her hand darted under her negligee. Slickie's snaked under the lefthand side of his jacket.

183

Then it hit me what was going to happen. She would bring out a small but deadly silver-plated automatic, but before she could level it, Slickie's cannon would make a red ruin of her midriff.

There I was, standing twenty feet away from both of them—and this poor girl couldn't reconstitute herself!

Swifter than thought I changed my arms back to upper dorsal tentacles and jerked back both Slickie's and the girl's elbow. They turned around, considerably startled, and saw me standing twenty feet away. I'd turned my tentacles back to arms before they'd noticed them. Their astonishment increased.

But I knew I had won only a temporary respite. Unless something happened, Slickie's trigger-blissful rage would swiftly be refocused on this foolish fragile creature. To save her, I had to divert his ire to myself.

"Get that little tramp out of here," I ordered Slickie from the corner of my mouth as I walked past him to the bar.

"Easy, Babe," he warned me.

I poured myself a liter of scotch—I had to open a second bottle to complete the measure—and downed it. I really didn't need it, but the assorted molecules were congenial building blocks and I was rather eager to get back to normal weight.

"Haven't you got that tramp out of here yet?" I demanded, eyeing him scornfully over my insouciant silver-filmed shoulder.

"Easy, Babe," he repeated, the vertical furrows creasing his brow to a depth of at least a centimeter and a half.

"That's telling her, Slickie," the blonde applauded.

"You two-timing rat!" I plagiarized, whipping up my silver skirt as if to wisk a gun from my nonexistent girdle.

His cannon coughed. Always a good sportsman, I moved an inch so that the bullet, slightly mis-aimed, took me exactly in the right eye, messily blowing off the back of my head. I winked at Slickie with my left eye and fell back through the doorway into the bedroom darkness.

I knew I had no time to spare. When a man's shot one girl he begins to lose his natural restraint. Lying on the floor, I reconstituted my eye and did a quick patch-job on the back of my head in seventeen seconds flat.

As I emerged from the bedroom, they were entering into a clinch, each holding a gun lightly against the other's back.

"Slickie," I said, pouring myself a scant half liter of scotch, "I told you about that tramp."

The ice-blonde squawked, threw up her hands as if she'd had a shot of strychnine, and ran out the door. I fancied I could feel the building tilt as she leaned on the elevator button.

I downed the scotch and advanced, shattering the paralyzed spacetime that Slickie seemed to be depending on as a defense.

"Slickie," I said, "let's get down to cases. I am indeed from Galaxy Center and we very definitely don't like your attitude. We don't care what your motives are, or whether they are derived from jumbled genes, a curdled childhood, or a sick society. We simply love you and we want you to reform." I grabbed him by a shivering shoulder that was now hardly higher than my waist, and dragged him into the bedroom, snatching up the rest of the scotch on the way. I switched on the light. The bedroom was a really lush lovenest. I drained the scotch—there was about a half liter left—and faced the cowering Slickie. "Now do to me," I told him uncompromisingly, "the thing you're always going to do to those girls, except you have to shoot them."

184

He frothed like an epileptic, snatched out his cannon and emptied its magazine into various parts of my torso, but since he hit only two of my five brains, I wasn't bothered. I reeled back bloodily through the blue smoke and fell into the bathroom. I felt real crazy—maybe I shouldn't have taken that last half liter. I reconstituted my torso faster even than I had my head, but my silver lamé frock was a mess. Not wanting to waste time and reluctant to use any more reconstituting energy, I stripped it off and popped into the off-the-shoulders evening dress the blonde had left lying over the edge of the bathtub. The dress wasn't a bad fit. I went back into the bedroom. Slickie was sobbing softly at the foot of the bed and gently beating his head against it.

"Slickie," I said, perhaps a shade too curtly, "about this love business—"

He sprang for the ceiling but didn't quite burst through it. Falling back, by chance on his feet, he headed for the hall. Now it wasn't in my orders from Galaxy Center that he run away and excite this world—in fact, my superiors had strictly forbidden such a happening. I had to stop Slickie. But I was a bit confused—perhaps fuddled by that last half liter. I hesitated—then he was too far away, had too big a start. To stop him, I knew I'd have to use tentacles. Swifter than thought I changed them and shot them out.

"Slickie," I cried reassuringly, dragging him to me.

Then I realized that in my excitement, instead of using my upper dorsal tentacles, I'd used the upper ventral ones I kept transmuted into my beautiful milk glands. I do suppose they looked rather strange to Slickie as they came out of the bosom of my off-the-shoulders evening dress and drew him to me.

Frightening sounds came out of him. I let him go and tried to resume my gorgeous shape, but now I was really confused (that last half liter!) and lost control of my transmutations. When I found myself turning my topmost tentacle into a milk gland I gave up completely and—except for a lung and vocal cords—resumed my normal shape. It was quite a relief. After all, I had done what Galaxy Center had intended I should. From now on, the mere sight of a brassière in a show window would be enough to give Slickie the shakes.

Still, I was bothered about the guy. As I say, he'd touched me.

I caressed him tenderly with my tentacles. Over and over again I explained that I was just a heptapus and that Galaxy Center had selected me for the job simply because my seven tentacles would transmute nicely into the seven extremities of the human female.

Over and over again I told him how I loved him.

It didn't seem to help. Slickie Millane continued to weep hysterically.

What's He Doing In There?

The Professor was congratulating Earth's first visitor from another planet on his wisdom in getting in touch with a cultural anthropologist before contacting any other scientists (or governments, God forbid!), and in learning English from radio and TV before landing from his orbit-parked rocket, when the Martian stood up and said hesitantly, "Excuse me, please, but where is it?"

That baffled the Professor and the Martian seemed to grow anxious—at least his long mouth curved upward, and he had earlier explained that its curling downward was his smile—and he repeated, "Please, where is it?"

He was surprisingly humanoid in most respects, but his complexion was textured so like the rich dark armchair he'd just been occupying that the Professor's pin-striped gray suit, which he had eagerly consented to wear, seemed an arbitrary interruption between him and the chair—a sort of Mother Hubbard dress on a phantom conjured from its shagreen leather.

The Professor's Wife, always a perceptive hostess, came to her husband's rescue, by saying with equal rapidity, "Top of the stairs, end of the hall, last door."

The Martian's mouth curled happily downward and he said, "Thank you very much," and was off.

Comprehension burst on the Professor. He caught up with his guest at the foot of the stairs.

"Here, I'll show you the way," he said.

"No, I can find it myself, thank you," the Martian assured him.

* * *

Something rather final in the Martian's tone made the Professor desist, and after watching his visitor sway up the stairs with an almost hypnotic softly jogging movement, he rejoined his wife in the study, saying wonderingly, "Who'd have thought it, by George! Function taboos as strict as our own!"

"I'm glad some of your professional visitors maintain 'em," his wife said darkly.

"But this one's from Mars, darling, and to find out he's—well, similar in an aspect of his life is as thrilling as the discovery that water is burned hydrogen. When I think of the day not far distant when I'll put his entries in the cross-cultural index . . ."

He was still rhapsodizing when the Professor's Little Son raced in.

"Pop, the Martian's gone to the bathroom!"

"Hush, dear. Manners."

"Now its perfectly natural, darling, that the boy should notice and be excited. Yes, Son, the Martian's not so very different from us."

"Oh, certainly," the Professor's Wife said with a trace of bitterness. "I don't imagine his turquoise complexion will cause any comment at all when you bring him to a faculty reception. They'll just figure he's had a hard night—and that he got that baby-elephant nose sniffing around for assistant professorships."

"Really, darling! He probably thinks of our noses as disagreeably amputated and paralyzed."

"Well, anyway, Pop, he's in the bathroom. I followed him when he squiggled upstairs."

"Now, Son, you shouldn't have done that. He's on a strange planet and it might make him nervous if he thought he was being spied on. We must show him every courtesy. By George, I can't wait to discuss these things with Ackerly-Ramsbottom! When I think of how much more this encounter has to give the anthropologist than even the physicist or astronomer . . ."

He was still going strong on his second rhapsody when he was interrupted by another high-speed entrance. It was the Professor's Coltish Daughter.

"Mom, Pop, the Martian's—"

"Hush, dear. We know."

The Professor's Coltish Daughter regained her adolescent poise, which was considerable. "Well, he's still in there," she said. "I just tried the door and it was locked."

"I'm glad it was!" the Professor said while his wife added, "Yes, you can't be sure what—" and caught herself. "Really, dear, that was very bad manners."

"I thought he'd come downstairs long ago," her daughter explained. "He's been in there an awfully long time. It must have been a half hour ago that I saw him gyre and gimbal upstairs in that real gone way he has, with Nosy here following him." The Professor's Coltish Daughter was currently soaking up both jive and *Alice*.

*   *   *

When the Professor checked his wristwatch, his expression grew troubled. "By George, he is taking his time! Though, of course, we don't know how much time Martians . . . I wonder."

"I listened for a while, Pop," his son volunteered. "He was running the water a lot."

"Running the water, eh? We know Mars is a water-starved planet. I suppose that in the presence of unlimited water, he might be seized by a kind of madness and . . . But he seemed so well adjusted."

Then his wife spoke, voicing all their thoughts. Her outlook on life gave her a naturally sepulchral voice.

"What's he doing in there?"

Twenty minutes and at least as many fantastic suggestions later, the Professor glanced again at his watch and nerved himself for action. Motioning his family aside, he mounted the stairs and tiptoed down the hall.

He paused only once to shake his head and mutter under his breath, "By George, I wish I had Fenchurch or von Gottschalk here. They're a shade better than I am on intercultural contracts, especially taboo-breakings and affronts . . ."

His family followed him at a short distance.

The Professor stopped in front of the bathroom door. Everything was quiet as death.

He listened for a minute and then rapped measuredly, steadying his hand by clutching its wrist with the other. There was a faint splashing, but no other sound.

Another minute passed. The Professor rapped again. Now there was no response at all. He very gingerly tried the knob. The door was still locked.

When they had retreated to the stairs, it was the Professor's Wife who once more voiced their thoughts. This time her voice carried overtones of supernatural horror. *"What's he doing in there?"*

"He may be dead or dying," the Professor's Coltish Daughter suggested briskly. "Maybe we ought to call the Fire Department, like they did for old Mrs. Frisbee."

The Professor winced. "I'm afraid you haven't visualized the complications, dear," he said gently. "No one but ourselves knows that the Martian is on Earth, or has even the slightest inkling that interplanetary travel has been achieved. Whatever we do, it will have to be on our own. But to break in on a creature engaged in—well, we don't know what primal private activity—is against all anthropological practice. Still—"

"Dying's a primal activity," his daughter said crisply.

"So's ritual bathing before mass murder," his wife added.

"Please! Still, as I was about to say, we do have the moral duty to succor him if, as you all too reasonably suggest, he has been incapacitated by a germ or virus or, more likely, by some simple environmental factor such as Earth's greater gravity."

"Tell you what, Pop—I can look in the bathroom window and see what he's doing. All I have to do is crawl out my bedroom window and along the gutter a little ways. It's safe as houses."

*   *   *

The Professor's question beginning with, "Son, how do you know—" died unuttered and he refused to notice the words his daughter was voicing silently at her brother. He glanced at his wife's sardonically composed face, thought once more of the Fire Department and of other and larger and even more jealous—or would it be skeptical?—government agencies, and clutched at the straw offered him.

Ten minutes later, he was quite unnecessarily assisting his son back through the bedroom window.

"Gee, Pop, I couldn't see a sign of him. That's why I took so long. Hey, Pop, don't look so scared. He's in there, sure enough. It's just that the bathtub's under the window and you have to get real close up to see into it."

"The Martian's taking a bath?"

"Yep. Got it full up and just the end of his little old schnozzle sticking out. Your suit, Pop, was hanging on the door."

The one word the Professor's Wife spoke was like a death knell.

"Drowned!"

"No, Ma, I don't think so. His schnozzle was opening and closing regular like."

"Maybe he's a shape-changer," the Professor's Coltish Daughter said in a burst of evil fantasy. "Maybe he softens in water and thins out after a while until he's like an eel and then he'll go exploring through the sewer pipes. Wouldn't it be funny if he went under the street and knocked on the stopper from underneath and crawled into the bathtub with President Rexford, or Mrs. President Rexford, or maybe right into the

189

middle of one of Janey Rexford's Oh-I'm-so-sexy bubble baths?"

"Please!" The Professor put his hand to his eyebrows and kept it there, cuddling the elbow in his other hand.

"Well, have you thought of something?" the Professor's Wife asked him after a bit. "What are you going to do?"

The Professor dropped his hand and blinked his eye hard and took a deep breath.

"Telegraph Fenchurch and Ackerly-Ramsbottom and then break in," he said in a resigned voice, into which nevertheless, a note of hope seemed also to have come. "First, however, I'm going to wait until morning."

And he sat down cross-legged in the hall a few yards from the bathroom door and folded his arms.

*　　*　　*

So the long vigil commenced. The Professor's family shared it and he offered no objection. Other and sterner men, he told himself, might claim to be able successfully to order their children to go to bed when there was a Martian locked in the bathroom, but he would like to see them faced with the situation.

Finally dawn began to seep from the bedrooms. When the bulb in the hall had grown quite dim, the Professor unfolded his arms.

Just then, there was a loud splashing in the bathroom. The Professor's family looked toward the door. The splashing stopped and they heard the Martian moving around. Then the door opened and the Martian appeared in the Professor's gray pin-stripe suit. His mouth curled sharply downward in a broad alien smile as he saw the Professor.

"Good morning!" the Martian said happily. "I never slept better in my life, even in my own little wet bed back on Mars."

He looked around more closely and his mouth straightened. "But where did you all sleep?" he asked. "Don't tell me you stayed dry all night! You *didn't* give up your only bed to me?"

His mouth curled upward in misery. "Oh, dear," he said, "I'm afraid I've made a mistake somehow. Yet I don't understand how. Before I studied you, I didn't know what your sleeping habits would be, but that question was answered for me—in fact, it looked so reassuringly homelike—when I saw those brief TV scenes of your females ready for sleep in their little tubs. Of course, on Mars, only the fortunate can always be sure of sleeping wet, but here, with your abundance of water, I thought there would be wet beds for all."

He paused. "It's true I had some doubts last night, wondering if I'd used the right words and all, but then when you rapped 'Good night' to me, I splashed the sentiment back at you and went to sleep in a wink. But I'm afraid that somewhere I've blundered and—"

"No, no, dear chap," the Professor managed to say. He had been waving his hand in a gentle circle for some time in token that he wanted to interrupt. "Everything is quite all right. It's true we stayed up all night, but please consider that as a watch—an honor guard, by George!—which we kept to indicate our esteem."

Try and Change the Past

No, I wouldn't advise anyone to try to change the past, at least not his *personal* past, although changing the *general* past is my business, my fighting business. You see, I'm a Snake in the Change War. Don't back off—human beings, even Resurrected ones engaged in timefighting, aren't built for outward wriggling and their poison is mostly psychological. "Snake" is slang for the soldiers on our side, like Hun or Reb or Ghib-belin. In the Change War we're tying to alter the past—and it's tricky, brutal work, believe me—at points all over the cosmos, anywhere and anywhen, so that history will be warped to make our side defeat the Spiders. But that's a much bigger story, the biggest in fact, and I'll leave it occupying several planets of microfilm and two asteroids of coded molecules in the files of the High Command.

Change one event in the past and you get a brand new future? Erase the conquests of Alexander by nudging a Neolithic pebble? Extirpate America by pulling up a shoot of Sumerian grain? Brother, that isn't the way it works at all! The space-time con-tinuum's built of stubborn stuff and change is anything but a chain-reaction. Change the past and you start a wave of changes moving futurewards, but it damps out mighty fast. Haven't you ever heard of temporal reluctance, or of the Law of Conservation of Reality?

Here's a little story that will illustrate my point: This guy was fresh recruited, the Resurrection sweat still wet in his armpits, when he got the idea he'd use the time-traveling power to go back and make a couple of little changes in his past, so that his life would take a happier course and maybe, he thought, he wouldn't have to die and get mixed up with Snakes and Spiders at all. It was as if a new-enlisted feuding hillbilly soldier should light out with the high-power rifle they issued him to go back to his mountains and pick off his pet enemies.

Normally it couldn't ever have happened. Normally, to avoid just this sort of thing, he'd have been shipped straight off to some place a few thousand or million years dis-tant from his point of enlistment and maybe a few light-years, too. But there was a local crisis in the Change War and a lot of routine operations got held up and one new recruit was simply forgotten.

Normally, too, he'd never have been left alone a moment in the Dispatching Room, never even have glimpsed the place except to be rushed through it on arrival and reshipment. But, as I say, there happened to be a crisis, the Snakes were shorthanded, and several soldiers were careless. Afterwards two N.C.'s were busted because of what happened and a First Looey not only lost his commission but was transferred outside the galaxy and the era. But during the crisis this recruit I'm telling you about had the opportunity and more to fool around with forbidden things and try out his schemes.

He also had all the details on the last part of his life back in the real world, on his death and its consequences, to mull over and be tempted to change. This wasn't anybody's carelessness. The Snakes give every candidate that information as part of the recruiting pitch. They spot a death coming and the Resurrection Men go back and recruit the person from a point a few minutes or at most a few hours earlier. They explain in uncomfortable detail what's going to happen and wouldn't he rather take the oath and put on scales? I never heard of anybody turning down that offer. Then they lift him from his lifeline in the form of a Doubleganger and from then on, brother, he's a Snake.

*   *   *

So this guy had a clearer picture of his death than of the day he bought his first car, and a masterpiece of morbid irony it was. He was living in a classy penthouse that had belonged to a crazy uncle of his—it even had a midget astronomical observatory, unused for years—but he was stony broke, up to the top hair in debt and due to be dispossessed next day. He'd never had a real job, always lived off his rich relatives and his wife's, but now he was getting a little too mature for his stern dedication to a life of sponging to be cute. His charming personality, which had been his only asset, was deader from overuse and abuse than he himself would be in a few hours. His crazy uncle would not have anything to do with him any more. His wife was responsible for a lot of the wear and tear on his social-butterfly wings; she had hated him for years, had screamed at him morning to night the way you can only get away with in a penthouse, and was going batty herself. He'd been playing around with another woman, who'd just given him the gate, though he knew his wife would never believe that and would only add a scornful note to her screaming if she did.

It was a lousy evening, smack in the middle of an August heat wave. The Giants were playing a night game with Brooklyn. Two long-run musicals had closed. Wheat had hit a new high. There was a brush fire in California and a war scare in Iran. And tonight a meteor shower was due, according to an astronomical bulletin that had arrived in the morning mail addressed to his uncle—he generally dumped such stuff in the fireplace unopened, but today he had looked at it because he had nothing else to do, either more useful or more interesting.

The phone rang. It was a lawyer. His crazy uncle was dead and in the will there wasn't a word about an Asteroid Search Foundation. Every penny of the fortune went to the no-good nephew.

This same character finally hung up the phone, fighting off a tendency for his heart to spring giddily out of his chest and through the ceiling. Just then his wife came screeching out of the bedroom. She'd received a cut, commiserating, tell-all note from the other woman; she had a gun and announced that she was going to finish him off.

The sweltering atmosphere provided a good background for sardonic catastrophe. The French doors to the roof were open behind him but the air that drifted through was muggy as death. Unnoticed, a couple of meteors streaked faintly across the night sky.

Figuring it would sure dissuade her, he told her about the inheritance. She screamed that he's just use the money to buy more other women—not an unreasonable prediction—and pulled the trigger.

The danger was minimal. She was at the other end of a big living room, her hand wasn't just shaking, she was waving the nickel-plated revolver as if it were a fan.

The bullet took him right between the eyes. He flopped down, deader than his hopes were before he got the phone call. He saw it happen because as a clincher the Resurrection Men brought him forward as a Doubleganger to witness it invisibly—also standard Snake procedure and not productive of time-complications, incidentally, since Doublegangers don't imprint on reality unless they want to.

They stuck around a bit. His wife looked at the body for a couple of seconds, went to her bedroom, blonded her graying hair by dousing it with two bottles of undiluted peroxide, put on a tarnished gold-lamé evening gown and a bucket of make-up, went back to the living room, sat down at the piano, played "Country Gardens" and then shot herself, too.

So that was the little skit, the little double blackout, he had to mull over outside the empty and unguarded Dispatching Room, quite forgotten by its twice-depleted skeleton crew while every available Snake in the sector was helping deal with the local crisis, which centered around the planet Alpha Centauri Four, two million years minus.

Naturally it didn't take him long to figure out that if he went back and gimmicked things so that the first blackout didn't occur, but the second still did, he would be sitting pretty back in the real world and able to devote his inheritance to fulfilling his wife's prediction and other pastimes. He didn't know much about Doublegangers yet and had it figured out that if he didn't die in the real world he'd have no trouble resuming his existence there—maybe it'd even happen automatically.

So this Snake—name kind of fits him, doesn't it?—crossed his fingers and slipped into the Dispatching Room. Dispatching is so simple a child could learn it in five minutes from studying the board. He went back to a point a couple of hours before the tragedy, carefully avoiding the spot where the Resurrection Men had lifted him from his lifeline. He found the revolver in a dresser drawer, unloaded it, checked to make sure there weren't any more cartridges around, and then went ahead a couple of hours, arriving just in time to see himself get the slug between the eyes same as before.

As soon as he got over his disappointment, he realized he'd learned something about Doublegangers he should have known all along, if his mind had been clicking. The bullets he'd lifted were Doublegangers, too; they had disappeared from the real world only at the point in space-time where he'd lifted them, and they had continued to exist, as real as ever, in the earlier and later sections of their lifelines—with the result that the gun was loaded again by the time his wife had grabbed it up.

So this time he set the board so he'd arrive just a few minutes before the tragedy. He lifted the gun, bullets and all, and waited around to make sure it stayed lifted. He figured—rightly—that if he left this space-time sector the gun would reappear in the dresser drawer, and he didn't want his wife getting hold of any gun, even one with a broken lifeline. Afterwards—after his own death was averted, that is—he figured he'd put the gun back in his wife's hand.

Two things reassured him a lot, although he'd been expecting the one and hoping for the other: his wife didn't notice his presence as a Doubleganger and when she went to grab the gun she acted as if it weren't gone and held her right hand as if there were a gun in it. If he'd studied philosophy, he'd have realized he was witnessing a proof of Leibnitz's Theory of Pre-established Harmony: that neither atoms nor human beings really affect each other, they just look as if they did.

But anyway he had no time for theories. Still holding the gun, he drifted out into the living room to get a box seat next to Himself for the big act. Himself didn't notice him any more than his wife had.

193

Sure enough, there was no shot this time, *and* no mysteriously appearing bullet hole—which was something he'd been afraid of. Himself just stood there dully while his wife made as if she were looking down at a dead body and went back to her bedroom.

He was pretty pleased: this time he actually *had* changed the past. Then Himself slowly glanced around at him, still with that dull look, and slowly came toward him. He was more pleased than ever because he figured now they'd melt together into one man and one lifeline again, and he'd be able to hurry out somewhere and establish an alibi, just to be on the safe side, while his wife suicided.

But it didn't quite happen that way. Himself's look changed from dull to desperate, he came up close . . . and suddenly grabbed the gun and quick as a wink put a thumb to the trigger and shot himself between the eyes. And flopped, same as ever.

* * *

Right there he was starting to learn a little—and it was an unpleasant shivery sort of learning—about the Law of Conservation of Reality. The four-dimensional space-time universe doesn't *like* to be changed, any more than it likes to lose or gain energy or matter. If it has to be changed, it'll adjust itself just enough to accept that change and no more. The Conservation of Reality is a sort of Law of Least Action, too. It doesn't matter how improbable the events involved in the adjustment are, just so long as they're possible at all and can be used to patch the established pattern. His death, at this point, was part of the established pattern. If he lived on instead of dying, billions of other compensatory changes would have to be made, covering many years, perhaps centuries, before the old pattern could be re-established, the snarled lifelines woven back into it—and the universe finally go on the same as if his wife had shot him on schedule.

This way the pattern was hardly effected at all. There were powder burns on his forehead that weren't there before, but there weren't any witnesses to the shooting in the first place, so the presence or absence of powder burns didn't matter. The gun was lying on the floor instead of being in his wife's hands, but he had the feeling that when the time came for her to die, she'd wake enough from the Pre-established Harmony trance to find it, just as Himself did.

So he'd learned a little about the Conservation of Reality. He also had learned a little about his own character, especially from Himself's last look and act. He'd got a hint that he had been trying to destroy himself for years by the way he'd lived, so that inherited fortune or accidental success couldn't save him, and if his wife hadn't shot him he'd have done it himself in any case. He'd got a hint that Himself hadn't merely been acting as an agent for a self-correcting universe when he grabbed the gun, he'd been acting on his own account, too—the universe, you know, operates by getting people to co-operate.

But although these ideas occurred to him, he didn't dwell on them, for he figured he'd had a partial success the second time. If he kept the gun away from Himself, if he dominated Himself, as it were, the melting-together would take place and everything else go forward as planned.

He had the dim realization that the universe, like a huge sleepy animal, knew what he was trying to do and was trying to thwart him. This feeling of opposition made him determined to outmaneuver the universe—not the first guy to yield to such a temptation, or course.

And up to a point his tactics worked. The third time he gimmicked the past, everything started to happen just as it did the second time. Himself dragged miserably over to him, looking for the gun, but he had it tucked away and was prepared to hold onto it. Encouragingly, Himself didn't grapple, the look of desperation changed to one of utter hopelessness, and Himself turned away from him and very slowly walked to the French doors and stood looking out into the sweating night. He figured Himself was just getting used to the idea of not dying. There wasn't a breath of air. A couple of meteors streaked across the sky. Then, mixed with the upseeping night sounds of the city, there was a low whirring whistle.

Himself shook a bit, as if he'd had a sudden chill. Then Himself turned around and slumped to the floor in one movement. Between his eyes was a black hole.

Then and there this Snake I'm telling you about decided never again to try and change the past, at least not his personal past. He'd had it, and he'd also acquired a healthy respect for a High Command able to change the past, albeit with difficulty. He scooted back to the Dispatching Room, where a sleepy and surprised Snake gave him a terrific chewing out and confined him to quarters. The chewing-out didn't bother him too much—he'd acquired a certain fatalism about things. A person's got to learn to accept reality as it is, you know—just as you'd best not be surprised at the way I disappear in a moment or two—I'm a Snake too, remember.

If a statistician is looking for an example of a highly improbable event, he can hardly pick a more vivid one than the chance of a man being hit by a meteorite. And, if he adds the condition that the meteorite hit him between the eyes so as to counterfeit the wound made by a 32-caliber bullet, the improbability becomes astronomical cubed. So how's a person going to outmaneuver a universe that finds it easier to drill a man through the head that way rather than postpone the date of his death?

Rump-Titty-Titty-Tum-Tah-Tee

Once upon a time, when just for an instant all the molecules in the world and in the collective unconscious mind got very slippery, so that just for an instant something could pop through from the past or the future or other places, six very important intellectual people were gathered in the studio of Simon Grue, the accidental painter.

There was Tally B. Washington, the jazz drummer. He was beating softly on a gray hollow African log and thinking of a composition he would entitle "Duet for Water Hammer and Whistling Faucet."

There were Lafcadio Smits, the interior decorator, and Lester Phlegius, the industrial designer. They were talking very intellectually together, but underneath they were wishing very hard that they had, respectively, a really catchy design for modernistic wallpaper and a really new motif for industrial advertising.

There were Gorius James McIntosh, the clinical psychologist, and Norman Saylor, the cultural anthropologist. Gorius James McIntosh was drinking whisky and wishing there were a psychological test that would open up patients a lot wider than the Rorschach or the TAT, while Norman Saylor was smoking a pipe but not thinking or drinking anything especially.

It was a very long, very wide, very tall studio. It had to be, so there would be room on the floor to spread flat one of Simon Grue's canvases, which were always big enough to dominate any exhibition with yards to spare, and room under the ceiling for a very tall, very strong scaffold.

The present canvas hadn't a bit of paint on it, not a spot or a smudge or a smear, except for the bone-white ground. On top of the scaffold were Simon Grue and twenty-seven big pots of paint and nine clean brushes, each eight inches wide. Simon Grue was about to have a new accident—a semi-controlled accident, if you please. Any minute now he'd plunge a brush in one of the cans of paint and raise it over his right shoulder and bring it forward and down with a great loose-wristed snap, as if he were cracking a bullwhip, and a great fissioning gob of paint would go *splaaAAT* on the canvas in a random, chance, arbitrary, spontaneous and therefore quintuply accidental pattern which would constitute the core of the composition and determine the form and rhythm for many, many subsequent splatters and maybe even a few contact brush strokes and impulsive smearings.

As the rhythm of Simon Grue's bouncy footsteps quickened, Norman Saylor glanced up, though not apprehensively. True, Simon had been known to splatter his friends as well as his canvases, but in anticipation of this Norman was wearing a faded shirt, old sneakers and the frayed tweed suit he'd sported as assistant instructor, while his fishing hat was within easy reach. He and his armchair were crowded close to a wall, as were the other four intellectuals. This canvas was an especially large one, even for Simon.

As for Simon, pacing back and forth atop his scaffold, he was experiencing the glorious intoxication and expansion of vision known only to an accidental painter in the great tradition of Wassily Kandinsky, Robert Motherwell and Jackson Pollock, when he is springily based a good twenty feet above a spotless, perfectly prepared canvas. At moments like this Simon was especially grateful for these weekly gatherings. Having his five especial friends on hand helped create the right intellectual milieu. He listened happily to the hollow rhythmic thrum of Tally's drumming, the multisyllabic rippling of Lester's and Lafcadio's conversation, the gurgle of Gorius' whisky bottle, and happily watched the mystic curls of Norman's pipe smoke. His entire being, emotions as well as mind, was a blank tablet, ready for the kiss of the universe.

Meanwhile the instant was coming closer and closer when all the molecules in the world and in the collective unconscious mind would get very slippery.

Tally B. Washington, beating on his African log, had a feeling of oppression and anticipation, almost (but not quite) a feeling of apprehension. One of Tally's ancestors, seven generations back, had been a Dahomey witch doctor, which is the African equivalent of an intellectual with artistic and psychiatric leanings. According to a very private family tradition, half joking, half serious, this five-greats-grandfather of Tally had discovered a Jumbo Magic which could "lay holt" of the whole world and bring it under its spell, but he had perished before he could try the magic or transmit it to his sons. Tally himself was altogether skeptical about the Jumbo Magic, but he couldn't help wondering about it wistfully from time to time, especially when he was beating on his African log and hunting for a new rhythm. The wistful feeling came to him right now, building on the feeling of oppression and anticipation, and his mind became a tablet blank as Simon's.

The slippery instant arrived.

Simon seized a brush and plunged it deep in the pot of black paint. Usually he used black for a final splatter if he used it at all, but this time he had the impulse to reverse himself.

All of a sudden Tally's wrists lifted high, hands dangling loosely, almost like a marionette's. There was a dramatic pause. Then his hands came down and beat out a phrase on the log, loudly and with great authority.

*Rump-titty-titty-tum-*TAH*-tee!*

Simon's wrist snapped and the middle air was full of free-falling paint which hit the canvas in a fast series of *splaaAAT's* which was an exact copy of Tally's phrase.

*Rump-titty-titty-tum-*TAH*-tee!*

Intrigued by the identity of the two sounds, and with their back hairs lifting a little for the same reason, the five intellectuals around the wall rose and stared, while Simon looked down from his scaffold like God after the first stroke of creation.

The big black splatter on the bone-white ground was itself an exact copy of Tally's phrase, sound made sight, music transposed into visual pattern. First there was a big roundish blot—that was the *rump.* Then two rather delicate, many-tongued splatters—those were the *titties.* Next a small *rump,* which was the *tum.* Following that a big blot like a bent spearhead, not so big as the *rump* but even more emphatic—the TAH. Last of all an indescribably curled and broken little splatter which somehow seemed exactly right for the *tee.*

The whole big splatter was as like the drummed phrase as an identical twin reared in a different environment and as fascinating as a primeval symbol found next to bison paintings in a Cro-Magnon cave. The six intellectuals could hardly stop looking at it and when they did, it was to do things in connection with it, while their minds were happily a-twitter with all sorts of exciting new projects.

There was no thought of Simon doing any more splattering on the new painting until this first amazing accidental achievement had been digested and pondered.

Simon's wide-angle camera was brought into play on the scaffold and negatives were immediately developed and prints made in the darkroom adjoining the studio. Each of Simon's friends carried at least one print when he left. They smiled at each other like men who share a mysterious but powerful secret. More than one of them drew his print from under his coat on the way home and hungrily studied it.

At the gathering next week there was much to tell. Tally had introduced the phrase at a private jam session and on his live jazz broadcast. The jam session had improvised on and developed the phrase for two solid hours and the musicians had squeaked with delight when Tally finally showed them the photograph of what they had been playing, while the response from the broadcast had won Tally a new sponsor with a fat pocket-book.

Gorius McIntosh had got phenomenal results from using the splatter as a Rorschach inkblot. His star patient had seen her imagined incestuous baby in it and spilled more in one session than in the previous hundred and forty. Stubborn blocks in two other analyses had been gloriously broken, while three catatonics at the state mental hospital had got up and danced.

Lester Phlegius rather hesitantly described how he was using "something like the splatter, really not too similar" (he said) as an attention-getter in a forthcoming series of Industrial-Design-for-Living advertisements.

Lafcadio Smits, who had an even longer and more flagrant history of stealing designs from Simon, brazenly announced that he had reproduced the splatter as a silk-screen pattern on linen. The pattern was already selling like hotcakes at five arty gift shops, while at this very moment three girls were sweating in Lafcadio's loft turning out more. He braced himself for a blast from Simon, mentally rehearsing the attractive deal he was prepared to offer, one depending on percentages of percentages, but the accidental painter was strangely abstracted. He seemed to have something weighing on his mind.

The new painting hadn't progressed any further than the first splatter.

Norman Saylor quizzed him about it semi-privately.

"I've developed a sort of artist's block," Simon confessed to him with relief. "Whenever I pick up a brush I get afraid of spoiling that first tremendous effect and I don't go on." He paused. "Another thing—I put down papers and tried some small test-splatters. They all looked almost exactly like the big one. Seems my wrist won't give out with anything esle." He laughed nervously. "How are you cashing in on the thing, Norm?"

The anthropologist shook his head. "Just studying it, trying to place in in the continuum of primitive signs and universal dream symbols. It goes very deep. But about this block and this . . . er . . . fancied limitation of yours—I'd just climb up there tomorrow morning and splatter away. The big one's been photographed, you can't lose that."

Simon nodded doubtfully and then looked down at his wrist and quickly grabbed it with his other hand, to still it. It had been twitching in a familiar rhythm.

If the tone of the gathering after the first week was enthusiastic, that after the second was euphoric. Tally's new drummed theme had given rise to a musical fad christened Drum 'n' Drag which promised to rival Rock 'n' Roll, while the drummer himself was in two days to appear as a guest artist on a network TV program. The only worry was that no new themes had appeared. All the Drum 'n' Drag pieces were based on duplications or at most developments of the original drummed phrase. Tally also mentioned with an odd reluctance that a few rabid cats had taken to greeting each other with a four-handed patty-cake that beat out *rump-titty-titty-tum*-TAH-*tee*.

Gorius McIntosh was causing a stir in psychiatric circles with his amazing successes in opening up recalcitrant cases, many of them hitherto thought fit for nothing but eventual lobotomy. Colleagues with M.D.s quite emphasizing the lowly "Mister" in his name, while several spontaneously addressed him as "Doctor" as they begged him for copies of the McSPAT (McIntosh's Splatter Pattern Apperception Test). His name had been mentioned in connection with the assistant directorship of the clinic where he was a humble psychologist. He also told how some of the state patients had taken to pommelling each other playfully while happily spouting some gibberish variant of the original phrase, such as *"Bump-biddy-biddy-bum*-BAH-*bee!"* The resemblance in behavior to Tally's hepcats was noted and remarked on by the six intellectuals.

The first of Lester Phlegius' attention-getters (identical with the splatter, of course) had appeared and attracted the most favorable notice, meaning chiefly that his customer's front office had received at least a dozen curious phone calls from the directors and presidents of cognate firms. Lafcadio Smits reported that he had rented a second loft, was branching out into dress materials, silk neckties, lampshades and wallpaper, and was deep in royalty deals with several big manufactures. Once again Simon Grue surprised him by not screaming robbery and demanding details and large simple percentages. The accidental painter seemed even more unhappily abstracted than the week before.

When he ushered them from his living quarters into the studio they understood why.

It was as if the original big splatter had whelped. Surrounding and overlaying it were scores of smaller splatters. They were all colors of a well-chosen artist's-spectrum, blending with each other and pointing each other up superbly. But each and every one of them was a perfect copy, reduced to one half or less, of the original big splatter.

Lafcadio Smits wouldn't believe at first that Simon had done them free-wrist from the scaffold. Even when Simon showed him details proving they couldn't have been stencilled, Lafcadio was still unwilling to believe, for he was deeply versed in methods of mass-producing the appearance of handwork and spontaneity.

But when Simon wearily climbed the scaffold and, hardly looking at what he was doing, flipped down a few splatters exactly like the rest, even Lafcadio had to admit that something miraculous and frightening had happened to Simon's wrist.

Gorius James McIntosh shook his head and muttered a remark about "stereotyped compulsive behavior at the artistic-creative level. Never heard of it getting *that* stereotyped, though."

Later during the gathering, Norman Saylor again consulted with Simon and also had a long confidential talk with Tally B. Washington, during which he coaxed out of the drummer the whole story of his five-greats-grandfather. When questioned about his own researches, the cultural anthropologist would merely say that they were "progressing." He did, however, have one piece of concrete advice, which he delivered to all the five others just before the gathering broke up.

"This splatter does have an obsessive quality, just as Gory said. It has that maddening feeling of incompleteness which cries for repetition. It would be a good thing if each of us, whenever he feels the thing getting too strong a hold on him, would instantly shift to some engrossing activity which has as little as possible to do with arbitrarily ordered sight and sound. Play chess or smell perfumes or eat candy or look at the moon through a telescope, or stare at a point of light in the dark and try to blank out your mind—something like that. Try to set up a countercompulsion. One of us might even hit on a counterformula—a specific antidote—like quinine for malaria."

If the ominous note of warning in Norman's statement didn't register on all of them just then, it did at some time during the next seven days, for the frame of mind in which the six intellectuals came to the gathering after the third week was one of paranoid grandeur and hysterical desperation.

Tally's TV appearance had been a huge success. He'd taken to the TV station a copy of the big splatter and although he hadn't intended to (he said) he'd found himself showing it to the M.C. and the unseen audience after his drum solo. The immediate response by phone, telegram and letter had been overwhelming but rather frightening, including a letter from a woman in Smallhills, Arkansas, thanking Tally for showing her "the wondrous picture of God."

Drum 'n' Drag had become a national and even international craze. The patty-cake greeting had become general among Tally's rapidly-growing horde of fans and it now included a staggering slap on the shoulder to mark the TAH. (Here Gorius McIntosh took a drink from his bottle and interrupted to tell of a spontaneous, rhythmic, lock-stepping procession at the state hospital with an even more violent TAH-blow. The mad march had been forcibly broken up by attendants and two of the patients treated at the infirmary for contusions.) *The New York Times* ran a dispatch from South Africa describing how police had dispersed a disorderly mob of University of Capetown students who had been chanting, "*Shlump Shliddy Shliddy Shlump* SHLAH *Shlee!*"—which the correspondents had been told was an antiapartheid cry phrased in pig-Afrikaans.

For both the drummed phrase and the big splatter had become a part of the news, either directly or by inferences that made Simon and his friends alternately cackle and shudder. An Indiana town was fighting a juvenile phenomenon called Drum Saturday. A radio-TV columnist noted that Blotto Cards were the latest rage among studio personnel; carried in handbag or breast pocket, whence they could be quickly whipped out and stared at, the cards were claimed to be an infallible remedy against boredom or sudden attacks of anger and the blues. Reports of a penthouse burglary included among the objects listed as missing "a recently-purchased spotted linen wallhanging"; the woman said she did not care about the other objects, but pleaded for the hanging's return, "as it was of great psychological comfort to my husband." Splatter-marked rain-coats were a highschool fad, the splattering being done ceremoniously at Drum 'n' Drag parties. An English prelate had preached a sermon inveighing against "this deafening new American craze with its pantherine overtones of mayhem." At a press interview Salvador Dali had refused to say anything to newsmen except the cryptic sentence, "The time has come."

In a halting, hiccupy voice Gorius McIntosh reported that things were pretty hot at the clinic. Twice during the past week he had been fired and triumphantly reinstated. Rather similarly at the state hospital Bump Parties had been alternately forbidden and then encouraged, mostly on the pleas of enthusiastic psychiatric aides. Copies of the McSPAT had come into the hands of general practitioners who, ignoring its original purpose, were using it as a substitute for electroshock treatment and tranquilizing drugs. A group of progressive psychiatrists calling themselves the Young Turks were circulating a statement that the McSPAT constituted the worst threat to classical

Freudian psychoanalysis since Alfred Adler, adding a grim scholarly reference to the Dancing Mania of the Middle Ages. Gorius finished his report by staring around almost frightenedly at his five friends and clutching the whisky bottle to his bosom.

Lafcadio Smits seemed equally shaken, even when telling about the profits of his pyramiding enterprises. One of his four lofts had been burglarized and another invaded at high noon by a red-bearded Greenwich Village Satanist protesting that the splatter was an illicitly procured Taoist magic symbol of direst power. Lafcadio was also receiving anonymous threatening letters which he believed to be from a criminal drug syndicate that looked upon Blotto Cards as his creation and as competitive to heroin and lesser forms of dope. He shuddered visibly when Tally volunteered the information that his fans had taken to wearing Lafcadio's splatter-patterned ties and shirts.

Lester Phlegius said that further copies of the issue of the costly and staid industrial journal carrying his attention-getter were unprocurable and that many had vanished from private offices and wealthy homes or, more often, simply had the crucial page ripped out.

Norman Saylor's two photographs of the big splatter had been pilfered from his locked third-floor office at the university, and a huge copy of the splatter, painted in a waterproof black substance, had appeared on the bottom of the swimming pool in the girls' gymnasium.

As they continued to share their experiences, it turned out that the six intellectuals were even more disturbed at the hold the drummed phrase and the big splatter had got on them individually and at their failure to cope with the obsession by following Norman's suggestions. Playing at a Sunday-afternoon bar concert, Tally had got snagged on the phrase for fully ten minutes, like a phonograph needle caught in one groove, before he could let go. What bothered him especially was that no one in the audience had seemed to notice and he had the conviction that if something hadn't stopped him (the drum skin ruptured) they would have sat frozen there until, wrists flailing, he died of exhaustion.

Norman himself, seeking escape in chess, had checkmated his opponent in a blitz game (where each player must move without hesitation) by banging down his pieces in the *rump-titty* rhythm—and his subconscious mind had timed it, he said, so that the last move came right on the *tee*; it was a little pawn-move after a big queen-check on the TAH. Lafacdio, turning to cooking, had found himself mixing salad with a *rump-titty* flourish. ("... and a madman to mix it, as the old Spanish recipe says," he finished with a despairing giggle.) Lester Phlegius, seeking release from the obsession in the companionship of a lady spiritualist with whom he had been carrying on a strictly Platonic love affair for ten years, found himself enlivening with the *rump-titty* rhythm the one chaste embrace they permitted themselves to each meeting. Phoebe had torn herself away and slapped him fullarm across the face. What had horrified Lester was that the impact had coincided precisely with the TAH.

Simon Grue himself, who hadn't stirred out of his apartment all week but wandered shivering from window to window in a dirty old bathrobe, had dozed in a broken armchair and had a terrifying vision. He had imagined himself in the ruins of Manhattan, chained to the broken stones (before dozing off he had wound both wrists heavily with scarves and cloths to cushion the twitching), while across the dusty jagged landscape all humanity tramped in an endless horde screeching the accursed phrase and every so often came a group of them carrying a two-story-high poster ("... like those Soviet parades," he said) with the big splatter staring blackly down from it. His nightmare had gone on to picture the dreadful infection spreading from the Earth by spaceship to planets revolving around other stars.

As Simon finished speaking Gorius McIntosh rose slowly from his chair, groping ahead of himself with his whisky bottle.

"That's it!" he said from between bared clenched teeth, grinning horribly. "That's what's happening to all of us. Can't get it out of our minds. Can't get it out of our muscles. Psychosomatic bondage!" He stumbled slowly across the circle of intellectuals toward Lester, who was sitting opposite him. "It's happening to me. A patient sits down across the desk and says with his eyes dripping tears, 'Help me, Doctor McIntosh,' and I see his problems clearly and I know just how to help him and I get up and I go around the desk to him"—he was standing right over Lester now, bottle raised high above the industrial designer's shoulder—"and I lean down so that my face is close to his and then I shout RUMP-TITTY-TITTY-TUM-TAH-TEE!"

At this point Norman Saylor decided to take over, leaving to Tally and Lafcadio the restraining of Gorius, who indeed seemed quite docile and more dazed than anything else now that his seizure was spent, at least temporarily. The cultural anthropologist strode to the center of the circle, looking very reassuring with his darkly billowing pipe and his strong jaw and his smoky tweeds, though he kept his hands clasped tightly together behind him, after snatching his pipe with one of them.

"Men," he said sharply, "my research on this thing isn't finished by a long shot, but I've carried it far enough to know that we are dealing with what may be called an ultimate symbol, a symbol that is the summation of all symbols. It has everything in it—birth, death, mating, murder, divine and demonic possession, all of life, the whole lot—to such a degree that after you've looked at it, or listened to it, or *made* it, for a time, you simply don't *need* life any more."

The studio was very quiet. The five other intellectuals looked at him. Norman rocked on his heels like any normal college professor, but his arms grew perceptibly more rigid as he clasped his hands even more tightly behind his back, fighting an exquistie compulsion.

"As I say, my studies aren't finished, but there's clearly no time to carry them further—we must act on such conclusions as I have drawn from the evidence assembled to date. Here's briefly how it shapes up: We must assume that mankind possesses an actual collective unconscious mind stretching thousands of years into the past and, for all I know, into the future. This collective unconscious mind may be pictured as a great dark space across which radio messages can sometimes pass with difficulty. We must also assume that the drummed phrase and with it the big splatter came to us by this inner radio from an individual living over a century in the past. We have good reason to believe that this individual is, or was, a direct male ancestor, in the seventh generation back, of Tally here. He was a witch doctor. He was acutely hungry for power. In fact, he spent his life seeking an incantation that would put a spell on the whole world. It appears that he found the incantation at the end, but died too soon to be able to use it—without ever being able to embody it in sound or sign. Think of his frustration!"

"Norm's right," Tally said, nodding somberly. "He was a mighty mean man, I'm told, and mighty persistent."

Norman's nod was quicker and also a plea for undivided attention. Beads of sweat were dripping down his forehead. "The thing came to us when it did—came to Tally specifically and through to him to Simon—because our six minds, reinforcing each other powerfully, were momentarily open to receive transmissions through the collective unconscious, and because there is—was—this sender at the other end long desirous of getting his message through to one of his descendants. We cannot say precisely where this sender is—a scientifically oriented person might say that he is in a shadowed portion of the space-time continuum while a religiously oriented person might aver that he is in Heaven or Hell."

"I'd plump for the last-mentioned," Tally volunteered. "He was that kind of man."

"Please, Tally," Norman said. "Wherever he is, we must operate on the hope that there is a counter formula or negative symbol—yang to this yin—which he wants, or wanted, to transmit too—something that will stop this flood of madness we have loosed on the world."

"That's where I must differ with you, Norm," Tally broke in, shaking his head more somberly than he had nodded it, "if Old Five-Greats ever managed to start something bad, he'd never want to stop it, especially if he knew how. I tell you he was mighty mighty mean and—"

"Please, Tally! Your ancestor's character may have changed with his new environment, there may be greater forces at work on him—in any case, our only hope is that he possesses and will transmit to us the counter formula. To achieve that, we must try to recreate, by artificial means, the conditions that obtained in this studio at the time of the first transmission."

A look of acute pain crossed his face. He unclasped his hands and brought them in front of him. His pipe fell to the floor. He looked at the large blister the hot bowl had raised in one palm. Then clasping his hands together in front of him, palm to palm, with a twisting motion that made Lafcadio wince, he continued rapping out the words.

"Men, we must act at once, using only such materials as can be rapidly assembled. Each of you must trust me implicitly. Tally, I know you don't use it any more, but can you still get weed, the genuine crushed leaf? Good, we may need enough for two or three dozen sticks. Gory, I want you to fetch the self-hypnotism rigmarole that's so effective—no, I don't trust your memory and we may need copies. Lester, if you're quite through satisfying yourself that Gory didn't break your collarbone with his bottle, you go with Gory and see that he drinks lots of coffee. On your way back several bunches of garlic, a couple of rolls of dimes, and a dozen red railway flares. Oh yes, and call up your mediumistic lady and do your damnedest to get her to join us here—her talents may prove invaluable. Laf, tear off to your home loft and get the luminous paint and the black velvet hangings you and your red-bearded ex-friend used—yes, I know about that association!—when you and he were dabbling with black magic. Simon and I will hold down the studio. All right, then—" A spasm crossed his face and the veins in his forehead and cords in his neck bulged and his arms were jerking with the struggle he was waging against the compulsion that threatened to overpower him. "All right, then—*Rump-titty-titty-tum*-GET-MOVING!"

*   *   *

An hour later the studio smelt like a fire in a eucalyptus grove. Such light from outside as got past the cabalistically figured hangings covering windows and skylight revealed the shadowy forms of Simon, atop the scaffold, and the other five intellectuals, crouched against the wall, all puffing their reefers, sipping the sour smoke industriously. Their marijuana-blanked minds were still reverberating to the last compelling words of Gory's rigmarole, read by Lester Phlegius in a sonorous bass.

Phoebe Saltonstall, who had refused reefers with a simple, "No thank you, I always carry my own peyote," had one wall all to herself. Eyes closed, she was lying along it on three small cushions, her pleated Grecian robe white as a winding sheet.

Round all four walls waist-high went a dimly luminous line with six obtuse angles in it besides the four corners; Norman said that made it the topological equivalent of a magician's pentalpha or pentagram. Barely visible were the bunches of garlic nailed to each door and the tiny silver discs scattered in front of them.

Norman flicked his lighter and the little blue flame added itself to the six glowing red points of the reefers. In a cracked voice he cried, "The time approaches!" and he shambled about rapidly setting fire to the twelve railway flares spiked into the floor through the big canvas.

In the hellish red glow they looked to each other like so many devils. Phoebe moaned and tossed. Simon coughed once as the dense clouds of smoke billowed up around the scaffold and filled the ceiling.

Norman Saylor cried, *"This is it!"*

Phoebe screamed thinly and arched her back as if in electroshock.

A look of sudden agonized amazement came into the face of Taliaferro Booker Washington, as if he'd been jabbed from below with a pin or hot poker. He lifted his hands with great authority and beat out a short phrase on his gray African log.

A hand holding a brightly-freighted eight-inch brush whipped out of the hellish smoke clouds above and sent down a great fissioning gout of paint that landed on the canvas with a sound that was an exact visual copy of Tally's short drummed phrase.

Immediately the studio became a hive of purposeful activity. Heavily-gloved hands jerked out the railway flares and plunged them into strategically located buckets of water. The hangings were ripped down and the windows thrown open. Two electric fans were turned on. Simon, half-fainting, slipped down the last feet of the ladder, was rushed to a window and lay across it gasping. Somewhat more carefully Phoebe Saltonstall was carried to a second window and laid in front of it. Gory checked her pulse and gave a reassuring nod.

Then the five intellectuals gathered around the big canvas and stared. After a while Simon joined them.

The new splatter, in Chinese red, was entirely different from the many ones under it and it was an identical twin of the new drummed phrase.

After a while the six intellectuals went about the business of photographing it. They worked systematically but rather listlessly. When their eyes chanced to move to the canvas they didn't even seem to see what was there. Nor did they bother to glance at the black-on-white prints (with the background of the last splatter touched out) as they shoved them under their coats.

Just then there was a rustle of draperies by one of the open windows. Phoebe Saltonstall, long forgotten, was sitting up. She looked around her with some distaste.

"Take me home, Lester," she said faintly but precisely.

Tally, half-way through the door, stopped. "You know," he said puzzledly, "I still can't believe that Old Five-Greats had the public spirit to do what he did. I wonder if she found out what it was that made him—"

Norman put his hand on Tally's arm and laid a finger of the other on his own lips. They went out together, followed by Lafcadio, Gorius, Lester and Phoebe. Like Simon, all five men had the look of drunkards in a benign convalescent stupor, and probably dosed with paraldehyde, after a bout of DTs.

The same effect was apparent as the new splatter and drummed phrase branched out across the world, chasing and eventually overtaking the first one. Any person who saw or heard it proceeded to repeat it once (make it, show it, wear it, if it were that sort of thing, in any case pass it on) and then forget it—and at the same time forget the first drummed phrase and splatter. All sense of compulsion or obsession vanished utterly.

Drum 'n' Drag died a-borning. Blotto Cards vanished from handbags and pockets, the McSPATS I and II from doctor's offices and psychiatric clinics. Bump Parties no longer plagued and enlivened mental hospitals. Catatonics froze again. The Young Turks went back to denouncing tranquilizing drugs. A fad of green-and-purple barber-pole stripes covered up splattermarks on raincoats. Satanists and drug syndicates presumably continued their activities unhampered except by God and the Treasury Department. Capetown had such peace as it deserved. Spotted shirts, neckties, dresses, lampshades, wallpaper, and linen wall hangings all became intensely passé. Drum Saturday was never heard of again. Lester Phlegius' second attention-getter got none.

Simon's big painting was eventually hung at one exhibition, but it got little attention even from critics, except for a few heavy sentences along the lines of "Simon Grue's latest elephantine effort fell with a thud as dull as those of the gobs of paint that in falling composed it." Visitors to the gallery seemed able only to give it one dazed look and then pass it by, as in not infrequently the case with modern paintings.

The reason for this was clear. On top of all the other identical splatters it carried one in Chinese red that was a negation of all symbols, a symbol that had nothing in it—the new splatter that was the identical twin of the new drummed phrase that was the negation and completion of the first, the phrase that had vibrated out from Tally's log through the red glare and come slapping down out of Simon's smoke cloud, the phrase that stilled and ended everything (and which obviously can only be stated here once): "Tah-*titty-titty-tee*-toe!"

The six intellectual people continued their weekly meetings almost as if nothing had happened, except that Simon substituted for splatterwork a method of applying the paint by handfuls with the eyes closed, later treading it in by foot. He sometimes asked his friends to join him in these impromptu marches, providing wooden shoes imported from Holland for the purpose.

One afternoon, several months later, Lester Phlegius brought a guest with him—Phoebe Saltonstall.

"Miss Saltonstall has been on a round-the-world cruise," he explained. "Her psyche was dangerously depleted by her experience in this apartment, she tells me, and a complete change was indicated. Happily now she's entirely recovered."

"Indeed I am," she said, answering their solicitous inquiries with a bright smile.

"By the way," Norman said, "at the time your psyche was depleted here, did you receive any message from Tally's ancestor?"

"Indeed I did," she said.

"Well, what did Old Five-Greats have to say?" Tally asked eagerly. "Whatever it was, I bet he was pretty crude about it!"

"Indeed he was," she said, blushing prettily. "So crude, in fact, that I wouldn't dare attempt to convey that aspect of his message. For that matter, I am sure that it was the utter fiendishness of his anger and the unspeakable visions in which his anger was clothed that so reduced my psyche." She paused.

"I don't know where he was sending from," she said thoughtfully. "I had the impression of a warm place, an intensely warm place, though of course I may have been reacting to the railway flares." Her frown cleared. "The actual message was short and simple enough:

"'Dear Descendant, They *made* me stop it. It was beginning to catch on *down here*.'"

The Haunted Future

My strangest case, bar none, from the Psychotic Years was the Green
Demon of New Angles.
—From the notebooks of Andreas Snowden

It would be hard to imagine a more peaceful and reassuring spot, a spot less likely to harbor or attract horrors, even in America of the Tranquil early twenty-first century, than the suburb—exurb, rather—of Civil Service Knolls. Cozy was the word for the place—a loose assembly of a half thousand homes snuggling down in the warm moonlight a mountain ridge away from the metropolis of New Angeles. With their fashionably rounded roofs the individual houses looked rather like giant mushrooms among the noble trees. They were like mushrooms too in the way they grew with the families they housed—one story for the newlyweds, two for the properly childrened and community-seasoned, three for those punchdrunk with reproduction and happy living. From under their eaves spilled soft yellow light of the exact shade that color analysts had pronounced most homelike.

There were no streets or roads, only the dark pine-scented asphalt disks of sideyard landing spots now holding the strange-vaned shapes of 'copters and flutteryplanes locked for the night, like sleeping dragonflies and moths. While for the ground-minded there was the unobtrusive subway entrance. Even the groceries came by underground tube straight to the kitchen in response to the housewife's morning dialing, delivery having at last gone underground with the other utilities. Well-chewed garbage vanished down rust-proof ducts in the close company of well-bred bacteria. There were not even any unsightly dirt paths worn in the thick springy lawns—the family hypnotherapist had implanted in the mind of every resident, each last baldie and toddler, the suggestion that pedestrians vary their routes and keep their steps light and rather few.

No nightclubs, no bars, no feelie pads, no mess parlors, no bongo haunts, no jukebox joints, no hamburg havens, no newsstands, no comic books, no smellorama, no hot rods, no weed, no jazz, no gin.

Yes, tranquil, secure and cozy were all good words for Civil Service Knolls—a sylvan monument to sane, civilized, progressive attitudes.

Yet fear was about to swoop there just the same. Not fear of war, missile-atomic or otherwise—the Cold Truce with Communism was a good fifty years old. Not fear of physical disease or any crippling organic infirmity—such ills were close to the vanishing

207

point and even funerals and deaths—again with the vital aid of the family hypnother-apist—were rather pleasant or at least reassuring occasions for the survivors. No, the fear that was about to infiltrate Civil Service Knolls was of the sort that must be called nameless.

A householder crossing a stretch of open turf as he strolled home from the subway thought he heard a *whish* directly overhead. There was nothing whatever blackly silhouetted against the wide stretch of moon-pale sky, yet it seemed to him that one of the moon-dimmed stars near the zenith quivered and shifted, as if there were an *eddy* in the air or sky. Heaven had wavered. And weren't there two extra stars there now?—two new stars in the center of the eddy—two dim red stars close-placed like eyes?

No, that was impossible, he must be seeing things—his own blasted fault for miss-ing his regular soothe session with the hypnotherapist! Just the same, he hurried his steps.

The eddy in the darkness overhead floated in pace with him awhile, then swooped. He heard a louder *whish*, then something brushed his shoulder and claws seemed to fasten there for an instant.

He gasped like someone about to vomit and leaped forward frantically.

From the empty moon-glowing darkness behind him came a cackle of grim laughter.

While the householder desperately pounded upon his own front door, the eddy in the darkness shot up the height of a sequois, then swooped on another section of Civil Service Knolls. It hovered for a while above the imposing two-story residence of Judistrator Wisant, took a swing around the three-story one of Securitor Harker, but in the end drifted down to investigate a faintly glowing upstairs window in another three-story house.

Inside the window an athletically handsome matron, mother of five, was leisurely preparing for bed. She was thinking, rather self-satisfiedly, that (1) she had completed all preparations for her family's participation in the Twilight Tranquility Festival tomorrow, high point of the community year; (2) she had thrown just the right amount of cold water on her eldest daughter's infatuation for the unsuitable boy visiting next door (and a hint to the hypnotherapist before her daughter's next session would do the rest); and (3) she truly didn't look five years older than her eldest daughter.

There was a tap at the window.

The matron started, pulling her robe around her, then craftily waved off the light. It had instantly occurred to her that the unsuitable boy might have had the audacity to try to visit her daughter illicitly and have mistaken bedroom windows—she had read in magazine articles that such wild lascivious young men actually existed in parts of America, though—thank Placidity!—not as regular residents of Civil Service Knolls.

She walked to the window and abruptly waved it to full transparency and then with a further series of quick sidewise waves brought the room's lights to photoflood brilliance.

At first she saw nothing but the thick foliage of the sycamore a few yards outside.

Then it seemed to her as if there were an *eddy* in the massed greenery. The leaves seemed to shift and swirl.

Then a face appeared in the eddy—a green face with the fanged grim of a devil and hotly glowing eyes that looked like twin peepholes into Hell.

The matron screamed, spun around and sprinted into the hall, shouting the local security number toward the phone, which her scream triggered into ear-straining awareness.

From beyond the window came peals of cold maniacal laughter.

Yes, fear had come to Civil Service Knolls—in fact, horror would hardly be too strong a term.

> *Some men lead perfect lives—poor devils!*
> —Notebooks of A.S.

Judistrator Wisant was awakened by a familiar insistent tingling in his left wrist. He reached out and thumbed a button. The tingling stopped. The screen beside the bed glowed into life with the handsome hatchet face of his neighbor Securitor Harker. He touched another button, activating the tiny softspeaker and micromike relays at his ear and throat.

"Go ahead, Jack," he murmured.

Two seconds after his head had left the pillow a faint light had sprung from the walls of the room. It increased now by easy stages as he listened to a terse secondhand account of the two most startling incidents to disturb Civil Service Knolls since that tragic episode ten years ago when the kindergarten hypnotherapist went crazy and called attention to her psychosis only by the shocking posthypnotic suggestions she implanted in the toddlers's minds.

Judistrator Wisant was a large, well-built, shaven-headed man. His body, half covered now by the lapping sheet, gave the impression of controlled strength held well in reserve. His hands were big and quiet. His face was a compassionate yet disciplined mask of sanity. No one ever met him and failed to be astounded when they learned afterward that it was his wife, Beth, who had been the aberrating school hypnotherapist and who was now a permanent resident of the nearby mental hospital of Serenity Shoals.

The bedroom was as bare and impersonal as a gymnasium locker room. Screen, player, two short bedside shelves of which one was filled with books and tapes and neatly stacked papers, an uncurtained darkened window leading to a small outside balcony and now set a little ajar, the double bed itself exactly half slept in—that about completed the inventory, except for two 3-D photographs on the other bedside shelf of two smiling, tragic-eyed women who looked enough alike to be sisters of about twenty-seven and seventeen. The photograph of the elder bore the inscription, "To my Husband, With all my Witchy Love. Beth," and of the younger, "To her Dear Daddikins from Gabby."

The topmost of the stacked papers was a back cover cut from a magazine demurely labeled *Individuality Unlimited: Monthly Bulletin.* The background was a cluster of shadowy images of weird and grim beings: vampires, werewolves, humanoid robots, witches, murderesses, "Martians," mask-wearers, naked brains with legs. A central banner shouted: NEXT MONTH: ACCENT THE MONSTER IN YOU. In the lower left-hand corner was a small sharp photo of a personable young man looking mysterious, with the legend "David Cruxon: Your Monster Mentor." Clipped to the page was a things-to-do-tomorrow memo in Joel Wisant's angular script: "10 ack emma: Individuality Unlimited hearing. Warn them on injunction."

Wisant's gaze shifted more than once to this item and to the two photographs as he patiently heard out Harker's account. Finally he said, "Thanks, Jack. No, I don't think it's a prankster—what Mr. Fredericks and Mrs. Ames report seeing is no jokeshop scare-your-friends illusion. And I don't think it's anything that comes in any way from Serenity Shoals, though the overcrowding there *is* a problem and we're going to have to do something about it. What's that? No, it's nobody fooling around in an antigravity harness—they're too restricted. And we know it's nothing from *outside*—that's impossible. No, the real trouble, I'm afraid, is that it's nothing at all—nothing material. Does the name Mattoon mean anything to you? . . .

"I'm not surprised, it was a hundred years ago. But a town went mad because of an imaginary prowler, there was an epidemic of insane fear. That sort of thing happening today could be much worse. Are you familiar with Report K? . . .

"No matter, I can give you the gist of it. You're cleared for it and ought to have it. But you *are* calling on our private line, aren't you? This stuff is top restricted . . .

"Report K is simply the *true* annual statistics on mental health in America. Adjusted ones showing no significant change have been issued through the usual channels. Jack, *the real incidence of new psychoses is up 15 percent in the last eight months.* Yes, it *is* pretty staggering and I *am* a close-mouthed old dog. No, it's been pretty well proved that it isn't nerve viruses or mind war, much as the Kremlin boys would like to see us flip and despite those irrational but persistent rumors of a Mind Bomb. Analysis is not complete, but the insanity surge seems to be due to a variety of causes—things that we've let get out of hand and must deal with drastically."

As Wisant said those last words he was looking at the "Accent the Monster" banner on the Individuality Unlimited Bulletin. His hand took a stylus, crossed out the "Warn them on" in his memo, underlined "injunction" three times and added an exclamation point.

Meanwhile he continued, "As far as Mr. Fredericks and Mrs. Ames are concerned, here's your procedure. First, instruct them to tell no one about what they thought they saw—tell them it's for the public safety—and direct them to see their hypnotherapists. Same instructions to family members and anyone to whom they may have talked. Second, find the names of their hypnotherapists, call *them* and tell them to get in touch with Dr. Andreas Snowden at Serenity Shoals—he's up on Report K and will know what reassurance techniques or memory-wiping to advise. I depend on Snowden a lot—for that matter he's going to be with us tomorrow when we go up against Individuality Unlimited. Third, don't let anything leak to the press—that's *vital*. We must confine this outbreak of delusions before any others are infected. I don't have to tell you, Jack, that I have a reason to feel very deeply about a thing like this." His gaze went to the photo of his wife. "That's right, Jack, we're sanitary engineers of the mind, you and I—we hose out mental garbage!"

A rather frosty smile came into his face and stayed there while he listened again to Harker.

After a bit he said, "No, I wouldn't think of missing the Tranquility Festival—in fact they've got me leading part of it. Always proud to—and these community occasions are very important in keeping people sane. Gabby? She's looking forward to it too, as only a pretty, sweet-minded girl of seventeen can who's been chosen Tranquility Princess. She really makes it for me. And now hop to it, Jack, while this old man grabs himself some more shut-eye. Remember that what you're up against is delusions and hallucinations, *nothing real.*"

Wisant thumbed off the phone. As his head touched the pillow and the light in the room started to die, he nodded twice, as if to emphasize his last remark.

Serenity Shoals, named with a happy unintended irony, is a sizable territory in America's newest frontier: the Mountains of Madness.
                                                            —Notebooks of A.S.

210

While the scant light that filtered past the window died, the eddy in the darkness swung away from the house of Judistrator Wisant and sped with a kind of desperation toward the sea. The houses and lawns gave out. The wooded knolls became lower and sandier and soon gave way to a wide treeless expanse of sand holding a half-dozen large institutional buildings and a tent city besides. The buildings were mostly dark, but with stripes of dimly lit windows marking stairwells and corridors; the tent city likewise had its dimly lit streets. Beyond them both the ghostly breakers of the Pacific were barely visible in the moonlight.

Serenity Shoals, which has been called a "sandbox for grownups," was one of twenty-first-century America's largest mental hospitals and now it was clearly filled beyond any planned capacity. Here dwelt the garden-variety schizos, manics, paranoids, brain-damaged, a few exotic sufferers from radiation-induced nerve sickness and space-flight-gendered gravitational dementia and cosmic shock, and a variety of other special cases—but really all of them were simply the people who for one reason or another found it a better or at least more bearable bargain to live with their imaginings rather than even pretend to live with what society called reality.

Tonight Serenity Shoals was restless. There was more noise, more laughter and chatter and weeping, more movement of small lights along the corridors and streets, more shouts and whistles, more unscheduled night parties and night wanderings of patients and night expeditions of aides, more beetlelike scurryings of sandcars with blinking headlights, more emergencies of all sorts. It may have been the general over-crowding, or the new batch of untrained nurses and aides, or the rumor that lobotomies were being performed again, or the two new snackbars. It may even have been the moonlight—Luna disturbing the "loonies" in the best superstitious tradition.

For that matter, it may have been the eddy in the darkness that was the cause of it all.

Along the landward side of Serenity Shoals, between it and the wasteland bordering Civil Service Knolls, stretched a bright new wire fence, unpleasantly but not lethally electrified—one more evidence that Serenity Shoals was having to cope with more than its quota.

Back and forth along the line of the fence, though a hundred yards above, the eddy in the darkness beat and whirled, disturbing the starlight. There was an impression of hopeless yearning about its behavior, as if it wanted to reach its people but could not pass over the boundary.

From the mangy terrace between the permanent buildings and the nominally temporary tents, Director Andreas Snowden durveyed his schizo-manic domain. He was an elderly man with sleepy eyes and unruly white hair. He frowned, sensing an extra element in the restlessness tonight. Then his brow cleared and smiling with tender cynicism, he recited to himself:

> *Give me your tired, your poor,*
> *Your huddled masses yearning to breathe free,*
> *The wretched refuse of your teeming shore.*
> *Send these, the homeless, tempest-tossed, to me.*

Applies a lot more to Serenity Shoals, he thought, *than to America these days. Though I ain't no bloody copper goddess bearing a lamp to dazzle the Dagos and I ain't got no keys to no golden doors.* (Dr. Snowden was always resolutely crude and ungrammatical in his private thoughts, perhaps in reaction to the relative gentility of his spoken utterances. He was also very sentimental.)

211

"Oh, hello, doctor!" The woman darting across the corner of the terrace had stopped suddenly. It was hard to see anything about her except that she was thin.

Dr. Snowden walked toward her. "Good evening, Mrs. Wisant," he said. "Rather late for you to be up and around, isn't it?"

"I know, doctor, but the thought rays are very thick tonight and they sting worse than the mosquitoes. Besides, I'm so excited I couldn't sleep anyhow. My daughter is coming here tomorrow."

"Is she?" Dr. Snowden asked gently. "Odd that Joel hasn't mentioned it to me. As it happens, I'm to see your husband tomorrow on a legal matter."

"Oh, Joel doesn't know she's coming," the lady assured him. "He'd never let her if he did. He doesn't think I'm good for her ever since I started blacking out on my visits home and . . . doing things. But it isn't a plot between me and Gabby, either—*she* doesn't know she's coming."

"So? Then how are you going to manage it, Mrs. Wisant?"

"Don't try to sound so normal, doctor!—especially when you know very well *I'm not*. I suppose *you* think that *I* think I will summon her by sending a thought ray. Not at all. I've practically given up using thought rays. They're not reliable and they carry yellow fever. No, doctor, I got Gabby to come here tomorrow ten years ago."

"Now how did you do that, Mrs. Wisant? Time travel?"

"Don't be so patronizing! I merely impressed it on Gabby's mind ten years ago—after all, I *am* a trained hypnotherapist—that she should come to me when she became a princess. Now Joel writes me she's been chosen Tranquility Princess for the festival tomorrow. You see?"

"Very interesting. But don't be disappointed if—"

"Stop being a wet blanket, doctor! Don't you have any trust in psychological techniques? I *know* she's coming. Oh, the daisies, the beautiful daisies . . ."

"Then that settles it. How are they treating you here these days?"

"I have no complaints, doctor—except I must say I don't like all these new nurses and aides. They're callow. They seem to think it's very queer of us to be crazy."

Dr. Snowden chuckled. "Some people are narrow-minded," he agreed.

"Yes, and so gullible, doctor. Just this afternoon two of the new nurses were goggling over a magazine ad about how people should improve their personalities by becoming monsters. I ask you!"

Dr. Snowden shrugged. "I doubt whether all of us are monster material. And now perhaps you'd better . . ."

"I suppose so. Good night, doctor."

As she was turning to go, Mrs. Wisant paused to slap her left forearm viciously.

"Thought ray?" Dr. Snowden asked.

Mrs. Wisant looked at him sardonically. "No," she said. "Mosquito!"

Dull security and the dead weight of perfection breed abberration even more surely than disorder and fear.

—Notebooks of A.S.

Gabrielle Wisant, commonly called Gabby though she was anything but that, was sleeping on her back in long pink pajamas, stretched out very straight and with her arms folded across her breasts, looking more like the stone funeral effigy of a girl than a living one—an effect which the unrumpled bedclothes heightened.

The unocculted window let in the first cold granular light of dawn. The room was feminine, but without any special character—it seemed secretive. It had one item in common with her father's: on a low bedside stand and next to a pad of pink notepaper was another sliced-off back cover of the Individuality Unlimited bulletin. Close beside the "David Cruxon: Your Monster Mentor" photo there was a note scrawled in green ink.

Gabs—How's this for kicks? Cruxon's Carny! or corny? Lunch with your MM same place but 130 pip emma. Big legal morning. Tell you then, Dave. (Signed and Sealed in the Monsterarium, 4 pip emma, 15 June)

The page was bowed up as if something about ten inches long were lying under it.

Gabrielle Wisant's eyes opened, though not another muscle of her moved, and they stayed that way, directed at the ceiling.

And then . . . then nothing overt happened, but it was as if the mind of Gabrielle Wisant—or the soul or spirit, call it what you will—rose from unimaginable depths to the surface of her eyes to take a long look around, like a small furtive animal that silently mounts to the mouth of its burrow to sniff the weather, ready to duck back at the slightest sudden noise or apprehension of danger—in fact, rather like the groundhog come up to see or not to see its shadow on Candlemas Day.

With a faculty profounder than physical sight, the mind of Gabby Wisant took a long questioning look around at her world—the world of a "pretty, sweet-minded girl of seventeen"—to decide if it was worth living in.

Sniffing the weather of America, she became aware of a country of suntanned, slimmed-down people with smoothed-out minds, who fed contentedly on decontaminated news and ads and inspiration pieces, like hamsters on a laboratory diet. *But what were they after? What did they do for kicks? What happened to the ones whose minds wouldn't smooth, or smoothed too utterly?*

She saw the sane, civilized, secure, superior community of Civil Service Knolls, a homestead without screeching traffic or violence, without jukeboxes or juvenile delinquency, a place of sensible adults and proper children, a place so tranquil it was going to have a Tranquility Festival tonight. *But just beyond it she saw Serenity Shoals with its lost thousands living in brighter darker worlds, including one who had planted posthypnotic suggestions in children's minds like tiny bombs.*

She saw a father so sane, so just, so strong, so perfectly controlled, so always right that he was not so much a man as a living statue—the statue she too tried to be every night while she slept. *And what was the statue really like under the marble? What were the heat and color of its blood?*

She saw a witty man named David Cruxon who pehaps loved her, but who was so mixed up between his cynicism and his idealism that you might say he canceled out. A knight without armor . . . and armor without a knight.

She saw no conventional monsters, no eddies in darkness—her mind had been hiding deep down below all night.

She saw the surface of her own mind, so sweetly smoothed by a succession of kindly hypnotherapists (and one beloved traitor who must not be named) that it was positively frightening, like a book of horrors bound in pink velvet with silk rosebuds, or the sluggish sea before a hurricane, or night softly silent before a scream. She wished she had the kind of glass-bottomed boat that would let her peer below, but that was the thing above all else she must not do.

She saw herself as Tranquility Princess some twelve hours hence, receiving the muted ovation under the arching trees, candlelight twinkling back from her flared and sequined skirt and just one leaf drifted down and caught in her fine-spun hair.

*   *   *

Princess . . . Princess . . . As if that word were somehow a signal, the mind of Gabby Wisant made its decision about the worth of the upper world and dove back inside, dove deep deep down. The groundhog saw its shadow black as ink and decided to dodge the dirty weather ahead.

The *thing* that instantly took control of Gabby Wisant's body when her mind went into hiding treated that body with a savage familiarity, certainly not as if it were a statue. It sprang to its haunches in the center of the bed, snuffing the air loudly. It ripped off the pink pajamas with a complete impatience or ignorance of magnetic clasps. It switched on the lights and occulted the windoor, making it a mirror, and leered approvingly at itself and ran its hands over its torso in fierce caresses. It snatched a knife with a six-inch thumb and smiled at the blood it drew and sucked it. Then it went through the inner door, utterly silent as to footsteps but breathing in loud, measured gasps like a careless tiger.

When Judistrator Wisant woke, his daughter was squatted beside him on the permanently undisturbed half of his bed, crooning to his scoutmaster's knife. She wasn't looking at him quite, or else she was looking at him sideways—he couldn't tell through the eyelash-blur of his slitted eyes.

He didn't move. He wasn't at all sure he could. He humped the back of his tongue to say "gabby," but he knew it would come out as a croak and he wasn't even sure he could manage that. He listened to his daughter—the crooning had changed back to faintly gargling tiger gasps—and he felt the cold sweat trickling down the sides of his face and over his naked scalp and stingingly into his eyes.

Suddenly his daughter lifted the knife high above her head, both hands locked around the hilt, and drove it down into the center of the empty, perfectly mounded pillow beside him. As it thudded home he realized with faint surprise that he hadn't moved although he'd tried to. It was as though he had contracted his muscles convulsively, but discovered that all the tendons had been cut without his knowing.

He lay there quite flaccid, watching his daughter through barely parted eyelids as she mutilated the pillow with slow savage slashes, digging in the point with a twist, and sawing off a corner. She must be sweating too—strands of her fine-spun pale gold hair clung wetly to her neck and slim shoulders. She was crooning once more, with a rippling low laugh and a soft growl for variety, and she was drooling a little. The hospital smell of the fresh-cut plastic came to him faintly.

Young male voices were singing in the distance. Judistrator Wisant's daughter seemed to hear them as soon as he did, for she stopped chopping at the pillow and held still, and then she started to sway her head and she smiled and she got off the bed with a long easy movements and went to the windoor and thumbed it wide open and stood on the balcony, the knife trailing laxly from her left hand.

The singing was louder now—young male voices rather dutifully joyous in a slow marching rhythm—and now he recognized the tune. It was "America the Beautiful" but the words were different. This verse began,

> *Oh beautiful for peaceful minds,*
> *Secure families . . .*

It occurred to Wisant that it must be the youths going out at dawn to gather the boughs and deck the Great Bower, a traditional preparatory step to the Twilight Tranquility Festival. He'd have deduced it instantly if his tendons hadn't been cut . . .

But then he found that he had turned his head toward the balcony and even turned his shoulders and lifted up on one elbow a little and opened his eyes wide.

His daughter put her knife between her teeth and clambered sure-footedly onto the railing and jumped to the nearest sycamore branch and hung there swinging, like a golden-haired, long-legged, naked ape.

> *And bring with thee*
> *Tranquility*
> *To Civil Service Knolls.*

She swung in along the branch to the trunk and laid her knife in a crotch and braced one foot there and started to swing the other and her free arm too in monkey circles.

He reached out and tried to thumb the phone button, but his hand was shaking in a four-inch arc.

He heard his daughter yell, "Yoohoo! Yoohoo, boys!"

The singing stopped.

Judistrator Wisant half scrabbled, half rolled out of bed and hurried shakingly—and he hoped noiselessly—through the door and down the hall and into his daughter's bedroom, shut the door behind him—and locked it, as he only discovered later—and grabbed her phone and punched out Securitor Harker's number.

The man he wanted answered almost immediately, a little cross with sleep.

Wisant was afraid he'd have trouble being coherent at all. He was startled to find himself talking with practically his normal confident authority and winningness.

"Wisant, Jack. Calling from home. Emergency. I need you and your squad on the double. Yes. Pick up Dr. Sims or Armstrong on the way but don't waste time. Oh—and I have your men bring ladders. Yes, and put in a quick call to Serenity Shoals for a 'copter. What? *My* authority. What? Jack, I don't want to say it now, I'm not using our private line. Well, all right, just let me think for a minute . . ."

Judistrator Wisant ordinarily never had trouble in talking his way around stark facts. And he wouldn't have had even this time, perhaps, if he hadn't just the moment before seen something that distracted him.

Then the proper twist of phrase came to him.

"Look, Jack," he said, "it's this way: Gabby has gone to join her mother. Get here *fast*."

He turned off the phone and picked up the disturbing item: the bulletin cover beside his daughter's bed. He read the note from Cruxon twice and his eyes widened and his jaw tightened.

His fear was all gone away somewhere. For the moment *all* his concerns were gone except this young man and his stupid smirking face and stupider title and his green ink.

He saw the pink pad and he picked up a dark crimson stylus and began to write rapidly in a script that was a shade larger and more angular than usual.

> *For 100 years even breakfast foods had been promoting delirious happiness and glorious peace of mind. To what end?*
> —Notebooks of A.S.

"Suppose you begin by backgrounding us in on what Individuality Unlimited is and how it came to be? I'm sure we all have a general idea and may know some aspects in detail, but the bold outline, from management's point of view, should be firmed. At the least it will get us talking."

This suggestion, coming from the judistrator himself, reflected the surface informality of the conference taking place in Wisant's airy chambers in central New Angeles. Dr. Andreas Snowden sat on the judistrator's right, doodling industriously. Securitor Harker sat on Wisant's left, while flanking the trio were two female secretaries in dark business suits similar to those men wore a century before, though of somewhat shapelier cut and lighter material.

Like all the other men in the room, Wisant was sensibly clad in singlet, business jerkin, Bermuda shorts and sandals. A folded pink paper sticking up a little from his breast pocket provided the only faintly incongruous detail. He had been just seven minutes late to the conference, perhaps a record for fathers who have seen their daughters 'coptered off to a mental hospital two hours earlier—though only Harker knew of and so could appreciate this ironman achievement.

A stocky man with shaggy pepper-and-salt hair and pugnacious brows stood up across the table from Wisant.

"Good idea," he said gruffly. "If we're going to be hanged, let's get the ropes around our necks. First I'd better identify us shifty-eyed miscreants. I'm Bob Diskrow, president and general manager." He then indicated the two men on his left: "Mr. Sobody, our vice-president in charge of research, and Dr. Gline, IU's chief psychiatrist." He turned to the right: "Miss Rawvetch, VP in charge of presentation—" (A big-boned blonde flashed her eyes. She was wearing a lavender business suit with pearl buttons, wing collars and ascot tie) "—and Mr. Cruxon, junior VP in charge of the . . . Monster Program." David Cruxon was identifiably the young man of the photograph, with the same very dark, crew-cut hair and sharply watchful eyes, but now he looked simply haggard rather than mysterious. At the momentary hesitation in Diskrow's voice he quirked a smile as rapid and almost as convulsive as a tic.

"I happen already to be acquainted with Mr. Cruxon," Wisant said with a smile, "though in no fashion prejudicial to my conducting this conference. He and my daughter know each other socially."

Diskrow stuck his hands in his pockets and rocked back on his heels reflectively.

Wisant lifted a hand. "One moment," he said. "There are some general considerations governing any judistrative conference of which I should remind us. They are in line with the general principle of government by Commission, Committee and Conference which has done so much to simplify legal problems in our times. This meeting is *private*. Press is excluded, politics are taboo. Any information you furnish about IU will be treated by us as strictly confidential and we trust you will return the courtesy regarding matters we may divulge. And this is a democratic conference. *Any* of us may speak freely.

"The suggestion has been made," Wisant continued smoothly, "that some practices of IU are against the public health and safety. After you have presented your case and made your defense—pardon my putting it that way—I may in my judicial capacity issue certain advisements. If you comply with those, the matter is settled. If you do not, the advisements immediately become injunctions and I, in my administrative capacity, enforce them—though you may work for their removal through the regular legal channels. Understood?"

Diskrow nodded with a wry grimace. "Understood. You got us in a combined hammerlock and body scissors. (Just don't sprinkle us with fire ants!) And now I'll give you that bold outline you asked for—and try to be bold about it."

He made a fist and stuck out a finger from it. "Let's get one thing straight at the start: Individuality Unlimited is no idealistic or mystical outfit with its head in orbit around the moon, and it doesn't pretend to be. We just manufacture and market a product the public is willing to fork out money for. That product is individuality." He rolled the word on his tongue.

"Over one hundred years ago people started to get seriously afraid that the Machine Age would turn them into a race of robots. That mass production and consumption, the mass media of a now instantaneous communication, the subtle and often subliminal techniques of advertising and propaganda, plus the growing use of group and hypnotherapy would turn them into a bunch of identical puppets. That wearing the same clothes, driving the same cars, living in look-alike suburban homes, reading the same pop books and listening to the same pop programs, they'd start thinking the same thoughts and having the same feelings and urges and end up with rubber-stamp personalities.

"Make no mistake, this fear was very real," Diskrow went on, leaning his weight on the table and scowling. "It was just about the keynote of the whole twentieth century (and of course to some degree it's still with us) The world was getting too big for any one man to comprehend, yet people were deeply afraid of groupthink, teamlife, hive living, hypoconformity, passive adjustment and all the rest of it. The sociologist and analyst told them they had to play 'roles' in their family life and that didn't help much, because a role is one more rubber stamp. Other cultures, like Russia, offered us no hope—they seemed further along the road to robot life than we were.

"In short, people were deathly afraid of loss of identity, loss of the sense of being unique human beings. First and always they dreaded depersonalization, to give it its right name.

"Now, that's where Individuality Unlimited, operating under its time-honored slogan 'Different Ways to Be Different,' got its start," Diskrow continued, making a scooping gesture, as if his right hand were IU gathering up the loose ends of existence. "At first our methods were pretty primitive or at least modest—we sold people individualized doodads to put on their cars and clothes and houses, we offered conversation kits and hobby guides, we featured Monthly Convention Crushers and Taboo Breakers that sounded very daring but really weren't"—Diskrow grinned and gave a little shrug—"and incidentally we came in for a lot of ribbing on the score that we were trying to mass-produce individuality and turn out uniqueness on an assembly line. Actually a lot of our work still involves randomizing pattern details and introducing automatic unpredictable variety into items as diverse as manufactured objects and philosophies of life.

"But in spite of the ribbing we kept going because we knew we had hold of a sound idea: that if a person can be made to *feel* he's different, if he is encouraged to take the initiative in expressing himself in even a rather trivial way, then his inner man wakes up and takes over and starts to operate under his own steam. What people basically need is a periodic shot in the arm. I bunk you not when I tell you that here IU has always done and is still doing a real public service. We don't necessarily give folks new personalities, but we renew the glow of those they have. As a result they become happier workers, better citizens. We make people individuality-certain."

"Uniqueness-convinced," Miss Rawvetch put in brightly.

"Depersonalization-secure," Dr. Gline chimed. He was a small man with a large

217

forehead and a permanent hunch to his shoulders. He added, "Only a man who is secure in his own individuality can be at one with the cosmos and really benefit from the tranquil awe-inspiring rhythms of the stars, the seasons and the sea."

At that windy remark David Cruxon quirked a second grimace and scribbled something on the pad in front of him.

Diskrow nodded approvingly at Gline. "Now, as IU began to see the thing bigger, it had to enter new fields and accept new responsibilities. Adult education, for example—one very genuine way of making yourself more of an individual is to acquire new knowledge and skills. Three-D shows—we needed them to advertise and dramatize our techniques. Art—self-expression and a style of one's own are master keys to individuality, though they don't unlock everybody's inner door. Philosophy—it was a big step forward for us when we were able to offer people 'A Philosophy of Life That's Yours Alone.' Religion—that too, of course, though only indirectly . . . strictly nonsectarian. Childhood lifeways—it's surprising what you can do in an individualizing way with personalized games, adult toys, imaginary companions and secret languages—and by recapturing and adapting something of the child's vivid sense of uniqueness. Psychology—indeed yes, for a person's individuality clearly depends on how his mind is organized and how fully its resources are used. Psychiatry too—it's amazing how a knowledge of the workings of abnormal minds can be used to suggest interesting patterns for the normal mind. Why—"

Dr. Snowden cleared his throat. The noise was slight but the effect was ominous. Diskrow hurried in to say, "Of course we were well aware of the serious step we were taking in entering this field so we added to our staff a large psychology department of which Dr. Gline is the distinguished current chief."

Dr. Snowden nodded thoughtfully at his professional colleague across the table. Dr. Gline blinked and hastily nodded back. Unnoticed, David Druxon got off a third derisive grin.

Diskrow continued: "But I do want to emphasize the psychological aspect of our work—yes, and the psychiatric too—because they've led us to such fruitful ideas as our program of 'Soft-Sell Your Superiority,' which last year won a Lasker Group Award of the American Public Health Association."

Miss Rawvetch broke in eagerly: "And which was dramatized to the public by that still-popular 3-D show, 'The Useless Five,' featuring the beloved characters of the Inferior Superman, the Mediocre Mutant, the Mixed-up Martian, the Clouded Esper and Rickety Robot."

Diskrow nodded. "*And* which also has led, by our usual reverse-twist technique, to our latest program of 'Accent the Monster in You.' Might as well call it our Monster Program." He gave Wisant a frank smile. "I guess that's the item that's been bothering you gentlemen and so I'm going to let you hear about it from the young man who created it—under Dr. Gline's close supervision. Dave, it's all yours."

Dave Cruxon stood up. He wasn't as tall as one would have expected. He nodded around rapidly.

"Gentlemen," he said in a deep but stridently annoying voice, "I had a soothing little presentation worked up for you. It was designed to show that IU's Monster Program is completely trivial and one hundred percent innocuous." He let that sink in, looked around sardonically, then went on with, "Well, I'm tossing that presentation in the junk-chewer!—because I don't think it does justice to the seriousness of the situation or to the great service IU is capable of rendering the cause of public health. I may step on some toes but I'll try not to break any phalanges."

Diskrow shot him a hard look that might have started out to be warning but ended up enigmatic. Dave grinned back at his boss, then his expression became grave.

"Gentlemen," he said, "a specter is haunting America—the specter of Depersonalization. Mr. Diskrow and Dr. Gline mentioned it but they passed over it quickly. I won't. Because depersonalization kills the mind. It doesn't mean just a weary sense of sameness and of life getting dull; it means forgetting who you are and where you stand, it means what we laymen still persist in calling insanity."

Several pairs of eyes went sharply to him at that word. Gline's chair creaked as he turned in it. Diskrow laid a hand on the psychiatrist's sleeve as if to say, "let him alone—maybe he's building toward a reverse angle."

"Why this very real and well-founded dread of depersonalization?" David Cruxon looked around. "I'll tell you why. It's not *primarily* the Machine Age, and it's not *primarily* because life is getting too complex to be easily grasped by any one person—though those are factors. No, it's because a lot of blinkered Americans, spoon-fed a sickeningly sweet version of existence, are losing touch with the basic facts of life and death, hate and love, good and evil. In particular, due to a lot too much hypno-soothing and suggestion techniques aimed at easy tranquility, they're losing a conscious sense of the black depths in their own natures—and that's what's making them fear depersonalization *and actually making them flip*—and that's what IU's Monster-in-You Program is really designed to remedy!"

There was an eruption of comments at that, with Diskrow starting to say, "Dave doesn't mean—", Gline beginning, "I disagree. I would *not* say—", and Snowden commencing, "Now if you bring in depth psychology—" but Dave added decibels to his voice and overrode them.

"Oh yes, superficially our Monster Program just consists of hints to our customers on how to appear harmlessly and handsomely sinister, but fundamentally it's going to give people a glimpse of the real Mr. Hyde in themselves—the deviant, the cripple, the outsider, the potential rapist and torture-killer—under the sugary hypno-soothed consciousness of Dr. Jekyll. In a story or play, people always love the villain best—though they'll seldom admit it—because the villain stands for the submerged, neglected and unloved dark half of themselves. In the Monster Program we're going to awaken that half for their own good. We're going to give some expression, for a change, to the natural love of adventure, risk, melodrama and sheer wickedness that's part of every man!"

"Dave, you're giving an unfair picture of your own program!" Diskrow was on his feet and almost bellowing at Cruxon. "I don't know why—maybe out of some twisted sense of self-criticism or some desire for martyrdom—but you are! Gentlemen, IU is not suggesting in its new program that people become real monsters in any way—"

"Oh, aren't we?"

"Dave, shut up and sit down! You've said too much already. I'll—"

"Gentlemen!" Wisant lifted a hand. "Let me remind you that this is a democratic conference. We can all speak freely. Any other course would be highly suspicious. So simmer down, gentlemen, simmer down." He turned toward Dave with a bland warm smile. "What Mr. Cruxon has to say interests me very much."

"I'm sure it does!" Diskrow fumed bitterly.

Dave said smoothly, "What I'm trying to get over is that people can't be pampered and soothed and wrapped away from the ugly side of reality and stay sane in the long run. Half truths kill the mind just as surely as lies. People live by the shock of reality—especially the reality of the submerged sections of their own minds. It's only when a

219

man knows the worst about himself and other men and the world that he can really take hold of the facts—brace himself against his atoms, you might say—and achieve true tranquility. People generally don't like tragedy and horror—not with the Sunday-school side of their minds, they don't—but deep down they have to have it. They have to break down the Pollyanna Partition and find what's really on the other side. An all-sugar diet is deadly. Life can be sweet, yes, but only when the contrast of horror brings out the taste. Especially the horror in a man's heart!"

"Very interesting indeed," Dr. Snowden put in quietly, even musingly, "and most lavishly expressed, if I may say so. What Mr. Cruxon has to tell us about the dark side of the human mind—the Id, the Shadow, the Death Wish, the Sick Negative: there have been many names—is of course an elementary truth. However . . ." He paused. Diskrow, still on his feet, looked at him with suspicious incredulity, as if to say, "Whose side are *you* pretending to be on?"

The smile faded from Snowden's face. "However," he continued, "it is an equally elementary truth that it is dangerous to unlock the dark side of the mind. Not every psychotherapist—not even every analyst"—here his gaze flickered toward Dr. Gline—is really competent to handle that ticklish operation. The untrained person who attempts it can easily find himself in the position of the sorcerer's apprentice. Nevertheless—"

"It's like the general question of human freedom," Wisant interrupted smoothly. "Most men are simply not qualified to use all the freedoms theoretically available to them." He looked at the IU people with a questioning smile. "For example, I imagine you all know something about the antigravity harness used by a few of our special military units? At least you know that such an item exists?"

Most of the people across the table nodded. Diskrow said, "Of course we do. We even had a demonstration model in our vaults until a few days ago." Seeing Wisant's eyebrows lift, he added impressively, "IU is often asked to help introduce new devices and materials to the public. As soon as the harness was released, we were planning to have Inferior Supe use it on 'The Useless Five' show. But then the directive came through restricting the item—largely on the grounds that it turned out to be extremely dangerous and difficult to operate—and we shipped back our model."

Wisant nodded. "Since you know that much, I can make my point about human freedom more easily. Actually (but I'll deny this if you mention it outside these chambers) the antigravity harness is not such a specialist's item. The average man can rather easily learn to operate one. In other words it is today technologically possible for us to put three billion humans in the air, flying like birds.

"But three billion humans in the air would add up to confusion, anarchy, an unimaginable aerial traffic jam. Hence—restriction and an emphasis on the dangers and extreme difficulties of using the harness. The freedom to swim through the air can't be given outright; it must be doled out gradually. The same applies to all freedoms—the freedom to love, the freedom to know the world, even the freedom to know yourself—especially your more explosive drives. Don't get me wrong now—such freedoms are fine if the person is conditioned for them." He smiled with frank pride. "That's our big job, you know: conditioning people for freedom. Using conditioning-for-freedom techniques, we ended juvenile delinquency and beat the Beat Generation. We—"

"Yes, you beat them all right!" Dave breaking in again suddenly, sounded raspingly angry. "You got all the impulses such movements expressed so well battened down, so well repressed and decontaminated, that now they're coming out as aberration, deep neurosis, mania. People are conforming and adjusting so well, they'e such carbon copies of each other, that now they're even all starting to flip at the same time. They were overprotected mentally and emotionally. They were shielded from the truth as if it were radioactive—and maybe in its way it is, because it can start chain reactions. They were treated like halfwits and that's what we're getting. Age of Tranquility! It's the Age of Psychosis! It's an open secret that the government and its Committee for Public Sanity have been doctoring the figures on mental disease for years. They're fifty, a hundred percent greater than the published ones—no one knows how much. What's this mysterious Report K we keep hearing about? Which of us hasn't had friends and family members flipping lately? Anyone can see the overcrowding at asylums, the bankruptcy of hypnotherapy. This is the year of the big payoff for generations of hysterical optimism, reassurance psychology and plain soft-soaping. It's the DTs after decades of soothing-syrup addition!"

"That's enough, Dave!" Diskrow shouted. "You're fired! You no longer speak for IU. Get out!"

"Mr. Diskrow!" Wisant's voice was stern. "I must point out to see that you're interfering with free inquiry, not to mention individuality. What your young colleague has to say interests me more and more. Pray continue, Mr. Cruxon." He smiled like a bit fat cat.

Dave answered smile with glare. "What's the use?" he said harshly. "The Monster Program's dead. You got me to cut its throat and now you'd like me to finish severing the neck, but what I did or didn't do doesn't matter a bit—you were planning to kill the Monster Program in any case. You don't want to do anything to stop the march of depersonalization. You like depersonalized people. As long as they're tranquil and manageable, you don't care—it's even O K by you if you have to keep 'em in flip factories and put the tranquility in with a needle. Government by the three Big C's of Commission, Committee and Conference! There's a fourth C, the biggest, and that's the one you stand for—government by Censorship! So long, everybody. I hope you're happy when your wives and kids start flipping—when *you* start flipping. I'm getting out."

Wisant waited until Dave got his thumb on the door, then he called, "One moment, Mr. Cruxon!" Dave held still though he did not turn around. "Miss Sturges," Wisant continued, "would you please give this to Mr. Cruxon?" He handed her the small folded sheet of pink paper from his breast pocket. Dave showed it in his pocket and went out.

"A purely personal matter between Mr. Cruxon and myself," Wisant explained, looking around with a smile. He swiftly reached across the table and snagged the scratchpad where Dave had been sitting. Diskrow seemed about to protest, then to think better of it.

"Very interesting," Wisant said after a moment, shaking his head. He looked up from the pad. "As you may recall, Mr. Cruxon only used his stylus once—just after Dr. Gline had said something about the awe-inspiring rhythms of the sea. Listen to what he wrote." He cleared his throat and read: "'*When the majestic ocean starts to sound like water slipping around in the bathtub, it's time to jump in.*'" Wisant shook his head. "I must say I feel concerned about that young man's safety . . . his *mental safety.*"

"I do too," Miss Rawvetch interjected, looking around with a helpless shrug. "My Lord, was there *anybody* that screwball forgot to antagonize?"

Dr. Snowden looked up quickly at Wisant. Then his gaze shifted out and he seemed to become abstracted.

Wisant continued: "Mr. Diskrow, I had best tell you now that in addition to my advisement against the Monster Program, I am going to have to issue an advisement that there be a review of the mental stability of IU's entire personnel. No personal reflection on any of you, but you can clearly see why."

Diskrow flushed but said nothing. Dr. Gline held very still. Dr. Snowden began to doodle furiously.

> *A monster is a master symbol of the secret and powerful, the dangerous and unknown, evoking the remotest mysteries of nature and human nature, the most dimly sensed enigmas of space, time and the hidden regions of the mind.*
>
> —Notebooks of A.S.

Masks of monsters brooded down from all the walls—full-lipped raven-browed Dracula, the cavern-eyed dome-foreheaded Phantom, the mighty patchwork visage of Dr. Frankenstein's charnel man with his filmy strangely compassionate eyes, and many earlier and later fruitions of the dark half of man's imagination. Along with them were numerous stills from old horror movies (both 3-D and flat), blown-up book illustrations, monster costumes and disguises including an Ape Man's hairy hide, and several big hand-lettered slogans such as "Accent Your Monster!" "Watch Out, Normality!" "America, Beware!" "Be Yourself—in Spades!" "Your Lady in Black," and "Mount to Your Monster!"

But Dave Cruxon did not look up at the walls of his "Monsterarium," Instead he smoothed out the pink note he had crumpled in his hand and read the crimson script for the dozenth time.

> *Please excuse my daughter for not attending lunch today, she being detained in consequence of a massive psychosis. (Signed and Sealed on the threshold of Serenity Shoals)*

The strangest thing about Dave Cruxon's reaction to the note was that he did not notice at all simply how weird it was, how strangely the central fact was stated, how queerly the irony was expressed, how like it was to an excuse sent by a pretentious mother to her child's teacher. All he had mind for was the central fact.

Now his gaze did move to the walls. Meanwhile his hands automatically but gently smoothed the note, then opened a drawer, reached far in and took out a thick sheaf of sheets of pink notepaper with crimson script, and started to add the new note to it. As he did so a brown flattened flower slipped out of the sheaf and crawled across the back of his hand. He jerked back his hands and stood staring at the pink sheets scattered over a large black blotter and at the wholly inanimate flower.

The phone tingled his wrist. He lunged at it.

"Dave Cruxon," he identified himself hoarsely.

"Serenity Shoals, Reception. I find we do have a patient named Gabrielle Wisant. She was admitted this morning. She cannot come to the phone at present or receive visitors. I would suggest, Mr. Cruxon, that you call again in about a week or that you get in touch with—"

Dave put back the phone. His gaze went back to the walls. After a while it became fixed on one particular mask on the far wall. After another while he walked slowly over to it and reached it down. As his fingers touched it, he smiled and his shoulders relaxed, as if it reassured him.

It was the face of a devil—a green devil.

He flipped a little smooth lever that could be operated by the tongue of the wearer and the eyes glowed brilliant red. Set unobtrusively in the cheeks just below the glowing eyes were the actual eyeholes of the mask—small, but each equipped with a fisheye lens so that the wearer would get a wide view.

He laid down the mask reluctantly and from a heap of costumes picked up what looked like a rather narrow silver breastplate or corselet, stiffly metallic but hinged at one side for the convenience of the person putting it on. To it were attached strong wide straps, rather like those of a parachute. A thin cable led from it to a small button-studded metal cylinder that fit in the hand. He smiled again and touched one of the buttons and the hinged breastplate rose toward the ceiling, dangling its straps and dragging upward his other hand and arm. He took his finger off the button and the breastplate sagged toward the floor. He set the whole assembly beside the mask.

Next he took up a wicked-looking pair of rather stiff gloves with horny claws set at the finger ends. He also handled and set aside a loose one-piece suit.

What distinguished both the gloves and the coverall was that they glowed whitely even in the moderately bright light of the Monsterarium.

Finally he picked up from the piled costumes what looked at first like a large handful of nothing—or rather as if he had picked up a loose cluster of lens and prisms made of so clear a material as to be almost invisible. In whatever direction he held it, the wall behind was distorted as if seen through a heat shimmer or as reflected in a crazy-house mirror. Sometimes his hand holding it disappeared partly and when he thrust his other arm into it, that arm vanished.

Actually what he was holding was a robe made of a plastic textile called light-flow fabric. Rather like lucite, the individual threads of the light-flow fabric carried or "piped" the light entering them, but unlike lucite they spilled such light after carrying it roughly halfway around a circular course. The result was that anything draped in a light-flow fabric became roughly invisible, especially against a uniform background.

Dave laid down the light-flow fabric rather more reluctantly than he had put down the mask, breastplate and other items. It was as if he had laid down a twisting shadow.

Then Dave clasped his hands behind him and began to pace. From time to time his features worked unpleasantly. The tempo of his pacing quickened. A smile came to his lips, worked into his cheeks, became a fixed, hard, graveyard grin.

Suddenly he stopped by the pile of costumes, struck an attitude, commanded hoarsely, "My hauberk, knave!" and picked up the silver breastplate and belted it around him. He tightened the straps around his thighs and shoulders, his movements now sure and swift.

Next, still grinning, he growled, "My surcoat, sirrah!" and donned the glowing coverall.

"Visard!" "Gauntlets!" He put on the green mask and the clawed gloves.

Then he took up the robe of light-flow fabric and started for the door, but he saw the scattered pink notes.

He brushed them off the black blotter, found a white stylus, and gripping it with two fingers and thumb extended from slits in the right-hand gauntlet, he wrote:

> *Dear Bobbie, Dr. Gee, et al.,*
> *By the time you read this, you will probably be hearing about me on the news channels. I'm doing one last bang-up public relations job for dear old IU. You can call it Cruxon's Crusade—the One-Man Witchcraft. I've tried out the equipment before, but only experimentally. Not this time! This time when I'm finished, no one will be able to bury the*

Monster Program. Wish me luck on my Big Hexperiment—you'll need it!—because the stench is going to be unendurable.
    Your little apprentice demon, D.C.

He threw the stylus away over his shoulder and slipped on the robe of light-flow fabric, looping part of it over his head like a cowl.

Some twenty minutes ago a depressed young man in business jerkin and shorts had entered the Monsterarium.

Now an exultant-hearted heat shimmer, with a reserve glow under its robe of invisibility, excited from it.

There is a batable ground between madness and sanity, though few tread it: laughter.
                                                    —Notebooks of A.S.

Andreas Snowden sat in Joel Wisant's bedroom trying to analyze his feelings of annoyance and uneasiness and dissatisfaction with himself—and also trying to decide if his duty lay here or back at Serenity Shoals.

The window was half open on fast-fading sunlight. Through it came a medley of hushed calls and commands, hurried footsteps, twittering female laughter and the sounds of an amateur orchestra self-consciously tuning up—the Twilight Tranquility Festival was about to begin.

Joel Wisant sat on the edge of the bed looking toward the wall. He was dressed in green tights, jerkin and peaked cap—a Robin Hood costume for the Festival. His face wore a grimly intent, distant expression. Snowden decided that here was a part of his reason for feeling annoyed—it is always irritating to be in the same room with someone who is communicating silently by micromike and softspeaker. He knew that Wisant was at the momment in touch with Security—not with Securitor Harker, who was downstairs and probably likewise engaged in silent phoning, but with the Central Security Station in New Angeles—but that was all he did know.

Wisant's face relaxed somewhat, though it stayed grim, and he turned quickly toward Snowden, who seized the opportunity to say, "Joel, when I came here this afternoon, I didn't know anything about—" but Wisant cut him short with:

"Hold it, Andy!—and listen to this. There have been at least a dozen new mass-hysteria outbreaks in the NA area in the past two hours." He rapped it out tersely. "Traffic is snarled on two ground routes and swirled in three 'copter lanes. If safety devices hadn't worked perfectly there'd have been a hatful of deaths and serious injuries. There've been panics in department stores, restaurants, offices and at least one church. The hallucinations are developing a certain amount of pattern, indicating case-to-case infection. People report something rushing invisibly through the air and buzzing them like a giant fly. I'm having the obvious lunatics held—those reporting hallucinations like green faces or devilish laughter. We can funnel 'em later to psychopathic or your place—I'll want your advice on that. The thing that bothers me most is that a garbled account of the disturbances had leaked out to the press. 'Green Demon Jolts City,' one imbecile blatted! I've given orders to have the involved 'casters and commentators picked up—got to try to limit the infection. Can you suggest any other measures I should take?"

"Why, no, Joel—it's rather out of my sphere, you know," Snowden hedged. "And I'm not too sure about your theory of infectius psychosis, though I've run across a little *folie à deux* in my time. But what I did want to talk to you about—"

"Out of your sphere, Andy? What do you mean by that?" Wisant interrupted curtly. "You're a psychologist, a psychiatrist—mass hysteria's right up your alley."

"Perhaps, but security operations aren't. And how can you be so sure, Joel, that there isn't something real behind these scares?"

"Green faces, invisible fliers, Satanic laughter? Don't be ridiculous, Andy. Why, these are just the sort of outbreaks Report K predicts. They're like the two cases here last night. Wake up, man! This is a major emergency."

"Well . . . perhaps it is. It still isn't up my alley. Get your loonies to Serenity Shoals and I'll handle them." Snowden raised his hand defensively. "Now wait a minute, Joel, there's something *I* want to say. I've had it on my mind ever since I heard about Gabby. I was shocked to hear about that, Joel—you should have told me about it earlier. Anyway, you had a big shock this morning. No, don't tell me differently—it's bound to shake a man to his roots when his daughter aberrates and does a symbolic murder on him or beside him. You simply shouldn't be driving yourself the way you are. You ought to have postponed the IU hearing this morning. It could have waited."

"What? And have taken a chance of more of that Monster material getting to the public?"

Snowden shrugged. "A day or two one way or the other could hardly have made any difference."

"I disagree," Wisant said sharply. "Even as it is, it's touched off this mass hysteria and—"

"If it is mass hysteria . . ."

Wisant shook his head impatiently. "—and we had to show Cruxon up as an irresponsible mischief-maker. You must admit that was a good thing."

"I suppose so," Snowden said slowly. "Though I'm rather sorry we stamped on him quite so hard—teased him into stamping on himself, really. He had hold of some very interesting ideas even if he was making bad use of them."

"How can you say that, Andy? Don't you psychologists ever take things seriously?" Wisant sounded deeply shocked. His face worked a little. "Look, Andy, I haven't told anybody this, but I think Cruxon was largely responsible for what happened to Gabby."

Snowden looked up sharply. "I keep forgetting you said they were acquainted. Joel, how deep did that go? Did they have dates? Do you think they were in love? Were they together much?"

"I don't know!" Wisant had started to pace. "Gabby didn't have dates. She wasn't old enough to be in love. She met Cruxon when he lectured to her communications class. After that she saw him in the daytime—only once or twice, I thought—to get material for her course. But there must have been things Gabby didn't tell me. I don't know how far they went, Andy, I don't know!"

He broke off because a plump woman in flowing Greek robes of green silk had darted into the room.

"Mr. Wisant, you're on in ten minutes!" she cried, hopping with excitement. Then she saw Snowden. "Oh, excuse me."

"That's quite all right, Mrs. Potter," Wisant told her. "I'll be there on cue."

She nodded happily, made an odd pirouette and darted out again. Simultaneously the orchestra outside, which sounded as if composed chiefly of flutes, clarinets and recorders, began warbling mysteriously.

Snowden took the opportunity to say quickly, "Listen to me, Joel. I'm worried about the way you're driving yourself after the shock you had this morning. I thought that when you came home here you'd quit, but now I find that it's just so you can participate in this community affair while keeping in touch at the same time with those NA scares. Easy does it, Joel—Harker and Security Central can handle those things."

Wisant looked at Snowden. "A man must attend to *all* his duties," he said simply. "This is *serious*, Andy, and any minute *you* may be involved whether you like it or not. What do you think the danger is of an outbreak at Serenity Shoals?"

"Outbreak?" Snowden said uneasily. "What do you mean?"

"I mean just that. You may think of your patients as children, Andy, but the cold fact is that you've got ten thousand dangerous maniacs not three miles from here under very inadequate guard. What if they are infected by the mass hysteria and stage an outbreak?"

Snowden frowned. "It's true we have some inadequately trained personnel these days. But you've got the wrong picture of the situation. Emotionally sick people don't stage mass outbreaks. They're not syndicate crooks with smuggled guns and dynamite."

"I'm not talking about plotted outbreaks. I'm talking about mass hysteria. If it can affect the sane, it can infect the insane. And I know the situation at Serenity Shoals has become very difficult—very difficult for you, Andy—with the overcrowding. I've been keeping in closer touch with that than you may know. I'm aware that you've petitioned that lobotomy, long-series electroshock and heavy narcotics be reintroduced in general treatment."

"You've got that wrong," Snowden said sharply. "A minority of doctors—a couple of them with political connections—have so petitioned. I'm dead set against it myself."

"But most families have given consent for lobotomies."

"Most families don't want to be bothered with the person who goes over the edge. They're willing to settle for anything that will 'soothe' him."

"Why do you headshrinkers always have to sneer at decent family feelings?" Wisant demanded stridently. "Now you're talking like Cruxon."

"I'm talking like myself! Cruxon was right about too much soothing syrup—especially the kind you put in with a needle or a knife."

Wisant looked at him puzzledly. "I don't understand you, Andy. You'll have to do something to control your patients as the overcrowding mounts. With this epidemic mass hysteria you'll have hundreds, maybe thousands of cases in the next few weeks. Serenity Shoals will become a—a Mind Bomb! I always thought of you as a realist, Andy."

Snowden answered sharply, "And I think that when you talk of thousands of new cases, you're extrapolating from too little data. 'Dangerous maniacs' and 'mind bombs' are theater talk—propaganda jargon. You can't mean that, Joel."

Wisant's face was white, possibly with suppressed anger, and he was trembling very slightly. "You won't say that, Andy, if your patients erupt out of Serenity Shoals and come pouring over the countryside in a great gush of madness."

Snowden stared at him. "You're afraid of them," he said softly. "That's it—you're afraid of my loonies. At the back of your mind you've got some vision of a stampede of droolers with butcher knives." Then he winced at his own words and slumped a little. "Excuse me, Joel," he said, "but really, if you think Serenity Shoals is such a dangerous place, why did you let your daughter go there?"

"Because *she* is dangerous," Wisant answered coldly. "I'm a realist, Andy."

Snowden blinked and then nodded wearily, rubbing his eyes. "I'd forgotten about this morning." He looked around. "Did it happen in this room?"

Wisant nodded.

"Where's the pillow she chopped up?" Snowden asked callously.

Wisant pointed across the room at a box that was not only wrapped and sealed as if it contained infectious material, but also corded and the cord tied in an elaborate bow. "I thought it should be carefully preserved," he said.

Snowden stared. "Did you wrap that box?"

"Yes. Why?"

Snowden said nothing.

Harker came in asking, "Been in touch with the Station the last five minutes, Joel? Two new outbreaks. A meeting of the League for Total Peace Through Total Disarmament reports that naked daggers appeared from nowhere and leaped through the air, chasing members and pinning the speaker to his rostrum by his jerkin. One man kept yelling about poltergeists—we got *him*. And the naked body of a man weighing three hundred pounds fell spang in the middle of the Congress of the SPECP—that's the Society for the Prevention of Emotional Cruelty to People. Turned out to be a week-old corpse stolen from City Hospital Morgue. Very fragrant. Joel, this mass-hysteria thing is broadening out."

Wisant nodded and opened a drawer beside his bed.

Snowden snorted. "A solid corpse is about as far from mass hysteria as you can get," he observed. "What do you want with that hot rod, Joel?"

Wisant did not answer. Harker showed surprise.

"You stuck a heat gun in your jerkin, Joel," Snowden persisted. "Why?"

Wisant did not look at him, but waved sharply for silence. Mrs. Potter had come scampering into the room, her green robes flying.

"You're on, Mr. Wisant, you're *on!*"

He nodded at her coolly and walked toward the door just as two unhappy-looking men in business jerkins and shorts appeared in it. One of them was carrying a rolled-up black blotter.

"Mr. Wisant we want to talk to you," Mr. Diskrow began. "I should say we *have* to talk to you. Dr. Gline and I were making some investigations at the IU offices—Mr. Cruxon's in particular—and we found—"

"Later," Wisant told them loudly as he strode by.

"Joel!" Harker called urgently, but Wisant did not pause or turn his head. He went out. The four men looked after him, puzzled.

*　　*　　*

The Twilight Tranquility Festival was approaching its muted climax. The Pixies and Fairies (girls) had danced their woodland ballet. The Leprechauns and Elves (boys) had made their Flashlight Parade. The Greenest Turf, the Growingest Garden, the Healthiest Tree, the Quietest 'Copter, the Friendliest House, the Rootedest Family and many other silently superlative exurban items had been identified and duly admired. The orchestra had played all manner of forest, brook and bird music. The Fauns and Pans (older boys) had sung "Tranquility So Masterful," "These Everlasting Knolls," the Safety Hymn, and "Come Let's Steal Quietly." The Sprites and Nymphs (older girls) had done their Candlelight Saraband. Representing religion, the local Zen Buddhist pastor (an old Caucasian Californian) had blessed the gathering with a sweet-sour wordlessness. And now the ever-popular Pop Wisant was going to give his yearly talk and award trophies. ("It's tremendous of him to give of himself this way," one

227

matron said, "after what he went through this morning. Did you know that she was stark naked? They wrapped a blanket around her to put her aboard the 'copter but she kept pulling it off.")

Freshly cut boughs attached to slim magnesium scaffolding made, along with the real trees, a vast leafy bower out of what had this morning been an acre of lawn. Proud mothers in green robes and dutiful fathers in green jerkins lined the walls, shepherding their younger children. Before them stood a double line of Nymphs and Sprites in virginal white ballet costumes, each holding a tall white candle tipped with blue-hearted golden flame.

Up to now it had been a rather more nervously gay Tranquility Festival than most of the mothers approved of. Even while the orchestra played there had been more than the usual quota of squeals, little shrieks, hysterical giggles, complaints of pinches and prods in the shadows, candles blown out, raids on the refreshment tables, small children darting into the bushes and having to be retrieved. But Pop Wisant's talk would smooth things out, the worriers told themselves.

And indeed as he strode between the ranked nymphs with an impassive smile and mounted the vine-wreathed podium, the children grew much quieter. In fact the hush that fell on the leafy Big Top was quite remarkable.

"Dear friends, charming neighbors and fellow old coots," he began—and then noticed that most of the audience were looking up at the green ceiling.

There had been no wind that evening, no breeze at all, but some of the boughs overhead were shaking violently. Suddenly the shaking died away. ("My, what a sudden gust that was," Mrs. Ames said to her husband. Mr. Ames nodded vaguely—he had somehow been thinking of the lines from Macbeth about Birnam Wood coming to Dunsinane.)

"Fellow householders and family members of Civil Service Knolls," Wisant began again, wiping his forehead. "In a few minutes several of you will be singled out for friendly recognition, but I think the biggest award ought to go to all of you collectively for one more year of working for tranquility . . ."

The shaking of the boughs had started up again and was traveling down the far wall. The eyes of at least half the audience were traveling with it. ("George!" Mrs. Potter said to her husband, "it looks as if a lot of crumpled cellophane were being dragged through the branches. It all wiggles." He replied, "I forgot my glasses." Mr. Ames muttered to himself, "The wood began to move. Liar and slave!")

Wisant resolutely kept his eyes away from the traveling commotion and continued, ". . . and for one more year of keeping up the good fight against violence, delinquency, irrationality . . ."

A rush of wind (looking like "curdled air," some said afterward) sped from the rear of the hall to the podium. Most of the candles were blown out, as if a giant had puffed at his giant birthday cake, and the Nymphs and Sprites squealed all the way down the double line.

The branches around Wisant shook wildly. ". . . emotionalism, superstition, and the evil powers of the imagination!" he finished with a shout, waving his arms as if to keep off bats or bees.

Twice after that he gathered himself to continue his talk, although his audience was in a considerable uproar, but each time his attention went back to a point a little above their heads. No one else saw anything where he was looking (except some "curdled air"), but Wisant seemed to see something most horrible, for his face paled, he began to back off as if the something were approaching him, he waved out his arms wildly as one might at a wasp or a bat, and suddenly he began to scream, "Keep it off me! Can't you see it, you fools? Keep it off!"

As he stepped off the podium backward he snatched something from inside his jerkin. There was a nasty *whish* in the air and those closest to him felt a wave of heat. There were a few shrill screams. Wisant fell heavily on the turf and did not move. A shining object skidded away from his hand. Mr. Ames picked it up. The pistol-shaped weapon was unfamiliar to him and he discovered only later that it was a heat gun.

The foliage of the Great Bower was still again, but a long streak of leaves in the ceiling had instantaneously turned brown. A few of these came floating down as if were autumn.

> *Sometimes I think of the whole world as one great mental hospital, its finest people only immates trying out as aides.*
> —Notebooks of A.S.

It is more fun than skindiving to soar through the air in an antigravity harness. That is, after you have got the knack of balancing your field. It is deeply thrilling to tilt your field and swoop down at a slant, or cut it entirely and just drop—and then right it or gun it and go bounding up like a rubber ball. The positive field around your head and shoulders creates an air cushion against the buffeting of the wind and your own speed.

But after a while the harness begins to chafe, your sense of balance gets tired, your gut begins to resent the slight griping effects of the field supporting you, and the solid ground which you first viewed with contempt comes to seem more and more inviting. David Cruxon discovered all of these things.

Also, it is great fun to scare people. It is fun to flash a green demon mask in their faces out of nowhere and see them blanch. Or to glow white in the dark and listen to them scream. It is fun to snarl traffic and panic pedestrians and break up solemn gatherings—the solemner the better—with rude or shocking intrusions. It is fun to know that your fellowman is little and puffed up and easily terrified and as in love with security as a baby with his bottle, and to prove it on him again and again. Yes, it is fun to be a practicing monster.

But after a while the best of Halloween pranks become monotonous, fear reactions begin to seem stereotyped, you start to see yourself in your victims, and you get ashamed of winning with loaded dice. David Cruxon discovered this too.

He had thought after he broke up the Tranquility Festival that he had hours of mischief left in him. The searing near-miss of Wisant's hot rod had left him exhilarated. (Only the light-flow fabric, diverting the infrared blast around him, had saved him from dangerous, perhaps fatal burns.) And now the idea of stampeding an insane asylum had an ironic attraction. And it *had* been good sport at first, especially when he invisibly buzzed two sandcars of aides into a panic so that they went careening over the dunes on their fat tires, headlight beams swinging frantically, and finally burst through the light fence on the landward side (giving rise to a rumor of an erupting horde of ravening madmen). *That* had been very good fun indeed, rather like harmlessly strafing war refugees, and after it Dave had shucked off his robe and hood of invisibility and put on a Glowing Phantom aerobatic display, diving and soaring over the dark tiny hills, swooping on little groups with menacing phosphorescent claws and peals of Satanic laughter.

But that didn't prove to be nearly as good fun. True, his victims squealed and sometimes ran, but they didn't seem to panic permanently like the aides. They seemed to stop after a few steps and come back to be scared again, like happily hysterical children. He began to wonder what could be going on in the minds down there if a Glowing Phantom was merely a welcome diversion. Then the feelings got hold of him that those people down there saw through him and sympathized with him. It was a strange feeling—both deflating and heartwarming.

But what really finished Dave off as a practicing monster was when they started to cheer him—cheer him as if he were their champion returning in triumph. Cruxon's Crusade—was that what he'd called it? And was this his Holy Land? As he asked himself that question he realized that he was drifting wearily down toward a hilltop on a long slow slant and he let his drift continue, landing with a long scuff.

Despite the cheers, he rather expected to be gibbered at and manhandled by the crowd that swiftly gathered around him. Instead he was patted on the back, congratulated for his exploits at New Angeles and asked intelligent questions.

*   *   *

Gabby Wisant's mind had fully determined to stay underground a long time. But that had been on the assumptions that her body would stay near Daddikins at Civil Service Knolls and that the thing that had taken control of her body would stay hungry and eager. Now those assumptions seemed doubtful, so her mind decided to risk another look round.

She found herself one of the scattered crowd of people wandering over sandhills in the dark. Some memories came to her, even of the morning, but not painfully enough to drive her mind below. They lacked pressure.

There was an older woman beside her—a rather silly and strangely affected woman by her talk, yet somehow likable—who seemed to be trying to look after her. By stages Gabby came to realize it must be her mother.

Most of the crowd were following the movements of something that glowed whitely as it swooped and whirled through the air, like a small demented comet far off course. After a bit she saw that the comet was a phosphorescent man. She laughed.

Some of the people started to cheer. She copied them. The glowing man landed on a little sandhill just ahead. Some of the crowd hurried forward. She followed them. She saw a young man stepping clumsily out of some glowing coveralls. The glow let her see his face.

"Dave, you idiot!" she squealed at him happily.

He smiled at her shamefacedly.

Dr. Snowden found Dave and Gabby and Beth Wisant on a dune just inside the break in the wire fence—the last of the debris from last night's storm. The sky was just getting light. The old man motioned back the aides with him and trudged up the sandy rise and sat down on a log.

"Oh, hello, doctor," Beth Wisant said. "Have you met Gabrielle? She came to visit me just like I told you."

Dr. Snowden nodded tiredly. "Welcome to Serenity Shoals, Miss Wisant. Glad to have you here."

Gabby smiled at him timidly. "I'm glad to be here too—I think. Yesterday . . ." Her voice trailed off.

"Yesterday you were a wild animal," Beth Wisant said loudly, "and you killed a pillow instead of your father. The doctor will tell you that's a very good sense."

Dr. Snowden said, "All of us have these somatic wild animals"—he looked at Dave—"these monsters."

Gabby said, "Doctor, do you think that Mama calling me so long ago can have had anything to do with what happened to me yesterday?"

"I see no reason why not," he replied, nodding. "Of course, there's a lot more than that that's mixed up about you."

"When *I* implant a suggestion, it works," Beth Wisant asserted.

Gabby frowned. "Part of the mixup is in the world, not me."

"The world is always mixed up," Dr. Snowden said. "It's a pretty crazy hodgepodge with sensible strains running through it, if you look for them very closely. That's one of the things we have to accept." He rubbed his eyes and looked up. "And while we're on the general topic of unpleasant facts, here's something else. Serenity Shoals has got itself one more new patient besides yourselves—Joel Wisant."

"Hum," said Beth Wisant. "Maybe now that I don't have him to go home to, I can start getting better."

"Poor Daddikins," Gabby said dully.

"Yes," Snowden continued, looking at Dave, "that last little show you put on at the Tranquility Festival—and then on top of it the news that there was an outbreak here—really broke him up." He shook his head. "Iron perfectionist. At the end he was even demanding that we drop an atomic bomb on Serenity Shoals—that was what swung Harker around to my side."

"An atom bomb!" Beth Wisant said. "The idea!"

Dr. Snowden nodded. "It does seem a little extreme."

"So you class me as a psychotic too," Dave said, a shade argumentatively. "Of course, I'll admit that after what I did—"

Dr. Snowden looked at him sourly. "I don't class you as psychotic at all—though a lot of my last-century colleagues would have taken great delight in tagging you as a psychopathic personality. I think you're just a spoiled and willful young man with no capacity to bear frustration. You're a self-dramatizer. You jumped into the ocean of aberration—that was the meaning of your note, wasn't it?—but the first waves tossed you back on the beach. Still, you got in here, which was your main object."

"How do you know that?" Dave asked.

"You'd be surprised," Dr. Snowden said wearily, "at how many more or less sane people want to get into mental hospitals these days—it's probably the main truth behind the Report K figures. They seem to think that insanity is the only great adventure left man in a rather depersonalizing age. They want to understand their fellowman at the depths, and here at least they get the opportunity." He looked at Dave meaningfully as he said that. Then he went on, "At any rate, Serenity Shoals is the safest place for you right now, Mr. Cruxon. It gets you out from under a stack of damage suits and maybe a lynch mob or two."

He stood up. "So come on then, all of you, down to Receiving," he directed, a bit grumpily. "Pick up that junk you've got there, Dave, and bring it along. We'll try to hang onto the harness—it might be useful in treating gravitational dementia. Come on, come on! I've wasted all night on you. Don't expect such concessions in the future. Serenity Shoals is no vacation resort—and no honeymoon resort either though"—he smiled flickeringly—"though some couples do try."

They followed him down to the sandy hill. The rising sun behind them struck gold from the drab buildings and faded tents ahead.

Dr. Snowden dropped back beside Dave. "Tell me one thing," he said quietly. "Was it fun being a green demon?"

Dave said, "That it was!"

Mariana

Mariana had been living in the big villa and hating the tall pine trees around it for what seemed like an eternity when she found the secret panel in the master control panel of the house.

The secret panel was simply a narrow blank of aluminum—she'd thought of it as room for more switches if they ever needed any, perish the thought!—between the air-conditioning controls and the gravity controls. Above the switches for the three-dimensional TV but below those for the robot butler and maids.

Jonathan had told her not to fool with the master control panel while he was in the city, because she would wreck anything electrical, so when the secret panel came loose under her aimlessly questing fingers and fell to the solid rock floor of the patio with a musical *twing* her first reaction was fear.

Then she saw it was only a small blank oblong of sheet aluminum that had fallen and that in the space it had covered was a column of six little switches. Only the top one was identified. Tiny glowing letters beside it spelled TREES and it was on.

* * *

When Jonathan got home from the city that evening she gathered her courage and told him about it. He was neither particularly angry nor impressed.

"Of course there's a switch for the trees," he informed her deflatingly, motioning the robot butler to cut his steak. "Didn't you know they were radio trees? I didn't want to wait twenty-five years for them and they couldn't grow in this rock anyway. A station in the city broadcasts a master pine tree and sets like ours pick it up and project it around homes. It's vulgar but convenient."

After a bit she asked timidly, "Jonathan, are the radio pine trees ghostly as you drive through them?"

"Of course not! They're solid as this house and the rock under it—to the eye and to the touch too. A person could even climb them. If you ever stirred outside you'd know these things. The city station transmits pulses of alternating matter at sixty cycles a second. The science of it is over your head."

She ventured one more question: "Why did they have the tree switch covered up?"

"So you wouldn't monkey with it—same as the fine controls on the TV. And so you wouldn't get ideas and start changing the trees. It would unsettle *me*, let me tell you, to come home to oaks one day and birches the next. I like consistency and I like pines." He looked at them out of the dining-room picture window and grunted with satisfaction.

She had been meaning to tell him about hating the pines, but that discouraged her and she dropped the topic.

About noon the next day, however, she went to the secret panel and switched off the pine trees and quickly turned around to watch them.

At first nothing happened and she was beginning to think that Jonathan was wrong again, as he so often was though would never admit, but then they began to waver and specks of pale green light churned across them and then they faded and were gone, leaving behind only an intolerably bright single point of light—just as when the TV is switched off. The star hovered motionless for what seemed a long time, then backed away and raced off toward the horizon.

Now that the pine trees were out of the way Mariana could see the real landscape. It was flat grey rock, endless miles of it, exactly the same as the rock on which the house was set and which formed the floor of the patio. It was the same in every direction. One black two-lane road drove straight across it—nothing more.

She disliked the view almost at once—it was dreadfully lonely and depressing. She switched the gravity to moon-normal and danced about dreamily, floating over the middle-of-the-room bookshelves and the grand piano and even having the robot maids dance with her, but it did not cheer her. About two o'clock she went to switch on the pine trees again, as she had intended to do in any case before Jonathan came home and was furious.

However, she found there had been changes in the column of six little switches. The TREES switch no longer had its glowing name. She remembered that it had been the top one, but the top one would not turn on again. She tried to force it from "off" to "on" but it would not move.

All the rest of the afternoon she sat on the steps outside the front door watching the black two-lane road. Never a car or a person came into view until Jonathan's tan roadster appeared, seeming at first to hang motionless in the distance and then to move only like a microscopic snail although she knew he always drove at top speed—it was one of the reasons she would never get in the car with him.

*   *   *

Jonathan was not as furious as she had feared. "Your own damn fault for meddling with it," he said curtly. "Now we'll have to get a man out here. Dammit, I hate to eat supper looking at nothing but those rocks! Bad enough driving through them twice a day."

She asked him haltingly about the barrenness of the landscape and the absence of neighbors.

"Well, you wanted to live *way out*," he told her. "You wouldn't ever have known about it if you hadn't turned off the trees."

"There's one other thing I've got to bother you with, Jonathan," she said. "Now the second switch—the one next below—has got a name that glows. It just says HOUSE. It's turned on—I haven't touched it! Do you suppose . . ."

"I want to look at this," he said, bounding up from the couch and slamming his martini-on-the-rocks tumbler down on the tray of the robot maid so that she rattled. "I bought this house as solid, but there are swindles. Ordinarily I'd spot a broadcast style in a flash, but they just might have slipped me a job relayed from some other planet or solar system. Fine thing if me and fifty other multi-megabuck men were spotted around in identical houses, each thinking his was unique."

"But if the house is based on rock like it is . . ."

"That would just make it easier for them to pull the trick, you dumb bunny!"

They reached the master control panel. "There it is," she said helpfully, jabbing out a finger . . . and hit the HOUSE switch.

For a moment nothing happened, then a white churning ran across the ceiling, the walls and furniture started to swell and bubble like cold lava, and then they were alone on a rock table big as three tennis courts. Even the master control panel was gone. The only thing that was left was a slender rod coming out of the grey stone at their feet and bearing at the top, like some mechanistic fruit, a small block with the six switches—that and an intolerably bright star hanging in the air where the master bedroom had been.

Mariana pushed frantically at the HOUSE switch, but it was unlabelled now and locked in the "off" position, although she threw her weight at it stiff-armed.

The upstairs star sped off like an incendiary bullet, but its last flashbulb glare showed her Jonathan's face set in lines of fury. He lifted his hands like talons.

"You little idiot!" he screamed, coming at her.

"No Jonathan, no!" she wailed, backing off, but he kept coming.

She realized that the block of switches had broken off in her hands. The third switch had a glowing name now: JONATHAN. She flipped it.

As his fingers dug into her bare shoulders they seemed to turn to foam rubber, then to air. His face and grey flannel suit seethed iridescently, like a leprous ghost's, then melted and ran. His star, smaller than that of the house but much closer, seared her eyes. When she opened them again there was nothing at all left of the star or Jonathan but a dancing dark after-image like a black tennis ball.

*   *   *

She was alone on an infinite flat rock plain under the cloudless, star-specked sky.

The fourth switch had its glowing name now: STARS.

It was almost dawn by her radium-dialled wristwatch and she was thoroughly chilled, when she finally decided to switch off the stars. She did not want to do it—in their slow wheeling across the sky they were the last sign of orderly reality—but it seemed the only move she could make.

She wondered what the fifth switch would say. ROCKS? AIR? Or even . . .?

She switched off the stars.

The Milky Way, arching in all its unalterable glory, began to churn, its component stars darting about like midges. Soon only one remained, brighter even than Sirius or Venus—until it jerked back, fading, and darted to infinity.

The fifth switch said DOCTOR and it was not on but off.

An inexplicable terror welled up in Mariana. She did not even want to touch the fifth switch. She set the block of switches down on the rock and backed away from it.

But she dared not go far in the starless dark. She huddled down and waited for dawn. From time to time she looked at her watch dial and at the night-light glow of the switch-label a dozen yards away.

It seemed to be growing much colder.

She read her watch dial. It was two hours past sunrise. She remembered they had taught her in third grade that the sun was just one more star.

She went back and sat down beside the block of switches and picked it up with a shudder and flipped the fifth switch.

The rock grew soft and crisply fragrant under her and lapped up over her legs and then slowly turned white.

She was sitting in a hospital bed in a small blue room with a white pin-stripe.

A sweet, mechanical voice came out of the wall, saying, "You have interrupted the wish-fulfilment therapy by your own decision. If you now recognize your sick depression and are willing to accept help, the doctor will come to you. If not, you are at liberty to return to the wish-fulfilment therapy and pursue it to its ultimate conclusion."

Mariana looked down. She still had the block of switches in her hands and the fifth switch still read DOCTOR.

The wall said, "I assume from your silence that you will accept treatment. The doctor will be with you immediately."

The inexplicable terror returned to Mariana with compulsive intensity.

She switched off the doctor.

She was back in the starless dark. The rocks had grown very much colder. She could feel icy feathers falling on her face—snow.

She lifted the block of switches and saw, to her unutterable relief, that the sixth and last switch now read, in tiny glowing letters: MARIANA.

The Beat Cluster

When the eviction order arrived, Fats Jordan was hanging in the center of the Big Glass Balloon, hugging his guitar to his massive black belly above his purple shorts.

The Big Igloo, as the large living-globe was more often called, was not really made of glass. It was sealingsilk, a cheap flexible material almost as transparent as fused silica and ten thousand times tougher—quite tough enough to hold a breathable pressure of air in the hard vacuum of space.

Beyond the spherical wall loomed the other and somewhat smaller balloons of the Beat Cluster, connected to each other and to the Big Igloo by three-foot-diameter cylindrical tunnels of triple-strength tinted sealingsilk. In them floated or swam about an assemblage of persons of both sexes in informal dress and undress and engaged in activities suitable to freefall: sleeping, sunbathing, algae tending ("rocking" spongy cradles of water, fertilizer and the green scummy "guk"), yeast culture (a rather similar business), reading, studying, arguing, stargazing, meditation, space-squash (played inside the globular court of an empty balloon), dancing, artistic creation in numerous media and the production of sweet sound (musical instruments don't depend on gravity).

Attached to the Beat Cluster by two somewhat larger sealingsilk tunnels and blocking off a good eighth of the inky, star-speckled sky, was the vast trim aluminum bulk of Research Satellite One, dazzling now in the untempered sunlight.

It was mostly this sunlight reflected by the parent satellite, however, that now illuminated Fats Jordan and the other "floaters" of the Beat Cluster. A huge sun-quilt was untidily spread (staying approximately where it was put, like all objects in freefall) against most of the inside of the Big Igloo away from the satellite. The sun-quilt was a patchwork of colors and materials on the inward side, but silvered on the outward side, as turned-over edges and corners showed. Similar "Hollywood Blankets" protected the other igloos from the undesirable heating effects of too much sunlight and, of course, blocked off the sun's disk from view.

Fats, acting as Big Daddy of the Space Beats, received the eviction order with thoughtful sadness.

"So we all of us gotta go down *there?*"

* * *

He jerked a thumb at the Earth, which looked about as big as a basketball held at arms-length, poised midway between the different silvers of the sun-quilt margin and the satellite. Dirty old Terra was in half phase: wavery blues and browns toward the sun, black away from it except for the tiny nebulous glows of a few big cities.

"That is correct," the proctor of the new Resident Civilian Administrator replied through thin lips. The new proctor was a lean man in silvery gray blouse, Bermuda shorts and moccasins. His hair was precision clipped—a quarter-inch blond lawn. He looked almost unbearably neat and hygienic contrasted with the sloppy long-haired floaters around him. He almost added, "and high time, too," but he remembered that the Administrator had enjoined him to be tactful—"firm, but tactful." He did not take this suggestion as including his nose, which had been wrinkled ever since he had entered the igloos. It was all he could do not to hold it shut with his fingers. Between the overcrowding and the loathsome Chinese gardening, the Beat Cluster *stank*.

And it was dirty. Even the satellite's precipitrons, working over the air withdrawn from the Beat Cluster via the exhaust tunnel, couldn't keep pace with the new dust. Here and there a film of dirt on the sealingsilk blurred the starfields. And once the proctor thought he saw the film *crawl*.

Furthermore, at the moment Fats Jordan was upside-down to the proctor, which added to the latter's sense of the unfitness of things. Really, he thought, these beat types were the curse of space. The sooner they were out of it the better.

"Man," Fats said mournfully, "I never thought they were going to enforce those old orders."

"The new Administrator has made it his first official act," the proctor said, smiling leanly. He went on, "The supply rocket was due to make the down-jump empty this morning, but the Administrator is holding it. There is room for fifty of your people. We will expect that first contingent at the boarding tube an hour before nightfall."

Fats shook his head mournfully and said, "Gonna be a pang, leavin' space."

His remark was taken up and echoed by various individuals spotted about in the Big Igloo.

*　　*　　*

"It's going to be a dark time," said Knave Grayson, merchant spaceman and sun-worshipper. Red beard and sheath-knife at his belt made him look like a pirate. "Do you realize the nights average twelve hours down there instead of two? And there are days when you never see Sol?"

"Gravity yoga will be a trial after freefall yoga," Guru Ishpingham opined, shifting from padmasana to a position that put his knees behind his ears in a fashion that made the proctor look away. The tall, though presently much folded and intertwined, Briton was as thin as Fats Jordan was stout. (In space the number of thins and fats tends to increase sharply, as neither overweight nor under-musculature carries the penalties it does on the surface of a planet.)

"And mobiles will be trivial after space stabiles," Erica Janes threw under her shoulder. The husky sculptress had just put the finishing touches to one of her three-dimensional free montages—and arrangement of gold, blue and red balls—and was snapping a stereophoto of it. "What really hurts," she added, "is that our kids will have to try to comprehend Newton's Three Laws of Motion in an environment limited by a gravity field. Elementary physics should never be taught anywhere in freefall."

"No more space diving, no more water sculpture, no more vacuum chemistry," chanted the Brain, fourteen-year-old fugitive from a brilliant but several times broken home down below.

"No more space pong, no more space pool," chimed in the Brainess, his sister. (Space billiards is played on the inner surface of a balloon smaller than that used for space-squash. The balls, when properly cued, follow it by reason of their slight centrifugal force.)

"Ah well, we all knew this bubble would someday burst," Gussy Friml summed up, pinwheeling lazily in her black leotards. (There is something particularly beautiful about girls in space, where gravity doesn't tug at their curves. Even fat folk don't sag in freefall. Luscious curves become truly remarkable.)

"*Yes!*" Knave Grayson agreed savagely. He'd seemed lost in brooding since his first remarks. Now as if he'd abruptly reached conclusions, he whipped out his knife and drove it through the taut sealingsilk at his elbow.

The proctor knew he shouldn't have winced so convulsively. There was only the briefest whistle of escaping air before the edge-tension in the sealingsilk closed the hole with an audible *snap.*

*   *   *

Knave smiled wickedly at the proctor. "Just testing," he explained. "I knew a roustabout who lost a foot stepping through sealingsilk. Edge-tension cut it off clean at the ankle. The foot's still orbiting around the satellite, in a brown boot with needle-sharp hobnails. This is one spot where a boy's got to remember not to put his finger in the dike."

At that moment Fats Jordan, who'd seemed lost in brooding too, struck a chilling but authoritative chord on his guitar.

    "Gonna be a *pang*
        "Leavin' space," (he sang)
    "Gonna be a *pang!*"

The proctor couldn't help wincing again. "That's all very well," he said sharply, "and I'm glad you're taking this realistically. But hadn't you better be getting a move on?"

Fats Jordan paused with his hand above the strings. "How do you mean, Mister Proctor?" he asked.

"I mean getting your first fifty ready for the down jump!"

"Oh, that," Fats said and paused reflectively. "Well, now, Mr. Proctor, that's going to take a little time."

The proctor snorted. "Two hours!" he said sharply and, grabbing at the nylon line he'd had the foresight to trail into the Beat Cluster behind him (rather like Theseus venturing into the Minotaur's probably equally smelly labyrinth), he swiftly made his way out of the Big Igloo, hand over hand, by way of the green tunnel.

The Brainess giggled. Fats frowned at her solemnly. The giggling was cut off. To cover her embarrassment the Brainess began to hum the tune to one of her semi-private songs:

        "Eskimos of space are we
        "In our igloos falling free.
        "We are space's Esquimaux,
        "Fearless vacuum-chewing hawks."

Fats tossed Gussy his guitar, which set him spinning very slowly. As he rotated, precessing a little, he ticked off points to his comrades on his stubby, ripe-banana-clustered fingers.

"Somebody gonna have to tell the research boys we're callin' off the art show an' the ballet an' terminatin' jazz Fridays. Likewise the Great Books course an' Saturday poker. Might as well inform our friends of Edison and Convair at the same time that they're gonna have to hold the 3D chess and 3D go tournaments at their place, unless they can get the new Administrator to donate them our quarters when we leave—which I doubt. I imagine he'll tote the Cluster off a ways and use the igloos for target practice. With the self-sealin' they should hold shape a long time.

"But don't exactly tell the research boys when we're goin' or why. Play it mysterioso.

"Meanwhile the gals gotta start sewin' us some ground clothes. Warm *and* decent. And we all gotta get our papers ready for the customs men, though I'm afraid most of us ain't kept nothin' but Davis passports. Heck, some of you are probably here on Nansen passports.

"An' we better pool our credits to buy wheelchairs and dollies groundside for such of us as are gonna need 'em." Fats looked back and forth dolefully from Guru Ishpingham's interwoven emaciation to his own hyper-portliness.

*   *   *

Meanwhile a space-diver had approached the Big Igloo from the direction of the satellite, entered the folds of a limp blister, zipped it shut behind him and unzipped the slit leading inside. The blister filled with a dull *pop* and the diver pushed inside through the lips. With a sharp effort he zipped them shut behind him, then threw back his helmet.

"Condition Red!" he cried. "The new Administrator's planning to ship us all ground-side! I got it straight from the Police Chief. The new A's taking those old deportation orders seriously and he's holding the—"

"We know all about that, Trace Davis," Fats interrupted him. "The new A's proctor's been here."

"Well, what are you going to *do* about it?" the other demanded.

"Nothin'," Fats serenely informed the flushed and shockheaded diver. "We're complyin'. You, Trace—" he pointed a finger—"get out of that suit. We're auctionin' it off 'long with the rest of our unworldly goods. The research boys'll be eager to bid on it. For fun-diving our spacesuits are the pinnacle."

A carrot-topped head thrust out of the blue tunnel. "Hey, Fats, we're broadcasting," its freckled owner called accusingly. "You're on in thirty seconds!"

"Baby, I clean forgot," Fats said. He sighed and shrugged. "Guess I gotta tell our downside fans the inglorious news. Remember all my special instructions, chillun. Share 'em out among you." He grabbed Gussy Friml's black ankle as it swung past him and shoved off on it, coasting toward the blue tunnel at about one fifth the velocity with which Gussy receded from him in the opposite direction.

"Hey, Fats," Gussy called to him as she bounced gently off the sun-quilt, "you got any general message for us?"

"Yeah," Fats replied, still rotating as he coasted and smiling as he rotated. "Make more guk, chillun. Yeah," he repeated as he disappeared into the blue tunnel, "take off the growth checks an' make mo' guk."

THE BEAT CLUSTER

*   *   *

Seven seconds later he was floating beside the spherical mike of the Beat Cluster's shortwave station. The bright instruments and heads of the Small Jazz Ensemble were all clustered in, sounding a last chord, while their foreshortened feet waved around the periphery. The half dozen of them, counting Fats, were like friendly fish nosing up to the single black olive of the mike. Fats had his eyes on the Earth, a little more than half night now and about as big as the snare drum standing out from the percussion rack Jordy had his legs scissored around. It was good, Fats thought, to see who you were talking to.

"Greetings, groundsiders," he said softly when the last echo had come back from the sealingsilk and died in the sun-quilt. "This is that ever-hateful voice from outer space, the voice of your old tormentor Fats Jordan, advertising no pickle juice." Fats actually said "advertising," not "advertisin'"—his diction always improved when he was on vacuum.

"And for a change, folks, I'm going to take this space to tell you something about us. No jokes this time, just tedious talk. I got a reason, a real serious reason, but I ain't saying what it is for a minute."

He contined, "You look mighty cozy down there, mighty cozy from where we're floating. Because we're way out here, you know. Out of this world, to quote the man. A good twenty thousand miles out, Captain Nemo.

"Or we're up here, if it sounds better to you that way. Way over your head. Up here with the stars and the flaming sun and the hot-cold vacuum, orbiting around Earth in our crazy balloons that look like a cluster of dingy glass grapes."

The band had begun to blow softly again, weaving a cool background to Fat's lazy phrases.

"Yes, the boys and girls are in space now, groundsiders. We've found the cheap way here, the back door. The wild ones who yesterday would have headed for the Village or the Quarter or Big Sur, the Left Bank or North Beach, or just packed up their Zen Buddhism and hit the road, are out here now, digging cool sounds as they fall round and round Dear Old Dirty. And folks, ain't you just a little glad we're gone?"

*   *   *

The band coasted into a phrase that was like the lazy swing of a hammock.

"Our cold-water flats have climbed. Our lofts have gone aloft. We've cut our pads loose from the cities and floated them above the stratosphere. It was a stiff drag for our motorcycles, Dad, but we made it. And ain't you a mite delighted to be rid of us? I know we're not all up here. But the worst of us are.

"You know, people once pictured the conquest of space entirely in terms of military outposts and machine precision." Here Burr's trumpet blew a crooked little battle cry. "They didn't leave any room in their pictures for the drifters and dreamers, the rebels and no-goods (like me, folks!) who are up here right now, orbiting with a few pounds of oxygen and a couple of gobs of guk (and a few cockroaches, sure, and maybe even a few mice, though we keep a cat) inside a cluster of smelly old balloons.

"That's a laugh in itself: the antique vehicle that first took man off the ground also being the first to give him cheap living quarters outside the atmosphere. Primitive

241

balloons floated free in the grip of the wind; we fall free in the clutch of gravity. A balloon's a symbol, you know, folks. A symbol of dreams and hopes and easily-punctured illusions. Because a balloon's a kind of bubble. But bubbles can be tough."

Led by Jordy's drums, the band worked into the Blue Ox theme from the Paul Bunyan Suite.

"Tough the same way the hemlock tents and sod huts of the American settlers were tough. We got out into space, a lot of us did, the same way the Irish and Finns got west. They built the long railroads. We built the big satellites."

Here the band shifted to the Axe theme.

"I was a welder myself. I came into space with a bunch of other galoots to help stitch together Research Satellite One. I didn't like the barracks they put us in, so I made myself a little private home of sealingsilk, a material which then was used only for storing liquids and gases—nobody'd even thought of it for human habitation. I started to meditate there in my bubble and I came to grips with a few half-ultimates and I got to like it real well in space. Same thing happened to a few of the other galoots. You know, folks, a guy who's wacky enough to wrestle sheet aluminum in vacuum in a spider suit may very well be wacky enough to get to really like stars and weightlessness and all the rest of it.

"When the construction job was done and the big research outfits moved it, we balloon men stayed on. It took some wangling but we managed. We weren't costing the Government much. And it was mighty convenient for them to have us around for odd jobs.

* * *

"That was the nucleus of our squatter cluster. The space roustabouts and rough-necks came first. The artists and oddballs, who have a different kind of toughness, followed. They got wind of what our life was like and they bought, bummed or conned their way up here. Some got space research jobs and shifted over to us at the ends of their stints. Others came up on awards trips and managed to get lost from their parties and accidentally find us. They brought their tapes and instruments with them, their sketchbooks and typers; some even smuggled up their own balloons. Most of them learned to do some sort of space work—it's good insurance on staying aloft. But don't get me wrong. We're none of us work-crazy. Actually we're the laziest cats in the cosmos: the ones who couldn't bear the thought of carrying their own weight around every day of their lives! We mostly only toil when we have to have money for extras or when there's a job that's just got to be done. We're the dreamers and funsters, the singers and studiers. We leave the 'to the stars by hard ways' business to our friends the space marines. When we use the 'ad astra per aspera' motto (was it your high school's too?) we change the last word to asparagus—maybe partly to honor the green guk we grow to get us oxygen (so we won't be chiseling too much gas from the Government) and to commemorate the food-yeasts and the other stuff we grow from our garbage.

"What sort of life do we have up here? How can we stand it cooped up in a lot of stinking balloons? Man, we're *free* out here, really free for the first time. We're floating, literally. Gravity can't bow our backs or break our arches or tame our ideas. You know, it's only out here that stupid people like us can really think. The weightlessness floats our thoughts and we can sort them. Ideas grow out here like nowhere else—it's the right environment for them.

"Anybody can get into space if he wants to hard enough. The ticket is a dream.

"That's our story, folks. We took the space road because it was the only frontier left. We had to come out, just because space was here, like the man who climbed the mountain, like the first man who skin-dove into the green deeps. Like the first man who envied a bird or a shooting star."

The music had softly soared with Fat's words. Now it died with them and when he spoke again it was without accompaniment, just a flat lonely voice.

"But that isn't quite the end of the story, folks. I told you I had something serious to impart—serious to us anyway. It looks like we're not going to be able to stay in space, folks. We've been told to get out. Because we're the wrong sort of people. Because we don't have the legal right to stay here, only the right that's conveyed by a dream.

"Maybe there's real justice in it. Maybe we've sat too long in the starbird seat. Maybe the beat generation doesn't belong in space. Maybe space belongs to soldiers and the civil service, with a slice of it for the research boys. Maybe there's somebody who wants to be in space more than we do. Maybe we deserve our comdownance. I wouldn't know.

"So get ready for a jolt, folks. We're coming back! If you *don't* want to see us, or if you think we ought to be kept safely cooped up here for security reasons—*your* security —you just might let the President know.

"This is the Beat Cluster, folks, signing off."

*   *

As Fats and the band pushed away from each other, Fats saw that the little local audience in the sending balloon had grown and that not all new arrivals were fellow floaters.

"Fats, what's this nonsense about you people privatizing your activities and excluding research personnel?" a grizzle-haired stringbean demanded. "You can't cut off recreation that way. I depend on the Cluster to keep my electron bugs happily abnormal. We even mention it downside in recruiting personnel—though we don't put it in print."

"I'm sorry, Mr. Thoms," Fats said. "No offense meant to you or to General Electric. But I got no time to explain. Ask somebody else."

"Whatdya mean, no offense?" the other demanded, grabbing at the purple shorts. "What are you trying to do, segregate the squares in space? What's wrong with research? Aren't we good enough for you?"

"Yes," put in Rumpleman of Convair, "and while you're doing that would you kindly throw some light on this directive we just received from the new A—that the Cluster's off-bounds to us and that all dating between research personnel and Cluster girls must stop? Did *you* put the new A up to that, Fats?"

"Not exactly," Fats said. "Look, boys, let up on me. I got work to do."

"Work!" Rumpleman snorted.

"Don't think you're going to get away with it," Thoms warned Fats. "We're going to protest. Why, the Old Man is frantic about the 3D chess tournament. He says the Brain's the only real competition he has up here." (The Old Man was Hubert WIllis, guiding genius of the open bevatron on the other side of the satellite.)

"The other research outfits are kicking up a fuss too," Trace Davis put in. "We spread the news like you said, and they say we can't walk out on them this way."

"Allied Microbiotics," Gussy Friml said, "wants to know who's going to take over the experiments on unshielded guk societies in freefall that we've been running for them in the Cluster."

Two of the newcomers had slightly more confidential messages for Fats.

Allison of Convair said, "I wouldn't tell you, except I think you've guessed, that I've been using the Beat Cluster as a pilot study in the psychology of anarchic human societies in freefall. If you cut yourself off from us, I'm in a hole."

"It's mighty friendly of you to feel that way," Fats said, "but right now I got to rush."

*   *   *

Space Marines Sergeant Gombert, satellite police chief, drew Fats aside and said, "I don't know why you're giving research a false impression of what's happening, but they'll find out the truth soon enough and I suppose you have your own sweet insidious reasons. Meanwhile I'm here to tell you that I can't spare the men to police your exodus. As you know, you old corner-cutter, this place is run more like a national park than a military post, in spite of its theoretical high security status. I'm going to have to ask you to handle the show yourself, using your best judgment."

"We'll certainly work hard at it, Chief," Fats said. "Hey, everybody, get cracking!"

"Understand," Gombert continued, his expression very fierce, "I'm wholly on the side of officialdom. I'll be officially overjoyed to see the last of you floaters. It just so happens that at the moment I'm short-handed."

"I understand," Fats said softly, then bellowed, "On the jump, everybody!"

But at sunset the new A's proctor was again facing him, rightside-up this time, in the Big Igloo.

"Your first fifty were due at the boarding tube an hour ago," the proctor began ominously.

"That's right," Fats assured him. "It just turns out we're going to need a little more time."

"What's holding you up?"

"We're getting ready, Mr. Proctor," Fats said. "See how busy everybody is?"

A half dozen figures were rhythmically diving around the Big Igloo, folding the sun-quilt. The sun's disk had dipped behind the Earth and only its wild corona showed, pale hair streaming across the star-fields. The Earth had gone into its dark phase, except for the faint unbalanced halo of sunlight bent by the atmosphere and for the faint dot-dot-dot of glows that were the Los Angeles-Chicago-New York line. Soft yellow lights sprang up here and there in the Cluster as it prepared for its short night. The transparent balloons seemed to vanish, leaving a band of people camped among the stars.

The proctor said, "We know you've been getting some unofficial sympathy from research and even the MP's. Don't depend on it. The new Administrator can create special deputies to enforce the deportation orders."

"He certainly can," Fats agreed earnestly, "but he don't need to. We're going ahead with it all, Mr. Proctor, as fast as we're able. F'rinstance, our groundclothes ain't sewed yet. You wouldn't want us arriving downside nine-tenths naked an' givin' the sat' a bad reputation. So just let us work an' don't joggle our elbow."

The proctor snorted. He said, "Let's not waste each other's time. You know, if you force us to do it, we can cut off your oxygen."

*   *   *

There was a moment's silence. Then from the side Trace Davis said loudly, "Listen to that! Listen to a man who'd solve the groundside housing problem by cutting off the water to the slums."

But Fats frowned at Trace and said quietly only, "If Mr. Proctor shut down on our air, he'd only be doing the satellite a disservice. Right now our algae are producing a shade more oxy than we burn. We've upped the guk production. If you don't believe me, Mr. Proctor, you can ask the atmosphere boys to check."

"Even if you do have enough oxygen," the proctor retorted, "you need our forced ventilation to keep your air moving. Lacking gravity convection, you'd suffocate in your own exhaled breath."

"We got our fans ready, battery driven," Fats told him.

"You've got no place to mount them, no rigid framework," the proctor objected.

"They'll mount on harnesses near each tunnel mouth," Fats said imperturbably. "Without gravity they'll climb away from the tunnel mouths and ride the taut harness. Besides, we're not above hand labor if it's necessary. We could use punkahs."

"Air's not the only problem," the proctor interjected. "We can cut off your food. You've been living on handouts."

"Right now," Fats said softly, "we're living half on yeasts grown from our own personal garbage. Living well, as you can see by a look at me. And if necessary we can do as much better than half as we have to. We're farmers, man."

"We can seal off the Cluster," the proctor snapped back, "and set you adrift. The orders allow it."

Fats replied, "Why not? It would make a very interesting day-to-day drama for the groundside public and for the food chemists—seeing just how long we can maintain a flourishing ecology."

The proctor grabbed at his nylon line. "I'm going to report your attitude to the new Administrator as hostile," he sputtered. "You'll hear from us again shortly."

"Give him our greetings when you do," Fats said. "We haven't had an opportunity to offer them. And there's one other thing," he called after the proctor, "I notice you hold your nose mighty rigid in here. It's a waste of energy. If you'd just steel yourself and take three deep breaths you'd never notice our stink again."

*　　*　　*

The proctor bumped into the tunnel side in his haste to be gone. Nobody laughed, which doubled the embarrassment. If they'd have laughed he could have cursed. Now he had to bottle up his indignation until he could discharge it in his report to the Administrator.

But even this outlet was denied him.

"Don't tell me a word," the new Administrator snapped at his proctor as the latter zipped into the aluminum office. "The deportation is canceled. I'll tell you about it, but if you tell anybody else I'll down-jump *you*. In the last twenty minutes I've had messages direct from the Space Marshal and the President. We must not disturb the Beat Cluster because of public opinion and because, although they don't know it, they're a pilot experiment in the free migration of people into space." ("Where else, Joel," the President had said, "do you think we're going to get people to go willingly off the Earth and achieve a balanced existence, using their own waste products? Besides, they're a floating labor pool for the satellites. And Joel, do you realize Jordan's broadcast is getting as much attention as the Russian landings on Ganymede?") The new Administrator groaned softly and asked the Unseen, "Why don't they tell a new man these things before he makes a fool of himself?"

Back in the Beat Cluster, Fats struck the last chord of "Glow Little Glow Worm." Slowly the full moon rose over the satellite, dimming the soft yellow lights that seemed to float in free space. The immemorial white globe of Luna was a little bit bigger than when viewed from Earth and its surface markings were more sharply etched. The craters of Tycho and Copernicus stood out by reason of the bright ray systems shooting out from them and the little dark smudge of the Mare Crisium looked like a curled black kitten. Fats led those around him into a new song:

> "Gonna be a *pang*
> "Leavin' space,
> "Gonna be a *pang!*
> "Gonna be a *pang*
> "Leavin' space,
> "So we won't go!"

The 64-Square Madhouse

I

Silently, so as not to shock anyone with illusions about well dressed young women, Sandra Lea Grayling cursed the day she had persuaded the *Chicago Space Mirror* that there would be all sorts of human interest stories to be picked up at the first international grandmaster chess tournament in which an electronic computing machine was entered.

Not that there weren't enough humans around, it was the interest that was in doubt. The large hall was crammed with energetic dark-suited men of whom a disproportionately large number were bald, wore glasses, were faintly untidy and indefinably shabby, had Slavic or Scandinavian features, and talked foreign languages.

They yakked interminably. The only ones who didn't were scurrying individuals with the eager-zombie look of officials.

Chess sets were everywhere—big ones on tables, still bigger diagram-type electric ones on walls, small peg-in sets dragged from side pockets and manipulated rapidly as part of the conversational ritual and still smaller folding sets in which the pieces were the tiny magnetized disks used for playing in free-fall.

There were signs featuring largely mysterious combination of letters: FIDE, WBM, USCF, USSF, USSR, and UNESCO. Sandra felt fairly sure about the last three.

The many clocks, bedside table size, would have struck a familiar note except that they had little red flags and wheels sprinkled over their faces and they were all in pairs, two clocks to a case. That Siamese-twin clocks should be essential to a chess tournament struck Sandra as a particularly maddening circumstance.

*   *   *

Her last assignment had been to interview the pilot pair riding the first American manned circum-lunar satellite—and the five alternate pairs who hadn't made the flight. This tournament hall seemed to Sandra much further out of this world.

Overheard scraps of conversation in reasonably intelligible English were not particularly helpful. Samples:

"They say the Machine has been programmed to play nothing but pure Barcza System and Indian Defenses—and the Dragon Formation if anyone pushes the King Pawn."

247

"Hah! In that case . . ."

"The Russians have come with ten trunkfuls of prepared variations and they'll gang up on the Machine at adjournments. What can one New Jersey computer do against four Russian grandmasters?"

"I heard the Russians have been programmed—with hypnotic cramming and somno-briefing. Votbinnik had a nervous breakdown."

"Why, the Machine hasn't even a *Hauptturnier* or an intercollegiate won. It'll over its head be playing."

"Yes, but maybe like Capa at San Sebastian or Morphy or Willie Angler at New York. The Russians will look like potzers."

"Have you studied the scores of the match between Moon Base and Circum-Terra?"

"Not worth the trouble. The play was feeble. Barely Expert Rating."

Sandra's chief difficulty was that she knew absolutely nothing about the game of chess—a point that she had slid over in conferring with the powers at the *Space Mirror*, but that now had begun to weigh on her. How wonderful it would be, she dreamed, to walk out this minute, find a quiet bar and get pie-eyed in an evil, ladylike way.

"Perhaps mademoiselle would welcome a drink?"

"You're durn tootin' she would!" Sandra replied in a rush, and then looked down apprehensively at the person who had read her thoughts.

It was a small sprightly elderly man who looked like a somewhat thinned down Peter Lorre—there was that same impression of the happy Slavic elf. What was left of his white hair was cut very short, making a silvery nap. His pince-nez had quite thick lenses. But in sharp contrast to the somberly clad men around them, he was wearing a pearl-gray suit of almost exactly the same shade as Sandra's—a circumstance that created for her the illusion that they were fellow conspirators.

"Hey, wait a minute," she protested just the same. He had already taken her arm and was piloting her toward the nearest flight of low wide stairs. "How did you know I wanted a drink?"

"I could see that mademoiselle was having difficulty swallowing," he replied, keeping them moving. "Pardon me for feasting my eyes on your lovely throat."

"I didn't suppose they'd serve drinks here."

"But of course." They were already mounting the stairs. "What would chess be without coffee or schnapps?"

"Okay, lead on," Sandra said. "You're the doctor."

"Doctor?" He smiled widely. "You know, I like being called that."

"Then the name is yours as long as you want it—Doc."

* * *

Meanwhile the happy little man had edged them into the first of a small cluster of tables, where a dark-suited jabbering trio was just rising. He snapped his fingers and hissed through his teeth. A white-aproned waiter materialized.

"For myself black coffee," he said. "For mademoiselle rhine wine and seltzer?"

"That'd go fine." Sandra leaned back. "Confidentially, Doc, I *was* having trouble swallowing . . . well, just about everything here."

He nodded. "You are not the first to be shocked and horrified by chess," he assured her. "It is a curse of the intellect. It is a game for lunatics—or else it creates them. But what brings a sane and beautiful young lady to this 64-square madhouse?"

Sandra briefly told him her story and her predicament. By the time they were served, Doc had absorbed the one and assessed the other.

"You have one great advantage," he told her. "You know nothing whatsoever of chess—so you will be able to write about it understandably for your readers." He swallowed half his demitasse and smacked his lips. "As for the Machine—you *do* know, I suppose, that it is not a humanoid metal robot, walking about clanking and squeaking like a late medieval knight in armor?"

"Yes, Doc, but . . ." Sandra found difficulty in phrasing the question.

"Wait." He lifted a finger. "I think I know what you're going to ask. You want to know why, if the Machine works at all, it doesn't work perfectly, so that it always wins and there is no contest. Right?"

Sandra grinned and nodded. Doc's ability to interpret her mind was as comforting as the bubbly, mildly astringent mixture she was sipping.

He removed his pince-nez, massaged the bridge of his nose and replaced them.

"If you had," he said, "a billion computers all as fast as the Machine, it would take them all the time there ever will be in the universe just to play through all the possible games of chess, not to mention the time needed to classify those games into branching families of wins for White, wins for Black and draws, and the additional time required to trace out chains of key-moves leading always to wins. So the Machine can't play chess like God. What the Machine can do is examine all the likely lines of play for about eight moves ahead—and then decide which is the best move on the basis of capturing enemy pieces, working toward checkmate, establishing a powerful central position and so on."

*   *   *

"That sounds like the way a man would play a game," Sandra observed. "Look ahead a little way and try to make a plan. You know, like getting out trumps in bridge or setting up a finesse."

"Exactly!" Doc beamed at her approvingly. "The Machine *is* like a man. A rather peculiar and not exactly pleasant man. A man who always abides by sound principles, who is utterly incapable of flights of genius, but who never makes a mistake. You see, you are finding human interest already, even in the Machine."

Sandra nodded. "Does a human chess player—a grandmaster, I mean—ever look eight moves ahead in a game?"

"Most assuredly he does! In crucial situations, say where there's a chance of winning at once by trapping the enemy king, he examines many more moves ahead than that—thirty or forty even. The Machine is probably programmed to recognize such situations and do something of the same sort, though we can't be sure from the information World Business Machines has released. But in most chess positions the possibilities are so very nearly unlimited that even a grandmaster can only look a very few moves ahead and must rely on his judgment and experience and artistry. The equivalent of those in the Machine is the directions fed into it before it plays a game."

"You mean the programming?"

"Indeed yes! The programming is the crux of the problem of the chess-playing computer. The first practical model, reported by Bernstein and Roberts of IBM in 1958 and which looked four moves ahead, was programmed so that it had a greedy worried tendency to grab at enemy pieces and to retreat its own whenever they were attacked. It had a personality like that of a certain kind of chess-playing dub—a dull-brained woodpusher afraid to take the slightest risk of losing material—but a dub who could almost always beat an utter novice. The WBM machine here in the hall operates about a million times as fast. Don't ask me how, I'm no physicist, but it depends on the new transistors and something they call hypervelocity, which in turn depends on keeping parts of the Machine at a temperature near absolute zero. However, the result is that the Machine can see eight moves ahead and is capable of being programmed much more craftily."

"A million times as fast as the first machine, you say, Doc? And yet it only sees twice as many moves ahead?" Sandra objected.

"There is a geometrical progression involved there," he told her with a smile. "Believe me, eight moves ahead is a lot of moves when you remember that the Machine is errorlessly examining every one of thousands of variations. Flesh-and-blood chess masters have lost games by blunders they could have avoided by looking only one or two moves ahead. The Machine will make no such oversights. Once again, you see, you have the human factor, in this case working for the Machine."

"Savilly, I have been looking allplace for you!"

A stocky, bull-faced man with a great bristling shock of blac, gray-flecked hair had halted abruptly by their table. He bent over Doc and began to whisper explosively in a guttural foreign tongue.

II

Sandra's gaze traveled beyond the balustrade. Now that she could look down at it, the central hall seemed less confusedly crowded. In the middle, toward the far end, were five small tables spaced rather widely apart and with a chessboard and men and a pair of the Siamese clocks set out on each. To either side of the hall were tiers of temporary seats, about half of them occupied. There were at least as many more people still wandering about.

On the far wall was a big electric scoreboard and also, above the corresponding tables, five large dully glassy chessboards, the White squares in light gray, the Black squares in dark.

One of the five wall chessboards was considerably larger than the other four—the one above the Machine.

Sandra looked with quickening interest at the console of the Machine—a bank of keys and some half-dozen panels of rows and rows of tiny telltale lights, all dark at the moment. A thick red velvet cord on little brass standards ran around the Machine at a distance of about ten feet. Inside the cord were only a few gray-smocked men. Two of them had just laid a black cable to the nearest chess table and were attaching it to the Siamese clock.

Sandra tried to think of a being who always checked everything, but only within limits beyond which his thoughts never ventured, and who never made a mistake . . .

"Miss Grayling! May I present to you Igor Jandorf."

She turned back quickly with a smile and a nod.

"I should tell you, Igor," Doc continued, "that Miss Grayling represents a large and influential Midwestern newspaper. Perhaps you have a message for her readers."

The shock-headed man's eyes flashed. "I most certainly do!" At that moment the waiter arrived with a second coffee and wine-and-seltzer. Jandorf seized Doc's new demitasse, drained it, set it back on the tray with a flourish and drew himself up.

* * *

"Tell your readers, Miss Grayling," he proclaimed, fiercely arching his eyebrows at her and actually slapping his chest, "that I, Igor Jandorf, will defeat the Machine by the living force of my human personality! Already I have offered to play it an informal game blindfold—I, who have played 50 blindfold games simultaneously! Its owners refuse me. I have challenged it also to a few games of rapid-transit—an offer no true grandmaster would dare ignore. Again they refuse me. I predict that the Machine will play like a great oaf—at least against *me*. Repeat: I, Igor Jandorf, by the living force of my human personality, will defeat the Machine. Do you have that? You can remember it?"

"Oh, yes," Sandra assured him, "but there are some other questions I very much want to ask you, Mr. Jandorf."

"I am sorry, Miss Grayling, but I must clear my mind now. In ten minutes they start the clocks."

While Sandra arranged for an interview with Jandorf after the day's playing session, Doc reordered his coffee.

"One expects it of Jandorf," he explained to Sandra with a philosophic shrug when the shock-headed man was gone. "At least he didn't take your wine-and-seltzer. Or did he? One tip I have for you: don't call a chess master Mister, call him Master. They all eat it up."

"Gee, Doc, I don't know how to thank you for everything. I hope I haven't offended Mis—Master Jandorf so that he doesn't—"

"Don't worry about that. Wild horses couldn't keep Jandorf away from a press interview. You know, his rapid-transmit challenge was cunning. That's a minor variety of chess where each player gets only ten seconds to make a move. Which I don't suppose would give the Machine time to look three moves ahead. Chess players would say that the Machine has a very slow sight of the board. This tournament is being played at the usual international rate of 15 moves an hour, and—"

"Is that why they've got all those crazy clocks?" Sandra interrupted.

"Oh, yes. Chess clocks measure the time each player takes in making his moves. When a player makes a move he presses a button that shuts his clock off and turns his opponent's on. If a player uses too much time, he loses as surely as if he were checkmated. Now since the Machine will almost certainly be programmed to take an equal amount of time on successive moves, a rate of 15 moves an hour means it will have 4 minutes a move—and it will need every second of them! Incidentally it was typical Jandorf bravado to make a point of a blindfold challenge—just as if the Machine weren't playing blindfold itself. Or *is* the Machine blindfold? How do you think of it?"

"Gosh, I don't know. Say, Doc, is it really true that Master Jandorf had played 50 games at once blindfolded? I can't believe that."

* * *

"Of course not!" Doc assured her. "It was only 49 and he lost two of those and drew five. Jandorf always exaggerates. It's in his blood."

"He's one of the Russians, isn't he?" Sandra asked. "Igor?"

Doc chuckled. "Not exactly," he said gently. "He is originally a Pole and now he has Argentinian citizenship. You have a program, don't you?"

Sandra started to hunt through her pocketbook, but just then two lists of names lit up on the big electric scoreboard.

THE PLAYERS

William Angler, USA
Bela Grabo, Hungary
Ivan Jal, USSR
Igor Jandorf, Argentina
Dr. S. Krakatower, France
Vassily Lysmov, USSR
The Machine, USA (programmed by Simon Great)
Maxim Serek, USSR
Moses Sherevsky, USA
Mikhail Votbinnik, USSR
Tournament Director: Dr. Jan Vanderhoef

FIRST ROUND PAIRINGS

Sherevski vs. Serek
Jal vs. Angler
Jandorf vs. Votbinnik
Lysmov vs. Krakatower
Grabo vs. Machine

"Cripes, Doc, they all sound like they were Russians," Sandra said after a bit. "Except this Willie Angler. Oh, he's the boy wonder, isn't he?"

Doc nodded. "Not such a boy any longer, though. He's ... Well, speak to the Devil's children ... Miss Grayling, I have the honor of presenting to you the only grandmaster ever to have been ex-chess-champion of the United States while still technically a minor—Master William Augustus Angler."

A tall, sharply-dressed young man with a hatchet face pressed the old man back into his chair.

"How are you, Savvy, old boy old boy?" he demanded. "Still chasing the girls, I see."

"Please, Willie, get off me."

"Can't take it, huh?" Angler straightened up somewhat. "Hey waiter! Where's that chocolate malt? I don't want it *next* year. About that *ex-*, though. I was swindled, Savvy. I was robbed."

"Willie!" Doc said with some asperity. "Miss Grayling is a journalist. She would like to have a statement from you as to how you will play against the Machine."

*   *   *

Angler grinned and shook his head sadly. "Poor old Machine," he said. "I don't know why they take so much trouble polishing up that pile of tin just so that I can give it a hit in the head. I got a hatful of moves it'll burn out all its tubes trying to answer. And if it gets too fresh, how about you and me giving its low-temperature section the hotfoot, Savvy? The money WBM's putting up is okay, though. That first prize will just fit the big hole in my bank account."

"I know you haven't the time now, Master Angler," Sandra said rapidly, "but if after the playing session you could grant me—"

"Sorry, babe," Angler broke in with a wave of dismissal. "I'm dated up for two months in advance. Waiter! I'm here, not there!" And he went charging off.

Doc and Sandra looked at each other and smiled.

"Chess masters aren't exactly humble people, are they?" she said.

Doc's smile became tinged with sad understanding. "You must excuse them, though," he said. "They really get so little recognition or recompense. This tournament is an exception. And it takes a great deal of ego to play greatly."

"I suppose so. So World Business Machines is responsible for this tournament?"

"Correct. Their advertising department is interested in the prestige. They want to score a point over their great rival."

"But if the Machine plays badly it will be a black eye for them," Sandra pointed out.

"True," Doc agreed thoughtfully. "WBM must feel very sure . . . It's the prize money they've put up, of course, that's brought the world's greatest players here. Otherwise half of them would be holding off in the best temperamental-artist style. For chess players the prize money is fabulous—$35,000, with $15,000 for first place, and all expenses paid for all players. There's never been anything like it. Soviet Russia is the only country that has ever supported and rewarded her best chess players at all adequately. I think the Russian players are here because UNESCO and FIDE (that's *Federation Internationale des Echecs*—the international chess organization) are also backing the tournament. And perhaps because the Kremlin is hungry for a little prestige now that its space program is sagging."

"But if a Russian doesn't take first place it will be a black eye for them."

Doc frowned. "True, in a sense. *They* must feel very sure . . . Here they are now."

III

Four men were crossing the center of the hall, which was clearing, toward the tables at the other end. Doubtless they just happened to be going two by two in close formation, but it gave Sandra the feeling of a phalanx.

"The first two are Lysmov and Votbinnik," Doc told her. "It isn't often that you see the current champion of the world—Votbinnik—and an ex-champion arm in arm. There are two other persons in the tournament who have held that honor—Jal and Vanderhoef the director, way back."

"Will whoever wins this tournament become champion?"

"Oh no. That's decided by two-player matches—a very long business—after elimination tournaments between leading contenders. This tournament is a round robin: each player plays one game with every other player. That means nine rounds."

"Anyway there *are* an awful lot of Russians in the tournament," Sandra said, consulting her program. "Four out of ten have USSR after them. And Bela Grabo, Hungary —that's a satellite. And Sherevsky and Krakatower are Russian-sounding names."

"The proportion of Soviet to American entries in the tournament represents pretty fairly the general difference in playing strength between the two countries," Doc said judiciously. "Chess mastery moves from land to land with the years. Way back it was the Moslems and the Hindus and Persians. Then Italy and Spain. A little over a hundred years ago it was France and England. Then Germany, Austria and the New World. Now it's Russia—including of course the Russians who have run away from Russia. But don't think there aren't a lot of good Anglo-Saxon types who are masters of the first water. In fact, there are a lot of them here around us, though perhaps you don't think so. It's just that if you play a lot of chess you get to looking Russian. Once it probably made you look Italian. Do you see that short bald-headed man?"

"You mean the one facing the Machine and talking to Jandorf?"

"Yes, Now that's one with a lot of human interest. Moses Sherevsky. Been champion of the United States many times. A very strict Orthodox Jew. Can't play chess on Fridays or on Saturdays before sundown." He chuckled. "Why, there's even a story going around that one rabbi told Sherevsky it would be unlawful for him to play against the Machine because it is technically a *golem*—the clay Frankenstein's monster of Hebrew legend."

Sandra asked, "What about Grabo and Krakatower?"

*　　*　　*

Doc gave a short scornful laugh. "Krakatower! Don't pay any attention to *him*. A senile has-been, it's a scandal he's been allowed to play in this tournament! He must have pulled all sorts of strings. Told them that his lifelong services to chess had won him the honor and that they had to have a member of the so-called Old Guard. Maybe he even got down on his knees and cried—and all the time his eyes on that expense money and the last-place consolation prize! Yet dreaming schizophrenically of beating them all! Please, don't get me started on Dirty Old Krakatower."

"Take it easy, Doc. He sounds like he would make an interesting article. Can you point him out to me?"

"You can tell him by his long white beard with coffeestains. I don't see it anywhere, though. Perhaps he's shaved it off for the occasion. It would be like that antique womanizer to develop senile delusions of youthfulness."

"And Grabo?" Sandra pressed, suppressing a smile at the intensity of Doc's animosity.

Doc's eyes grew thoughtful. "About Bela Grabo (why are three out of four Hungarians named Bela?) I will tell you only this: That he is a very brilliant player and that the Machine is very lucky to have drawn him as its first opponent."

He would not amplify his statement. Sandra studied the scoreboard again.

"This Simon Great who's down as programming the Machine. He's a famous physicist, I suppose?"

"By no means. That was the trouble with some of the early chess-playing machines —they were programmed by scientists. No, Simon Great is a psychologist who at one time was a leading contender for the world's chess championship. I think WBM was surprisingly shrewd to pick him for the programming job. Let me tell you— No, better yet—"

Doc shot to his feet, stretched an arm on high and called out sharply, "Simon!"

A man some four tables away waved back and a moment later came over.

"What is it, Savilly?" he asked. "There's hardly any time, you know."

*   *   *

The newcomer was of middle-height, compact of figure and feature, with graying hair cut short and combed sharply back.

Doc spoke his piece for Sandra.

Simon Great smiled thinly. "Sorry," he said, "but I am making no predictions and we are giving out no advance information on the programming of the Machine. As you know, I have had to fight the Players' Committee tooth and nail on all sorts of points about that and they have won most of them. I am not permitted to re-program the Machine at adjournments—only between games (I did insist on that and get it!) And if the Machine breaks down during a game, its clock keeps running on it. My men are permitted to make repairs—if they can work fast enough."

"That makes it very tough on you," Sandra put in. "The Machine isn't allowed any weaknesses."

Great nodded soberly. "And now I must go. They've almost finished the count-down, as one of my technicians keeps on calling it. Very pleased to have met you, Miss Grayling—I'll check with our PR man on that interview. Be seeing you, Savvy."

The tiers of seats were filled now and the central space almost clear. Officials were shooing off a few knots of lingerers. Several of the grandmasters, including all four Russians, were seated at their tables. Press and company cameras were flashing. The four smaller wallboards lit up with the pieces in the opening position—white for White and red for Black. Simon Great stepped over the red velvet cord and more flash bulbs went off.

"You know, Doc," Sandra said, "I'm a dog to suggest this, but what if this whole thing were a big fake? What if Simon Great were really playing the Machine's moves? There would surely be some way for his electricians to rig—"

Doc laughed happily—and so loudly that some people at the adjoining tables frowned.

"Miss Grayling, that is a wonderful idea! I will probably steal it for a short story. I still manage to write and place a few in England. No, I do not think that is at all likely. WBM would never risk such a fraud. Great is completely out of practice for actual tournament play, though not for chess-thinking. The difference in style between a computer and a man would be evident to any expert. Great's own style is remembered and would be recognized—though, come to think of it, his style was often described as being machine-like . . ." For a moment Doc's eyes became thoughtful. Then he smiled again. "But no, the idea is impossible. Vanderhoef as Tournament Director has played two or three games with the Machine to assure himself that it operates legitimately and has grandmaster skill."

"Who won?" Sandra asked.

Doc shrugged. "The scores weren't released. It was very hush-hush. But about your idea, Miss Grayling—did you ever read about Maelzel's famous chessplaying automaton of the 19th Century? That one too was supposed to work by machinery (cogs and gears, not electricity) but actually it had a man hidden inside it—your Edgar Poe exposed the fraud in a famous article. In *my* story I think the chess robot will break down while it is being demonstrated to a millionaire purchaser and the young inventor will have to win its game for it to cover up and swing the deal. Only the millionaire's daughter, who is really a better player than either of them . . . yes, yes! Your Ambrose Bierce too wrote a story about a chessplaying robot of the clickety-clank-grr kind who murdered his creator, crushing him like an iron grizzly bear when the man won a game from him. Tell me, Miss Grayling, do you find yourself imagining this Machine putting out angry tendrils to strangle its opponents, or beaming rays of death and hypnotism at them? I can imagine . . ."

While Doc chattered happily on about chessplaying robots and chess stories, Sandra found herself thinking about him. A writer of some sort evidently and a terrific chess buff. Perhaps he was an actual medical doctor. She'd read something about two or three coming over with the Russian squad. But Doc certainly didn't sound like a Soviet citizen.

He was older than she'd first assumed. She could see that now that she was listening to him less and looking at him more. Tired, too. Only his dark-circled eyes shone with unquenchable youth. A useful old guy, whoever he was. An hour ago she'd been sure she was going to muff this assignment completely and now she had it laid out cold. For the umpteenth time in her career Sandra shied away from the guilty thought that she wasn't a writer at all or even a reporter, she just used dime-a-dozen female attractiveness to rope a susceptible man (young, old, American, Russian) and pick his brain . . .

She realized suddenly that the whole hall had become very quiet.

Doc was the only person still talking and people were looking at them disapprovingly. All five wall-boards were lit up and the changed position of a few pieces showed that opening moves had been made on four of them, including the Machine's. The central space between the tiers of seats were completely clear now, except for one man hurrying across it in their direction with the rapid yet quiet, almost tip-toe walk that seemed to mark all the officials. *Like morticians' assistants*, she thought. He rapidly mounted the stairs and halted on their table, his eyebrows went up, and he made a beeline for Doc. Sandra wondered if she should warn him that he was about to be shushed.

The official laid a hand on Doc's shoulder. "Sir!" he said agitatedly. "Do you realize that they've started your clock, Dr. Krakatower?"

*   *   *

Sandra became aware that Doc was grinning at her. "Yes, it's true enough, Miss Grayling," he said. "I trust you will pardon the deception, though it was hardly one, even technically. Every word I told you about Dirty Old Krakatower is literally true. Except the long white beard—he never wore a beard after he was 35—that part was an out-and-out lie! Yes, yes! I will be along in a moment! Do not worry, the spectators will get their money's worth out of me! And WBM did not with its expense account buy my soul—that belongs to the young lady here."

Doc rose, lifted her hand and kissed it. "Thank you, mademoiselle, for a charming interlude. I hope it will be repeated. Incidentally, I should say that besides . . . (Stop pulling at me, man!—there can't be five minutes on my clock yet!) . . . that besides being Dirty Old Krakatower, grandmaster emeritus, I am also the special correspondent of

256

the *London Times*. It is always pleasant to chat with a colleague. Please do not hesitate to use in your articles any of the ideas I tossed out, if you find them worthy—I sent in my own first dispatch two hours ago. Yes, yes, I come! Au revoir, mademoiselle!"

He was at the bottom of the stairs when Sandra jumped up and hurried to the balustrade.

"Hey, Doc!" she called.

He turned.

"Good luck!" she shouted and waved.

He kissed his hand to her and went on.

People glared at her then and a horrified official came hurrying. Sandra made big frightened eyes at him, but she couldn't hide her grin.

IV

Sitzfleisch (which roughly means endurance—"sitting flesh" or "buttock meat") is the quality needed above all others by tournament chess players—and their audiences.

After Sandra had watched the games (the players' faces, rather—she had a really good pair of zoomer glasses) for a half hour or so, she had gone to her hotel room, written her first article (interview with the famous Dr. Krakatower), sent it in and then come back to the hall to see how the games had turned out.

They were still going on, all five of them.

The press section was full, but two boys and a girl of high-school age obligingly made room for Sandra on the top tier of seats and she tuned in on their whispered conversation. The jargon was recognizably related to that which she'd gotten a dose of on the floor, but gamier. Players did not sacrifice pawns, they sacked them. No one was ever defeated, only busted. Pieces weren't lost but blown. The Ruy Lopez was the Dirty Old *Rooay*—and incidentally a certain set of opening moves named after a long-departed Spanish churchman, she now discovered from Dave, Bill and Judy, whose sympathetic help she won by frequent loans of her zoomer glasses.

The four-hour time control point—two hours and 30 moves for each player—had been passed while she was sending in her article, she learned, and they were well on their way toward the next control point—an hour more and 15 moves for each player—after which unfinished games would be adjourned and continued at a special morning session. Sherevsky had had to make 15 moves in two minutes after taking an hour earlier on just one move. But that was nothing out of the ordinary, Dave had assured her in the same breath, Sherevsky was always letting himself get into "fantastic time-pressure" and then wriggling out of it brilliantly. He was apparently headed for a win over Serek. *Score one for the USA over the USSR*, Sandra thought proudly.

Votbinnik had Jandorf practically in *Zugzwang* (his pieces all tied up, Bill explained) and the Argentinian would be busted shortly. Through the glasses Sandra could see Jandorf's thick chest rise and fall as he glared murderously at the board in front of him. By contrast Votbinnik looked like a man lost in reverie.

Dr. Krakatower had lost a pawn to Lysmov but was hanging on grimly. However, Dave would not give a plugged nickle for his chances against the former world's champion, because "those old ones always weaken in the sixth hour."

257

"You for-get the bio-logical mir-acle of Doc-tor Las-ker," Bill and Judy changed as one.

"Shut up," Dave warned them. An official glared angrily from the floor and shook a finger. Much later Sandra discovered that Dr. Emanuel Lasker was a philosopher-mathematician who, after holding the world's championship for 26 years, had won a very strong tournament (New York 1924) at the age of 56 and later almost won another (Moscow 1935) at the age of 67.

*　　*　　*

Sandra studied Doc's face carefully through her glasses. He looked terribly tired now, almost a death's head. Something tightened in her chest and she looked away quickly.

The Angler-Jal and Grabo-Machine games were still ding-dong contests, Dave told her. If anything, Grabo had a slight advantage. The Machine was "on the move," meaning that Grabo had just made a move and was waiting the automaton's reply.

The Hungarian was about the most restless "waiter" Sandra could imagine. He twisted his long legs constantly and writhed his shoulders and about every five seconds he ran his hands back through his unkempt tassle of hair.

Once he yawned self-consciously, straightened himself and sat very compactly. But almost immediately he was writhing again.

The Machine had its own mannerisms, if you could call them that. Its dim, unobtrusive telltale lights were winking on and off in a fairly rapid, random pattern. Sandra got the impression that from time to time Grabo's eyes were trying to follow their blinking, like a man watching fireflies.

Simon Great sat impassively behind a bare table next to the Machine, his five gray-smocked technicians grouped around him.

A flushed-faced, tall, distinguished-looking elderly gentleman was standing by the Machine's console. Dave told Sandra it was Dr. Vanderhoef, the Tournament Director, one-time champion of the world.

"Another old potzer like Krakatower, but with sense enough to know when he's licked," Bill characterized harshly.

"Youth, ah, un-van-quish-able youth," Judy chanted happily by herself. "Flashing like a meteor across the chess fir-ma-ment. Morphy, Angler, Judy Kaplan . . ."

"Shut up! They really will throw us out," Dave warned her and the explained in whispers to Sandra that Vanderhoef and his assistants had the nervous-making job of feeding into the Machine the moves made by its opponent, "so everyone will know it's on the level, I guess." He added, "It means the Machine loses a few seconds every move, between the time Grabo punches the clock and the time Vanderhoef gets the move fed into the Machine."

Sandra nodded. The players were making it as hard on the Machine as possible, she decided with a small rush of sympathy.

*　　*　　*

Suddenly there was a tiny movement of the gadget attached from the Machine to the clocks on Grabo's table and a faint *click*. But Grabo almost leapt out of his skin.

Simultaneously a red castle-topped piece (one of the Machine's rooks, Sandra was informed) moved four squares sideways on the big electric board above the Machine. An official beside Dr. Vanderhoef went over to Grabo's board and carefully moved the corresponding piece. Grabo seemed about to make some complaint, then apparently thought better of it and plunged into brooding cogitation over the board, elbows on the table, both hands holding his head and fiercely massaging his scalp.

The Machine let loose with an unusually rapid flurry of blinking. Grabo straightened up, seemed again about to make a complaint, then once more to repress the impulse. Finally he moved a piece and punched his clock. Dr. Vanderhoef immediately flipped four levers on the Machine's console and Grabo's move appeared on the electric board.

Grabo sprang up, went over to the red velvet cord and motioned agitatedly to Vanderhoef.

There was a short conference, inaudible at the distance, during which Grabo waved his arms and Vanderhoef grew more flushed. Finally the latter went over to Simon Great and said something, apparently with some hesitancy. But Great smiled obligingly, sprang to his feet, and in turn spoke to his technicians, who immediately fetched and unfolded several large screens and set them in front of the Machine, masking the blinking lights. *Blindfolding it,* Sandra found herself thinking.

Dave chuckled. "That's already happened once while you were out," he told Sandra. "I guess seeing the lights blinking makes Grabo nervous. But then *not* seeing them makes him nervous. Just watch."

"The Machine has its own mysterious pow-wow-wers," Judy chanted.

"That's what you think," Bill told her. "Did you know that Willie Angler has hired Evil Eye Bixel out of Brooklyn to put the whammy on the Machine? S'fact."

". . . pow-wow-wers unknown to mere mortals of flesh and blood—"

"Shut up!" Dave hissed. "Now you've done it. Here comes old Eagle Eye. Look, I don't know you two. I'm with this lady here."

Bela Grabo was suffering acute tortures. He had a winning attack, he knew it. The Machine was counter-attacking, but unstrategically, desperately, in the style of a Frank Marshall complicating the issue and hoping for a swindle. All Grabo had to do, he knew, was keep his head and *not blunder*—not throw away a queen, say, as he had to old Vanderhoef at Brussels, or overlook a mate in two, as he had against Sherevsky at Tel Aviv. The memory of those unutterably black moments and a dozen more like them returned to haunt him. Never if he lived a thousand years would he be free of them.

For the tenth time in the last two minutes he glanced at his clock. He had fifteen minutes in which to make five moves. He wasn't in time-pressure, he must remember that. He mustn't make a move on impulse, he mustn't let his treacherous hand leap out without waiting for instructions from its guiding brain.

First prize in this tournament meant incredible wealth—transportation money and hotel bills for more than a score of future tournaments. But more than that, it was one more chance to blazon before the world his true superiority rather than the fading reputation of it. ". . . Bela Grabo, brilliant but erratic . . ." Perhaps his last chance.

When, in the name of Heaven, was the Machine going to make its next move? Surely it had already taken more than four minutes! But a glance at its clock showed him that hardly half that time had gone by. He decided he had made a mistake in asking again for the screens. It was easier to watch those damned lights blink than have them blink in his imagination.

Oh, if chess could only be played in intergalactic space, in the black privacy of one's

259

thoughts. But there had to be the physical presence of the opponent with his (possibly deliberate) unnerving mannerisms—Lasker and his cigar, Capablanca and his red necktie, Nimzowitsch and his nervous contortions (very like Bela Grabo's, though the latter did not see it that way). And now this ghastly flashing, humming, stinking, button-banging metal monster!

Actually, he told himself, he was being asked to play two opponents, the Machine and Simon Great, a sort of consultation team. It wasn't fair!

*   *   *

The Machine hammered its button and rammed its queen across the electric board. In Grabo's imagination it was like an explosion.

Grabo held onto his nerves with an effort and plunged into a maze of calculations.

Once he came to, like a man who has been asleep, to realized that he was wondering whether the lights were still blinking behind the screens while he was making his move. Did the Machine really analyze at such times or were the lights just an empty trick? He forced his mind back to the problems of the game, decided on his move, checked the board twice for any violent move he might have missed, noted on his clock that he'd taken five minutes, checked the board again very rapidly and then put out his hand and made his move—with the fiercely suspicious air of a boss compelled to send an extremely unreliable underling on an all-important errand.

Then he punched his clock, sprang to his feet, and once more waved for Vanderhoef.

Thirty seconds later the Tournament Director, very red-faced now, was saying in a low voice, almost pleadingly, "But Bela, I cannot keep asking them to change the screens. Already they have been up twice and down once to please you. Moving them disturbs the other players and surely isn't good for your own peace of mind. Oh, Bela, my dear Bela—"

Vanderhoef broke off. Grabo knew he had been going to say something improper but from the heart, such as, "For God's sake don't blow this game out of nervousness now that you have a win in sight"—and this sympathy somehow made the Hungarian furious.

"I have other complaints which I will make formally after the game," he said harshly, quivering with rage. "It is a disgrace the way that mechanism punches the timeclock button. It will crack the case! The Machine never stops humming! And it stinks of ozone and hot metal, as if it were about to explode!"

"It *cannot* explode, Bela. Please!"

"No, but it threatens to! And you know a threat is always more effective than an actual attack! As for the screens, they must be taken down at once, I demand it!"

"Very well, Bela, very well, it will be done. Compose yourself."

Grabo did not at once return to his table—he could not have endured to sit still for the moment—but paced along the line of tables, snatching looks at the other games in progress. When he looked back at the big electric board, he saw that the Machine had made a move although he hadn't heard it punch the clock.

He hurried back and he studied the board without sitting down. Why, the Machine had made a *stupid* move, he saw with a rush of exaltation. At that moment the last screen being folded started to fall over, but one of the gray-smocked men caught it deftly. Grabo flinched and his hand darted out and moved a piece.

He heard someone gasp. Vanderhoef.

* * *

It got very quiet. The four soft clicks of the move being fed into the Machine were like the beat of a muffled drum.

There was a buzzing in Grabo's ears. He looked down at the board in horror.

The Machine blinked, blinked once more and then, although barely twenty seconds had elapsed, moved a rook.

On the glassy gray margin above the Machine's electric board, large red words flamed on:

CHECK! AND MATE IN THREE

Up in the stands Dave squeezed Sandra's arm. "He's done it! He's let himself be swindled."

"You mean the Machine has beaten Grabo?" Sandra asked.

"What else?"

"Can you be sure? Just like that?"

"Of cour . . . Wait a second . . . Yes, I'm sure."

"Mated in three like a potzer," Bill confirmed.

"The poor old boob," Judy sighed.

Down on the floor Bela Grabo sagged. The assistant director moved toward him quickly. But then the Hungarian straightened himself a little.

"I resign," he said softly.

The red words at the top of the board were wiped out and briefly replaced, in white, by:

THANK YOU FOR A GOOD GAME

And then a third statement, also in white, flashed on for a few seconds:

YOU HAD BAD LUCK

Bela Grabo clenched his fists and bit his teeth. Even *the Machine* was being sorry for him!

He stiffly walked out of the hall. It was a long, long walk.

V

Adjournment time neared. Serek, the exchange down but with considerable time on his clock, sealed his forty-sixth move against Sherevsky and handed the envelope to Vanderhoef. It would be opened when the game was resumed at the morning session. Dr. Krakatower studied the position on his board and then quietly tipped over his king. He sat there for a moment as if he hadn't the strength to rise. Then he shook himself a

261

little, smiled, got up, clasped hands briefly with Lysmov and wandered over to watch the Angler-Jal game.

Jandorf had resigned his gave to Votbinnik some minutes ago, rather more surlily.

After a while Angler sealed a move, handing it to Vanderhoef with a grin just as the little red flag dropped on his clock, indicating he'd used every second of his time.

Up in the stands Sandra worked her shoulders to get a kink out of her back. She'd noticed several newsmen hurrying off to report in the Machine's first win. She was thankful that her job was limited to special articles.

"Chess is a pretty intense game," she remarked to Dave.

He nodded. "It's a killer. I don't expect to live beyond forty myself."

"Thirty," Bill said.

"Twenty-five is enough time to be a meteor," said Judy.

Sandra thought to herself: *the Unbeat Generation.*

* * *

Next day Sherevsky played the Machine to a dead-level ending. Simon Great offered a draw for the Machine (over an unsuccessful interfering protest from Jandorf that this constituted making a move for the Machine) but Sherevsky refused and sealed his move.

"He wants to have it proved to him that the Machine can play end games," Dave commented to Sandra up in the stands. "I don't blame him."

At the beginning of today's session Sandra had noticed that Bill and Judy were following each game in a very new-looking book they shared jealously between them. *Won't look new for long,* Sandra had thought.

"That's the 'Bible' they got there," Dave had explained. "MCO—*Modern Chess Openings*. It lists all the best open-moves in chess, thousands and thousands of variations. That is, what masters *think* are the best moves. The moves that have won in the past, really. We chipped in together to buy the latest edition—the 13th—just hot off the press," he had finished proudly.

Now with the Machine-Sherevsky ending the center of interest, the kids were consulting another book, one with grimy, dog-eared pages.

"That's the 'New Testament'—*Basic Chess Endings*," Dave said when he noticed her looking. "There's so much you must know in endings that it's amazing the Machine can play them at all. I guess as the pieces get fewer it starts to look deeper."

Sandra nodded. She was feeling virtuous. She had got her interview with Jandorf and then this morning one with Grabo ("How it Feels to Have a Machine Out-Think You") The latter had made her think of herself as a real vulture of the press, circling over the doomed. The Hungarian had seemed in a positively suicidal depression.

One newspaper article made much of the Machine's "psychological tactics," hinting that the blinking lights were designed to hypnotize opponents. The general press coverage was somewhat startling. A game that in America normally rated only a fine-print column in the back sections of a very few Sunday papers was now getting boxes on the front page. The defeat of a man by a machine seemed everywhere to awaken nervous feelings of insecurity, like the launching of the first sputnik.

Sandra had rather hesitantly sought out Dr. Krakatower during the close of the morning session of play, still feeling a little guilty from her interview with Grabo. But Doc had seemed happy to see her and quite recovered from last night's defeat, though when she had addressed him as "Master Krakatower" he had winced and said, "Please, not that!" Another session of coffee and wine-and-seltzer had resulted in her getting an introduction to her first Soviet grandmaster, Serek, who had proved to be unexpectedly charming. He had just managed to draw his game with Sherevsky (to the great amazement of the kibitzers, Sandra learned) and was most obliging about arranging for an interview.

Not to be outdone in gallantry, Doc had insisted on escorting Sandra to her seat in the stands—at the price of once more losing a couple of minutes on his clock. As a result her stock went up considerably with Dave, Bill and Judy. Thereafter they treated anything she had to say with almost annoying deference—Bill especially, probably in penance for his thoughtless cracks at Doc. Sandra later came to suspect that the kids had privately decided that she was Dr. Krakatower's mistress—probably a new one because she was so scandalously ignorant of chess. She did not disillusion them.

Doc lost again in the second round—to Jal.

In the third round Lysmov defeated the Machine in 27 moves. There was a flaring of flashbulbs, a rush of newsmen to the phones, jabbering in the stands and much comment and analysis that was way over Sandra's head—except she got the impression that Lysmov had done something tricky.

The general emotional reaction in America, as reflected by the newspapers, was not too happy. One read between the lines that for the Machine to beat a man was bad, but for a Russian to beat an American machine was worse. A widely-read sports columnist, two football coaches, and several rural politicians announced that chess was a morbid game played only by weirdies. Despite these thick-chested he-man statements, the elusive mood of insecurity deepened.

Besides the excitement of the Lysmov win, a squabble had arisen in connection with the Machine's still-unfinished end game with Sherevsky, which had been continued through one morning session and was now headed for another.

Finally there were rumors that World Business Machines was planning to replace Simon Great with a nationally famous physicist.

Sandra begged Doc to try to explain it all to her in kindergarten language. She was feeling uncertain of herself again and quite subdued after being completely rebuffed in her efforts to get an interview with Lysmov, who had fled her as if she were a threat to his Soviet virtue.

Doc on the other hand was quite vivacious, cheered by his third-round draw with Jandorf.

"Most willingly, my dear," he said. "Have you ever noticed that kindergarten language can be far honester than the adult tongues? Fewer fictions. Well, several of us hashed over the Lysmov game until three o'clock this morning. Lysmov wouldn't though. Neither would Votbinnik or Jal. You see, I have my communication problems with the Russians too.

"We finally decided that Lysmov had managed to guess with complete accuracy both the depth at which the Machine is analyzing in the opening and middle game (ten moves ahead instead of eight, we think—a prodigious achievement!) and also the main value scale in terms of which the Machine selects its move.

"Having that information, Lysmov managed to play into a combination which would give the Machine a maximum plus value in its value scale (win of Lysmov's queen, it was) after ten moves but a checkmate for Lysmov on his second move *after* the first ten. A human chess master would have seen a trap like that, but the Machine could not, because Lysmov was maneuvering in an area that did not exist for the

Machine's perfect but limited mind. Of course the Machine changed its tactics after the first three moves of the ten had been played—it could see the checkmate then—but by that time it was too late for it to avert a disastrous loss of material. It was tricky of Lysmov, but completely fair. After this we'll all be watching for the opportunity to play the same sort of trick on the Machine.

*　　*　　*

"Lysmov was the first of us to realize fully that *we are not playing against a metal monster but against a certain kind of programming.* If there are any weaknesses we can spot in that programming, we can win. Very much in the same way that we can again and again defeat a flesh-and-blood player when we discover that he consistently attacks without having an advantage in position or is regularly overcautious about launching a counter-attack when he himself is attacked without justification."

Sandra nodded eagerly. "So from now on your chances of beating the Machine should keep improving, shouldn't they? I mean as you find out more and more about the programming."

Doc smiled. "You forget," he said gently, "that Simon Great can change the programming before each new game. Now I see why he fought so hard for that point."

"Oh. Say, Doc, what's this about the Sherevsky end game?"

"You are picking up the language, aren't you?" he observed. "Sherevsky got a little angry when he discovered that Great had the Machine programmed to analyze steadily on the next move after an adjournment until the game was resumed next morning. Sherevsky questioned whether it was fair for the Machine to 'think' all night while its opponent had to get some rest. Vanderhoef decided for the Machine, though Sherevsky may carry the protest to FIDE.

"Bah— I think Great wants us to get heated up over such minor matters, just as he is happy (and oh so obliging!) when we complain about how the Machine blinks or hums or smells. It keeps our minds off the main business of trying to outguess his programming. Incidentally, that is one thing we decided last night—Sherevsky, Willie Angler, Jandorf, Serek, and myself—that we are all going to have to learn to play the Machine without letting it get on our nerves and without asking to be protected from it. As Willie puts it, 'So suppose it sounds like a boiler factory even—okay, you can think in a boiler factory.' Myself, I am not so sure of that, but his spirit is right."

Sandra felt herself perking up as a new article began to shape itself in her mind. She said, "And what about WBM replacing Simon Great?"

Again Doc smiled. "I think, my dear, that you can safely dismiss that as just a rumor. I think that Simon Great has just begun to fight."

VI

Round Four saw the Machine spring the first of its surprises.

It had finally forced a draw against Sherevsky in the morning session, ending the long second-round game, and now was matched against Votbinnik.

The Machine opened Pawn to King Four, Votbinnik replied Pawn to King Three.

"The French Defense, Binny's favorite," Dave muttered and they settled back for the Machine's customary four-minute wait.

Instead the Machine moved at once and punched its clock.

Sandra, studying Votbinnik through her glasses, decided that the Russian grand-master looked just a trifle startled. Then he made his move.

Once again the Machine responded instantly.

There was a flurry of comment from the stands and a scurrying-about of officials to shush it. Meanwhile the Machine continued to make its moves at better than rapid-transit speed, although Votbinnik soon began to take rather more time on his.

The upshot was that the Machine made eleven moves before it started to take time to 'think' at all.

Sandra clamored so excitedly to Dave for an explanation that she had two officials waving at her angrily.

As soon as he dared, Dave whispered, "Great must have banked on Votbinnik play-ing the French—almost always does—and fed all the variations of the French into the Machine's 'memory' from MCO and maybe some other books. So long as Votbinnik stuck to a known variation of the French, why, the Machine could play from memory without analyzing at all. Then when a strange move came along—one that wasn't in its memory—only on the twelfth move yet!—the Machine went back to analyzing, only now it's taking longer and going deeper because it's got more time—six minutes a move, about. The only thing I wonder is why Great didn't have the Machine do it in the first three games. It seems so obvious."

Sandra ticketed that in her mind as a question for Doc. She slipped off to her room to write her "Don't Let a Robot Get Your Goat" article (drawing heavily on Doc's observations) and got back to the stands twenty minutes before the second time-control point. It was becoming a regular routine.

Votbinnik was a knight down—almost certainly busted, Dave explained.

"It got terrifically complicated while you were gone," he said. "A real Votbinnik position."

"Only the Machine out-binniked him," Bill finished.

Judy hummed Beethoven's "Funeral March for the Death of a Hero."

Nevertheless Votbinnik did not resign. The Machine sealed a move. Its board blacked out and Vanderhoef, with one of his assistants standing beside him to witness, privately read the move off a small indicator on the console. Tomorrow he would feed the move back into the Machine when play was resumed at the morning session.

Doc sealed a move too although he was two pawns down in his game against Grabo and looked tired to death.

"They don't give easily, do they?" Sandra observed to Dave. "They must really love the game. Or do they hate it?"

"When you get to psychology it's all beyond me," Dave replied. "Ask me something else."

Sandra smiled. "Thank you, Dave," she said. "I will."

*   *   *

Come the morning session, Votbinnik played on for a dozen moves then resigned.

A little later Doc managed to draw his game with Grabo by perpetual check. He caught sight of Sandra coming down from the stands and waved to her, then made the motions of drinking.

Now he looks almost like a boy, Sandra thought as she joined him.

"Say, Doc," she asked when they had secured a table, "why is a rook worth more than a bishop?"

He darted a suspicious glance at her. "That is not your kind of question," he said sternly. "Exactly what have you been up to?"

Sandra confessed that she had asked Dave to teach her how to play chess.

"I knew those children would corrupt you," Doc said somberly. "Look, my dear, if you learn to play chess you won't be able to write your clever little articles about it. Besides, as I warned you the first day, chess is a madness. Women are ordinarily immune, but that doesn't justify you taking chances with your sanity."

"But I've kind of gotten interested, watching the tournament," Sandra objected. "At least I'd like to know how the pieces move."

"Stop!" Doc commanded. "You're already in danger. Direct your mind somewhere else. Ask me a sensible, down-to-earth journalist's question—something completely irrational!"

"Okay, why didn't Simon Great have the Machine set to play the openings fast in the first three games?"

"Hah! I think Great plays Lasker-chess in his programming. He hides his strength and tries to win no more easily than he has to, so he will have resources in reserve. The Machine loses to Lysmov and immediately starts playing more strongly—the psychological impression made on the other players by such tactics is formidable."

"But the Machine isn't ahead yet?"

"No, of course not. After four rounds Lysmov is leading the tournament with $3\frac{1}{2} - \frac{1}{2}$, meaning $3\frac{1}{2}$ in the win column and $\frac{1}{2}$ in the loss column . . ."

"How do you half win a game of chess? Or half lose one?" Sandra interrupted.

"By drawing a game—playing to a tie. Lysmov's $3\frac{1}{2} - \frac{1}{2}$ is notational shorthand for three wins and a draw. Understand? My dear, I don't usually have to explain things to you in such detail."

"I just didn't want you to think I was learning too much about chess."

"Ho! Well, to get on with the score after four rounds, Angler and Votbinnik both have $3 - 1$, while the Machine is bracketed at $2\frac{1}{2} - 1\frac{1}{2}$ with Jal. But the Machine has created an impression of strength, as if it were all set to come from behind with a rush." He shook his head. "At the moment, my dear," he said, "I feel very pessimistic about the chances of neurons against relays in this tournament. Relays don't panic and fag. But the oddest thing . . ."

"Yes?" Sandra prompted.

"Well, the oddest thing is that the Machine doesn't play 'like a machine' at all. It uses dynamic strategy, the kind we sometimes call 'Russian,' complicating each position as much as possible and creating maximum tension. But that too is a matter of the programming . . ."

*   *   *

Doc's foreboding was fulfilled as round followed hard-fought round. In the next five days (there was a weekend recess) the Machine successively smashed Jandorf,

Serek and Jal and after seven rounds was out in front by a full point.

Jandorf, evidently impressed by the Machine's flawless opening play against Vot- binnik, chose an inferior line in the Ruy Lopez to get the Machine "out of the books." Perhaps he hoped that the Machine would go on blindly making book moves, but the Machine did not oblige. It immediately slowed its play, "thought hard" and annihilated the Argentinian in 25 moves.

Doc commented, "The Wild Bull of the Pampas tried to use the living force of his human personality to pull a fast one and swindle the Machine. Only the Machine didn't swindle."

Against Jal, the Machine used a new wrinkle. It used a variable amount of time on moves, apparently according to how difficult it "judged" the position to be.

When Serek got a poor pawn-position the Machine simplified the game relentlessly, suddenly discarding its hitherto "Russian" strategy. "It plays like anything but a machine," Doc commented. "We know the reason all too well—Simon Great—but doing something about it is something else again. Great is hitting at our individual weaknesses wonderfully well. Though I think I could play brilliant psychological chess myself if I had a machine to do the detail work." Doc sounded a bit wistful.

The audiences grew in size and in expensiveness of wardrobe, though most of the cafe society types made their visits fleeting ones. Additional stands were erected. A hard-liquor bar was put in then taken out. The problem of keeping reasonable order and quiet became an unending one for Vanderhoef, who had to ask for more "hushers." The number of scientists and computer men in attendance increased. Navy, Army and Space Force uniforms were more in evidence. Dave and Bill turned up one morning with a three-dimensional chess set of transparent plastic and staggered Sandra by assuring her that most bright young space scientists were moderately adept at this 512-square game.

Sandra heard that WBM had snagged a big order from the War Department. She also heard that a Syndicate man had turned up with a book on the tournament, taking bets from the more heavily heeled types and that a detective was circulating about, trying to spot him.

The newspapers kept up their front-page reporting, most of the writers personal- izing the Machine heavily and rather too cutely. Several of the papers started regular chess columns and "How to Play Chess" features. There was a flurry of pictures of movie starlets and such sitting at chess boards. Hollywood revealed plans for two chess movies: "They Made Her a Black Pawn" and "The Monster From King Rook Square." Chess novelties and costume jewelry appeared. The United States Chess Federation proudly reported a phenomenal rise in membership.

*　　*　　*

Sandra learned enough chess to be able to blunder through a game with Dave without attempting more than one illegal move in five, to avoid the Scholar's Mate most of the time and to be able to checkmate with two rooks though not with one. Judy had asked her, "Is *he* pleased that you're learning chess?"

Sandra had replied, "No, he thinks it is a madness." The kids had all whooped at that and Dave had said, "How right he is!"

Sandra was scraping the bottom of the barrel for topics for her articles, but then it occurred to her to write about the kids, which worked out nicely, and that led to a

267

humorous article "Chess Is for Brains" about her own efforts to learn the game, and for the nth time in her career she thought of herself as practically a columnist and was accordingly elated.

After his two draws, Doc lost three games in a row and still had the Machine to face and then Sherevsky. His 1 —6 score gave him undisputed possession of last place. He grew very depressed. He still made a point of squiring her about before the playing sessions, but she had to make most of the conversation. His rare flashes of humor were rather macabre.

"They have Dirty Old Krakatower locked in the cellar," he muttered just before the start of the next to the last round, "and now they send the robot down to destroy him."

"Just the same, Doc," Sandra told him, "good luck."

Doc shook his head. "Against a man luck might help. But against a Machine?"

"It's not the Machine you're playing, but the programming. Remember?"

"Yes, but it's the Machine that doesn't make the mistake. And a mistake is what I need most of all today. Somebody else's."

Doc must have looked very dispirited and tired when he left Sandra in the stands, for Judy (Dave and Bill not having arrived yet) asked in a confidential, womanly sort of voice, "What do you do for him when he's so unhappy?"

"Oh, I'm especially passionate," Sandra heard herself answer.

"Is that good for him?" Judy demanded doubtfully.

"Sh!" Sandra said, somewhat aghast at her irresponsibility and wondering if *she* were getting tournament-nerves. "Sh, they're starting the clocks."

VII

Krakatower had lost two pawns when the first time-contol point arrived and was intending to resign on his 31st move when the Machine broke down. Three of its pieces moved on the electric board at once, then the board went dark and all the lights on the console went out except five which started winking like angry red eyes. The gray-smocked men around Simon Great sprang silently into action, filing around back of the console. It was the first work anyone had seen them do except move screens around and fetch each other coffee. Vanderhoef hovered anxiously. Some flash bulbs went off. Vanderhoef shook his fist at the photographers. Simon Great did nothing. The Machine's clock ticked on. Doc watched for a while and then fell asleep.

When Vanderhoef jogged him awake, the Machine had just made its next move, but the repair-job had taken 50 minutes. As a result the Machine had to make 15 moves in ten minutes. At 40 seconds a move it played like a dub whose general lack of skill was complicated by a touch of insanity. On his 43rd move Doc shrugged his shoulders apologetically and announced mate in four. There were more flashes. Vanderhoef shook his fist again. The machine flashed:

YOU PLAYED BRILLIANTLY.
CONGRATULATIONS!

Afterwards Doc said sourly to Sandra, "And *that* was one big lie—a child could have beat the Machine with that time advantage. Oh, what an ironic glory the gods reserved for Krakatower's dotage—to vanquish a broken-down computer! Only one good thing about it—that it didn't happen while it was playing one of the Russians, or someone would surely have whispered *sabotage*. And that is something of which they do not accuse Dirty Old Krakatower, because they are sure he has not got the brains even to think to sprinkle a little magnetic oxide powder in the Machine's memory box. Bah!"

Just the same he seemed considerably more cheerful.

Sandra said guilelessly, "Winning a game means nothing to you chess players, does it, unless you really do it by your own brilliancy?"

Doc looked solemn for a moment, then he started to chuckle. "You are getting altogether too smart, Miss Sandra Lea Grayling," he said. "Yes, yes—a chess player is happy to win in any barely legitimate way he can, by an earthquake if necessary, or his opponent sickening before he does from the bubonic plague. So—I confess it to you—I was very happy to chalk up my utterly undeserved win over the luckless Machine."

"Which incidentally makes it anybody's tournament again, doesn't it, Doc?"

*   *   *

"Not exactly." Doc gave a wry little headshake. "We can't expect another fluke. After all, the Machine has functioned perfectly seven games out of eight, and you can bet the WBM men will be checking it all night, especially since it has no adjourned games to work on. Tomorrow it plays Willie Angler, but judging from the way it beat Votbinnik and Jal, it should have a definite edge on Willie. If it beats him, then only Votbinnik has a chance for a tie and to do that he must defeat Lysmov. Which will be most difficult."

"Well," Sandra said, "don't you think that Lysmov might just kind of let himself be beaten, to make sure a Russian gets first place or at least ties for it?"

Doc shook his head emphatically. "There are many things a man, even a chess master, will do to serve his state, but party loyalty doesn't go that deep. Look, here is the standing of the players after eight rounds." He handed Sandra a penciled list.

ONE ROUND TO GO

Player	Wins	Losses
Machine	5½	2½
Votbinnik	5½	2½
Angler	5	3
Jal	4½	3½
Lysmov	4½	3½
Serek	4½	3½
Sherevsky	4	4
Jandorf	2½	5½
Grabo	2	6
Krakatower	2	6

LAST ROUND PAIRINGS

Machine vs. Angler
Votbinnik vs. Lysmov
Jal vs. Serek
Sherevsky vs. Krakatower
Jandorf vs. Grabo

After studying the list for a while, Sandra said, "Hey, even Angler could come out first, couldn't he, if he beat the Machine and Votbinnik lost to Lysmov?"

"Could, could—yes. But I'm afraid that's hoping for too much, barring another breakdown. To tell the truth, dear, the Machine is simply too good for all of us. If it were only a little faster (and these technological improvements always come) it would outclass us completely. We are at that fleeting moment of balance when genius is almost good enough to equal mechanism. It makes me feel sad, but proud too in a morbid fashion, to think that I am in at the death of grandmaster chess. Oh, I suppose the game will always be played, but it won't ever be quite the same." He blew out a breath and shrugged his shoulders.

"As for Willie, he's a good one and he'll give the Machine a long hard fight, you can depend on it. He might conceivably even draw."

He touched Sandra's arm. "Cheer up, my dear," he said. "You should remind yourself that a victory for the Machine is still a victory for the USA."

*   *   *

Doc's prediction about a long hard fight was decidedly not fulfilled.

Having White. the Machine opened Pawn to King Four and Angler went into the Sicilian Defense. For the first twelve moves on each side both adversaries pushed their pieces and tapped their clocks at such lightning speed (Vanderhoef feeding in Angler's moves swiftly) that up in the stands Bill and Judy were still flipping pages madly in their hunt for the right column in MCO.

The Machine made its thirteenth move, still at blitz tempo.

"Bishop takes Pawn, check, and mate in three!" Willie announced very loudly, made the move, banged his clock and sat back.

There was a collective gasp-and-gabble from the stands.

Dave squeezed Sandra's arm hard. Then for once, forgetting that he was Dr. Caution, he demanded loudly of Bill and Judy, "Have you two idiots found that column yet? *The Machine's thirteenth move is a boner!*"

Pinning down the reference with a fingernail, Judy cried, "Yes! Here is it on page 161 in footnote (e) (2) (B). Dave, *that same thirteenth move for White is in the book!* But Black replies Knight to Queen Two, not Bishop takes Pawn, check. And three moves later the book gives White a plus value."

"What the heck, it can't be," Bill asserted.

"But it *is*. Check for yourself. *That boner is in the book.*"

"Shut up, everybody!" Dave ordered, clapping his hands to his face. When he dropped them a moment later his eyes gleamed. I got it now! Angler figured they were using the latest edition of MCO to program the Machine on openings, he found an editorial error and then he deliberately played the Machine into that variation!"

Dave practically shouted his last words, but that attracted no attention as at that moment the whole hall was the noisiest it had been throughout the tournament. It simmered down somewhat as the Machine flashed a move.

Angler replied instantly.

The Machine replied almost as soon as Angler's move was fed into it.

Angler moved again, his move was fed into the Machine and the Machine flashed:

I AM CHECKMATED.
CONGRATULATIONS!

VIII

Next morning Sandra heard Dave's guess confirmed by both Angler and Great. Doc had spotted them having coffee and a malt together and he and Sandra joined them.

Doc was acting jubilant, having just drawn his adjourned game with Sherevsky, which meant, since Jandorf had beaten Grabo, that he was in undisputed possession of Ninth Place. They were all waiting for the finish of the Votbinnik-Lysmov game, which would decide the final standing of the leaders. Willie Angler was complacent and Simon Great was serene and at last a little more talkative.

"You know, Willie," the psychologist said, "I was afraid that one of you boys would figure out something like that. That was the chief reason I didn't have the Machine use the programmed openings until Lysmov's win forced me to. I couldn't check every opening line in MCO and the *Archives* and *Shakhmaty*. There wasn't time. As it was, we had a dozen typists and proofreaders busy for weeks preparing that part of the programming and making sure it was accurate as far as following the books went. Tell the truth now, Willie, how many friends did you have hunting for flaws in the latest edition of MCO?"

Willie grinned. "Your unlucky 13th. Well, that's my secret. Though I've always said that anyone joining the Willie Angler Fan Club ought to expect to have to pay some day for the privilege. They're sharp, those little guys, and I work their tails off."

Simon Great laughed and said to Sandra, "Your young friend Dave was pretty sharp himself to deduce what had happened so quickly. Willie, you ought to have him in the Bleeker Street Irregulars."

Sandra said, "I get the impression he's planning to start a club of his own."

Angler snorted. "That's the one trouble with *my* little guys. They're all waiting to topple me."

Simon Great said, "Well, so long as Willie is passing up Dave, I want to talk to him. It takes real courage in a youngster to question authority."

"How should he get in touch with you?" Sandra asked.

While Great told her, Willie studied them frowningly.

"Si, are you planning to stick in this chess-programming racket?" he demanded.

Simon Great did not answer the question. "You try telling me something, Willie," he said. "Have you been approached the last couple of days by IBM?"

271

"You mean asking me to take over your job?"

"I said *IBM*, Willie."

"Oh." Willie's grim became a tight one. "I'm not talking."

*   *   *

There was a flurry of sound and movement around the playing tables. Willie sprang up.

"Lysmov's agreed to a draw!" he informed them a moment later. "The gangster!"

"Gangster because he puts you in equal first place with Votbinnik, both of you ahead of the Machine?" Great inquired gently.

"Ahh, he could have beat Binny, giving me sole first. A Russian gangster!"

Doc shook a finger. "Lysmov could also have *lost* to Votbinnik, Willie, putting you in second place."

"Don't think evil thoughts. So long, pals."

As Angler clattered down the stairs, Simon Great signed the waited for more coffee, lit a fresh cigarette, took a deep drag and leaned back.

"You know," he said, "it's a great relief not to have to impersonate the hyperconfident programmer for awhile. Being a psychologist has spoiled me for that sort of thing. I'm not as good as I once was at beating people over the head with my ego."

"You didn't do too badly," Doc said.

"Thanks. Actually, WBM is very much pleased with the Machine's performance. The Machine's flaws made it seem more real and more newsworthy, especially how it functioned when the going got tough—those repairs the boys made under time pressure in your game, Savilly, will help sell WBM computers or I miss my guess. In fact nobody could have watched the tournament for long without realizing there were nine smart rugged men out there, ready to kill that computer if they could. The Machine passed a real test. And then the whole deal dramatizes what computers are and what they can and can't do. And not just at the popular level. The WBM research boys are learning a lot about computer and programming theory by studying how the Machine and its programmer behave under tournament stress. It's a kind of test unlike that provided by any other computer work. Just this morning, for instance, one of our big mathematicians told me that he is beginning to think that the Theory of Games *does* apply to chess, because you can bluff and counterbluff with your programming. And *I'm* learning about human psychology."

Doc chuckled. "Such as that even human thinking is just a matter of how you program your own mind?—that we're all like the Machine to that extent?"

"That's one of the big points, Savilly. Yes."

Doc smiled at Sandra. "You wrote a nice little newsstory, dear, about how Man conquered the Machine by a palpitating nose and won a victory for international amity."

"Now the story starts to go deeper."

*   *   *

"A lot of things go deeper," Sandra replied, looking at him evenly. "Much deeper than you ever expect at the start."

The big electric scoreboard lit up.

FINAL STANDING

Player	Wins	Losses
Angler	6	3
Votbinnik	6	3
Jal	5½	3½
Machine	5½	3½
Lysmov	5	4
Serek	4½	4½
Sherevsky	4½	4½
Jandorf	3½	5½
Krakatower	2½	6½
Grabo	2	7

"It was a good tournament," Doc said. "And the Machine has proven itself a grand-master. It must make you feel good, Simon, after being out of tournament chess for twenty years."

The psychologist nodded.

"Will you go back to psychology now?" Sandra asked him.

Simon Great smiled. "I can answer that question honestly, Miss Grayling, because the news is due for release. No. WBM is pressing for entry of the Machine in the Inter-zonal Candidates' Tournament. They want a crack at the World's Championship."

Doc raised his eyebrows. "That's news indeed. But look, Simon, with the knowledge you've gained in this tournament won't you be able to make the Machine almost a sure winner in every game?"

"I don't know. Players like Angler and Lysmov may find some more flaws in its functioning and dream up some new stratagems. Besides, there's another solution to the problems raised by having a single computer entered in a grandmaster tournament."

Doc sat up straight. "You mean having more programmer-computer teams than just one?"

"Exactly. The Russians are bound to give their best players computers, considering the prestige the game has in Russia. And I wasn't asking Willie that question about IBM just on a hunch. Chess tournaments are a wonderful way to test rival computers and show them off to the public, just like cross-country races were for the early auto-mobiles. The future grandmaster will inevitably be a programmer-computer team, a man-machine symbiotic partnership, probably with more freedom each way than I was allowed in this tournament—I mean the man taking over the play in some positions, the machine in others."

"You're making my head swim," Sandra said.

*   *   *

"Mine is in the same storm-tossed ocean," Doc assured her. "Simon, that will be very fine for the masters who can get themselves computers—either from their govern-ments or from hiring out to big firms. Or in other ways. Jandorf, I'm sure, will be able to interest some Argentinian millionaire in a computer for him. While I . . . oh, I'm too old . . . still, when I start to think about it . . . But what about the Bela Grabos? Incidentally, did you know that Grabo is contesting Jandorf's win? Claims Jandorf discussed the position with Serek. I think they exchanged about two words."

Simon shrugged, "The Bela Grabos will have to continue to fight their own battles, if necessary satisfying themselves with the lesser tournaments. Believe me, Savilly, from now on grandmaster chess without one or more computers entered will lack sauce."

Dr. Krakatower shook his head and said, "Thinking gets more expensive every year."

From the floor came the harsh voice of Igor Jandorf and the shrill one of Bela Grabo raised in anger. Three words came through clearly: ". . . I challenge you . . ."

Sandra said, "Well, there's something you can't build into a machine—ego."

"Oh, I don't know about that," said Simon Great.

The Man Who Made Friends With Electricity

When Mr. Scott showed Peak House to Mr. Leverett, he hoped he wouldn't notice the high-tension pole outside the bedroom window, because it had twice before queered promising rentals—so many elderly people were foolishly nervous about electricity. There was nothing to be done about the pole except try to draw prospective tenants' attention away from it—electricity follows the hilltops and these lines supplied more than half the juice used in Pacific Knolls.

But Mr. Scott's prayers and suave misdirections were in vain—Mr. Leverett's sharp eyes lit on the "negative feature" the instant they stepped out on the patio. The old New Englander studied the short thick wooden column, the 18-inch ridged glass insulators, the black transformer box that stepped down voltage for this house and a few others lower on the slope. His gaze next followed the heavy wires swinging off rhythmically four abreast across the empty grey-green hills. Then he cocked his head as his ears caught the low but steady frying sound, varying from a crackle to a buzz of electrons leaking off the wires through the air.

"Listen to that!" Mr. Leverett said, his dry voice betraying excitement for the first time in the tour. "Fifty thousand volts if there's five! A power of power!"

"Must be unusual atmospheric conditions today—normally you can't hear a thing," Mr. Scott responded lightly, twisting the truth a little.

"You don't say?" Mr. Leverett commented, his voice dry again, but Mr. Scott knew better than to encourage conversation about a negative feature. "I want you to notice this lawn," he launched out heartily. "When the Pacific Knolls Golf Course was subdivided, the original owner of Peak House bought the entire eighteenth green and—"

For the rest of the tour Mr. Scott did his state-certified real estate broker's best, which in Southern California is no mean performance, but Mr. Leverett seemed a shade perfunctory in the attention he accorded it. Inwardly Mr. Scott chalked up another defeat by the damn pole.

On the quick retrace, however, Mr. Leverett insisted on their lingering on the patio. "Still holding out," he remarked about the buzz with an odd satisfaction. "You know, Mr. Scott, that's a restful sound to me. Like wind or a brook or the sea. I hate the clatter of machinery—that's the *other* reason I left New England—but this is like a sound of nature. Downright soothing. But you say it comes seldom?"

Mr. Scott was flexible—it was one of his great virtues as a salesman.

"Mr. Leverett," he confessed simply, "I've never stood on this patio when I didn't hear that sound. Sometimes it's softer, sometimes louder, but it's always there. I play it down, though, because most people don't care for it."

"Don't blame you," Mr. Leverett said. "Most people are a pack of fools or worse. Mr. Scott, are any of the people in the neighboring houses Communists to your knowledge?"

"No, sir!" Mr. Scott responded without an instant's hesitation. "There's not a Communist in Pacific Knolls. And that's something, believe me, I'd never shade the truth on."

"Believe you," Mr. Leverett said. "The east's packed with Communists. Seem scarcer out here. Mr. Scott, you've made yourself a deal. I'm taking a year's lease on Peak House as furnished and at the figure we last mentioned."

"Shake on it!" Mr. Scott boomed. "Mr. Leverett, you're the kind of person Pacific Knolls wants."

They shook. Mr. Leverett rocked on his heels, smiling up at the softly crackling wires with a satisfaction that was already a shade possessive.

"Fascinating thing, electricity," he said. "No end to the tricks it can do with it. For instance, if a man wanted to take off for elsewhere in an elegant flash, he'd only have to wet down the lawn good and take twenty-five foot of heavy copper wire in his two bare hands and whip the other end of it over those lines. Whang! Every bit as good as Sing Sing and a lot more satisfying to a man's inner needs."

Mr. Scott experienced a severe though momentary sinking of heart and even for one wildly frivolous moment considered welshing on the verbal agreement he'd just made. He remembered the red-haired lady who'd rented an apartment from him solely to have a quiet place in which to take an overdose of barbiturates. Then he reminded himself that Southern California is, according to a wise old saw, the home (actual or aimed-at) of the peach, the nut and the prune; and while he'd had a few dealings with real or would-be starlets, he'd had enough of crackpots and retired grouches. Even if you piled fanciful death wishes and a passion for electricity atop rabid anti-communist and anti-machine manias, Mr. Leverett's personality was no more than par for the S. Cal. course.

Mr. Leverett said shrewdly, "You're worrying now, aren't you, I might be a suicider? Don't. Just like to think my thoughts. Speak them out too, however peculiar."

Mr. Scott's last fears melted and he became once more his pushingly congenial self as he invited Mr. Leverett down to the office to sign the papers.

Three days later he dropped by to see how the new tenant was making out and found him in the patio ensconced under the buzzing pole in an old rocker.

"Take a chair and sit," Mr. Leverett said, indicating one of the tubular modern pieces. "Mr. Scott, I want to tell you I'm finding Peak House every bit as restful as I hoped. I listen to the electricity and let my thoughts roam. Sometimes I hear voices in the electricity—the wires talking, as they say. You've heard of people who hear voices in the wind?"

"Yes, I have," Mr. Scott admitted a bit uncomfortably and then, recalling that Mr. Leverett's check for the first quarter's rent was safely cleared, was emboldened to speak his own thoughts. "But wind is a sound that varies a lot. That buzz is pretty monotonous to hear voices in."

"Pshaw," Mr. Leverett said with a little grin that made it impossible to tell how seriously he meant to be taken. "Bees are highly intelligent insects, entomologists say they even have a language, yet they do nothing but buzz. I hear voices in the electricity."

He rocked silently for a while after that and Mr. Scott sat.

"Yep, I hear voices in the electricity," Mr. Leverett said dreamily. "Electricity tells me how it roams the forty-eight states—even the forty-ninth by way of Canadian power lines. Electricity goes everywhere today—into our homes, every room of them, into our offices, into government buildings and military posts. And what it doesn't learn that way it overhears by the trace of it that trickles through our phone lines and over our air waves. Phone electricity's the little sister of power electricity, you might say, and little pitchers have big ears. Yep, electricity knows everything about us, our every last secret. Only it wouldn't think of telling most people what it knows, because they believe electricity is a cold mechanical force. It isn't—it's warm and pulsing and sensitive and friendly underneath, like any other live thing."

Mr. Scott, feeling a bit dreamy himself now, thought what good advertising copy that would make—imaginative stuff, folksy but poetic.

"*And* electricity's got a mite of viciousness too," Mr. Leverett continued. "You got to tame it. Know its ways, speak it fair, show no fear, make friends with it. Well now, Mr. Scott," he said in a brisker voice, standing up, "I know you've come here to check up on how I'm caring for Peak House. So let me give *you* the tour."

And in spite of Mr. Scott's protests that he had no such inquisitive intention, Mr. Leverett did just that.

Once he paused for an explanation: "I've put away the electric blanket and the toaster. Don't feel right about using electricity for menial jobs."

As far as Mr. Scott could see, he had added nothing to the furnishings of Peak House beyond the rocking chair and a large collection of Indian arrow heads.

Mr. Scott must have talked about the latter when he got home, for a week later his nine-year-old son said to him, "Hey, Dad, you know that old guy you unloaded Peak House onto?"

"Rented is the only proper expression, Bobby."

"Well, I went up to see his arrow heads. Dad, it turns out he's a snake-charmer!"

Dear God, thought Mr. Scott, *I knew there was going to be something really impossible about Leverett. Probably like hilltops because they draw snakes in hot weather.*

"He didn't charm a real snake, though, Dad, just an old extension cord. He squatted down on the floor—this was after he showed me those crumby arrow heads—and waved his hands back and forth over it and pretty soon the end with the little box on it started to move around on the floor and all of a sudden it lifted up, like a cobra out of a basket. It was real spooky!"

"I've seen that sort of trick," Mr. Scott told Bobby. "There's a fine thread attached to the end of the wire pulling it up."

"I'd have seen a thread, Dad."

"Not if it were the same color as the background," Mr. Scott explained. Then he had a thought. "By the way Bobby, was the other end of the cord plugged in?"

"Oh it was, Dad! He said he couldn't work the trick unless there was electricity in the cord. Because you see, Dad, he's really an electricity-charmer. I just said snake-charmer to make it more exciting. Afterwards we went outside and he charmed electricity down out of the wires and made it crawl all over his body. You could see it crawl from part to part."

"But how could you see that?" Mr. Scott demanded, struggling to keep his voice casual. He had a vision of Mr. Leverett standing dry and sedate, entwined by glimmering blue serpents with flashing diamond eyes and fangs that sparked.

"By the way it would make his hair stand on end, Dad. First on one side of his head, then on the other. Then he said, 'Electricity, crawl down my chest,' and a silk handkerchief hanging out of his top pocket stood out stiff and sharp. Dad, it was almost as good as the Museum of Science and Industry!"

Next day Mr. Scott dropped by Peak House, but he got no chance to ask his carefully thought-out questions, for Mr. Leverett greeted him with, "Reckon your boy told you about the little magic show I put on for him yesterday. I like children, Mr. Scott. Good Republican children like yours, that is."

"Why yes, he did," Mr. Scott admitted, disarmed and a bit flustered by the other's openness.

"I only showed him the simplest tricks, of course. Kid stuff."

"Of course," Mr. Scott echoed. "I guessed you must have used a fine thread to make the extension cord dance."

"Reckon you know all the answers, Mr. Scott," the other said, his eyes flashing. "But come across to the patio and sit for a while."

The buzzing was quite loud that day, yet after a bit Mr. Scott had to admit to himself that it *was* a restful sound. And it had more variety than he'd realized—mounting crackles, fading sizzles, hisses, hums, clicks, sighs: If you listened to it long enough, you probably would begin to hear voices.

Mr. Leverett, silently rocking, said, "Electricity tells me about all the work it does and all the fun it has—dances, singing, big crackling band concerts, trips to the stars, foot races that make rockets seem like snails. Worries, too. You know that electric breakdown they had in New York? Electricity told me why. Some of its folks went crazy —overwork, I guess—and just froze. It was a while before they could send others in from outside New York and heal the crazy ones and start them moving again through the big copper web. Electricity tells me it's fearful the same thing's going to happen in Chicago and San Francisco. Too much pressure.

"Electricity doesn't *mind* working for us. It's generous-hearted and it loves its job. But it would be grateful for a little more consideration—a little more recognition of its special problems.

"It's got its savage brothers to contend with, you see—the wild electricity that rages in storms and haunts the mountaintops and comes down to hunt and kill. Not civilized like the electricity in the wires, though it will be some day.

"For civilized electricity's a great teacher. Shows us how to live clean and in unity and brother-love. Power fails one place, electricity's rushing in from everywhere to fill the gap. Serves Georgia same as Vermont, Los Angeles same as Boston. Patriotic too—only revealed its greatest secrets to true-blue Americans like Edison and Franklin. Did you know it killed a Swede when he tried that kite trick? Yep, electricity's the greatest power for good in all the U.S.A."

Mr. Scott thought sleepily of what a neat little electricity cult Mr. Leverett could set up, every bit as good as Science of Mind or Krishna Venta or the Rosicrucians. He could imagine the patio full of earnest seekers while Krishna Leverett—or maybe High Electro Leverett—dispensed wisdom from his rocker, interpreting the words of the humming wires. Better not suggest it, though—in Southern California such things had a way of coming true.

Mr. Scott felt quite easy at heart as he went down the hill, though he did make a point of telling Bobby not to bother Mr. Leverett any more.

But the prohibition didn't apply to himself. During the next months Mr. Scott made a point of dropping in at Peak House from time to time for a dose of "electric wisdom." He came to look forward to these restful, amusingly screwy breaks in the hectic round. Mr. Leverett appeared to do nothing whatever except sit in his rocker on the patio, yet stayed happy and serene. There was a lesson for anybody in that, if you thought about it.

Occasionally Mr. Scott spotted amusing side effects of Mr. Leverett's eccentricity. For instance, although he sometimes let the gas and water bills go, he always paid up phone and electricity on the dot.

And the newspapers eventually did report short but severe electric breakdowns in Chicago and San Francisco. Smiling a little frowningly at the coincidences, Mr. Scott decided he could add fortune-telling to the electricity cult he'd imagined for Mr. Leverett. "Your life's story foretold in the wires!"—more novel, anyway, than crystal balls or Talking with God.

Only once did the touch of the gruesome, that had troubled Mr. Scott in his first conversation with Mr. Leverett, come briefly back, when the old man chuckled and observed, "Recall what I told you about whipping a copper wire up there? I've thought of a simpler way, just squirt the hose at those H-T lines in a hard stream, gripping the metal nozzle. Might be best to use the hot water and throw a box of salt in the heater first." When Mr. Scott heard that he was glad that he'd warned Bobby against coming around.

But for the most part Mr. Leverett maintained his mood of happy serenity.

When the break in that mood came, it did so suddenly, though afterwards Mr. Scott realized there had been one warning note sounded when Mr. Leverett had added onto a rambling discourse, "By the way, I've learned that power electricity goes all over the world, just like the ghost electricity in radios and phones. It travels to foreign shores in batteries and condensers. Roams the lines in Europe and Asia. Some of it even slips over into Soviet territory. Wants to keep tabs on the Communists, I guess. Electric freedom-fighters."

On his next visit Mr. Scott found a great change. Mr. Leverett had deserted his rocking chair to pace the patio on the side away from the pole, though every now and then he would give a quick funny look up over his shoulder at the dark muttering wires.

"Glad to see you, Mr. Scott. I'm real shook up. Reckon I better tell someone about it so if something happens to me they'll be able to tell the FBI. Though I don't know what *they'll* be able to do.

"Electricity just told me this morning it's got a world government—it had the nerve to call it that—and that it doesn't care a snap for either us *or* the Soviets and that there's Russian electricity in our wires and American electricity in theirs—it shifts back and forth with never a quiver of shame.

"When I heard that you could have knocked me down with a paper dart.

"What's more, electricity's determined to stop any big war that may come, no matter how rightful that war be or how much in defense of America. If the buttons are pushed for the atomic missiles, electricity's going to freeze and refuse to budge. And it'll flash out and kill anybody who tries to set them off another way.

"I pleaded with electricity, I told it I'd always thought of it as American and true— reminded it of Franklin and Edison—finally I commanded it to change its ways and behave decent, but it just chuckled at me with never a spark of love or loyalty.

"Then it threatened me back! It told me if I tried to stop it, if I revealed its plans it would summon down its savage brothers from the mountains and with their help it would seek me out and kill me! Mr. Scott, I'm all alone up here with electricity on my window sill. What am I going to do?"

Mr. Scott had considerable difficulty soothing Mr. Leverett enough to make his escape. In the end he had to promise to come back in the morning bright and early— silently vowing to himself that he'd be damned if he would.

His task was not made easier when the electricity overhead, which had been especially noisy this day, rose in a growl and Mr. Leverett turned and said harshly, "Yes, I hear!"

That night the Los Angeles area had one of its very rare thunderstorms, accompanied by gales of wind and torrents of rain. Palms and pines and eucalyptus were torn down, earth cliffs crumbled and sloshed, and the great square concrete spillways ran brimful from the hills to the sea.

The lightning was especially fierce. Several score Angelinos, to whom such a display was a novelty, phoned civil defense numbers to report or inquire fearfully about atomic attack.

Numerous freak accidents occurred. To the scene of one of these Mr. Scott was summoned next morning bright and early by the police—because it had occurred on a property he rented and because he was the only person known to be acquainted with the deceased.

The previous night Mr. Scott had awakened at the height of the storm when the lightning had been blinding as a photoflash and the thunder had cracked like a mile-long whip just above the roof. At that time he had remembered vividly what Mr. Leverett had said about electricity threatening to summon its wild giant brothers from the hills. But now, in the bright morning, he decided not to tell the police about that or say anything to them at all about Mr. Leverett's electricity mania—it would only complicate things to no purpose and perhaps make the fear at his heart more crazily real.

Mr. Scott saw the scene of the freak accident before anything was moved, even the body—except there was now, of course, no power in the heavy corroded wire wrapped tight as a bullwhip around the skinny shanks with only the browned and blackened fabric of cotton pyjamas between.

The police and the power-and-light men reconstructed the accident this way: At the height of the storm one of the high-tension lines had snapped a hundred feet away from the house and the end, whipped by the wind and its own tension, had struck back freakishly through the open bedroom window of Peak House and curled once around the legs of Mr. Leverett, who had likely been on his feet at the time, killing him instantly.

One had to strain that reconstruction, though, to explain the additional freakish elements in the accident—the facts that the high-tension wire had struck not only through the bedroom window, but then through the bedroom door to catch the old man in the hall, and that the black shiny cord of the phone was wrapped like a vine twice around the old man's right arm, as if to hold him back from escaping until the big wire had struck.

Bazaar of the Bizarre

The strange stars of the World of Nehwon glinted thickly above the black-roofed city of Lankhmar, where swords clink almost as often as coins. For once there was no fog.

In the Plaza of Dark Delights, which lies seven blocks south of the Marsh Gate and extends from the Fountain of Dark Abundance to the Shrine of the Black Virgin, the shop-lights glinted upward no more brightly than the stars glinted down. For there the vendors of drugs and the peddlers of curiosa and the hawkers of assignations light their stalls and crouching places with foxfire, glowworms, and firepots with tiny single windows, and they conduct their business almost as silently as the stars conduct theirs.

There are plenty of raucous spots a-glare with torches in nocturnal Lankhmar, but by immemorial tradition soft whispers and a pleasant dimness are the rule in the Plaza of Dark Delights. Philosophers often go there solely to meditate, students to dream, and fanatic-eyed theologians to spin like spiders abstruse new theories of the devil and of the other dark forces ruling the universe. And if any of these find a little illicit fun by the way, their theories and dreams and theologies and demonologies are undoubtedly the better for it.

Tonight, however, there was a glaring exception to the darkness rule. From a low doorway with a trefoil arch new-struck through an ancient wall, light spilled into the Plaza. Rising above the horizon of the pavement like some monstrous moon a-shine with the ray of a murderous sun, the new doorway dimmed almost to extinction the stars of the other merchants of mystery.

Eerie and unearthly objects for sale spilled out of the doorway a little way with the light, while beside the doorway crouched an avid-faced figure clad in garments never before seen on land or sea . . . in the World of Nehwon. He wore a hat like a small red pail, baggy trousers, and outlandish red boots with upturned toes. His eyes were as predatory as a hawk's, but his smile as cynically and lasciviously cajoling as an ancient satyr's.

Now and again he sprang up and pranced about, sweeping and resweeping with a rough long broom the flagstones as if to clean path for the entry of some fantastic emperor, and he often paused in his dance to bow low and loutingly, but always with upglancing eyes, to the crowd gathering in the darkness across from the doorway and to wing his hand from them toward the interior of the new shop in a gesture of invitation at once servile and sinister.

No one of the crowd had yet plucked up courage to step forward into the glare and enter the shop, or even inspect the rarities set out so carelessly yet temptingly before it.

But the number of fascinated peerers increased momently. There were mutterings of censure at the dazzling new method of merchandising—the infraction of the Plaza's custom of darkness—but on the whole the complaints were outweighed by the gasps and murmurings of wonder, admiration, and curiosity kindling ever hotter.

*   *   *

The Gray Mouser slipped into the Plaza at the Fountain end as silently as if he had come to slit a throat or spy on the spies of the Overlord. His ratskin moccasins were soundless. His sword Scalpel in its mouseskin sheath did not swish ever so faintly against either his tunic or cloak, both of gray silk curiously coarse of weave. The glances he shot about him from under his gray silk hood half thrown back were freighted with menace and a freezing sense of superiority.

Inwardly the Mouser was feeling very much like a schoolboy—a schoolboy in dread of rebuke and a crushing assignment of homework. For in the Mouser's pouch of rat-skin was a note scrawled in dark brown squid-ink on silvery fish-skin by Sheelba of the Eyeless Face, inviting the Mouser to be at this spot at this time.

Sheelba was the Mouser's supernatural tutor and—when the whim struck Sheelba —guardian, and it never did to ignore his invitations, for Sheelba had eyes to track down the unsociable though he did not carry them between his cheeks and forehead.

But the tasks Sheelba would set the Mouser at times like these were apt to be peculiarly onerous and even noisome—such as procuring nine white cats with never a black hair among them, or stealing five copies of the same book of magic runes from five widely separated sorcerous libraries or obtaining specimens of the dung of our kings living or dead—so the Mouser had come early, to get the bad news as soon as possible, and he had come alone, for he certainly did not want his comrade Fafhrd to stand snickering by while Sheelba delivered his little wizardly homilies to a dutiful Mouser . . . and perchance thought of extra assignments.

Sheelba's note, invisibly graven somewhere inside the Mouser's skull, read merely, *When the star Akul bedizens the Spire of Rhan, be you by the Fountain of Dark Abundance,* and the note was signed only with the little featureless oval which is Sheelba's sigil.

The Mouser glided now through the darkness to the Fountain, which was a squat black pillar from the rough rounded top of which a single black drop welled and dripped every twenty elephant's heartbeats.

The Mouser stood beside the Fountain and, extending a bent hand, measured the altitude of the green star Akul. It had still to drop down the sky seven finger widths more before it would touch the needle-point of the slim star-silhouetted distant minaret of Rhan.

The Mouser crouched doubled-up by the black pillar and then vaulted lightly atop it to see if that would make any great difference in Akul's attitude. It did not.

He scanned the nearby darkness for motionless figures . . . especially that of one robed and cowled like a monk—cowled so deeply that one might wonder how he saw to walk. There were no figures at all.

The Mouser's mood changed. If Sheelba chose not to come courteously before-hand, why he could be boorish too! He strode off to investigate the new bright arch-doored shop, of whose infractious glow he had become inquisitively aware at least a block before he had entered the Plaza of Dark Delights.

*   *   *

Fafhrd the Northerner opened one wine-heavy eye and without moving his head scanned half the small firelit room in which he slept naked. He shut that eye, opened the other, and scanned the other half.

There was no sign of the Mouser anywhere. So far so good! If his luck held, he would be able to get through tonight's embarrassing business without being jeered at by the small gray rogue.

He drew from under his stubbly cheek a square of violet serpenthide pocked with tiny pores so that when he held it between his eyes and the dancing fire it made stars. Studied for a time, these stars spelled out obscurely the message: *When Rhan-dagger stabs the darkness in Akul-heart, seek you the Source of the Black Drops.*

Drawn boldly across the prickholes in an orange-brown like dried blood—in fact spanning the violet square—was one of the sigils of Ningauble of the Seven Eyes.

Fafhrd had no difficulty in interpreting the Source of the Black Drops as the Fountain of Dark Abundance. He had become wearily familiar with such cryptic poetic language during his boyhood as a scholar of the singing skalds.

Ningauble stood to Fafhrd very much as Sheelba stood to the Mouser except that the seven-eyed one was a somewhat more pretentious archimage, whose taste in the thaumaturgical tasks he set Fafhrd ran in larger directions, such as the slaying of dragons, the sinking of four-masted magic ships, and the kidnapping of ogre-guarded enchanted queens.

Also, Ningauble was given to quiet realistic boasting, especially about the grandeur of his vast cavern-home, whose stony serpent-twisting back corridors led, he often averred, to all spots in space and time—provided Ningauble instructed one beforehand exactly how to step those rocky crooked low-ceilinged passageways.

Fafhrd was driven by no great desire to learn Ningauble's formulas and enchantments, as the Mouser was driven to learn Sheelba's, but the septinocular one had enough holds on the Northerner, based on the latter's weaknesses and past misdeeds, so that Fafhrd had always to listen patiently to Ningauble's wizardly admonishments and vaunting sorcerous chit-chat—but *not*, if humanly or inhumanly possible, while the Gray Mouser was present to snigger and grin.

Meanwhile, Fafhrd standing before the fire, had been whipping, slapping, and belting various garments and weapons and ornaments onto his huge brawny body with its generous stretches of thick short curling red-gold hairs. When he opened the outer door and, also booted and helmeted now, glanced down the darkling alleyway preparatory to leaving and noted only the hunch-backed chestnut vendor a-squat by his brazier at the next corner, one would have sworn that when he did stride forth toward the Plaza of Dark Delights it would be with the clankings and thunderous tread of a siege-tower approaching a thick-walled city.

Instead the lynx-eared old chestnut vendor, who was also a spy of the Overlord, had to swallow down his heart when it came sliding crookedly up his throat as Fafhrd rushed past him, tall as a pine tree, swift as the wind, and silent as a ghost.

*   *   *

The Mouser elbowed aside two gawkers with shrewd taps on the floating rib and strode across the dark flagstones toward the garishly bright shop with its doorway like an upended heart. It occurred to him they must have had masons working like fiends to have cut and plastered that archway so swiftly. He had been past here this afternoon and noted nothing but blank wall.

The outlandish porter with the red cylinder hat and twisty red shoe-toes came frisking out to the Mouser with his broom and then went curtsying back as he reswept a path for this first customer with many an obsequious bow and smirk.

But the Mouser's visage was set in an expression of grim and all-skeptical disdain. He paused at the heaping of objects in front of the door and scanned it with disapproval. He drew Scalpel from its thin gray sheath and with the tip of the long blade flipped back the cover on the topmost of a pile of musty books. Without going any closer he briefly scanned the first page, shook his head, rapidly turned a half dozen more pages with Scalpel's tip, using the sword as if it were a teacher's wand to point out words here and there—because they were ill-chosen, to judge from his expression—and then abruptly closed the book with another sword-flip.

Next he used Scalpel's tip to lift a red cloth hanging from a table behind the books and peer under it suspiciously, to rap contemptuously a glass jar with a human head floating in it, to touch disparagingly several other objects and to waggle reprovingly at a footchained owl which hooted at him solemnly from its high perch.

He sheathed Scalpel and turned toward the porter with a sour, lifted-eyebrow look which said—nay, shouted—plainly, "Is *this* all you have to offer? Is this garbage your excuse for defiling the Dark Plaza with glare?"

Actually the Mouser was mightily interested by every least item which he had glimpsed. The book, incidentally, had been in a script which he not only did not understand, but did not even recognize.

Three things were very clear to the Mouser: first, that this stuff offered here for sale did not come Nehwon's farthest outback; second, that all this stuff was, in some way which he could not yet define, extremely dangerous; third, that all this stuff was monstrously fascinating and that he, the Mouser, did not intend to stir from this place until he had personally scanned, studied, and, if need be, tested every last intriguing item and scrap.

At the Mouser's sour grimace, the porter went into a convulsion of wheedling and fawning caperings, seemingly torn between a desire to kiss the Mouser's foot and to point out with flamboyant caressing gestures every object in his shop.

He ended by bowing so low that his chin brushed the pavement, sweeping an ape-long arm toward the interior of the shop, and gibbering in atrocious Lankhmarese, "Every object to pleasure the flesh and senses and imagination of man. Wonders undreamed. Very cheap, very cheap! Yours for a penny! The Bazaar of the Bizarre. Please to inspect, oh king!"

The Mouser yawned a very long yawn with the back of his hand to his mouth, next he looked around him again with the weary, patient, worldly smile of a duke who knows he must put up with many boredoms to encourage business in his demesne, finally he shrugged faintly and entered the shop.

Behind him the porter went into a jigging delirium of glee and began to resweep the flagstones like a man maddened with delight.

Inside, the first thing the Mouser saw was a stack of slim books bound in gold-lined fine-grained red and violet leather.

The second was a rack of gleaming lenses and slim brass tubes calling to be peered through.

The third was a slim dark-haired girl smiling at him mysteriously from a gold-barred cage that swung from the ceiling.

Beyond that cage hung others with bars of silver and strange green, ruby, orange, ultramarine, and purple metals.

Fafhrd saw the Mouser vanish into the shop just as his left hand touched the rough chill pate of the Fountain of Dark Abundance and as Akul pointed precisely on Rhantop as if it were that needlespire's green-lensed pinnacle-lantern.

He might have followed the Mouser, he might have done no such thing, he certainly would have pondered the briefly glimpsed event, but just then there came from behind him a low "Hssssst!"

Fafhrd turned like a giant dancer and his longsword Graywand came out of its sheath swiftly and rather more silently than a snake emerges from its hole.

Ten arm lengths behind him, in the mouth of an alleyway darker than the Dark Plaza would have been without its new commercial moon, Fafhrd dimly made out two robed and deeply cowled figures poised side by side.

One cowl held darkness absolute. Even the face of a Negro of Klesh might have been expected to shoot ghostly bronze gleams. But here there were none.

In the other cowl there nested seven very faint pale greenish glows. They moved about restlessly, sometimes circling each other, swinging mazily. Sometimes one of the seven horizontally oval gleams would grow a little brighter, seemingly as it moved forward toward the mouth of the cowl—or a little darker, as it drew back.

Fafhrd sheathed Graywand and advanced toward the figures. Still facing him, they retreated slowly and silently down the alley.

Fafhrd followed as they receded. He felt a stirring of interest . . . and of other feelings. To meet his own supernatural mentor alone might be only a bore and a mild nervous strain; but it would be hard for anyone entirely to repress a shiver of awe at encountering at one and the same time both Ningauble of the Seven Eyes and Sheelba of the Eyeless Face.

Moreover, that those two bitter wizardly rivals would have joined forces, that they should apparently by operating together in amity . . . Something of great note must be afoot! There was no doubting that.

*　　*　　*

The Mouser meantime was experiencing the smuggest, most mindteasing, most exotic enjoyments imaginable. The sleekly leather-bound gold-stamped books turned out to contain scripts stranger far than that in the book whose pages he had flipped outside—scripts that looked like skeletal beasts, cloud swirls, and twisty-branched bushes and trees—but for a wonder he could read them all without the least difficulty.

The books dealt in the fullest detail with such matters as the private life of devils, the secret histories of murderous cults, and—these were illustrated—the proper dueling techniques to employ against sword-armed demons and the erotic tricks of lamias, succubi, bacchantes, and hamadryads.

The lenses and brass tubes, some of the latter of which were as fantastically crooked as if they were periscopes for seeing over the walls and through the barred windows of other universes, showed at first only delightful jeweled patterns, but after a bit the Mouser was able to see through them into all sorts of interesting places: the treasure-room of dead kings, the bedchambers of living queens, council-crypts of rebel angels, and the closets in which the gods hid plans for worlds too frighteningly fantastic to risk creating.

As for the quaintly clad slim girls in their playfully widely-barred cages, well, they were pleasant pillows on which to rest eyes momentarily fatigued by book-scanning and tube-peering.

Ever and anon one of the girls would whistle softly at the Mouser and the point cajolingly or imploringly or with languorous hintings at a jeweled crank set in the wall whereby her cage, suspended on a gleaming chain running through gleaming pulleys, could be lowered to the floor.

At these invitations the Mouser would smile with a bland amorousness and nod and softly wave a hand from the fingerhinge as if to whisper, "Later . . . later. Be patient."

After all, girls had a way of blotting out all lesser, but not thereby despicable, delights. Girls were for dessert.

Ningauble and Sheelba receded down the dark alleyway with Fafhrd following them until the latter lost patience and, somewhat conquering his unwilling awe, called out nervously, "Well, are you going to keep on fleeing me backward until we all pitch into the Great Salt Marsh? What do you want of me? What's it all about?"

But the two cowled figures had already stopped, as he could perceive by the starlight and the glow of a few high windows, and now it seemed to Fafhrd that they had stopped a moment before he had called out. A typical sorcerers' trick for making one feel awkward! He gnawed his lip in the darkness. It was ever thus!

"Oh My Gentle Son . . ." Ningauble began in his most sugary-priestly tones, the dim puffs of his seven eyes now hanging in his cowl as steadily and glowing as mildly as the Pleiades seen late on a summer night through a greenish mist rising from a lake freighted with blue vitriol and corrosive gas of salt.

"I asked what's it all about!" Fafhrd interruped harshly. Already convicted of impatience, he might as well go the whole hog.

"Let me put it as a hypothetical case," Ningauble replied imperturbably. "Let us suppose, My Gentle Son, that there is a man in a universe and that a most evil force comes to this universe from another universe, or perhaps from a congeries of universes, and that this man is a brave man who wants to defend his universe and who counts his life as a trifle and that moreover he has to counsel him a very wise and prudent and public-spirited uncle who knows all about these matters which I have been hypothecating—"

"The Devourers menace Lankhmar!" Sheelba rapped out in a voice as harsh as a tree cracking and so suddenly that Fafhrd almost started—and for all we know, Ningauble too.

Fafhrd waited a moment to avoid giving false impressions and then switched his gaze to Sheelba. His eyes had been growing accustomed to the darkness and he saw much more now than he had seen at the alley's mouth, yet he still saw not one jot more than absolute blackness inside Sheelba's cowl.

"Who are the Devourers?" he asked.

It was Ningauble, however, who replied, "The Devourers are the most accomplished merchants in all the many universes—so accomplished, indeed, that they sell only trash. There is a deep necessity in this, for the Devourers must occupy all their cunning in perfecting their methods of selling and so have not an instant to spare in considering the worth of what they sell. Indeed, they dare not concern themselves with such matters for a moment, for fear of losing their golden touch—and yet such are their skills that their wares are utterly irresistible, indeed the finest wares in all the many universes—if you follow me?"

Fafhrd looked hopefully toward Sheelba, but since the latter did not this time interrupt with some pithy summation, he nodded to Ningauble.

Ningauble continued, his seven eyes beginning to weave a bit, judging from the movements of the seven green glows, "As you might readily deduce, the Devourers possess all the mightiest magics garnered from the many universes, whilst their assault groups are led by the most aggressive wizards imaginable, supremely skilled in all methods of battling, whether it be with the wits, or the feelings, or with the beweaponed body.

"The method of the Devourers is to set up shop in a new world and first entice the bravest and the most adventuresome and the supplest-minded of its people—who have so much imagination that with just a touch of suggestion they themselves do most of the work of selling themselves.

"When these are safely ensnared, the Devourers proceed to deal with the remainder of the population: meaning simply that they sell and sell and sell!—sell trash and take good money and even finer things in exchange."

Ningauble sighed windily and a shade piously. "All this is very bad, My Gentle Son," he continued, his eye-glows weaving hypnotically in his cowl, "but natural enough in universes administered by such gods as we have—natural enough and perhaps endurable. However"—he paused—"there is worse to come! The Devourers want not only the patronage of all beings in all universes, but—doubtless because they are afraid someone will some day raise the ever-unpleasant question, of the true worth of things —they want all their customers reduced to a state of slavish and submissive suggestibility, so that they are fit for nothing whatever but to gawk at and buy the trash the Devourers offer for sale. This means of course that eventually the Devourers' customers will have nothing wherewith to pay the Devourers for their trash, but the Devourers do not seem to be concerned with this eventuality. Perhaps they feel that there is always a new universe to exploit. And perhaps there is!"

"Monstrous!" Fafhrd commented. "But what do the Devourers gain from all these furious commercial sorties, all this mad merchandising? What do they really want?"

Ningauble replied, "The Devourers want only to amass cash and to raise little ones like themselves to amass more cash and they want to compete with each other at cash-amassing. (Is that coincidentally a city, do you think, Fafhrd? Cashamash?) And the Devourers want to brood about their great service to the many universes—it is their claim that servile customers make the most obedient subjects for the gods—and to complain about how the work of amassing cash tortures their minds and upsets their digestions. Beyond this, each of the Devourers also secretly collects and hides away forever, to delight no eyes but his own, all the finest objects and thoughts created by true men and women (and true wizards and true demons) and bought by the Devourers at bankruptcy prices and paid for with trash or—this is their ultimate preference—with nothing at all."

"Monstrous indeed!" Fafhrd repeated. "Merchants are ever an evil mystery and these sound the worst. But what has all this to do with me?"

"Oh My Gentle Son," Ningauble responded, the piety in his voice now tinged with a certain clement disappointment, "you force me once again to resort to hypothecating. Let us return to the supposition of this brave man whose whole universe is direly menaced and who counts his life a trifle and to the related supposition of this brave man's wise uncle, whose advice the brave man invariably follows—"

"The Devourers have set up shop in the Plaza of Dark Delights!" Sheelba interjected so abruptly in such iron-harsh syllables that this time Fafhrd actually did start. "You must obliterate this outpost tonight!"

Fafhrd considered that for a bit, then said, in a tentative sort of voice, "You will both accompany me, I presume, to aid me with your wizardly sendings and castings in what I can see must be a most perilous operation, to serve me as a sort of sorcerous artillery and archery corps while I play assault battalion—"

"Oh My Gentle Son . . ." Ningauble interrupted in tones of deepest disappointment, shaking his head so that his eye-glows jogged in his cowl.

"You must do it alone!" Sheelba rasped.

"Without any help at all?" Fafhrd demanded. "No! Get someone else. Get this doltish brave man who always follows his scheming uncle's advice as slavishly as you tell me the Devourers' customers respond to their merchandising. Get *him!* but as for me—No, I say!"

"Then leave us, coward!" Sheelba decreed dourly, but Ningauble only sighed and said quite apologetically, "It was intended that you have a comrade in this quest, a fellow soldier against noisome evil—to wit, the Gray Mouser. But unfortunately he came too early to his appointment with my colleague here and was enticed into the shop of the Devourers and is doubtless now deep in their snares, if not already extinct. So you can see that we do take thought for your welfare and have no wish to overburden you with solo quests. However, My Gentle Son, if it still be your firm resolve . . ."

Fafhrd let out a sigh more profound than Ningauble's. "Very well," he said in gruff tones admitting defeat, "I'll do it for you. Someone will have to pull that poor little gray fool out of the pretty-pretty fire—or the twinkly-twinkly water!—that tempted him. But how do I go about it?" He shook a big finger at Ningauble. "And no more Gentle-Sonning!"

Ningauble paused. Then he said only, "Use your own judgment."

Sheelba said, "Beware the Black Wall!"

Ningauble said to Fafhrd, "Hold, I have a gift for you," and held out to him a ragged ribbon a yard long, pinched between the cloth of the wizard's long sleeve so that it was impossible to see the manner of hand that pinched. Fafhrd took the tatter with a snort, crumpled it into a ball, and thrust it into his pouch.

"Have a greater care with it," Ningauble warned. "It is the Cloak of Invisibility, somewhat worn by many magic usings. Do not put it on until you near the Bazaar of the Devourers. It has two minor weaknesses: it will not make you altogether invisible to a master sorcerer if he senses your presence and takes certain steps. Also, see to it that you do not bleed during this exploit, for the cloak will not hide blood."

"I've a gift too!" Sheelba said, drawing from out of his black cowl-hole—with sleeve-masked hand, as Ningauble had done—something that shimmered faintly in the dark like . . .

Like a spiderweb.

Sheelba shook it, as if to dislodge a spider, or perhaps two.

"The Blindfold of True Seeing," he said as he reached it toward Fafhrd. "It shows all things as they really are! Do not lay it across your eyes until you enter the Bazaar. On no account, as you value your life or your sanity, wear it now!"

Fafhrd took it from him most gingerly, the flesh of his fingers crawling. He was inclined to obey the taciturn wizard's instructions. At this moment he truly did not much care to see the true visage of Sheelba of the Eyeless Face.

*   *   *

The Gray Mouser was reading the most interesting book of them all, a great compendium of secret knowledge written in a script of astrologic and geomantic signs, the meaning of which fairly leaped off the page into his mind.

To rest his eyes from that—or rather to keep from gobbling the book too fast—he peered through a nine-elbowed brass tube at a scene that could only be the blue heaven-pinnacle of the universe where angels flew shimmeringly like dragonflies and where a few choice heroes rested from their great mountain-climb and spied down critically on the antlike labors of the gods many levels below.

To rest his eye from *that*, he looked up between the scarlet (bloodmetal?) bars of the inmost cage at the most winsome, slim, fair, jet-eyed girl of them all. She knelt, sitting on her heels, with her upper body leaned back a little. She wore a red velvet tunic and had a mop of golden hair so thick and pliant that she could sweep it in a neat curtain over her upper face, down almost to her pouting lips. With the slim fingers of one hand she would slightly part these silky golden drapes to peer at the Mouser playfully, while with those of the other she rattled golden castanets in a most languorously slow rhythm, though with occasional swift staccato bursts.

The Mouser was considering whether it might not be as well to try a turn or two on the ruby-crusted golden crank next to his elbow, when he spied for the first time the glimmering wall at the back of the shop. What could its material be? he asked himself. Tiny diamonds countless as the sand set in smoky glass? Black opal? Black pearl? Black moonshine?

Whatever it was, it was wholly fascinating, for the Mouser quickly set down his book, using the nine-crooked spy-tube to mark his place—a most engrossing pair of pages on dueling where were revealed the Universal Party and its five false variants and also the three true forms of the Secret Thrust—and with only a finger-wave to the ensorceling blonde in red velvet he walked quickly toward the back of the shop.

As he approached the Black Wall he thought for an instant that he glimpsed a silver wraith, or perhaps a silver skeleton, walking toward him out of it, but then he saw that it was only his own darkly handsome reflection, pleasantly flattered by the lustrous material. What had momentarily suggested silver ribs was the reflection of the silver lacings on his tunic.

He smirked at his image and reached out a finger to touch *its* lustrous finger when —Lo, a wonder!—his hand went into the wall with never a sensation at all save a faint tingling coolth promising comfort like the sheets of a fresh-made bed.

He looked at his hand inside the wall and—Lo, another wonder—it was all a beautiful silver faintly patterned with tiny scales. And though his own hand indubitably, as he could tell by clenching it, it was scarless now and a mite slimmer and longer fingered—altogether a more handsome hand than it had been a moment ago.

He wriggled his fingers and it was like watching small silver fish dark about—fingerlings!

What a droll conceit, he thought, to have a dark fishpond or rather swimming pool set on its side indoors, so that one could walk into the fracious erect fluid quietly and gracefully, instead of all the noisy, bouncingly ahletic business of diving!

And how charming that the pool should be filled not with wet soppy cold water, but with a sort of moon-dark essence of sleep! An essence with beautifying cosmetic properties too—a sort of mudbath without the mud. The Mouser decided he must have a swim in this wonder pool at once, but just then his gaze lit on a long high black couch toward the other end of the dark liquid wall, and beyond the couch a small high table set with viands and a crystal pitcher and goblet.

He walked along the wall to inspect these, his handsome reflection taking step for step with him.

He trailed his hand in the wall for a space and then withdrew it, the scales instantly vanishing and the familiar old scars returning.

The couch turned out to be a narrow high-sided black coffin lined with quilted black satin and piled at one end with little black satin pillows. It looked most invitingly comfortable and restful—not quite as inviting as the Black Wall, but very attractive just the same; there was even a rack of tiny black books nested in the black satin for the occupant's diversion and also a black candle, unlit.

The collation on the little ebony table beyond the coffin consisted entirely of black foods. By sight and then by nibbling and sipping the Mouser discovered their nature: thin slices of a very dark rye bread crusted with poppy seeds and dripped with black butter; slivers of charcoal-seared steak; similarly broiled tiny thin slices of calf's liver sprinkled with dark spices and liberally pricked with capers; the darkest grape jellies; truffles cut paper thin and mushrooms fried black; pickled chestnuts; and of course, ripe olives and black fish eggs—caviar. The black drink, which foamed when he poured it, turned out to be stout laced with the bubbly wine of Ilthmar.

He decided to refresh the inner Mouser—the Mouser who lived a sort of blind soft greedy undulating surface-like between his lips and his belly—before taking a dip in the Black Wall.

*　　*　　*

Fafhrd re-entered the Plaza of Dark Delights walking warily and with the long tatter that was the Cloak of Invisibility trailing from between left forefinger and thumb and with the glimmering cobweb that was the Blindfold of True Seeing pinched even more delicately by its edge between the same digits of his right hand. He was not yet altogether certain that the trailing gossamer hexagon was completely free of spiders.

Across the Plaza he spotted the bright-mouthed shop—the shop he had been told was an outpost of the deadly Devourers—through a ragged gather of folk moving about restlessly and commenting and speculating to one another in harsh excited undertones.

The only feature of the shop Fafhrd could make out at all clearly at this distance was the red-capped red-footed baggy-trousered porter, not capering now but leaning on his long broom beside the trefoil-arched doorway.

With a looping swing of his left arm Fafhrd hung the Cloak of Invisibility around his neck. The ragged ribband hung to either side down his chest in its wolfskin jerkin only halfway to his wide belt which supported longsword and short-axe. It did not vanish his body to the slightest degree that he could see and he doubted it worked at all. Like many another thaumaturge, Ningauble never hesitated to give one useless charms, not for any treacherous reason, necessarily, but simply to improve one's morale. Fafhrd strode boldly toward the shop.

The Northerner was a tall, broad-shouldered, formidable-looking man—doubly formidable by his barbaric dress and weaponing in supercivilized Lankhmar—and so he took it for granted that the ordinay run of city folk stepped out of his way; indeed it had never occurred to him that they should not.

He got a shock. All the clerks, seedy bravos, scullery folk, students, slaves, second-rate merchants and second-class courtesans who would automatically have moved aside for him (though the last with a saucy swing of the hips) now came straight at him, so that he had to dodge and twist and stop and even sometimes dart back to avoid being toe-tramped and bumped. Indeed one fat pushy proud-stomached fellow almost carried away his cobweb, which he could see now by the light of the shop was free of spiders— or if there were any spiders still on it, they must be very small.

He had so much to do dodging Fafhrd-blind Lankhmarians that he could not spare one more glance for the shop until he was almost at the door. And then before he took his first close look, he found that he was tilting his head so that his left ear touched the shoulder below it and that he was laying Sheelba's spiderweb across his eyes.

The touch of it was simply like the touch of any cobweb when one runs face into it walking between close-set bushes at dawn. Everything shimmered a bit as if seen through a fine crystal grating. Then the least shimmering vanished, and with it the delicate clinging sensation, and Fafhrd's vision returned to normal—as far as he could tell.

It turned out that the doorway to the Devourers' shop was piled with garbage— garbage of a particularly offensive sort: old bones, dead fish, butcher's offal, moldering gravecloths folded in uneven squares like badly bound uncut books, broken glass and potsherds, splintered boxes, large stinking dead leaves orange-spotted with blight, bloody rags, tattered discarded loincloths, large worms nosing about, centipedes a-scuttle, cockroaches a-stagger, maggots a-crawl—and less agreeable things.

Atop all perched a vulture which had lost most of its feathers and seemed to have expired of some avian eczema. At lest Fafhrd took it for dead, but then it opened one white-filmed eye.

The only conceivably salable object outside the shop—but it was a most notable exception—was the tall black iron statue, somewhat larger than life-size, of a lean swordsman of dire yet melancholy visage. Standing on its square pedestal beside the door, the statue leaned forward just a little on its long two-handed sword and regarded the Plaza dolefully.

The statue almost teased awake a recollection in Fafhrd's mind—a recent recollection, he fancied—but then there was a blank in his thoughts and he instantly dropped the puzzle. On raids like this one, relentlessly swift action was paramount. He loosened his axe in its loop, noiselessly whipped out Graywand and, shrinking away from the piled and crawling garbage just a little, entered the Bazaar of the Bizarre.

*   *   *

The Mouser, pleasantly replete with tasty black food and heady black drink, drifted to the Black Wall and thrust in his right arm to the shoulder. He waved it about, luxuriating in the softly flowing coolth and balm—admiring its fine silver scales and more than human handsomeness. He did the same with his right leg, swinging it like a dancer exercising at the bar. Then he took a gentle deep breath and drifted farther in.

*   *   *

Fafhrd on entering the Bazaar saw the same piles of gloriously bound books and racks of gleaming brass spy-tubes and crystal lenses as had the Mouser—a circumstance which seemed to overset Ningauble's theory that the Devourers sold only trash.

He also saw the eight beautiful cages of jewel-gleaming metals and the gleaming chains that hung them from the ceiling and went to the jeweled wall cranks.

Each cage held a gleaming, gloriously hued, black- or light-haired spider big as a rather small person and occasionally waving a long jointed claw-handed leg, or softly opening a little and then closing a pair of fanged down-swinging mandibles, while staring steadily at Fahrd with eight watchful eyes set in two jewel-like rows of four.

Set a spider to catch a spider, Fafhrd thought, thinking of his cobweb, and then wondered what the thought meant.

He quickly switched to more practical questions then, but he had barely asked himself whether before proceeding further he should kill the very expensive-looking spiders, fit to be the coursing beasts of some jungle empress—another count against Ning's trash-theory!—when he heard a faint splashing from the back of the shop. It reminded him of the Mouser taking a bath—the Mouser loved baths, slow luxurious ones in hot soapy scented oil-dripped water, the small gray sybarite!—and so Fafhrd hurried off in that direction with many a swift upward overshoulder glance.

He was detouring the last cage, a scarlet-metaled one holding the handsomest spider yet, when he noted a book set down with a crooked spy-tube in it—exactly as the Mouser would keep his place in a book by closing it on a dagger.

Fafhrd paused to open the book. Its lustrous white pages were blank. He put his impalpably cobwebbed eye to the spy-tube. He glimpsed a scene that could only be the smoky red hell-nadir of the universe, where dark devils scuttled about like centipedes and where chained folk gazing yearningly upward and the damned writhed in the grip of black serpents whose eyes shone and whose fangs dripped and whose nostrils breathed fire.

As he dropped tube and book, he heard the faint sonorous quick dull report of bubbles being expelled from a fluid at its surface. Staring instantly toward the dim back of the shop, he saw at last the pearl-shimmering Black Wall and a silver skeleton eyed with great diamonds receding into it. However, this costly bone-man—once more Ning's trash-theory disproved!—still had one arm sticking partway out of the wall and this arm was not bone, whether silver, white, brownish or pink, but live-looking flesh covered with proper skin.

As the arm sank into the wall, Fafhrd sprang forward as fast as he ever had in his life and grabbed the hand just before it vanished. He knew then he had hold of his friend, for he would recognize anywhere the Mouser's grip, no matter how enfeebled. He tugged, but it was as if the Mouser were mired in black quicksand. He laid Graywand down and grasped the Mouser by the wrist too and braced his feet against the rough black flags and gave a tremendous heave.

The silver skeleton came out of the wall with a black splash, metamorphosing as it did into a vacant-eyed Gray Mouser who without a look at his friend and rescuer went staggering off in a curve and pitched head over heels into the black coffin.

But before Fafhrd could hoist his comrade from this new gloomy predicament, there was a swift clash of footsteps and there came racing into the shop, somewhat to Fafhrd's surprise, the tall black iron statue. It had forgotten or simply stepped off its pedestal, but it had remembered its two-handed sword, which it brandished about most fiercely while shooting searching black glances like iron darts at every shadow and corner and nook.

The black gaze passed Fafhrd without pausing, but halted at Graywand lying on the floor. At the sight of the longsword the statue started visibly, snarled its iron lips, narrowed its black eyes. It shot glances more ironly stabbing than before, and it began to move about the shop in sudden zigzag rushes, sweeping its darkly flashing sword in low scythe-strokes.

At that moment the Mouser peeped moon-eyed over the edge of the coffin, lifted a limp hand and waved it at the statue, and in a soft sly foolish voice cried, "Yoo-hoo!"

The statue paused in its searchings and scythings to glare at the Mouser in mixed contempt and puzzlement.

"Ho, slave!" he cried to the statue with maudlin gaiety, "your wares are passing passable. I'll take the girl in red velvet." He pulled a coin from his pouch, goggled at it closely, then pitched it at the statue. "That's one penny. And the nine-crooked spy-tube. That's another penny." He pitched it. "And *Gron's Grand Compendium of Exotic Love*—another penny for you! Yes, and here's one more for supper—very tasty, 'twas. Oh and I almost forgot—here's for tonight's lodging!" He pitched a fifth large copper coin at the demonic black statue and, smiling blissfully, flopped back out of sight. The black quilted satin could be heard to sigh as he sank in it.

Four-fifths of the way through the Mouser's penny-pitching Fafhrd decided it was useless to try to unriddle his comrade's nonsensical behavior and that it would be far more to the point to make use of this diversion to snatch up Graywand. He did so on the instant, but by that time the black statue was fully alert again, if it had ever been otherwise. Its gaze switched to Graywand the instant Fafhrd touched the longsword and it stamped its foot, which rang against the stone, and cried a harsh metallic "Ha!"

Apparently the sword became invisible as Fafhrd grasped it, for the black statue did not follow him with its iron eyes as he shifted position across the room. Instead it swiftly laid down its own mighty blade and caught up a long narrow silver trumpet and set it to its lips.

Fafhrd thought it wise to attack before the statue summoned reinforcements. He rushed straight at the thing, swinging back Graywand for a great stroke at the neck—and steeling himself for an arm-numbing impact.

The statue blew and instead of the alarm blare Fafhrd had expected, there silently puffed out straight at him a great cloud of white powder that momentarily blotted out everything, as if it were the thickest of fogs from Hlal the River.

Fafhrd retreated, choking and coughing. The demon-blown fog cleared quickly, the white powder falling to the stony floor with unnatural swiftness, and he could see again to attack, but now the statue apparently could see him too, for it squinted straight at him and cried its metallic "Ha!" again and whirled its sword around its iron head preparatory to the charge—rather as if winding itself up.

Fafhrd saw that his own hands and arms were thickly filmed with the white powder, which apparently clung to him everywhere except his eyes, doubtless protected by Sheelba's cobweb.

The iron statue came thrusting and slashing in. Fafhrd took the great sword on his, chopped back, and was parried in return. And now the combat assumed the noisy deadly aspects of a conventional longsword duel, except that Graywand was notched whenever it caught the chief force of a stroke, while the statue's somewhat longer weapon remained unmarked. Also, whenever Fafhrd got through the other's guard with a thrust—it was almost impossible to reach him with a slash—it turned out that the other had slipped his lean body or head aside with unbelievably swift and infallible anticipations.

It seemed to Fafhrd—at least at the time—the most fell, frustrating, and certainly the most wearisome combat in which he had ever engaged, so he suffered some feelings of hurt and irritation when the Mouser reeled up in his coffin again and learned and leaned an elbow on the black-satin-quilted side and rested chin on fist and grinned hugely at the battlers and from time to time laughed wildly and shouted such enraging nonsense as, "Use Secret Thrust Two-and-a-Half, Fafhrd—it's all in the book!" or "Jump in the oven!—there'd be a master stroke of strategy!" or—this to the statue—"Remember to sweep under his feet, you rogue!"

Backing away from one of Fafhrd's sudden attacks, the statue bumped the table holding the remains of the Mouser's repast—evidently its anticipatory abilities did not extend to its rear—and scraps of black food and white potsherds and jags of crystal shattered across the floor.

The Mouser leaned out of his coffin and waved a finger waggishly. "You'll have to sweep that up!" he cried and went off into a gale of laughter.

Backing away again, the statue bumped the black coffin. The Mouser only clapped the demonic figure comradely on the shoulder and called, "Set to it again, clown! Brush him down! Dust him off!"

But the worst was perhaps when, during a brief pause while the combatants gasped and eyed each other dizzily, the Mouser waved coyly to the nearest giant spider and called his inane "Yoo-hoo!" again, following it with, "I'll see you, dear, after the circus."

Fafhrd, parrying with weary desperation a fifteenth or a fiftieth cut at his head, thought bitterly, *This comes of trying to rescue small heartless madmen who would howl at their grandmothers hugged by bears. Sheelba's cobweb has shown me the gray one in his true idiot nature.*

The Mouser had first been furious when the sword-skirling clashed him awake from his black satin dreams, but as soon as he saw what was going on he became enchanted at the wildly comic scene.

For, lacking Sheelba's cobweb, what the Mouser saw was only the zany red-capped porter prancing about in his tip-curled red shoes and aiming with his broom great strokes at Fafhrd, who looked exactly as if he had climbed a moment ago out of a barrel of meal. The only part of the Northerner not whitely dusted was a mask-like stretch across his eyes.

What made the whole thing fantastically droll was that miller-white Fafhrd was going through all the motions—and emotions!—of a genuine combat with excruciating precision, parrying the broom as if it were some great jolting scimitar or two-handed broadsword even. The broom would go sweeping up and Fafhrd would gawk at it, giving a marvellous interpretation of apprehensive goggling despite his strangely shadowed eyes. Then the broom would come sweeping down and Fafhrd would brace himself and seem to catch it on his sword only with the most prodigious effort—and then pretend to be jolted back by it!

The Mouser had never suspected Fafhrd had such a perfected theatric talent, even if it were acting of a rather mechanical sort, lacking the broad sweeps of true dramatic genius, and he whooped with laughter.

Then the broom brushed Fafhrd's shoulder and blood sprang out.

Fafhrd, wounded at last and thereby knowing himself unlikely to out-endure the black statue—although the latter's iron chest was working now like a bellows—decided on swifter measures. He loosened his hand-axe again in its loop and at the next pause in the fight, both battlers having outguessed each other by retreating simultaneously, whipped it up and hurled it at his adversary's face.

Instead of seeking to dodge or ward off the missile, the black statue lowered its sword and merely wove its head in a tiny circle.

The axe closely circled the lean black head, like a silver woodtailed comet whipping around a black sun, and came back straight at Fafhrd like a boomerang—and rather more swiftly than Fafhrd had sent it.

But time slowed for Fafhrd then and he half ducked and caught it left-handed as it went whizzing past his cheek.

His thoughts too went for a moment fast as his actions. He thought of how his adversary, able to dodge every frontal attack, had not avoided the table or the coffin behind him. He thought of how the Mouser had not laughed now for a dozen clashes and he looked at him and saw him, though still dazed-seeming, strangely pale and sober-faced, appearing to stare with horror at the blood running down Fafhrd's arm.

So crying as heartily and merrily as he could, "Amuse yourself! Join in the fun, clown!—here's your slap-stick," Fafhrd tossed the axe toward the Mouser.

Without waiting to see the result of that toss—perhaps not daring to—he summoned up his last reserves of speed and rushed at the black statue in a circling advance that drove it back toward the coffin.

Without shifting his stupid horrified gaze, the Mouser stuck out a hand at the last possible moment and caught the axe by the handle as it spun lazily down.

As the black statue retreated near the coffin and poised for what promised to be a stupendous counter-attack, the Mouser leaned out and, now grinning foolishly again, sharply rapped its black pate with the axe.

The iron head split like a coconut, but did not come apart. Fafhrd's hand-axe, wedged in it deeply, seemed to turn all at once to iron like the statue and its black haft was wrenched out of the Mouser's hand as the statue stiffened up straight and tall.

The Mouser stared at the split head woefully, like a child who hadn't known knives cut.

The statue brought its great sword flat against its chest, like a staff on which it might lean but did not, and it fell rigidly forward and hit the floor with a ponderous clank.

At that stony-metallic thundering, white wildfire ran across the Black Wall, lightning the whole shop like a distant levin-bolt, and iron-basalt thundering echoed from deep within it.

Fafhrd sheathed Graywand, dragged the Mouser out of the black coffin—the fight hadn't left him the strength to lift even his small friend—and shouted in his ear. "Come on! Run!"

The Mouser ran for the Black Wall.

Fafhrd snagged his wrist as he went by and plunged toward the arched door, dragging the Mouser after him.

The thunder faded out and there came a low whistle, cajolingly sweet.

Wildfire raced again acros the Black Wall behind them—much more brightly this time, as if a lightning storm were racing toward them.

The white glare striking ahead imprinted one vision indelibly on Fafhrd's brain: the giant spider in the inmost cage pressed against the bloodred bars to gaze down at them. It had pale legs and a velvet red body and a mask of sleek thick golden hair from which eight jet eyes peered, while its fanged jaws hanging down in the manner of the wide blades of a pair of golden scissors rattled together in a wild staccato rhythm like castanets.

That moment the cajoling whistle was repeated. It too seemed to be coming from the red and golden spider.

But strangest of all to Fafhrd was to hear the Mouser, dragged unwillingly along behind him, cry out in answer to the whistling, "Yes, darling, I'm coming. Let me go, Fafhrd! Let me climb to her! Just one kiss! Sweetheart!"

"Stop it, Mouser," Fafhrd growled, his flesh crawling in mid-plunge. "It's a giant spider!"

"Wipe the cobwebs out of your eyes, Fafhrd," the Mouser retorted pleadingly and most unwittingly to the point. "It's a gorgeous girl! I'll never see her ticklesome like— and I've paid for her! *Sweetheart!*"

Then the booming thunder drowned his voice and any more whistling there might have been, and the wildfire came again, brighter than day, and another great thunder-clap right on its heels, and the floor shuddered and the whole shop shook, and Fafhrd dragged the Mouser through the trefoil-arched doorway, and there was another great flash and clap.

The flash showed a semicircle of Lankhmarians peering ashen-faced overshoulder as they retreated across the Plaza of Dark Delights from the remarkable indoor thunderstorm that threatened to come out after them.

Fafhrd spun around. The archway had turned to blank wall.

The Bazaar of the Bizarre was gone from the World of Nehwon.

The Mouser, sitting on the dank flags where Fafhrd had dragged him, babbled wailfully, "The secrets of time and space! The lore of the gods! The mysteries of Hell! Black nirvana! Red and gold Heaven! Five pennies gone forever!"

Fafhrd set his teeth. A mighty resolve, rising from his many recent angers and bewilderments, crystallized in him.

Thus far he had used Sheelba's cobweb—and Ningauble's tatter too—only to serve others. Now he would use them for himself! He would peer at the Mouser more closely and at every person he knew. He would study even his own reflection! But most of all, he would stare Sheelba and Ning to their wizardly cores!

There came from overhead a low "Hssst!"

As he glanced up he felt something snatched from around his neck and, with the faintest tingling sensation, from off his eyes.

For a moment there was a shimmer traveling upward and through it he seemed to glimpse distortedly, as through thick glass, a black face with a cobwebby skin that entirely covered mouth and nostrils and eyes.

Then that dubious flash was gone and there were only two cowled heads peering down at him from over the wall top. There was chuckling laughter.

Then both cowled heads drew back out of sight and there was only the edge of the roof and the sky and the stars and the blank wall.

237 Talking Statues, Etc.

During the last five years of his life, when his theatrical career was largely over, the famous actor Francis Legrande spent considerable time making portraits of himself: plaster heads and busts, some larger statues, oil paintings, sketches in various media, and photographic self-studies. Most of them showed him in roles in which he had starred on the stage and screen. Legrande had always been a versatile craftsman and the results were artistically adequate.

After his death, his wife devoted herself to caring for the self-portraits along with other tangible and intangible memories of the great man. Keeping them alive, as it were, or at least dusted and cleaned and even pampered with an occasional change of air and prospect. There were 237 of them on view, distributed throughout Legrande's studio, the living room and halls and bedrooms of the house, and in the garden.

Legrande had a son, Francis Legrande II, who had no more self content or success in life than most sons of prominent and widely admired men. After the collapse of his third marriage and his eleventh job, young Francis—who was well over forty—retreated for a time to his father's house.

His relations with his mother were amicable but limited: they said loud cheery things to each other when they met, but after a bit they began to keep their daily orbits separate—by accident, as it were.

Young Francis was drinking rather too heavily and trying hard to control it, yet without any definite program for the future—a poor formula for quiet nerves.

After six weeks his father's selfportraits began to talk to him. It came as no great surprise, since they had been following him with their eyes for at least a week, and for the past two days they had been frowing and smiling at him—critically, he was certain —glaring and smirking—and this morning the air was full of ominous hangoverish noises on the verge of intelligibility.

He was alone in the studio. In fact he was alone in the whole house, since his mother was calling on a neighbor. There came a tiny but nerve-rasping dry grating sound, exactly as if chalk were coughing or plaster had cleared its throat. He quickly glanced at a white bust of his father as Julius Caesar and he distinctly saw the plaster lips part a little and the tip of a plaster tongue come out and quickly run around them. Then—

FATHER: I irritate you, don't I? Or perhaps I should say *we* irritate you?

SON (*startled but quickly accepting the situation and deciding to speak frankly*): Well, yes, you do. Most sons are bugged by their fathers—any psychologist who knows his stuff will tell you that. By the actual father or by his memory. If the father happens to be a famous man, the son is that much more intimidated and inhibited and overawed. And if, in addition, the father leaves behind dozens of faces of himself, created by himself, if he insists on going on living after death . . . *(He shrugs.)*

FATHER: *(smiling compassionately from a painting of himself as Jesus of Nazareth):* In short, you hate me.

SON: Oh, I wouldn't go as far as that. It's more that you weary me. Seeing you around everywhere, all the time, I get bored.

FATHER: *(in dark colors, as Strindberg's Captain):* You get bored? You've only been here six weeks. Think of me having nothing to look at for ten whole years but your mother.

SON: *(with a certain satisfaction):* I always thought your affection and devotion to mother were overdone.

FATHER: *(a head of Don Juan, interrupting):* But it *has* been a dull time. There have been exactly three beautiful girls inside this house during the last decade, and one of those was collecting for Community Chest and only stayed five minutes. And none of them got undressed.

FATHER: *(as Socrates):* And then there are so many of me to be bored and just one of you. I've sometimes wished I hadn't been quite so enthusiastic about multiplying myself.

SON *(wincing from a crick in the neck got from swiveling his head rapidly from portrait to portrait):* Serves you right! Two hundred and thirty-seven self-portraits!

FATHER: Actually there are about 450, but the others are put away.

SON: Good Lord! Are they alive too?

FATHER: Well, yes, in an imprisoned drugged sort of way . . . *(From various cabinets and drawers comes a low but tumultuous groaning and muttering.)*

SON *(rushing out of the studio into the living room in a sudden spasm of terror which he tries to conceal by speaking loudly and contemptuously):* What collosal vanity! Four hundred and fifty self-portraits! What narcissism!

FATHER *(from a full-length painting of King Lear over the fireplace):* I don't think it was vanity, son, not chiefly. All my life I was used to making up my face and getting into costume. Spending half an hour at it, or if there were something special like a beard *(the portrait touches its long white one with wrinkle-painted fingers)* an hour or more. When I retired from the stage, I still had the make-up habit, the itch to work my face over. I took it out in doing self-portraits. It was as simple as that.

SON: I might have known you'd have an innocent fine-sounding explanation. You always did.

FATHER: In an average acting year I made myself up at least two hundred and fifty times. So even 237 self-portraits are less than a year at the dressing-room table, and 450 less than two years.

SON: You'd never have been able to do so many portraits except you cheated. You worked from photographs and life-masks of yourself.

FATHER *(self-painted as Leonarde da Vinci):* Son, great artists have been cheating that way for five thousand years.

SON: All right, all right!

FATHER *(being very fair about it):* I'll admit that in addition the self-portraits let me relive my triumphs and keep up the illusion I was still acting.

SON *(cruelly):* You never stopped! On the stage or off you were always acting.

FATHER *(as Moses):* That's hardly just. I never talked a great deal. I was never domineering and *(pointedly)* I never ranted.

SON (*stung*): That's right!—offstage you preferred the quiet starring roles to the windy ones. Your favorite was a sickeningly noble, serene, infallible, pipesmoking older hero—a modern Brutus, a worldly Christ, a less folksy Will Rogers. But no matter how restrained your offstage characterizations, you managed to stay stage center.

FATHER (*shrugging pen-and-ink shoulders*): Laymen always accuse actors of acting. Because we can portray genuine emotion, we're supposed to be unable to feel it. It's the oldest charge made against us.

SON: And it's true!

FATHER (*very kindly, from a jaunty portrait of Cyrano de Bergerac*): My child, I do believe you're jealous of me.

SON (*pacing wildly and waving his arms*): Certainly I am! What son wouldn't be?—surrounded, stifled, suffocated by a father disguised as all the great men who ever were or are or will be! All the great sages! All the great adventurers! All the great lovers!

FATHER (*gently, from the gape-mouth of a gaunt plaster head of Lazarus lifting from a plaster gravehole*): But there's no reason to be jealous of me any longer, son. I'm dead.

SON: You don't act as if you were! You're alive 237 times—450, if we count your reserve battalions. You're all over the place!

FATHER (*as Peer Gynt*): Oh son, these are only poor phantoms, roused for a moment from the nightmarish waking-sleep of Hell. Only powerless ghosts . . . (*All the portraits cry out softly and confusedly and there comes again the muttering and groaning of the ones shut away in darkness.*)

SON (*overcome by another gust of terror and banging the door as he rushes out into the garden*): They are not! They're all facets of your perfection, damn you! Your miserable perfection, which you spent a lifetime polishing.

FATHER (*from a gauntcheeked bas relief of Don Quixote on the patio wall*): Every human being believes he is perfect in his way, even the most miserable scoundrel or dreamer.

SON; Not to the degree you believed you were perfect. You practiced perfection in front of the mirror. You rehearsed it. You watched your least word and gesture and you never made a slip.

FATHER (*incredulous*): Did I actually seem like that to you?

SON: Seem? My God, if you knew how I prayed for you to make a mistake. Just one, just once. Make it and own up to it. But you never did.

FATHER (*shaking a green-tarnished bronze head across a screen of leaves*): I never suspected you felt that way. Naturally a parent pretends to his child to be a little more perfect than he actually is. To admit any of his real weaknesses would be too much like encouraging vice. He wants to be sure his child is law-abiding during the formative years—later he may be able to stand the truth. Children can't distinguish between black and the palest shade of gray. It's the parent's duty to set as good an example as he can, even if he has to cover up some things and cheat a bit, until the child has mature judgment.

SON: And as a result the child is utterly crushed by this great white marble image of perfection!

FATHER: I suppose that conceivably could happen. Do you mean to tell me, son, that you didn't know your father was as other men?—that he had every last one of their weaknesses?

SON (*a hope dawning*): You really mean that? You're honestly saying . . . (*Then, recovering himself*) Oh, oh, I smell another of your lily-white, high-sounding explanations coming.

FATHER (*still from bronze head, which is that of Hamlet*): No, son! I could accuse me of such things that it were better my mother had not borne me. I was very proud, revengeful, ambitious, with more offenses at my beck than I had thoughts to put them in, imagination to give them shape, or time to act them in. I itched to excell at everything. Because my life depended on being the best actor, I was bitterly jealous of everyone's least accomplishments, even your own. I hid my scorn of all mankind under a mask of tolerant serenity—which I had trouble keeping in place, believe me. I lived for applause. During my last years I was bitterly resentful that ill-advised friends and greedy managers did not force me to come out of retirement and make farewell tours. I wronged your mother by lusting after other women, and myself by never having the nerve to yield to temptation—

SON: What, never?

FATHER: Well, hardly ever.

SON: Dad, that's terrific!

FATHER (*modestly*): Well, inspired by the great characters I portray, I sometimes get carried away. A little of them rubs off on me.

SON (*rather breathless*): This puts a different complexion on everything. What a relief! Dad, I feel wonderful. (*He laughs, a touch hysterically.*)

FATHER: Wait, son, I did worse than that. I watched your mother's personality fade, I watched her change into a mere adjunct of myself, and I let it happen, merely because life was a trifle easier for me that way. I watched you blunder along under a load of anxiety and guilt and I never tried to get close to you or tell you the truth about myself, which might have helped you, simply because it would have been difficult and uncomfortable for me to have done so and because I—

SON (*concerned*): Now you are going too far, Dad. You mustn't blame yourself for—

FATHER (*ignoring the sympathy*): —and because I actually enjoyed your awed embittered admiration. You were such a gullible audience! And then during the last years, instead of turning outward, I lost interest in almost everything except the self-portraits. I poured all of myself into them, finally the life-force itself, so that now I live on in them—a solitary self-created Hell. A human being's punishment for his misdeeds is having to watch and sometimes suffer their consequences . . . but to have to watch them minute after minute from 237 vantage points, unable to take the slightest action, unable even to comment, without the boon of a moment's forgetfulness, a moment's nirvana . . . (*His voice grows ghostly.*) Ten years! Thirty-six hundred interminable twilights. Thirty-six hundred empty dawns. To have to watch this house and garden die. To watch your mother mooning about day after day, wasting herself on memories and sentimental bric-a-brac. To watch you narrow your life down as I did mine, but before you've even lived it, and all your sodden drinking. To have to observe in all its loathsome detail the soul-rotting, snail-slow creep of inanition . . .

SON (*angry again, in spite of himself, and once more quite frightened*): Well don't bellyache to me about it. It's your own fault that there are 237 of you, all corroding with life-force—another man would have been satisfied with being damned just once. There's nothing I can do for you.

FATHER (*grinning evilly from the head of Mephistopheles peering from between bushes opposite Hamlet*): But there is. Break us, burn us, melt us down. Give us oblivion. Smash us!

SON (*rushing back into house, partly to grab up poker from fireplace and partly because, all in all, the talking portraits in the house are less eerie than those hidden about the garden*): By God, I'd like to! I don't know how often I've thought of this house as a musty old museum, the lumber room of one man's vanity.

FATHER *(a chorus)*: Strike!

SON *(hesitating with poker lifted above his head)*: But they'd think I was crazy. They'd believe that envy of you pushed me over the line into psychosis. They'd probably put me away.

FATHER *(as Leonardo again)*: Nonsense! They'd merely say that you were ridding the world of some amateurish daubs and thumb-scoopings. *Smash us!*

SON *(veering into argument)*: Amateurish is too strong a word. They're not that bad, certainly.

FATHER *(pleased)*: You think my work has enduring professional quality?

SON *(frowns)*: No, that would be going too far in the opposite direction.

FATHER: *Smash us!*

SON *(raised the poker, but again hesitates)*: There's another thing: mother would never forgive me.

FATHER: *Don't bring your mother into this!*

SON: Why not? For that matter, if you've really been wanting oblivion for ten years, why didn't you ask mother to smash you? Or at least to put you all away, where you'd have something nearer oblivion, I gather. Or *give* you all away to people who would either destroy you or provide you with more diverse environments and a more interesting shadowlife.

FATHER: Son, I've never been able to make things like that clear to your mother. Somehow the more she fitted herself to me, the less she was really in touch with me. She was as close to me and yet as far beyond my ken as . . . my gall bladder. I've tried to talk to her, but she doesn't hear. I don't think she even sees my self-portraits any more, but only the image of me—her own creation—which she carries in her mind. But *you*, at long last, hear me. And I tell you: *smash us!*

FATHER *(as plaster head of Don Juan, calling from studio)*: Think of the fiery impetuous philanderer imprisoned in the icy rigid statue he invites for dinner. Three girls glimpsed in ten years! *Smash us!*

FATHER *(as the painted Leonardo)*: You were always scared to take action, I wasn't! —I expressed myself, even in these miserable self-portraits. Now it's your turn—and your opportunity. *Smash us!*

FATHER *(as Peer Gynt)*: Plunge me back in the crucible. Melt me down.

FATHER *(as Beethoven)*: Strike a great healing discord!

FATHER *(as Jean Valjean)*: Explode the prison!

FATHER *(as St. John the Divine)*: Unleash the apocalypse!

FATHER *(a muffled chorus of photographs)*: Break our glass, shred us, touch a match to us. Destroy us!

FATHER *(all 237 with the dark undertones of the imprisoned ones)*: SMASH US!

SON *(swings up the poker a third time, then lowers its tip to the floor with a smile, his manner suddenly easy)*: No. Why should I let myself be agitated by a bunch of old pictures and sculptures, even if they do talk? How would destroying them change me? And why should I be intimidated by a dead father, even if he lives on in various obscure ways? It's ridiculous.

FATHER *(once more King Lear)*: Have you lost your respect for us? Are you not at least filled with supernatural terror at this morning's events?

SON *(shaking his head)*: No, I think it's just my hangover talking with a strong psychotic accent—or 237 accents. And if it really *is* you, Dad, somehow talking from somewhere, I think you mean me well and so I'm not frightened. And finally, to be very honest with you, I don't think you *really* want to be destroyed, Dad, even in effigy—or effigies. I think you've just been getting your feelings off your chest, especially your boredom.

FATHER (*as Peer Gynt, smiling an inscrutable smile, perhaps of relief, perhaps of triumph, perhaps of resignation*): Well, if you can't bring yourself to destroy us, at least stir up this old house, stir up your own life.

SON (*nodding*): There's something to that, all right, Dad.

FATHER: If you don't take the initiative—and moderate your drinking, too—we'll probably start talking again some morning or night, and not nearly as pleasantly, or even sanely. So stir things up.

SON (*seriously*): I'll remember that, Dad.

FATHER (*calling as Don Juan, from studio*): Invite some—(*The voice breaks off abruptly.*)

SON *looks around at the portraits. They have suddenly all gone mum. He can detect no movement in any of them, or changes in their features. The front door opens and his mother comes in excitedly with an opened letter in her hand.*

MOTHER: Francis, I've just received the most interesting request. The Merrivale Young Ladies' Academy wants a bust of your father for their library or lounge room. I think we should grant their request—that it, if you agree.

SON (*poking elaborately at the ashes in the fireplace, to account for the poker*): Why not? (*Then getting an inspiration and growing wily*) How about the Hamlet head?

MOTHER: Out of the question—that's his masterpiece. Besides, it's rivetted to its pillar in the garden.

SON: Well, then the Lear.

MOTHER: Certainly not, it's my favorite. Besides, it's a painting, not a bust.

SON (*baiting his trap*): Well, I suppose you could give them . . . No, it's not good enough.

MOTHER (*instantly contentious*): What's not good enough?

SON (*as if reluctantly*): I was going to say the bust of Don Juan, but—

MOTHER: I think that's a very fine piece of work—and an excellent choice in this instance.

SON: Perhaps you're right about that, mother. In any case, I bow to your judgment.

MOTHER: Thank you, Francis. I've never given any of the statues away before, but I think I should begin to. I'll write Merrivale Young Ladies' Academy they may have the bust of Don Juan. (*Starts out.*)

SON: I think you'll feel happier when you've done this, mother. And I think father will feel happier too.

MOTHER (*pausing in doorway*): What's happened to you, Francis? You're usually so cynical about these matters.

SON (*shrugs*): I don't know. Maybe I'm growing. (*As his mother leaves, he begins to smile. Suddenly he whirls toward the portrait of Peer Gynt. It had seemed to wink, but now it presents only its fixed painted expression. Francis Legrande II continues to smile as he hears someone in the studio begin faintly to hum an air from Don Giovanni.*")

When the Change-Winds Blow

I was halfway between Arcadia and Utopia, flying a long archeologic scout, looking for coleopt hives, lepidopteroid stiltcities, and ruined villas of the Old Ones.

On Mars they've stuck to the fanciful names the old astronomers dreamed onto their charts. They've got an Elysium and an Ophir too.

I judged I was somewhere near the Acid Sea, which by a rare coincidence does become a poisonous shallow marsh, rich in hydrogen ions, when the northern icecap melts.

But I saw no sign of it below me, nor any archeologic features either—only the endless dull rosy plain of felsite dust and iron-oxide powder slipping steadily west under my flier, with here and there a shallow canyon or low hill, looking for all the world (Earth? Mars?) like parts of the Mojave.

The sun was behind me, its low light flooding the cabin. A few stars glittered in the dark blue sky. I recognized the constellations of Sagittarius and Scorpio, the red pinpoint of Antares.

I was wearing my pilot's red spacesuit. They've enough air on Mars for flying now, but not for breathing if you fly even a few hundred yards above the surface.

Beside me sat my copilot's green spacesuit, which would have had someone in it if I were more sociable or merely mindful of flying regulations. From time to time it swayed and jogged just a little.

And things were feeling eerie, which isn't how they ought to feel to someone who loves solitude as much as I do, or pretend to myself I do. But the Martian landscape is even more spectral than that of Arabia or the American Southwest—lonely and beautiful and obsessed with death and immensity and sometimes it strikes through.

From some old poem the words came, ". . . and strange thoughts grow, with a certain humming in my ears, about the life before I lived this life."

I had to stop myself from leaning forward and looking around into the faceplate of the green spacesuit to see if there weren't someone there now. A thin man. Or a tall slim woman. Or a black crabjointed Martian coleopteroid, who needs a spacesuit about as much as a spacesuit does. Or . . . who knows?

It was very still in the cabin. The silence did almost hum. I had been listening to Deimos Station, but now the outer moonlet had dropped below the southern horizon. They'd been broadcasting a suggestions program about dragging Mercury away from the sun to make it the moon of Venus—and giving both planets rotation too—so as to stir up the thick smoggy furnace-hot atmosphere of Venus and make it habitable.

303

Better finish fixing up Mars first, I'd thought.

But then almost immediately the rider to that thought had come: No, I *want Mars to stay lonely. That's why I came here. Earth got crowded and look what happened.*

Yet there are times on Mars when it would be pleasant, even to an old solitary like me, to have a companion. That is if you could be sure of picking your companion.

Once again I felt the compulsion to peer inside the green spacesuit.

Instead I scanned around. Still only the dust-desert drawing toward sunset: almost featureless, yet darkly rosy as an old peach. "True peach, rosy and flawless . . . Peach-blossom marble all, the rare, the ripe as fresh-poured wine of nighty pulse . . ." *What* was *that poem?*—my mind nagged.

On the seat beside me, almost under the thigh of the green spacesuit, vibrating with it a little, was a tape: *Vanished Churches and Cathedrals of Terra.* Old buildings are an abiding interest with me, of course, and then some of the hills or hives of the black coleopts are remarkably suggestive of Earth towers and spires, even to details like lancet windows and flying buttresses, so much that it's been suggested there is an imitative element, perhaps telepathic, in architecture of those strange beings who despite their humanoid intelligence are very like social insects. I'd been scanning the book at my last stop, hunting out coleopt-hill resemblances, but then a cathedral interior had reminded me of the Rockefeller Chapel at the University of Chicago and I'd slipped the tape out of the projector. That chapel was where Monica had been, getting her Ph.D. in physics on a bright June morning, when the fusion blast licked the southern end of Lake Michigan, and I didn't want to think about Monica. Or rather I wanted too much to think about her.

"What's done is done, and she is dead beside, dead long ago . . ." Now I recognized the poem!—Browning's *The Bishop Orders His Tomb at St. Praxed's Church.* That was a distant cry!—Had there been a view of St. Praxed's on the tape?—The 16th Century . . . and the dying bishop pleading with his sons for a grotesquely grand tomb—a frieze of satyrs, nymphs, the Savior, Moses, lynxes—while he thinks of their mother, his mistress . . .

"Your tall pale mother with her talking eyes . . . Old Grandolf envied me, so fair she was!"

Robert Browning and Elizabeth Barrett and their great love . . .

Monica and myself and our love that never got started . . .

Monica's eyes talked. She was tall and slim and proud . . .

Maybe if I had more character, or only energy, I'd find myself someone else to love —a new planet, a new girl!—I wouldn't stay uselessly faithful to that old romance, I wouldn't go courting loneliness, locked in a dreaming life-in-death on Mars . . .

"Hours and long hours in the dead night, I ask, 'Do I live, am I dead?'"

But for me the loss of Monica is tied up, in a way I can't untangle, with the failure of Earth, with my loathing of what Terra did to herself in her pride of money and power and success (communist and capitalist alike) with that unneccessary atomic war that came just when they thought they had everything safe and solved, as they felt before the one in 1914. It didn't wipe out an Earth by any means, only about a third, but it wiped out my trust in human nature—and the divine too, I'm afraid—and it wiped out Monica . . .

"And as she died so must we die ourselves, and thenst ye may perceive the world's a dream."

A dream? Maybe we lack a Browning to make read those moments of modern history gone over the Niagara of the past, to find them again needle-in-haystack, atom-in-whirlpool, and etch them perfectly, the moments of starflight and planet-landing etched as he had etched the moments of the Renaissance.

Yet—the world (Mars? Terra?) only a dream? Well maybe. A bad dream sometimes, that's for sure! I told myself as I jerked my wandering thoughts back to the flier and the unchanging rosy desert under the small sun.

Apparently I hadn't missed anything—my second mind had been faithfully watching and instrument-tending while my first mind rambled in imaginings and memories.

But things were feeling eerier than ever. The silence did hum now, brassily, as if a great peal of bells had just clanged, or were about to. There was menace now in the small sun about to set behind me, bringing the Martian night and what Martian were-things there may be that they don't know of yet. The rosy plain had turned sinister. And for a moment I was sure that if I looked into the green spacesuit, I would see a dark wraith thinner than any coleopt, or else's a bone-brown visage fleshlessly grinning—the King of Terrors.

"Swift as a weaver's shuttle fleet our years: Man goeth to the grave, and where is he?"

You know, the weird and the supernatural didn't just evaporate when the world got crowded and smart and technical. They moved outward—to Luna, to Mars, to the Jovian satellites, to the black tangled forest of space and the astronomic marches and the unimaginably distant bulls-eye windows of the stars. Out to the realms of the unknown, where the unexpected still happens every other hour and the impossible every other day—

And right at that moment I saw the impossible standing 400 feet tall and cloaked in lacy gray in the desert ahead of me.

And while my first mind froze for seconds that stretched toward minutes and my central vision stayed blankly fixed on that upwardly bifurcated incredibility with its dark hint of rainbow caught in the gray lace, my second mind and my periferal vision brought my flier down to a swift, dream-smooth, skimmering landing on its long skis in the rosy dust. I brushed a control and the cabin walls swung silently downward to either side of the pilot's seat, and I stepped down through the dream-easy Martian gravity to the peach-dark pillowy floor, and I stood looking at the wonder, and my first mind began to move at last.

There could be no doubt about the name of this, for I'd been looking at a taped view of it not five hours before—this was the West Front of Chartres Cathedral, that Gothic masterpiece, with its plain 12th Century spire, the *Clocher Vieux*, to the north and between them the great rose window fifty feet across and below that the ion-crowded triple-arched West Porch.

Swiftly now my first mind moved to one theory after another of this grotesque miracle and rebounded from them almost as swiftly as if they were like magnetic poles.

I was hallucinating from the taped pictures. Yes, maybe the world's a dream. That's always a theory and never a useful one.

A transparency of Chartres had got pasted against my faceplate. Shake my helmet. No.

I was seeing a mirage that had traveled across fifty million miles of space . . . and some years of time too, for Chartres had vanished with the Paris Bomb that near-missed toward Le Mans, just as Rockefeller Chapel had gone with the Michigan Bomb and St. Praxed's with the Rome.

The thing was a mimic-structure built by the coleopteroids to a plan telepathized from a memory picture of Chartres in some man's mind. But most memory pictures don't have anywhere near such precision and I never heard of the coleopts mimicking stained glass though they do build spired nests a half thousand feet high.

It was all one of those great hypnotism-traps the Arean jingoists are forever claiming the coleopts are setting us. Yes, and the whole universe was built by demons to deceive only me—and possibly Adolf Hitler—as Descartes once hypothesized. *Stop it.*

They'd moved Hollywood to Mars as they'd earlier moved it to Mexico and Spain and Egypt and the Congo to cut expenses, and they'd just finished an epic of the Middle Ages—The *Hunchback of Notre Dame,* no doubt, with some witless producer substituting Notre Dame of Chartres for Notre Dame of Paris because his leading mistress liked its looks better and the public wouldn't know the difference. Yes, and probably hired hordes of black coleopts at next to nothing to play monks, wearing robes and humanoid masks. And why not a coleopt to play Quasimodo?—improve race relations. *Don't hunt for comedy in the incredible.*

Or they'd been giving the Martian tour to the last mad president of La Belle France to quiet his nerves and they'd propped up a fake cathedral of Chartres, all west facade, to humor him, just like the Russians had put up papier-mache villages to impress Peter III's German wife. The Fourth Republic on the fourth planet! *No, don't get hysterical. This thing is here.*

*   *   *

Or maybe—and here my first mind lingered—past and future forever exist somehow, somewhere (the Mind of God? the fourth dimension?) in a sort of suspended animation, with little trails of somnambulant change running through the future as our willed present actions change it and perhaps, who knows, other little trails running through the past too?—for there may be professional timetravelers. And maybe, once in a million millennia, an amateur accidentally finds a Door.

A Door to Chartres. But when?

As I lingered on those thoughts, staring at the gray prodigy—"Do I live, am I dead?" —there came a moaning and a rustling behind me and I turned to see the green spacesuit diving out of the flier toward me, but with its head ducked so I still couldn't see inside the faceplate. I could no more move than in a nightmare. But before the suit reached me, I saw that there was with it, perhaps carrying it, a wind that shook the flier and swept up the feather-soft rose dust in great plumes and waves. And then the wind bowled me over—one hasn't much anchorage in Mars gravity—and I was rolling away from the flier with the billowing dust and the green spacesuit that went somersaulting faster and higher than I, as if it were empty, but then wraiths are light.

The wind was stronger than any wind on Mars should be, certainly than any unheralded gust, and as I went tumbling deliriously on, cushioned by my suit and the low gravity, clutching futilely toward the small low rocky outcrops through whose long shadows I was rolling, I found myself thinking with the serenity of fever that this wind wasn't blowing across Mars-space only but through time too.

A mixture of space-wind and time-wind—what a puzzle for the physicist and drawer of vectors! It seemed unfair—I thought as I tumbled—like giving a psychiatrist a patient with psychosis overlaid by alcoholism. But reality's always mixed and I knew from experience that only a few minutes in an anechoic, lightness, null-G chamber will set the most normal mind veering uncontrollably into fantasy—or is it always fantasy?

One of the smaller rocky outcrops took for an instant the twisted shape of Monica's dog Brush as he died—not in the blast with here, but of fallout, three weeks later, hairless and swollen and oozing. I winced.

Then the wind died and the West Front of Chartres was shooting vertically up above me and I found myself crouched on the dust-drifted steps of the south bay with the great sculpture of the Virgin looking severely out from above the high doorway at the Martian desert and the figures of the four liberal arts ranged below her—Grammar, Rhetoric, Music, and Dialectic—and Aristotle with frowning forehead dipping a stone pen into stone ink.

The figure of Music hammering her little stone bells made me think of Monica and how she'd studied piano and Brush had barked when she practiced. Next I remembered from the tape that Chartres is the legendary resting place of St. Modesta, a beautiful girl tortured to death for her faith by her father Quirnus in the Emperor: Diocletian's day. Modesta—Music—Monica.

The double door was open a little and the green spacesuit was sprawled on its belly there, helmet lifted, as if peering inside at floor level.

I pushed to my feet and walked up the rose-mounded steps. *Dust blowing through time? Grotesque. Yet was I more than dust? "Do I live, am I dead?"*

I hurried faster and faster, kicking up the fine powder in peach-red swirls, and almost hurled myself down on the green, spacesuit to turn it over and peer into the faceplate. But before I could quite do that I had looked into the doorway and what I saw stopped me. Slowly I got to my feet again and took a step beyond the prone green spacesuit and then another step.

Instead of the great Gothic nave of Chartres, long as a football field, high as a sequois, alive with stained light, there was a smaller, darker interior—churchly, too, but Romanesque, even Latin, with burly granite columns and rich red marble steps leading up toward an altar where mosaics glittered through another open door like a theatrical spot in the wings, struck on the wall opposite me and revealed a gloriously ornate tomb where a sculptured mortuary figure—a bishop by his miter and crook—lay above a crowded bronze frieze on a bright green jasper slab with a blue lapis-lazuli globe of Earth between his stone knees and nine thin columns of peach-blossom marble rising around him to the canopy . . .

But of course: this was the bishop's tomb of Browning's poem. This was St. Praxed's church, powdered by the Rome Bomb, the church sacred to the martyred Praxed, daughter of Pudens, pupil of St. Peter tucked even further into the past than Chartres' martyed Modesta. Napoleon had planned to liberate those red marble steps and take them to Paris. But with this realization came almost instantly the companion memory: that although St. Praxed's church had been real, the tomb of Browning's bishop had existed only in Browning's imagination and the minds of his readers.

Can it be, I thought, that not only do the past and future exist forever, but also all the possibilities that were never and will never be realized . . . somehow, somewhere (the fifth dimension? the Imagination of God?) as if in a dream within a dream . . . Crawling with change too, as artists or anyone thinks of them . . . Change-winds mixed with the time-winds with space-winds . . .

In that moment I became aware of two dark-clad figures in the aisle beside the tomb and studying it—a pale man with dark beard covering his cheeks and a pale woman with dark straight hair covering hers under a filmy veil. There was movement near their feet and a fat dark sluglike beast, almost hairless, crawled away from them into the shadows.

I didn't like it. I didn't like that beast. I didn't like it disappearing. For the first time I felt actively frightened.

And then the woman moved too, so that her dark wide floor-brushing skirt jogged, and in a very British voice she called, "Flush! Come here, Flush!" and I remembered that was the name of the dog Elizabeth Barrett had taken with her from Wimpole Street when she ran off with Browning.

Then the voice called again, anxiously, but the British had gone out of it now; in fact it was a voice I knew, a voice that froze me inside, and the dog's name had changed to Brush, and I looked up, and the gaudy tomb was gone and the walls had grayed and receded, but not so far as those of Chartres, only so far as those of the Rockefeller Chapel, and there coming toward me down the center aisle, tall and slim in a black academic robe with the three velvet doctor's bars on the sleeves, with the brown of science edging the hood, was Monica.

I think she saw me, I think she recognized me through my faceplate, I think she smiled at me fearfully, wonderingly.

Then there was a rosy glow behind her, making a hazily-gleaming nimbus of her hair, like the glory of a saint. But then the glow became too bright, intolerably so, and something struck me, driving me back through the doorway, whirling me over and over, so that all I saw were swirls of rose dust and star-pricked sky.

I think what struck at me was the ghost of the front of an atomic blast.

In my mind was the thought: St. Praxed, St. Modesta, and Monica the atheist saint martyred by the bomb.

Then all winds were gone and I was picking myself up from the dust near the flier.

I scanned around through ebbing dust-swirls. The cathedral was gone. No hill or structure anywhere relieved the flatness of the Martian horizon.

Leaning against the flier, as if lodged there by the wind yet on its feet, was the green spacesuit, its back toward me, its head and shoulders sunk in an attitude mimicking profound dejection.

I moved toward it quickly. I had the thought that it might have gone with me to bring someone back.

It seemed to shrink from me a little as I turned it around. The faceplate was empty. There on the inside, below the transparency, distorted by my angle of view was the little complex console of dials and levers, but no face above them.

I took the suit up very gently in my arms, carrying it as if it were a person, and I started toward the door of the cabin.

It's in the things we've lost that we exist most fully.

There was a faint green flash from the sun as its last silver vanished on the horizon. All the stars came out.

Gleaming green among them and brightest of all, low in the sky where the sun had gone, was the Evening Star—Earth.

Four Ghosts in Hamlet

Actors are a superstitious lot, probably because chance plays a big part in the success of a production of a company or merely an actor—and because we're still a little closer than other people to the gypsies in the way we live and think. For instance, it's bad luck to have peacock feathers on stage or say the last line of a play at rehearsals or whistle in the dressing room (the one nearest the door gets fired) or sing God Save the Sovereign on a railway train (a Canadian company got wrecked that way).

Shakespearean actors are no exceptions. They simply travel a few extra superstitions, such as the one which forbids reciting the lines of the Three Witches, or anything from *Macbeth*, for that matter, except at performances, rehearsals, and on other legitimate occasions. This might be a good rule for outsiders too—then there wouldn't be the endless flood of books with titles taken from the text of *Macbeth*—you know, *Brief Candle, Tomorrow and Tomorrow, The Sound and the Fury, A Poor Player, All Our Yesterdays*, and those are all just from one brief soliloquy.

And our company, the Governor's company, has a rule against the Ghost in *Hamlet* dropping his greenish cheesecloth veil over his helmet-framed face until the very moment he makes each of his entrances. Hamlet's dead father mustn't stand veiled in the darkness of the wings.

This last superstition commemorates something which happened not too long ago, an actual ghost story. Sometimes I think it's the greatest ghost story in the world—though certainly not from my way of telling it, which is gossipy and poor, but from the wonder blazing at its core.

It's not only a true tale of the supernatural, but also very much a story about people, for after all—and before everything else—ghosts are people.

The ghostly part of the story first showed itself in the tritest way imaginable: three of our actresses (meaning practically all the ladies in a Shakespearean company) took to having sessions with a Ouija board in the hour before curtain time and sometimes even during a performance when they had long offstage waits, and they became so wrapped up in it and conceited about it and they squeaked so excitedly at the revelations which the planchette spelled out—and three or four times almost missed entrances because of it—that if the Governor weren't such a tolerant commander-in-chief, he would have forbidden them to bring the board to the theater. I'm sure he was tempted to and might have, except that Props pointed out to him that our three ladies probably wouldn't enjoy Ouija sessions one bit in the privacy of a hotel room, that much of the fun in operating a Ouija board is in having a half-exasperated, half-intrigued floating audience, and that when all's done the basic business of all ladies is glamour, whether of personal charm or of actual witchcraft, since the word means both.

Props—that is, our property man, Billy Simpson—was fascinated by their obsession, as he is by any new thing that comes along, and might very well have broken our Shakespearean taboo by quoting the Three Witches about them, except that Props has no flair for Shakespearean speech at all, no dramatic ability whatsoever, in fact he's the one person in our company who never acts even a bit part or carries a mute spear on stage, though he has other talents which make up for this deficiency—he can throw together a papier-mâché bust of Pompey in two hours, or turn out a wooden prop dagger all silvery-bladed and hilt-gilded, or fix a zipper, and that's not all.

As for myself, I was very irked at the ridiculous alphabet board, since it seemed to occupy most of Monica Singleton's spare time and satisfy all her hunger for thrills. I'd been trying to promote a romance with her—a long touring season becomes deadly and cold without some sort of heart-tickle—and for a while I'd made progress. But after Ouija came along, I became a ridiculous Guildenstern mooning after an unattainable unseeing Ophelia—which were the parts I and she actually played in *Hamlet*.

I cursed the idiot board with its childish corner-pictures of grinning suns and smirking moons and windblown spirits, and I further alienated Monica by asking her why wasn't it called a Nenein, or No-No board (Ninny board!) instead of a Yes-Yes board? Was that, I inquired, because all spiritualists are forever accentuating the positive and behaving like a pack of fawning yes-men?—yes, we're here; yes, we're your uncle Harry; yes, we're happy on this plane; yes, we have a doctor among us who'll diagnose that pain in your chest; and so on.

Monica wouldn't speak to me for a week after that.

I would have been even more depressed except that Props pointed out to me that no flesh-and-blood man can compete with ghosts in a girl's affections, since ghosts being imaginary have all the charms and perfections a girl can dream of, but that all girls eventually tire of ghosts, or if their minds don't, their bodies do. This eventually did happen, thank goodness, in the case of myself and Monica, though not until we'd had a grisly, mind-wrenching experience—a night of terrors before the nights of love.

So Ouija flourished and the Governor and the rest of us put up with it one way or another, until there came that three-night-stand in Wolverton, when its dismal uncanny old theater tempted our three Ouija-women to ask the board who was the ghost haunting the spooky place and the swooping planchette spelled out the name S-H-A-K-E-S-P-E-A-R-E . . .

But I am getting ahead of my story. I haven't introduced our company except for Monica, Props, and the Governor—and I haven't identified the last of those three.

We call Gilbert Usher the Governor out of sheer respect and affection. He's about the last of the old actor-managers. He hasn't the name of Gielgud or Olivier or Evans or Richardson, but he's spent most of a lifetime keeping Shakespeare alive, spreading that magical areligious gospel in the more remote counties and the Dominions and the United States, like Benson once did. Our other actors aren't names at all—I refuse to tell you mine!—but with the exception of myself they're good troupers, or if they don't become that the first season, they drop out. Gruelingly long seasons, much uncomfortable traveling, and small profits are our destiny.

This particular season had got to that familiar point where the plays are playing restlessness sets in. Robert Dennis, our juvenile, was writing a novel of theatrical life (he said) mornings at the hotel—up at seven to slave at it, our Robert claimed. Poor old Guthrie Boyd had started to drink again, and drink quite too much, after an abstemious two months which had astonished everyone.

Francis Farley Scott, our leading man, had started to drop hints tht he was going to

310

organize a Shakespearean repertory company of his own next year and he began to have conspiratorial conversations with Gertrude Grainger, our leading lady, and to draw us furtively aside one by one to made us hypothetical offers, no exact salary named. F.F. is as old as the Governor—who is our star, of course—and he has no talents at all except for self-infatuation and a somewhat grandiose yet impressive fashion of acting. He's portly like an opera tenor and quite bald and he travels with an assortment of thirty toupees, ranging from red to black shot with silver, which he alternates with shameless abandon—they're for wear offstage, not on. It doesn't matter to him that the company knows all about his multi-colored artificial toppings, for we're part of his world of illusion, and he's firmly convinced that the stage-struck local ladies he squires about never notice, or at any rate mind the deception. He once gave me a lecture on the subtleties of suiting the color of your hair to the lady you're trying to fascinate—her own age, hair color, and so on.

Every year F.F. plots to start a company of his own—it's a regular midseason routine with him—and every year it comes to nothing, for he's as lazy and impractical as he is vain. Yet F.F. believes he could play any part in Shakespeare or all of them at once in a pinch; perhaps the only F.F. Scott Company which would really satisfy him would be one in which he would be the only actor—a Shakespearean monologue; in fact, the one respect in which F.F. is not lazy is in his eagerness to double as many parts as possible in any single play.

F.F.'s yearly plots never bother the Governor a bit—he keeps waiting wistfully for F.F. to fix him with an hypnotic eye and in a hoarse whisper ask *him* to join the Scott company.

And I of course was hoping that now at last Monica Singleton would stop trying to be the most exquisite ingenue that ever came tripping Shakespeare's way (rehearsing her parts even in her sleep, I guessed, though I was miles from being in a position to know that for certain) and begin to take note and not just advantage of my devoted attentions.

But then old Sybil Jameson bought the Ouija board and Gertrude Grainger dragooned an unwilling Monica into placing her fingertips on the planchette along with theirs "just for a lark." Next day Gertrude announced to several of us in a hushed voice that Monica had the most amazing undeveloped mediumistic talent she'd ever encountered, and from then on the girl was a Ouija-addict. Poor tight-drawn Monica, I suppose she had to explode out of her self-imposed Shakespearean discipline somehow, and it was just too bad it had to be the board instead of me. Though come to think of it, I shouldn't have felt quite so resentful of the board, for she might have exploded with Robert Dennis, which would have been infinitely worse, though we were never quite sure of Robert's sex. For that matter I wasn't sure of Gertrude's and suffered agonies of uncertain jealousy when she captured my beloved. I was obsessed with the vision of Gertrude's bold knees pressing Monica's under the Ouija board, though with Sybil's bony ones for chaperones, fortunately.

Francis Farley Scott, who was jealous too because this new toy had taken Gertrude's mind off their annual plottings, said rather spitefully that Monica must be one of those grabby girls who have to take command of whatever they get their fingers on, whether it's a man or a planchette, but Props told me he'd bet anything that Gertrude and Sybil had "followed" Monica's first random finger movements like the skillfulest dancers guiding a partner while seeming to yield, in order to coax her into business and make sure of their third.

Sometimes I thought that F.F. was right and sometimes Props and sometimes I thought that Monica had a genuine supernatural talent, though I don't ordinarily believe in such things, and that last really frightened me, for such a person might give up live men for ghosts forever. She was such a sensitive, subtle, wraith-cheeked girl and she could get so keyed up and when she touched the planchette her eyes got such an empty look, as if her mind had traveled down into her fingertips or out to the ends of time and space. And once the three of them gave me a character reading from the board which embarrassed me with its accuracy. The same thing happened to several other people in the company. Of course, as Props pointed out, actors can be pretty good character analysts whenever they stop being egomaniacs.

After reading characters and foretelling the future for several weeks, our Three Weird Sisters got interested in reincarnation and began asking the board and then telling us what famous or infamous people we'd been in past lives. Gertrude Grainger had been Queen Boadicea, I wasn't surprised to hear. Sybil Jameson had been Cassandra. While Monica was once mad Queen Joanna of Castile and more recently a prize hysterical patient of Janet at the Salpetriere—touches which irritated and frightened me more than they should have. Billy Simpson—Props—had been an Egyptian silversmith under Queen Hatshepsut and later a servant of Samuel Pepys; he heard this with a delightful chuckle. Guthrie Boyd had been the Emperor Claudius and Robert Dennis had been Caligula. For some reason I had been both John Wilkes Booth and Lambert Simnel, which irritated me considerably, for I saw no romance but only neurosis in assassinating an American president and dying in a burning barn, or impersonating the Earl of Warwick, pretending unsuccessfully to the British throne, being pardoned for it—of all things!—and spending the rest of my life as a scullion in the kitchen of Henry VII and his son. The fact that both Booth and Simnel had been actors of a sort—a poor sort—naturally irritated me the more. Only much later did Monica confess to me that the board had probably made those decisions because I had had such a "tragic, dangerous, defeated look"—a revelation which surprised and flattered me.

Francis Farley Scott was flattered too, to hear he'd once been Henry VIII—he fancied all those wives and he wore his golden blond toupee after the show that night—until Gertrude and Sybil and Monica announced that the Governor was a reincarnation of no less than William Shakespeare himself. That made F.F. so jealous that he instantly sat down at the prop table, grabbed up a quill pen, and did an impromptu rendering of Shakespeare composing Hamlet's "To be or not to be" soliloquy. It was an effective performance, though with considerably more frowning and eye-rolling and trying of lines for sound than I imagine Willy S. himself used originally, and when F.F. finished, even the Governor, who'd been standing unobserved in the shadows beside Props, applauded with the latter.

Governor kidded the pants off the idea of himself as Shakespeare. He said that if Willy S. were ever reincarnated it ought to be as a world-famous dramatist who was secretly in his spare time the world's greatest scientist and philosopher and left clues to his identity in his mathematical equations—that way he'd get his own back at Bacon, rather the Baconians.

Yet I suppose if you had to pick someone for a reincarnation of Shakespeare, Gilbert Usher wouldn't be a bad choice. Insofar as a star and director ever can be, the Governor is gentle and self-effacing—as Shakespeare himself must have been, or else there would never have arisen that ridiculous Bacon-Oxford-Marlowe-Elizabeth-take-your-pick-who-wrote-Shakespeare controversy. And the Governor has a sweet melancholy about him, though he's handsomer and despite his years more athletic than one imagines Shakespeare being. And he's generous to a fault, especially where old actors who've done brave fine things in the past are concerned.

This season his mistake in that last direction had been in hiring Guthrie Boyd to play some of the more difficult older leading roles, including a couple F.F. usually handles: Brutus, Othello, and besides those Duncan in *Macbeth*, Kent in *King Lear*, and the Ghost in *Hamlet*.

Guthrie was a bellowing hard-drinking bear of an actor, who'd been a Shakespearean star in Australia and successfully smuggled some of his reputation west—he learned to moderate his bellowing, while his emotions were always simple and sincere, though explosive—and finally even spent some years in Hollywood. But there his drinking caught up with him, probably because of the stupid film parts he got, and he failed six times over. His wife divorced him. His children cut themselves off. He married a starlet and she divorced him. He dropped out of sight.

Then after several years the Governor ran into him. He'd been rusticating in Canada with a stubborn teetotal admirer. He was only a shadow of his former self, but there was some substance to the shadow—and he wasn't drinking. The Governor decided to take a chance on him—although the company manager Harry Grossman was dead set against it—and during rehearsals and the first month or so of performances it was wonderful to see how old Guthrie Boyd came back, exactly as if Shakespeare were a restorative medicine.

It may be stuffy or sentimental of me to say so, but you know, I think Shakespeare's good for people. I don't know of an actor, except myself, whose character hasn't been strengthened and his vision widened and charity quickened by working in the plays. I've heard that before Gilbert Usher became a Shakespearean, he was a more ruthlessly ambitious and critical man, not without malice, but the plays mellowed him, as they've mellowed Props's philosophy and given him a zest for life.

Because of his contact with Shakespeare, Robert Dennis is a less strident and pettish swish (if he is one), Gertrude Grainger's outbursts of cold rage have an undercurrent of queenly make-believe, and even Francis Farley Scott's grubby little seductions are probably kinder and less insultingly illusionary.

In fact I sometimes think that what civilized serenity the British people possess, and small but real ability to smile at themselves, is chiefly due to their good luck in having had William Shakespeare born one of their company.

But I was telling how Guthrie Boyd performed very capably those first weeks, against the expectations of most of us, so that we almost quit holding our breaths—or sniffing at his. His Brutus was workmanlike, his Kent quite fine—that bluff rough honest part suited him well—and he regularly got admiring notices for his Ghost in *Hamlet*. I think his years of living death as a drinking alcoholic had given him an understanding of loneliness and frozen abilities and despair that he put to good use—probably unconsciously—in interpreting that small role.

He was really a most impressive figure in the part, even just visually. The Ghost's basic costume is simple enough—a big all-enveloping cloak that brushes the ground-cloth, a big dull helmet with the tiniest battery light inside its peak to throw a faint green glow on the Ghost's features, and over the helmet a veil of greenish cheesecloth that registers as mist to the audience. He wears a suit of stage armor under the cloak, but that's not important and at a pinch he can do without it, for his cloak can cover his entire body.

The Ghost doesn't switch on his helmet-light until he makes his entrance, for fear of it being glimpsed by an edge of the audience, and nowadays because of that superstition or rule I told you about, he doesn't drop the cheesecloth veil until the last second either, but when Guthrie Boyd was playing the part that rule didn't exist and I have a vivid recollection of him standing in the wings, waiting to go on, a big bearish inscrutable figure about as solid and unsupernatural as a bushy seven-foot evergreen covered by a gray tarpaulin. But then when Guthrie would switch on the tiny light and stride smoothly and silently on stage and his hollow distant tormented voice boom out, there'd be a terrific shivery thrill, even for us backstage, as if we were listening to words that really had traveled across black windy infinite gulfs from the Afterworld or the Other Side.

At any rate Guthrie was a great Ghost, and adequate or a bit better than that in most of his other parts—for those first nondrinking weeks. He seemed very cheerful on the whole, modestly buoyed up by his comeback, though sometimes something empty and dead would stare for a moment out of his eyes—the old drinking alcoholic wondering what all this fatiguing sober nonsense was about. He was especially looking forward to our three-night stand at Wolverton, although that was still two months in the future then. The reason was that both his children—married and with families now, of course —lived and worked at Wolverton and I'm sure he set great store on proving to them in person his rehabilitation, figuring it would lead to a reconciliation and so on.

But then came his first performance as Othello. (The Governor, although the star, always played Iago—an equal role, though not the title one.) Guthrie was almost too old for Othello, of course, and besides that, his health wasn't good—the drinking years had taken their toll of his stamina and the work of rehearsals and of first nights in eight different plays after years away from the theater had exhausted him. But somehow the old volcano inside him got seething again and he gave a magnificent performance. Next morning the papers raved about him and one review rated him even better than the Governor.

That did it, unfortunately. The glory of his triumph was too much for him. The next night—*Othello* again—he was drunk as a skunk. He remembered most of his lines—though the Governor had to throw him about every sixth one out of the side of his mouth—but he weaved and wobbled, he planked a big hand on the shoulder of every other character he addressed to keep from falling over, and he even forgot to put in his false teeth the first two acts, so that his voice was mushy. To cap that, he started really to strangle Gertrude Grainger in the last scene, until that rather brawny Desdemona, unseen by the audience, gave him a knee in the gut; then, after stabbing himself, he flung the prop dagger high in the flies so that it came down with two lazy twists and piercing the groundcloth buried its blunt point deep in the soft wood of the stage floor not three feet from Monica, who plays Iago's wife Emilia and so was lying dead on the stage at that point in the drama, murdered by her villainous husband—and might have been dead for real if the dagger had followed a slightly different trajectory.

Since a third performance of *Othello* was billed for the following night, the Governor had no choice but to replace Guthrie with Francis Farley Scott, who did a good job (for him) of covering up his satisfaction at getting his old role back. F.F., always a plushy and lascivious-eyed Moor, also did a good job with the part, coming in that way without even a brush-up rehearsal, so that one critic, catching the first and third shows, marveled how we could change big roles at will, thinking we'd done it solely to demonstrate our virtuosity.

Of course the Governor read the riot act to Guthrie and carried him off to a doctor, who without being prompted threw a big scare into him about his drinking and his heart, so that he just might have recovered from his lapse, except that two nights later we did *Julius Caesar* and Guthrie, instead of being satisfied with being workmanlike, decided to recoup himself with a really rousing performance. So he bellowed and groaned and bugged his eyes as I suppose he had done in his palmiest Australian days. His optimistic self-satisfaction between scenes was frightening to behold. Not too terrible a performance, truly, but the critics all panned him and one of them said, "Guthrie Boyd played Brutus—a bunch of vocal cords wrapped up in a toga."

That tied up the package and knotted it tight. Thereafter Guthrie was medium pie-eyed from morning to night—and often more than medium. The Governor had to yank him out of Brutus too (F.F. again replacing), but being the Governor he didn't sack him. He put him into a couple of bit parts—Montano and the Soothsayer—in *Othello* and *Caesar* and let him keep on at the others and he gave me and Joe Rubens and some-times Props the job of keeping an eye on the poor old sot and making sure he got to the theater by the half hour and if possible not too plastered. Often he played the Ghost or the Doge of Venice in his street clothes under cloak or scarlet robe, but he played them. And many were the nights Joe and I made the rounds of half the local bars before we corraled him. The Governor sometimes refers to Joe Rubens and me in mild derision as "the American element" in his company, but just the same he depends on us quite a bit; and I certainly don't mind being one of his trouble-shooters—it's a joy to serve him.

All this may seem to contradict my statement about our getting to the point, about this time, where the plays were playing smoothly and the monotony setting in. But it doesn't really. There's always something going wrong in a theatrical company—any-thing else would be abnormal; just as the Samoans say no party is a success until some-body's dropped a plate or spilled a drink or tickled the wrong woman.

Besides, once Guthrie had got Othello and Brutus off his neck, he didn't do too badly. The little parts and even Kent he could play passably whether drunk or sober. King Duncan, for instance, and the Doge in *The Merchant* are easy to play drunk because the actor always has a couple of attendants to either side of him, who can guide his steps if he weaves and even hold him up if necessary—which can turn out to be an effective dramatic touch, registering as the infirmity of extreme age.

And somehow Guthrie continued to give that same masterful performance as the Ghost and get occasional notices for it. In fact Sybil Jameson insisted he was a shade better in the Ghost now that he was invariably drunk; which could have been true. And he still talked about the three-night-stand coming up in Wolverton, though now as often with gloomy apprehension as with proud fatherly anticipation.

Well, the three-night-stand eventually came. We arrived at Wolverton on a non-playing evening. To the surprise of most of us, but especially Guthrie, his son and daughter were there at the station to welcome him with their respective spouses and all their kids and numerous in-laws and a great gaggle of friends. Their cries of greeting when they spotted him were almost an organized cheer and I looked around for a brass band to strike up.

I found out later that Sybil Jameson, who knew them, had been sending them all his favorable notices, so that they were eager as weasels to be reconciled with him and show him off as blatantly as possbile.

When he saw his children's and grandchildren's faces and realized the cries for him, old Guthrie got red in the face and beamed like the sun, and they closed in around him and carried him off in triumph for an evening of celebrations.

Next day I heard from Sybil, whom they'd carried off with him, that everything had gone beautifully. He'd drunk like a fish, but kept marvellous control, so that no one but she noticed, and the warmth of the reconciliation of Guthrie to everyone, complete strangers included, had been wonderful to behold. Guthrie's son-in-law, a pugnacious chap, had got angry when he'd heard Guthrie wasn't to play Brutus the third night, and he declared that Gilbert Usher must be jealous of his magnificent father-in-law. Everything was forgiven twenty times over. They'd even tried to put old Sybil to bed with Guthrie, figuring romantically, as people will about actors, that she must be his mistress. All this was very fine, and of course wonderful for Guthrie, and for Sybil too in a fashion, yet I suppose the unconstrained nightlong bash, after two months of uninterrupted semi-controlled drunkenness, was just about the worst thing anybody could have done to the old boy's sodden body and laboring heart.

Meanwhile on that first evening I accompanied Joe Rubens and Props to the theater we were playing at Wolverton to make sure the scenery got stacked right and the costume trunks were all safely arrived and stowed. Joe is our stage manager besides doing rough or Hebraic parts like Caliban and Tubal—he was a professional boxer in his youth and got his nose smashed crooked. Once I started to take boxing lessons from him, figuring an actor should know everything, but during the third lesson I walked into a gentle right cross and although it didn't exactly stun me there were bells ringing faintly in my head for six hours afterwards and I lived in a world of faery and that was the end of my fistic career. Joe is actually a most versatile actor—for instance, he understudies the Governor in Macbeth, Lear, Iago, and of course Shylock—though his brutal moon-face is against him, especially when his make-up doesn't include a beard. But he dotes on being genial and in the States he often gets a job by day playing Santa Claus in big department stores during the month before Christmas.

The Monarch was a cavernous old place, very grimy backstage, but with a great warren of dirty little dressing rooms and even a property room shaped like an L stage left. Its empty shelves were thick with dust.

There hadn't been a show in the Monarch for over a year, I saw from the yellowing sheets thumbtacked to the callboard as I tore them off and replaced them with a simple black-crayoned HAMLET: TONIGHT AT 8:30.

Then I noticed, by the cold inadequate working lights, a couple of tiny dark shapes dropping down from the flies and gliding around in wide swift circles—out into the house too, since the curtain was up. Bats, I realized with a little start—the Monarch was really halfway through the lich gate. The bats would fit very nicely with *Macbeth*, I told myself, but not so well with *The Merchant of Venice*, while with *Hamlet* they should neither help nor hinder, provided they didn't descent in nightfighter squadrons; it would be nice if they stuck to the Ghost scenes.

I'm sure the Governor had decided we'd open at Wolverton with *Hamlet* so that Guthrie would have the best chance of being a hit in his children's home city.

Billy Simpson, shoving his properties table into place just in front of the dismal L of the prop room, observed cheerfully, "It's a proper haunted house. The girls'll find some rare ghosts here, I'll wager, if they work their board."

Which turned out to be far truer than he realized at the time—I think.

"Bruce!" Joe Rubens called to me. "We better buy a couple of rat traps and set them out. There's something scuttling back of the drops."

But when I entered the Monarch next night, well before the hour, by the creaky thick metal stage door, the place had been swept and tidied a bit. With the groundcloth down and the *Hamlet* set up, it didn't look too terrible, even though the curtain was still unlowered, dimly showing the house and its curves of empty seats and the two faint green exit lights with no one but myself to look at them.

There was a little pool of light around the callboard stage right, and another glow the other side of the stage beyond the wings, and lines of light showing around the edges of the door of the second dressing room, next to the star's.

I started across the dark stage, sliding my shoes softly so as not to trip over a cable or stage-screw and brace, and right away I got the magic electric feeling I often do in an empty theater the night of a show. Only this time there was something additional, something that started a shiver crawling down my neck. It wasn't, I think, the thought of the bats which might now be swooping around me unseen, skirling their inaudibly shrill trumpet calls, or even of the rats which *might* be watching sequin-eyed from behind trunks and flats, although not an hour ago Joe had told me that the traps he'd actually procured and set last night had been empty today.

No, it was more as if all of Shakespeare's characters were invisibly there around me—all the infinite possibilities of the theater. I imagined Rosalind and Flastaff and Prospero standing arm-in-arm watching me with different smiles. And Caliban grinning down from where he silently swung in the flies. And side by side, but unsmiling and not arm-in-arm: Macbeth and Iago and Dick the Three Eyes—Richard III. And all the rest of Shakespeare's myriad-minded good-evil crew.

I passed through the wings opposite and there in the second pool of light Billy Simpson sat behind his table with the properties for *Hamlet* set out on it: the skulls, the foils, the lantern, the purses, the parchmentry letters, Ophelia's flowers, and all the rest. It was odd Props having everything ready quite so early and a bit odd too that he should be alone, for Props has the un-actorish habit of making friends with all sorts of locals, such as policemen and porters and flower women and newsboys and shop-keepers and tramps who claim they're indigent actors, and even inviting them backstage with him—a fracture of rules which the Governor allows since Props is such a sensible chap. He has a great liking for people, especially low people, Props has, and for all the humble details of life. He'd make a good writer, I'd think, except for his utter lack of dramatic flair and story-skill—a sort of prosiness that goes with his profession.

And now he was sitting at his table, his stooped shoulders almost inside the doorless entry to the empty-shelfed prop room—no point in using it for a three-night-stand—and he was gazing at me quizzically. He has a big forehead—the light was on that—and a tapering chin—that was in shadow—and rather large eyes, which were betwixt the light and the dark. Sitting there like that, he seemed to me for a moment (mostly because of the outspread props, I guess) like the midnight Master of the Show in *The Rubaiyat* round whom all the rest of us move like shadow shapes.

Usually he has a quick greeting for anyone, but tonight he was silent, and that added to the illusion.

"Props," I said, "this theater's got a supernatural smell."

His expression didn't change at all, but he solemnly sniffed the air in several little whiffles adding up to one big inhalation, and as he did so he threw his head back, bring-ing his weakish chin into the light and shattering the illusion.

"Dust," he said after a moment. "Dust and old plush and scenery waterpaint and sweat and drains and gelatin and greasepaint and powder and a breath of whisky. But the supernatural . . . no, I can't smell that. Unless . . ." And he sniffed again, but shook his head.

I chuckled at his materialism—although that touch about whisky did seem fanciful, since I hadn't been drinking and Props never does and Guthrie Boyd was nowhere in evidence. Props has a mind like a notebook for sensory details—and for the minutiae of human habits too. It was Props, for instance, who told me about the actual notebook in which John McCarthy (who would be playing Fortinbras and the Player King in a couple of hours) jots down the exact number of hours he sleeps each night and keeps totting them up, so he knows when he'll have to start sleeping extra hours to average the full nine he thinks he must get each night to keep from dying.

It was also Props who pointed out to me that F.F. is much more careless gumming his offstage toupees to his head than his theater wigs—a studied carelessness, like that in tying a bowtie, he assured me; it indicated, he said, a touch of contempt for the whole offstage world.

Props isn't *only* a detail-worm, but it's perhaps because he is one that he has sympathy for all human hopes and frailties, even the most trivial, like my selfish infatuation with Monica.

Now I said to him, "I didn't mean an actual smell, Billy. But back there just now I got the feeling anything might happen tonight."

He nodded slowly and solemnly. With anyone but Props I'd have wondered if he weren't a little drunk. Then he said, "You were on a stage. You know, the science-fiction writers are missing a bet there. We've got time machines right now. Theaters. Theaters are time machines and spaceships too. They take people on trips through the future and the past and the elsewhere and the might-have-been—yes, and if it's done well enough, give them glimpses of Heaven and Hell."

I nodded back at him. Such grotesque fancies are the closet Props ever comes to escaping from prosiness.

I said, "Well, let's hope Guthrie gets aboard the spaceship before the curtain up-jets. Tonight we're depending on his children having the sense to deliver him here intact. Which from what Sybil says about them is not to be taken for granted."

Props stared at me owlishly and slowly shook his head. "Guthrie got here about ten minutes ago," he said, "and looking no drunker than usual."

"That's a relief," I told him, meaning it.

"The girls are having a Ouija session," he went on, as if he were determined to account for all of us from moment to moment. "They smelt the supernatural here, just as you did, and they're asking the board to name the culprit." Then he stooped so that he looked almost hunchbacked and he felt for something under the table.

I nodded. I'd guessed the Ouija part from the lines of light showing around the door of Gertrude Grainger's dressing room.

Props straightened up and he had a pint bottle of whisky in his hand. I don't think a loaded revolver would have dumbfounded me as much. He unscrewed the top.

"There's the Governor coming in," he said tranquilly, hearing the stage door creak and evidently some footsteps my own ears missed. "That's seven of us in the theater before the hour."

He took a big slow swallow of whisky and recapped the bottle, as naturally as if it were a nightly action. I goggled at him without comment. What he was doing was simply unheard of—for Billy Simpson.

At that moment there was a sharp scream and a clatter of thin wood and something twangy and metallic falling and a scurry of footsteps. Our previous words must have cocked a trigger in me, for I was at Gertrude Grainger's dressing-room door as fast as I could sprint—no worry this time about tripping over cables or braces in the dark.

I yanked the door open and there by the bright light of the bulbs framing the mirror were Gertrude and Sybil sitting close together with the Ouija board face down on the floor in front of them along with a flimsy wire-backed chair, overturned. While pressing back into Gertrude's costumes hanging on the rack across the little room, almost as if she wanted to hide behind them like bedclothes, was Monica, pale and staring-eyed. She didn't seem to recognize me. The dark-green heavily brocaded costume Gertrude wears as the Queen in *Hamlet,* into which Monica was chiefly pressing herself, accentuated her pallor. All three of them were in their streetclothes.

I went to Monica and put an arm around her and gripped her hand. It was cold as ice. She was standing rigidly.

While I was doing that Gertrude stood up and explained in rather haughty tones what I told you earlier: about them asking the board who the ghost was haunting the Monarch tonight and the planchette spelling out S-H-A-K-E-S-P-E-A-R-E . . .

"I don't know why it started you so, dear," she ended crossly, speaking to Monica. "It's very natural his spirit should attend performances of his plays."

I felt the slim body I clasped relax a little. That relieved me. I was selfishly pleased at having got an arm around it, even under such public and unamorous circumstances, while at the same time my silly mind was thinking that if Props had been lying to me about Guthrie Boyd having come in no more drunken than usual (this new Props who drank straight whisky in the theater could lie too, I supposed), why then we could certainly use William Shakespeare tonight, since the Ghost in *Hamlet* is the one part in all his plays Shakespeare himself is supposed to have acted on the stage.

"I don't know why myself now," Monica suddenly answered from beside me, shaking her head as if to clear it. She became aware of me at last, started to pull away, then let my arm stay around her.

The next voice that spoke was the Governor's. He was standing in the doorway, smiling faintly, with Props peering around his shoulder. Props would be as tall as the Governor if he ever straightened up, but his stoop takes almost a foot off his height.

The Governor said softly, a comic light in his eyes, "I think we should be content to bring Shakespeare's plays to life, without trying for their author. It's hard enough on the nerves just to *act* Shakespeare."

He stepped forward with one of his swift, naturally graceful movements and kneeling on one knee he picked up the fallen board and planchette. "At all events I'll take these in charge for tonight. Feeling better now, Miss Singleton?" he asked as he straightened and stepped back.

"Yes, quite all right," she answered flusteredly, disengaging my arm and pulling away from me rather too quickly.

He nodded. Gertrude Grainger was staring at him coldly, as if about to say something scathing, but she didn't. Sybil Jameson was looking at the floor. She seemed embarrassed, yet puzzled too.

I followed the Governor out of the dressing room and told him, in case Props hadn't, about Guthrie Boyd coming to the theater early. My momentary doubt of Props's honesty seemed plain silly to me now, although his taking that drink remained an astonishing riddle.

Props confirmed me about Guthrie coming in, though his manner was a touch abstracted.

The Governor nodded his thanks for the news, then twitched a nostril and frowned. I was sure he'd caught a whiff of alcohol and didn't know to which of us two to attribute it—or perhaps even to one of the ladies, or to an earlier passage of Guthrie this way.

He said to me, "Would you come into my dressing room for a bit, Bruce?"

I followed him, thinking he'd picked me for the drinker and wondering how to answer—best perhaps simply silently accept the fatherly lecture—but when he'd turned on the lights and I'd shut the door, his first question was, "You're attracted to Miss Singleton, aren't you, Bruce?"

When I nodded abruptly, swallowing my morsel of surprise, he went on softly but emphatically, "Then why don't you quit hovering and playing Galahad and really go after her? Ordinarily I must appear to frown on affairs in the company, but in this case it would be the best way I know of to break up those Ouija sessions, which are obviously harming the girl."

I managed to grin and tell him I'd be happy to obey his instructions—and do it entirely on my own initiative too.

He grinned back and started to toss the Ouija board on his couch, but instead put it and the planchette carefully down on the end of his long dressing table and put a second question to me.

"What do you think of some of this stuff they're getting over the board, Bruce?"

I said, "Well, that last one gave me a shiver, all right—I suppose because . . ." and I told him about sensing the presence of Shakespeare's characters in the dark. I finished, "But of course the whole idea is nonsense," and I grinned.

He didn't grin back.

I continued impulsively, "There was one idea they had a few weeks back that impressed me, though it didn't seem to impress you. I hope you won't think I'm trying to butter you up, Mr. Usher. I mean the idea of you being a reincarnation of William Shakespeare."

He laughed delightedly and said, "Clearly you don't yet know the difference between a player and a playwright, Bruce. Shakespeare striding about romantically with head thrown back?—and twirling a sword and shaping his body and voice to every feeling handed him? Oh no! I'll grant he might have played the Ghost—it's a part within the scope of an average writer's talents, requiring nothing more than that he stand still and sound off sepulchrally."

He paused and smiled and went on. "No, there's only one person in this company who might be Shakespeare come again, and that's Billy Simpson. Yes, I mean Props. He's a great listener and he knows how to put himself in touch with everyone and then he's got that rat-trap mind for every hue and scent and sound of life, inside or out the mind. And he's very analytic. Oh, I know he's got no poetic talent, but surely Shakespeare wouldn't have that in *every* reincarnation. I'd think he'd need about a dozen lives in which to gather material for every one in which he gave it dramatic form. Don't you find something very poignant in the idea of a mute inglorious Shakespeare spending whole humble lifetimes collecting the necessary stuff for one great dramatic burst? Think about it some day."

I was doing that already and finding it a fascinating fantasy. It crystalized so perfectly the feeling I'd got seeing Billy Simpson behind his property table. And then Props did have a high-foreheaded poet-schoolmaster's face like that given Shakespeare in the posthumous engravings and woodcuts and portraits. Why, even their initials were the same. It made me feel strange.

Then the Governor put his third question to me.

"He's drinking tonight, isn't he? I mean Props, not Guthrie."

I didn't say anything, but my face must have answered for me—at least to such a student of expressions as the Governor—for he smiled and said, "You needn't worry. I wouldn't be angry with him. In fact, the only other time I know of that Props drank spirits by himself in the theater, I had a great deal to thank him for." His lean face grew thoughtful. "It was long before your time, in fact it was the first season I took out a company of my own. I had barely enough money to pay the printer for the three-sheets and get the first-night curtain up. After that it was touch and go for months. Then in mid-season we had a run of bad luck—a two-night heavy fog in one city, an influenza

320

scare in another, Harvey Wilkins' Shakespearean troupe two weeks ahead of us in a third. And when in the next town we played it turned out the advance sale was very light—because my name was unknown there and the theater was an unpopular one—I realized I'd have to pay off the company while there was still money enough to get them home, if not the scenery.

"That night I caught Props swigging, but I hadn't the heart to chide him for it—in fact I don't think I'd have blamed anyone, except perhaps myself, for getting drunk that night. But then during the performance the actors and even the union stagehands we travel with began coming to my dressing room by ones and twos and telling me they'd be happy to work without salary for another three weeks, if I thought that might give us a chance of recouping. Well, of course I grabbed at their offers and we got a spell of brisk pleasant weather and we hit a couple of places starved for Shakespeare, and things worked out, even to paying all the back salary owed before the season was ended.

"Later on I discovered it was Props who had put them all up to doing it."

Gilbert Usher looked up at me and one of his eyes was wet and his lips were working just a little. "I couldn't have done it myself," he said, "for I wasn't a popular man with my company that first season—I'd been riding everyone much too hard and with nasty sarcasms—and I hadn't yet learned how to ask anyone for help when I really needed it. But Billy Simpson did what I couldn't, though he had to nerve himself for it with spirits. He's quick enough with his tongue in ordinary circumstances, as you know, particularly when he's being the friendly listener, but apparently when something very special is required of him, he must drink himself to the proper pitch. I'm wondering . . ."

His voice trailed off and then he straightened up before his mirror and started to unknot his tie and she said to me briskly, "Better get dressed now, Bruce. And then look in on Guthrie, will you?"

My mind was churning some rather strange thoughts as I hurried up the iron stairs to the dressing room I shared with Robert Dennis. I got on my Guildenstern make-up and costume, finishing just as Robert arrived; as Laertes, Robert makes a late entrance and so needn't hurry to the theater on *Hamlet* nights. Also, although we don't make a point of it, he and I spend as little time together in the dressing room as we can.

Before going down I looked into Guthrie Boyd's. He wasn't thee, but the lights were on and the essentials of the Ghost's costume weren't in sight—impossible to miss that big helmet!—so I assumed he'd gone down ahead of me.

It was almost the half hour. The house lights were on, the curtain down, more stage lights on too, and quite a few of us about. I noticed that Props was back in the chair behind his table and not looking particularly different from any other night—perhaps the drink had been a once-only aberration and not some symptom of a crisis in the company.

I didn't make a point of hunting for Guthrie. When he gets costumed early he generally stands back in a dark corner somewhere, wanting to be alone—perchance to sip, aye, there's the rub!—or visits with Sybil in her dressing room.

I spotted Monica sitting on a trunk by the switchboard, where backstage was brightest lit at the moment. She looked ethereal yet springlike in her blonde Ophelia wig and first costume, a pale green one. Recalling my happy promise to the Governor, I bounced up beside her and asked her straight out about the Ouija business, pleased to have something to the point besides the plays to talk with her about—and really not worrying as much about her nerves as I suppose I should have.

She was in a very odd mood, both agitated and abstracted, her gaze going back and forth between distant and near and very distant. My questions didn't disturb her at all, in fact I got the feeling she welcomed them, yet she genuinely didn't seem able to tell me much about why she'd been so frightened at the last name the board had spelled. She told me that she actually did get into a sort of dream state when she worked the board and that she'd screamed before she'd quite comprehended what had shocked her so; then her mind had blacked out for a few seconds, she thought.

"One thing though, Bruce," she said. "I'm not going to work the board any more, at least when the three of us are alone like that."

"That sounds like a wise idea," I agreed, trying not to let the extreme heartiness of my agreement show through.

She stopped peering around as if for some figure to appear that wasn't in the play and didn't belong backstage, and she laid her hand on mine and said, "Thanks for coming so quickly when I went idiot and screamed."

I was about to improve this opportunity by telling her that the reason I'd come so quickly was that she was so much in my mind, but just then Joe Rubens came hurrying up with the Governor behind him in his Hamlet black to tell me that neither Guthrie Boyd nor his Ghost costume was to be found anywhere in the theater.

What's more, Joe had got the phone numbers of Guthrie's son and daughter from Sybil and rung them up. The one phone hadn't answered, while on the other a female voice—presumably a maid's—had informed him that everyone had gone to see Guthrie Boyd in *Hamlet*.

Joe was already wearing his cumbrous chain-mail armor for Marcellus—woven cord silvered—so I knew I was elected. I ran upstairs and in the space of time it took Robert Dennis to guess my mission and advise me to try the dingiest bars first and have a drink or two myself in them, I'd put on my hat, overcoat, and wristwatch and left him.

So garbed and as usual nervous about people looking at my ankles, I sallied forth to comb the nearby bars of Wolverton. I consoled myself with the thought that if I found Hamlet's father's ghost drinking his way through them, no one would ever spare a glance for my own costume.

Almost on the stroke of curtain I returned, no longer giving a damn what anyone thought about my ankles. I hadn't found Guthrie or spoken to a soul who'd seen a large male imbiber—most likely of Irish whisky—in great-cloak and antique armor, with perhaps some ghostly green light cascading down his face.

Beyond the curtain the overture was fading to its sinister close and the backstage lights were all down, but there was an angry hushed-voice dispute going on stage left, where the Ghost makes all his entrances and exits. Skipping across the dim stage in front of the blue-lit battlements of Elsinore—I still in my hat and overcoat—I found the Governor and Joe Rubens and with them John McCarthy all ready to go on as the Ghost in his Fortinbras armor with a dark cloak and some green gauze over it.

But alongside them was Francis Farley Scott in a very similar get-up—no armor, but a big enough cloak to hide his King costume and a rather more impressive helmet than John's.

They were all very dim in the midnight glow leaking back from the dimmed-down blue floods. The five of us were the only people I could see on this side of the stage.

F.F. was arguing vehemently that he must be allowed to double the Ghost with King Claudius because he knew the part better than John and because—this was the important thing—he could imitate Guthrie's voice perfectly enough to deceive his children and perhaps save their illusions about him. Sybil had looked through the curtain hole and seen them and all of their yesterday crowd, with new recruits besides, occupying all of the second, third, and fourth rows center, chattering with excitement and beaming with anticipation. Harry Grossman had confirmed this from the front of the house.

I could tell that the Governor was vastly irked at F.F. and at the same time touched by the last part of his argument. It was exactly the sort of sentimental heroic rationalization with which F.F. cloaked his insatiable yearnings for personal glory. Very likely he believed it himself.

John McCarthy was simply ready to do what the Governor asked him. He's an actor untroubled by inward urgencies—except things like keeping a record of the hours he sleeps and each penny he spends—though with a natural facility for portraying on stage emotions which he doesn't feel one iota.

The Governor shut up F.F. with a gesture and got ready to make his decision, but just then I saw that there was a sixth person on this side of the stage.

Standing in the second wings beyond our group was a dark figure like a tarpaulined Christmas tree topped by a big helmet of unmistakable general shape despite its veiling. I grabbed the Governor's arm and pointed at it silently. He smothered a large curse and strode up to it and rasped, "Guthrie, you old Son of a B! Can you go on?" The figure gave an affirmative grunt.

Joe Rubens grimaced at me as if to say "Show business!" and grabbed a spear from the prop table and hurried back across the stage for his entrance as Marcellus just before the curtain lifted and the first nervous, superbly atmospheric lines of the play rang out, loud at first, but then going low with unspoken apprehension.

"Who's there?"

"Nay, answer me; stand, and unfold yourself."

"Long live the king!"

"Bernardo?"

"He."

"You come most carefully upon your hour."

"'Tis now struck twelve; get thee to bed, Francisco."

"For this relief much thanks; 'tis bitter cold and I am sick at heart."

"Have you had quiet guard?"

"Not a mouse stirring."

With a resigned shrug, John McCarthy simply sat down. F.F. did the same, though *his* gesture was clench-fisted and exasperated. For a moment it seemed to me very comic that two Ghosts in *Hamlet* should be sitting in the wings, watching a third perform. I unbuttoned my overcoat and slung it over my left arm.

The Ghost's first two appearances are entirely silent ones. He merely goes on stage, shows himself to the soldiers, and comes off again. Nevertheless there was a determined little ripple of handclapping from the audience—the second, third, and fourth rows center greeting their patriarchal hero, it seemed likely. Guthrie didn't fall down at any rate and he walked reasonably straight—an achievement perhaps rating applause, if anyone out there knew the degree of intoxication Guthrie was probably burdened with at this moment—a cask-bellied Old Man of the Sea on his back.

The only thing out of normal was that he had forgot to turn on the little green light in the peak of his helmet—an omission which hardly mattered, certainly not on his first appearance. I hurried up to him when he came off and told him about it in a whisper as he moved off toward a dark backstage corner. I got in reply, through the inscrutable green veil, an exhalation of whisky and three affirmative grunts: one, that he knew it; two, that the light was working; three, that he'd remember to turn it on next time.

Then the scene had ended and I darted across the stage as they changed to the room-of-state set. I wanted to get rid of my overcoat. Joe Rubens grabbed me and told me about Guthrie's green light not being on and I told him that was all taken care of.

"Where the hell was he all the time we were hunting for him?" Joe asked me.

"I don't know," I answered.

By that time the second scene was playing, with F.F., his Ghostcoverings shed, playing the King as well as he always does (it's about his best part) and Gertrude Grainger looking very regal beside him as the Queen, her namesake, while there was another flurry of applause, more scattered this time, for the Governor in his black doublet and tights beginning about his seven hundredth performance of Shakespeare's longest and meatiest role.

Monica was still sitting on the trunk by the switchboard, looking paler than ever under her make-up, it seemed to me, and I folded my overcoat and silently persuaded her to use it as a cushion. I sat beside her and she took my hand and we watched the play from the wings.

After a while I whispered to her, giving her hand a little squeeze, "Feeling better now?"

She shook her head. Then leaning toward me, her mouth close to my ear, she whispered rapidly and unevenly, as if she just had to tell someone, "Bruce, I'm frightened. There's something in the theater. I don't think that was Guthrie playing the Ghost."

I whispered back, "Sure it was. I talked with him."

"Did you see his face?" she asked.

"No, but I smelled his breath," I told her and explained to her about him forgetting to turn on the green light. I continued, "Francis and John were both ready to go on as the Ghost, though, until Guthrie turned up. Maybe you glimpsed one of them before the play started and that gave you the idea that it was Guthrie."

Sybil Jameson in her Player costume looked around at me warningly. I was letting my whispering get too loud.

Monica put her mouth so close that her lips for an instant brushed my ear and she mouse-whispered, "I don't mean another *person* playing the Ghost—not that exactly. Bruce, there's *something* in the theater."

"You've got to forget that Ouija nonsense," I told her sharply. "And buck up now," I added, for the curtain had just gone down on Scene Two and it was time for her to get on stage for her scene with Laertes and Polonius.

I waited until she was launched into it, speaking her lines brightly enough, and then I carefully crossed the stage behind the backdrop. I was sure there was no more than nerves and imagination to her notions, though they'd raised shivers on me, but just the same I wanted to speak to Guthrie again and see his face.

When I'd completed my slow trip (you have to move rather slowly, so the drop won't ripple or bulge), I was dumbfounded to find myself witnessing the identical backstage scene that had been going on when I'd got back from my tour of the bars. Only now there was a lot more light because the scene being played on stage was a bright one. And Props was there behind his table, watching everything like the spectator he basically is. But beyond him were Francis Farley Scott and John McCarthy in their improvised Ghost costumes again, and the Governor and Joe with them, and all of them carrying on that furious lip-reader's argument, now doubly hushed.

I didn't have to wait to get close to them to know that Guthrie must have disappeared again. As I made my way toward them, watching their silent antics, my silly mind became almost hysterical with the thought that Guthrie had at last discovered that invisible hole every genuine alcoholic wishes he had, into which he could decorously disappear and drink during the times between his absolutely necessary appearances in the real world.

As I neared them, Donald Fryer (our Horatio) came from behind me, having made the trip behind the backdrop faster than I had, to tell the Governor in hushed gasps that Guthrie wasn't in any of the dressing rooms or anywhere else stage right.

Just at that moment the bright scene ended, the curtain came down, the drapes before which Ophelia and the others had been playing swung back to reveal again the battlements of Elsinore, and the lighting shifted back to the midnight blue of the first scene, so that for the moment it was hard to see at all. I heard the Governor say decisely, "*You* play the Ghost," his voice receding as he and Joe and Don hurried across the stage to be in place for their proper entrance. Seconds later there came the dull soft hiss of the main curtain opening and I heard the Governor's taut resonant voice saying, "The air bites shrewdly; it's very cold," and Don responding as Horatio with, "It is a nipping and an eager air."

By that time I could see again well enough—see Francis Farley Scott and John McCarthy moving side by side toward the back wing through which the Ghost enters. They were still arguing in whispers. The explanation was clear enough: each thought the Governor had pointed at him in the sudden darkness—or possibly in F.F.'s case was pretending he so thought. For a moment the comic side of my mind, grown a bit hysterical by now, almost collapsed me with the thought of twin Ghosts entering the stage side by side. Then once again, history still repeating itself, I saw beyond them that other bulkier figure with the unmistakable shrouded helmet. They must have seen it too for they stopped dead just before my hands touched a shoulder of each of them. I circled quickly past them and reached out my hands to put them lightly on the third figure's shoulders, intending to whisper, "Guthrie, are you okay?" It was a very stupid thing for one actor to do to another—startling him just before his entrance—but I was made thoughtless by the memory of Monica's fears and by the rather frantic riddle of where Guthrie could possibly have been hiding.

But just then Horatio gasped, "Look, my lord, it comes," and Guthrie moved out of my light grasp onto the stage without so much as turning his head—and leaving me shaking because where I'd touched the rough buckram-braced fabric of the Ghost's cloak I'd felt only a kind of insubstantially beneath instead of Guthrie's broad shoulders.

I quickly told myself that was because Guthrie's cloak had stood out from his shoulders and his back as he had moved. I had to tell myself something like that. I turned around. John McCarthy and F.F. were standing in front of the dark prop table and by now my nerves were in such a state that their paired forms gave me another start. But I tiptoed after them into the downstage wings and watched the scene from there.

The Governor was still on his knees with his sword held hilt up like a cross doing the long speech that begins, "Angels and ministers of grace defend us!" And of course the Ghost had his cloak drawn around him so you couldn't see what was under it—and the little green light still wasn't lit in his helmet. Tonight the absence of that theatric touch made him a more frightening figure—certainly to me, who wanted so much to see Guthrie's ravaged old face and be reassured by it. Though there was still enough comedy left in the ragged edges of my thoughts that I could imagine Guthrie's pugnacious son-in-law whispering angrily to those around him that Gilbert Usher was so jealous of his great father-in-law that he wouldn't let him show his face on the stage.

Then came the transition to the following scene where the Ghost has led Hamelt off alone with him—just a five-second complete darkening of the stage while a scrim is dropped—and at last the Ghost spoke those first lines of "Mark me" and "My hour is almost come, When I to sulphurous and tormenting flames Must render up myself."

If any of us had any worries about the Ghost blowing up on his lines or slurring them drunkenly, they were taken care of now. Those lines were delivered with the greatest authority and effect. And I was almost certain that it was Guthrie's rightful voice—at least I was at first—but doing an even better job than the good one he had always done of getting the effect of distance and otherworldliness and hopeless alienation from all life on Earth. The theater became as silent as death, yet at the same time I could imagine the soft pounding of a thousand hearts, thousands of shivers crawling— and I *knew* that Francis Farley Scott, whose shoulder was pressed against mine, was trembling.

Each word the Ghost spoke was like a ghost itself, mounting the air and hanging poised for an impossible extra instant before it faded towards eternity.

Those great lines came: "I am thy father's spirit; Doomed for a certain term to walk the night . . ." and just at that moment the idea came to me that Guthrie Boyd might be dead, that he might have died and be lying unnoticed somewhere between his children's home and the theater—no matter what Props had said or the rest of us had seen—and that his ghost might have come to give a last performance. And on the heels of that shivery impossibility came the thought that similar and perhaps even eerier ideas must be frightening Monica. I knew I had to go to her.

So while the Ghost's words swooped and soared in the dark—marvellous black-plumed birds—I again made that nervous cross behind the backdrop.

Everyone stage right was standing as frozen and absorbed—motionless loomings —as I'd left John and F.F. I spotted Monica at once. She'd moved forward from the switchboard and was standing, crouched a little, by the big floodlight that throws some dimmed blue on the backdrop and across the back of the stage. I went to her just as the Ghost was beginning his exit stage left, moving backward along the edge of the light from the flood, but not quite in it, and reciting more lonely and eerily than I'd ever heard them before those memorable last lines:

> "Fare thee well at once!
> "The glow-worm shows the matin to be near,
> "And 'gins to pale his uneffectual fire;
> "Adieu, adieu! Hamlet, remember me."

One second passed, then another, and then there came two unexpected bursts of sound at the same identical instant: Monica screamed and a thunderous applause started out front, touched off by Guthrie's people, of course, but this time swiftly spreading to all the rest of the audience.

I imagine it was the biggest hand the Ghost ever got in the history of the theater. In fact, I never heard of him getting a hand before. It certainly was a most inappropriate place to clap, however much the performance deserved it. It broke the atmosphere and the thread of the scene.

Also, it drowned out Monica's scream, so that only I and a few of those behind me heard it.

At first I thought I'd made her scream, by touching her as I had Guthrie, suddenly, like an idiot, from behind. But instead of dodging away she turned and clung to me, and kept clinging too even after I'd drawn her back and Gertrude Grainger and Sybil

Jameson had closed in to comfort her and hush her gasping sobs and try to draw her away from me.

By this time the applause was through and Governor and Don and Joe were taking up the broken scene and knitting together its finish as best they could, while the floods came up little by little, changing to rosy, to indicate dawn breaking over Elsinore.

Then Monica mastered herself and told us in quick whispers what had made her scream. The Ghost, she said, had moved for a moment into the edge of the blue flood-light, and she had seen for a moment through his veil, and what she had seen had been a face like Shakespeare's. Just that and no more. Except that at the moment when she told us—later she became less certain—she was sure it was Shakespeare himself and no one else.

I discovered that when you hear something like that you don't exclaim or get outwardly excited. Or even inwardly, exactly. It rather shuts you up. I know I felt at the same time extreme awe and a renewed irritation at the Ouija board. I was deeply moved, yet at the same time pettishly irked, as if some vast adult creature had disordered the toy world of my universe.

It seemed to hit Sybil and even Gertrude the same way. For the moment we were shy about the whole thing, and so, in her way, was Monica, and so were the few others who had overheard in part or all what Monica had said.

I knew we were going to cross the stage in a few more seconds when the curtain came down on that scene, ending the first act, and stagelights came up. At least I knew that I was going across. Yet I wasn't looking forward to it.

When the curtain did come down—with another round of applause from out front —and we started across, Monica beside me with my arm still tight around her, there came a choked-off male cry of horror from ahead to shock and hurry us. I think about a dozen of us got stage left about the same time, including of course the Governor and the others who had been on stage.

F.F. and Props were standing inside the doorway to the empty prop room and look-ing down into the hidden part of the L. Even from the side, they both looked pretty sick. Then F.F. knelt down and almost went out of view, while Props hunched over him with his natural stoop.

As we craned around Props for a look—myself among the first, just beside the Governor—we saw something that told us right away that this Ghost wasn't ever going to be able to answer that curtain call they were still fitfully clapping for out front, although the house lights must be up by now for the first intermission.

Guthrie Boyd was lying on his back in his street clothes. His face looked grey, the eyes staring straight up. Swirled beside him lay the Ghost's cloak and veil and the helmet and an empty fifth of whisky.

Between the two conflicting shocks of Monica's revelation and the body in the prop room, my mind was in a useless state. And from her helpless incredulous expres-sion I knew Monica felt the same. I tried to put things together and they wouldn't fit anywhere.

F.F. looked up at us over his shoulder. "He's not breathing," he said. "I think he's gone." Just the same he started loosing Boyd's tie and shirt and pillowing his head on the cloak. He handed the whisky bottle back to us through several hands and Joe Rubens got rid of it.

The Governor sent out front for a doctor and within two minutes Harry Grossman was bringing us one from the audience who'd left his seat number and bag at the box office. He was a small man—Guthrie would have made two of him—and a bit awestruck,

327

I could see, though holding himself with greater professional dignity because of that, as we made way for him and then crowded in behind.

He confirmed F.F.'s diagnosis by standing up quickly after kneeling only for a few seconds where F.F. had. Then he said hurriedly to the Governor, as if the words were being surprised out of him against his professional caution, "Mr. Usher, if I hadn't heard this man giving that great performance just now, I'd think he'd been dead for an hour or more."

He spoke low and not all of us heard him, but I did and so did Monica, and there was Shock Three to go along with the other two, raising in my mind for an instant the grisly picture of Guthrie Boyd's spirit, or some other entity, willing his dead body to go through with the last performance. Once again I unsuccessfully tried to fumble together the parts of this night's mystery.

The little doctor looked around at us slowly and puzzledly. He said, "I take it he just wore the cloak over his street clothes?" He paused. Then, "He *did* play the Ghost?" he asked us.

The Governor and several others nodded, but some of us didn't at once and I think F.F. gave him a rather peculiar look, for the doctor cleared his throat and said, "I'll have to examine this man as quickly as possible in a better place and light. Is there—?" The Governor suggested the couch in his dressing room and the doctor designated Joe Rubens and John McCarthy and Francis Farley Scott to carry the body. He passed over the Governor, perhaps out of awe, but Hamlet helped just the same, his black garb most fitting.

It was odd the doctor picked the older men—I think he did it for dignity. And it was odder still that he should have picked two ghosts to help carry a third, though he couldn't have known that.

As the designated ones moved forward, the doctor said, "Please stand back, the rest of you."

It was then that the very little thing happened which made all the pieces of this night's mystery fall into place—for me, that is, and for Monica too, judging from the way her hand trembled in then tightened around mine. We'd been given the key to what had happened. I won't tell you what it was until I've knit together the ends of this story.

The second act was delayed perhaps a minute, but after that we kept to schedule, giving a better performance than usual—I never knew the Graveyard Scene to carry so much feeling or the bit with Yorick's skull to be so poignant.

Just before I made my own first entrance, Joe Rubens snatched off my street hat—I'd had it on all this while—and I played all of Guildenstern wearing a wristwatch, though I don't imagine anyone noticed.

F.F. played the Ghost as an off-stage voice when he makes his final brief appearance in the Closet Scene. He used Guthrie's voice to do it, imitating him very well. It struck me afterwards as ghoulish—but right.

Well before the play ended, the doctor had decided he could say that Guthrie had died of a heart seizure, not mentioning the alcoholism. The minute the curtain came down on the last act, Harry Grossman informed Guthrie's son and daughter and brought them backstage. They were much moved, though hardly deeply smitten, seeing they'd been out of touch with the old boy for a decade. However, they quickly saw it was a Grand and Solemn Occasion and behaved accordingly, especially Guthrie's pugnacious son-in-law.

Next morning the two Wolverton papers had headlines about it and Guthrie got his biggest notices ever in the Ghost. The strangeness of the event carried the item around the world—a six-line filler, capturing the mind for a second or two, about how a once-famous actor had died immediately after giving a performance as the Ghost in *Hamlet*, though in some versions, of course, it became Hamlet's Ghost.

The funeral came on the afternoon of the third day, just before our last performance in Wolverton, and the whole company attended along with Guthrie's children's crowd and many other Wolvertonians. Old Sybil broke down and sobbed.

Yet to be a bit callous, it was a neat thing that Guthrie died where he did, for it saved us the trouble of having to send for relatives and probably take care of the funeral outselves. And it did give old Guthrie a grand finish, with everything outside the company thinking him a hero-martyr to the motto The Show Must Go On. And of course we knew too that in a deeper sense he'd really been that.

We shifted around in our parts and doubled some to fill the little gaps Guthrie had left in the plays, so that the Governor didn't have to hire another actor at once. For me, and I think for Monica, the rest of the season was very sweet. Gertrude and Sybil carried on with the Ouija sessions alone.

And now I must tell you about the very little thing which gave myself and Monica's a satisfying solution to the mystery of what had happened that night.

You'll have realized that it involved Props. Afterwards I asked him straight out about it and he shyly told me that he really couldn't help me there. He'd had this unaccountable devilish compulsion to get drunk and his mind had blanked out entirely from well before the performance until he found himself standing with F.F. over Guthrie's body at the end of the first act. He didn't remember the Ouija-scare or a word of what he'd said to me about theaters and time machines—or so he always insisted.

F.F. told us that after the Ghost's last exit he'd seen him—very vaguely in the dimness—lurch across backstage into the empty prop room and that he and Props had found Guthrie lying there at the end of the scene. I think the queer look F.F.—the old reality-fuddling rogue!—gave the doctor was to hint to him that *he* had played the Ghost, though that wasn't something I could ask him about.

But the very little thing— When they were picking up Guthrie's body and the doctor told the rest of us to stand back, Props turned as he obeyed and straightened his shoulders and looked directly at Monica and myself, or rather a little over our heads. He appeared compassionate yet smilingly serene as always and for a moment transfigured, as if he were the eternal observer of the stage of life and this little tragedy were only part of an infinitely vaster, endlessly interesting pattern.

I realized at that instant that Props could have done it, that he'd very effectively guarded the doorway to the empty prop room during our searches, that the Ghost's costume could be put on or off in seconds (though Prop's shoulders wouldn't fill the cloak like Guthrie's), and that I'd never once before or during the play seen him and the Ghost at the same time. Yes, Guthrie had arrived a few minutes before me . . . and died . . . and Props, nerved to it by drink, had covered for him.

While Monica, as she told me later, knew at once that here was the great-browed face she'd glimpsed for a moment through the greenish gauze.

Clearly there had been four ghosts in *Hamlet* that night—John McCarthy, Francis Farley Scott, Guthrie Boyd, and the fourth who had really played the role. Mentally blacked out or not, knowing the lines from the many times he'd listened to *Hamlet* - performed in this life, or from buried memories of times he'd taken the role in the days of Queen Elizabeth the First, Billy (or Willy) Simpson, or simply Willy S., had played the Ghost, a good trouper responding automatically to an emergency.

Gonna Roll The Bones

Suddenly Joe Slattermill knew for sure he'd have to get out quick or else blow his top and knock out with the shrapnel of his skull the props and patches holding up his decaying home, that was like a house of big wooden and plaster wallpaper cards except for the huge fireplace and ovens and chimney across the kitchen from him.

Those were stone-solid enough, though. The fireplace was chinhigh, at least twice that long, and filled from end to end with roaring flames. Above were the square doors of the ovens in a row—his Wife baked for part of their living. Above the ovens was the wall-long mantelpiece, too high for his mother to reach or Mr. Guts to jump any more, set with all sorts of ancestral curios, but any of them that weren't stone or glass or china had been so dried and darkened by decades of heat that they looked like nothing but shrunken human heads and black golf balls. At one end were clustered his Wife's square gin bottles. Above the mantelpiece hung one old chromo, so high and so darkened by soot and grease that you couldn't tell whether the swirls and fat cigar shape were a whaleback steamer ploughing through a hurricane or a spaceship plunging through a storm of light-driven dust motes.

As soon as Joe curled his toes inside his boots, his Mother knew what he was up to. "Going bumming," she mumbled with conviction. "Pants pockets full of cartwheels of house money, too, to spend on sin." And she went back to munching the long shreds she stripped fumblingly with her right hand off the turkey carcass set close to the terrible heat, her left hand ready to fend off Mr. Guts, who stared at her yellow-eyed, gaunt-flanked, with long mangy tail a-twitch. In her dirty dress, streaky as the turkey's sides, Joe's Mother looked like a bent brown bag and her fingers were lumpy twigs.

Joe's Wife knew as soon or sooner, for she smiled thin-eyed at him over her shoulder from where she towered at the centermost oven. Before she closed its door, Joe glimpsed that she was baking two long, flat, narrow, fluted loaves and one high, round-domed one. She was thin as death and disease in her violet wrapper. Without looking, she reached out a yard-long, skinny arm for the nearest gin bottle and downed a warm slug and smiled again. And without a word spoken, Joe knew she'd said, "You're going out and gamble and get drunk and lay a floozy and come home and beat me and go to jail for it," and he had a flash of the last time he'd been in the dark gritty cell and she'd come by moonlight, which showed the green and yellow lumps on her narrow skull where he'd hit her, to whisper to him through the tiny window in the back and slip him a half pint through the bars.

And Joe knew for certain that this time it would be that bad and worse, but just the same he heaved up himself and his heavy, muffledly clanking pockets and shuffled straight to the door, muttering, "Guess I'll roll the bones, up the pike a stretch and back," swinging his bent, knobbly-elbowed arms like paddlewheels to make a little joke about his words.

When he'd stepped outside, he held the door open a hand's breadth behind him for several seconds. When he finally closed it, a feeling of deep misery struck him. Earlier years, Mr. Guts would have come streaking along to seek fights and females on the roofs and fences, but not the big tom was content to stay home and hiss by the fire and snatch for turkey and dodge a broom, quarrelling and comforting with two house-bound women. Nothing had followed Joe to the door but his Mother's chomping and her gasping breaths and the clink of the gin bottle going back on the mantel and the creaking of the floor boards under his feet.

The night was up-side down deep among the frosty stars. A few of them seemed to move, like the white-hot jets of spaceships. Down below it looked as if the whole town of Ironmine had blown or buttoned out the light and gone to sleep, leaving the streets and spaces to the equally unseen breezes and ghosts. But Joe was still in the hemisphere of the musty dry odour of the worm-eaten carpentry behind him, and as he felt and heard the dry grass of the lawn brush his calves, it occurred to him that something deep down inside him had for years been planning things so that he and the House and his Wife and Mother and Mr. Guts would all come to an end together. Why the kitchen heat hadn't touched off the tindery place ages ago was a physical miracle.

Hunching his shoulders, Joe stepped out, not up the pike, but down the dirt road that led past Cypress Hollow Cemetery to Night Town.

The breezes were gentle, but unusually restless and variable tonight, like leprechaun squalls. Beyond the drunken, whitewashed cemetery fence dim in the starlight, they rustled the scraggly trees of Cypress Hollow and made it seem they were stroking their beards of Spanish moss. Joe sensed that the ghosts were just as restless as the breezes, uncertain where and whom to haunt, or whether to take the night off, drifting together in sorrowfully lecherous companionship. While among the trees the red-green vampire lights pulsed faintly and irregularly, like sick fireflies or a plague-stricken space fleet. The feeling of deep misery stuck with Joe and deepened and he was tempted to turn aside and curl up in any convenient tomb or around some half-toppled head board and cheat his Wife and the other two behind him out of a shared doom. He thought: Gonna roll the bones, gonna roll 'em up and go to sleep. But while he was deciding, he got past the sagged-open gate and the rest of the delirious fence and Shantyville too.

At first Night Town seemed dead as the rest of Ironmine, but then he noticed a faint glow, sick as the vampire lights but more feverish, and with it a jumping music, tiny at first as a jazz for jitterbugging ants. He stepped along the springy sidewalk, wistfully remembering the days when the spring was all in his own legs and he'd bound into a fight like a bobcat or a Martian sand-spider. God, it had been years now since he had fought a real fight, or felt *the power*. Gradually the midget music got raucous as a bunny-hug for grizzly bears and loud as a polka for elephants, while the glow became a riot of gas flares and flambeaux and corpse-blue mercury tubes and jiggling pink neon ones that all jeered at the stars where the spaceships roved. Next thing, he was facing a three-storey false front flaring everywhere like a devil's elbow, with a pale blue topping of St. Elmo's fire. There were wide swinging doors in the center of it, spilling light above and below. Above the doorway, golden calcium light scrawled over and over again, with wild curlicues and flourishes, "The Boneyard," while a fiendish red kept printing out, "Gambling."

So the new place they'd all been talking about for so long had opened at last! For the first time that night, Joe Slattermill felt a stirring of real life in him and the faintest caress of excitement.

Gonna roll the bones, he thought.

He dusted off his blue-green work clothes with big, careless swiped and slapped his pockets to hear the clank. Then he threw back his shoulders and grinned his lips sneeringly and pushed through the swinging doors as if giving a foe the straight-armed heel of his palm.

Inside, The Boneyard seemed to cover the area of a township and the bar looked as long as the railroad tracks. Round pools of light on the green poker tables alternated with hourglass shapes of exciting gloom, through which drink girls and change-girls moved like white-legged witches. By the jazz-stand in the distance, belly dancers made *their* white hourglass shapes. The gamblers were thick and hunched down as mushrooms, all bald from agonizing over the fall of a card or a die or the dive of an ivory ball, while the Scarlet Women were like fields of poinsettia.

The calls of the croupiers and the slaps of dealt cards were as softly yet fatefully staccato as the rustle and beat of the jazz drums. Every tight-locked atom of the place was controlledly jumping. Even the dust motes jiggled tensely in the cones of light.

Joe's excitement climbed and he felt sift through him, like a breeze that heralds a gale, the faintest breath of a confidence which he knew could become a tornado. All thoughts of his House and Wife and Mother dropped out of his mind, while Mr. Guts remained only as a crazy young tom walking stiff-legged around the rim of his consciousness. Joe's own leg muscles twitched in sympathy and he felt them grow supplely strong.

He coolly and searchingly looked the place over, his hand going out like it didn't belong to him to separate a drink from a passing, gently bobbing tray. Finally his gaze settled on what he judged to be the Number One Crap Table. All the Big Mushrooms seemed to be there, bald as the rest but standing tall as toadstools. Then through a gap in them Joe saw on the other side of the table a figure still taller, but dressed in a long dark coat with collar turned up and a dark slouch hat pulled low, so that only a triangle of white face showed. A suspicion and a hope rose in Joe and he headed straight for the gap in the Big Mushroom.

As he got nearer, the white-legged and shiny-topped drifters eddying out of his way, his suspicion received confirmation after confirmation and his hope budded and swelled. Back from one end of the table was the fattest man he'd ever seen, with a long cigar and a silver vest and a gold tie clasp at least eight inches wide that just said in thick script, "Mr. Bones." Back a little from the other end was the nakedest change-girl yet and the only one he'd seen whose tray, slung from her bare shoulders, and indenting her belly just below her breasts, was stacked with gold in gleaming little towers and with jet-black chips. While the dice-girl, skinnier and taller and longer armed than his Wife even, didn't seem to be wearing much but a pair of long white gloves. She was all right if you went for the type that isn't much more than pale skin over bones with breasts like china doorknobs.

Beside each gambler was a high round table for his chips. The one by the gap was empty. Snapping his fingers at the nearest silver change-girl, Joe traded all his greasy dollars for an equal number of pale chips and tweaked her left nipple for luck. She playfully snapped her teeth towards his fingers.

Not hurrying but not wasting any time, he advanced and carelessly dropped his modest stacks on the empty table and took his place in the gap. He noted that the second Big Mushroom on his right had the dice. His heart but no other part of him gave an extra jump. Then he steadily lifted his eyes and looked straight across the table.

The coat was a shimmering elegant pillar of black satin with jet buttons, the upturned collar of fine dull plush black as the darkest cellar, as was the slouch hat with down-turned brim and a band of only a thin braid of black horse-hair. The arms of the coat were long, lesser satin pillars, ending in slim, longfingered hands that moved swiftly when they did, but held each position of rest with a statue's poise.

Joe still couldn't see much of the face except for smooth lower forehead with never a bead or trickle of sweat—the eyebrows were like straight snippets of the hat's braid—and gaunt aristocratic cheeks and narrow but somewhat flat nose. The complexion of the face wasn't as white as Joe had first judged. There was a faint touch of brown in it, like ivory that's just begun to age, or Venusian soapstone. Another glance at the hands confirmed this.

Behind the man in black was a knot of just about the flashiest and nastiest customers, male or female, Joe had ever seen. He knew from one look that each bediamonded, pomaded bully had a belly gun beneath the flap of his flowered vest and a blackjack in his hip pocket, and each snake-eyed sporting girl a stiletto in her garter and a pearl-handled silver-plated derringer under the sequinned silk in the hollow between her jutting breasts.

Yet at the same time Joe knew they were just trimmings. It was the man in black, their master, who was the deadly one, the kind of man you knew at a glance you couldn't touch and live. If without asking you merely laid a finger on his sleeve, no matter how lightly and respectfully, an ivory hand would move faster than thought and you'd be stabbed or shot. Or maybe just the touch would kill you, as if every black article of his clothing were charged from his ivory skin outwards with a high-voltage, high-amperage ivory electricity. Joe looked at the shadowed face again and decided he wouldn't care to try it.

For it was the eyes that were the most impressive feature. All great gamblers have dark-shadowed deep-set eyes. But this one's eyes were sunk so deep you couldn't even be sure you were getting a gleam of them. They were inscrutability incarnate. They were unfathomable. They were like black holes.

But all this didn't disappoint Joe one bit, though it did terrify him considerably. On the contrary, it made him exult. His first suspicion was completely confirmed and his hope spread into full flower.

This must be one of those really big gamblers who hit Ironmine only once a decade at most, come from the Big City on one of the river boats that ranged the watery dark like luxurious comets, spouting long thick tails of sparks from their sequoia-tall stacks with top foliage of curvy-snipped sheet iron. Or like silver space-liners with dozens of jewel-flamed jets, their portholes atwinkle like ranks of marshalled asteroids.

For that matter, maybe some of those really big gamblers actually came from other planets where the nighttime pace was hotter and the sporting life a delirium of risk and delight.

Yes, this was the kind of man Joe had always yearned to pit his skill against. He felt *the power* begin to tingle in his rock-still fingers, just a little.

Joe lowered his gaze to the crap table. It was almost as wide as a man is tall, at least twice as long, unusually deep, and lined with black, not green, felt, so that it looked like a giant's coffin. There was something familiar about its shape which he couldn't place. Its bottom, thought not its sides or ends, had a twinkling iridescence, as if it had been lightly sprinkled with very tiny diamonds. As Joe lowered his gaze all the way and looked directly down, his eyes barely over the table, he got the crazy notion that it went down all the way through the world, so that the diamonds were the stars on the other side, visible despite the sunlight there, just as Joe was always able to see the stars by day up the shaft of the mine he worked in, and so that if a cleaned-out gambler, dizzy with defeat, toppled forward into it, he'd fall forever, towards the bottom-most bottom, be it Hell or some black galaxy. Joe's thoughts swirled and he felt the cold, hard-fingered clutch of fear at his crotch. Someone was crooning beside him, "Come on, Big Dick."

Then the dice, which had meanwhile passed to the Big Mushroom immediately on his right, came to rest near the table's center, contradicting and wiping out Joe's vision. But instantly there was another oddity to absorb him. The Ivory dice were large and unusually round-cornered with dark red spots that gleamed like real rubies, but the spots were arranged in such a way that each face looked like a miniature skull. For instance, the seven thrown just now, by which the Big Mushroom to his right had lost his point, which had been ten, consisted of a two with the spots evenly spaced towards one side, like eyes, instead of towards opposite corners, and of a five with the same red eyespots but a central red nose and two spots close together below that to make teeth.

The long, skinny, white-gloved arm of the dice-girl snaked out like an albino cobra and scooped up the dice and whisked them on to the rim of the table right in front of Joe. He inhaled silently, picked up a single chip from his table and started to lay it beside the dice, then realized that wasn't the way things were done here, and put it back. He would have liked to examine the chip more closely, though. It was curiously lightweighted and pale tan, about the colour of cream with a shot of coffee in it, and it had embossed on its surface a symbol he could feel, though not see. He didn't know what the symbol was, that would have taken more feeling. Yet its touch had been very good, setting the power tingling full blast in his shooting hand.

Joe looked casually yet swiftly at the faces around the table, not missing the Big Gambler across from him, and said quietly, "Roll a penny," meaning of course one pale chip, or a dollar.

There was a hiss of indignation from all the Big Mushrooms and the moonface of big-bellied Mr. Bones grew purple as he started forward to summon his bouncers.

The Big Gambler raised a black-satined forearm and sculptured hand, palm down. Instantly Mr. Bones froze and the hissing stopped faster than that of a meteor prick in self-sealing space steel. Then in a whispery, cultured voice, without the faintest hint of derision, the man in black said, "Get on him, gamblers."

Here, Joe thought, was a final confirmation of his suspicion, had it been needed. The really great gamblers were always perfect gentleman and generous to the poor.

With only the tiny, respectful hint of a guffaw, one of the Big Mushrooms called to Joe, "You're faded."

Joe picked up the ruby-featured dice.

Now ever since he had first caught two eggs on one plate, won all the marbles in Ironmine, and juggled six alphabet blocks so they finally fell in a row on the rug spelling "Mother," Joe Slattermill had been almost incredibly deft at precision throwing. In the mine he could carom a rock off a wall of ore to crack a rat's skull fifty feet away in the dark and he sometimes amused himself by tossing little fragments of rock back into the holes from which they had fallen, so that they stuck there, perfectly fitted in, for at least a second. Sometimes, by fast tossing, he could fit seven or eight fragments into the hole from which they had fallen, like putting together a puzzle block. If he could ever have got into space, Joe would undoubtedly have been able to pilot six Moon-skimmers at once and do figure eights through Saturn's rings blindfolded.

Now the only real difference between precision-tossing rocks or alphabet blocks and dice is that you have to bounce the latter off the end wall of a crap table, and that just made it a more interesting test of skill for Joe.

Rattling the dice now, he felt the power in his fingers and palm as never before.

He made a swift low roll, so that the bones ended up exactly in front of the white-gloved dice-girl. His natural seven was made up, as he'd intended, of a four and a three. In red-spot features they were like the five, except that both had only one tooth and the three no nose. Sort of baby-faced skulls. He had won a penny—that is, a dollar.

"Roll two cents," said Joe Slattermill.

This time, for variety, he made his natural with an eleven. The six was like the five, except it had three teeth, the bestlooking skull of the lot.

"Roll a nickel less one."

Two Big Mushrooms divided that bet with a covert smirk at each other.

Now Joe rolled a three and an ace. His point was four. The ace, with its single spot off center towards a side, still somehow looked like a skull—maybe of a Lilliputian Cyclops.

He took a while making his point, once absent-mindedly rolling three successive tens the hard way. He wanted to watch the dice-girl scoop up the cubes. Each time it seemed to him that her snake-swift fingers went under the dice while they were still flat on the felt. Finally he decided it couldn't be an illusion. Although the dice couldn't penetrate the felt, her white-gloved fingers somehow could, dipping in a flash through the black, diamond-sparkling material as if it weren't there.

Right away the thought of a crap-table-size hole through the earth came back to Joe. This would mean that the dice were rolling and lying on a perfectly transparent flat surface, impenetrable for them but nothing else. Or maybe it was only the dice-girl's hands that could penetrate the surface, which would turn into a mere fantasy Joe's earlier vision of a cleaned-out gambler taking the Big Dive down that dreadful shaft, which made the deepest mine a mere pin dent.

Joe decided he had to know which was true. Unless absolutely unavoidable, he didn't want to take the chance of being troubled by vertigo at some crucial stage of the game.

He made a few more meaningless throws, from time to time crooning for realism, "Come on, Little Joe." Finally he settled on his plan. When he did at last make his point—the hard way, with two twos—he caromed the dice off the far corner so that they landed exactly in front of him. Then, after a minimum pause for his throw to be seen by the table, he shot his left hand down under the cubes, just a flicker ahead of the dice-girl's strike, and snatched them up.

Wow! Joe had never had a harder time in his life making his face and manner conceal what his body felt, not even when the wasp had stung him on the neck just as he had been for the first time putting his hand under the skirt of his prudish, fickle, demanding Wife-to-be. His fingers and the back of his hand were in as much agony as if he'd stuck them into a blast furnace. No wonder the dice-girl wore white gloves. They must be asbestos. And a good thing he hadn't used his shooting hand, he thought as he ruefully watched the blisters rise.

He remembered he'd been taught in school what Twenty-Mile Mine also demonstrated: that the earth was fearfully hot under its crust. The crap-table-size hole must pipe up that heat, so that any gambler taking the Big Dive would fry before he'd fallen a furlong and come out less than a cinder in China.

As if his blistered hand weren't bad enough, the Big Mushrooms were all hissing at

336

him again and Mr. Bones had purpled once more and was opening his melon-size mouth to shout for his bouncers.

Once again a lift of the Big Gambler's hand saved Joe. The whispery, gentle voice called, "Tell him, Mr. Bones."

The latter roared towards Joe, "No gambler may pick up the dice he or any other gambler has shot. Only my dice-girl may do that. Rule of the house!"

Joe snapped Mr. Bones the barest nod. He said coolly, "Rolling a dime less two," and when that still peewee bet was covered, he shot Phoebe for his point and then fooled around for quite a while, throwing anything but a five or a seven, until the throbbing in his left hand should fade and all his nerves feel rock-solid again. There had never been the slightest alteration in the power in his right hand; he felt that strong as ever, or stronger.

Midway of this interlude, the Big Gambler bowed slightly but respectfully towards Joe, hooding those unfathomable eye sockets, before turning around to take a long black cigarette from his prettiest and evilest-looking sporting girl. Courtesy in the smallest matters, Joe thought, another mark of the master devotee of games of chance. The Big Gambler sure had himself a flash crew, all right, though in idly looking them over again as he rolled, Joe noted one bummer towards the back who didn't fit in—a raggedly-elegant chap with the elflocked hair and staring eyes and TB-spotted cheeks of a poet.

As he watched the smoke trickling up from under the black slouch hat, he decided that either the lights across the table had dimmed or else the Big Gambler's complexion was yet a shade darker than he'd thought at first. Or it might even be—wild fantasy— that the Big Gambler's skin was slowly darkening tonight, like a meerschaum pipe being smoked a mile a second. That was almost funny to think of—there was enough heat in this place, all right, to darken meerschaum, as Joe knew from sad experience, but so far as he was aware it was all under the table.

None of Joe's thoughts, either familiar or admiring, about the Big Gambler decreased in the slightest degree his certainty of the supreme menace of the man in black and his conviction that it would be death to touch him. And if any doubts had stirred in Joe's mind, they would have been squelched by the chilling incident which next occurred.

The Big Gambler had just taken into his arms his prettiest-evilest sporting girl and was running an aristocratic hand across her haunch with perfect gentility, when the poet chap, green-eyed from jealousy and lovesickness, came leaping forward like a wildcat and aimed a long gleaming dagger at the black satin back.

Joe couldn't see how the blow could miss, but without taking his genteel right hand off the sporting girl's plush rear end, the Big Gambler shot out his left arm like a steel spring straightening. Joe couldn't tell whether he stabbed the poet chap in the throat, or judo-chopped him there, or gave him the Martian double-finger, or just touched him, but anyhow the fellow stopped as dead as if he'd been shot by a silent elephant gun or an invisible ray pistol and he slammed down on the floor. A couple of darkies came running up to drag off the body and nobody paid the least attention, such episodes apparently being taken for granted at The Boneyard.

It gave Joe quite a turn and he almost shot Phoebe before he intended to.

But by now the waves of pain had stopped running up his left arm and his nerves were like metal-wrapped new guitar strings, so three rolls later he shot a five, making his point, and set in to clean out the table.

He rolled nine successive naturals, seven sevens and two elevens, pyramiding his first wager of a single chip to a stake of over four thousand dollars. None of the Big Mushrooms had dropped out yet, but some of them were beginnign to look worried and a couple were sweating. The Big Gambler still hadn't covered any part of Joe's bets, but he seemed to be following the play with interest from the cavernous depths of his eye sockets.

Then Joe got a devilish thought. Nobody could beat him tonight, he knew, but if he held on to the dice until the table was cleaned out, he'd never get a chance to see the Big Gambler exercise *his* skill, and he was truly curious about that. Besides, he thought, he ought to return courtesy for courtesy and have a crack at being a gentleman himself.

"Pulling out forty-one dollars less a nickel," he announced. "Rolling a penny."

This time there wasn't any hissing and Mr. Bones's moonface didn't cloud over. But Joe was conscious that the Big Gambler was staring at him disappointedly, or sorrowfully, or maybe just speculatively.

Joe immediately crapped out by throwing boxcars, rather pleased to see the two best-looking tiny skulls grining rubytoothed side by side, and the dice passed to the Big Mushroom on his left.

"Knew when his streak was over," he heard another Big Mushroom mutter with grudging admiration.

The play worked rather rapidly around the table, nobody getting very hot and the stakes never more than medium high. "Shoot a fin." "Rolling a sawbuck." "An Andrew Jackson." "Rolling thirty bucks." Now and then Joe covered part of a bet, winning more than he lost. He had over seven thousand dollars, real money, before the bones got around to the Big Gambler.

That one held the dice for a long moment on his statue-steady palm while he looked at them reflectively, though not the hint of a furrow appeared in his almost brownish forehad down which never a bead of sweat trickled. He murmured, "Rolling a double sawbuck," and when he had been faded, he closed his fingers, lightly rattled the cubes—the sound was like seeds inside a small gourd only half dry—and negligently cast the dice towards the end of the table.

It was a throw like none Joe had ever seen before at any crap table. The dice travelled flat through the air without turning over, struck the exact juncture of the table's end and bottom, and stopped there dead, showing a natural seven.

Joe was distinctly disappointed. On one of his own throws he was used to calculating something like, "Launch three-up, five north, two and a half rolls in the air, hit on the six-five-three corner, three-quarter roll and a one-quarter side-twist right, hit end on the one-two edge, one-half reverse roll and three-quarter side-twist left, land on five face, roll over twice, come up two," and that would be for just one of the dice, and a really commonplace throw, without extra bounces.

By comparison, the technique of the Big Gambler had been ridiculously, abysmally, horrifyingly simple. Joe could have duplicated it with the greatest ease, of course. It was no more than an elementary form of his old pastime of throwing fallen rocks back into their holes. But Joe had never once thought of pulling such a babyish trick at the crap table. It would make the whole thing too easy and destroy the beauty of the game.

Another reason Joe had never used the trick was that he'd never dreamed he'd be able to get away with it. By all the rules he'd ever heard of, it was a most questionable throw. There was the possibility that one or the other die hadn't completely reached the end of the table, or lay a wee bit cocked against the end. Besides, he reminded himself, weren't both dice supposed to rebound off the end, if only for a fraction of an inch?

However, as far as Joe's very sharp eyes could see, both dice lay perfectly flat and sprang up against the end wall. Morever, everyone else at the table seemed to accept the throw, the dice-girl had scooped up the cubes, and the Big Mushrooms who had faded the man in black were paying off. As far as the rebound business went, well, The Boneyard appeared to put a slightly different interpretation on that rule, and Joe believed in never questioning House Rules except in dire extremity—both his Mother and Wife had long since taught him it was the least troublesome way.

Besides, there hadn't been any of his own money riding on that roll.

In a voice like wind through Cypress Hollow or on Mars, the Big Gambler announced, "Roll a century." It was the biggest bet yet tonight, ten thousand dollars, and the way the Big Gambler said it made it seem something more than that. A hush fell on The Boneyard, they put the mutes on the jazz horns, the croupiers' calls became more confidential, the cards fell softlier, even the roulette balls seemed to be trying to make less noise as they rattled into their cells. The crowd around the Number One Crap Table quietly thickened. The Big Gambler's flash boys and girls formed a double semi-circle around him, ensuring him lots of elbow room.

That century bet, Joe realized, was thirty bucks more than his own entire pile. Three or four of the Big Mushrooms had to signal each other before they'd agreed how to fade it.

The Big Gambler shot another natural seven with exactly the same flat, stop-dead throw.

He bet another century and did it again.

And again.

And again.

Joe was getting mighty concerned and pretty indignant too. It seemed unjust that the Big Gambler should be winning such huge bets with such machinelike, utterly unromantic rolls. Why, you couldn't even call them rolls, the dice never turned over an iota, in the air or after. It was the sort of thing you'd expect from a robot, and a very dully programmed robot at that. Joe hadn't risked any of his own chips fading the Big Gambler, of course, but if things went on like this he'd have to. Two of the Big Mushrooms had already retired sweatingly from the table, confessing defeat, and no one had taken their places. Pretty soon there'd be a bet the remaining Big Mushrooms couldn't entirely cover between them, and then he'd have to risk some of his own chips or else pull out of the game himself—and he couldn't do that, not with the power surging in his right hand like chained lightning.

Joe waited and waited for someone else to question one of the Big Gambler's shots, but no one did. He realized that, despite his efforts to look imperturbable, his face was slowly reddening.

With a little lift of his left hand, the Big Gambler stopped the dice-girl as she was about to snatch at the cubes. The eyes that were like black wells directed themselves at Joe, who forced himself to look back into them steadily. He still couldn't catch the faintest gleam in them. All at once he felt the lightest touch-on-neck of a dreadful suspicion.

With the utmost civility and amiability, the Big Gambler whispered, "I believe that the fine shooter across from me has doubts about the validity of my last throw, though he is too much of a gentleman to voice them. Lottie, the card test."

The wraith-tall, ivory dice-girl plucked a playing card from below the table and with a venomous flash of her little white teeth spun it low across the table through the air at Joe. He caught the whirling pasteboard and examined it briefly. It was the thinnest, stiffest, flattest, shiniest playing card Joe had ever handled. It was also the Joker, if that meant anything. He spun it back lazily into her hand and she slid it very gently, letting it descend by its own weight, down the end wall against which the two dice lay. It came to rest in the tiny hollow their rounded edges made against the black felt. She deftly moved it about without force, demonstrating that there was no space between either of the cubes and the table's end at any point.

"Satisfied?" the Big Gambler asked. Rather against his will Joe nodded. The Big Gambler bowed to him. The dice-girl smirked her short, thin lips and drew herself up, flaunting her white-china-doorknob breasts at Joe.

Casually, almost with an air of boredom, the Big Gambler returned to his routine of shooting a century and making a natural seven. The Big Mushrooms wilted fast and one by one tottered away from the table. A particularly pink-faced Toadstool was brought extra cash by a gasping runner, but it was no help, he only lost the additional centuries. While the stacks of pale and black chips beside the Big Gambler grew skyscraper-tall.

Joe got more and more furious and frightened. He watched like a hawk or spy satellite the dice nesting against the end wall, but never could spot justification for calling for another card test, or nerve himself to question the House Rules at this late date. It was maddening, in fact insanitizing, to know that if only he could get the cubes once more he could shoot circles around that black pillar of sporting aristocracy. He damned himself a googelplex of ways for the idiotic, conceited, suicidal impulse that had led him to let go of the bones when he'd had them.

To make matters worse, the Big Gambler had taken to gazing steadily at Joe with those eyes like coal mines. Now he made three rolls running without even glancing at the dice or the end wall, as far as Joe could tell. Why, he was getting as bad as Joe's Wife or Mother—watching, watching, watching Joe.

But the constant staring of those eyes that were not eyes was mostly throwing a terrific scare into him. Supernatural terror added itself to his certainty of the deadlines of the Big Gambler. Just who, Joe kept asking himself, had he got into a game with tonight? There was curiosity and there was dread—a dreadful curiosity as strong as his desire to get the bones and win. His hair rose and he was all over goose bumps, though the power was still pulsing in his hand like a braked locomotive or a rocket wanting to lift from the pad.

At the same time the Big Gambler stayed just that—a black satin-coated, slouch-hatted elegance, suave, courtly, lethal. In fact, almost the worst thing about the spot Joe found himself in was that, after admiring the Big Gambler's perfect sportsmanship all night, he must now be disenchanted by his machinelike throwing and try to catch him out on any technicality he could.

The remorseless mowing down of the Big Mushrooms went on. The empty spaces outnumbered the Toadstools. Soon there were only three left.

The Boneyard had grown still as Cypress Hollow or the Moon. The jazz had stopped and the gay laughter and the shuffle of feet and the squeak of goosed girls and the clink of drinks and coins. Everybody seemed to be gathered around the Number One Crap Table, rank on silent rank.

Joe was racked by watchfulness, sense of injustice, selfcontempt, wild hopes, curiosity and dread. Especially the last two.

The complexion of the Big Gambler, as much as you could see of it, continued to darken. For one wild moment Joe found himself wondering if he'd got into a game with a nigger, maybe a witch-craft-drenched Voodoo Man whose white make-up was wearing off.

Pretty soon there came a century wager which the two remaining Big Mushrooms couldn't fade between them. Joe had to make up a sawbuck from his miserably tiny pile or get out of the game. After a moment's agonizing hesitation, he did the former.

And lost his ten.

The two Big Mushrooms reeled back into the hushed crowd.

Pit-black eyes bored into Joe. A whisper: "Rolling your pile."

Joe felt well up in him the shameful impulse to confess himself licked and run home. At least his six thousand dollars would make a hit with his Wife and Ma.

But he just couldn't bear to think of the crowd's laughter, or the thought of living with himself knowing that he'd had a final chance, however slim, to challenge the Big Gambler and passed it up.

He nodded.

The Big Gambler shot. Joe leaned out over and down the table, forgetting his vertigo, as he followed the throw with eagle or space-telescopic eyes.

"Satisfied?"

Joe knew he ought to say, "Yes," and slink off with head held as high as he could manage. It was the gentlemanly thing to do. But then he reminded himself that he wasn't a gentleman, but just a dirty, working-stiff miner with a talent for precision hurling.

He also know that it was probably very dangerous for him to say anything but, "Yes," surrounded as he was by enemies and strangers. But then he asked himself what right had he, a miserable, mortal, homebound failure, to worry about danger.

Besides, one of the ruby-grinning dice looked just the tiniest hair out of line with the other.

It was the biggest effort yet of Joe's life, but he swallowed and managed to say, "No. Lottie, the card test."

The dice-girl fairly snarled and reared up and back as if she were going to spit in his eyes, and Joe had a feeling her spit was cobra venom. But the Big Gambler lifted a finger at her in reproof and she skimmed the card at Joe, yet so low and viciously that it disappeared under the black felt for an instant before flying up into Joe's hand.

It was hot to the touch and singed a pale brown all over, though otherwise unimpaired. Joe gulped and spun it back high.

Sneering poisoned daggers at him, Lottie let it glide down the end wall . . . and after a moment's hesitation, it slithered behind the die Joe had suspected.

A bow and then the whisper: "You have sharp eyes, sir. Undoubtedly that die failed to reach the wall. My sincerest apologies and . . . your dice, sir."

Seeing the cubes on the black rim in front of him almost gave Joe apoplexy. All the feelings racking him, including his curiosity, rose to an almost unbelivable pitch of intensity, and when he'd said, "Rolling my pile," and the Big Gambler had replied, "You're faded," he yielded to an uncontrollable impulse and cast the two dice straight at the Big Gambler's ungleaming, midnight eyes.

They went right through into the Big Gambler's skull and bounced around inside there, rattling like big seeds in a big gourd not quite yet dry.

Throwing out a hand, palm back, to either side, to indicate that none of his boys or girls or anyone else must make a reprisal on Joe, the Big Gambler dryly gargled the two cubical bones, then spat them out so that they landed in the center of the table, the one die flat, the other leaning against it.

"Cocked dice, sir," he whispered as graciously as if no indignity whatever had been done him. "Roll again."

Joe shook the dice reflectively, getting over the shock. After a little bit he decided that though he could now guess the Big Gambler's real name, he'd still give him a run for his money.

A little corner of Joe's mind wondered how a live skeleton hung together. Did the bones still have gristle and thews, were they wired, was it done with force-fields, or was each bone a calcium magnet clinging to the next?—this tying in somehow with the generation of the deadly ivory electricity.

In the great hush of The Boneyard, someone cleared his throat, a Scarlet Woman tittered hysterically, a coin fell from the nakedest change-girl's tray with a golden clink and rolled musically across the floor.

"Silence," the Big Gambler commanded and in a movement almost too fast to follow whipped a hand inside the bosom of his coat and out to the crap table's rim in front of him. A short-barrelled silver revolver lay softly gleaming there. "Next creature, from the humblest nigger night-girl to you, Mr. Bones, who utters a sound while my worthy opponent rolls, gets a bullet in the head."

Joe gave him a courtly bow back, it felt funny, and then decided to start his run with a natural seven made up of an ace and a six. He rolled and this time the Big Gambler, judging from the movements of his skull, closely followed the course of the cubes with his eyes that weren't there.

The dice landed, rolled over, and lay still. Incredulously, Joe realized that for the first time in his crap-shooting life he'd made a mistake. Or else there was a power in the Big Gambler's gaze greater than that in his own right hand. The six cube had come down okay, but the ace had taken an extra half roll and come down six too.

"End of the game," Mr. Bones boomed sepulchrally.

The Big Gambler raised a brown skeletal hand. "Not necessarily," he whispered. His black eyepits aimed themselves at Joe like the mouths of siege guns. "Joe Slattermill, you still have something of value to wager, if you wish. Your life."

At that a giggling and a hysterical tittering and a guffawing and a braying and a shrieking burst uncontrollablyout of the whole Boneyard. Mr. Bones summed up the sentiments when he bellowed over the rest of the racket. "Now what use or value is there in the life of a bummer like Joe Slattermill? Not two cents, ordinary money."

The Big Gambler laid a hand on the revolver gleaming before him and all the laughter died.

"I have no use for it," the Big Gambler whispered. "Joe Slattermill, on my part I will venture all my winnings of tonight, and throw in the world and everything in it for a side bet. You will wager you life, and on the side your soul. You to roll the dice. What's your pleasure?"

Joe Slattermill quailed, but then the drama of the situation took hold of him. He thought it over and realized he certainly wasn't going to give up being stage center in a spectacle like this to go home broke to his Wife and Mother and decaying House and the dispirited Mr. Guts. Maybe, he told himself encouragingly, there wasn't a power in the Big Gambler's gaze, maybe Joe had just made his one and only crap-shooting error. Besides, he was more inclined to accept Mr. Bones's assessment of the value of his life than the Big Gambler's.

"It's a bet," he said.

"Lottie, give him the dice."

Joe concentrated his mind as never before, the power tingled triumphantly in his hand, and he made his throw.

The dice never hit the felt. They went swooping down, then up, in a crazy curve far out over the end of the table, and then came streaking back like tiny red-glinting meteors towards the face of the Big Gambler, where they suddenly nested and hung in his black eye sockets, each with the single red gleam of an ace showing.

Snake eyes.

The whisper, as those red-glinting dice-eyes stared mockingly at him: "Joe Slattermill, you've crapped out."

Using thumb and middle finger—or bone rather—of either hand, the Big Gambler removed the dice from his eye sockets and dropped them in Lottie's white-gloved hand.

"Yes, you've crapped out, Joe Slattermill," he went on tranquilly. "And now you can shoot yourself"—he touched the silver gun—"or cut your throat"—he whipped a gold-handled bowie knife out of his coat and laid it beside the revolver—"or poison yourself" —the two weapons were joined by a small black bottle with white skull and crossbones on it—"or Miss Flossie here can kiss you to death." He drew forward beside him his prettiest, evilest-looking sporting girl. She preened herself and flounced her short violet skirt and gave Joe a provocative, hungry look, lifting her carmine upper lip to show her long white canines.

"Or else," the Big Gambler added, nodding significantly towards the black-bottomed crap table, "you can take the Big Dive."

Joe said evenly, "I'll take the Big Dive."

He put his right foot on his empty chip table, his left on the black rim, fell forward . . . and suddenly kicking off from the rim, launched himself in a tiger spring straight across the crap table at the Big Gambler's throat, solacing himself with the thought that certainly the poet chap hadn't seemed to suffer long.

As he flashed across the exact center of the table he got an instant photograph of what really lay below, but his brain had no time to develop that snapshot, for the next instant he was ploughing into the Big Gambler.

Stiffened brown palm edge caught him in the temple with a lightning-like judo chop . . . and the brown fingers or bones flew all apart like puff paste. Joe's left hand went through the Big Gambler's chest as if there were nothing there but black satin coat, while his right hand, straight-armedly clawing at the slouch-hatted skull, crunched it to pieces. Next instant Joe was sprawled on the floor with some black clothes and brown fragments.

He was on his feet in a flash and snatching at the Big Gambler's tall stacks. He had time for one left-handed grab. He couldn't see any gold or silver or any black chips, so he stuffed his left pants pocket with a handful of the pale chips and ran.

Then the whole population of The Boneyard was on him and after him. Teeth, knives and brass knuckles flashed. He was punched, clawed, kicked, tripped and stamped on with spike heels. A goldplated trumpet with a bloodshot-eyed black face behind it bopped him on the head. He got a white flash of the golden dice-girl and made a grab for her, but she got away. Someone tried to mash a lighted cigar in his eye. Lottie, writhing and flailing like a white boa constrictor, almost got a simultaneous strangle hold and scissors on him. From a squat wide-mouth bottle Flossie, snarling like a feline fiend, threw what smelt like acid past his face. Mr. Bones peppered shots around him from the silver revolver. He was stabbed at, gouged, rabbit-punched, scrag-mauled, slugged, kneed, bitten, bearhugged, butted, beaten and had his toes trampled.

But somehow none of the blows or grabs had much real force. It was like fighting ghosts. In the end it turned out that the whole population of The Boneyard, working together, had just a little more strength than Joe. He felt himself being lifted by a multitude of hands and pitched out through the swinging doors so that he thudded

343

down on his rear end on the board sidewalk. Even that didn't hurt much. It was more like a kick of encouragement.

He took a deep breath and felt himself over and worked his bones. He didn't seem to have suffered any serious damage. He stood up and looked around. The Boneyard was dark and silent as the grave, or the planet Pluto, or all the rest of Ironmine. As his eyes got accustomed to the starlight and occasional roving spaceship-gleam, he saw a padlocked sheet-iron door where the swinging ones had been.

He found he was chewing on something crusty that he'd somehow carried in his right hand all the way through the final fracas. Mighty tasty, like the bread his Wife baked for best customers. At that instant his brain developed the photograph it had taken when he had glanced down as he flashed across the center of the crap table. It was a thin wall of flames moving sideways across the table and just beyond the flames the faces of his Wife, Mother, and Mr. Guts, all looking very surprised. He realized that what he was chewing was a fragment of the Big Gambler's skull, and he remembered the shape of the three loaves his Wife had started to bake when he left the House. And he understood the magic she'd made to let him get a little ways away and feel half a man, and then come diving home with his fingers burned.

He spat out what was in his mouth and pegged the rest of the bit of giant-popover skull across the street.

He fished in his left pocket. Most of the pale poker chips had been mashed in the fight, but he found a whole one and explored its surface with his fingertips. The symbol embossed on it was a cross. He lifted it to his lips and took a bite. It tasted delicate, but delicious. He ate it and felt his strength revive. He patted his bulging left pocket. At least he'd started out well provisioned.

Then he turned and headed straight for home, but he took the long way, around the world.

The Inner Circles

After the supper dishes were done there was a general movement from the Adler kitchen to the Adler living room.

It was led by Gottfried Helmuth Adler, commonly known as Gott. He was thinking how they should be coming from a dining room, yes, with colored maids, not from a kitchen. In a large brandy snifter he was carrying what had been left in the shaker from the martinis, a colorless elixir weakened by melted ice yet somewhat stronger than his wife was supposed to know. This monster drink was a regular part of Gott's carefully thought-out program for getting safely through the end of the day.

"After the seventeenth hour of creation God got sneaky," Gott Adler once put it to himself.

He sat down in his leather-upholstered easy chair, flipped open Plutarch's *Lives* left-handed, glanced down through the lower halves of his executive bifocals at the paragraph in the biography of Caesar he'd been reading before dinner, then, without moving his head, looked through the upper halves back toward the kitchen.

After Gott came Jane Adler, his wife. She sat down at her drawing table, where pad, pencils, knife, art gum, distemper paints, waters, brushes and rags were laid out neatly.

Then came little Heinie Adler, wearing a spaceman's transparent helmet with a large hole in the top for ventilation. He went and stood beside this arrangement of objects: first a long wooden box about knee-high with a smaller box on top and propped against the latter a toy control panel of blue and silver plastic, on which only one lever moved at all; next facing the panel, a child's wooden chair; then back of the chair another long wooden box lined up with the first.

"Goodbye Mama, goodbye Papa," Heinie called. "I'm going to take a trip in my spaceship."

"Be back in time for bed," his mother said.

"Hot jets!" murmured his father.

Heinie got in, touched the control panel twice, and then sat motionless in the little wooden chair, looking straight ahead.

A fourth person came into the living room from the kitchen—the Man in the Black Flannel Suit. He moved with the sick jerkiness and had the slack putty-gray features of a figure of the imagination that hasn't been fully developed. (There was a fifth person in the house, but even Gott didn't know about him yet.)

The man in the Black Flannel Suit made a stiff gesture at Gott and gaped his mouth to talk to him, but the latter silently writhed his lips in a "Not yet, you fool!" and nodded curtly toward the sofa opposite his easy chair.

"Gott," Jane said, hovering a pencil over the pad, "you've lately taken to acting as if you were talking to someone who isn't there."

"I have, my dear?" her husband replied with a smile as he turned a page, but not lifting his face from his book. "Well, talking to oneself is the sovereign guard against madness."

"I thought it worked the other way," Jane said.

"No," Gott informed her.

Jane wondered what she should draw and saw she had very faintly sketched on a small scale the outlines of a child, done in sticks-and-blobs like Paul Klee or kindergarten art. She could do another "Children's Clubhouse," she supposed, but where should she put it this time?

The old electric clock with brass fittings that stood on the mantel began to wheeze shrilly, "Mystery, mystery, mystery, mystery." It struck Jane as a good omen for her picture. She smiled.

Gott took a slow pull from his goblet and felt the scentless vodka bite just enough and his skin shiver and the room waver pleasantly for a moment with shadows chasing across it. Then he swung the pupils of his eyes upward and looked across at the Man in the Black Flannel Suit, noting with approval that he was sitting rigidly on the sofa. Gott conducted his side of the following conversation without making a sound or parting his lips more than a quarter of an inch, just flaring his nostrils from time to time.

BLACK FLANNEL: Now if I may have your attention for a space, Mr. Adler—

GOTT: Speak when you're spoken to! Remember, I created you.

BLACK FLANNEL: I respect your belief. Have you been getting any messages?

GOTT: The number 6669 turned up three times today in orders and estimates. I received an airmail advertisement beginning "Are you ready for big success?" though the rest of the ad didn't signify. As I opened the envelope the minute hand of my desk clock was pointing at the faceless statue of Mercury on the Commerce Building. When I was leaving the office my secretary droned at me, "A representative of the Inner Circle will call on you tonight," though when I questioned her, she claimed that she'd said, "Was the letter to Innes-Burkel and Company all right?" Because she is aware of my deafness, I could hardly challenge her. In any case she sounded sincere. If those were messages from the Inner Circle, I received them. But seriously I doubt the existence of that clandestine organization. Other explanations seem to me more likely—for instance, that I am developing a psychosis. I do not believe in the Inner Circle.

BLACK FLANNEL: (smiling shrewdly—his features have grown tightly handsome though his complexion is still putty gray): Psychosis is for weak minds. Look, Mr. Adler, you believe in the Mafia, the FBI, and the Communist Underground. You believe in upper-echelon control groups in unions and business and fraternal organizations. You know the workings of big companies. You are familiar with industrial and political espionage. You are not wholly unacquainted with the secret fellowships of munitions manufacturers, financiers, dope addicts and procurers and pornography connoisseurs and the brotherhoods and sisterhoods of sexual deviates and enthusiasts. Why do you boggle at the Inner Circle?

GOTT (coolly): I do not wholly believe in all of those other organizations. And the Inner Circle still seems to me more of a wish-dream than the rest. Besides, you may want me to believe in the Inner Circle in order at a later date to convict me of insanity.

BLACK FLANNEL (drawing a black briefcase from behind his legs and unzipping it on his knees): Then you do not wish to hear about the Inner Circle?

GOTT (inscrutably): I will listen for the present. Hush!

Heinie was calling out excitedly, "I'm in the stars, Papa! They're so close they burn!" He said nothing more and continued to stare straight ahead.

"Don't touch them," Jane warned without looking around. Her pencil made a few faint five-pointed stars. The Children's Clubhouse would be on a boundary of space, she decided—put it in a tree on the edge of the Old Ravine. She said, "Gott, what do you suppose Heinie sees out there beside stars?"

"Blue-eyed angels, probably," her husband answered, smiling again but still not taking his head out of his book.

BLACK FLANNEL (*consulting a sheet of crackling black paper he has slipped from his briefcase, though as far as Gott can see there is no printing, typing, writing, or symbols of any sort in any color ink on the black bond*): The Inner Circle is the world's secret elite, operating behind and above all figureheads, workhorses, wealthy dolts, and those talented exhibitionists we name genius. The Inner Circle has existed *sub rose niger* for thousands of years. It controls human life. It is the repository of all great abilities, and the key to all ultimate delights.

GOTT (*tolerantly*): You make it sound plausible enough. Everyone half believes in such a cryptic power gang, going back to Sumeria.

BLACK FLANNEL: The membership is small and very select. As you are aware, I am a kind of talent scout for the group. Qualifications for admission (*he slips a second sheet of black bond from his briefcase*) include a proven great skill in achieving and wielding power over men and women, an amoral zest for all of life, a seasoned blend of ruthlessness and reliability, plus wide knowledge and lightning wit.

GOTT (*contemptuously*): Is that all?

BLACK FLANNEL (*flatly*): Yes. Initiation is binding for life—and for the afterlife: one of our mottos is Ferdinand's dying cry in *The Duchess of Malfi.* "I will vault credit and affect high pleasures after death." The penalty for revealing organizational secrets is not death alone but extinction—all memory of the person is erased from public and private history; his name is removed from records; all knowledge of and feeling for him is deleted from the minds of his wives, mistresses, and children: it is as if he had never existed. That, by the by, is a good example of the powers of the Inner Circle. It may interest you to know, Mr. Adler, that as a result of the retaliatory activities of the Inner Circle, the names of three British kings have been expunged from history. Those who have suffered a like fate include two popes, seven movie stars, a brilliant Flemish artist superior to Rembrandt . . . (*As he spins out an apparently interminable listing, the Fifth Person creeps in on hands and knees from the kitchen. Gott cannot see him at first, as the sofa is between Gott's chair and the kitchen door. The Fifth Person is the Black Jester, who looks rather like a caricature of Gott but has the same putty complexion as the Man in the Black Flannel Suit. The Black Jester wears skin-tight clothing of that color, silver-embroidered boots and gloves, and a black hood edged with silver bells that do not tinkle. He carries a scepter topped with a small death's-head that wears a black hood like his own edged with tinier silver bells, soundless as the larger ones.*)

THE BLACK JESTER (*suddenly rearing up like a cobra from behind the sofa and speaking to the Man in the Black Flannel Suit over the latter's shoulder*): Ho! So you're still teasing his rickety hopes with that shit about the Inner Circle? Good sport, brother!—you play your fish skillfully.

GOTT (*immensely startled, but controlling himself with some courage*): Who are you? How dare you bring your brabblement into my court?

THE BLACK JESTER: Listen to the old cock crow innocent! As if he didn't know he'd himself created both of us, time and again, to stave off boredom, madness or suicide.

347

GOTT (*firmly*): I never created *you.*

THE BLACK JESTER: Oh yes you did, old cock. Truly your mind has never birthed anything but twins—for every good, a bad; for every breath, a fart; and for every white, a black.

GOTT (*flares his nostrils and glares a death spell which hums toward the newcomer like a lazy invisible bee*).

THE BLACK JESTER (*pales and staggers backward as the death-spell strikes, but shakes it off with an effort and glares back murderously at Gott*): Old cock-father, I'm beginning to hate you at last.

Just then the refrigerator motor went on in the kitchen, and its loud rapid rocking sound seemed to Jane to be a voice saying, "Watch your children, they're in danger. Watch your children they're in danger."

"I'm no ladybug," Jane retorted tartly in her thoughts, irked at the worrisome interruption now that her pencil was rapidly developing the outlines of the Clubhouse in the Tree with the moon risen across the ravine between clouds in the late afternoon sky. Nevertheless she looked at Heinie. He hadn't moved. She could see how the plastic helmet was open at neck and top, but it made her think of suffocation just the same.

"Heinie, are you still in the stars?" she asked.

"No, now I'm landing on a moon," he called back. "Don't talk to me, Mama, I've got to watch the road."

Jane at once wanted to imagine what roads in space might look like, but the refrigerator motor had said "children," not "child," and she knew that the language of machinery is studded with tropes. She looked at Gott. He was curled comfortably over his book, and as she watched, he turned a page and touched his lips to the martini water. Nevertheless, she decided to test him.

"Gott, do you think this family is getting too ingrown?" she said. "We used to have more people around."

"Oh, I think we have quite a few as it is," he replied, looking up at the empty sofa, beyond it, and then around at her expectantly, as if ready to join in any conversation she cared to start. But she simply smiled at him and returned relieved to her thoughts and her picture. He smiled back and bowed his head again to his book.

BLACK FLANNEL (*ignoring the Black Jester*): My chief purpose in coming here tonight, Mr. Adler, is to inform you that the Inner Circle has begun a serious study of your qualifications for membership.

THE BLACK JESTER: At *his* age? After *his* failures? Now we curtsy forward toward the Big Lie!

BLACK FLANNEL (*in a pained voice*): Really! (*then once more to Gott*) Point One: you have gained for yourself the reputation of a man of strong patriotism, deep company loyalty, and realistic self-interest, sternly contemptuous of all youthful idealism and rebelliousness. Point Two: you have cultivated constructive hatreds in your business life, deliberately knifing colleagues when you could, but allying yourself to those on the rise. Point Three and most important: you have gone some distance toward creating the master illusion of a man who has secret sources of information, secret new techniques for thinking more swiftly and acting more decisively than others, secret superior connections and contacts—in short, a dark new strength which all others envy even as they cringe from it.

THE BLACK JESTER (*in a kind of counterpoint as he advances around the sofa*): But he's come down in the world since he lost his big job. National Motors was at least a step in the right direction, but Hagbolt-Vincent has no company planes, no company

348

apartments, no company shooting lodges, no company call girls! Besides, he drinks too much. The Inner Circle is not for drunks on the downgrade.

BLACK FLANNEL: Please! You're spoiling things.

THE BLACK JESTER: *He's* spoiled. (*Closing in on Gott.*) Just look at him now. Eyes that need crutches for near and far. Ears that mis-hear the simplest remark.

GOTT: Keep off me, I tell you.

THE BLACK JESTER (*ignoring the warning*): Fat belly, flaccid sex, swollen ankles. And a mouthful of stinking cavities!—did you know he hasn't dared visit his dentist for five years? Here, open up and show them! (*Thrusts black-gloved hand toward Gott's face.*)

Gott, provoked beyond endurance, snarled aloud, "Keep off, damn you!" and shot out the heavy book in his left hand and snapped it shut on the Black Jester's nose. Both black figures collapsed instantly.

Jane lifted her pencil a foot from the pad, turned quickly, and demanded, "My God, Gott, what was that?"

"Only a winter fly, my dear," he told her soothingly. "One of the fat ones that hide in December and breed all the black clouds of spring." He found his place in Plutarch and dipped his face close to study both pages and the trough between them. He looked around slyly at Jane and said, "I didn't squush her."

The chair in the spaceship rutched. Jane asked, "What is it, Heinie?"

"A meteor exploded, Mama. I'm all right. I'm out in space again, in the middle of the road."

Jane was impressed by the time it had taken the sound of Gott's book clapping shut to reach the spaceship. She began lightly to sketch blob-children in swings hanging from high limbs in the Tree, swinging far out over the ravine into the stars.

Gott took a pull of martini water, but he felt lonely and impotent. He peeped over the edge of his Plutarch at the darkness below the sofa and grinned with new hope as he saw the huge glat blob of black putty the Jester and Flannel had collapsed into. *I'm on a black kick,* he thought, *why black?*—choosing to forget that he had first started to sculpt figures of the imagination from the star-specked blackness that pulsed under his eyelids while he lay in the dark abed: tiny black heads like wrinkled peas on which any three points of light made two eyes and a mouth. He'd come a long way since then. Now with strong rays from his eyes he rolled all the black putty he could see into a womanlong bolster and hoisted it onto the sofa. The bolster helped with blind sensuous hitching movements, especially where it bent at the middle. When it was lying full length on the sofa he began with cruel strength to sculpt it into a figure of a high-breasted exaggeratedly sexual girl.

Jane found she'd sketched some flies into the picture, buzzing around the swingers. She rubbed them out and put in more stars instead. But there would be flies in the ravine, she told herself, because people dumped garbage down the other side; so she drew one large fly in the lower left-hand corner of the picture. He could be the observer. She said to herself firmly, *No black clouds of spring in this picture* and changed them to hints of Road in Space.

Gott finished the Black Girl with two twisting tweaks to point her nipples. Her waist was barely thick enough not to suggest an actual wasp or a giant amazon ant. Then he gulped martini water and leaned forward just a little and silently but very strongly blew the breath of life into her across the eight feet of living-room air between them.

The phrase "black clouds of spring" made Jane think of dead hopes and drowned talents. She said out loud, "I wish you'd start writing in the evenings again, Gott. Then I wouldn't feel so guilty."

"These days, my dear, I'm just a dull businessman, happy to relax in the heart of his family. There's not an atom of art in me," Gott informed her with quiet conviction, watching the Black Girl quiver and writhe as the creativity-wind from his lips hit her. With a sharp twinge of fear it occurred to him that the edges of the wind might leak over to Jane and Heinie, distorting them like heat shimmers, changing them nastily. Heinie especially was sitting so still in his little chair light-years away. Gott wanted to call to him, but he couldn't think of the right bit of spaceman's lingo.

THE BLACK GIRL (*sitting up and dropping her hand coquettishly to her crotch*): He-he! Now ain't this something, Mr. Adler! First time you've ever had me in your home.

GOTT (*eyeing her savagely over Plutarch*): Shut up!

THE BLACK GIRL (*unperturbed*): Before this it was only when you were away on trips or, once or twice lately, at the office.

GOTT (*flaring his nostrils*): Shut up, I say! You're less than dirt.

THE BLACK GIRL (*smirking*): But I'm interesting dirt, ain't I? You want we should do it in front of her? I could come over and flow inside your clothes and—

GOTT: One more word and I uncreate you! I'll tear you apart like a boiled crow. I'll squunch you back to putty.

THE BLACK GIRL (*still serene, preening her nakedness*): Yes, and you'll enjoy every red-hot second of it, won't you?

Affronted beyond bearing, Gott sent chopping rays at her over the Plutarch parapet, but at that instant a black figure, thin as a spider, shot up behind the sofa and reaching over the Black Girl's shoulder brushed aside the chopping rays with one flick of a whip-like arm. Grown from the black putty Gott had overlooked under the sofa, the figure was that of an old conjure woman, stick-thin with limbs like wires and breasts like dangling ropes, face that was a pack of spearheads with black ostrich plumes a-quiver above it.

GOTT (*frightened, but not showing it*): Keep your arms and legs on, Mother. Flossie and I were only teasing each other. Vicious play is a specialty of your house, isn't it?

With a deep groaning cry the furnace fan switched on in the basement and began to say over and over again in a low rapid rumble, "Oh, my God, my God, my God. Demons, demons, demons, demons." Jane heard the warning very clearly, but she didn't want to lose the glow of her feelings. She asked, "Are you all right out there in space, Heinie?" and thought he nodded "Yes." She began to color the Clubhouse in the Tree—blue roof, red walls, a little like Chagall.

THE BLACK CRONE (*continuing a tirade*): Understand this, Mr. Adler, you don't own us, we own you. Because you gotta have the girls to live, you're the girls' slave.

THE BLACK GIRL: He-he! Shall I call Susie and Belle? They've never been here either, and they'd enjoy this.

THE BLACK CRONE: Later, if he's humble. You understand me, Slave? If I tell you have your wife cook dinner for the girls or wash their feet or watch you snuggle with them, then you gotta do it. And your boy gotta run our errands. Come over here now and sit by Flossie while I brand you with dry ice.

Gott quaked, for the Crone's arms were lengthening toward him like snakes, and he began to sweat, and he murmured, "God in Heaven," and the smell of fear went out of him to the walls—millions of stinking molecules.

A cold wind blew over the fence of Heinie's space road and the stars wavered and then fled before it like diamond leaves.

Jane caught the murmur and the fear-whiff too, but she was coloring the Clubhouse windows a warm rich yellow; so what she said in a rather loud, rapt, happy voice was: "I think Heaven is like a children's clubhouse. The only people there are the ones you remember from childhood—either because you were in childhood with them or they told you about their children honestly. The *real* people."

At the word *real* the Black Crone and the Black Girl strangled and began to bend and melt like a thin candle and a thicker one over a roaring fire.

Heinie turned his spaceship around and began to drive it bravely homeward through the unspeckled dark, following the ghostly white line that marked the center of the road. He thought of himself as the cat they'd had. Papa had told him stories of the cat coming back—from downtown, from Pittsburgh, from Los Angeles, from the moon. Cats could do that. He was the cat coming back.

Jane put down her brush and took up her pencil once more. She'd noticed that the two children swinging out farthest weren't attached yet to their swings. She started to hook them up, then hesitated. Wasn't it all right for some of the children to go sailing out to the stars? Wouldn't it be nice for some evening world—maybe the late-afternoon moon—to have a shower of babies? She wished a plane would crawl over the roof of the house and drone out an answer to her question. She didn't like to have to do all the wondering by herself. It made her feel guilty.

"Gott," she said, "why don't you at least finish the last story you were writing? The one about the Elephants' Graveyard." Then she wished she hadn't mentioned it, because it was an idea that had scared Heinie.

"Some day," her husband murmured. Jane thought.

Gott felt weak with relief, though he was forgetting why. Balancing his head carefully over his book, he drained the next to the last of the martini water. It always got stronger toward the bottom. He looked at the page through the lower halves of his executive bifocals and for a moment the word "Caesar" came up in letters an inch high, each jet serif showing its tatters and the white paper its ridgy fibers. Then, still never moving his head, he looked through the upper halves and saw the long thick blob of dull black putty on the wavering blue couch and automatically gathered the putty together and with thumb-and-palm rays swiftly shaped the Old Philosopher in the Black Toga, always an easy figure to sculpt since he was never finished, but rough-hewn in the style of Rodin or Daumier. It was always good to finish up an evening with the Old Philosopher.

The white line in space tried to fade. Heinie steered his ship closer to it. He remembered that in spite of Papa's stories, the cat had never come back.

Jane held her pencil poised over the detached children swinging out from the clubhouse. One of them had a leg kicked over the moon.

THE PHILOSOPHER (*adjusting his craggy toga and yawning*): The topic for tonight's symposium is that vast container of all, the Void.

GOTT (*condescendingly*): The Void? That's interesting. Lately I've wished to merge with it. Life wearies me.

A smiling dull black skull, as crudely shaped as the Philosopher, looked over the latter's shoulder and then rose higher on a rickety black bone framework.

DEATH (*quietly, to Gott*): Really?

GOTT (*greatly shaken, but keeping up a front*): I *am* on a black kick tonight. Can't even do a white skeleton. Disintegrate, you two. You bore me almost as much as life.

351

DEATH: Really? If you did not cling to life like a limpet, you would have crashed your car, to give your wife and son the insurance, when National Motors fired you. You planned to do that. Remember?

GOTT (with hysterical coolness): Maybe I should have cast you in brass or aluminum. Then you'd at least have brightened things up. But it's too late now. Disintegrate quickly and don't leave any scraps around.

DEATH: Much too late. Yes, you planned to crash your car and doubly indemnify your dear ones. You had the spot picked, but your courage failed you.

GOTT (blustering): I'll have you know I am not only Gottfried but also Helmuth—Hell's Courage Adler!

THE PHILOSOPHER (confused but trying to keep in the conversation): A most swashbuckling sobriquet.

DEATH: Hell's courage failed you on the edge of the ravine. (Pointing at Gott a three-fingered thumbless hand like a black winter branch.) Do you wish to die now?

GOTT (blacking out visually): Cowards die many times. (Draining the last of the martini water in absolute darkness.) The valiant taste death once. Caesar.

DEATH (a voice in darkness): Coward. Yet you summoned me—and even though you fashioned me poorly, I am indeed Death—and there are others besides yourself who take long trips. Even longer ones. Trips in the Void.

THE PHILOSOPHER (another voice): Ah, yes, the Void. Imprimis—

DEATH: Silence.

In the great obedient silence Gott heard the unhurried click of Death's feet as he stepped from behind the sofa across the bare floor toward Heinie's spaceship. Gott reached up in the dark and clung to his mind.

Jane heard the slow clicks too. They were the kitchen clock ticking out, "Now. Now. Now. Now. Now."

Suddenly Heinie called out, "The line's gone. Papa, Mama, I'm lost."

Jane said sharply, "No, you're not, Heinie. Come out of space at once."

"I'm not in space now. I'm in the Cats' Graveyard."

Jane told herself it was insane to feel suddenly so frightened. "Come back from wherever you are, Heinie," she said calmly. "Its time for bed."

"I'm lost, Papa," Heinie cried. "I can't hear Mama any more."

"Listen to your mother, Son," Gott said thickly, groping in the blackness for other words.

"All the Mamas and Papas in the world are dying," Heinie wailed.

Then the words came to Gott, and when he spoke his voice flowed. "Are your atomic generators turning over, Heinie? Is your space-warp lever free?"

"Yes, Papa, but the line's gone."

"Forget it. I've got a fix on you through subspace and I'll coach you home. Swing her two units to the right and three up. Fire when I give the signal. Are you ready?"

"Yes, Papa."

"Roger. Three, two, one, fire and away! Dodge that comet! Swing left around that planet! Never mind the big dust cloud! Home on the third beacon. Now! Now! Now!"

Gott had dropped his Plutarch and come lurching blindly across the room, and as he uttered the last Now! the darkness cleared, and he caught Heinie up from his space-chair and staggered with him against Jane and steadied himself there without upsetting her paints, and she accused him laughingly. "You beefed up the martini water again," and Heinie pulled off his helmet and crowed, "Make a big hug," and they clung to each other and looked down at the half-colored picture where a children's clubhouse sat in a tree over a deep ravine and blob children swung out from it against the cool pearly moon and the winding roads in space and the next to the last child hooked onto his swing with one hand and with the other caught the last child of all, while from the picture's lower lefthand corner a fat, black fly looked on enviously.

Searching with his eyes as the room swung toward equilibrium, Gottfried Helmuth Adler saw Death peering at him through the crack between the hinges of the open kitchen door.

Laboriously, half passing out again, Gott sneered his face at him.

Ship of Shadows

"Issiot! Ffool! Lushsh!" hissed the cat and bit Spar somewhere.

The fourfold sting balanced the gut-wretchedness of his looming hangover, so that Spar's mind floated as free as his body in the blackness of Windrush, in which shone only a couple of running lights dim as churning dream-glow and infinitely distant as the Bridge or the Stern.

The vision came of a ship with all sails set creaming through blue, wind-ruffled sea against a blue sky. The last two nouns were not obscene now. He could hear the whistle of the salty wind through shrouds and stays, its drumming against the taut sails, and the creak of the three masts and all the rest of the ship's wood.

What was wood? From somewhere came the answer: plastic alive-o.

And what force flattened the water and kept it from breaking up into great globules and the ship from spinning away, keel over masts, in the wind?

Instead of being blurred and rounded like reality, the vision was sharp-edged and bright—the sort Spar never told, for fear of being accused of second sight and so of witchcraft.

Windrush was a ship too, was often called the Ship. But it was a strange sort of ship, in which the sailors lived forever in the shrouds inside cabins of all shapes made of translucent sails welded together.

The only other things the two ships shared were the wind and the unending creaking. As the vision faded, Spar began to hear the winds of Windrush softly moaning through the long passageways, while he felt the creaking in the vibrant shroud to which he was clipped wrist and ankle to keep him from floating around in the Bat Rack.

Sleepday's dreams had begun good, with Spar having Crown's three girls at once. But Sleepday night he had been half-waked by the distant grinding of Hold Three's big chewer. Then werewolves and vampires had attacked him, solid shadows diving in from all six sides, while witches and their familiars tittered in the black shadowy background. Somehow he had been protected by the cat, familiar of a slim witch whose bared teeth had been an ivory blur in the larger silver blur of her wild hair. Spar pressed his rubbery gums together. The cat had been the last of the supernatural creatures to fade. Then had come the beautiful vision of the ship.

His hangover hit him suddenly and mercilessly. Sweat shook off him until he must be surrounded by a cloud of it. Without warning his gut reversed. His free hand found a floating waste tube in time to press its small trumpet to his face. He could hear his acrid vomit gurgling away, urged by a light suction.

355

His gut reversed again, quick as the flap of a safety hatch when a gale blows up in the corridors. He thrust the waste tube inside the leg of his short, loose slopsuit and caught the dark stuff, almost as watery and quite as explosive as his vomit. Then he had the burning urge to make water.

Afterward, feeling blessedly weak, Spar curled up in the equally blessed dark and prepared to snooze until Keeper woke him.

"Ssot!" hissed the cat. "Sleep no more! Ssee! Ssee shsharply!"

In his left shoulder, through the worn fabric of his slopsuit, Spar could feel four sets of prickles, like the touch of small thorn clusters in the Gardens of Apollo or Diana. He froze.

"Sspar," the cat hissed more softly, quitting to prickle. "I wishsh you all besst. Mosst ashshuredly."

Spar warily reached his right hand across his chest, touched short fur softer than Suzy's, and stroked gingerly.

The cat hissed very softly, almost purring, "Ssturdy Sspar! Ssee ffar! Ssee fforever! Fforessee! Afftssee!"

Spar felt a surge of irritation at this constant talk of seeing—bad manners in the cat! —He decided that this was no witch cat left over from his dream, but a stray which had wormed its way through a wind tube into the Bat Rack, setting off his dream. There were quite a few animal strays in these days of the witch panic and the depopulation of the Ship, or at least of Hold Three.

Dawn struck the Bow then, for the violet fore-corner of the Bat Rack began to glow. The running lights were drowned in a growing white blaze. Within twenty heart-beats Windrush was bright as it ever would be on Workday or any other morning.

Out along Spar's arm moved the cat, a black blur to his squinting eyes. In teeth Spar could not see, it held a smaller gray blur. Spar touched the latter. It was even shorter furred, but cold.

As if irked, the cat took off from his bare forearm with a strong push of hind legs. It landed expertly on the next shroud, a wavery line of gray that vanished in either direction before reaching a wall.

Spar unclipped himself, curled his toes around his own pencil-thin shroud, and squinted at the cat.

The cat stared back with eyes that were green blurs which almost coalesced in the black blur of its outsize head.

Spar asked, "Your child? Dead?"

The cat loosed its gray burden, which floated beside its head.

"Chchild!" All the former scorn and more were back in the sibilant voice. "It izz a rat I sslew her, issiot!"

Spar's lips puckered in a smile. "I like you, cat. I will call you Kim."

"Kim-shlim!" the cat spat. "I'll call you Lushsh! Or ssot!"

The creaking increased, as it always did after dayspring and noon. Shrouds twanged. Walls crackled.

Spar swiftly swiveled his head. Though reality was by its nature a blur, he could unerringly spot movement.

Keeper was slowly floating straight at him. On the round of his russet body was mounted the great, pale round of his face, its bright pink target-center drawing attention from the tiny, wide-set, brown blurs of his eyes. One of his fat arms ended in the bright gleam of pliofilm, the other in the dark gleam of steel. Far beyond him was the dark red aft corner of the Bat Rack, with the great gleaming torus, or doughnut, of the bar midway between.

"Lazy, pampered he-slut," Keeper greeted. "All Sleepday you snored while I stood guard, and now I bring your morning pouch of moonmist to your sleeping shroud.

"A bad night, Spar," he went on, his voice growing sententious. "Werewolves, vampires, and witches loose in the corridors. But I stood them off, not to mention rats and mice. I heard through the tubes that the vamps got Girlie and Sweetheart, the silly sluts! Vigilance, Spar! Now suck your moonmist and start sweeping. The place stinks."

He stretched out the pliofilm-gleaming hand.

His mind hissing with Kim's contemptuous words, Spar said, "I don't think I'll drink this morning, Keeper. Corn gruel and moonbrew only. No, water."

"What, Spar?" Keeper demanded. "I don't believe I can allow that. We don't want you having convulsions in front of the customers. Earth strangle me!—what's that?"

Spar instantly, launched himself at Keeper's steel-gleaming hand. Behind him his shroud twanged. With one hand he twisted a cold, thick barrel. With the other he pried a plump finger from a trigger.

"He's not a witch cat, only a stray," he said as they tumbled over and kept slowly rotating.

"Unhand me, underling!" Keeper blustered. "I'll have you in irons. I'll tell Crown."

"Shooting weapons are as much against the law as knives or needles," Spar countered boldly, though he already was feeling dizzy and sick. "It's you should fear the brig." He recognized beneath the bullying voice the awe Keeper always had of his ability to move swiftly and surely, though half-blind.

They bounced to rest against a swarm of shrouds. "Loose me, I say," Keeper demanded, struggling weakly. "Crown gave me this pistol. And I have a permit for it from the Bridge." The last at least, Spar guessed, was a lie. Keeper continued, "Besides, it's only a line-shooting gun reworked for heavy, elastic ball. Not enough to rupture a wall, yet sufficient to knock out drunks—or knock in the head of a witch cat!"

"Not a witch cat, Keeper," Spar repeated, although he was having to swallow hard to keep from spewing. "Only a well-behaved stray, who has already proved his use to us by killing one of the rats that have been stealing our food. His name is Kim. He'll be a good worker."

The distant blur of Kim lengthened and showed thin blurs of legs and tail, as if he were standing out rampant from his line. "Asset izz I," he boasted. "Ssanitary. Uzze wasste tubes. Sslay ratss, micece! Sspy out witchchess, vampss ffor you!"

"He speaks!" Keeper gasped. "Witchcraft!"

"Crown has a dog who talks," Spar answered with finality. "A talking animal's no proof of anything."

All this while he had kept firm hold of barrel and finger. Now he felt through their grappled bodies a change in Keeper, as though inside his blubber the master of the Bat Rack were transforming from stocky muscle and bone into a very thick, sweet syrup that could conform to and flow around anything.

"Sorry, Spar," he whispered unctuously. "It was a bad night and Kim startled me. He's black like a witch cat. An easy mistake on my part. We'll try him out as catcher. He must earn his keep! Now take your drink."

The pliant double pouch filling Spar's palm felt like the philosopher's stone. He lifted it toward his lips, but at the same time his toes unwittingly found a shroud, and he dove swiftly toward the shing torus, which had a hole big enough to accommodate four barmen at a pinch.

Spar collapsed against the opposite inside of the hole. With a straining of its shrouds, the torus absorbed his impact. He had the pouch to his lips, its cap unscrewed, but had not squeezed. He shut his eyes and with a tiny sob blindly thrust the pouch back into the moonmist cage.

Working chiefly by touch, he took a pouch of corn gruel from the hot closet, snitching at the same time a pouch of coffee and thrusting it into an inside pocket. Then he took a pouch of water, opened it, shoved in five salt tablets, closed it, and shook and squeezed it vigorously.

Keeper, having drifted behind him, said into his ear, "So you drink anyhow. Moonmist not good enough, you make yourself a cocktail. I should dock it from your scrip. But all drunks are liars, or become so."

Unable to ignore the taunt, Spar explained, "No, only salt water to harden my gums."

"Poor Spar, what'll you ever need hard gums for? Planning to share rats with your new friend? Don't let me catch you roasting them in my grill! I should dock you for the salt. To sweeping, Spar!" Then, turning his head toward the violet fore-corner and speaking loudly: "And you! Catch mice!"

Kim had already found the small chewer tube and thrust the dead rat into it, gripping tube with foreclaws and pushing rat with aft. At the touch of the rat's cadaver against the solid wrist of the tube, a grinding began there which would continue until the rat was macerated and slowly swallowed away toward the great cloaca which fed the Gardens of Diana.

Three times Spar manfully swished salt water against his gums and spat into a waste tube, vomiting a little after the first gargle. Then, facing away from the Keeper as he gently squeezed the pouches, he forced into his throat the coffee—dearer than moonmist, the drink distilled from moonbrew—and some of the corn gruel.

He apologetically offered the rest to Kim, who shook his head. "Jusst had a mousse."

Hastily Spar made his way to the green starboard corner. Outside the hatch he heard some drunks calling with weary and mournful anger, "Unzip!"

Grasping the heads of two long waste tubes, Spar began to sweep the air, working out from the green corner in a spiral, quite like an orb spider building her web.

From the torus, where he was idly polishing its thin titanium, Keeper upped the suction on the two tubes, so that reaction sped Spar in his spiral. He need use his body only to steer course and to avoid shrouds in such a way that his tubes didn't tangle.

Soon Keeper glanced at his wrist and called, "Spar, can't you keep track of the time? Open up!" He threw a ring of keys which Spar caught, though he could see only the last half of their flight. As soon as he was well headed toward the green door, Keeper called again and pointed aft and aloft. Spar obediently unlocked and unzipped the dark and also the blue hatch, though there was no one at either, before opening the green. In each case he avoided the hatch's gummy margin and the sticky emergency hatch hinged close beside.

In tumbled three brewos, old customers, snatching at shrouds and pushing off from each other's bodies in their haste to reach the torus, and meanwhile cursing Spar.

"Sky strangle you!"

"Earth bury you!"

"Seas sear you!"

"Language, boys!" Keeper reproved. "Though I'll agree my helper's stupidity and sloth tempt a man to talk foul."

Spar threw the keys back. The brewos lined up elbow to elbow around the torus, three grayish blobs with heads pointing toward the blue corner.

Keeper faced them. "Below, below!" he ordered indignantly. "You think you're gents?"

"But you're serving no one aloft yet."

"There's only us three."

"No matter," Keeper replied. "Propriety, suckers! Unless you mean to buy the pouch, invert."

With low grumbles the brewos reversed their bodies so that their heads pointed toward the black corner.

Himself not bothering to invert, Keeper tossed them a slim and twisty faint red blur with three branches. Each grabbed a branch and stuck it in his face.

The pudge of his fat hand on glint of valve, Keeper said, "Let's see your scrip first."

With angry mumbles each unwadded something too small for Spar to see clearly, and handed it over. Keeper studied each item before feeding it to the cashbox. Then he decreed, "Six seconds of moonbrew. Suck fast," and looked at his wrist and moved the other hand.

One of the brewos seemed to be strangling, but he blew out through his nose and kept sucking bravely.

Keeper closed the valve.

Instantly one brewo splutteringly accused, "You cut us off too soon. That wasn't six."

The treacle back in his voice, Keeper explained. "I'm squirting it to you four and two. Don't want you to drown. Ready again?"

The brewos greedily took their second squirt and then, at times wistfully sucking their tubes for remnant drops, began to shoot the breeze. In his distant circling, Spar's keen ears heard most of it.

"A dirty Sleepday, Keeper."

"No, a good one, brewo—for a drunken sucker to get his blood sucked by a lust-tickling vamp."

"I was dossed safe at Pete's, you fat ghoul."

"Pete's safe? That's news!"

"Dirty Atoms to you! But vamps did get Girlie and Sweetheart. Right in the starboard main drag, if you can believe it. By Cobalt Ninety, Windrush is getting lonely! Third Hold, anyhow. You can swim a whole passageway by day without meeting a soul."

"How do you know that about the girls?" the second brewo demanded. "Maybe they've gone to another hold to change their luck."

"Their luck's run out. Suzy saw them snatched."

"Not Suzy," Keeper corrected, now playing umpire. "But Mable did. A proper fate for drunken sluts."

"You've got no heart, Keeper."

"True enough. That's why the vamps pass me by. But speaking serious, boys, the werethings and witches are running too free in Three. I was awake all Sleepday guarding. I'm sending a complaint to the Bridge."

"You're kidding."

"You wouldn't."

Keeper solemnly nodded his head and crossed his left chest. The brewos were impressed.

Spar spiraled back toward the green corner, sweeping farther from the wall. On his way he overtook the black blob of Kim, who was circling the periphery himself, industriously leaping from shroud to shroud and occasionally making dashes along them.

A fair-skinned, plump shape twice circled by blue—bra and culottes—swam in through the green hatch.

"Morning, Spar," a soft voice greeted. "How's it going?"

"Fair and foul," Spar replied. The golden cloud of blonde hair floating loose touched his face. "I'm quitting moonmist, Suzy."

"Don't be too hard on yourself, Spar. Work a day, loaf a day, play a day, sleep a day—that way it's best."

"I know. Workday, Loafday, Playday, Sleepday. Ten days make a terranth, twelve terranths make a sunth, twelve sunths make a starth, and so on, to the end of time. With corrections, some tell me. I wish I knew what all those names mean."

"You're too serious. You should— Oh, a kitten! How darling!"

"Kitten-shmitten!" the big-headed black blur hissed as it leaped past them. "Izz cat. Izz Kim."

"Kim's our new catcher," Spar explained. "He's serious too."

"Quit wasting time on old Toothless Eyeless, Suzy," Keeper called, "and come all the way in."

As Suzy complied with a sigh, taking the easy route of the ratlines, her soft taper fingers brushed Spar's crumpled cheek. "Dear Spar . . ." she murmured. As her feet passed his face, there was a jingle of her charm-anklet—all goldwashed hearts, Spar knew.

"Hear about Girlie and Sweetheart?" a brewo greeted ghoulishly. "How'd you like your carotid or outside iliac sliced, your—?"

"Shut up, sucker!" Suzy wearily cut him off. "Gimme a drink, Keeper."

"Your tab's long, Suzy. How you going to pay?"

"Don't play games, Keeper, please. Not in the morning, anyhow. You know all the answers, especially to that one. For now, a pouch of moonbrew, dark. And a little quiet."

"Pouches are for ladies, Suzy. I'll serve you aloft. You got to meet your marks, but—"

There was a shrill snarl which swiftly mounted to a scream of rage. Just inside the aft hatch, a pale figure in vermilion culottes and bra—no, wider than that, jacket or short coat—was struggling madly, somersaulting and kicking.

Entering carelessly, like too swiftly, the slim girl had got parts of herself and her clothes stuck to the hatch's inside margin and the emergency hatch.

Breaking loose by frantic main force while Spar dove toward her and the brewos shouted advice, she streaked toward the torus, jerking at the ratlines, black hair streaming behind her.

Coming up with a *bong* of hip against titanium, she grabbed together her vermilion —yes, clutch coat—with one hand and thrust the other across the rocking bar.

Drifting in close behind, Spar heard her say, "Double pouch of moonmist, Keeper. Make it fast."

"The best of mornings to you, Rixende," Keeper greeted. "I would gladly serve you goldwater, except, well—" The fat arms spread. "—Crown doesn't like his girls coming to the Bat Rack by themselves. Last time he gave me strict orders to—"

"What the smoke! It's on Crown's account I came here, to find something he lost. Meanwhile, moonmist. Double!" She pounded on the bar until reaction started her aloft, and she pulled back into place with Spar's unthanked help.

"Softly, softly, lady," Keeper gentled, the tiny brown blurs of his eyes vanishing with his grinning. "What if Crown comes in while you're squeezing?"

"He won't!" Rixende denied vehemently, though glancing past Spar quickly—black blur, blur of pale face, black blur again. "He's got a new girl. I don't mean Phanette or Doucette, but a girl you've never seen. Name of Almodie. He'll be busy with the skinny bitch all morning. And now uncage that double moonmist, you dirty devil!"

"Softly, Rixie. All in good time. What is it Crown lost?"

"A little black bag. About so big." She extended her slender hand, fingers merged. "He lost it here last Playday night, or had it lifted."

"Hear that, Spar?" Keeper said.

"No little black bags," Spar said very quickly. "But you did leave your big orange one here last night, Rixende. I'll get it." He swung inside the torus.

"Oh, damn both bags. Gimme that double!" the black-haired girl demanded frantically. "Earth Mother!"

Even the brewos gasped. Touching hands to the sides of his head, Keeper begged: "No big obscenities, please. They sound worse from a dainty girl, gentle Rixende."

"Earth Mother, I said! Now cut the fancy, Keeper, and give, before I scratch your face off and rummage your cages!"

"Very well, very well. At once, at once. But how will you pay? Crown told me he'd get my license revoked if I ever put you on his tab again. Have you scrip? Or . . . coins?"

"Use your eyes! Or you think this coat's got inside pockets." She spread it wide, flashing her upper body, then clutched it tight again. "Earth Mother! Earth Mother! Earth Mother!" The brewos babbled scandalized. Suzy snorted mildly in boredom.

With one fat hand-blob, Keeper touched Rixende's wrist where a yellow blur circled it closely. "You've got gold," he said in hushed tones, his eyes vanishing again, this time in greed.

"You know damn well they're welded on. My anklets too."

"But these?" His hand went to a golden blur close beside her head.

"Welded too. Crown had my ears pierced."

"But . . ."

"Oh, you atom-dirty devil! I get you, all right. Well, then, *all right!*" The last words ended in a scream more of anger than pain as she grabbed a gold blur and jerked. Blood swiftly blobbed out. She thrust forward her fisted hand. "Now *give!* Gold for a double moonmist."

Keeper breathed hard but said nothing as he scrabbled in the moonmist cage, as if knowing he had gone too far. The brewos were silent too. Suzy sounded completely unimpressed as she said, "*And* my dark." Spar found a fresh dry sponge and expertly caught up the floating scarlet blobs with it before pressing it to Rixende's torn ear.

Keeper studied the heavy gold pendant, which he held close to his face. Rixende milked the double pouch pressed to her lips and her eyes vanished as she sucked blissfully. Spar guided Rixende's free hand to the sponge, and she automatically took over the task of holding it to her ear. Suzy gave a hopeless sigh, then reached her whole plump body across the bar, dipped her hand into a cool cage, and helped herself to a double of dark.

A long, wiry, very dark brown figure in skintight dark violent jumpers mottled with silver arrowed in from the dark red hatch at a speed half again as great as Spar ever dared and without brushing a single shroud by accident or intent. Midway the newcomer did a half somersault as he passed Spar; his long, narrow bare feet hit the titanium next to Rixende. He accordioned up so expertly that the torus hardly swayed.

One very dark brown arm snaked around her. The other plucked the pouch from her mouth, and there was a snap as he spun the cap shut.

A lazy musical voice inquired, "What'd we tell you would happen, baby, if you ever again took a drink on your own?"

The Bat Rack held very still. Keeper was backed against the opposite side of the hole, one hand behind him. Spar had his arm in his lost-and-found nook behind the moonbrew and moonmist cages and kept it there. He felt fearsweat beading on him. Suzy kept her dark close to her face.

A brewo burst into violent coughing, choked it to a wheezing end, and gasped subserviently. "Excuse me, coroner. Salutations."

Keeper chimed dully, "Morning . . . Crown."

Crown gently pulled the clutch coat off Rixende's far shoulder and began to stroke her. "Why, you're all gooseflesh, honey, and rigid as a corpse. What frightened you? Smooth down, skin. Ease up, muscles. Relax, Rix, and we'll give you a squirt."

His hand found the sponge, stopped, investigated, found the wet part, then went toward the middle of his face. He sniffed.

"Well, boys, at least we know none of you are vamps," he observed softly. "Else we'd found you sucking at her ear."

Rixende said very rapidly in a monotone, "I didn't come for a drink, I swear to you. I came to get that little bag you lost. Then I was tempted. I didn't know I would be. I tried to resist, but Keeper led me on. I—"

"Shut up," Crown said quietly. "We were just wondering how you paid him. Now we know. How were you planning to buy your third double? Cut off a hand or a foot? Keeper . . . show me your other hand. We said show it. That's right. Now unfist."

Crown plucked the pendant from Keeper's opened handblob. His yellow-brown eye-blurs on Keeper all the while, he wagged the precious bauble back and forth, then tossed it slowly aloft.

As the golden blur moved toward the open blue hatch at unchanging pace, Keeper opened and shut his mouth twice, then babbled, "I didn't tempt her, Crown, honest. I didn't. I didn't know she was going to hurt her ear. I tried to stop her, but—"

"We're not interested," Crown said. "Put the double on our tab." His face never leaving Keeper's, he extended his arm aloft and pinched the pendant just before it straightlined out of reach.

"Why's this home of jollity so dead?" Snaking a long leg across the bar as easily as an arm, Crown pinched Spar's ear between his big and smaller toes, pulled him close and turned him round. "How're you coming along with the saline, baby? Gums hardening? Only one way to test it." Gripping Spar's jaw and lip with his other toes, he thrust the big one into Spar's mouth. "Come on, bite me, baby."

Spar bit. It was the only way not to vomit. Crown chuckled. Spar bit hard. Energy flooded his shaking frame. His face grew hot and his forehead throbbed under its drenching of fear-sweat. He was sure he was hurting Crown, but the Coroner of Hold Three only kept up his low, delighted chuckle and when Spar gasped, withdrew his foot.

"My, my, you're getting strong, baby. We almost felt that. Have a drink on us."

Spar ducked his stupidly wide-open mouth away from the thin jet of moonmist. The jet struck him in his eye and stung so that he had to knot his fists and clamp his aching gums together to keep from crying out.

"Why's this place so dead, I ask again? No applause for baby and now baby's gone temperance on us. Can't you give us just one tiny laugh?" Crown faced each in turn. "What's the matter? Cat got your tongues?"

"Cat? We have a cat, a new cat, came just last night, working as catcher," Keeper suddenly babbled. "It can talk a little. Not as well as Hellhound, but it talks. It's very funny. It caught a rat."

"What'd you do with the rat's body, Keeper?"

"Fed it to the chewer. That is, Spar did. Or the cat."

"You mean to tell us that you disposed of a corpse without notifying us? Oh, don't go pale on us, Keeper. That's nothing. Why, we could accuse you of harboring a witch cat. You say he came last night, and that was a wicked night for witches. Now don't go green on us too. We were only putting you on. We were only looking for a small laugh.

"Spar! Call your cat! Make him say something funny."

Before Spar could call, or even decide whether he'd call Kim or not, the black blur appeared on a shroud near Crown, green eye-blurs fixed on the yellow-brown ones.

"So you're the joker, eh? Well . . . joke."

Kim increased in size. Spar realized it was his fur standing on end.

"Go ahead, Joke . . . like they tell us you can. Keeper, you wouldn't be kidding us about this cat being able to talk?

"Spar! Make your cat joke!

"Don't bother. We believe he's got his own tongue too. That the matter, Blackie?" He reached out his hand. Kim lashed at it and sprang away. Crown only gave another of his low chuckles.

Rixende began to shake uncontrollably. Crown examined her solicitously yet leisurely, using his outstretched hand to turn her head toward him, so that any blood that might have been coming from it from the cat's slash would have gone into the sponge.

"Spar swore the cat could talk," Keeper babbled. "I'll—"

"Quiet," Crown said. He put the pouch to Rixende's lips, squeezed until her shaking subsided and it was empty, then flicked the crumpled pliofilm toward Spar.

"And now about that little black bag, Keeper," Crown said flatly.

"Spar!"

The latter dipped into his lost-and-found nook, saying quickly, "No little black bags, coroner, but we did find this one the lady Rixende forgot last Playday night," and he turned back holding out something big, round, gleamingly orange, and closed with drawstrings.

Crown took and swung it slowly in a circle. For Spar, who couldn't see the strings, it was like magic. "Bit too big, and a mite the wrong shade. We're certain we lost the little black bag here, or had it lifted. You making the Bat Rack a tent for dips, Keeper?"

"Spar—?"

"We're asking you, Keeper."

Shoving Spar aside, Keeper groped frantically in the nook, pulling aside the cages of moonmist and moonbrew pouches. He produced many small objects. Spar could distinguish the largest—an electric hand-fan and a bright red footglove. They hung around Keeper in a jumble.

Keeper was panting and had scrabbled his hands for a full minute in the nook without bringing out anything more, when Crown said, his voice lazy again, "That's enough. The little black bag was of no importance to us in any case."

Keeper emerged with a face doubly blurred, surrounded by a haze of sweat. He pointed an arm at the orange bag.

"It might be inside that one!"

Crown opened the bag, began to search through it, changed his mind, and gave the whole bag a flick. Its remarkably numerous contents came out and moved slowly aloft at equal speeds, like an army on the march in irregular order. Crown scanned them as they went past.

"No, not here." He pushed the bag toward Keeper. "Return Rix's stuff to it and have it ready for us the next time we dive in—"

Putting his arm around Rixende, so that it was his hand that held the sponge to her ear, he turned and kicked off powerfully for the aft hatch. After he had been out of sight for several seconds, there was a general sigh; the three brewos put out new scrip-wads to pay for another squirt. Suzy asked for a second double dark, which Spar handed her quickly, while Keeper shook off his daze and ordered Spar, "Gather up all the floating trash, especially Rixie's, and get that back in her purse. On the jump, lubber!" Then he used the electric hand-fan to cool and dry himself.

It was a mean task Keeper had set Spar, but Kim came to help, darting after objects too small for Spar to see. Once he had them, in his hands, Spar could readily finger or sniff which was which.

When his impotent rage at Crown had faded, Spar's thoughts went back to Sleep-day night. Had his vision of vamps and werewolves been dream only?—now that he knew the werethings had been abroad in force. If only he had better eyes to distinguish illusion from reality! Kim's "Ssee! Ssee shsharply!" hissed in his memory. What would it be like to see sharply? Everything brighter? Or closer?

After a weary time the scattered objects were gathered and he went back to sweeping and Kim to his mouse hunt. As Workday morning progressed, the Bat Rack gradually grew less bright, though so gradually it was hard to tell.

A few more customers came in, but all for quick drinks, which Keeper served them glumly; Suzy judged none of them worth cottoning up to.

As time slowly passed, Keeper grew steadily more fretfully angry, as Spar had known he would after groveling before Crown. He tried to throw out the three brewos, but they produced more crumpled scrip, which closest scrutiny couldn't prove counterfeit. In revenge he short-squirted them and there were arguments. He called Spar off his sweeping to ask him nervously, "That cat of yours—he scratched Crown, didn't he? We'll have to get rid of him; Crown said he might be a witch cat, remember?" Spar made no answer. Keeper set him renewing the glue of the emergency hatches, claiming that Rixende's tearing free from the aft one had shown it must be drying out. He gobbled appetizers and drank moonmist with tomato juice. He sprayed the Bat Rack with some abominable synthetic scent. He started counting the boxed scrip and coins but gave up the job with a slam of self-locking drawer almost before he'd begun. His grimace fixed on Suzy.

"Spar!" he called. "Take over! And over-squirt the brewos on your peril!"

Then he locked the cash box, and giving Suzy a meaningful jerk of his head toward the scarlet starboard hatch, he pulled himself toward it. With an unhappy shrug toward Spar, she wearily followed.

As soon as the pair were gone, Spar gave the brewos an eight-second squirt, waving back their scrip, and placed two small serving cages—of fritos and yeast balls—before them. They grunted their thanks and fell to. The light changed from healthy bright to corpse white. There was a faint, distant roar, followed some seconds later by a brief crescendo of creakings. The new light made Spar uneasy. He served two more suck-and-dives and sold a pouch of moonmist at double purser's prices. He started to eat an appetizer, but just then Kim swam in to proudly show him a mouse. He conquered his nausea, but began to dread the onset of real withdrawal symptoms.

A potbellied figure clad in sober black dragged itself along the ratlines from the green hatch. On the aloft side of the bar there appeared a visage in which the blur of white hair and beard hid leather-brown flesh, though accentuating the blurs of gray eyes.

"Doc!" Spar greeted, his misery and unease gone, and instantly handed out a chill pouch of three-star moonbrew. Yet all he could think to say in his excitement was the banal, "A bad Sleepday night, eh, Doc? Vamps and—"

"—And other doltish superstitions, which was every sunth, but never wane," an amiable, cynical old voice cut in. "Yet, I suppose I shouldn't rob you of your illusions, Spar, even the terrifying ones. You've little enough to live by, as it is. And there *is* viciousness astir in Windrush. Ah, that smacks good against my tonsils."

Then Spar remembered the important thing. Reaching deep inside his slopsuit, he brought out, in such a way as to hide it from the brewos below, a small flat narrow black bag.

"Here, Doc," he whispered, "you lost it last Playday. I kept it safe for you."

"Dammit, I'd lose my jumpers, if I ever took them off," Doc commented, hushing his voice when Spar put finger to lips. "I suppose I started mixing moonmist with my moonbrew—again?"

"You did, Doc. But you didn't lose your bag. Crown or one of his girls lifted it, or snagged it when it sat loose beside you. And then I . . . I, Doc, lifted it from Crown's hip pocket. Yes, and kept that secret when Rixende and Crown came in demanding it this morning."

"Spar, my boy, I am deeply in your debt," Doc said. "More than you can know. Another three-star, please. Ah, nectar. Spar, ask any reward of me, and if it lies merely within the realm of the first transfinite infinity, I will grant it."

To his own surprise, Spar began to shake—with excitement. Pulling himself forward halfway across the bar, he whispered hoarsely, "Give me good eyes, Doc!" adding impulsively, "and teeth!"

After what seemed a long while, Doc said in a dreamy, sorrowful voice. "In the Old Days, that would have been easy. They'd perfected eye transplants. They could regenerate cranial nerves, and sometimes restore scanning power to an injured cerebrum. While transplanting tooth buds from a stillborn was intern's play. But now . . . Oh, I might be able to do what you ask in an uncomfortable, antique, inorganic fashion, but . . ." He broke off on a note that spoke of the misery of life and the uselessness of all effort.

"The Old Days," one brewo said from the corner of his mouth to the brewo next to him. "Witch talk!"

"Witch-smitch!" the second brewo replied in like fashion. "The flesh mechanic's only senile. He dreams all four days, not just Sleepday."

The third brewo whistled against the evil eye a tune like the wind.

Spar tugged at the long-armed sleeve of Doc's black jumper. "Doc, you promised. I want to see sharp, bite sharp!"

Doc laid his shrunken hand commiseratingly on Spar's forearm. "Spar," he said softly, "seeing sharply would only make you very unhappy. Believe me, I *know*. Life's easier to bear when things are blurred, just as it's best when thoughts are blurred by brew or mist. And while there are people in Windrush who yearn to bite sharply, you are not their kind. Another three-star, if you please."

"I quit moonmist this morning, Doc," Spar said somewhat proudly as he handed over the fresh pouch.

Doc answered with sad smile, "Many quit moonmist every Workday morning and change their minds when Playday comes around."

"Not me, Doc! Besides," Spar argued, "Keeper and Crown and his girls and even Suzy all see sharply, and they aren't unhappy."

"I'll tell you a secret, Spar," Doc replied. "Keeper and Crown and the girls are all zombies. Yes, even Crown with his cunning and power. To them Windrush is the universe."

"It isn't, Doc?"

Ignoring the interruption, Doc continued, "But you wouldn't be like that, Spar. You'd want to know more. And that would make you far unhappier than you are."

"I don't care, Doc," Spar said. He repeated accusingly, "You promised."

The gray blurs of Doc's eyes almost vanished as he frowned in thought. Then he said, "How would this be, Spar? I know moonmist brings pains and sufferings as well as easings and joys. But suppose that every Workday morning and Loafday noon I should bring you a tiny pill that would give you all the good effects of moonmist and none of the bad. I've one in this bag. Try it now and see. And every Playday night I would bring you without fail another sort of pill that would make you sleep soundly with never a nightmare. Much better than eyes and teeth. Think it over."

As Spar considered that, Kim drifted up. He eyed Doc with his close-set green blurs. "Resspectfful greetingsss, ssir," he hissed. "Name izz Kim."

Doc answered, "The same to you, sir. May mice be ever abundant." He softly stroked the cat, beginning with Kim's chin and chest. The dreaminess returned to his voice. "In the Old Days, all cats talked, not just a few sports. The entire feline tribe. And many dogs, too—pardon me, Kim. While as for dolphins and whales and apes . . ."

Spar said eagerly, "Answer me one question, Doc. If your pills give happiness without hangover, why do you always drink moonbrew yourself and sometimes spike it with moonmist?"

"Because for me—" Doc began and then broke off with a grin. "You trapped me, Spar. I never thought you used your mind. Very well, on your own mind be it. Come to my office this Loafday—you know the way? Good!—and we'll see what we can do about your eyes and teeth. And now a double pouch for the corridor."

He paid in bright coins, thrust the big squinchy three-star in a big pocket, and said, "See you, Spar. So long, Kim," and tugged himself toward the green hatch, zigzagging.

"Ffarewell, ssir," Kim hissed after him.

Spar held out the small black bag. "You forgot it again, Doc."

As Doc returned with a weary curse and pocketed it, the scarlet hatch unzipped and Keeper swam out. He looked in a good humor now and whistled the tune of "I'll Marry the Man on the Bridge" as he began to study certain rounds on scrip-till and moonbrew valves, but when Doc was gone he asked Spar suspiciously, "What was that you handed the old geezer?"

"His purse," Spar replied easily. "He forgot it just now." He shook his loosely fisted hand and it chinked. "Doc paid in coins, Keeper." Keeper took them eagerly. "Back to sweeping, Spar."

As Spar dove toward the scarlet hatch to take up larboard tubes, Suzy emerged and passed him with face averted. She sidled up to the bar and unsmilingly snatched the pouch of moonmist Keeper offered her with mock courtliness.

Spar felt a brief rage on her behalf, but it was hard for him to keep his mind on anything but his coming appointment with Doc. When Workday night fell swiftly as a hurled knife, he was hardly aware of it and felt none of his customary unease. Keeper turned on full all the lights in the Bat Rack. They shone brightly while beyond the translucent walls there was a milky churning.

Business picked up a little. Suzy made off with the first likely mark. Keeper called Spar to take over the torus, while he himself got a much-erased sheet of paper and, holding it to a clipboard held against his bent knees, wrote on it laboriously, as if he were thinking out each word, perhaps each letter, often wetting his pencil in his mouth. He became so absorbed in his difficult task that without realizing he drifted off toward the black below hatch, rotating over and over. The paper got dirtier and dirtier with his scrawlings and smudgings, new erasures, saliva and sweat.

The short night passed more swiftly than Spar dared hope, so that the sudden glare of Loafday dawn startled him. Most of the customer's made off to take their siestas.

Spar wondered what excuse to give Keeper for leaving the Bat Rack, but the problem was solved for him. Keeper folded the grimy sheet, and sealed it with hot tape. "Take this to the Bridge, loafer, to the Exec. Wait." He took the repacked orange bag from its nook and pulled on the cords to make sure they were drawn tight. "On your way deliver this at Crown's Hole. With all courtesy and subservience, Spar! Now, on the jump!"

Spar slid the sealed message into his only pocket with working zipper and drew that tight. Then he dove slowly toward the aft hatch, where he almost collided with Kim. Recalling Keeper's talk of getting rid of the cat, he caught hold of him around the slim furry chest under the forelegs and gently thrust him inside his slopsuit, whispering, "You'll take a trip with me, little Kim." The cat set his claws in the thin material and steadied himself.

For Spar, the corridor was a narrow cylinder ending in mist either way and decorated by lengthwise blurs of green and red. He guided himself chiefly by touch and memory, this time remembering that he must pull himself against the light wind hand-over-hand along the centerline. After curving past the larger cylinders of the fore-and-aft gangways, the corridor straightened. Twice he worked his way around centrally slung fans whirring so softly that he recognized them chiefly by the increase in breeze before passing them and the slight suction after.

Soon he began to smell soil and green stuff growing. With a shiver he passed a black round that was the elastic-curtained door to Hold Three's big chewer. He met no one—odd even for Loafday. Finally he saw the green of the Gardens of Apollo and beyond it a huge black screen, in which hovered toward the aft side a small, smoky-orange circle that always filled Spar with inexplicable sadness and fear. He wondered in how many black screens that doleful circle was portrayed, especially in the starboard end of Windrush. He had seen it in several.

So close to the gardens that he could make out wavering green shoots and the silhouette of a floating farmer, the corridor right-angled below. Two dozen pulls along the line and he floated by an open hatch, which both memory for distance and the strong scent of musky, mixed perfumes told him was the entry to Crown's Hole. Peering in, he could see the intermelting and silver spirals of the decor of the great globular room. Directly opposite the hatch was another large black screen with the red-mottled dun disk placed similarly off-center.

From under Spar's chin, Kim hissed very softly, but urgently, "Sstop! Ssilencce, on your liffe!" The cat had poked his head out of the slopsuit's neck. His ears tickled Spar's throat. Spar was getting used to Kim's melodrama, and in any case the warning was hardly needed. He had just seen the half-dozen floating naked bodies and would have held still if only from embarrassment. Not that Spar could see genitals any more than ears at the distance. But he could see that save for hair, each body was of one texture: one very dark brown and the other five—or was it four? no, five—fair. He didn't recognize the two with platinum and golden hair, who also happened to be the two palest. He wondered which was Crown's new girl, name of Almodie. He was relieved that none of the bodies were touching.

367

There was the glint of metal by the golden-haired girl, and he could just discern the red blur of a slender, five-forked tube which went from the metal to the five other faces. It seemed strange that even with a girl to play bartender, Crown should have moonbrew served in such plebeian fashion in his palatial Hole. Of course the tube might carry moonwine, or even moonmist.

Or was Crown planning to open a rival bar to the Bat Rack? A poor time, these days, and a worse location, he mused as he tried to think of what to do with the orange bag.

"Sslink off!" Kim urged still more softly.

Spar's fingers found a snap-ring by the hatch. With the faintest of clicks he secured it around the draw-cords of the pouch and then pulled back the way he had come.

But faint as the click had been, there was a response from Crown's Hole—a very deep, long growl.

Spar pulled faster at the centerline. As he rounded the corner leading inboard, he looked back.

Jutting out from Crown's hatch was a big, prick-eared head narrower than a man's and darker even than Crown's.

The growl was repeated.

It was ridiculous he should be so frightened of Hellhound, Spar told himself as he jerked himself and his passenger along. Why, Crown sometimes even brought the big dog to the Bat Rack.

Perhaps it was that Hellhound never growled in the Bat Rack, only talked in a hundred or so monosyllables.

Besides, the dog couldn't pull himself along the centerline at any speed. He lacked sharp claws. Though he might be able to bound forward, caroming from one side of the corridor to another.

This time the center-slit black curtains of the big chewer made Spar veer violently. He was a fine one—going to get new eyes today and frightened as a child!

"Why did you try to scare me back there, Kim?" he asked angrily.

"I ssaw shsheer evil, issiot!"

"You saw five folk sucking moonbrew. And a harmless dog. This time you're the fool, Kim; you're the idiot!"

Kim shut up, drawing in his head, and refused to say another word. Spar remembered about the vanity and touchiness of all cats. But by now he had other worries. What if the orange bag were stolen by a passerby before Crown noticed it? And if Crown did find it, wouldn't he know Spar, forever Keeper's errandboy, had been peeping? That all this should happen on the most important day of his life! His verbal victory over Kim was small consolation.

Also, although the platinum-haired girl had interested him most of the two strange ones, something began to bother him about the girl who'd been playing bartender, the one with golden hair like Suzy's, but much slimmer and paler—he had the feeling he'd seen her before. And something about her had frightened him.

When he reached the central gangways, he was tempted to go to Doc's office before the Bridge. But he wanted to be able to relax at Doc's and take as much time as needed, knowing all errands were done.

Reluctantly he entered the windy violet gangway and dove at a fore angle for the first empty space on the central gang-line, so that his palms were only burned a little before he had firm hold of it and was being sped fore at about the same speed as the wind. Keeper was a miser, not to buy him handgloves, let alone footgloves!—but he had to pay sharp attention to passing the shroud-slung roller bearings that kept the thick, moving line centered in the big corridor. It was an easy trick to catch hold of the line ahead of the bearing and then get one's hand out of the way, but it demanded watchfulness.

There were few figures traveling on the line and fewer still being blown along the corridor. He overtook a doubled-up one tumbling over and over and crying out in an old cracked voice, "Jacob's Ladder, Tree of Life, Marriage Lines . . ."

He passed the squeeze in the gangway marking the division between the Third and Second Holds without being stopped by the guard there and then he almost missed the big blue corridor leading aloft. Again he slightly burned his palms making the transfer from one moving gang-line to another. His fretfulness increased.

"Sspar, you issiot—!" Kim began.

"Ssh!—we're in officers' territory," Spar cut him off, glad to have that excuse for once more putting down the impudent cat. And true enough, the blue spaces of Windrush always did fill him with awe and dread.

Almost too soon to suit him, he found himself swinging from the gang-line to a stationary monkey jungle of tubular metal just below the deck of the Bridge. He worked his way to the aloft-most bars and floated there, waiting to be spoken to.

Much metal, in many strange shapes, gleamed in the Bridge, and there were irregularly pulsing rainbow surfaces, the closest of which sometimes seemed ranks and files of tiny lights going on and off—red, green, all colors. Aloft of everything was an endless velvet-black expanse very faintly blotched by churning, milky glintings.

Among the metal objects and the rainbows, floated figures all clad in the midnight blue of officers. They sometimes gestured to each other, but never spoke a word. To Spar, each of their movements was freighted with profound significance. These were the gods of Windrush, who guided everything, if there were gods at all. He felt reduced to importance to a mouse, which would be chased off chittering if it once broke silence.

After a particularly tense flurry of gestures, there came a brief distant roar and a familiar creaking and crackling. Spar was amazed, yet at the same time realized he should have known that the Captain, the Navigator, and the rest were responsible for the familiar diurnal phenomena.

It also marked Loafday noon. Spar began to fret. His errands were taking too long. He began to lift his hand tentatively toward each passing figure in midnight blue. None took the least note of him.

Finally he whispered, "Kim—?"

The cat did not reply. He could hear a purring that might be a snore. He gently shook the cat. "Kim, let's talk."

"Shshut off! I ssleep! Ssh!" Kim resettled himself and his claws and recommenced his purring snore—whether natural or feigned, Spar could not tell. He felt very despondent.

The lunths crept by. He grew desperate and weary. He must not miss his appointment with Doc! He was nerving himself to move farther aloft and speak, when a pleasant, young voice said, "Hello, grandpa, what's on your mind?"

Spar realized that he had been raising his hand automatically and that a person as dark-skinned as Crown, but clad in midnight blue, had at last taken notice. He unzipped the note and handed it over. "For the Exec."

"That's my department." A trilled crackle—fingernail slitting the note? A larger crackle—note being opened. A brief wait. Then, "Who's Keeper?"

"Owner of the Bat Rack, sir. I work there."

"Bat Rack?"

"A moonbrew mansion. Once called the Happy Torus, I've been told. In the Old Days, Wine Mess Three, Doc told me."

"Hmm. Well, what's all this mean, gramps? And what's your name?"

Spar stared miserably at the dark-mottled gray square. "I can't read, sir. Name's Spar."

"Hmm. Seen any . . . er . . . supernatural beings in the Bat Rack?"

"Only in my dreams, sir."

"Mmm. Well, we'll have a look in. If you recognize me, don't let on. I'm Ensign Drake, by the way. Who's your passenger, grandpa?"

"Only my cat, Ensign," Spar breathed in alarm.

"Well, take the black shaft down." Spar began to move across the monkey jungle in the direction pointed out by the blue arm-blur.

"And next time remember animals aren't allowed on the Bridge."

As Spar traveled below, his warm relief that Ensign Drake had seemed quite human and compassionate was mixed with anxiety as to whether he still had time to visit Doc. He almost missed the shift to the gang-line grinding aft in the dark red main-drag. The corpse-light brightening into the false dawn of later afternoon bothered him. Once more he passed the tumbling bent figure, this time croaking, "Trinity, Trellis, Wheat Ear . . ."

He was fighting down the urge to give up his visit to Doc and pull home to the Bat Rack, when he noticed he had passed the second squeeze and was in Hold Four with the passageway to Doc's coming up. He dove off, checked himself on a shroud and began the hand-drag to Doc's office, as far larboard as Crown's Hole was starboard.

He passed two figures clumsy on the line, their breaths malty in anticipation of Playday. Spar worried that Doc might have closed his office. He smelled soil and greenery again, from the Gardens of Diana.

The hatch was shut, but when Spar pressed the bulb, it unzipped after three honks, and the white-haloed gray-eyed face peered out.

"I'd just about given up on you, Spar."

"I'm sorry, Doc. I had to—"

"No matter. Come in, come in. Hello, Kim—take a look around if you want."

Kim crawled out, pushed off from Spar's chest, and soon was engaged in a typical cat's tour of inspection.

And there was a great deal to inspect, as even Spar could see. Every shroud in Doc's office seemed to have objects clipped along its entire length. There were blobs large and small, gleaming and dull, light and dark, translucent and solid. They were silhouetted against a wall of the corpse-light Spar feared, but had no time to think of now. At one end was a band of even brighter light.

"Careful, Kim!" Spar called to the cat as he landed against a shroud and began to paw his way from blob to blob.

"He's all right," Doc said. "Let's have a look at you, Spar. Keep your eyes open."

Doc's hands held Spar's head. The gray eyes and leathery face came so close they were one blur.

"Keep them open, I said. Yes, I know you have to blink them, that's all right. Just as I thought. The lenses are dissolved. You've suffered the side-effect which one in ten do who are infected with the Lethean rickettsia."

"Styx ricks, Doc?"

"That's right, though the mob's got hold of the wrong river in the Underworld. But

370

we've all had it. We've all drunk the water of Lethe. Though sometimes when we grow very old we begin to remember the beginning. Don't squirm."

"Hey, Doc, is it because I've had the Styx ricks I can't remember anything back before the Bat Rack?"

"It could be. How long have you been at the Rack?"

"I don't know, Doc. Forever."

"Before I found the place, anyhow. When the Rumdum closed here in Four. But that's only a starth ago."

"But I'm awful old, Doc. Why don't I start remembering?"

"You're not old, Spar. You're just bald and toothless and etched by moonmist and your muscles have shriveled. Yes, and your mind has shriveled too. Now open your mouth."

One of Doc's hands went to the back of Spar's neck. The other probed. "Your gums are tough, anyhow. That'll make it easier."

Spar wanted to tell about the salt water, but when Doc finally took his hand out of Spar's mouth, it was to say, "Now open wide as you can."

Doc pushed into his mouth something big as a handbag and hot. "Now bite down hard."

Spar felt as if he had bitten fire. He tried to open his mouth, but hands on his head and jaw held it closed. Involuntarily he kicked and clawed air. His eyes filled with tears.

"Stop writhing! Breathe through your nose. It's not that hot. Not hot enough to blister, anyhow."

Spar doubted that, but after a bit decided it wasn't quite hot enough to bake his brain through the roof of his mouth. Besides, he didn't want to show Doc his cowardice. He held still. He blinked several times and the general blur became the blurs of Doc's face and the cluttered room silhouetted by the corpse-glare. He tried to smile, but his lips were already stretched wider than their muscles could ever have done. That hurt too; he realized now that the heat was abating a little.

Doc was grinning for him. "Well, you would ask an Old drunkard to use techniques he'd only read about. To make it up on you, I'll give you teeth sharp enough to sever shrouds. Kim, please get away from that bag."

The black blur of the cat was pushing off from a black blur twice his length. Spar mumbled disapprovingly at Kim through his nose and made motions. The larger blur was shaped like Doc's little bag, but bigger than a hundred of them. It must be massive too, for in reaction to Kim's push it had bent the shroud to which it was attached and—the point—the shroud was very slow in straightening.

"That bag contains my treasure, Spar," Doc explained, and when Spar lifted his eyebrows twice to signal another question, went on, "No, not coin and gold and jewels, but a second transfinite infinitude—sleep and dreams and nightmares for every soul in a thousand Windrushes." He glanced at his wrist. "Time enough now. Open your mouth." Spar obeyed, though it cost him new pain.

Doc withdrew what Spar had bittend on, wrapped in it gleam, and clipped it to the nearest shroud. Then he looked in Spar's mouth again.

"I guess I did make it a bit too hot," he said. He found a small pouch, set it to Spar's lips, and squeezed it. A mist filled Spar's mouth and all pain vanished.

Doc tucked the pouch in Spar's pocket. "If the pain returns, use it again."

But before Spar could thank Doc, the latter had pressed a tube to his eye. "Look, Spar, what do you see?"

Spar cried out, he couldn't help it, and jerked his eye away.

"What's wrong, Spar?"

"Doc, you gave me a dream," Spar said hoarsely. "You won't tell anyone, will you? And it tickled."

"What was the dream like?" Doc asked eagerly.

"Just a picture, Doc. The picture of a goat with the tail of a fish. Doc, I saw the fish's"—his mind groped—"scales! Everything had . . . edges! Doc, is *that* what they mean when they talk about seeing sharply?"

"Of course, Spar. This is good. It means there's no cerebral or retinal damage. I'll have no trouble making up field glasses—that it, if there's nothing seriously wrong with my antique pair. So you still see things sharp-edged in dreams—that's natural enough. But why were you afraid of me telling?"

"Afraid of being accused of witchcraft, Doc. I thought seeing things like that was clairvoyance. The tube tickled my eye a little."

"Isotopes and insanity! It's supposed to tickle. Let's try the other eye."

Again Spar wanted to cry out, but he restrained himself, and this time he had no impulse to jerk his eye away, although there was again the faint tickling. The picture was that of a slim girl. He could tell she was female because of her general shape. But he could see her edges. He could see . . . details. For instance, her eyes weren't mist-bounded colored ovals. They had points at both ends, which were china-white . . . triangles. And the pale violet round between the triangles had a tiny black round at its center.

She had silvery hair, yet she looked young, he thought, though it was hard to judge such matters when you could see edges. She made him think of the platinum-haired girl he'd glimpsed in Crown's Hole.

She wore a long, gleaming white dress, which left her shoulders bare, but either art or some unknown force had drawn her hair and her dress toward her feet. In her dress it made . . . folds.

"What's her name, Doc? Almodie?"

"No. Virgo. The Virgin. You can see her edges?"

"Yes, Doc. Sharp. I get it!—like a knife. And the goatfish?"

"Capricorn," Doc answered, removing the tube from Spar's eye.

"Doc, I know Capricorn and Virgo are the names of lunths, terranths, sunths, and starths, but I never knew they had pictures. I never knew they *were* anything."

"You— Of course, you've never seen watches, or stars, let alone the constellations of the zodiac."

Spar was about to ask what all *those* were, but then he saw that the corpse-light was all gone, although the ribbon of brighter light had grown very wide.

"At least in this stretch of your memory," Doc added. "I should have your new eyes and teeth ready next Loafday. Come earlier if you can manage. I may see you before that at the Bat Rack, Playday Night or earlier."

"Great, Doc, but now I've got to haul. Come on, Kim! Sometimes business heavies up Loafday night, Doc, like it was Playday night come at the wrong end. Jump in, Kim."

"Sure you can make it back to the Bat Rack all right, Spar? It'll be dark before you get there."

"Course I can, Doc."

But when night fell, like a heavy hood jerked down over his head, halfway down the first passageway, he would have gone back to ask Doc, to guide him, except he feared Kim's contempt, even though the cat still wasn't talking. He pulled ahead rapidly, though the few running lights hardly let him see the centerline.

The fore gangway was even worse—completely empty and its lights dim and flickering. Seeing by blurs bothered him now that he knew what seeing sharp was like. He was beginning to sweat and shake and cramp from his withdrawal from alcohol, and his thoughts were a tumult. He wondered if *any* of the weird things that had happened since meeting Kim were real or dream. Kim's refusal—or inability?—to talk any more was disquieting. He began seeing the misty rims of blurs that vanished when he looked straight toward them. He remembered Keeper and the brewos talking about vamps and witches.

Then, instead of waiting for the Bat Rack's green hatch, he dove off into the passageway leading to the aft one. This passageway had no lights at all. Out of it he thought he could hear Hellhound growling, but couldn't be sure because the big chewer was grinding. He was scrabbling with panic when he entered the Bat Rack through the dark red hatch, remembering barely in time to avoid the new glue.

The place was jumping with light and excitement and dancing figures, and Keeper at once began to shout abuse at him. He dove into the torus and began taking orders and serving automatically, working entirely by touch and voice, because withdrawal now had his vision swimming—a spinning blur of blurs.

After a while that got better, but his nerves got worse. Only the unceasing work kept him going—and shut out Keeper's abuse—but he was getting too tired to work at all. As Playday dawned, with the crowd around the torus getting thicker all the while, he snatched a pouch of moonmist and set it to his lips.

Claws dug his chest. "Issiot! Ssot! Sslave of ffear!"

Spar almost went into convulsions, but put back the moonmist. Kim came out of the slopsuit and pushed off contemptuously, circled the bar and talked to various of the drinkers, soon became a conversation piece. Keeper started to boast about him and quit serving. Spar worked on and on and on through sobriety more nightmarish than any drunk he could recall. And far, far longer.

Suzy came in with a mark and touched Spar's hand when he served her dark to her. It helped.

He thought he recognized a voice from below. It came from a kinky-haired, slop-suited brewo he didn't know. But then he heard the man again and thought he was Ensign Drake. There were several brewos he didn't recognize.

The place started really jumping. Keeper upped the music. Singly or in pairs, somersaulting dancers bounded back and forth between shrouds. Others toed a shroud and shimmied. A girl in black did splits on one. A girl in white dove through the torus. Keeper put it on her boyfriend's check. Brewos tried to sing.

Spar heard Kim recite:

"Izz a cat.

"Kilzz a rat.

"Greetss each guy,

"Thin or ffat.

"Ssay dolls, hi!"

Playday night fell. The pace got hotter. Doc didn't come. But Crown did. Dancers parted and a whole section of drinkers made way aloft for him and his girls and Hellhound, so that they had a third of the torus to themselves, with no one below in that third either. To Spar's surprise they all took coffee except the dog, who when asked by Crown, responded, "Bloody Mary," drawing out the words in such deep tones that they were little more than a low "Bluh-Muh" growl.

"Iss that sspeech, I assk you?" Kim commented from the other side of the torus.

373

Drunks around him choked down chuckles.

Spar served the pouched coffee piping hot with felt holders and mixed Hellhound's drink in a self-squeezing syringe with sipping tube. He was very groggy and for the moment more afraid for Kim than himself. The face blurs tended to swim, but he could distinguish Rixende by her black hair, Phanette and Doucette by their matching red-blonde hair and oddly red-mottled fair skins, while Almodie *was* the platinum-haired pale one, yet she looked horribly right between the dark brown, purple-vested blur to one side of her and the black, narrower, prick-eared silhouette to the other.

Spar heard Crown whisper to her, "Ask Keeper to show you the talking cat." The whisper was very low and Spar wouldn't have heard it except that Crown's voice had a strange excited vibrancy Spar had never known in it before.

"But won't they fight then?—I mean Hellhound," she answered in a voice that sent silvery tendrils around Spar's heart. He yearned to see her face through Doc's tube. She would look like Virgo, only more beautiful. Yet, Crown's girl, she could be no virgin. It was a strange and horrible world. Her eyes *were* violet. But he was sick of blurs. Almodie sounded very frightened, yet she continued, "Please don't, Crown." Spar's heart was captured.

"But that's the whole idea, baby. And nobody don't's us. We thought we'd schooled you to that. We'd teach you another lesson here, except tonight we smell high fuzz—lots of it. Keeper!—our new lady wishes to hear your cat talk. Bring it over."

"I really don't . . ." Almodie began and went no further.

Kim came floating across the torus while Keeper was shouting in the opposite direction. The cat checked himself against a slender shroud and looked straight at Crown. "Yess?"

"Keeper, shut that junk off." The music died abruptly. Voices rose, then died abruptly too. "Well, cat, talk."

"Shshall ssing insstead," Kim announced and began an eerie caterwauling that had a pattern but was not Spar's idea of music.

"It's an abstraction," Almodie breathed delightedly. "Listen, Crown, that was a diminished seventh."

"A demented third, I'd say," Phanette commented from the other side.

Crown signed them to be quiet.

Kim finished with a high trill. He slowly looked around at his baffled audience and then began to groom his shoulder.

Crown gripped a ridge of the torus with his left hand and said evenly, "Since you will not talk to us, will you talk to our dog?"

Kim stared at Hellhound sucking his Bloody Mary. His eyes widened, their pupils slitted, his lips writhed back from needle-like fangs.

He hissed, "Schschweinhund!"

Hellhound launched himself, hind paws against the palm of Crown's left hand, which threw him forward toward the left, where Kim was dodging. But the cat switched directions, rebounding hindward from the next shroud. The dog's white-jagged jaws snapped sideways a foot from their mark as his great-chested black body hurtled past.

Hellhound landed with four paws in the middle of a fat drunk, who puffed out his wind barely before his swallow, but the dog took off instantly on reverse course. Kim bounced back and forth betwen shrouds. This time hair flew when jaws snapped, but also a rigidly spread paw slashed.

Crown grabbed Hellhound by his studded collar, restraining him from another dive. He touched the dog below the eye and smelled his fingers. "That'll be enough, boy," he said. "Can't go around killing musical geniuses." His hand dropped from his nose to below the torus and came up loosely fisted. "Well, cat, you've talked with our dog. Have you a word for us?"

"Yess!" Kim drifted to the shroud nearest Crown's face. Spar pushed off to grab him back, while Almodie gazed at Crown's fist and edged a hand toward it.

Kim loudly hissed, "Hellzz sspawn! Ffiend!"

Both Spar and Almodie were too late. From between two of Crown's fisted fingers a needle-stream jetted and struck Kim in his open mouth.

After what seemed to Spar a long time, his hand interrupted the stream. Its back burned acutely.

Kim seemed to collapse into himself, then launched himself away from Crown, toward the dark, open-jawed.

Crown said, "That's mace, an antique weapon like Greek fire, but well-known to our folk. The perfect answer to a witch cat."

Spar sprang at Crown, grappled his chest, tried to butt his jaw. They moved away from the torus at half the speed with which Spar had sprung.

Crown got his head aside. Spar closed his gums on Crown's throat. There was a *snick.* Spar felt wind on his bare back. Then a cold triangle pressed his flesh over his kidneys. Spar opened his jaws and floated limp. Crown chuckled.

A blue fuzz-glare, held by a brewo, made everyone in the Bat Rack look more corpse-like than larboard light. A voice commanded, "Okay, folks, break it up. Go home. We're closing the place."

Sleepday dawned, drowning the fuzz-glare. The cold triangle left Spar's back. There was another *snick.* Saying, "Bye-bye, baby," Crown pushed off through the white glare toward four women's faces and one dog's. Phanette's and Doucette's faintly red-mottled ones were close beside Hellhound's, as if they might be holding his collar.

Spar sobbed and began to hunt Kim. After a while Suzy came to help him. The Bat Rack emptied. Spar and Suzy cornered Kim. Spar grasped the cat around the chest. Kim's forelegs embraced his wrist, claws pricking. Spar got out the pouch Doc had given him and shoved its mouth between Kim's jaws. The claws dug deep. Taking no note of that, Spar gently sprayed. Gradually the claws came out and Kim relaxed. Spar hugged him gently. Suzy bound up Spar's wounded wrist.

Keeper came up followed by two brewos, one of them Ensign Drake, who said, "My partner and I will watch today by the aft and starboard hatches." Beyond them the Bat Rack was empty.

Spar said, "Crown has a knife." Drake nodded.

Suzy touched Spar's hand and said, "Keeper, I want to stay here tonight. I'm scared."

Keeper said, "I can offer you a shroud."

Drake and his mate dove slowly toward their posts.

Suzy squeezed Spar's hand. He said, rather heavily, "I can offer you my shroud, Suzy."

Keeper laughed and, after looking toward the Bridge men, whispered, "I can offer you mine, which, unlike Spar, I own. And moonmist. Otherwise, the passageways."

Suzy sighed, paused, then went off with him.

Spar miserably made his way to the fore-corner. Had Suzy expected him to fight Keeper? The sad thing was that he no longer wanted her, except as a friend. He loved Crown's new girl. Which was sad too.

He was very tired. Even the thought of new eyes tomorrow didn't interest him. He clipped his ankle to a shroud and tied a rag over his eyes. He gently clasped Kim, who had not spoken. He was asleep at once.

He dreamed of Almodie. She looked like Virgo, even to the white dress. She held Kim, who looked sleek as polished black leather. She was coming toward him, smiling. She kept coming without getting closer.

Much later—he thought—he woke in the drip of withdrawal. He sweat and shook, but that was minor. His nerves were jumping. Any moment, he was sure, they would twitch all his muscles into a stabbing spasm of sinew-snapping agony. His thoughts were moving so fast he could hardly begin to understand one in ten. It was like speeding through a curving, ill-lit passageway ten times faster than the main drag. If he touched a wall, he would forget even what little Spar knew, forget he was Spar. All around him black shrouds whipped in perpetual sine curves.

Kim was no longer by him. He tore the rag from his eyes. It was dark as before. Sleepday night. But his body stopped speeding and his thoughts slowed. His nerves still crackled, and he still saw the black snakes whipping, but he knew them for illusion. He even made out the dim glows of three running lights.

Then he saw two figures floating toward him. He could barely make out their eye-blurs, green in the smaller, violet in the other, whose face was spreadingly haloed by silvery glints. She was pale and whiteness floated around her. And, instead of a smile, he could see the white horizontal blur of bared teeth. Kim's teeth too were bared.

Suddenly he remembered the golden-haired girl who he'd thought was playing bartender in Crown's Hole. She was Suzy's one-time friend Sweetheart, snatched last Sleepday by vamps.

He screamed, which in Spar was a hoarse, retching bellow, and scrabbled at his clipped ankle.

The figures vanished. Below, he thought.

Lights came on. Someone dove and shook Spar's shoulder. "What happened, gramps?"

Spar gibbered while he thought what to tell Drake. He loved Almodie and Kim. He said, "Had a nightmare. Vamps attacked me."

"Description?"

"An old lady and a . . . a . . . little dog."

The other officer dove in. "The black hatch is open."

Drake said, "Keeper told us that was always locked. Follow through, Fenner." As the other dove below, "You're sure this was a nightmare, gramps? A *little* dog? And an *old* woman?"

Spar said, "Yes," and Drake dove after his comrade, out through the black hatch.

Workday dawned. Spar felt sick and confused, but he set about his usual routine. He tried to talk to Kim, but the cat was as silent as yesterday afternoon. Keeper bullied and found many tasks—the place was a mess from Playday. Suzy got away quickly. She didn't want to talk about Sweetheart or anything else. Drake and Fenner didn't come back.

Spar swept and Kim patrolled, out of touch. In the afternoon Crown came in and talked with Keeper while Spar and Kim were out of earshot. They mightn't have been there for all notice Crown took of them.

Spar wondered about what he had seen last night. It might really have been a dream, he decided. He was no longer impressed by his memory-identification of Sweetheart. Stupid of him to have thought that Almodie and Kim, dream or reality, were vamps. Doc had said vamps were superstitions. But he didn't think much. He still had withdrawal symptoms, only less violent.

When Loafday dawned, Keeper gave Spar permission to leave the Bat Rack without his usual prying questions. Spar looked around for Kim, but couldn't see his black blob. Besides, he didn't really want to take the cat.

He went straight to Doc's office. The passageways weren't as lonely as last Loafday. For a third time he passed the bent figure croaking, "Seagull, Kestrel, Cathedral . . ."

Doc's hatch was unzipped, but Doc wasn't there. Spar waited a long while, uneasy in the corpse-light. It wasn't like Doc to leave his office unzipped and unattended. And he hadn't turned up at the Bat Rack last night, as he'd half promised.

Finally Spar began to look around. One of the first things he noticed was that the big black bag, which Doc had said contained his treasure, was missing.

Then he noticed the gleaming pliofilm bag in which Doc had put the mold of Spar's gums, now held something different. He unclipped it from its shroud. There were two items in it.

He cut a finger on the first, which was half circle, half pink and half gleaming. He felt out its shape more cautiously then, ignoring the tiny red blobs welling from his finger. It had an irregular depression in its pink top and bottom. He put it in his mouth. His gums mated with the depressions. He opened his mouth, then closed it, careful to keep his tongue back. There was a *snick* and a dull *click*. He had teeth!

His hands were shaking, not just from withdrawal, as he felt the second item.

It was two thick rounds joined by a short bar and with a thicker long bar ending in a semicircle going back from each.

He thrust a finger into one of the rounds. It tickled, just as the tube had tickled his eyes, only more intensely, almost painfully.

Hands shaking worse than ever, he fitted the contraption to his face. The semi-circles went around his ears, the rounds circled his eyes, not closely enough to tickle.

He could see sharply! *Everything* had edges, even his spread-fingered hands and the . . . clot of blood on one finger. He cried out—a low, wondering wail—and scanned the office. At first the scores and dozens of sharp-edged objects, each as distinct as the pictures of Capricorn and Virgo had been, were too much for him. He closed his eyes.

When his breathing was a little evener and his shaking less, he opened them cautiously and began to inspect the objects clipped to the shrouds. Each one was a wonder. He didn't know the purpose of half of them. Some of them with which he was familiar by use or blurred sight startled him greatly in their appearance—a comb, a brush, a book with pages (that infinitude of ranked black marks), a wrist watch (the tiny pictures around the circular margin of Capricorn and Virgo, and of the Bull and the Fishes, and so on, and the narrow bars radiating from the center and swinging swiftly or slowly or not at all—and pointing to the signs of the zodiac.

Before he knew it, he was at the corpse-glow wall. He faced it with a new courage, though it forced from his lips another wondering wail.

The corpse-glow didn't come from everywhere, though it took up the central quarter of his field of vision. His fingers touched taut, transparent pliofilm. What he saw beyond—a great way beyond, he began to think—was utter blackness with a great many tiny . . . points of bright light in it. Points were even harder to believe in than edges, he had to believe what he saw.

But centrally, looking much bigger than all the blackness, was a vast corpse-white round pocked with faint circles and scored by bright lines and mottled with slightly darker areas.

It didn't look as if it were wired for electricity, and it certainly didn't look afire.

After a while Spar got the weird idea that its light was reflected from something much brighter *behind* Windrush.

It was infinitely strange to think of so much *space* around Windrush. Like thinking of a reality containing reality.

And if Windrush were between the hypothetical brighter light and the pocked white round, its shadow ought to be on the latter. Unless Windrush were almost infinitely small. Really these speculations were utterly too fantastic to deal with.

Yet could anything be too fantastic? Werewolves, witches, points, edges, size and space beyond any but the most insane belief.

When he had first looked at the corpse-white object, it had been round. And he had heard and felt the creakings of Loafday noon, without being conscious of it at the time. But now the round had its fore edge evenly sliced off, so that it was lopsided. Spar wondered if the hypothetical incandescence behind Windrush were moving, or the white round. Such thoughts, especially the last, were dizzying almost beyond endurance.

He made for the open door, wondering if he should zip it behind him, decided not to. The passageway was another amazement, going off and off and off, and narrowing as it went. Its walls bore . . . arrows, the red pointing to larboard, the way from which he'd come, the green pointing starboard, the way he was going. The arrows were what he'd always seen as dash-shaped blurs. As he pulled himself along the strangely definite dragline, the passageway stayed the same diameter, all the way up to the violet main drag.

He wanted to jerk himself as fast as the green arrows to the starboard end of Windrush to verify the hypothetical incandescence and see the details of the orange-dun round that always depressed him.

But he decided he ought first to report Doc's disappearance to the Bridge. He might find Drake there. And report the loss of Doc's treasure too, he reminded himself.

Passing faces fascinated him. Such a welter of noses and ears! He overtook the croaking, bent shape. It was that of an old woman whose nose almost met her chin. She was doing something twitchy with her fingers to two narrow sticks and a roll of slender, fuzzy line. He impulsively dove off the dragline and caught hold of her, whirling them around.

"What are you doing, grandma?" he asked.

She puffed with anger. "Knitting," she answered indignantly.

"What are the words you keep saying?"

"Names of knitting patterns," she replied, jerking loose from him and blowing on. "Sand Dunes, Lightning, Soldiers Marching . . ."

He started to swim for the dragline, then saw he was already at the blue shaft leading aloft. He grabbed hold of its speeding centerline, not minding the burn, and speeded to the Bridge.

When he got there, he saw there was a multitude of stars aloft. The oblong rainbows were all banks of multi-colored lights winking on and off. But the silent officers—they looked very old, their faces stared as if they were sleep-swimming, their gestured orders were mechanical. He wondered if they knew where Windrush was going—or anything at all, beyond the Bridge of Windrush.

A dark, young officer with tightly curly hair floated to him. It wasn't until he spoke that Spar knew he was Ensign Drake.

"Hello, gramps. Say, you look younger. What are those things around your eyes?"

"Field glasses. They help me see sharp."

378

"But field glasses have tubes. They're a sort of binocular telescope."

Spar shrugged and told about the disappearance of Doc and his big, black treasure bag.

"But you say he drank a lot and he told you his treasures were dreams? Sounds like he was wacky and wandered off to do his drinking somewhere else."

"But Doc was a regular drinker. He always came to the Bat Rack."

"Well, I'll do what I can. Say, I've been pulled off the Bat Rack investigation. I think that character Crown got at someone higher up. The old ones are easy to get at—not so much greed as going by custom, taking the easiest course. Fenner and I never did find the old woman and the little dog, or any female and animal . . . or anything."

Spar told about Crown's earlier attempt to steal Doc's little black bag.

"So you think the two cases might be connected. Well, as I say, I'll do what I can."

Spar went back to the Bat Rack. It was very strange to see Keeper's face in detail. It looked old and its pink target center was a big red nose crisscrossed by veins. His brown eyes were not so much curious as avid. He asked about the things around Spar's eyes. Spar decided it wouldn't be wise to tell Keeper about seeing sharply.

"They're a new kind of costume jewelry, Keeper. Blasted Earth, I don't have any hair on my head, ought to have something."

"Language, Spar! It's like a drunk to spend precious scrip on such a grotesque bauble."

Spar neither reminded Keeper that all the scrip he'd earned at the Bat Rack amounted to no more than a wad as big as his thumb-joint, nor that he'd quit drinking. Nor did he tell him about his teeth, but kept them hidden behind his lips.

Kim was nowhere in sight. Keeper shrugged. "Gone off somewhere. You know the way of strays, Spar."

Yes, thought Spar, *this one's stayed put too long.*

He kept being amazed that he could see *all* of the Bat Rack sharply. It was a hexagon criscrossed by shrouds and made up of two pyramids put together square base to square base. The apexes of the pyramids were the violet fore and dark red aft corners. The four other corners were the starboard green, the black below, the larboard scarlet, and the blue aloft, if you named them from aft in the way the hands of a watch move.

Suzy drifted in early Playday. Spar was shocked by her blowsy appearance and bloodshot eyes. But he was touched by her signs of affection and he felt the strong friendship between them. Twice when Keeper wasn't looking he switched her nearly empty pouch of dark for a full one. She told him that, yes, she'd once known Sweetheart and that, yes, she'd heard people say Mable had seen Sweetheart snatched by vamps.

Business was slow for Playday. There were no strange brewos. Hoping against fearful, gut-level certainty, Spar kept waiting for Doc to come in zigzagging along the ratlines and comment on the new gadgets he'd given Spar and spout about the Old Days and his strange philosophy.

Playday night Crown came in with his girls, all except Almodie. Doucette said she'd had a headache and stayed at the Hole. Once again, all of them ordered coffee, though to Spar all of them seemed high.

Spar covertly studied their faces. Though nervous and alive, they all had something in their stares akin to those he'd seen in most of the officers on the Bridge. Doc had said they were all zombies. It was interesting to find out that Phanette's and Doucette's red-mottled appearance was due to . . . freckles, tiny reddish star-clusters on their white skins.

"Where's that famous talking cat?" Crown asked Spar.

Spar shrugged. Keeper said, "Strayed. For which I'm glad. Don't want a little feline who makes fights like last night."

Keeping his yellow-brown irised eyes on Spar, Crown said, "We believe it was that fight last Playday gave Almodie her headache, so she didn't want to come back tonight. We'll tell her you got rid of the witch cat."

"I'd have got rid of the beast if Spar hadn't," Keeper put in. "So you think it was a witch cat, coroner?"

"We're certain. What's that stuff on Spar's face?"

"A new sort of cheap eye jewelry, coroner, such as attracts drunks."

Spar got the feeling that this conversation had been prearranged, that there was a new agreement between Crown and Keeper. But he just shrugged again. Suzy was looking angry, but she said nothing.

Yet she stayed behind again after the Bat Rack closed. Keeper put no claim on her, though he leered knowingly before disappearing with a yawn and a stretch through the scarlet hatch. Spar checked that all six hatches were locked and shut off the lights, though that made no difference in the morning glare, before returning to Suzy, who had gone to his sleeping shroud.

Suzy asked, "You didn't get rid of Kim?"

Spar answered, "No, he just strayed, as Keeper said at first. I don't know where Kim is."

Suzy smiled and put her arms around him. "I think your new eye-things are beautiful," she said.

Spar said, "Suzy, did you know that Windrush isn't the Universe? That it's a ship going through space around a white round marked with circles, a round much bigger than all Windrush?"

Suzy replied, "I know Windrush is sometimes called the Ship. I've seen that round —in pictures. Forget all wild thoughts, Spar, and lose yourself in me."

Spar did so, chiefly from friendship. He forgot to clip his ankle to the shroud. Suzy's body didn't attract him. He was thinking of Almodie.

When it was over, Suzy slept. Spar put the rag around his eyes and tried to do the same. He was troubled by withdrawal symptoms only a little less bad than last Sleepday's. Because of that little, he didn't go to the torus for a pouch of moonmist. But then there was a sharp jab in his back, as if a muscle had spasmed there, and the symptoms got much worse. He convulsed, once, twice, then just as the agony became unbearable, blanked out.

Spar woke, his head throbbing, to discover that he was not only clipped, but lashed to his shroud, his wrists stretched in one direction, his ankles in the other, his hands and his feet both numb. His nose rubbed the shroud.

Light made his eyelids red. He opened them a little at a time and saw Hellhound poised with bent hind legs against the next shroud. He could see Hellhound's great stabbing teeth very clearly. If he had opened his eyes a little more swiftly, Hellhound would have dove at his throat.

He rubbed his sharp metal teeth together. At least he had more than gums to meet an attack on his face.

Beyond Hellhound he saw black and transparent spirals. He realized he was in Crown's Hole. Evidently the last jab in his back had been the injection of a drug.

But Crown had not taken away his eye jewelry, nor noted his teeth. He had thought of Spar as old Eyeless Toothless.

Between Hellhound and the spirals, he saw Doc lashed to a shroud and his big black bag clipped next to him. Doc was gagged. Evidently he had tried to cry out. Spar decided not to. Doc's gray eyes were open and Spar thought Doc was looking at him.

Very slowly Spar moved his numb fingers on top of the knot lashing his wrists to the shroud and slowly contracted all his muscles and pulled. The knot slid down the shroud a millimeter. So long as he did something slowly enough, Hellhound could not see it. He repeated his action at intervals.

Even more slowly he swung his face to the left. He saw nothing more than that the hatch to the corridor was zipped shut, and that beyond the dog and Doc, between the black spirals, was an empty and unfurnished cabin whose whole starboard side was stars. The hatch to that cabin was open, with its black-striped emergency hatch wavering beside it.

With equal slowness he swung his face to the right, past Doc and past Hellhound, who was eagerly watching him for signs of life or waking. He had pulled down the knot on his wrists two centimeters.

The first thing he saw was a transparent oblong. In it were more stars and, by its aft edge, the smoky orange round. At last he could see the latter more clearly. The smoke was on top, the orange underneath and irregularly placed. The whole was about as big as Spar's palm could have covered, if he had been able to stretch out his arm to full length. As he watched, he saw a bright flash in one of the orange areas. The flash was short, then it turned to a tiny black round pushing out through the smoke. More than ever, Spar felt sadness.

Below the transparency, Spar saw a horrible tableau. Suzy was strapped to a bright metal rack guyed by shrouds. She was very pale and her eyes were closed. From the side of her neck went a red sipping-tube which forked into five branches. Four of the branches went into the red mouths of Crown, Rixende, Phanette, and Doucette. The fifth was shut by a small metal clip, and beyond it Almodie floated cowering, hands over her eyes.

Crown said softly, "We want it all. Strip her, Rixie."

Rixende clipped shut the end of her tube and swam to Suzy. Spar expected her to remove the blue culottes and bra, but instead she simply began to massage one of Suzy's legs, pressing always from ankle toward waist, driving her remaining blood nearer her neck.

Crown removed his sipping tube from his lips long enough to say, "Ahh, good to the last drop." Then he had mouthed the blood that had spurted out in the interval and had the tube in place again.

Phanette and Doucette convulsed with soundless giggles.

Almodie peered between her parted fingers, out of her mass of platinum hair, then scissored them shut again.

After a while Crown said, "That's all we'll get. Phan and Doucie, feed her to the big chewer. If you meet anyone in the passageway, pretend she's drunk. Afterward we'll get Doc to dose us high, and give him a little brew if he behaves, then we'll drink Spar."

Spar had his wrist knot more than halfway to his teeth. Hellhound kept watching eagerly for movement, unable to see movement that slow. Slaver made tiny gray globes beside his fangs.

Phanette and Doucette opened the hatch and steered Suzy's dead body through it.

Embracing Rixende, Crown said expansively toward Doc, "Well, isn't it the right thing, old man? Nature bloody in tooth and claw, a wise one said. They've poisoned everything there." He pointed toward the smoky orange round sliding out of sight.

"They're still fighting, but they'll soon all be dead. So death should be the rule too for this gimcrack, so-called survival ship. Remember they are aboard her. When we've drunk the blood of everyone aboard Windrush, including their blood, we'll drink our own, if our own isn't theirs."

Spar thought, *Crown thinks too much in they's.* The knot was close to his teeth. He heard the big chewer start to grind.

In the empty next cabin, Spar saw Drake and Fenner, clad once more as brewos, swimming toward the open hatch.

But Crown saw them too. "Get 'em, Hellhound," he directed, pointing. "It's our command."

The big black dog bulleted from his shroud through the open hatch. Drake pointed something at him. The dog went limp.

Chuckling softly, Crown took by one tip a swastika with curved, gleaming, razor-sharp blades and sent it spinning off. It curved past Spar and Doc, went through the open hatch, missed Drake and Fenner—and Hellhound—and struck the wall of stars.

There was a rush of wind, then the emergency hatch smacked shut. Spar saw Drake, Fenner, and Hellhound, wavery through the transparent pliofilm, spew blood, bloat, burst bloodily open. The empty cabin they had been in disappeared. Windrush had a new wall and Crown's Hole was distorted.

Far beyond, growing ever tinier, the swastika spun toward the stars.

Phanette and Doucette came back. "We fed in Suzy. Someone was coming, so we beat it." The big chewer stopped grinding.

Spar bit cleanly through his wrist lashings and immediately doubled over to bite his ankles loose.

Crown dove at him. Pausing to draw knives, the four girls did the same.

Phanette, Doucette, and Rixende went limp. Spar had the impression that small black balls had glanced from their skulls.

There wasn't time to bite his feet loose, so he straightened. Crown hit his chest as Almodie bit his feet.

Crown and Spar giant-swung around the shroud. Then Almodie had cut Spar's ankles loose. As they spun off along the tangent, Spar tried to knee Crown in the groin, but Crown twisted and evaded the blow as they moved toward the inboard wall.

There was the *snick* of Crown's knife unfolding. Spar saw the dark wrist and grabbed it. He butted at Crown's jaw. Crown evaded. Spar set his teeth in Crown's neck and bit.

Blood covered Spar's face, spurted over it. He spat out a hunk of flesh. Crown convulsed. Spar fought off the knife. Crown went limp. That the pressure in a man should work against him.

Spar shook the blood from his face. Through its beads, he saw Keeper and Kim side by side. Almodie was clutching his ankles. Phanette, Doucette, Rixende floated.

Keeper said proudly, "I shot them with my gun for drunks. I knocked them out. Now I'll cut their throats, if you wish."

Spar said, "No more throat-cutting. No more blood." Shaking off Almodie's hands, he took off for Doc, picking up Doucette's floating knife by the way.

He slashed Doc's lashings and cut the gag from his face.

Meanwhile Kim hissed, "Sstole and ssecreted Keeper's sscrip from the boxx. Ashshured him you sstole it, Sspar. You and Ssuzzy. Sso he came. Keeper izz a shshlemiel."

Keeper said, "I saw Suzy's foot going into the big chewer. I knew it by its anklet of hearts. After that I had the courage to kill Crown or anyone. I loved Suzy."

Doc cleared his throat and croaked, "Moonmist." Spar found a triple pouch and Doc sucked it all. Doc said, "Crown spoke the truth. Windrush is a plastic survival ship from Earth. Earth"—he motioned toward the dull orange round disappearing aft in the window—"poisoned herself with smog pollution and nuclear war. She spent gold for war, plastic for survival. Best forgotten. Windrush went mad. Understandably. Even without the Lethean rickettsia, or Styx ricks, as you call it. Thought Windrush was the cosmos. Crown kidnapped me to get my drugs, kept me alive to know the doses."

Spar looked at Keeper. "Clean up here," he ordered. "Feed Crown to the big chewer."

Almodie pulled herself from Spar's ankles to his waist. "There was a second survival ship. Circumluna. When Windrush went mad, my father and mother—and you—were sent here to investigate and cure. But my father died and you got Styx ricks. My mother died just before I was given to Crown. She sent you Kim."

Kim hissed, "My fforebear ccame from Ccircumluna to Windrushsh, too. Great-grandmother. Taught me the ffiguress for Windrushsh . . . Radiuss from moon-ccenter, two thoussand five hundred miless. Period, ssixx hourss—sso, the sshort dayss. A terranth izz the time it takess Earth to move through a cconsstellation, and sso on."

Doc said, "So, Spar, you're the only one who remembers without cynicism. You'll have to take over. It's all yours, Spar."

Spar had to agree.

Endfray of the Ofay

Alerted by their watchmen, who were mostly Seminoles, the Red-Necked Ofays of the Okefinokee Reservation came hurtling out of their soggy holes and nests with such violence that the alligators and water moccasins went hurtling back into theirs. Reptiles can take only so much excitement.

With hoarse cackles of happiness, the emaciated whites and their Red Indian fellow-reservationists floundered about snatching at the little transparent packets of hominy grits, chitterlings, and moonshine originally intended for the poor Black trash of Appalachia, but now miraculously diverted and falling like manna from the sweaty southern sky.

Along with the hillbilly ambrosia and nectar, a faint cry haunting as the flight of the flamingo lingered in those same dismal hot heavens: 'Compliments of the Endfray of the Ofay!'

The Red-Necked Ofays paused in their snatching to lift a ragged cheer.

This was not the first exploit of the mysterious marauder who had thus far left no clue to his identity except a cry from the sky. Most folks now attributed to him the signs, 'Whitey lives!' which a month ago had begun to appear scrawled big in shiver-somely daring spots, such as the front wall of the Black House in Memphis. Then a week ago a boisterous party of Luxor Blacks on a sweep-and-annoy excursion through the Bayous Reservation had had their persons and swamp buggies deluged with Yazoo mud, 'Courtesy of the Endfray of the Ofay!' Many intellectual and fashionable Blacks had secretly approved this literally dirty trick, since the chivvying and terrorizing of helpless Ofays was beginning to be considered uncouth behavior. Then only yesterday a 17-year-old white concubine of the Caliph of Harlem had been kidnapped by the Endfray and levitated back to her tribe in the Great Barrens Reservation. Reactionary and moralistic Blacks, long detesting the Caliph for his contempt of the strict rules against miscegenation, had openly praised the act. In fact, only the rescued and wind-blown white girl had been completely unhappy about the whole business. But no Blacks could be expected to approve the food drop, which not only upset the national economy, but also violated the even stricter laws against interfering, by helping the weak, with the divine principle of survival of the fittest.

The Black wardens of the Okefinokee melted with their furious and frightened messages the wires to Memphis, Cairo, Thebes, Luxor (once Vicksburg and Natchez) and the other great Government cities of the American Nile.

Within ten seconds two squadrons of Black Angels based on Karnak had scrambled and another was screaming down through the stratosphere.

At her palatial HQ in Memphis, Her Serene Darkness noted the disturbance and ordered that samples of the food packets be recovered and rushed to her. She did not, nevertheless, shift one black iota of her essential concentration off the great war that was being fought between North America and Africa to Make the World Safe for Black Supremacy, by determining which Blacks really were supreme.

Ten seconds more and all three squadrons of Black Angels were reversing course west as quickly as their already great velocity would permit, and then shifting into overdrive.

Word had come that there had been another drop of mysteriously diverted viands —this time on the Death Valley Reservation of the Bearded and Beaded Ofays.

Once again there had come that weird cry from the sky: 'Compliments of the End-fray of the Ofay!'

Along with the packets of fruit and saffron-tinted, precooked rice and vegetables, there were falling foam-packaged Tibetan prayer wheels, smuggled no man might say how through the Nirvana Screen.

The starving descendants of ancient hippies, beats, cultists and movie moguls had come boiling up out of the furnace-hot mouths of *their* caves and holes. Even outside the reservations, holes were a popular residence in those exciting times when Black atom bombs were in the air and when all mankind was preoccupied, to a degree at least equal to his interest in space, with Earth's molten, slow-churning mantle, rich in mohole-minable radioactives and also a source of strange and mighty powers when properly tickled by CDEF (Coleman-Dufresne Electrogravitomagnetic Fields) or by magic spells. For in the new world sorcery and science walked arm in arm, sometimes so closely that none might tell which was which, or who was holding the other up. And the density and darkness of Earth's interior suited the Black Age. Russia, which ever since Dostoyevsky Day had shifted her fundamentally introspective and peasant interests from the sky to the East European plains and Siberian steppes, had used CDEF (and possibly some Tungu chants) to carry by slow convection and concentrate vast subcritical masses of fissionable radioactives underneath all the world's continents. Increased CDEF tickling would produce unimaginably destructive earthquakes—the so-called mantle bombs that were the USSR's doomsday answer to aggression. Africa and North America utilized the same methods to enrich the radioactives they took from their mohole mines. Australia had employed CDEF and bone-pointing Aboriginal magic to accelerate continental drift, so that the great down-under island, shoving Tasmania before it, was now separated from Antarctica by only a narrow strait. Australia enjoyed a Canadian climate and was hemmed by extremely rich fisheries. While the great Buddhist hegemony of Sino-India had used CDEF (possibly) and yoga and zen (certainly) to create the Nirvana Screen.

In response to the echoing cry from the dry sky, the Beaded and Bearded Ofays touched fingertips to foreheads and briefly meditated their gratitude.

In the fringes of her awareness, Her Serene Darkness noted this food-drop also, and she gave the same order.

Over the Pacific, a tiny westward-speeding vehicle reversed course instantaneously, and so of course without circling, to return momentarily to a point over Death Valley and shout down, 'The Endfray thanks you for your prayers.'

The Ofays below rejoiced, while by the psionic grapevine that tenuously links unfortunates, a little hope was kindled in the Swarthy Ofays of the Chihuahua Reservation, the Stunted Ofays of the Jersey Flats, the Giant Ofays of the Panhandle Reservation, the Long-Haired Ofays of the Tules, and even in the Wild or Unfenced Honkies of the Rocky Mountains, the Black Hills, and the Badlands.

The Endfray's linear hoop wasted enough time to let the Black Angels zero in on him, her, it or them, with their radars and telescopes. With hardly a millisecond's delay, they aimed and activated their deadly lasers, rocket bombs and constriction fields.

*   *   *

The Endfray went zigzagging west again just in time. His evasive tactics were masterly. He seemed able to anticipate each move of his pursuers. Mini-atomics burst into searing violet spheres about him, red laser-needles lanced past him, space itself was squeezed and wrenched, but he bobbed along unharmed like a ping-pong ball in a tornado.

For an instant one Black Angel telescoped him clearly. The fleeing vehicle was incredibly tiny, the size and shape of a chunky dwarf's spaceshit, snow white in hue, and across it went the red letters 'Endfray of the Ofay'. There were no jets or antennae. It flashed out of sight perhaps a microsecond before a laser pierced the space it had occupied.

Yet despite or perhaps because of the Endfray's ingenious doublings and dartings, the Black Angels were gaining on him. He veered south, but Australia sent up a line of warning star rockets. He veered north, but when he neared the moored, melancholy black balloons marking the Russian border, they moaned, 'Nyet, nyet', at him and he once more reversed course and sought the Equator.

The blue of the sky ahead became grainy and glittering like a holograph. It extended down to sea level, blotting out Borneo and the western shore of Celebes.

Without hesitation the Endfray plunged, at precisely 120 degrees east longitude, into the Nirvana Screen.

Changing their fatalistic death chants, the pilots of the Black Angels sent their slim ebon ships after him.

Without perceptible passage of time, pursued and pursuers emerged over the Indian Ocean at 60 degrees east longitude.

The same thing would have happened in reverse if they had been traveling east, or at 45 degrees north latitude and the Equater of they had been traveling along a north–south vector. It was the Orient's master mystery, greater than the rope trick. Truth to tell, no one outside knew for sure whether India and China still existed inside the Nirvana Screen, or not. Explanations ran the gamut from spacewarp to mass hypnosis and the Nigerian null-spell. While what the superscientific and/or superpsychic Buddhists of the Fourth Dimensional Path might do if they ever came out, chilled even Earth's blackest blood.

Africa loomed, the continent that was the home of the biggest animals, the biggest magics and the biggest bombs in the world. The Endfray climbed steeply. Already at greater altitude, the Black Angels rode the hypotenuse of a collision course.

Ninety miles from intercept, magnibombs mashed the stratosphere everywhere around the Endfray and coalesced into one massive incandescence.

Veering off with hardly nanoseconds to spare, the Black Angels' wing commander bounced home his message off the most convenient orbital relay: 'Target destroyed by African antispacecraft fire.'

387

*   *   *

But before it was received at Memphis, there was dropping on the Fierce Fuzzy or Bluecoated Ofays of the Chicago Craters Reservation, a shower of packeted food—wienerschnitzel, corned beef and cabbage, Irish whiskey, beer—and foam-crated roller skates, the latter diverted from a shipment intended for the greater gladiatorial ring at Cairo. While down the slants of rain from the dismal sky there resounded, 'Compliments of the Endfray of the Ofay!'

No one knew why the Chicago Craters Ofays were called fuzzy, or simply referred to as 'the fuzz', since all of them were totally bald from residual radioactivity. It was one of recent history's many mysteries, about which thought was discouraged. But anyone could figure out that roller skates would be an excellent means of transportation on crater glass. And by now everyone, Black or White, knew that the Endfray was an impudent and unbearable affront to absolute authority.

Her Serene Darkness made a decision and took her mind completely off the war. She could safely do this because her uncles were good generals and because her psionic intelligence organization was the world's best, with vast powers of telepathy, clairvoyance, clairaudience, telekinesis and teleportation, from the orbiting espers each shut-eyed in her capsule to the Blacks in Blackness: whole psionic families which had lived for generations in deep-buried, absolutely anechoic, a-aptical psy-spy-proof environments, their only connections with the upper world being inbound nutrient-pipes and oxypipes and quartz-cable ultraviolet conductors and outbound waste-pipes and report lines. Psionic Intelligence's chief task was to spot and course-chart bombs lobbed over from Africa and up from Argentina and Brazil, where Africa had an enormous beachhead and then either turn them back by telekinesing their controls, or else guide atomic interceptors to them. Her Darkness was certain that her espers were the world's finest because she had been their working chief before taking over her largely conscious, nonpsionic imperial duties.

Now like an arboreal black leopard—slim, flashing-eyed and dangerous—she gazed down the Watusi-Hottentot gap between her and her pages.

'Summon me my psychiawitches and sorceresps,' she commanded.

The patter of sprinting bare feet faded from the tesselated floor, which was a great, diagrammatic map of Earth and the spaces around. Turning her beautiful, small head on her slender, long neck, Her Darkness gazed out between the narrow pillars of Vermont marble fretted with California gold at the rippling blue Mississippi, and she meditated.

A page entered and knelt to her, lifting a golden tray on which gleamed glassy packets, samples from the Endfray's food-drops. She silently indicated where to set it.

A tall, glossy warrior in HQ harness folded his arms in the Communications doorway and intoned, 'Acapulco, Halifax and Port of Spain have sustained medium to severe damage from nuclear nearmisses. Our rockets intercepted, but not in good time. Orbital warnings on the three African attacks were late and inadequate.'

'What from the Blacks in Blackness?' Her Serenity inquired.

'No warning whatever from that quarter.'

She nodded dismissal and returned to her meditations.

Yet it seemed hardly picoseconds before the Presence Pavilion was once more full and silent, except for the faint susurrus of the most respectful breathing and the pounding of frightened hearts.

*   *   *

Slowly, one by one, Her Darkness gave her assembled psychiawitches and sorceresps the leopard look which her populace expected of her and loved, especially when they did not have to face it.

Those gathered in the pavilion were almost as tall as she and even more gorgeously clad, but they crouched away from her and ducked their heads like terrified children.

Then she asked in a voice that set them shivering, 'Why is our newest and insolentest enemy uncaught by you, nay, unreported even,' and without waiting for an answer commanded, 'Read me the mind of the Endfray. Ice it and slice it, dice it and rice it. Skewer him in space, nail him in time. Sound him from his lowest note to the top of his compass. Tell me his source, his nature and his fate.'

Instantly a sorceresp of the Seventh Rank babbled, 'He is a dwarf white trained and equipped in a secret laboratory in a branch of the Carlsbad Caverns underlying the White Sands Reservation of the Bulge-Brained Ofays. His aim, unquestionably, is the formenting of an Ofay revolt, a Honky insurrection. He is now hovering seventeen miles above Aswan-St. Paul.'

Without intervening pause, the Second Psychiawitch chittered, 'He is an African agent of Pygmy extraction, a marauder skilled in teleportation and telepathy. His means of aerial locomotion is a deceit; he uses slowed-down teleportation, not speeded-up field flight. Under cover of the magnibomb blast, he landed unharmed in the territory of our hateful enemies and is now making report to His Terrible Tenebrosity in his shelter-palace beneath Mogadishu.'

'The Endfray is not one, but many,' another took up. 'He is radioactive atoms over the Somali coast. He also speeds east intact over Old Cleveland on the Dead Sea. Another of these duplicates—'

'By Bast and by Ptah, the Endfray is extraterrestrial,' yet another cut in. 'A seven-tentacled amphibian from the fourth planet of pulsing Altair, he is the forerunner of an invasion which—'

'By Serapis and Harpocrates, she is an Indian witch, sister to Kali, able to penetrate the Nirvana Screen and let others through. She—'

'The Endfray is a group-minded nation of Black Martian Ants. Only such tiny creatures could survive the changes of momentum that—'

'The Endfray is a fantasm! That's why no material weapon can—'

'That'll be enough!' interposed Her Serene Darkness. 'When I want improvisations, I'll summon me my artists.' The faint, jeering notes of an electronic calliope on a distant pleasure barge seemed an overtone of her scornful contralto voice. 'Facts I desire. Where is the Endfray? Take scent and search!' And picking up the gold tray, she scattered its contents across the room in one sweep.

*   *   *

The soaring, transparent food-packets were snatched, sniffed, fingered, held to ear and forehead, passed hand to hand. There were faint growlings and eager whimperings as the assembly transformed into a pack.

Her Serenity directed, 'Each search that part of earth or space on which she stands,' referring to the diagrammatic floor map. 'Let not one oozy sea cranny or fissure of damp clay cave be overlooked, and forget not the far side of the moon. Except you . . . and you,' she added, beckoning the First Psychiawitch and also the sorceresp of the Seventh-Rank who had been first to answer. 'The rest, to work!'

'How many minutes have we for our task?' the Second Psychiawitch ventured. The eyes of most of the others had already closed or gone blank as the minds behind them clairvoyantly scanned.

'I give you each one hundred seconds.' Then, turning to the Seven-Rank sorceresp, 'You spoke of an Ofay revolt. Where? When?'

'One is planned, Your Darkness. It will begin in Los Alamos and be timed to coincide with an all-out African assault ordered by His Terrible Tenebrosity.'

'Ridiculous!' the First Psychiawitch interjected in a whisper. 'Not even His Idiocy would be so stupid as to think the reservation Ofays might be roused to helpful revolution, or the wild Honkies organized for any purpose. Nor would even His Vileness stoop to use such foul and tawdry means.'

In the Communications doorway there appeared a warrior, impassive but white-eyed. Her Serenity showed him her finger. He intoned, 'The Blacks in Blackness report that Africa has launched from Casablanca a vehicle with a two-hundred-million-pound firststage thrust. Window clouds surround it. Its course bends west.'

'Two hundred million?'

'Aye. Ten times that of any known Afric or Americ launching vehicle.'

'It is the revolt-sign!' the Seventh-Rank sorceresp wailed.

'From its size, it's more likely itself our death-sign, if our interceptors let it get over our land,' the First Psychiawitch remarked coolly.

'Silence,' Her Darkness said, not unkindly. Then, to the room, 'The hundred seconds are up. Where is the Endfray?'

*   *   *

In the hundred and seventy-odd faces, eyes opened and/or came alive with spirit, looking toward Her Serenity with a professional confidence which, as the seconds passed and not one of them spoke, transformed, again into fear.

'Has any one of you not completed search?' Her Darkness inquired. 'Or failed to make it as thorough as I commanded?'

Heads rotated from side to side. Lips formed, 'No.'

'Then the Endfray is nowhere,' the First Psychiawitch whispered in a voice that was not meant to carry, but did.

One cried, 'It is as I said. He is a fantasm, invisible to psionic search.'

'No, it is as *I* said!' another took up. 'He is from Altair, and returned there in the twinkling of a self-teleportive thought. We have not searched Altair, only space out to Pluto.'

'When the possible seems to fail, only weak brains grasp at the impossible,' Her Serenity interposed. 'Stellar teleportation takes perceptible time and leaves perceptible clues, as you well know. While fantasms make no teleportive food-drops and leave no psychic scent. No, to solve our problem we must use an apothegm of Sherlock Holmes.'

Eyes grew puzzled, while the First Psychiawitch murmured, 'Who is that?'

'Sherlock Holmes was a Cryptoblack of vast deductive intelligence, who lived in—' Her Darkness rapidly starred herself, moving fingertips to the seven cardinal points— 'the Tabooed Times.'

Everyone else copied Her Darkness and starred herself at once, to ward off any ill hap which might come from mention of a forbidden area of the continuum.

Her Serenity continued, 'The Sherlockian apothegm I have in mind is this: when all other explanations are proven false, then the least likely explanation must be the true one. You have not searched *all* of habitable Earth and Solar space.'

The psychiatrist standing on Memphis said hesitantly, 'But, begging Your Serenity's pardon, I have searched every closet of your secret quarters, including the apartments housing your harem and your laboratories of magic and the vault guarding your secret fortune.'

'It is well that you have,' Her Darkness replied, smiling most dangerously. 'But those are not the sole forbidden or esp-proof volumes of Earth.'

'You are thinking of the mantle and core?' one asked.

'I said, "habitable",' Her Darkness snapped. 'Can you not guess the other spot I have in mind?'

A sorceresp standing just south of Louisville cried out, 'I scent the Endfray over Bowling Green! His vector, southwest by west. He speeds. Already he overpasses Clarksville.'

The psychiawitch standing between her and the one on Memphis took up with, 'And now I catch his scent in turn. He comes on fast. He is over Paris, Milan, Bells, Brownsville, Covington—'

'And now—' the one on Memphis began.

The air screamed. The gold-chased pillars shook, and the purple silken awning snapped and flapped as something white flashed through the pavilion, tumbling by its blast everyone but Her Serenity.

The scream, which had abruptly dropped in pitch as the disturbance went by, and then faded somewhat, now rose again in pitch and volume.

'He returns to buzz us once more,' the First Psychiawitch gasped from the floor.

Her Dark Serenity—hair unspiraled and straight on end, eyes like a mad tiger's, fists clenched, knees bent, slender feet a-stamp—incanted rapidly,

> 'Null Kull, null Rull,
> Null time, null space,
> Null motion and null Grace.
> By Hanged Man, Spades, and Lovers
> Be winged-clogged, all that hovers
> Paralysis know, and fear—'

The screaming knifed. The pillars began to shake. Something white—

'—And drop down here!'

Silence returned with a roar. Something white lay on the tesselated floor—a squat and rigid spacesuit like a white oil drum with stubby cylindrical arms and legs, but windowless and without sign of head.

Her Serenity drew and expelled three gasping but controlled breaths. Her hair recurled with faintest rustlings. Those around craned, leaned in, and peered, though without rising fully from the floor where they had been sent sprawling.

Holding out her right hand prone, Her Serenity commanded, 'Arise!'

Like the reversed motion picture of a rigid fall, the white spacesuit swung erect as if its heels were hinged to the floor.

'Emerge!' Her Serenity continued.

The suit did not open, but out of it, as if walking through a white wall, there stepped a handsome black boy who looked nine years old. He wore a loincloth. Though his eyes were shut tight, his face was animated, and he smiled as he looked up.

'My Empress—' he began.

Her slender hands, snaking forward to capture him, clamped tight on air.

A chuckle came from the far end of the pavilion, where the black boy had rematerialized midway between awning and floor. Heads switched around to watch him where he stood on air.

Two sorceresps pointed at him, the one a wand, the other a yellow thighbone.

Three warriors appeared at the Force door, bearing silvery, cone-nosed hand weapons. Her Darkness snapped her fingers.

Still shut-eyed, the black boy chuckled again. The three warriors swayed like ticked bowling pins, arms tight to sides, legs tight together, bound by the constriction fields their weapons had projected backfiring on them. While pointed wand and thighbone hung limp as cooked spaghetti from the hands of the sorceresps.

'Any more games?' the black boy inquired hopefully. If he'd been chubbier, he'd have seemed like a wingless cupid.

'Who are you?' Her Darkness demanded far more coolly than she felt.

'The Endfray, of course, Empress,' he replied, looking at her as directly as if his eyes had been open. 'At your service, providing—I humbly beg your pardon—the service suits me.'

'Yet you have helped the Honkies, aided the Ofays—why?' Her Darkness asked automatically. She was still half in shock.

The Endfray's grin widened and he quirked his face. Finally, 'Just for fun,' he said. 'No, that's not true. Fact is, you see, I like stories of wars and battles, and—'

'As any young Black should,' Her Serenity interrupted approvingly. She was regaining her sense of command, and her mind was beginning to work again.

At her feet the First Psychiawitch took fire from her and cried out, 'Indeed yes! Brave battles! Complete courage! Stark strength! Merciless might! Violence and victory!'

The Endfray hung his head. His expression became an odd mixture of embarrassment and defiance. 'But you see, Empress, I always like the losing side best. Being with the winners is no fun. But siding with the losers, when all the odds are against them— And you got to admit, it's hard to imagine a losinger side than the Ofays.'

'Accommodation! Tomism! Honky-love!' the Second Psychiawitch cried scandalized.

'Don't you know the first sign of high intelligence is the faculty of violence?' the First Psychiawitch demanded.

'Inside the Nirvana Screen, they think it's the ability to sit still,' the Endfray countered.

'Strength is virtue. Weakness is sin,' the Leading Sorceresp chanted.

'But you got to remember we were the losingest once, we were the weak ones, we—' the Endfray continued stubbornly, but his voice was drowned in cries of horror at his unprefaced and unstarred reference to the Tabooed Times.

The warrrior appearing at the Communications doorway did not stand on ceremony, but roared over the din, 'Our psionic trackers have lost touch with the African super-missile south of the Azores! The Blacks in Blackness have broken off their reports.'

* * *

There was shocked silence, in which the Endfray's voice sounded out clearly. His grin was gone. 'Yes,' he said, 'and now, big as a metal moon, it's approaching Bermuda. Our interceptors rise to destroy it. Counter-missiles shoot from it and become balls of white flame. Our interceptors puff into nothingness. It still comes on.'

The Leading Sorceresp pointed at him a shaking arm. 'He is an African agent,' she screeched, 'sent to disrupt our counsels at this moment of crisis.'

'That's not true, Empress,' the Endfray protested. 'I've stuck with America because *we* are the losingest side of this war. We are the weak ones. Africa's going to win, unless I—'

Once again his voice was lost, this time in a din of outrage that broke off only when Her Dark Serenity threw up her arms and cried, 'Fools! Have you not yet guessed who the Endfray is? Have you not yet solved the Sherlockian riddle? The only spot you haven't psionically searched is psi-proof Mammoth Cave, immemorial home of the Blacks in Blackness and just by Bowling Green. He is clearly one of them, and their best tracker too, highest product of our breeding for psionicity. When he was out on his mad mission to the Ofays, three bombs got through. When he returned home and you could not find him, we got reports on the launching of the African super-missile. When he started here, those reports stopped. And did it not occur to you that he keeps his eyes shut because he has never before been in an environment of optical light? You are all idiots! Endfray, how goes it?'

'The big one zoomed in over Savannah and Macon. Its last counter-missiles blasted those of our coastal and backup defenses. Ten seconds ago it was about to break up over Birmingham and shower all the cities of the Nile with a hundred hydrogen heads.'

'Was?'

'Of course, "was", Empress. While all these here were squawking, I jiggered its control and put it into a permanent 93-minute circular orbit around Terra. I'm going to keep it there too. I'm sorry, Empress, but in spite of you being very bright and right about me, I don't trust you with that big a bomb. Or His Terrible Tenebrosity, of course. War's romantic, but destruction's too realistic.'

Her Darkness turned on him. 'You have your nerve!'

His embarrassment returned. 'I *told* you I'm sorry, Empress.'

She paused and turned toward the Communications doorway, where a warrior had appeared. 'The super-missile still speeds west,' he rapped out. 'Twenty of our interceptors have risen from Colorado Springs and thirty from Frisco to destroy it.'

'Imbeciles! Would you break it up, to do destruction, while it is still over our continent?'

'Don't worry, Empress,' the Endfray said.

A second warrior appeared behind the first. 'Our fifty interceptors have escaped control and formed themselves into two goose wings slanting back from the super-missile. Their radar blips are unmistakable.'

The Endfray grinned. 'And now, my Empress, I got to be going. That flock needs looking after.'

* * *

A third warrior appeared behind the second. 'A bliplet, tiny but unmistakable, has added itself to the fifty blips and one superblip.'

'We know,' Her Dark Serenity said a shade wearily, waving her hand in dismissal.

393

Then, to the First Psychiawitch, who was at last pushing herself up from the floor, 'What exactly, Sister, means the word Endfray?'

'O Your Dread Serenity,' the other replied, 'now that the taboos are lifting, it comes to me. I take it to be a word of Swine Roman, or Pig Latin if you prefer, a secret language of the Evil Days when Santan-Dis-Ahriman ruled. It was formed from English by putting the last part of a word first and then adding a long A. Even as Ofay means foe, Endfray means friend.'

'Friend of the Foe,' Her Darkness intoned tiredly. 'I might have deduced all from his name alone.' Her eyebrows lifted. 'Or Ender of the Fray. Frayender.'

'However you name him, he appears to have a lost-cause fixation and a comic-book mentality,' the First Psychiawitch intellectualized.

'Stop,' Her Serenity protested, raising a listless palm. 'We've heard enough about Honkies for today. Dismiss all.'

Russia noted the super-bomb orbiting with its entourage and set off a warning earthquake that quivered all Antarctica. Australia in turn dropped in the Bering Sea a warning bomb that upset a sealer and sent a small tsunami foaming over the beaches of Kamchatka.

But that night the Ofays in their reservations went to sleep for the first time in a century with hope and even a little confidence in their hearts. Someone cared.

*   *   *

Next day North America and Africa agreed to a bombing halt. It was madness to continue a war which only built up the Endfray's orbiting armory. They diverted all their research—scientific, psionic and sorcerous—to a hunt for a means of knocking the Endfray out of the high sky. But secretly Her Dark Serenity decided that he would make her ideal successor. She pondered plans to win him over. So did His Terrible Tenebrosity.

The Endfray turned his major attention to the plight of the Untouchables behind the Nirvana Screen. There was a cause even more lost than that of the Ofays.

And he still had, for a lost-cause ace in the hole, the Boars and other white trash of the Blancostans and concentration camps of Rhodesia and South Africa.

America The Beautiful

I am returning to England. I am shorthanding this, July 5, 2000, aboard the Dallas-London rocket as it arches silently out of the diffused violet daylight of the stratosphere into the eternally star-spangled purpling night of the ionosphere.

I have refused the semester instructorship in poetry at UTD, which would have munificently padded my honorarium for delivering the Lanier Lectures and made me for four months second only to the Poet in Residence.

And I am almost certain that I have lost Emily, although we plan to meet in London in a fortnight if she can wangle the stopover on her way to take up her Peace Corps command in Niger.

I am not leaving America because of the threat of a big war. I believe that this new threat, like all the rest, is only another move, even if a long and menacing queen's move, in the game of world politics, while the little wars go endlessly on in Chad, Czechoslovakia, Sumatra, Siam, Baluchistan, and Bolivia as America and the Communist League firm their power boundaries.

And I am certainly not leaving America because of any harassment as a satellitic neutral possible spy. There may have been surveillance of my actions and lectures, but if so it was an impalpable as the checks they must have made on me in England before granting me visiting clearance. The U.S. intelligence agencies have become almost incredibly deft in handling such things. And I was entertained in America more than royally—I was made to feel at home by a family with a great talent for just that.

No, I am leaving because of the shadows. The shadows are everywhere in America, but which I saw most clearly in Professor Grissim's serene and lovely home. The shadows which would irresistibly have gathered behind my instructor's lectern, precisely as I was learning to dress with an even trimmer and darker reserve while I was a guest at the Grissims' and even to shower more frequently. The shadows which revealed themselves to me deepest of all around Emily Grissim, and which I could do nothing to dispel.

I think that you, or at least I, can see the shadows in America more readily these days because of the very clean air there. Judging only from what I saw with my own eyes in Texas, the Americans have completely licked their smog problem. Their gently curving freeways purr with fast electric cars, like sleek and disciplined silver cats. Almost half the nation's power comes from atomic reactors, while the remaining coal-burning plants loose back into the air at most a slight shimmer of heat. Even the streams and rivers run blue and unsmirched again, while marine life is returning to the eastern Great Lakes. In brief, America is beautiful, for with the cleanliness, now greater than that of the Dutch, has come a refinement in taste, so that all buildings are grace-fully shaped and disposed, while advertisements, though molding minds more surely than ever, are restrained and almost finically inoffensive.

The purity of the atmosphere was strikingly brought to my notice when I debarked at Dallas rocketport and found the Grissims waiting for me outdoors, downwind of the landing area. They made a striking group, all of them tall, as they stood poised yet familiarly together: the professor with his grizzled hair still close-trimmed in military fashion, for he had served almost as long as a line officer and in space services as he had now as a university physicist; his slim, white-haired wife; Emily, like her mother in the classic high-waisted, long-skirted Directoire style currently fashionable; and her brother Jack, in his dress pale grays with sergeant's stripes, on furlough from Siam.

Their subdued dress and easy attitudes reminded me of a patrician Roman's toga dropping in precise though seemingly accidental folds. The outworn cliché about America being Rome to England's Greece came irritatingly to my mind.

Introductions were made by the professor, who had met my father at Oxford and later seen much of him during the occupation of Britain throughout the Three Years' Alert. I was surprised to find their diction almost the same as my own. We strolled to their electric station wagon, the doors of which opened silently at our approach.

I should have been pleased by the simple beauty of the Grissims, as by that of the suburban landscape through which we now sped, especially since my poetry is that of the Romantic Revival, which looks back to Keats and Shelley more even than to Shakespeare. Instead, it rubbed me the wrong way. I became uneasy and within ten minutes found myself beginning to talk bawdy and make nasty little digs at America.

They accepted my rudeness in such an unshocked, urbane fashion, demonstrating that they understood though did not always agree with me, and they went to such trouble to assure me that not all America was like this, there were still many ugly stretches, that I soon felt myself a fool and shut up. It was I who was the crass Roman, I told myself, or even barbarian.

Thereafter Emily and her mother kept the conversation going easily and soon coaxed me back into it, with the effect of smoothing the grumbling and owlish young British poet's ruffled feathers.

The modest one storey, shaded by slow-shedding silvery eucalyptus and mutated chaparral, which was all that showed of the Grissim home, opened to receive our fumeless vehicle. I was accompanied to my bedroom-and-study, served refreshments, and left there to polish up my first lecture. The scene in the view window was so faith-fully transmitted from the pickup above, the air fresher if possible than that outdoors, that I found it hard to keep in mind I was well underground.

It was at dinner that evening, when my hosts made such a nicely concerted effort to soothe my nervousness over my initial lecture, and largely succeeded, that I first began truly to like and even respect the Grissims.

It was at the same instant, in that pearly dining room, that I first became aware of the shadows around them.

Physical shadows? Hardly, though at times they really seemed that. I recall thinking, my mind still chiefly on my lecture, something like, *These good people are so wedded to the way of war, the perpetual little wars and the threat of the big one, and have been so successful in masking the signs of its strains in themselves, that they have almost forgotten that those strains are there. And they love their home and country, and the security of their taut way of life, so deeply that they have become unaware of the depth of that devotion.*

My lecture went off that night. The audience was large, respectful, and seemingly even attentive. The number of African and Mexican faces gave the lie to what I'd been told about integration being a sham in America. I should have been pleased, and I temporarily was, at the long, mutedly drumming applause I was given and at the many intelligent, flattering comments I received afterward. And I should have stopped seeing the shadows then, but I didn't.

Next morning Emily toured me around city and countryside on a long silvery scooter, I riding pillion behind her. I remember the easy though faintly formal way in which she drew my arms around her waist and laid her hand for a moment on one of mine, meanwhile smiling cryptically over-shoulder. Besides that smile, I remember a charming Spanish-American graveyard in pastel stucco, the towering Kennedy shrine, the bubbling, iridescent tubes of algae farming converging toward the horizon, and rockets taking off in the distance with their bright, smokeless exhausts. Emily was almost as unaffected as a British girl and infinitely more competent, in a grand style. That one day the shadows vanished altogether.

They returned at evening when after dinner we gathered in the living room for our first wholly unhurried and relaxed conversation, my lectures being spaced out in a leisurely—to Americans, not to me—one day in two schedule.

We sat in a comfortable arc before the wide fireplace, where resinous woods burned yellow and orange. Occasionally Jack would put on another log. From time to time, a light shower of soot dropped back from the precipitron in the chimney, the tiny particles as they fell flaring into brief white points of light, like stars.

A little to my surprise, the Grissims drank as heavily as the English, though they carried their liquor very well. Emily was the exception to this family pattern, contenting herself with a little sherry and three long, slim reefers, which she drew from an elegant foil package covered with gold script and Lissajous curves, and which she inhaled sippingly, her lips rapidly shuddering with a very faint, low, trilling sound.

Professor Grissim set the pattern by deprecating the reasons for America's domestic achievements, which I had led off by admitting were far greater than I'd expected. They weren't due to any peculiar American drive, he said, and certainly not to any superior moral fiber, but simply to technology and computerized civilization given their full head and unstinting support. The powerful sweep of those two almost mathematical forces had automatically solved such problems as overpopulation, by effortless and aesthetic contraception, and stagnant or warped brain potential, by unlimited semiautomated education and psychiatry—just as on a smaller scale the drug problem had largely been resolved by the legalization of marijuana and peyote, following the simple principle of restricting only the sale of quickly addictive chemicals and those provably damaging to nervous tissue—"Control the poisons, but let each person learn to control his intoxicants, especially now that we have metabolic rectifiers for the congenitally alcoholic."

I was also told that American extremism, both of the right and left, which had seemed such a big thing in mid-century, had largely withered away or at least been muted by the great surge of the same forces which were making America ever more beautiful and prosperous. Cities were no longer warrens of discontent. Peace marches and Minutemen rallies alike, culminating in the late sixties, had thereafter steadily declined.

While impressed, I did not fall into line, but tried to point out some black holes in this glowing picture. Indeed, feeling at home with the Grissims now and having learned that nothing I could say would shock them into anger and confusion, I was able to be myself fully and to reveal frankly my anti-American ideas, though of course more politely and, I hoped, more tellingly than yesterday—it seemed an age ago—driving from the rocketport.

In particular, I argued that many or most Americans were motivated by a subtle, even sophisticated puritanism, which made them feel that the world was not safe unless they were its moral arbiters, and that this puritanism was ultimately based on the same swollen concern about property and money—industry, in its moral sense—that one found in the Swiss and Scottish Presbyterians and most of the early Protestants.

"You're puritans with a great deal of style and restraint and wide vision," I said. "Yet you're puritans just the same, even though your puritanism is light years away from that of the Massachusettes theocrats and the harsh rule Calvin tried to impose on Geneva. In fact," I added uncautiously, "your puritanism is not so much North European as Roman."

Smiles crinkled briefly at that and I kicked myself for having myself introduced into the conversation that hackneyed comparison.

At this point Emily animatedly yet cooly took up the argument for America, pointing out the nation's growing tolerance and aestheticism, historically distinguishing Puritanism from Calvinism, and also reminding me that the Chinese and Russians were far more puritanical than any other peoples on the globe—and not in a sophisticated or subtle way either.

I fought back, as by citing the different impression I'd got of the Russians during my visits in the Soviet Union and by relaying the reports of close colleagues who had spent time in China. But on the whole Emily had the best of me. And this was only partly due to the fact that the longer I sparred with her verbally, the less concerned I became to win my argument, and the more to break her calm and elicit some sharp emotional reaction from her, to see that pale skin flush, to make those reefer-serene eyes blaze with anger. But I wasn't successful there either.

At one point Jack came to her aid, mildly demonstrating for American broad-mindedness by describing to us some of the pleasure cities of southern Asia he'd visited on R.&R.

"Bangkok's a dismal place now, of course," he began by admitting, "with the Com-g'rillas raiding up to and even into it, and full of fenced-off bombed and booby-trapped areas. Very much like the old descriptions of Saigon in the sixties. As you walk down the potholed streets, you listen for the insect hum of a wandering antipersonnel missile seeking human heat, or the faint flap-flap of an infiltrator coming down on a whirligig parachute. You brace your thoughts against the psychedelic strike of a mind bomb. Out of the black alley ahead there may charge a fifty-foot steel centipede, the remote-controlled sort we use for jungle fighting, captured by the enemy and jiggered to renegade.

"But most of old Bangkok's attractive features—and the entrepreneurs and girls and other entertainers that go with them—have been transferred en masse to Kandy and Trincomalee in Ceylon." And he went on to describe the gaily orgiastic lounges and bars, the fresh pastel colors, the spicy foods and subtly potent drinks, the clean little laughing harlots supporting their families well during the ten years of their working life between fifteen and twenty-five, the gilded temples, the slim dancers with movements stylized as their black eyebrows, the priests robed in orange and yellow.

I tried to fault him in my mind for being patronizing, but without much success.

"Buddhism's an attractive way of life," he finished, "except that it doesn't know how to wage war. But if you're looking only for nirvana, I guess you don't need to know that." For an instant his tough face grew bleak, as if he could do with a spot of nirvana himself, and the shadows gathered around him and the others more thickly.

During the following off-lecture evenings we kept up our fireplace talks and Emily and I returned more than once to our debate over puritanism, while the rest listened to us with faint, benevolent smiles, that at times seemed almost knowing. She regularly defeated me.

Then on the sixth night she delivered her crowning argument, or celebrated her victory, or perhaps merely followed an impulse. I had just settled myself in bed when the indirect lightning of my "doorbell" flooded the room with brief flashes, coming at three-second intervals, of a rather ghastly white light. Blinking, I fumbled on the bedside table for the remote control of the room's appliances, including tri-V and door, and thumbed the button for the latter.

The door moved aside and there, silhouetted against the faint glow of the hall, was the dark figure of Emily, like a living shadow. She kept her finger, however, on the button long enough for two more silent flashes to illuminate her briefly. She was wearing a narrow kimono—Jack's newest gift, she later told me—and her platinum hair, combed straight down like an unrippling waterfall, almost exactly matched the silvery, pale gray silk. Without quite overdoing it, she had made up her face somewhat like a temple dancer's—pale powder, almost white; narrow slanting brows, almost black; green eyeshadow with a pinch of silvery glitter; and the not-quite-jarring sensual note of crimson lips.

She did not come into my room, but after a pause during which I sat up jerkily and she became again a shadow, she beckoned to me.

I snatched up my dressing gown and followed her as she moved noiselessly down the hall. My throat was dry and constricted, my heart was pounding a little, with apprehension as well as excitement. I realized that despite my near week with the Grissims, a part of my mind was still thinking of the professor and his wife as a strait-laced colonel and his lady from a century ago, when so many retired army officers lived in villas around San Antonio, as they do now too around the Dallas-Ft. Worth metropolitan area.

Emily's bedroom was not the austere silver cell or self-shrine I had sometimes imagined, especially when she was scoring a point against me, but an almost cluttered museum-workshop of present interests and personal memorabilia. She'd even kept her kindergarten study-machine, her first CO_2 pistol, and a hockey stick, along with mementos from her college days and her Peace Corps tours.

But those I noticed much later. Now pale golden light from a rising full moon, coming through the great view window, brimmed the room. I had just enough of my wits left to recall that the real moon was new, so that this must be a tape of some past night. I never even thought of the Communist and American forts up there, with their bombs earmarked for Earth. Then, standing straight and tall and looking me full in the eyes, like some Amazonia athlete, or Phryne before her judges, Emily let her kimono glide down from her shoulders.

In the act of love she was energetic, but tender. No, the word is courteous, I think. I very happily shed a week of tensions and uncertainties and self-inflicted humiliations.

"You still think I'm a puritan, don't you?" she softly asked me afterward, smiling at me sideways with the smeared remains of her crimson mouth, her gray eyes enigmatic blurs of shadow.

"Yes, I do," I told her forthrightly. "The puritan playing the hetaera, but still the puritan."

She answered lazily, "I think you like to play the Hun raping the vestal virgin."

That made me talk dirty to her. She listened attentively—almost famishedly, I thought, for a bit—but her final comment was "You do that very well, dear," just before using her lips to stop mine, which would otherwise have sulphurously cursed her insufferable poise.

Next morning I started to write a poem about her but got lost in analysis and speculation. Tried too soon, I thought.

Although they were as gracious and friendly as ever, I got the impression that the other Grissims had quickly become aware of the change in Emily's and my relationship. Perhaps it was that they showed a slight extra fondness toward me. I don't know how they guessed—Emily was as cool as always in front of them, while I kept trying to play myself, as before. Perhaps it was that the argument about puritanism was never resumed.

Two evenings afterward the talk came around to Jack's and Emily's elder brother Jeff, who had fallen during the Great Retreat from Jammu and Kashmir to Baluchistan. It was mentioned that during his last furlough they had been putting up an exchange instructor from Yugoslavia, a highly talented young sculptress. I gathered that she and Jeff had been quite close.

"I'm glad Jeff knew her love," Emily's mother said calmly, a tear behind her voice, though not on her cheeks. "I'm very glad he had that." The professor unobtrusively put his hand on hers.

I fancied that this remark was directed at me and was her way of giving her blessing to Emily's and my affair. I was touched and at the same time irritated—and also irritated at myself for feeling irritated. Her remark had brought back the shadows, which darkened further when Jack said a touch grimly and for once with a soldier's callousness, though grinning at me to remove any possible offense, "Remember not to board any more lady artists or professors, mother, at least when I'm on leave. Bad luck."

By now I was distinctly bothered by my poetry block. The last lectures were going swimmingly and I ought to have been feeling creative, but I wasn't. Or rather, I was feeling creative but I couldn't create. I had also begun to notice the way I was fitting myself to the Grissim family—muting myself, despite all the easiness among us. I couldn't help wondering if there weren't a connection between the two things. I had received the instructorship offer, but was delaying my final answer.

After we made love together that night—under a sinking crescent moon, the real night this time, repeated from above—I told Emily about my first trouble only. She pressed my hand. "Never stop writing poetry, dear," she said. "America needs poetry. This family—"

That broken sentence was as close as we ever got to talking about marriage. Emily immediately recovered herself with an uncharacteristically ribald "Cheer up. I don't even charge a poem for admission."

Instead of responding to that cue, I worried my subject. "I should be able to write poetry here," I said. "America is beautiful, the great golden apple of the Hesperides, hanging in the west like the setting sun. But there's a worm in the core of that apple, a great scaly black dragon."

When Emily didn't ask a question, I went on, "I remember an advertisement. 'Join all your little debts into one big debt.' Of course they didn't put it so boldly, they made it sound wonderful. But you Americans are like that. You've collected all your angers into one big anger. You've removed your angers from things at home—where you seem to have solved your problems very well, I must admit—and directed those angers at the Communist League. Or instead of angers, I could say fears. Same thing."

Emily still didn't comment, so I continued, "Take the basic neurotic. He sets up a program of perfection for himself—a thousand obligations, a thousand ambitions. As long as he works his program, fulfilling those obligations and ambitions, he does very well. In fact, he's apt to seem like a genius of achievement to those around him, as America does to me. But there's one big problem he always keeps out of his program and buries deep in his unconscious—the question of who he really is and what he really wants—and in the end it always throws him."

Then at last Emily said, speaking softly at first, "There's something I should tell you, dear. Although I talk a lot of it from the top of my mind, deep down I loathe discussing politics and international relations. As my old colonel used to tell me, 'It doesn't matter much which side you fight on, Emily, so long as you have the courage to stand up and be counted. You pledge your life, your fortune, and your sacred honor, and you live up to that pledge!' And now, dear, I want to sleep."

Crouching on the edge of her bed before returning to my room, and listening to her breathing regularize itself, I thought, "Yes, you're looking for nirvana too. Like Jack." But I didn't wake her to say it, or any of the other things that were boiling up in my brain.

Yet the things I left unsaid must have stayed and worked in my mind, for at our next fireside talk—four pleasant Americans, one Englishman with only one more lecture to go—I found myself launched into a rather long account of the academic Russian family I stayed with while delivering the Pushkin Lectures in Leningrad, where the smog and the minorities problems have been licked too. I stressed the Rosanovs' gentility, their friendliness, the tolerance and sophistication which had replaced the old rigid insistence on *kulturny* behavior, and also the faint melancholy underlying and somehow vitiating all they said. In short, I did everything I knew to underline their similarity to the Grissims. I ended by saying "Professor Grissim, the first night we talked, you said America's achievement had been due almost entirely to the sweep of science, technology, and computerized civilization. The people of the Communist League believe that too—in fact, they made their declaration of faith earlier than America."

"It's very strange," he mused, nodding. "So like, yet so unlike. Almost as if the chemical atoms of the East were subtly different from those of the West. The very electrons—"

"Professor, you don't actually think—"

"Of course not. A metaphor only."

But whatever he thought, I don't believe he felt it only as a metaphor.

Emily said sharply to me, "You left out one more similarity, the most important. That they hate the Enemy with all their hearts and will never trust or understand him."

I couldn't find an honest and complete answer to that, though I tried.

The next day I made one more attempt to turn my feelings into poetry, dark poetry, and I failed. I made my refusal of the instructorship final, confirmed my reservation on the Dallas-London rocket for day after tomorrow, and delivered the last of the Lanier Lectures.

The Fourth of July was a quiet day. Emily took me on a repeat of our first scooter jaunt, but although I relished the wind on my face and our conversation was passably jolly and tender, the magic was gone. I could hardly see America's beauty for the shadows my mind projected on it.

Our fireside conversation that night was as brightly banal. Midway we all went outside to watch the fireworks. It was a starry night, very clear of course, and the fireworks seemed vastly remote—transitory extra starfields of pink and green and amber. Their faint cracks and booms sounded infinitely distant, and needless to say, there was not a ribbon or whiff of chemical smoke. I was reminded of my last night in Leningrad with the Rosanovs after the Pushkin Lectures. We'd all strolled down the Kirovskiy Prospekt to the Bolshaya Neva, and across its glimmering waters watched the Vladivostok mail rocket take off from the Field of Mars up its ringed electric catapult taller far than the Eiffel Tower. That had been on a May Day.

Later that night I went for the first time by myself to Emily's door and pressed its light-button. I was afraid she wouldn't stop by for me and I needed her. She was in a taut and high-strung mood, unwilling to talk in much more than monosyllables, yet unable to keep still, pacing like a restless feline. She wanted to play in the view window the tape of a real battle in Bolivia with the original sounds too, muted down. I vetoed that and we settled for an authentic forest fire recorded in Alaska.

Sex and catastrophe fit. With the wild red light pulsing and flaring in the bedroom, casting huge wild shadows, and with the fire's muted roar and hurricane crackle and explosions filling our ears, we made love with a fierce and desperate urgency that seemed almost—I am eternally grateful for the memory—as if it would last forever. Sex and a psychedelic trip also have their meeting point.

Afterward I slept like a sated tiger. Emily waited until dawn to wake me and shoo me back to my bedroom.

Next day all the Grissims saw me off. As we strolled from the silver station wagon to the landing area, Emily and I dropped a little behind. She stopped, hooked her arms around me, and kissed me with a devouring ferocity. The others walked on, too well bred ever to look back. The next moment she was her cool self again, sipping a reefer.

Now the rocketship is arching down. The stars are paling. There is a faint whistling as the air molecules of the stratosphere begin to carom off the titanium skin. We had only one flap, midway of freefall section of the trip, when we briefly accelerated and then decelerated to match, perhaps in order to miss a spy satellite or one of the atomic-headed watchdog rockets eternally circling the globe. The direction comes, "Secure seat harnesses."

I just don't know. Maybe I should have gone to America drunk as Dylan Thomas, but purposefully, bellowing my beliefs like the word or the thunderbolts of God. Maybe then I could have fought the shadows. No . . .

I hope Emily makes it to London. Perhaps there, against a very different background, with shadows of a different sort . . .

In a few more seconds the great jet will begin to brake, thrusting its hygienic, aseptic exhaust of helium down into the filthy cancerous London smog, and I will be home.

Ill Met In Lankhmar

Silent as specters, the tall and the fat thief edged past the dead, noose-strangled, watch-leopard, out the thick, lock-picked door of Jengao the Gem Merchant, and strolled east on Cash Street through the thin black night-smog of Lankhmar.

East on Cash it had to be, for west at Cash and Silver was a police post with unbribed guardsmen restlessly grounding and rattling their pikes.

But tall, tight-lipped Slevyas, master thief candidate, and fat, darting-eyed Fissif, thief second class, with a rating of talented in double-dealing, were not in the least worried. Everything was proceeding according to plan. Each carried thonged in his pouch a smaller pouch of jewels of the first water only, for Jengao, now breathing stertoriously inside and senseless from the slugging he'd suffered, must be allowed, nay, nursed and encouraged to build his business again and so ripen it for another plucking. Almost the first law of the Thieves' Guild was never to kill the hen that laid eggs with a ruby in the yolk.

The two thieves also had the relief of knowing that they were going straight home now, not to a wife, Arath forbid!—or to parents and children, all gods forfend!—but to Thieves' House, headquarters and barracks of the almighty Guild, which was father to them both and mother too, though no woman was allowed inside its ever-open portal on Cheap Street.

In addition there was the comforting knowledge that although each was armed only with his regulation silver-hilted thief's knife, they were nevertheless most strongly convoyed by three reliable and lethal bravoes hired for the evening from the Slayers' Brotherhood, one moving well ahead of them as point, the other two well behind as rear guard and chief striking force.

And if all that were not enough to make Slevyas and Fissif feel safe and serene, there danced along soundlessly beside them in the shadow of the north curb a small, malformed or at any rate somewhat large-headed shape that might have been a very small dog, a somewhat undersized cat, or a very big rat.

True, this last guard was not an absolutely unalloyed reassurance. Fissif strained upward to whisper softly in Slevyas' long-lobed ear, "Damned if I like being dogged by that familiar of Hristomilo, no matter what security he's supposed to afford us. Bad enough that Krovas did employ or let himself be cowed into employing a sorcerer of most dubious, if dire, reputation and aspect, but that—"

"Shut your trap!" Slevyas hissed still more softly.

Fissif obeyed with a shrug and employed himself in darting his gaze this way and that, but chiefly ahead.

Some distance in that direction, in fact just short of Gold Street, Cash was bridged by an enclosed second-story passageway connecting the two buildings which made up the premises of the famous stone-masons and sculptors Rokkermas and Slaarg. The firm's buildings themselves were fronted by very shallow porticoes supported by unnecessarily large pillars of varied shape and decoration, advertisements more than structural members.

From just beyond the bridge came two low, brief whistles, a signal from the point bravo that he had inspected that area for ambushes and discovered nothing suspicious and that Gold Street was clear.

Fissif was by no means entirely satisfied by the safety signal. To tell the truth, the fat thief rather enjoyed being apprehensive and even fearful, at least up to a point. So he scanned most closely through the thin, sooty smog the frontages and overhangs of Rokkermas and Slaarg.

On this side the bridge was pierced by four small windows, between which were three large niches in which stood—another advertisement—three life-size plaster statues, somewhat eroded by years of weather and dyed varyingly tones of dark gray by as many years of smog. Approaching Jengao's before the burglary, Fissif had noted them. Now it seemed to him that the statue to the right had indefinably changed. It was that of a man of medium height wearing cloak and hood, who gazed down with crossed arms and brooding aspect. No, not indefinably quite—the statue was a more uniform dark gray now, he fancied, cloak, hood, and face; it seemed somewhat sharper featured, less eroded; and he would almost swear it had grown shorter!

Just below the niches, moreover, there was a scattering of gray and raw white rubble which he didn't recall having been there earlier. He strained to remember if during the excitement of the burglary, the unsleeping watchcorner of his mind had recorded a distant crash, and now he believed it had. His quick imagination pictured the possibility of a hole behind each statue, through which it might be given a strong push and so tumbled onto passersby, himself and Slevyas specifically, the right-hand statue having been crashed to test the device and then replaced with a near twin.

He would keep close watch on all the statues as he and Slevyas walked under. It would be easy to dodge if he saw one start to over-balance. Should he yank Slevyas out of harm's way when that happened? It was something to think about.

His restless attention fixed next on the porticoes and pillars. The latter, thick and almost three yards tall, were placed at irregular intervals as well as being irregularly shaped and fluted, for Rokkermas and Slaarg were most modern and emphasized the unfinished look, randomness, and the unexpected.

Nevertheless it seemed to Fissif, that there was an intensification of unexpectedness, specifically that there was one more pillar under the porticoes than when he had last passed by. He couldn't be sure which pillar as the newcomer, but he was almost certain there was one.

The enclosed bridge was clsoe now. Fissif glanced up at the right-hand statue and noted other differences from the one he'd recalled. Although shorter, it seemed to hold itself more strainingly erect, while the frown carved in its dark gray face was not so much one of philosophic brooding as sneering contempt, self-conscious cleverness, and conceit.

Still, none of the three statues toppled forward as he and Slevyas walked under the bridge. However, something else happened to Fissif at that moment.

One of the pillars winked at him.

The Gray Mouser turned round in the right-hand niche, leaped up and caught hold of the cornice, silently vaulted to the flat roof, and crossed it precisely in time to see the two thieves emerge below.

Without hesitation he leaped forward and down, his body straight as a crossbow bolt, the soles of his ratskin boots aimed at the shorter thief's fat-buried shoulder blades, though leading him a little to allow for the yard he'd walk while the Mouser hurtled toward him.

In the instant that he leaped, the tall thief glanced up over-shoulder and whipped out a knife, though making no move to push or pull Fissif out of the way of the human projectile speeding toward him.

More swiftly than one would have thought he could manage, Fissif whirled round then and thinly screamed, "Slivikin!"

The ratskin boots took him high in the belly. It was like landing on a big cushion. Writhing aside from Slevyas' thrust, the Mouser somersaulted forward, and as the fat thief's skull hit a cobble with a dull *bong* he came to his feet with dirk in hand, ready to take on the tall one.

But there was no need. Slevyas, his eyes glazed, was toppling too.

One of the pillars had sprung forward, trailing a voluminous robe. A big hood had fallen back from a youthful face and long-haired head. Brawny arms had emerged from the long, loose sleeves that had been the pillar's topmost section. While the big fist ending one of the arms had dealt Slevyas a shrewd knockout punch on the chin.

Fafhrd and the Gray Mouser faced each other across the two thieves sprawled senseless. They were poised for attack, yet for the moment neither moved.

Fafhrd said, "Our motives for being here seem identical."

"Seem? Surely must be!" the Mouser answered curtly, fiercely eyeing this potential new foe, who was taller by a head than the tall thief.

"You said?"

"I said, 'Seem? Surely must be!'"

"How civilized of you!" Fafhrd commented in pleased tones.

"Civilized?" the Mouser demanded suspiciously, gripping his dirk tighter.

"To care, in the eye of action, exactly what's said," Fafhrd explained. Without letting the Mouser out of his vision, he glanced down. His gaze traveled from the pouch of one fallen thief to that of the other. Then he looked up at the Mouser with a broad, ingenuous smile.

"Fifty-fifty?" he suggested.

The Mouser hesitated, sheathed his dirk, and rapped out, "A deal!" He knelt abruptly, his fingers on the drawstrings of Fissif's pouch. "Loot you Slivikin," he directed.

It was natural to suppose that the fat thief had been crying his companion's name at the end.

Without looking up from where he knelt, Fafhrd remarked, "That . . . ferret they had with them. Where did it go?"

"Ferret?" the Mouser answered briefly. "It was a marmoset!"

"Marmoset," Fafhrd mused. "That's a small tropical monkey, isn't it? Well, might have been—I've never been south—but I got the impression that—"

The silent, two-pronged rush which almost overwhelmed them at that instant really surprised neither of them. Each had unconsciously been expecting it.

The three bravoes racing down upon them in concerted attack, all with swords poised to thrust, had assumed that the two highjackers would be armed at most with knives and as timid in weapons-combat as the general run of thieves and counter-thieves. So it was they who were thrown into confusion when with the lightning speed of youth the Mouser and Fafhrd sprang up, whipped out fearsomely long swords, and faced them back to back.

The Mouser made a very small parry in carte so that the thrust of the bravo from the east went past his left side by only a hair's breadth. He instantly riposted. His adversary, desperately springing back, parried in turn in carte. Hardly slowing, the tip of the Mouser's long, slim sword dropped under that parry with the delicacy of a princess curtsying and then leaped forward and a little upward and went between two scales of the bravo's armored jerkin and between his ribs and through his heart and out his back as if all were angel food cake.

Meanwhile Fafhrd, facing the two bravoes, from the west, swept aside their low thrusts with somewhat larger, down-sweeping parries in seconde and low prime, then flipped up his sword, as long as the Mouser's but heavier, so that it slashed through the neck of his right-hand adversary, half decapitating him. Then dropping back a swift step, he readied a thrust for the other.

But there was no need. A narrow ribbon of bloodied steel, followed by a gray glove and arm, flashed past him from behind and transfixed the last bravo with the identical thrust the Mouser had used on the first.

The two young men wiped their swords. Fafhrd brushed the palm of his open right hand down his robe and held it out. The Mouser pulled off his right-hand gray glove and shook it. Without word exchanged, they knelt and finished looting the two unconscious thieves, securing the small bags of jewels. With an oily towel and then a dry one, the Mouser sketchily wiped from his face the greasy ash-soot mixture which had darkened it.

Then, after only a questioning eye-twitch east on the Mouser's part and a nod from Fafhrd, they swiftly walked on in the direction Slevyas and Fissif and their escort had been going.

After reconnoitering Gold Street, they crossed it and continued east on Cash at Fafhrd's gestured proposal.

"My woman's at the Golden Lamprey," he explained.

"Let's pick her up and take her home to meet my girl," the Mouser suggested.

"Home?" Fafhrd inquired politely.

"Dim Lane," the Mouser volunteered.

"Silver Eel?"

"Behind it. We'll have some drinks."

"I'll pick up a jug. Never have too much juice."

"True. I'll let you."

Fafhrd stopped, again wiped right hand on robe, and held it out. "Name's Fafhrd."

Again the Mouser shook it. "Gray Mouser," he said a touch defiantly, as if challenging anyone to laugh at the sobriquet.

"Gray Mouser, eh?" Fafhrd remarked. "Well, you killed yourself a couple of rats tonight."

"That I did." The Mouser's chest swelled and he threw back his head. Then with a comic twitch of his nose and a sidewise half-grin he admitted, "You'd have got your second man easily enough. I stole him from you to demonstrate my speed. Besides, I was excited."

Fafhrd chuckled. "You're telling me? How do you suppose I was feeling?"

Once more the Mouser found himself grinning. What the deuce did this big fellow have that kept him from putting on his usual sneers?

Fafhrd was asking himself a similar question. All his life he'd mistrusted small men, knowing his height awakened their instant jealousy. But this clever little chap was somehow an exception. He prayed to Kos that Vlana would like him.

On the northeast corner of Cash and Whore a slow-burning torch shaded by a broad, gilded spiral cast a cone of light up into the thickening black night-smog and another cone down on the cobbles before the tavern door. Out of the shadows into the second cone stepped Vlana, handsome in a narrow black velvet dress and red stockings, her only ornaments a silver-hilted dagger in a silver sheath and a silver-worked black pouch, both on a plain black belt.

Fafhrd introduced the Gray Mouser, who behaved with an almost fawning courtesy. Vlana studied him boldly, then gave him a tentative smile.

Fafhrd opened under the torch the small pouch he'd taken off the tall thief. Vlana looked down into it. She put her arms around Fafhrd, hugged him tight and kissed him soundly. Then she thrust the jewels into the pouch on her belt.

When that was done, he said, "Look, I'm going to buy a jug. You tell her what happened, Mouser."

When he came out of the Golden Lamprey he was carrying four jugs in the crook of his left arm and wiping his lips on the back of his right hand. Vlana frowned. He grinned at her. The Mouser smacked his lips at the jugs. They continued east on Cash. Fafhrd realized that the frown was for more than the jugs and the prospect of stupidly drunken male revelry. The Mouser tactfully walked ahead.

When his figure was little more than a blob in the thickening smog, Vlana whispered harshly, "You had two members of the Thieves' Guild knocked out cold and you didn't cut their throats?"

"We slew three bravoes," Fafhrd protested by way of excuse.

"My quarrel is not with the Slayers' Brotherhood, but that abominable guild. You swore to me that whenever you had the chance—"

"Vlana! I couldn't have the Gray Mouser thinking I was an amateur counter-thief consumed by hysteria and blood lust."

"Well, he told me that *he'd* have slit their throats in a wink, if he'd known I wanted it that way."

"He was only playing up to you from courtesy."

"Perhaps and perhaps not. But you know and you didn't—"

"Vlana, shut up!"

Her frown became a rageful glare, then suddenly she laughed widely, smiled twitchingly as if she were about to cry, mastered herself and smiled more lovingly. "Pardon me, darling," she said. "Sometimes you must think I'm going mad and sometimes I believe I am."

"Well, don't," he told her shortly. "Think of the jewels we've won instead. And behave yourself with our new friends. Get some wine inside you and relax. I mean to enjoy myself tonight. I've earned it."

She nodded and clutched his arm in agreement and for comfort and sanity. They hurried to catch up with the dim figure ahead.

The Mouser, turning left, led them a half square north on Cheap Street to where a narrower way went east again. The black mist in it looked solid.

"Dim Lane," the Mouser explained.

Vlana said, "Dim's too weak—too *transparent* a word for it tonight," with an uneven laugh in which there were still traces of hysteria and which ended in a fit of strangled coughing.

She gasped out, "Damn Lankhmar's night-smog! What a hell of a city!"

"It's the nearness here of the Great Salt Marsh," Fafhrd explained.

And he did indeed have part of the answer. Lying low betwixt the Marsh, the Inner Sea, the River Hlal, and the southern grain fields watered by canals fed by the Hlal, Lankhmar with its innumerable smokes was the prey of fogs and sooty smogs.

About halfway to Carter Street, a tavern on the north side of the lane emerged from the murk. A gape-jawed serpentine shape of pale metal crested with soot hung high for a sign. Beneath it they passed a door curtained with begrimed leather, the slit in which spilled out noise, pulsing torchlight, and the reek of liquor.

Just beyond the Silver Eel the Mouser led them through an inky passageway outside the tavern's east wall. They had to go single file, feeling their way along rough, slimly bemisted brick.

"Mind the puddle," the Mouser warned. "It's deep as the Outer Sea."

The passageway widened. Reflected torchlight filtering down through the dark mist allowed them to make out only the most general shape of their surroundings. Crowding close to the back of the Silver Eel rose a dismal, rickety building of darkened brick and blackened, ancient wood. From the fourth story attic under the ragged-guggered roof, faint lines of yellow light shone around and through three tightly latticed windows. Beyond was a narrow alley.

"Bones Alley," the Mouser told them.

By now Vlana and Fafhrd could see a long, narrow wooden outside stairway, steep yet sagging and without a rail, leading up to the lighted attic. The Mouser relieved Fafhrd of the jugs and went up it quite swiftly.

"Follow me when I've reached the top," he called back. "I think it'll take your weight, Fafhrd, but best one of you at a time."

Fafhrd gently pushed Vlana ahead. She mounted to the Mouser where he now stood in an open doorway, from which streamed yellow light that died swiftly in the night-smog. He was lightly resting a hand on a big, empty, wrought-iron lamp-hook firmly set in a stone section of the outside wall. He bowed aside, and she went in.

Fafhrd followed, placing his feet as close as he could to the wall, his hands ready to grab for support. The whole stairs creaked ominously and each step gave a little as he shifted his weight onto it. Near the top, one step gave way with the muted crack of half-rotted wood. Gently as he could, he sprawled himself hand and knee on as many steps as he could get, to distribute his weight, and cursed sulphurously.

"Don't fret, the jugs are safe," the Mouser called down gayly.

Fafhrd crawled the rest of the way and did not get to his feet until he was inside the doorway. When he had done so, he almost gasped with surprise.

It was like rubbing the verdigris from a cheap brass ring and revealing a rainbow-fired diamond of the first water. Rich drapes, some twinkling with embroidery of silver and gold, covered the walls except where the shuttered windows were—and the shutters of those were gilded. Similar but darker fabrics hid the low ceiling, making a gorgeous canopy in which the flecks of gold and silver were like stars. Scattered about were plump cushions and low tables, on which burned a multitude of candles. On shelves against the walls were neatly stacked like small logs a vast reserve of candles, numerous scrolls, jugs, bottles, and enameled boxes. In a large fireplace was set a small metal stove, neatly blacked, with an ornate firepot. Also set beside the stove was a tidy pyramid of thin, resinous torches with frayed ends—fire-kindlers and other pyramids of small, short logs and gleamingly black coal.

On a low dais by the fireplace was a couch covered with cloth of gold. On it sat a thin, pale-faced, delicately handsome girl clad in a dress of thick violet silk worked with silver and belted with a silver chain. Silver pins headed with amethysts held in place her high-piled black hair. Round her shoulders was drawn a wrap of snow-white serpent fur. She was leaning forward with uneasy-seeming graciousness and extending a narrow white hand which shook a little to Vlana, who knelt before her and now gently took the proffered hand and bowed her head over it, her own glossy, straight, dark-brown hair making a canopy, and pressed its back to her lips.

Fafhrd was happy to see his woman playing up properly to this definitely odd, though delightful situation. Then looking at Vlana's long, red-stockinged leg stretched far behind her as she knelt on the other, he noted that the floor was everywhere strewn —to the point of double, treble, and quadruple overlaps—with thick-piled, close-woven, many-hued rugs of the finest quality imported from the Eastern Lands. Before he knew it, his thumb had shot toward the Gray Mouser.

"You're the Rug Robber!" he proclaimed. "You're the Carpet Crimp!—and the Candle Corsair too!" he continued, referring to two series of unsolved thefts which had been on the lips of all Lankhmar when he and Vlana had arrived a moon ago.

The Mouser shrugged impassive-faced at Fafhrd, then suddenly grinned, his slitted eyes a-twinkle, and broke into an impromptu dance which carried him whirling and jigging around the room and left him behind Fafhrd, where he deftly reached down the hooded and longsleeved huge robe from the latter's stooping shoulders, shook it out, carefully folded it, and set it on a pillow.

The girl in violet nervously patted with her free hand the cloth of gold beside her, and Vlana seated herself there, carefully not too clse, and the two women spoke together in low tones, Vlana taking the lead.

The Mouser took off his own gray, hooded cloak and laid it beside Fafhrd's. Then they unbelted their swords, and the Mouser set them atop folded robes and cloak.

Without those weapons and bulking garments, the two men looked suddenly like youths, both with clar, close-shaven faces, both slender despite the swelling muscles of Fafhrd's arms and calves, he with long red-gold hair falling down his back and about his shoulders, the Mouser with dark hair cut in bangs, the one in brown leather tunic worked with copper wire, the other in jerkin of coarsely woven gray silk.

They smiled at each other. The feeling each had of having turned boy all at once made their smiles embarrassed. The Mouser cleared his throat and, bowing a little, but looking still at Fafhrd, extended a loosely spread-fingered arm toward the golden couch and said with a preliminary stammer, though otherwise smoothly enough, "Fafhrd, my good friend, permit me to introduce you to my princess. Ivrian, my dear receive Fafhrd graciously if you please, for tonight he and I fought back to back against three and we conquered."

Fafhrd advanced, stooping a little, the crown of his red-gold hair brushing the be-starred canopy, and knelt before Ivrian exactly as Vlana had. The slender hand extended to him looked steady now, but was still quiveringly a-tremble, he discovered as soon as he touched it. He handled it as if it were silk woven of the white spider's gossamer, barely brushing it with his lips, and still felt nervous as he mumbled some compliments.

He did not sense that the Mouser was quite as nervous as he, if not more so, praying hard that Ivrian would not overdo her princess part and snub their guests, or collapse in trembling or tears, for Fafhrd and Vlana were literally the first beings that he had brought into the luxurious nest he had created for his aristocratic beloved—save the two love birds that twittered in a silver cage hanging to the other side of the fireplace from the dais.

Despite his shrewdness and cynicism, it never occurred to the Mouser that it was chiefly his charming but preposterous coddling of Ivrian that was making her doll-like.

But now as Ivrian smiled at last, the Mouser relaxed with relief, fetched two silver cups and two silver mugs, carefully selected a bottle of violet wine, then with a grin at Fafhrd uncorked instead one of the jugs the Northerner had brought, and near-brimmed the four gleaming vessels and served them all four.

With no trace of stammer this time, he toasted, "To my greatest theft to date in Lankhmar, which willy-nilly I must share fifty-fifty with"—He couldn't resist the sudden impulse—"with this great, long-haired, barbarian lout here!" And he downed a quarter of his mug of pleasantly burning wine fortified with brandy.

Fafhrd quaffed off half of his, then toasted back, "To the most boastful and finical little civilized chap I've ever deigned to share loot with," quaffed off the rest, and with a great smile that showed white teeth, held out his empty mug.

The Mouser gave him a refill, topped off his own, then set that down to go to Ivrian and pour into her lap from their small pouch the gems he'd filched from Fissif. They gleamed in their new, enviable location like a small puddle of rainbow-hued quicksilver.

Ivrian jerked back a-tremble, almost spilling them, but Vlana gently caught her arm, steadying it. At Ivrian's direction, Vlana fetched a blue-enameled box inlaid with silver, and the two of them transferred the jewels from Ivrian's lap into its blue velvet interior. Then they chatted on.

As he worked through his second mug in smaller gulps, Fafhrd relaxed and began to get a deeper feeling of his surroundings. The dazzling wonder of the first glimpse of this throne room in a slum faded, and he began to note the ricketiness and rot under the grand overlay.

Black, rotten wood showed here and there between the drapes and loosed its sick, ancient stinks. The whole floor sagged under the rugs, as much as a span at the center of the room. Threads of night-smog were coming through the shutters, making evanescent black arabesques against the gilt. The stones of the large fireplace had been scrubbed and varnished, yet most of the mortar was gone from between them; some sagged, others were missing altogether.

The Mouser had been building a fire there in the stove. Now he pushed in all the way the yellow-flaring kindler he'd lit from the fire-pot, hooked the little black door shut over the mounting flames, and turned back into the room. As if he'd read Fafhrd's mind, he took up several cones of incense, set their peaks a-smolder at the fire-pot, and placed them about the room in gleaming, shallow brass bowls. Then he stuffed silken rags in the widest shutter-cracks, took up his silver mug again, and for a moment gave Fafhrd a very hard look.

Next moment he was smiling and lifting his mug to Fafhrd, who was doing the same. Need of refills brought them close together. Hardly moving his lips, the Mouser explained, "Ivrian's father was a duke. I slew him. A most cruel man, cruel to his daughter too, yet a duke, so that Ivrian is wholly unused to fending for herself. I pride myself that I maintain her in grander state than her father did with all his servants."

Fafhrd nodded and said amiably, "Surely you've thieved together a charming little place."

From the couch Vlana called in her husky contralto, "Gray Mouser, your Princess would hear an account of tonight's adventure. And might we have more wine?"

Ivrian called, "Yes, please, Mouser."

The Mouser looked to Fafhrd for the go-ahead, got the nod, and launched into his story. But first he served the girls wine. There wasn't enough for their cups, so he opened another jug and after a moment of thought uncorked all three, setting one by the couch, one by Fafhrd where he sprawled now on the pillowy carpet, and reserving one for himself. Ivrian looked apprehensive at this signal of heavy drinking ahead, Vlana cynical.

The Mouser told the tale of counter-thievery well, acting it out in part, and with only the most artistic of embellishments—the ferret-marmoset before escaping ran up his body and tried to scratch out his eyes—and he was interrupted only twice.

When he said, "And so with a whish and a snick I bared Scalpel—" Fafhrd remarked, "Oh, so you've nicknamed your sword as well as yourself?"

The Mouser drew himself up. "Yes, and I call my dirk Cat's Claw. Any objections? Seem childish to you?"

"Not at all. I call my own sword Graywand. Pray continue."

And when he mentioned the beastie of uncertain nature that had gamboled along with the thieves (and attacked his eyes!), Ivrian paled and said with a shudder, "Mouser! That sounds like a witch's familiar!"

"Wizard's," Vlana corrected. "Those gutless Guild-villains have no truck with women, except as fee'd or forced vehicles for their lust. But Krovas, their current king, is noted for taking *all* precautions, and might well have a warlock in his service."

"That seems most likely; it harrows me with dread," the Mouser agreed with ominous gaze and sinister voice, eagerly accepting any and all atmospheric enhancements of his performance.

When he was done, the girls, eyes flashing and fond, toasted him and Fafhrd for their cunning and bravery. The Mouser bowed and eye-twinklingly smiled about, then sprawled him down with a weary sigh, wiping his forehead with a silken cloth and downing a large drink.

After asking Vlana's leave, Fafhrd told the adventurous tale of their escape from Cold Corner—he from his clan, she from an acting troupe—and of their progress to Lankhmar, where they lodged now in an actors' tenement near the Plaza of Dark Delights. Ivrian hugged herself to Vlana and shivered large-eyed at the witchy parts of his tale.

The only proper matter he omitted from his account was Vlana's fixed intent to get a monstrous revenge on the Thieves' Guild for torturing to death her accomplices and harrying her out of Lankhmar when she'd tried freelance thieving in the city before they met. Nor of course did he mention his own promise—foolish, he thought now—to help her in this bloody business.

After he'd done and got his applause, he found his throat dry despite his skald's training, but when he sought to wet it, he discovered that his mug was empty and his jug too, though he didn't feel in the least drunk—he had talked all the liquor out of him, he told himself, a little of the stuff escaping in each glowing word he'd spoken.

The Mouser was in like plight and not drunk either—though inclined to pause mysteriously and peer toward infinity before answering question or making remark. This time he suggested, after a particularly long infinity-gaze, that Fafhrd accompany him to the Eel while he purchsed a fresh supply.

"But we've a lot of wine left in *our* jug," Ivrian protested. "Or at least a little," she amended. It did sound empty when Vlana shook it. "Besides, you've wine of all sorts here."

"Not this sort, dearest, and first rule is never mix 'em," the Mouser explained, wagging a finger. "That way lies unhealth, aye, and madness."

"My dear," Vlana said, sympathetically patting her wrist, "at some time in any good

411

party all the men who are really men simply have to go out. It's extremely stupid, but it's their nature and can't be dodged, believe me."

"But, Mouser, I'm scared. Fafhrd's tale frightened me. So did yours—I'll hear that familiar a-scratch at the shutters when you're gone, I know I will!"

"Darlingest," the Mouser said with a small hiccup, "there is all the Inner Sea, all the Land of the Eight Cities, and to boot all the Trollstep Mountains in their sky-scraping grandeur between you and Fafhrd's Cold Corner and its silly sorcerers. As for familiars, pish!—they've never in the world been anything but the loathy, all-too-natural pets of stinking old women and womanish old men."

Vlana said merrily, "Let the sillies go, my dear. 'Twill give us chance for a private chat, during which we'll take 'em apart from wine-fumey head to restless foot."

So Ivrian let herself be persuaded, and the Mouser and Fafhrd slipped off, quickly shutting the door behind them to keep out the nigh-smog, and the girls heard their light steps down the stairs.

Waiting for the four jugs to be brought up from the Eel's cellar, the two newly met comrades ordered a mug each of the same fortified wine, or one near enough, and ensconced themselves at the least noisy end of the long serving counter in the tumultuous tavern. The Mouser deftly kicked a rat that thrust head and shoulders from his hole.

After each had enthusiastically complimented the other on his girl, Fafhrd said diffidently, "Just between ourselves, do you think there might be anything to your sweet Ivrian's notion that the small dark creature with Slivikin and the other Guild-thief was a wizard's familiar, or at any rate the cunning pet of a sorcerer, trained to act as go-between and report disasters to his master or to Krovas?"

The Mouser laughed lightly. "You're building bugbears—formless baby ones unlicked by logic—out of nothing, dear barbarian brother, if I may say so. How could that vermin make useful report? I don't believe in animals that talk—except for parrots and such birds, which only . . . parrot.

"Ho, there, you back of the counter! Where are my jugs? Rats eaten the boy who went for them days ago? Or he simply starved to death while on his cellar quest? Well, tell him to get a swifter move on and brim us again!

"No, Fafhrd, even granting the beastie to be directly or indirectly a creature of Krovas, and that it raced back to Thieves' House after our affray, what would that tell them there? Only that something had gone wrong with the burglary at Jengao's."

Fafhrd frowned and muttered stubbornly, "The furry slinker might, nevertheless, somehow convey our appearances to the Guild masters, and they might recognize us and come after us and attack us in our homes."

"My dear friend," the Mouser said condolingly, "once more begging your indulgence, I fear this potent wine is addling your wits. If the Guild knew our looks or where we lodged, they'd have been nastily on our necks days, weeks, nay, months ago. Or conceivably you don't know that their penalty for freelance thieving within the walls of Lankhmar is nothing less than death, after torture, if happily that can be achieved."

"I know all about that, and my plight is worse even than yours," Fafhrd retorted, and after pledging the Mouser to secrecy, told him the tale of Vlana's vendetta against the Guild and her deadly serious dreams of an all-encompassing revenge.

During his story the four jugs came up from the cellar, but the Mouser only ordered that their earthenware mugs be refilled.

Fahfrd finished, "And so, in consequence of a promise given by an infatuated and unschooled boy in a southern angle of the Cold Waste, I find myself now as a sober—well, at other times—man being constantly asked to make war on a power as great as that of Lankhmar's overlord, for as you may know the Guild has locals in all other cities and major towns of this land. I love Vlana dearly and she is an experienced thief herself, but on this one topic she has a kink in her brains, a hard knot neither logic nor persuasion can even begin to loosen."

"Certes t'would be insanity to assault the Guild direct, your wisdom's perfect there," the Mouser commented. "If you cannot break your most handsome girl of this mad notion, or coax her from it, then you must stoutly refuse e'en her least request in that direction."

"Certes I must," Fafhrd agreed with great emphasis and conviction. "I'd be an idiot taking on the Guild. Of course, if they should catch me, they'd kill me in any case for freelancing and highjacking. But wantonly to assault the Guild direct, kill one Guild-thief needlessly—lunacy entire!"

"You'd not only be a drunken, drooling idiot, you'd questionless be stinking in three nights at most from that emperor of diseases, Death. Malicious attacks on her person, blows directed at the organization, the Guild requites tenfold what she does other rule-breaking, freelancing included. So, at least giving-in to Vlana in this one matter."

"Agreed!" Fafhrd said loudly, shaking the Mouser's iron-thewed hand in a near crusher grip.

"And now we should be getting back to the girls," the Mouser said.

"After one more drink while we settle the score. Ho, boy!"

"Suits."

Vlana and Ivrian, deep in excited talk, both started at the pounding rush of foot-steps up the stairs. Racing behemoths could hardly have made more noise. The creaking and groaning were prodigious, and there were the crashes of two treads breaking. The door flew open and their two men rushed in through a great mushroom top of night-smog which was neatly sliced off its black stem by the slam of the door.

"I told you we'd be back in a wink," the Mouser cried gayly to Ivrian, while Fafhrd strode forward, unmindful of the creaking floor, crying, "Dearest heart, I've missed you sorely," and caught up Vlana despite her voiced protests and pushing-off and kissed and hugged her soundly before setting her back on the couch again.

Oddly, it was Ivrian who appeared to be angry at Fafhrd then, rather than Vlana, who was smiling fondly if somewhat dazedly.

"Fafhrd, sir," she said boldly, her little fists set on her narrow hips, her tapered chin held high, her dark eyes blazing, "my beloved Vlana has been telling me about the unspeakably atrocious things the Thieves' Guild did to her and to her dearest friends. Pardon my frank speaking to one I've only met, but I think it quite unmanly of you to refuse her the just revenge she desires and fully deserves. And that goes for you too, Mouser, who boasted to Vlana of what you would have done had you but known, all the while intending only empty ingratiation. You who in like case did not scruple to slay my very own father!"

It was clear to Fafhrd that while he and the Gray Mouser had idly boozed in the Eel, Vlana had been giving Ivrian a doubtless empurpled account of her grievances against the Guild and playing mercilessly on the naive girl's bookish, romantic sympathies and high concept of knightly honor. It was also clear to him that Ivrian was more than a little drunk. A three-quarters empty flask of violet wine of far Kiraay sat on the low table next to the couch.

Yet he could think of nothing to do but spread his big hands helplessly and bow his head, more than the low ceiling made necessary, under Ivrian's glare, now reinforced by that of Vlana. After all, they *were* in the right. He *had* promised.

So it was the Mouser who first tried to rebut.

"Come now, pet," he cried lightly as he danced about the room, silk-stuffing more cracks against the thickening night-smog and stirring up and feeding the fire in the stove, "and you too, beauteous Lady Vlana. For the past month Fafhrd has by his high-jackings been hitting the Guild-thieves where it hurts them most—in their purses a-dangle between their legs. Come, drink we up all." Under his handling, one of the new jugs came uncorked with a pop, and he darted about brimming silver cups and mugs.

"A merchant's revenge!" Ivrian retorted with scorn, not one whit appeased, but rather enangered anew. "At the least you and Fafhrd must bring Vlana the head of Krovas!"

"What would she *do* with it? What *good* would it be except to spot the carpets?" the Mouser plaintively inquired, while Fafhrd, gathering his wits at last and going down on one knee, said slowly, "Most respected Lady Ivrian, it is true I solemnly promised my beloved Vlana I would help her in her revenge, but if Mouser and I should bring Vlana the head of Krovas, she and I would have to flee Lankhmar on the instant, every man's hand against us. While you infallibly would lose this fairyland Mouser has created for love of you and be forced to do likewise, be with him a beggar on the run for the rest of your natural lives."

While Fahrd spoke, Ivrian snatched up her new-filled cup and drained it. Now she stood up straight as a soldier, her pale face flushed, and said scathingly, "*You count the costs!* You speak to me of *things—*" She waved at the many-hued splendor around her, "—of mere property, however costly—when *honor* is at stake. You gave Vlana *your word.* Oh, is knighthood wholly dead?"

Fafhrd could only shrug again and writhe inside and gulp a little easement from his silver mug.

In a master stroke, Vlana tried gently to draw Ivrian down to her golden seat again. "Softly, dearest," she pled. "You have spoken nobly for me and my cause, and believe me, I am most grateful. Your words revived in me great, fine feelings dead these many years. But of us here, only you are truly an aristocrat attuned to the highest properties. We other three are naught but thieves. Is it any wonder some of us put safety above honor and word-keeping, and most prudently avoid risking our lives? Yes, we are three thieves and I am outvoted. So please speak no more of honor and rash, dauntless bravery, but sit you down and—"

"You mean, they're both *afraid* to challenge the Thieves' Guild, don't you?" Ivrian said, eyes wide and face twisted by loathing. "I always thought my Mouser was a noble-man first and a thief second. Thieving's nothing. My father lived by cruel thievery done on rich wayfarers and neighbors less powerful than he, yet he was an aristocrat. Oh, you're *cowards*, both of you! *Poltroons!*" she finished, turning her eyes flashing with cold scorn first on the Mouser, then on Fafhrd.

The latter could stand it no longer. He sprang to his feet, face flushed, fists clenched at his sides, quite unmindful of his down-clattered mug and the ominous creak his sudden action drew from the sagging floor.

"*I am not a coward!*" he cried. "I'll dare Thieves' House and fetch you Krovas' head and toss it with blood a-drip at Vlana's feet. I swear that by my sword Graywand here at my side!"

He slapped his left hip, found nothing there but his tunic, and had to content himself with pointing tremble-armed at his belt and scabbarded sword where they lay atop his neatly folded robe—and then picking up, refilling splashily, and draining his mug.

The Gray Mouser began to laugh in high, delighted tuneful peals. All stared at him. He came dancing up beside Fafhrd, and still smiling widely, asked, "Why not? Who speaks of fearing the Guild-thieves? Who becomes upset at the prospect of this ridiculously easy exploit, when all of us know that all of them, even Krovas and his ruling clique, are but pygmies in mind and skill compared to me or Fafhrd here? A wondrously simple, foolproof scheme has just occurred to me for penetrating Thieves' House, every closet and cranny. Stout Fafhrd and I will put it into effect at once. Are you with me, Northerner?"

"Of course I am," Fafhrd responded gruffly, at the same time frantically wondering what madness had gripped the little fellow.

"Give me a few heartbeats to gather needed props, and we're off!" the Mouser cried. He snatched from shelf and unfolded a stout sack, then raced about, thrusting into it coiled ropes, bandage rolls, rags, jars of ointment and unction and unguent, and other oddments.

"But you can't go tonight," Ivrian protested, suddenly grown pale and uncertain-voiced. "You're both . . . in no condition to."

"You're both drunk," Vlana said harshly. "Silly drunk—and that way you'll get naught in Thieves' House but your deaths. Fafhrd! Control yourself!"

"Oh, no," Fafhrd told her as he buckled on his sword. "You wanted the head of Krovas heaved at your feet in a great splatter of blood, and that's what you're going to get, like it or not!"

"Softly, Fafhrd," the Mouser interjected, coming to a sudden stop and drawing tight the sack's mouth by its strings. "And softly you too, Lady Vlana, and my dear princess. Tonight I intend but a scouting expedition. No risks run, only the information gained needful for planning our murderous strike tomorrow or the day after. So no head-choppings whatsoever tonight. Fafhrd, you hear me? Whatever may hap, hist's the word. And don your hooded robe."

Fafhrd shrugged, nodded, and obeyed.

Ivrian seemed somewhat relieved. Vlana too, though she said, "Just the same you're both drunk."

"All to the good!" the Mouser assured her with a mad smile. "Drink may slow a man's sword-arm and soften his blows a bit, but it sets his wits ablaze and fires his imagination, and those are the qualities we'll need tonight."

Vlana eyed him dubiously.

Under cover of this confab Fafhrd made quietly yet swiftly to fill once more his and the Mouser's mugs, but Vlana noted it and gave him such a glare that he set down mugs and uncorked jug so swiftly his robe swirled.

The Mouser shouldered his sack and drew open the door. With a casual wave at the girls, but no word spoken, Fafhrd stepped out on the tiny porch. The night-smog had grown so thick he was almost lost to view. The Mouser waved four fingers at Ivrian, then followed Fafhrd.

"Good fortune go with you," Vlana called heartily.

"Oh, be careful, Mouser," Ivrian gasped.

The Mouser, his figure slight against the loom of Fafhrd's, silently drew shut the door.

Their arms automatically gone around each other, the girls waited for the inevitable creaking and groaning of the stairs. It delayed and delayed. The night-smog that had entered the room dissipated and still the silence was unbroken.

"What can they be doing out there?" Ivrian whispered. "Plotting their course?"

Vlana impatiently shook her head, then disentangled herself, tiptoed to the door, opened it, descended softly a few steps, which creaked most dolefully, then returned, shutting the door behind her.

"They're gone," she said in wonder.

"I'm frightened!" Ivrian breathed and sped across the room to embrace the taller girl.

Vlana hugged her tight, then disengaged an arm to shoot the door's three heavy bolts.

In Bones Alley the Mouser returned to his pouch the knotted line by which they'd descended from the lamp hook. He suggested, "How about stopping at the Silver Eel?"

"You mean and just *tell* the girls we've been to Thieves' House?" Fafhrd asked.

"Oh, no," the Mouser protested. "But you missed your stirrup cup upstairs—and so did I."

With a crafty smile Fafhrd drew from his robe two full jugs.

"Palmed 'em, as 'twere, when I set down the mugs. Vlana sees a lot, but not all."

"You're a prudent, far-sighted fellow," the Mouser said admiringly. "I'm proud to call you comrade."

Each uncorked and drank a hearty slug. Then the Mouser led them west, they veering and stumbling only a little, and then north into an even narrower and more noisome alley.

"Plague Court," the Mouser said.

After several preliminary peepings and peerings, they staggered swiftly across wide, empty Crafts Street and into Plague Court again. For a wonder it was growing a little lighter. Looking upward, they saw stars. Yet there was no wind blowing from the north. The air was deathly still.

In their drunken preoccupation with the project at hand and mere locomotion, they did not look behind them. There the night-smog was thicker than ever. A high-circling nighthawk would have seen the stuff converging from all sections of Lankhmar in swift-moving black rivers and rivulets, heaping, eddying, swirling, dark and reeking essence of Lankhmar from its branding irons, braziers, bonfires, kitchen fires and warmth fires, kilns, forges, breweries, distilleries, junk and garbage fires innumerable, sweating alchemist's and sorcerers' dens, crematoriums, charcoal burners' turfed mounds, all those and many more . . . converging purposefully on Dim Lane and particularly on the Silver Eel and the rickety house behind it. The closer to that center it got, the more substantial the smog became, eddy-strands and swirl-tatters tearing off and clinging like black cobwebs to rough stone corners and scraggly surfaced brick.

But the Mouser and Fafhrd merely exclaimed in mild, muted amazement at the stars and cautiously zigzagging across the Street of the Thinkers, called Atheist Avenue by moralists, continued up Plague Court until it forked.

The Mouser chose the left branch, which trended northwest.

"Death Alley."

After a curve and recurve, Cheap Street swung into sight about thirty paces ahead. The Mouser stopped at once and lightly threw his arm against Fafhrd's chest.

Clearly in view across Cheap Street was the wide, low, open doorway of Thieves' House, framed by grimy stone blocks. There led up to it two steps hollowed by the treading of centuries. Orange-yellow light spilled out from bracketed torches inside.

There was no porter or guard in sight, not even a watchdog on a chain. The effect was ominous.

"Now how do we get into the damn place?" Fafhrd demanded in a hoarse whisper. "That doorway stinks of traps."

The Mouser answered, scornful at last, "Why, we'll walk straight through that doorway you fear." He frowned. "Tap and hobble, rather. Come on, while I prepare us."

As he drew the skeptically grimacing Fafhrd back down Death Alley until all Cheap Street was again cut off from view, he explained, "We'll pretend to be beggars, members of *their* guild, which is but a branch of the Thieves' Guild and reports in to the Beggarmasters at Thieves' House. We'll be new members, who've gone out by day, so it'll not be expected that the Night Beggarmaster will know our looks."

"But we don't look like beggars," Fafhrd protested. "Beggars have awful sores and limbs all a-twist or lacking altogether."

"That's just what I'm going to take care of now," the Mouser chuckled, drawing Scalpel. Ignoring Fafhrd's backward step and wary glance, the Mouser gazed puzzledly at the long tapering strip of steel he'd bared, then with a happy nod unclipped from his belt Scalpel's scabbard furbished with ratskin, sheathed the sword and swiftly wrapped it up, hilt and all, spirally, with the wide ribbon of a bandage roll dug from his sack.

"There!" he said, knotting the bandage ends. "Now I've a tapping cane."

"What's that?" Fafhrd demanded. "And why?"

The Mouser laid a flimsy black rag across his own eyes and tied it fast behind his head.

"Because I'll be blind, that's why." He took a few shuffling steps, tapping the cobbles ahead with wrapped sword—gripping it by the quillons, or cross guard, so that the grip and pommel were up his sleeve—and groping ahead with his other hand. "That look all right to you?" he asked Fafhrd as he turned back. "Feels perfect to me. Bat-blind!—eh? Oh, don't fret, Fafhrd—the rag's but gauze. I can see through it—fairly well. Besides, I don't have to convince anyone inside Thieves' House I'm actually blind. Most Guild-beggars fake it, as you must know. Now what to do with you? Can't have you blind also—too obvious, might wake suspicion." He uncorked his jug and sucked inspiration. Fafhrd copied this action, on principle.

The Mouser smacked his lips and said, "I've got it! Fafhrd, stand on your right leg and double up your left behind you at the knee. Hold!—don't fall on me! Avaunt! But steady yourself by my shoulder. That's right. Now get that left foot higher. We'll disguise your sword like mine, for a crutch cane—it's thicker and'll look just right. You can also steady yourself with your other hand on my shoulder as you hop—the halt leading the blind. But higher with that left foot! No, it just doesn't come off—I'll have to rope it. But first unclip your scabbard."

Soon the Mouser had Graywand and its scabbard in the same state as Scalpel and was tying Fafhrd's left ankle to his thigh, drawing the rope cruelly tight, though Fafhrd's wine-numbed nerves hardly registered it. Balancing himself with his steel-cored crutch cane as the Mouser worked, he swigged from his jug and pondered deeply.

Brilliant as the Mouser's plan undoubtedly was, there did seem to be drawback to it.

"Mouser," he said, "I don't know as I like having our swords tied up, so we can't draw 'em in emergency."

"We can still use 'em as clubs," the Mouser countered, his breath hissing between his teeth as he drew the last knot hard. "Besides, we'll have our knives. Say, pull your belt around until your knife is behind your back, so your robe will hide it sure. I'll do the same with Cat's Claw. Beggars don't carry weapons, at least in view. Stop drinking now, you've had enough. I myself need only a couple swallows more to reach my finest pitch."

"And I don't know as I like going hobbled into that den of cutthroats. I can hop amazingly fast, it's true, but not as fast as I can run. Is it really wise, think you?"

"You can slash yourself loose in an instant," the Mouser hissed with a touch of impatience and anger. "Aren't you willing to make the least sacrifice for art's sake?"

"Oh, very well," Fafhrd said, draining his jug and tossing it aside. "Yes, of course I am."

"Your complexion's too hale," the Mouser said, inspecting him critically. He touched up Fafhrd's features and hands with pale gray grease paint, then added wrinkles with dark. "And your garb's too tidy." He scooped dirt from between the cobbles and smeared it on Fafhrd's robe, then tried to put a rip in it, but the material resisted. He shrugged and tucked his lightened sack under his belt.

"So's yours," Fafhrd observed, and crouching on his right leg got a good handful of muck himself. Heaving himself up with a mighty effort, he wiped the stuff off on the Mouser's cloak and gray silken jerkin too.

The small man cursed, but, "Dramatic consistency," Fafhrd reminded him. "Now come on, while our fires and our stinks are still high." And grasping hold of the Mouser's shoulder, he propelled himself rapidly toward Cheap Street, setting his bandaged sword between cobbles well ahead and taking mighty hops.

"Slow down, idiot," the Mouser cried softly, shuffling along with the speed almost of a skater to keep up, while tapping his (sword) cane like mand. "A cripple's supposed to be *feeble*—that's what draws the sympathy."

Fafhrd nodded wisely and slowed somewhat. The ominous empty doorway slid again into view. The Mouser tilted his jug to get the last of his wine, swallowed awhile, then choked sputteringly. Fafhrd snatched and drained the jug, then tossed it over shoulder to shatter noisily.

They hop-shuffled across Cheap Street and without pause up the two worn steps and through the doorway, past the exceptionally thick wall. Ahead was a long, straight, high-ceilinged corridor ending in a stairs and with doors spilling light at intervals and wall-set torches adding their flare, but empty all its length.

They had just got through the doorway when cold steel chilled the neck and pricked a shoulder of each of them. From just above, two voices commanded in unison, "Halt!"

Although fired—and fuddled—by fortified wine, they each had wit enough to freeze and then very cautiously look upward.

Two gaunt, scarred, exceptionally ugly faces, each topped by a gaudy scarf binding back hair, looked down at them from a big, deep niche just above the doorway. Two bent, gnarly arms thrust down the swords that still pricked them.

"Gone out with the noon beggar-batch, eh?" one of them observed. "Well, you'd better have a high take to justify your tardy return. The Night Beggarmaster's on a Whore Street furlough. Report above to Krovas. Gods, you stink! Better clean up first, or Krovas will have you bathed in live steam. Begone!"

The Mouser and Fafhrd shuffled and hobbled forward at their most authentic. One niche-guard cried after them, "Relax, boys! You don't have to put it on here."

"Practice makes perfect," the Mouser called back in a quavering voice. Fafhrd's fingerends dug his shoulder warningly. They moved along somewhat more naturally, so far as Fafhrd's tied-up leg allowed. Truly, thought Fafhrd, Kos of the Dooms seemed to be leading him direct to Krovas and perhaps head-chopping *would* be the order of the night. And now he and the Mouser began to hear voices, mostly curt and clipped ones, and other noises.

They passed some doorways they'd liked to have paused at, yet the most they dared do was slow down a bit more.

Very interesting were some of those activities. In one room young boys were being trained to pick pouches and slit purses. They'd approach from behind an instructor, and if he heard scuff of bare foot or felt touch of dipping hand—or, worst, heard *clunk* of dropped leaden mockcoin—that boy would be thwacked.

In a second room, older thieves were doing laboratory work in lock picking. One group was being lectured by a grimy-handed graybeard, who was taking apart a most complex lock piece by weighty piece.

In a third, thieves were eating at long tables. The odors were tempting, even to men full of booze. The Guild did well by its members.

In a fourth, the floor was padded in part and instruction was going on in slipping, dodging, ducking, tumbling, tripping, and otherwise foiling pursuit. A voice like a sergeant-major's rasped, "Nah, nah, nah! You couldn't give your crippled grandmother the slip. I said duck, not genuflect to holy Arth. Now this time—"

By that time the Mouser and Fafhrd were halfway up the end stairs, Fafhrd vaulting somewhat laboriously as he grasped curving banister and swaddled sword.

The second floor duplicated the first, but was as luxurious as the other had been bare. Down the long corridor lamps and filagreed incense pots pendent from the ceiling alternated, diffusing a mild light and spicy smell. The walls were richly draped, the floor thick-carpeted. Yet this corridor was empty too and, moreover, *completely* silent. After a glance at each other, they started off boldly.

The first door, wide open, showed an untennanted room full of racks of garments, rich and plain, spotless and filthy, also wig stands, shelves of beards and such. A disguising room, clearly.

The Mouser darted in and out to snatch up a large green flask from the nearest table. He unstoppered and sniffed it. A rotten-sweet gardenia-reek contended with the nose-sting of spirits of wine. The Mouser sloshed his and Fafhrd's fronts with this dubious perfume.

"Antidote to muck," he explained with the pomp of a physician, stoppering the flask. "Don't want to be parboiled by Krovas. No, no, no."

Two figures appeared at the far end of the corridor and came toward them. The Mouser hid the flask under his cloak, holding it between elbow and side, and he and Fafhrd continued boldly onward.

The next three doorways they passed were shut by heavy doors. As they neared the fifth, the two approaching figures, coming on arm-in-arm, became distinct. Their clothing was that of noblemen, but their faces those of thieves. They were frowning with indignation and suspicion, too, at the Mouser and Fafhrd.

Just then, from somewhere between the two man-pairs, a voice began to speak words in a strange tongue, using the rapid monotone priests employ in a routine service, or some sorcerers in their incantations.

The two richly clad thieves slowed at the seventh doorway and looked in. Their progress ceased altogether. Their necks strained, their eyes widened. They paled. Then all of a sudden they hastened onward, almost running, and by-passed Fafhrd and the Mouser as if they were furniture. The incantatory voice drummed on without missing a beat.

The fifth doorway was shut, but the sixth was open. The Mouser peeked in with one eye, his nose brushing the jamb. Then he stepped forward and gazed inside with entranced expression, pushing the black rag onto his forehead for better vision. Fafhrd joined him.

It was a large room, empty so far as could be told of human and animal life, but filled with most interesting things. From knee-high up, the entire far wall was a map of the city of Lankhmar. Every building and street seemed depicted, down to the meanest hovel and narrowest court. There were signs of recent erasure and redrawing at many spots, and here and there little colored hieroglyphs of mysterious import.

The floor was marble, the ceiling blue as lapis lazuli. The side walls were thickly hung, the one with all manner of thieves' tools, from a huge, thick, pry-bar that looked as if it could unseat the universe, to a rod so slim it might be an elf-queen's wand and seemingly designed to telescope out and fish from a distance for precious gauds on milady's spindle-legged, ivory-topped vanity table. The other wall had padlocked to it all sorts of quaint, gold-gleaming and jewel-flashing objects, evidently mementos chosen for their oddity from the spoils of memorable burglaries, from a female mask of thin gold, breathlessly beautiful in its features and contours but thickly set with rubies simulating the spots of the pox in its fever stage, to a knife whose blade was wedged-shaped diamonds set side by side and this diamond cutting-edge looking razor-sharp.

In the center of the room was a bare round table of ebony and ivory squares. About it were set seven straight-backed but well-padded chairs, the one facing the map and away from the Mouser and Fafhrd being higher backed and wider armed than the others—a chief's chair, likely that of Krovas.

The Mouser tiptoed forward, irresistibly drawn, but Fafhrd's left hand clamped down on his shoulder.

Scowling his disapproval, the Northerner brushed down the black rag over the Mouser's eyes again and with his crutch-hand thumbed ahead, then set off in that direction in most carefully calculated, silent hops. With a shrug of disappointment the Mouser followed.

As soon as they had turned away from the doorway, a neatly black-bearded, crop-haired head came like a serpent's around the side of the highest-backed chair and gazed after them from deep-sunken yet glinting eyes. Next a snake-supple, long hand followed the head out, crossed thin lips with ophidian forefinger for silence, and then finger-beckoned the two pairs of dark-tunicked men who were standing to either side of the doorway, their backs to the corridor wall, each of the four gripping a curvy knife in one hand and a dark leather, lead-weighted bludgeon in the other.

When Fafhrd was halfway to the seventh doorway, from which the monotonous yet sinister recitation continued to well, there shot out through it a slender, whey-faced youth, his narrow hands clapped over his mouth, under terror-wide eyes, as if to shut in screams or vomit, and with a broom clamped in an armpit, so that he seemed a bit like a young warlock about to take to the air. He dashed past Fafhrd and the Mouser and away, his racing footsteps sounding rapid-dull on the carpeting and hollow-sharp on the stairs before dying away.

Fafhrd gazed back at the Mouser with a grimace and shrug, then squatting one-legged until the knee of his bound-up leg touched the floor, advanced half his face past the doorjamb. After a bit, without otherwise changing position, he beckoned the Mouser to approach. The latter slowly thrust half his face past the jamb, just above Fafhrd's.

What they saw was a room somewhat smaller than that of the great map and lit by central lamps that burnt blue-white instead of customary yellow. The floor was marble, darkly colorful and complexly whorled. The dark walls were hung with astrological and anthropomantic charts and instruments of magic and shelved with cryptically labeled porcelain jars and also with vitreous flasks and glass pipes of the oddest shapes, some filled with colored fluids, but many gleamingly empty. At the foot of the walls, where the shadows were thickest, broken and discarded stuff was irregularly heaped, as if swept out of the way and forgot, and here and there opened a large rathole.

In the center of the room and brightly illuminated by contrast was a long table with thick top and many stout legs. The Mouser thought fleetingly of a centipede and then of the bar at the Eel, for the table top was densely stained and scarred by many a split elixir and many a deep black burn by fire or acid or both.

In the midst of the table an alembic was working. The lamp's flame—deep blue, this one—kept a-boil in the large crystal cucurbit a dark, viscid fluid with here and there diamond glints. From out of the thick, seething stuff, strands of a darker vapor streamed upward to crowd through the cucurbit's narrow mouth and stain—oddly, with bright scarlet—the transparent head and then, dead black now, flow down the narrow pipe from the head into a spherical crystal receiver, larger even than the cucurbit, and there curl and weave about like so many coils of living black cord—an endless, skinny, ebon serpent.

Behind the left end of the table stood a tall, yet hunchbacked man in black robe and hood, which shadowed more than hid a face of which the most prominent features were a long, thick, pointed nose with out-jutting, almost chinless mouth. His complexion was sallow-gray like sandy clay. A short-haired, bristly, gray beard grew high on his wide cheeks. From under a receding forehead and bushy gray brows, wide-set eyes looked intently down at an age-browned scroll, which his disgustingly small clubhands, knuckled big, short backs gray-bristled, ceaselessly unrolled and rolled up again. The only move his eyes ever made, besides the short side-to-side one as he read the lines he was rapidly intoning, was an occasional glance at the alembic.

On the other end of the table, beady eyes darting from the sorcerer to the alembic and back again, crouched a small black beast, the first glimpse of which made Fafhrd dig fingers painfully into the Mouser's shoulder and the latter almost gasp, but not from the pain. It was most like a rat, yet it had a higher forehead and closer-set eyes, while its forepaws, which it constantly rubbed together in what seemed restless glee, looked like tiny copies of the sorcerer's clubhands.

Simultaneously yet independently, Fafhrd and the Mouser each became certain it was the beast which had gutter-escorted Slivikin and his mate, then fled, and each recalled what Ivrian had said about a witch's familiar and Vlana about the likelihood of Krovas employing a warlock.

The tempo of the incantation quickened; the blue-white flames brightened and hissed audibly; the fluid in the cucurbit grew thick as lava; great bubbles formed and loudly broke; the black rope in the receiver writhed like a nest of snakes; there was an increasing sense of invisible presences; the supernatural tension grew almost unendurable, and Fafhrd and the Mouser were hard put to keep silent the open-mouthed gapes by which they now breathed, and each feared his heartbeat could be heard yards away.

Abruptly the incantation peaked and broke off, like a drum struck very hard, then instantly silenced by palm and fingers outspread against the head. With a bright flash and dull explosion, cracks innumerable appeared in the cucurbit; its crystal became white and opaque, yet it did not shatter or drip. The head lifted a span, hung there, fell back. While two black nooses appeared among the coils in the receiver and suddenly narrowed until there were only two big black knots.

The sorcerer grinned, let the end of the parchment roll up with a snap, and shifted his gaze from the receiver to his familiar, while the latter chittered shrilly and bounded up and down in rapture.

"Silence, Slivikin! Comes now *your* time to race and strain and sweat," the sorcerer cried, speaking pidgin Lankhmarese now, but so rapidly and in so squeakingly high-pitched a voice that Fafhrd and the Mouser could barely follow him. They did, however, both realize they had been completely mistaken as to the identity of Slivikin. In moment of disaster, the fat thief had called to the witch-beast for help rather than to his human comrade.

"Yes, master," Slivikin squeaked back no less clearly, in an instant revising the Mouser's opinions about talking animals. He continued in the same fife-like, fawning tones, "Harkening in obedience, Hristomilo."

Hristomilo ordered in whiplash pipings, "To your appointed work! See to it you summon an ample sufficiency of feasters!—I want the bodies stripped to skeletons, so the bruises of the enchanted smog and all evidence of death by suffocation will be vanished utterly. But forget not the loot! On your mission, now—depart!"

Slivikin, who at every command had bobbed his head in manner reminiscent of his bouncing, now squealed, "I'll see it done!" and gray lightning-like, leaped a long leap to the floor and down an inky rathole.

Hristomilo, rubbing together his disgusting clubhands much as Slivikin had his, cried chucklingly, "What Slevyas lost, my magic has re-won!"

Fafhrd and the Mouser drew back out of the doorway, partly for fear of being seen, partly in revulsion from what they had seen and heard, and in poignant if useless pity for Slevyas, whoever he might be, and for the other unknown victims of the rat-like and conceivably rat-related sorcerer's deathspells, poor strangers already dead and due to have their flesh eaten from their bones.

Fafhrd wrested the green bottle from the Mouser and, though almost-gagging on the rotten-flowery reek, gulped a large, stinging mouthful. The Mouser couldn't quite bring himself to do the same, but was comforted by the spirits of wine he inhaled.

Then he saw, beyond Fafhrd, standing before the doorway to the map room, a richly clad man with gold-hilted knife jewel-scabbarded at his side. His sunken-eyed face was prematurely wrinkled by responsibility, overwork, and authority, and framed by neatly cropped black hair and beard. Smiling, he silently beckoned them with a serpentine gesture.

The Mouser and Fafhrd obeyed, the latter returning the green bottle to the former, who recapped it and thrust it under his left elbow with well-concealed irritation.

Each guessed their summoner was Krovas, the Guild's Grandmaster. Once again Fafhrd marveled, as he hobbledehoyed along, reeling and belching, how Kos or the Fates were guiding him to his target tonight. The Mouser, more alert and more apprehensive too, was reminding himself that they had been directed by the nich-guards to report to Krovas, so that the situation, if not developing quite in accord with his own misty plans, was still not deviating disastrously.

Yet not even his alertness, nor Fafhrd's primeval instincts, gave them forewarning as they followed Krovas into the map room.

Two steps inside, each of them was shoulder-grabbed and bludgeon-menaced by a pair of ruffians further armed with knives tucked in their belts.

"All secure, Grandmaster," one of the ruffians rapped out.

Krovas swung the highest-backed chair around and sat down, eyeing them coolly.

"What brings two stinking, drunken beggar-guildsmen into the top-restricted precincts of the masters?" he asked quietly.

The Mouser felt the sweat of relief bead his forehead. The disguises he had brilliantly conceived were still working, taking in even the head man, though he had spotted Fafhrd's tipsiness. Resuming his blind-man manner, he quavered, "We were directed by the guard above the Cheap Street door to report to you in person, great Krovas, the Night Beggarmaster being on furlough for reasons of sexual hygiene. Tonight we've made good haul!" And fumbling in his purse, ignoring as far as possible the tightened grip on his shoulders, he brought out a golden coin and displayed it tremble-handed.

"Spare me your inexpert acting," Krovas said sharply. "I'm not one of your marks. And take that rag off your eyes."

The Mouser obeyed and stood to attention again insofar as his pinioning would permit, and smiling the more seeming carefree because of his reawakening uncertainties. Conceivably he wasn't doing quite as brilliantly as he'd thought.

Krovas leaned forward and said placidly yet piercingly, "Granted you were so ordered, why were you spying into a room beyond this one when I spotted you?"

"We saw brave thieves flee from that room," the Mouser answered pat. "Fearing that some danger threatened the Guild, my comrade and I investigated, ready to scotch it."

"But what we saw and heard only perplexed us, great sir," Fafhrd appended quite smoothly.

"I didn't ask you, sot. Speak when you're spoken to," Krovas snapped at him. Then, to the Mouser, "You're an overweening rogue, most presumptuous for your rank. Beggars claim to protect thieves indeed! I'm of a mind to have you both flogged for your spying, and again for your drunkenness, aye, and once more for your lies."

In a flash the Mouser decided that further insolence—and lying, too—rather than fawning, was what the situation required. "I am a most presumptuous rogue indeed, sir," he said smugly. Then he set his face solemn. "But now I see the time has come when I must speak darkest truth entire. The Day Beggarmaster suspects a plot against your own life, sir, by one of your highest and closest lieutenants—one you trust so well you'd not believe it, sir. He told us that! So he set me and my comrade secretly to guard you and sniff out the verminous villain."

"More and clumsier lies!" Krovas snarled, but the Mouser saw his face grow pale. The Grandmaster half rose from his seat. "Which lieutenant?"

The Mouser grinned and relaxed. His two captors gazed sideways at him curiously, losing their grip a little. Fafhrd's pair seemed likewise intrigued.

The Mouser then asked coolly, "Are you questioning me as a trusty spy or a pinioned liar? If the latter, I'll not insult you with one more word."

Krovas' face darkened. "Boy!" he called. Through the curtains of an inner doorway, a youth with the dark complexion of a Kleshite and clad only in a black loincloth sprang to kneel before Krovas, who ordered, "Summon first my sorcerer, next the thieves Slevyas and Fissif," whereupon the dark youth dashed into the corridor.

Krovas hesitated a moment in thought, then shot a hand toward Fafhrd. "What do you know of this, drunkard? Do you support your mate's crazy tale?"

Fafhrd merely sneered his face and folded his arms, the still-slack grip of his captors permitting it, his sword-crutch hanging against his body from his lightly gripping hand. Then he scowled as there came a sudden shooting pain in his numbed, bound-up left leg, which he had forgotten.

Krovas raised a clenched fist and himself wholly from his chair, in prelude to some fearsome command—likely that Fafhrd and the Mouser be tortured, but at that moment Hristomilo came gliding into the room, his feet presumably taking swift, but very short steps—at any rate his black robe hung undisturbed to the marble floor despite his slithering speed.

There was a shock at his entrance. All eyes in the map room followed him, breaths were held, and the Mouser and Fafhrd felt the horny hands that gripped them shake just a little. Even Krovas' tense expression became also guardedly uneasy.

Outwardly oblivious to this reaction to his appearance, Hristomilo, smiling thin-lipped, halted close to one side of Krovas' chair and inclined his hood-shadowed rodent face in the ghost of a bow.

Krovas asked sharply yet nervously, gesturing toward the Mouser and Fafhrd, "Do you know these two?"

Hristomilo nodded decisively. "They just now peered a befuddled eye each at me," he said, "whilst I was about that business we spoke of. I'd have shooed them off, reported them, save such action would have broken my spell, put my words out of time with the alembic's workings. The one's a Northerner, the other's features have a southern cast—from Tovilyis or near, most like. Both younger than their now-looks. Freelance bravoes, I'd judge 'em, the sort the Brotherhood hires as extras when they get at once several big guard and escort jobs. Clumsily disguised now, of course, as beggars."

Fafhrd by yawning, the Mouser by pitying headshake tried to convey that all this was so much poor guesswork. The Mouser even added a warning glare, brief as lightning, to suggest to Krovas that the conspiring lieutenant might be the Grandmaster's own sorcerer.

"That's all I can tell you without reading their minds," Hristomilo concluded. "Shall I fetch my lights and mirrors?"

"Not yet." Krovas faced the Mouser and said, "Now speak truth, or have it magicked from you and then be whipped to death. Which of my lieutenants were you set to spy on by the Day Beggarmaster? But you're lying about that commission, I believe?"

"Oh, no," the Mouser denied it guilelessly. "We reported our every act to the Day Beggarmaster and he approved them, told us to spy our best and gather every scrap of fact and rumor we could about the conspiracy."

"And he told me not a word about it!" Krovas rapped out. "If true, I'll have Blannat's head for this! But you're lying, aren't you?"

As the Mouser gazed with wounded eyes at Krovas, a portly man limped past the doorway with help of a gilded staff. He moved with silence and aplomb.

But Krovas saw him. "Night Beggarmaster!" he called sharply. The limping man stopped, turned, came crippling majestically through the door. Krovas stabbed a finger at the Mouser, then Fafhrd. "Do you know these two, Flim?"

The Night Beggarmaster unhurriedly studied each for a space, then shook his head with its turban of cloth of gold. "Never seen either before. What are they? Fink beggars?"

"But Flim wouldn't know us," the Mouser explained desperately, feeling everything collapsing in on him and Fafhrd. "All our contacts were with Bannat alone."

Flim said quietly, "Bannat's been abed with the swamp ague this past ten-day. Meanwhile I have been Day Beggarmaster as well as Night."

At that moment Slevyas and Fissif came hurrying in behind Flim. The tall thief bore on his jaw a bluish lump. The fat thief's head was bandaged above his darting eyes. He pointed quickly at Fafhrd and the Mouser and cried, "There are the two that slugged us, took our Jengao loot, and slew our escort."

The Mouser lifted his elbow and the green bottle crashed to shards at his feet on the hard marble. Gardenia-reek sprang swiftly through the air.

But more swiftly still the Mouser, shaking off the careless hold of his startled guards, sprang toward Krovas, clubbing his wrapped-up sword.

With startling speed Flim thrust out his gilded staff, tripping the Mouser, who went heels over head, midway seeking to change his involuntary somersault into a voluntary one.

Meanwhile Fafhrd lurched heavily against his left-hand captor, at the same time swinging bandaged Graywand strongly upward to strike his right-hand captor under the jaw. Regaining his one-legged balance with a mighty contortion, he hopped for the loot-wall behind him.

Slevyas made for the wall of thieves' tools, and with a muscle-cracking effort wrenched the great pry-bar from its padlocked ring.

Scrambling to his feet after a poor landing in front of Krovas' chair, the Mouser found it empty and the Thief King in a half-crouch behind it, gold-hilted dagger drawn, deep-sunk eyes coldly battle-wild. Spinning around, he saw Fafhrd's guards on the floor, the one sprawled senseless, the other starting to scramble up, while the great Northerner, his back against the wall weird jewelry, menaced the whole room with wrapped-up Graywand and with his long knife, jerked from its scabbard behind him.

Likewise drawing Cat's Claw, the Mouser cried in trumpet-voice of battle, "Stand aside, all! He's gone mad! I'll hamstring his good leg for you!" And racing through the press and between his own two guards, who still appeared to hold him in some awe, he launched himself with flashing dirk at Fafhrd, praying that the Northerner, drunk now with battle as well as wine and poisonous perfume, would recognize him and guess his stratagem.

Graywand slashed well above his ducking head. His new friend not only guessed, but was playing up—and not just missing by accident, the Mouser hoped. Stooping low by the wall, he cut the lashings on Fafhrd's left leg. Graywand and Fafhrd's long knife continued to spare him. Springing up, he headed for the corridor, crying over-shouldered to Fafhrd, "Come on!"

Hristomilo stood well out of his way, quietly observing. Fissif scuttled toward safety. Krovas stayed behind his chair, shouting, "Stop them! Head them off!"

The three remaining ruffian guards, at last beginning to recover their fighting-wits, gathered to oppose the Mouser. But menacing them with swift feints of his dirk, he slowed them and darted between—and then just in the nick of time knocked aside with a downsweep of wrapped-up Scalpel Flim's gilded staff, thrust once again to trip him.

All this gave Slevyas time to return from the tools-wall and aim at the Mouser a great swinging blow with the massive pry-bar. But even as that blow started, a very long, bandaged and scabbarded sword on a very long arm thrust over the Mouser's shoulder and solidly and heavily poked Slevyas high on the chest, jolting him backwards, so that the pry-bar's swing was short and sang past harmlessly.

Then the Mouser found himself in the corridor and Fafhrd beside him, though for some weird reason still only hopping. The Mouser pointed toward the stairs. Fafhrd nodded, but delayed to reach high, still on one leg only, and rip off the nearest wall a dozen yards of heavy drapes, which he threw across the corridor to baffle pursuit.

They reached the stairs and started up the next flight, the Mouser in advance. There were cries behind, some muffled.

"Stop hopping, Fafhrd!" the Mouser ordered querulously. "You've got two legs again."

"Yes, and the other's still dead," Fafhrd complained. "Ahh! Now feeling begins to return to it."

A thrown knife whished between them and dully clinked as it hit the wall point-first and stone powder flew. Then they were around the bend.

Two more empty corridors, two more curving flights, and then they saw above them on the last landing a stout ladder mounting to a dark, square hole in the roof. A thief with hair bound back by a colorful handkerchief—it appeared to be the door guards' identification—menaced the Mouser with drawn sword, but when he saw there were two of them, both charging him determinedly with shining knives and strange staves or clubs, he turned and ran down the last empty corridor.

The Mouser, followed closely by Fafhrd, rapidly mounted the ladder and vaulted up through the hatch into the star-crusted night.

He found himself near the unrailed edge of a slate roof which slanted enough to have made it look most fearsome to a novice roof-walker, but safe as houses to a veteran.

Turning back at a bumping sound, he saw Fafhrd prudently hoisting the ladder. Just as he got it free, a knife flashed up close past him out of the hatch.

It clattered down near them and slid off the roof. The Mouser loped south across the slates and was halfway from the hatch to that end of the roof when the faint chink came of the knife striking the cobbles of Murder Alley.

Fafhrd followed more slowly, in part perhaps from a lesser experience of roofs, in part because he still limped a bit to favor his left leg, and in part because he was carrying the heavy ladder balanced on his right shoulder.

"We won't need that," the Mouser called back.

Without hesitation Fafhrd heaved it joyously over the edge. By the time it crashed in Murder Alley, the Mouser was leaping down two yards and across a gap of one to the next roof, of opposite and lesser pitch. Fafhrd landed beside him.

The Mouser led them at almost a run through a sooty forest of chimneys, chimney pots, ventilators with tails that made them always face the wind, black-legged cisterns, hatch covers, bird houses, and pigeon traps across five roofs, until they reached the Street of the Thinkers at a point where it was crossed by a roofed passageway much like the one at Rokkermas and Slaarg's.

While they crossed it wat a crouching lope, something hissed close past them and clattered ahead. As they leaped down from the roof of the bridge, three more somethings hissed over their heads to clatter beyond. One rebounded from a square chimney almost to the Mouser's feet. He picked it up, expecting a stone, and was surprised by the greater weight of a leaden ball big as two doubled-up fingers.

"They," he said, jerking thumb overshoulder, "lost no time in getting slingers on the roof. When roused, they're good."

Southeast then through another black chimney-forest toward a point on Cheap Street where upper stories overhung the street so much on either side that it would be easy to leap the gap. During this roof-traverse, an advancing front of night-smog, dense enough to make them cough and wheeze, engulfed them and for perhaps sixty heartbeats the Mouser had to slow to a shuffle and feel his way, Fafhrd's hand on his shoulder. Just short of Cheap Street they came abruptly and completely out of the smog and saw the stars again, while the black front rolled off northward behind them.

"Now what the devil was that?" Fafhrd asked and the Mouser shrugged.

A nighthawk would have seen a vast thick hoop of black night-smog blowing out in all directions from a center near the Silver Eel.

East of Cheap Street the two comrades soon made their way to the ground, landing back in Plague Court.

Then at last they looked at each other and their trammeled swords and their filthy faces and clothing made dirtier still by roof-soot, and they laughed and laughed and laughed, Fafhrd roaring still as he bent over to massage his left leg above and below knee. This hooting self-mockery continued while they unwrapped their swords—the Mouser as if his were a surprise package—and clipped their scabbards once more to their belts. Their exertions had burnt out of them the last mote and atomy of strong wine and even stronger stenchful perfume, but they felt no desire whatever for more drink, only the urge to get home and eat hugely and guzzle hot, bitter gahveh, and tell their lovely girls at length the tale of their mad adventure.

They loped on side by side.

Free of night-smog and drizzled with starlight, their cramped surroundings seemed much less stinking and oppressive than when they had set out. Even Bones Alley had a freshness to it.

They hastened up the long, creaking, broken-treaded stairs with an easy carefulness, and when they were both on the porch, the Mouser shoved at the door to open it with surprise-swiftness.

It did not budge.

"Bolted," he said to Fafhrd shortly. He noted now there was hardly any light at all coming through the cracks around the door, nor had any been noticeable through the lattices—at most, a faint orange-red glow. Then with sentimental grin and in fond voice in which only the ghost of uneasiness lurked, he said, "They've gone to sleep, the unworrying wenches!" He knocked loudly thrice and then cupping his lips called softly at the door crack, "Hola, Ivrian! I'm home safe. Hail, Vlana! Your man's done you proud, felling Guild-thieves innumerable with one foot tied behind his back!"

There was no sound whatever from inside—that is, if one discounted a rustling so faint it was impossible to be sure of it.

Fafhrd was wrinkling his nostrils. "I smell vermin."

The Mouser banged on the door again. Still no response.

Fafhrd motioned him out of the way, hunching his big shoulder to crash the portal.

The Mouser shook his head and with a deft tap, slide, and a tug removed a brick that a moment before had looked to be a firm-set of the wall beside the door. He reached in all his arm. There was the scrape of a bolt being withdrawn, then another, than a third. He swiftly recovered his arm and the door swung fully inward at touch.

But neither he nor Fafhrd rushed in at once, as both had intended to, for the indefinable scent of danger and the unknown came puffing out along with an increased reek of filthy beast and a slight, sickening sweet scent that though female was no decent female perfume.

They could see the room faintly by the orange glow coming from the small oblong of the open door of the little, well-blacked stove. Yet the oblong did not sit properly upright but was unnaturally a-tilt—clearly the stove had been half overset and now leaned against a side wall of the fireplace, its small door fallen open in that direction.

By itself alone, that unnatural angle conveyed the entire impact of a universe overturned.

The orange glow showed the carpets oddly rucked up with here and there ragged black circles a palm's breadth across, the neatly stacked candles scattered about below their shelves along with some of the jars and enameled boxes, and—above all—two black, low, irregular, longish heaps, the one by the fireplace, the other half on the golden couch, half at its foot.

From each heap there stared at the Mouser and Fafhrd innumerable pairs of tiny, rather widely set, furnace-red eyes.

On the thickly carpeted floor on the other side of the fireplace was a silver cobweb —a fallen silver cage, but no love birds sang from it.

There was the faint scrape of metal as Fafhrd made sure Graywand was loose in his scabbard.

As if that tiny sound had beforehand been chosen as the signal for attack, each instantly whipped out sword and they advanced side by side into the room, warily at first, testing the floor with each step.

At the screech of the swords being drawn, the tiny furnace-red eyes had winked and shifted restlessly, and now with the two men's approach they swiftly scattered pattering, pair by red pair, each pair at the forward end of a small, low, slender, hairless-tailed black body, and each making for one of the black circles in the rugs, where they vanished.

Indubitably the black circles were ratholes newly gnawed up through the floor and rugs, while the red-eyed creatures were black rats.

Fafhrd and the Mouser sprang forward, slashing and chopping at them in a frenzy, cursing and human-snarling besides.

They sundered few. The rats fled with preternatural swiftness, most of them disappearing down holes near the walls and the fireplace.

Also Fafhrd's first frantic chop went through the floor and on his third step, with an ominous crack and splintering, his leg plunged through the floor to his hip. The Mouser darted past him, unmindful of further crackings.

Fafhrd heaved out his trapped leg, not even noting the splinter-scratches it got and as unmindful as the Mouser of the continuing creakings. The rats were gone. He lunged after his comrade, who had thrust a bunch of kindlers into the stove, to make more light.

The horror was that, although the rats were all gone, the two longish heaps remained, although considerably diminished and, as now shown clearly by the yellow flames leaping from the tilted black door, changed in hue—no longer were the heaps red-beaded black, but a mixture of gleaming black and dark brown, a sickening purple-blue, violet and velvet black and snow-serpent white, and the reds of stockings and blood and bloody flesh and bone.

Although hands and feet had been gnawed bone-naked, and bodies tunneled heart-deep, the two faces had been spared. But that was not good, for they were purple-blue from death by strangulation, lips drawn back, eyes bulging, all features contorted in agony. Only the black and very dark brown hair gleamed unchanged—that and the white, white teeth.

As each man stared down at his love, unable to look away despite the waves of horror and grief and rage washing higher from the black depression ringing each throat and drift off, dissipating toward the open door behind them—two strands of night-smog.

With a crescendo of crackings the floor sagged three spans more in the center before arriving at a new temporary stability.

Edges of centrally tortured minds noted details: That Vlana's silver-hilted dagger skewered to the floor a rat, which, likely enough, overeager had approached too closely before the night-smog had done its magic work. That her belt and pouch were gone. That the blue-enameled box inlaid with silver, in which Ivrian had put the Mouser's share of the highjacked jewels, was gone too.

The Mouser and Fafhrd lifted to each other white, drawn faces, which were quite mad, yet completely joined in understanding and purpose. No need for Fafhrd to explain why he stripped off his robe and hood, or why he jerked up Vlana's dagger, snapped the rat off it with a wrist-flick, and thrust it in his belt. No need for the Mouser to tell why he searched out a half dozen jars of oil and after smashing three of them in front of the flaming stove, paused, thought, and stuck the other three in the sack at his wrist, adding to them the remaining kindlers and the fire-pot, brimmed with red coals, its top lashed down tight.

Then, still without word exchanged, the Mouser reached into the fireplace and without a wince at the burning metal's touch, deliberately tipped the flaming stove forward, so that it fell door-down on oil-soaked rugs. Yellow flames sprang up around him.

They turned and raced for the door. With louder crackings than any before, the floor collapsed. They desperately scrambled their way up a steep hill of sliding carpets and reached door and porch just before all behind them gave way and the flaming rugs and stove and all the firewood and candles and the golden couch and all the little tables and boxes and jars—and the unthinkably mutilated bodies of their first loves—cascaded into the dry, dusty, cobweb-choked room below, and the great flames of a cleansing or at least obliterating cremation began to flare upward.

They plunged down the stairs, which tore away from the wall and collapsed in the dark as they reached the ground. They had to fight their way over the wreckage to get to Bones Alley.

By then the flames were darting their bright lizard-tongues out of the shuttered attic windows and the boarded-up ones in the story just below. By the time they reached Plague Court, running side by side at top speed, the Silver Eel's fire alarm was clanging cacophonously behind them.

They were still sprinting when they took the Death Alley fork. Then the Mouser grappled Fafhrd and forced him to a halt. The big man struck out, cursing insanely, and only desisted—his white face still a lunatic's—when the Mouser cried panting, "Only ten heartbeats to arm us!"

He pulled the sack from his belt and keeping tight hold of its neck, crashed it on the cobbles—hard enough to smash not only the bottles of oil, but also the fire-pot, for the sack was soon flaming at its base.

Then he drew gleaming Scalpel and Fafhrd Graywand, and they raced on, the Mouser swinging his sack in a great circle beside him to fan its flames. It was a veritable ball of fire burning his left hand as they dashed across Cheap Street and into Thieves' House, and the Mouser, leaping high, swung it up into the great niche above the doorway and let go of it.

The niche-guards screeched in surprise and pain at the fiery invader of their hidey-hole.

Student thieves poured out of the door ahead at the screeching and foot-pounding, and then poured back as they saw the fierce point of flames and the two demonfaced on-comers brandishing their long, shining swords.

One skinny little apprentice—he could hardly have been ten yers old—lingered too long. Graywand thrust him pitilessly through, as his big eyes bulged and his small mouth gaped in horror and plea to Fafhrd for mercy.

Now from ahead of them there came a weird, wailing call, hollow and hair-raising, and doors began to thud shut instead of spewing forth the armed guards Fafhrd and the Mouser prayed would appear to be skewered by their swords. Also, despite the long, bracketed torches looking newly renewed, the corridor was darkening.

The reason for this last became clear as they plunged up the stairs. Strands of night-smog appeared in the stairwell, materializing from nothing, or the air.

The strands grew longer and more tangible. They touched and clung nastily. In the corridor above they were forming from wall to wall and from ceiling to floor, like a gigantic cobweb, and were becoming so substantial that the Mouser and Fafhrd had to slash them to get through, or so their two maniac minds believed. The black web muffled a little a repetition of the eerie, wailing call, which came from the seventh door ahead and this time ended in a gleeful chittering and cackling as insane as the emotions of the two attackers.

Here, too, doors were thudding shut. In an ephemeral flash of rationality, it occurred to the Mouser that it was not he and Fafhrd the thieves feared, for they had not been seen yet, but rather Hristomilo and his magic, even though working in defense of Thieves' House.

Even the map room, whence counterattack would most likely erupt, was closed off by a huge oaken, iron-studded door.

They were now twice slashing the black, clinging, ropethick spiderweb for every single step they drove themselves forward. While midway between the map and magic rooms, there was forming on the inky web, ghostly at first but swiftly growing more substantial, a black spider as big as a wolf.

The Mouser slashed heavy cobweb before it, dropped back two steps, then hurled himself at it in a high leap. Scalpel thrust through it, striking amidst its eight new-formed jet eyes, and it collapsed like a daggered bladder, loosing a vile stink.

Then he and Fafhrd were looking into the magic room, the alchemist's chamber. It was much as they had seen it before, except some things were doubled, or multiplied even further.

On the long table two blue-boiled cucurbits bubbled and roiled, their heads shooting out a solid, writhing rope more swiftly than moves the black swamp-cobra, which can run down a man—and not into twin receivers, but into the open air of the room (if any of the air in Thieves' House could have been called open then) to weave a barrier between their swords and Hristomilo, who once more stood tall though hunch-backed over his sorcerous, brown parchment, though this time his exultant gaze was chiefly fixed on Fafhrd and the Mouser, with only an occasional downward glance at the text of the spell he drummingly intoned.

While at the other end of the table, in web-free space, there bounced not only Slivikin, but also a huge rat matching him in size in all members except the head.

From the ratholes at the foot of the walls, red eyes glittered and gleamed in pairs.

With a bellow of rage Fafhrd began slashing at the black barrier, but the ropes were replaced from the cucurbit heads as swiftly as he sliced them, while the cut ends, instead of drooping slackly, now began to strain hungrily toward him like constrictive snakes or stranglevines.

He suddenly shifted Graywand to his left hand, drew his long knife and hurled it at the sorcerer. Flashing toward its mark, it cut through three strands, was deflected and slowed by a fourth and fifth, almost halted by a sixth, and ended hanging futilely in the curled grip of a seventh.

Hristomilo laughed cackingly and grinned, showing his huge upper incisors, while Slivikin chittered in ecstasy and bounded the higher.

The Mouser hurled Cat's Claw with no better result—worse, indeed, since his action gave two darting smog-strands time to curl hamperingly around his sword-hand and stranglingly around his neck. Black rats came racing out of the big holes at the cluttered base of the walls.

Meanwhile other strands snaked around Fafhrd's ankles, knees and left arm, almost toppling him. But even as he fought for balance, he jerked Vlana's dagger from his belt and raised it over his shoulder, its silver hilt glowing, its blade brown with dried rat's-blood.

The grin left Hristomilo's face as he saw it. The sorcerer screamed strangely and importuningly then, and drew back from his parchment and the table, and raised clawed clubhands to ward off doom.

Vlana's dagger sped unimpeded through the black web—its strands even seemed to part for it—and betwixt the sorcerer's warding hands, to bury itself to the hilt in his right eye.

He screamed thinly in dire agony and clawed at his face.

The black web writhed as if in death spasm.

The cucurbits shattered as one, spilling their lava on the scarred table, putting out the blue flames even as the thick wood of the table began to smoke a little at the lava's edge. Lava dropped with *plops* on the dark marble floor.

With a faint, final scream Hristomilo pitched forward, hands clutched to his eyes above his jutting nose, silver dagger-hilt protruding between his fingers.

The web grew faint, like wet ink washed with a gush of clear water.

The Mouser raced forward and transfixed Slivikin and the huge rat with one thrust of Scalpel before the beasts knew what was happening. They too died swiftly with thin screams, while all the other rats turned tail and fled back down their holes swift almost as black lightning.

Then the last trace of night-smog or sorcery-smoke vanished, and Fafhrd and the Mouser found themselves standing alone with three dead bodies amidst a profound silence that seemed to fill not only this room but all Thieves' House. Even the cucurbit-lava had ceased to move, was hardening, and the wood of the table no longer smoked.

Their madness was gone and all their rage, too—vented to the last red atomy and glutted to more than satiety. They had no more urge to kill Krovas or any other thieves than to swat flies. With horrified inner-eye Fafhrd saw the pitiful face of the child-thief he'd skewered in his lunatic anger.

Only their grief remained with them, diminished not one whit, but rather growing greater—that and an ever more swiftly growing revulsion from all that was around them: the dead, the disordered magic room, all Thieves' House, all of the city of Lankhmar to its last stinking alleyway.

With a hiss of disgust the Mouser jerked Scalpel from the rodent cadavers, wiped it on the nearest cloth, and returned it to its scabbard. Fafhrd likewise sketchily cleansed and sheathed Graywand. The the two men picked up their knife and dirk from where they'd dropped to the floor when the web had dematerialized, though neither glanced at Vlana's dagger where it was buried. But on the sorcerer's table they did notice Vlana's black velvet, silver-worked pouch and belt, and Ivrian's blue-enameled box inlaid with silver. These they took.

With no more word than they had exchanged back at the Mouser's burnt nest behind the Eel, but with a continuing sense of their unity of purpose, their identity of intent, and of their comradeship, they made their way with shoulders bowed and with slow, weary steps which only very gradually quickened out of the magic room and down the thick-carpeted corridor, past the map room's wide door now barred with oak and iron, and past all the other shut, silent door, down the echoing stairs, their footsteps speeding a little; down the bare-floored lower corridor past its closed, quiet doors, their footsteps resounding loudly no matter how softly they sought to tread; under the deserted, black-scorched guard-niche, and so out into Cheap Street, turning left and north because that was the nearest way to the Street of the Gods, and there turning right and east—not a waking soul in the wide street except for one skinny, bent-backed apprentice lad unhappily swabbing the flagstones in front of a wine shop in the dim pink light beginning to seep from the east, although there were many forms asleep, a-snore and a-dream in the gutters and under the dark porticoes—yes, turning right and east down the Street of the Gods, for that way was the Marsh Gate, leading to Causey Road across the Great Salt Marsh; and the Marsh Gate was the nearest way out of the great and glamorous city that was now loathsome to them, a city of beloved, unfaceable ghosts—indeed, not to be endured for one more stabbing, leaden heartbeat than was necessary.

The Bait

Fafhrd the Northerner was dreaming of a great mound of gold.

The Gray Mouser the Southern, ever cleverer in his forever competitive fashion, was dreaming of a heap of diamonds. He hadn't tossed out all of the yellowish ones yet, but he guessed that already his glistening pile must be worth more than Fafhrd's glowing one.

How he knew in his dream what Fafhrd was dreaming was a mystery to all beings in Newhon, except perhaps Sheelba of the Eyeless Face and Ninguable of the Seven Eyes, respectively the Mouser's and Fafhrd's sorcerer-mentors. Maybe, a vast, black basement mind shared by two was involved.

Simultaneously they awoke, Fafhrd a shade more slowly, and sat up in bed.

Standing midway between the feet of their cots was an object that fixed their attention. It weighed about eighty pounds, was about four feet eight inches tall, had long straight black hair pendent from head, had ivory-white skin, and was as exquisitely formed as a slim chesspiece of the King of Kings carved from a single moonstone. It looked thirteen, but the lips smiled a cool self-infatuated seventeen, while the gleaming deep eye-pools were first blue melt of the Ice Age. Naturally, she was naked.

"She's mine!" the Gray Mouser said, always quick from the scabbard.

"No, she's mine!" Fafhrd said almost simultaneously, but conceding by that initial "No" that the Mouser had been first, or at least he had expected the Mouser to be first.

"I belong to myself and to no one else, save two or three virile demidevils," the small naked girl said, though giving them each in turn a most nymphish lascivious look.

"I'll fight you for her," the Mouser proposed.

"And I you," Fafhrd confirmed, slowly drawing Graywand from its sheath beside his cot.

The Mouser likewise slipped Scalpel from its rat-skin container.

The two heroes rose from their cots.

At this moment, two personages appeared a little behind the girl—from thin air, to all appearances. Both were at least nine feet tall. They had to bend, not to bump the ceiling. Cobwebs tickled their pointed ears. The one on the Mouser's side was black as wrought iron. He swiftly drew a sword that looked forged from the same material.

At the same time, the other newcomer—bone-white, this one—produced a silver-seeming sword, likely steel plated within.

The nine-footer opposing the Mouser aimed a skull-spitting blow at the top of his head. The Mouser parried in prime and his opponent's weapon shrieked off to the left.

Whereupon, smartly swinging his rapier widdershins, the Mouser slashed off the black fiend's head, which struck the floor with a horrid clank.

The white afreet opposing Fafhrd trusted to a downward thrust. But the Northerner, catching him through, the silvery sword missing Fafhrd's right temple by the thinness of a hair.

With a petulant stamp of her naked heel, the nymphet vanished into thin air, or perhaps Limbo.

The Mouser made to wipe off his blade on the cot-clothes, but discovered there was no need. He shrugged. "What a misfortune for you, comrade," he said in a voice of mocking woe. "Now you will not be able to enjoy the delicious chit as she disports herself on your heap of gold."

Fafhrd moved to cleanse Graywand on *his* sheets, only to note that it too was altogether unbloodied. He frowned. "Too bad for you, best of friends," he sympathized. "Now you won't be able to possess her as she writhes with girlish abandon on your couch of diamonds, their glitter striking opalescent tones from her pale flesh."

"Mauger that effeminate artistic garbage, how did you know that I was dreaming diamonds?" the Mouser demanded.

"How did I?" Fafhrd asked himself wonderingly. At last he begged the question with, "The same way, I suppose, that you knew I was dreaming of gold."

The two excessively long corpses chose that moment to vanish, and the severed head with them.

Fafhrd said sagely, "Mouser, I begin to believe that supernatural forces were involved in this morning's haps."

"Or else hallucinations, oh great philosopher," the Mouser countered somewhat peevishly.

"Not so," Fafhrd corrected, "forsee, they've left their weapons behind."

"True enough," the Mouser conceded, rapaciously eyeing the wrought iron and tin plated blades on the floor. "Those will fetch a fancy price on Curio Court."

The Great Gong of Lankhmar, sounding distantly through the walls, boomed out the twelve funeral strokes of noon, when burial parties plunge spade into earth.

"An after-omen," Fafhrd pronounced. "Now we know the source of the supernal force. The Shadowland, terminus of all funerals."

"Yes," the Mouser agreed. "Prince Death, that eager boy, has had another go at us."

Fafhrd splashed cool water onto his face from a great bowl set against the wall. "Ah well," he spoke through the splashes, "'Twas a pretty bait at least. Truly, there's nothing like a nubile girl, enjoyed or merely glimpsed naked, to give one an appetite for breakfast."

"Indeed yes," the Mouser replied, as he tightly shut his eyes and briskly rubbed his face with a palm full of white brandy. "She was just the sort of immature dish to kindle your satyrish taste for maids newly budded."

In the silence that came as the splashing stopped, Fafhrd inquired innocently, "*Whose* satyrish taste?"

Midnight by the Morphy Watch

Being world's chess champion (crowned or uncrowned) puts a more deadly and maddening strain on a man even than being President of the United States. We have a prime example enthroned right now. For more than ten years the present champion was clearly the greatest chess player in the world, but during that time he exhibited such willful and seemingly self-destructive behavior—refusing to enter crucial tournaments, quitting them for crankish reasons while holding a commanding lead, entertaining what many called a paranoid delusion that the world was plotting to keep him from reaching the top—that many informed experts wrote him off as a contender for the highest honors. Even his staunchest supporters experienced agonizing doubts— until he finally silenced his foes and supremely satisfied his friends by decisively winning the crucial and ultimate match on a fantastic polar island.

Even minor players bitten by the world's-championship bug—or the fantasy of it—experience a bit of that terrible strain, occasionally in very strange and even eerie fashion . . .

Stirf Ritter-Rebil was indulging in one of his numerous creative avocations— wandering at random through his beloved downtown San Francisco with its sometimes dizzily slanting sidewalks, its elusive narrow courts and alleys, and its kaleidoscope of ever-changing store and restaurant-fronts amongst the ones that persist as landmarks. To divert his gaze, there were interesting almond and black faces among the paler ones. There was the dangerous surge of traffic threatening to invade the humpy sidewalks.

The sky was a careless silvery grey, like an expensive whore's mink coat covering bizarre garb or nakedness. There were even wisps of fog, that Bay Area benison. There were bankers and hippies, con men and corporation men, queers of all varieties, beggars and sports, murderers and saints (at least in Ritter's freewheeling imagination). And there were certainly alluring girls aplenty in an astounding variety of packages—and pretty girls are the essential spice in any really tasty ragout of people. In fact there may well have been Martians and time travelers.

Ritter's ramble had taken on an even more dream-like, whimsical quality than usual—with an unflagging anticipation of mystery, surprise, and erotic or diamond-studded adventure around the very next corner.

He frequently thought of himself by his middle name, Ritter, because he was a sporadically ardent chess player now in the midst of a sporad. In German "Ritter" means "knight," yet Germans do not call a knight a Ritter, but a springer, or jumper (for its crookedly hopping move), a matter for inexhaustible philological, historical, socioracial speculation. Ritter was also a deeply devoted student of the history of chess, both in its serious and anecdotal aspects.

He was a tall, white-haired man, rather thin, saved from the look of mere age by ravaged handsomeness, an altogether youthful though worldly and sympathetically cynical curiosity in his gaze (when he wasn't daydreaming), and a definitely though unobtrusively theatrical carriage.

He was more daydreamingly lost than usual on this particular ramble, though vividly aware of all sorts of floating, freakish, beautiful and grotesque novelties about him. Later he recollected that he must have been fairly near Portsmouth Square and not terribly far from the intersection of California and Montgomery. At all events, he was fascinatedly looking into the display window of a secondhand store he'd never recalled seeing before. It must be a new place, for he knew all the stores in the area, yet it had the dust and dinginess of an *old* place—its owner must have moved in without refurbishing the premises or even cleaning them up. And it had a delightful range of items for sale, from genuine antiques to mod facsimiles of same. He noted in his first scanning glance, and with growing delight, a Civil War saber, a standard promotional replica of the starship *Enterprise,* a brand-new deck of tarots, an authentic shrunken head like a black globule of detritus from a giant's nostril, some fancy roach-clips, a silver lusterware creamer, a Sony tape recorder, a last year's whiskey jug in the form of a cable car, a scatter of Gene McCarthy and Nixon buttons, a single brass Lucas "King of the Road" headlamp from a Silver Ghost Rolls Royce, an electric toothbrush, a 1920's radio, a last month's copy of the *Phoenix,* and three dime-a-dozen plastic chess sets.

*   *   *

And then, suddenly, all these were wiped from his mind. Unnoticed were the distant foghorns, the complaining prowl of slowed traffic, the shards of human speech behind him mosaicked with the singsong chatter of Chinatown, the reflection in the plate glass of a girl in a grandmother dress selling flowers, and of opening umbrellas as drops of rain began to sprinkle from the mist. For every atom of Stirf Ritter-Rebil's awareness was burningly concentrated on a small figure seeking anonymity among the randomly set-out chessmen of one of the plastic sets. It was a squat, tarnished silver chess pawn in the form of a barbarian warrior. Ritter knew it was a chess pawn—and what's more, he knew to what fabulous historic set it belonged, because he had seen one of its mates in a rare police photograph given him by a Portuguese chess-playing acquaintance. He knew that he had quite without warning arrived at a once-in-a-lifetime experience.

Heart pounding but face a suave mask, he drifted into the store's interior. In situations like this it was all-essential not to let the seller know what you were interested in or even that you were interested at all.

The shadowy interior of the place lived up to its display window. There was the same piquant clutter of dusty memorables and among them several glass cases housing presumably choicer items, behind one of which stood a gaunt yet stocky elderly man whom Ritter sensed was the proprietor, but pretended not even to notice.

But his mind was so concentrated on the tarnished silver pawn he *must* possess that it was a stupefying surprise when his automatically flitting gaze stopped at a second and even greater once-in-a-lifetime item in the glass case behind which the proprietor stood. It was a dingy, old-fashioned gold pocket watch with the hours not in Roman numerals as they should have been in so venerable a timepiece, but in the form of dull gold and silver chess pieces as depicted in game-diagrams. Attached to the watch

436

by a bit of thread was a slim, hexagonal gold key.

Ritter's mind almost froze with excitement. Here was the big brother of the skulking barbarian pawn. Here, its true value almost certainly unknown to its owner, was one of the supreme rarities of the world of chess-memorabilia. Here was no less than the gold watch Paul Morphy, meteorically short-reigned King of American chess, had been given by an adoring public in New York City on May 25, $859, after the triumphal tour of London and Paris which had proven him to be perhaps the greatest chess genius of all time.

Ritter veered as if by lazy chance toward the case, his eyes resolutely fixed on a dull silver ankh at the opposite end from the chess watch.

He paused like a sleepwalker across from the proprietor after what seemed like a suitable interval and—hoping the pounding of his heart wasn't audible—made a desultory inquiry about the ankh. The proprietor replied in as casual fashion, though getting the item out for his inspection.

Ritter brooded over the silver love-cross for a bit, then shook his head and idly asked about another item and still another, working his insidious way toward the Morphy watch.

The proprietor responded to his queries in a low, bored voice, though in each case dutifully getting the item out to show Ritter. He was a very old and completely bald man with a craggy Baltic cast to his features. He vaguely reminded Ritter of someone.

Finally Ritter was asking about an old silver railroad watch next to the one he still refused to look at directly.

Then he shifted to another old watch with a complicated face with tiny windows showing the month and the phases of the moon, on the other side of the one that was keeping his heart a-pound.

His gambit worked. The proprietor at last dragged out the Morphy watch, saying softly, "Here is an odd old piece that might interest you. The case is solid gold. It threatens to catch your interest, does it not?"

Ritter at last permitted himself a second devouring glance. It confirmed the first the first. Beyond a shadow of a doubt this was the genuine relic that had haunted his thoughts for two thirds of a lifetime.

What he said was "It's odd, all right. What are those funny little figures it has in place of hours?"

"Chessmen," the other explained. "See, that's a King at six o'clock, a pawn at five, a Bishop at four, a Knight at three, a Rook at two, a Queen at one, another King at midnight, and then repeat, eleven to seven, around the dial."

"Why midnight rather than noon?" Ritter asked stupidly. He knew why.

The proprietor's wrinkled fingernail indicated a small window just above the center of the face. In it showed the letters P.M. "That's another rare feature," he explained. "I've handled very few watches that knew the difference between night and day."

"Oh, and I suppose those squares on which the chessmen are placed and which go around the dial in two and a half circles make a sort of checkerboard?"

"Chessboard," the other corrected. "Incidentally, there are exactly sixty-four squares, the right number."

Ritter nodded. "I suppose you're asking a fortune for it," he remarked, as if making conversation.

The other shrugged, "Only a thousand dollars."

Ritter's heart skipped a beat. He had more than ten times that in his bank account. A trifle, considering the stake.

But he bargained for the sake of appearances. At one point he argued, "But the watch doesn't run, I suppose."

"But it still has its hands," the old Balt with the hauntingly familiar face countered. "And it still has its works, as you can tell by the weight. They could be repaired, I imagine. A French movement. See, there's the hexagonal winding-key still with it."

A price of seven hundred dollars was finally agreed on. He paid out the fifty dollars he always carried with him and wrote a check for the remainder. After a call to his bank, it was accepted.

The watch was packed in a small box in a nest of fluffy cotton. Ritter put it in a pocket of his jacket and buttoned the flap.

He felt dazed. The Morphy watch, the watch Paul Morphy had kept his whole short life, despite his growing hatred of chess, the watch he had willed to his French admirer and favorite opponent Jules Arnous de Riviere, the watch that had then mysteriously disappeared, the watch of watches—was his!

He felt both weightless and dizzy as he moved toward the street, which blurred a little.

As he was leaving he noticed in the window something he'd forgotten—he wrote a check for fifty dollars for the silver barbarian pawn without bargaining.

He was in the street, feeling glorious and very tired. Faces and umbrellas were alike blurs. Rain pattered on his face unnoticed, but there came a stab of anxiety.

He held still and very carefully used his left hand to transfer the heavy little box —and the pawn in a twist of paper—to his trouser pocket, where he kept his left hand closed around them. Then he felt secure.

He flagged down a cab and gave his home address.

The passing scene began to come unblurred. He recognized Rimini's Italian Restaurant where his own chess game was now having a little renaissance after five years of foregoing tournament chess because he knew he was too old for it. A chess-smitten young cook there, indulged by the owner, had organized a tourney. The entrants were mostly young people. A tall, moody girl he thought of as the Czarina, who played a remarkable game, and a likable, loudmouthed young Jewish lawyer he thought of as Rasputin, who played almost as good a game and talked a better one, both stood out. On impulse Ritter had entered the tournament because it was such a trifling one that it didn't really break his rule against playing chess. And, his old skills reviving nicely, he had done well enough to have a firm grip on third place, right behind Rasputin and the Czarina.

But now that he had the Morphy watch . . .

Why the devil should he think that having the Morphy watch should improve his chess game? he asked himself sharply. It was as silly as faith in the power of the relics of saints.

In his hand inside his left pocket the watch box vibrated eagerly, as if it contained a big live insect, a golden bee or beetle. But that, of course, was his imagination.

Stirf Ritter-Rebil (a proper name, he always felt, for a chess player, since they specialize in weird ones, from Euwe to Znosko-Borovsky, from Noteboom to Dus-Chotimirski) lived in a one-room and bath, five blocks west of Union Square and packed with files, books, and also paintings wherever the wall space allowed, of his dead wife and parents, and of his son. Now that he was older, he liked living with clues to all of his life in view. There was a fine view of the Pacific and the Golden Gate and their fogs to the west, over a sea of roofs. On the orderly cluttered tables were two fine chess sets with positions set up.

Ritter cleared a space beside one of them and set in its center the box and packet. After a brief pause—as if for propitiatory prayer, he gingerly took out the Morphy watch and centered it for inspection with the unwrapped silver pawn behind it.

Then, wiping and adjusting his glasses and from time to time employing a large magnifying glass, he examined both treasures exhaustively.

The outer edge of the dial was circled with a ring or wheel of twenty-four squares, twelve pale and twelve dark alternating. On the pale squares were the figures of chessmen indicating the hours, placed in the order the old Balt had described. The Black pieces went from midnight to five and were of silver set with tiny emeralds or bright jade, as his magnifying glass confirmed. The White pieces went from six to eleven and were of gold set with minute rubies or amethysts. He recalled that descriptions of the watch always mentioned the figures as being colored.

Inside that came a second circle of twenty-four pale and dark squares.

Finally, inside *that*, there was a two-thirds circle of sixteen squares below the center of the dial.

In the corresponding space above the center was the little window showing P.M.

The hands on the dial were stopped at 11:57—three minutes to midnight.

With a paper knife he carefully pried open the hinged back of the watch, on which were floridly engraved the initials PM—which he suddenly realized also stood for Paul Morphy.

On the inner golden back covering the works was engraved "France H&H"—the old Balt was right again—while scratched in very tiny—he used his magnifier once more—were a half dozen sets of numbers, most of the sevens having the French slash. Pawnbrokers' marks. Had Arnous de Riviere pawned the treasure? Or later European owners? Oh well, chess players were an impecunious lot. There was also a hole by which the watch could be wound with its hexagonal key. He carefully wound it but of course nothing happened.

He closed the back and brooded on the dial. The sixty-four squares—twenty-four plus twenty-four plus sixteen—made a fantastic circular board. One of the many variants of chess he had played once or twice was cylindrical.

"*Les échecs fantasques,*" he quoted. "It's a cynical madman's allegory with its doddering monarch, vampire queen, gangster knights, double-faced bishops, ramming rooks and inane pawns, whose supreme ambition is to change their sex and share the dodderer's bed."

With a sigh of regret he tore his gaze away from the watch and took up the pawn behind it. Here was a grim little fighter, he thought, bringing the tarnished silver figure close to his glasses. Naked long-sword clasped against his chest, point down, iron skullcap low on forehead, face merciless as Death's. What did the golden legionaries look like?

Then Ritter's expression grew grim, too, as he decided to do something he'd had in mind ever since glimpsing the barbarian pawn in the window. Making a long arm, he slid out a file drawer and after flipping a few tabs drew out a folder marked "Death of Alekhine." The light was getting bad. He switched on a big desk lamp against the night.

Soon he was studying a singularly empty photograph. It was of an unoccupied old armchair with a peg-in chess set open on one of the flat wooden arms. Behind the chess set stood a tiny figure. Bringing the magnifying glass once more into play, he confirmed what he had expected: that it was a precise mate to the barbarian pawn he had bought today.

He glanced through another item from the folder—an old letter on onionskin paper in a foreign script with cedillas under half the "C's" and tildes over half the "A's."

It was from his Portuguese friend, explaining that the photo was a reproduction of one in the Lisbon police files.

The photo was of the chair in which Alexander Alekhine had been found dead of a heart attack on the top floor of a cheap Lisbon rooming house in 1946.

Alekhine had won the World's Chess Championship from Capablanca in 1927. He had held the world's record for the greatest number of games played simultaneously and blindfolded—thirty-two. In 1946 he was preparing for an official match with the Russian champion Botvinnik, although he had played chess for the Axis in World War II. Though at times close to psychosis, he was considered the profoundest and most brilliant attacking player who had ever lived.

Had he also, Ritter asked himself, been one of the players to own the Morphy silver-and-gold chess set and the Morphy watch?

He reached for another file folder, labeled "Death of Steinitz." This time he found a brownish daguerreotype showing an empty, narrow, old-fashioned hospital bed with a chessboard and set on a small table beside it. Among the chess pieces, Ritter's magnifier located another one of the unmistakable barbarian pawns.

Wilhelm Steinitz, called the Father of Modern Chess, had held the world's championship for twenty-eight years, until his defeat by Emmanuel Lasker in 1894. Steinitz had had two psychotic episodes and been hospitalized for them in the last years of his life, during the second of which he had believed he could move the chess pieces by electricity and challenged God to a match, offering God the odds of Pawn and Move. It was after the second episode that the daguerreotype had been taken which Ritter had acquired many years ago from the aged Emmanuel Lasker.

Ritter leaned back wearily from the table, took off his glasses and knuckled his tired eyes. It was later than he'd imagined.

He thought about Paul Morphy retiring from chess at the age of twenty-one after beating every important player in the world and issuing a challenge, never accepted, to take on any master at the odds of Pawn and Move. After that contemptuous gesture in 1859 he had brooded for twenty-five years, mostly a recluse in his family home in New Orleans, emerging only fastidiously dressed and becaped for an afternoon promenade and regular attendance at the opera. He suffered paranoid episodes during which he believed his relatives were trying to steal his fortune and, of all things, his clothes. And he never spoke of chess or played it, except for an occasional game with his friend Maurian at the odds of Knight and Move.

Twenty-five years of brooding in solitude without the solace of playing chess, but with the Morphy chess set and the Morphy watch in the same room, testimonials to his world mastery.

Ritter wondered if those circumstances—with Morphy constantly thinking of chess, he felt sure—were not idea for the transmission of the vibrations of thought, and feeling into inanimate objects, in this case the golden Morphy set and watch.

Material objects intangibly vibrating with twenty-five years of the greatest chess thought and then by strange chance (chance alone?) falling into the hands of two other periodically psychotic chess champions, as the photographs of the pawns hinted.

An absurd fancy, Ritter told himself. And yet one to the pursuit of which he had devoted no small part of his life.

And now the richly vibrant objects were in *his* hands. What would be the effect of that on *his* game?

But to speculate in that direction was doubly absurd.

A wave of tiredness went through him. It was close to midnight.

He heated a small supper for himself, consumed it, drew the heavy window drapes tight, and undressed.

He turned back the cover of the big couch next to the table, switched off the light, and inserted himself into bed.

It was Ritter's trick to put himself to sleep by playing through a chess opening in his thoughts. Like any talented player, he could readily contest one blindfold game, though he could not quite visualize the entire board and often had to count moves square by square, especially with the bishops. He selected Breyer's Gambit, an old favorite of his.

He made a half dozen moves. Then suddenly the board was brightly illuminated in his mind, as if a light had been turned on there. He had to stare around to assure himself that the room was still dark as pitch: There was only the bright board inside his head.

His sense of awe was lost in luxuriant delight. He moved the mental pieces rapidly, yet saw deep into the possibilities of each position.

Far in the background he heard a church clock on Franklin boom out the dozen strokes of midnight. After a short while he announced mate in five by White. Black studied the position for perhaps a minute, then resigned.

Lying flat on his back he took several deep breaths. Never before had he played such a brilliant blindfold game—or game with sight even. That it was a game with himself didn't seem to matter—his personality had split neatly into two players.

He studied the final position for a last time, returned the pieces to their starting positions in his head, and rested a bit before beginning another game.

It was then he heard the ticking, a nervous sound five times as fast as the distant clock had knelled. He lifted his wristwatch to his ear. Yes, it was ticking rapidly too, but this was another ticking, louder.

He sat up silently in bed, leaned over the table, switched on the light.

The Morphy watch. That was where the louder ticks were coming from. The hands stood at twelve ten and the small window showed A.M.

For a long while he held that position—mute, motionless, aghast, wondering, fearing, doubting, dreaming dreams no mortal ever dared to dream before.

Let's see. Edgar Allan Poe had died when Morphy was twelve years old and beating his uncle, Ernest Morphy, then chess king of New Orleans.

It seemed impossible that a stopped watch with works well over one hundred years old should begin to run. Doubly impossible that it should begin to run at approximately the right time—his wristwatch and the Morphy watch were no more than a minute apart.

Yet the works might be in better shape than either he or the old Balt had guessed; watches did capriciously start and stop running. Coincidences were only coincidences.

Yet he felt profoundly uneasy. He pinched himself and went through the other childish tests.

He said aloud, "I am Stirf Ritter-Rebil, an old man who lives in San Francisco and plays chess, and who yesterday discovered an unusual curio. But really, everything is perfectly normal . . ."

Nevertheless, he suddenly got the feeling of "A man-eating lion is a-prowl." It was the childish form terror still took for him on rare occasions. For a minute or so everything seemed *too* still, despite the ticking. The stirring of the heavy drapes at the window gave him a shiver, and the walls seemed thin, their protective power nil.

Gradually the sense of a killer lion moving outside them faded and his nerves calmed.

He switched off the light, the bright mental board returned, and the ticking became reassuring rather than otherwise. He began another game with himself, playing for Black the Classical Defense to the Ruy Lopez, another of his favorites.

This game proceeded as brilliantly and vividly as the first. There was the sense of a slim, man-shaped glow standing beside the bright board in the mental dark. After a while the shape grew amorphous and less bright, then split into three. However, it bothered him little, and when he at last announced mate in three for Black, he felt great satisfaction and profound fatigue.

Next day he was in exceptionally good spirits. Sunlight banished all night's terrors as he went about his ordinary business and writing chores. From time to time he reassured himself that he could still visualize a mental chessboard very clearly, and he thought now and again about the historical chess mystery he was in the midst of solving. The ticking of the Morphy watch carried an exciting, eager note. Toward the end of the afternoon he realized he was keenly anticipating visiting Rimini's to show off his newfound skill.

He got out an old gold watch chain and fob, snapped it to the Morphy watch, which he carefully wound again, pocketed them securely in his vest, and set out for Rimini's. It was a grand day—cool, brightly sunlit, and a little windy. His steps were brisk. He wasn't thinking of all the strange happenings but of *chess*. It's been said that a man can lose his wife one day and forget her that night, playing *chess*.

Rimini's was a good, dark, garlic-smelling restaurant with an annex devoted to drinks, substantial free pasta appetizers and, for the nonce, chess. As he drifted into the long L-shaped room, Ritter became pleasantly aware of the row of boards, chessmen, and the intent, mostly young, faces bent above them.

Then Rasputin was grinning at him calculatedly and yapping at him cheerfully. They were due to play their tournament game. They checked out a set and were soon at it. Beside them the Czarina also contested a crucial game, her moody face askew almost as if her neck were broken, her bent wrists near her chin, her long fingers pointing rapidly at her pieces as she calculated combinations, like a sorceress putting a spell on them.

Ritter was aware of her, but only peripherally. For last night's bright mental board had returned, only now it was superimposed on the actual board before him. Complex combinations sprang to mind effortlessly. He beat Rasputin like a child. The Czarina caught the win from the corner of her eye and growled faintly in approval. She was winning her own game; Ritter beating Rasputin bumped her into first place. Rasputin was silent for once.

A youngish man with a black moustache was sharply inspecting Ritter's win. He was the California state champion, Martinez, who had recently played a simultaneous at Rimini's. He now suggested a casual game to Ritter, who nodded somewhat abstractedly.

They contested two very hairy games—a Sicilian Defense by Martinez in which Ritter advanced all his pawns in front of his castled King in a wild-looking attack, and a Ruy Lopez by Martinez that Ritter answered with the Classical Defense, going to great lengths to preserve his powerful King's Bishop. The mental board stayed superimposed, and it almost seemed to Ritter that there was a small faint halo over the piece he must next move or capture. To his mild astonishment he won both games.

A small group of chess-playing onlookers had gathered around their board. Martinez was looking at him speculatively, as if to ask, "Now just where did you spring from, old man, with your power game? I don't recall ever hearing of you."

Ritter's contentment would have been complete, except that among the kibitzers, toward the back there was a slim young man whose face was always shadowed when Ritter glimpsed it. Ritter saw him in three different places, though never in movement and never for more than an instant. Somehow he seemed one onlooker too many. This disturbed Ritter obscurely, and his face had a thoughtful, abstracted expression when he finally quit Rimini's for the faintly drizzling evening streets. After a block he looked around, but so far as he could tell, he wasn't being followed. This time he walked the whole way to his apartment, passing several landmarks of Dashiell Hammet, Sam Spade, and *The Maltese Falcon.*

Gradually, under the benison of the foggy droplets, his mood changed to one of exaltation. He had just now played some beautiful chess, he was in the midst of an amazing historic chess mystery he'd always yearned to penetrate, and somehow the Morphy watch was working *for* him—he could actually hear its muffled ticking in the street, coming up from his waist to his ear.

Tonight his room was a most welcome retreat, *his* place, like an extension of his mind. He fed himself. Then he reviewed, with a Sherlock Holmes smile, what he found himself calling "The Curious Case of the Morphy Timepiece." He wished he had a Dr. Watson to hear him expound. First, the appearance of the watch after Morphy returned to New York on the *Persia* in 1859. Over paranoid years Morphy had imbued it with psyhic energy and vast chessic wisdom. Or else—mark this, Doctor—he had set up the conditions whereby subsequent owners of the watch would *think* he had done such, for the supernatural is not our bailiwick, Watson. Next (after de Riviere) great Steinitz had come into possession of it and challenged God and died mad. Then, after a gap, paranoid Alekhine had owned it and devised diabolically brilliant, hyper-Morphian strategies of attack, and died all alone after a thousand treacheries in a miserable Lisbon flat with a pegin chess set and the telltale barbarian pawn next to his corpse. Finally, after a hiatus of almost thirty years (where had the watch and set been then? Who'd had their custody? Who was the old Balt?) the timepiece and a pawn had come into his own possession. A unique case, Doctor. There isn't even a parallel in Prague in 1863.

The nighted fog pressed against the windowpane and now and again a little rain pattered. San Francisco was a London City and had its own resident great detective. One of Dashiell Hammett's hobbies had been chess, even though there was no record of Spade having played the game.

From time to time Ritter studied the Morphy watch as it glowed and ticked on the table space he'd cleared. P.M. once more, he noted. The time: White Queen, ruby glittering, past Black King, microscopically emerald studded—I mean five minutes past midnight, Doctor. The witching hour, as the superstitiously minded would have it.

But to bed, to bed, Watson. We have much to do tomorrow—and, paradoxically, tonight.

Seriously, Ritter was glad when the golden glow winked out on the watch face, though the strident ticking kept on, and he wriggled himself into his couch-bed and arranged himself for thought. The mental board flashed on once more and he began to play. First he reviewed all the best games he'd ever played in his life—there weren't very many—discovering variations he'd never dreamed of before. Then he played through all his favorite games in the history of chess, from MacDonnell-La Bourdonnais to Fischer-Spassky, not forgetting Steinitz-Zukertort and Alekhine-Bogolyubov. They were richer masterpieces than ever before—the mental board saw deeply. Finally he

443

split his mind again and challenged himself to an eight-game blindfold match, Black against White. Against all expectation, Black won with three wins, two losses, and three draws.

But the night was not all imaginative and ratiocinative delight. Twice there came periods of eerie silence, which the ticking of the watch in the dark made only more complete, and two spells of the man-eating lion a-prowl that raised his hair at the roots. Once again there loomed the slim, faint, man-shaped glows, one short and stocky, with a limp, the other fairly tall, stocky too, and restless. These inner intruders bothered Ritter increasingly—who were they? And wasn't there beginning to be a faint fourth? He recalled the slim young elusive watcher with shadowed face of his games with Martinez and wondered if there was a connection.

Disturbing stuff—and most disturbing of all, the apprehension that his mind might be racked apart and fragmented abroad with all its machine-gun thinking, that it already extended by chessic veins from one chess-playing planet to another, to the ends of the universe?

He was profoundly glad when toward the end of his self-match, his brain began to dull and slow. His last memory was of an attempt to invent a game to be played on the circular board on the watch dial. He thought he was succeeding as his mind at last went spiraling off into unconsciousness.

Next day he awoke restless, scratchy, and eager—and with the feeling that the three or four dim figures had stood around his couch all night vibrating like strobe lights to the rhythm of the Morphy watch.

Coffee heightened his alert nervousness. He rapidly dressed, snapped the Morphy watch to its chain and fob, pocketed the silver pawn, and went out to hunt down the store where he'd purchased the two items.

In a sense he never found it, though he tramped and minutely scanned Montgomery, Kearny, Grant, Stockton, Clay, Sacramento, California, Pine, Bush, and all the rest.

What he did find at long last was a store window with a grotesque pattern of dust on it that he was certain was identical with that on the window through which he had first glimpsed the barbarian pawn day before yesterday.

Only now the display space behind the window was empty and the whole store too, except for a tall, lanky Black with a fabulous Afro hair-do, sweeping up.

Ritter struck up a conversation with the man as he worked, and slowly winning his confidence, discovered he was one of three partners opening a store there that would be stocked solely with African imports.

Finally, after the Black had fetched a great steaming pail of soapy water and a long-handled roller mop and begun to efface forever the map of dust by which Ritter had identified the place, the man at last grew confidential.

"Yeah," he said, "there *was* a queer old character had a secondhand store here until yesterday that had every crazy thing you could dig for sale, some junk, some real fancy. Then he cleared everything out into two big trucks in a great rush, with me breathing down his neck every minute because he'd been supposed to do it the day before.

"Oh, but he was a fabulous cat, though," the Black went on with a reminiscing grin as he sloshed away the last peninsulas and archipelagos of the dust map. "One time he said to me, 'Excuse me while I rest,' and—you're not going to belive this—he went into a corner and stood on his head. I'm telling you he did, man. I'd like to bust a gut. I thought he'd have a stroke—and he did get a bit lavender in the face—but after three minutes exact—I timed him—he flipped back onto his feet neat as you could ask and went on with his work twice as fast as before, supervising his carriers out of their skulls. Wow, that was an event."

Ritter departed without comment. He had got the final clue he'd been seeking to the identity of the old Balt and likewise the fourth and most shadowy form that had begun to haunt his mental chessboard.

Casually standing on his head, saying "It threatens to catch your interest"—why, it had to be Aaron Nimzovich, most hypereccentric player of them all and Father of Hypermodern Chess, who had been Alekhine's most dangerous but ever-evaded challenger. Why, the old Balt had even looked exactly like an aged Nimzovich—hence Ritter's constant sense of a facial familiarity. Of course, Nimzovich had supposedly died in the 1930's in his home city of Rig in the U.S.S.R., but what were life and breath to the forces with which Ritter was now embroiled?

It seemed to him that there were four dim figures stalking him relentlessly as lions right now in the Chinatown crowds, while despite the noise he could hear and feel the ticking of the Morphy watch at his waist.

He fled to the Danish Kitchen at the St. Francis Hotel and consumed cup on cup of good coffee and two orders of Eggs Benedict, and had his mental chessboard flashing on and off in his mind like a strobe light, and wondered if he shouldn't hurl the Morphy watch into the Bay to be rid of the influence racking his mind apart and destroying his sense of reality.

But then with the approach of evening, the urge toward *chess* gripped him more and more imperiously and he headed once again for Rimini's.

Rasputin and the Czarina were there and also Martinez again, and with the last a distinguished silver-haired man whom Martinez introduced as the South American international master, Pontebello, suggesting that he and Ritter have a quick game.

The board glowed again with the superimposed mental one, the halos were there once more, and Ritter won as if against a tyro.

At that, chess fever seized him entirely and he suggested he immediately play four simultaneous blindfold games with the two masters and the Czarina and Rasputin, Pontebello acting also as referee.

There were incredulous looks a-plenty at that, but he *had* won those two games from Martinez and now the one from Pontebello, so arrangements were quickly made, Ritter insisting on an actual blindfold. All the other players crowded around to observe.

The simul began. There were now four mental boards glowing in Ritter's mind. It did not matter—now—that there were four dim forms with them, one by each. Ritter played with a practiced brilliance, combinations bubbled, he called out his moves crisply and unerringly. And so he beat the Czarina and Rasputin quickly. Pontebello took a little longer, and he drew with Martinez by perpetual check.

There was silence as he took off the blindfold to scan a circle of astonished faces and four shadowed ones behind them. He felt the joy of absolute chess mastery. The only sound he heard was the ticking, thunderous to him, of the Morphy watch.

Pontebello was the first to speak. To Ritter, "Do you realize, master, what you've just done?" To Martinez, "Have you the scores of all four games?" To Ritter again, "Excuse me, but you look pale, as if you've seen a ghost." "Four," Ritter corrected quietly. "Those of Morphy, Steinitz, Alekhine, and Nimzovich."

"Under the circumstances, most appropriate," commented Pontebello, while Ritter sought out again the four shadowed faces in the background. They were still there, though they had shifted their positions and withdrawn a little into the varied darknesses of Rimini's.

Amid talk of scheduling another blindfold exhibition and writing a multiple-signed letter describing tonight's simul to the U.S. Chess Federation—not to mention Pontebello's searching queries as to Ritter's chess career—he tore himself away and made for home through the dark streets, certain that four shadowy figures stalked behind him. The call of the mental *chess* in his own room was not to be denied.

Ritter forgot no moment of that night, for he did not sleep at all. The glowing board in his mind was an unquenchable beacon, an all-demanding mandala. He contested two matches with himself, then one each with Morphy, Steinitz, Alekhine, and Nimzovich, winning the first two, drawing the third, and losing the last by a half point. Nimzovich was the only one to speak, saying, "I am both dead and alive, as I'm sure you know. Please don't smoke, or threaten to."

He stacked eight mental boards and played two games of three-dimensional chess, Black winning both. He traveled to the ends of the universe, finding chess everywhere he went, and contesting a long game, more complex than 3-D chess, on which the fate of the universe depended. He drew it.

And all through the long night the four with him in the room and the man-eating lion stared in through the window with black-and-white checkered mask and silver mane. While the Morphy watch ticked like a death-march drum. All figures vanished when the dawn came creeping, though the mental board stayed bright and busy into full daylight and showed no signs of vanishing ever. Ritter felt overpoweringly tired, his mind racked to atoms, on the verge of death.

But he knew what he had to do. He got a small box and packed into it, in cotton wool, the silver barbarian pawn, the old photograph and daguerreotype, and a piece of paper on which he scribbled only:

Morphy, 1859–1884
de Riviere, 1884–?
Steinitz, ?–1900
Alekhine, ?–1946
Nimzovich, 1946–now
Ritter-Rebil, 3 days

Then he packed the watch in the box too, it stopped ticking, its hands were still at last, and in Ritter's mind the mental board winked out.

He took one last devouring gaze at the grotesque, glittering dial. Then he shut the box, wrapped and sealed and corded it, boldly wrote on it in black ink "Chess Champion of the World" and added the proper address.

He took it to the post office on Van Ness and sent it off by registered mail. Then he went home and slept like the dead.

*   *   *

Ritter never received a response. But he never got the box back either. Sometimes he wonders if the subsequent strange events in the Champion's life might have had anything to do with the gift.

And on even rarer occasions he wonders what would have happened if he had faced the challenge of death and let his mind be racked to bits, if that was what was to happen.

But on the whole he is content. Questions from Martinez and the others he has put off with purposefully vague remarks.

He still plays chess at Rimini's. Once he won another game from Martinez, when the latter was contesting a simul against twenty-three players.

Belsen Express

George Simister watched the blue flames writhe beautifully in the gate, like dancing girls drenched with alcohol and set afire, and congratulated himself on having survived well through the middle of the Twentieth Century without getting involved in military service, world-saving, or any activities that interfered with the earning and enjoyment of money.

Outside rain dripped, a storm snarled at the city from the outskirts, and sudden gusts of wind produced in the chimney a sound like the mourning of doves. Simister shimmied himself a fraction of an inch deeper in his easy chair and took a slow sip of diluted scotch—he was sensitive to most cheaper liquors. Simister's physiology was on the delicate side; during his childhood certain tastes and odors, playing on an elusive heart weakness, had been known to make him faint.

The outspread newspaper started to slip from his knee. He detained it, let his glance rove across the next page, noted a headline about an uprising in Prague like that in Hungary in 1956 and murmured, "Damn Slavs," noted another about border fighting around Israel and muttered, "Damn Jews," and let the paper go. He took another sip of his drink, yawned, and watched a virginal blue flame flutter frightenedly the length of the log before it turned to a white smoke ghost. There was a sharp *knock-knock*.

Simister jumped and then got up and hurried tight-lipped to the front door. Lately some of the neighborhood children had been trying to annoy him probably because his was the most respectable and best-kept house on the block. Doorbell ringing, obscene sprayed scrawls, that sort of thing. And hardly children—young rowdies rather, who needed rough handling and a trip to the police station. He was really angry by the time he reached the door and swung it wide. There was nothing but a big wet empty darkness. A chilly draft spattered a couple of cold drops on him. Maybe the noise had come from the fire. He shut the door and started back to the living room, but a small pile of books untidily nested in wrapping paper on the hall table caught his eye and he grimaced.

They constituted a blotchily addressed parcel which the postman had delivered by mistake a few mornings ago. Simister could probably have deciphered the address, for it was clearly on his street, and rectified the postman's error, but he did not choose to abet the activities of illiterates with leaky pens. And the delivery must have been a mistake for the top book was titled *The Scourge of the Swastika* and the other two had similar titles, and Simister had an acute distaste for books that insisted on digging up that satisfactorily buried historical incident known as Nazi Germany.

The reason for this distaste was a deeply hidden fear that George Simister shared with millions, but that he had never revealed even to his wife. It was a quite unrealistic and now completely anachronistic fear of the Gestapo.

It had begun years before the Second World War, with the first small reports from Germany of minority persecutions and organized hoodlumism—the sense of something reaching out across the dark Atlantic to threaten his life, his security, and his confidence that he would never have to suffer pain except in a hospital.

Of course it had never got at all close to Simister, but it had exercised an evil tyranny over his imagination. There was one nightmarish series of scenes that had slowly grown in his mind and then had kept bothering him for a long time. It began with a thunderous knocking, of boots and rifle butts rather than fists, and a shouted demand: "Open up! It's the Gestapo." Next he would find himself in a stream of frantic people being driven toward a portal where a division was made between those reprieved and those slated for immediate extinction. Last he would be inside a closed motor van jammed so tightly with people that it was impossible to move. After a long time the van would stop, but the motor would keep running, and from the floor, leisurely seeking the crevices between the packed bodies, the entrapped exhaust fumes would begin to mount.

Now in the shadowy hall the same horrid movie had a belated showing. Simister shook his head sharply, as if he could shake the scenes out, reminding himself that the Gestapo was dead and done with for more than ten years. He felt the angry impulse to throw in the fire the books responsible for the return of his waking nightmare. But he remembered that books are hard to burn. He stared at them uneasily, excited by thoughts of torture and confinement, concentration and death camps, but knowing the nasty aftermath they left in his mind. Again he felt a sudden impulse, this time to bundle the books together and throw them in the trash can. But that would mean getting wet, it could wait until tomorrow. He put the screen in front of the fire which had died and was smoking like a cramatory, and went up to bed.

Some hours later he waked with the memory of a thunderous knocking.

He started up, exclaiming, "Those damned kids!" The drawn shades seemed abnormally dark—probably they'd thrown a stone through the street lamp.

He put one foot on the chilly floor. It was now profoundly still. The storm had gone off like a roving cat. Simister strained his ears. Beside him his wife breathed with irritating evenness. He wanted to wake her and explain about the young delinquents. It was criminal that they were permitted to roam the streets at this hour. Girls with them too, likely as not.

The knocking was not repeated. Simister listened for footsteps going away, or for the creaking of boards that would betray a lurking presence on the porch.

After awhile he began to wonder if the knocking might not have been part of a dream, or perhaps a final rumble of actual thunder. He lay down and pulled the blankets up to his neck. Eventually his muscles relaxed and he got to sleep.

At breakfast he told his wife about it.

"George, it may have been burglars," she said.

"Don't be stupid, Joan. Burglars don't knock. If it was anything it was those damned kids."

"Whatever it was, I wish you'd put a bigger bolt on the front door."

"Nonsense. If I'd known you were going to act this way I wouldn't have said anything. I told you it was probably just the thunder."

But next night at about the same hour it happened again.

This time there could be little question of dreaming. The knocking still rever-berated in his ears. And there had been words mixed with it, some sort of yapping in a foreign language. Probably the children of some of those European refugees who had settled in the neighborhood.

Last night they'd fooled him by keeping perfectly still after banging on the door, but tonight he knew what to do. He tiptoed across the bedroom and went down the stairs rapidly, but quietly because of his bare feet. In the hall he snatched up something to hit them with, then in one motion unlocked and jerked open the door.

There was no one.

He stood looking at the darkness. He was puzzled as to how they could have got away so quickly and silently. He shut the door and switched on the light. Then he felt the thing in his hand. It was one of the books. With a feeling of disgust he dropped it on the others. He must remember to throw them out first thing tomorrow.

But he overslept and had to rush. The feeling of disgust or annoyance, or some-thing akin, must have lingered, however, for he found himself sensitive to things he wouldn't ordinarily have noticed. People especially. The swollen-handed man seemed deliberately surly as he counted Simister's pennies and handed him the paper. The tight-lipped woman at the gate hesitated suspiciously, as if he were trying to pass off a last month's ticket.

And when he was hurrying up the stairs in response to an approaching rumble, he brushed against a little man in an oversize coat and received in return a glance that gave him a positive shock.

Simister vaguely remembered having seen the little man several times before. He had the thin nose, narrowset eyes and receding chin that is by a stretch of the imagina-tion described as "rat-faced." In the movies he'd have played a stool pigeon. The flapping overcoat was rather comic.

But there seemed to be something at once so venomous and sly, so time-bidingly vindictive, in the glance he gave Simister that the latter was taken aback and almost missed the train.

He just managed to squeeze through the automatically closing door of the smoker after the barest squint at the sign to assure himself that the train was an express. His heart was pounding in a way that another time would have worried him, but now he was immersed in a savage pleasure at having thwarted the man in the oversize coat. The latter hadn't hurried fast enough and Simister had made no effort to hold open the door for him.

As a smooth surge of electric power sent them sliding away from the station Simister pushed his way from the vestibule into the car and snagged a strap. From the next one already swayed his chief commuting acquaintance, a beefy, suspiciously red-nosed, irritating man named Holstrom, now reading a folded newspaper one-handed. He shoved a headline in Simister's face. The latter knew what to expect.

"Atomic Weapons for West Germany," he read tonelessly. Holstrom was always trying to get him into outworn arguments about totalitarianism, Nazi Germany, racial prejudice and the like. "Well, what about it?"

Holstrom shrugged. "It's a natural enough step, I suppose, but it started me think-ing about the top Nazis and whether we really got all of them."

"Of course," Simister snapped.

"I'm not so sure," Holstrom said. "I imagine quite a few of them got away and are still hiding out somewhere."

But Simister refused the bait. The question bored him. Who talked about the Nazis any more? For that matter, the whole trip this morning was boring; the smoker was overcrowded; and when they finally piled out at the downtown terminus, the rude jostling increased his irritation.

The crowd was approaching an iron fence that arbitrarily split the stream of hurrying people into two sections which reunited a few steps farther on. Beside the fence a new guard was standing, or perhaps Simister hadn't noticed him before. A cocky-looking young fellow with close-cropped blonde hair and cold blue eyes.

Suddenly it occurred to Simister that he habitually passed to the right of the fence, but that this morning he was being edged over toward the left. This trifling circumstance, coming on top of everything else, made him boil. He deliberately pushed across the stream, despite angry murmurs and the hard stare of the guard.

He had intended to walk the rest of the way, but his anger made him forgetful and before he realized it he had climbed aboard a bus. He soon regretted it. The bus was even more crowded than the smoker and the standees were morose and lumpy in their heavy overcoats. He was tempted to get off and waste his fare, but he was trapped in the extreme rear and moreover shrank from giving the impression of a man who didn't know his own mind.

Soon another annoyance was added to the ones already plaguing him—a trace of exhaust fumes was seeping up from the motor at the rear. He immediately began to feel ill. He looked around indignantly, but the others did not seem to notice the odor, or else accepted it fatalistically.

In a couple of blocks the fumes had become so bad that Simister decided he must get off at the next stop. But as he started to push past her, a fat woman beside him gave him such a strangely apathetic stare that Simister, whose mind was perhaps a little clouded by nausea, felt almost hypnotized by it, so that it was several seconds before he recalled and carried out his intention.

Ridiculous, but the woman's face stuck in his mind all day.

In the evening he stopped at a hardware store. After supper his wife noticed him working in the front hall.

"Oh, you're putting on a bolt," she said.

"Well, you asked me to, didn't you?"

"Yes, but I didn't think you'd do it."

"I decided I might as well." He gave the screw a final turn and stepped back to survey the job. "Anything to give you a feeling of security."

Then he remembered the stuff he had been meaning to throw out that morning. The hall table was bare.

"What did you do with them?" he asked.

"What?"

"Those fool books."

"Oh, those. I wrapped them up again and gave them to the postman."

"Now why did you do that? There wasn't any return address and I might have wanted to look at them."

"But you said they weren't addressed to us and you hate all that war stuff."

"I know, but—" he said and then stopped, hopeless of making her understand why he particularly wanted to feel he had got rid of that package himself, and by throwing it in the trash can. For that matter, he didn't quite understand his feelings himself. He began to poke around the hall.

"I did return the package," his wife said sharply. "I'm not losing my memory."

"Oh, all right!" he said and started for bed.

That night no knocking awakened him, but rather a loud crashing and rending of wood along with a harsh metallic *ping* like a lock giving.

In a moment he was out of bed, his sleep-sodden nerves jangling with anger. Those hoodlums! Rowdy pranks were perhaps one thing, deliberate destruction of property certainly another. He was halfway down the stairs before it occurred to him that the sound he had heard had a distinctly menacing aspect. Juvenile delinquents who broke down doors would hardly panic at the appearance of an unarmed householder.

But just then he saw that the front door was intact.

Considerably puzzled and apprehensive, he searched the first floor and even ventured into the basement, racking his brains as to just what could have caused such a noise. The water heater? Weight of the coal bursting a side of the bin? Those objects were intact. But perhaps the porch trellis giving way?

That last notion kept him peering out of the front window several moments. When he turned around there was someone behind him.

"I didn't mean to startle you," his wife said. "What's the matter, George?"

"I don't know. I thought I heard a sound. Something being smashed."

He expected that would send her into one of her burglar panics, but instead she kept looking at him.

"Don't stand there all night," he said. "Come on to bed."

"George, is something worrying you? Something you haven't told me about?"

"Of course not. Come on."

Next morning Holstrom was on the platform when Simister got there and they exchanged guesses as to whether the dark rainclouds would burst before they got downtown. Simister noticed the man in the oversize coat loitering about, but he paid no attention to him.

Since it was a bank holiday there were empty seats in the smoker and he and Holstrom secured one. As usual the latter had his newspaper. Simister waited for him to start his ideological sniping—a little uneasily for once; usually he was secure in his prejudices, but this morning he felt strangely vulnerable.

It came. Holstrom shook his head. "That's a bad business in Czechoslovakia. Maybe we were a little too hard on the Nazis."

To his surprise Simister found himself replying with both nervous hypocrisy and uncharacteristic vehemence. "Don't be ridiculous! Those rats deserved a lot worse than they got!"

As Holstrom turned toward him saying, "Oh, so you've changed your mind about the Nazis," Simister thought he heard someone just behind him say at the same time in a low, distinct, pitiless voice: "I heard you."

He glanced around quickly. Leaning forward a little, but with his face turned sharply away as if he had just become interested in something passing the window, was the man in the oversize coat.

"What's wrong?" Holstrom asked.

"What do you mean?"

"You've turned pale. You look sick."

"I don't feel that way."

"Sure? You know, at our age we've got to begin to watch out. Didn't you once tell me something about your heart?"

Simister managed to laugh that off, but when they parted just outside the train he was conscious that Holstrom was still eyeing him rather closely.

As he slowly walked through the terminus his face began to assume an abstracted look. In fact he was lost in thought to such a degree that when he approached the iron fence, he started to pass it on the left. Luckily the crowd was thin and he was able to cut across to the right without difficulty. The blonde young guard looked at him closely —perhaps he remembered yesterday morning.

Simister had told himself that he wouldn't again under any circumstances take the bus, but when he got outside it was raining torrents. After a moment's hesitation he climbed aboard. It seemed even more crowded than yesterday, if that were possible, with more of the same miserable people, and the damp air made the exhaust odor particularly offensive.

The abstracted look clung to his face all day long. His secretary noticed, but did not comment. His wife did, however, when she found him poking around in the hall after supper.

"Are you still looking for that package, George?" Her tone was flat.

"Of course not," he said quickly, shutting the table drawer he'd opened.

She waited. "Are you sure you didn't order those books?"

"What gave you that idea?" he demanded. "You know I didn't."

"I'm glad," she said. "I looked through them. There were pictures. They were nasty."

"You think I'm the sort of person who'd buy books for the sake of nasty pictures?"

"Of course not, dear, but I thought you might have seen them and they were what had depressed you."

"Have I been depressed?"

"Yes. Your heart hasn't been bothering you, has it?"

"No."

"Well, what is it then?"

"I don't know." Then with considerable effort he said, "I've been thinking about war and things."

"War! No wonder you're depressed. You shouldn't think about things you don't like, especially when they aren't happening. What started you?"

"Oh, Holstrom keeps talking to me on the train."

"Well, don't listen to him."

"I won't."

"Well, cheer up then."

"I will."

"And don't let anyone make you look at morbid pictures. There was one of some people who had been gassed in a motor van and then laid out—"

"Please, Joan! Is it any better to tell me about them than to have me look at them?"

"Of course not, dear. That was silly of me. But do cheer up."

"Yes."

The puzzled, uneasy look was still in her eyes as she watched him go down the front walk next morning. It was foolish, but she had the feeling that his gray suit was really black—and he had whimpered in his sleep. With a shiver at her fancy she stepped inside.

That morning George Simister created a minor disturbance in the smoker, it was remembered afterwards, though Holstrom did not witness the beginning of it. It seems that Simister had run to catch the express and had almost missed it, due to a collision with a small man in a large overcoat. Someone recalled that trifling prelude because of the amusing circumstance that the small man, although he had been thrown to his knees and the collision was chiefly Simister's fault, was still anxiously begging Simister's pardon after the latter had dashed on.

Simister just managed to squeeze through the closing door while taking a quick squint at the sign. It was then that his queer behavior started. He instantly turned around and unsuccessfully tried to force his way out again, even inserting his hands in the crevice between the door frame and the rubber edge of the sliding door and yanking violently.

Apparently as soon as he noticed the train was in motion, he turned away from the door, his face pale and set, and roughly pushed his way into the interior of the car.

There he made a beeline for the little box in the wall containing the identifying signs of the train and the miniature window which showed in reverse the one now in use, which read simply EXPRESS. He stared at it as if he couldn't believe his eyes and then started to turn the crank, exposing in turn all the other white signs on the roll of black cloth. He scanned each one intently, oblivious to the puzzled or outraged looks of those around him.

He had been through all the signs once and was starting through them again before the conductor noticed what was happening and came hurrying. Ignoring his expostulations, Simister asked him loudly if this was really the express. Upon receiving a curt affirmative, Simister went on to assert that he had in the moment of squeezing aboard glimpsed another sign in the window—and he mentioned a strange name. He seemed both very positive and very agitated about it, the conductor said. The latter asked Simister to spell the name. Simister haltingly complied: "B . . . E . . . L . . . S . . . E . . . N . . ." The conductor shook his head, then his eyes widened and he demanded, "Say, are you trying to kid me? That was one of those Nazi death camps." Simister slunk toward the other end of the car.

It was there that Holstrom saw him, looking "as if he'd just got a terrible shock." Holstrom was alarmed—and as it happened felt a special private guilt—but could hardly get a word out of him, though he made several attempts to start a conversation, choosing uncharacteristically neutral topics. Once, he remembered, Simister looked up and said, "Do you suppose there are some things a man simply can't escape, no matter how quietly he lives or how carefully he plans?" But his face immediately showed he had realized there was at least one very obvious answer to this question, and Holstrom didn't know what to say. Another time he suddenly remarked, "I wish we were like the British and didn't have standing in buses," but he subsided as quickly. As they neared the downtown terminus Simister seemed to brace up a little, but Holstrom was still worried about him to such a degree that he went out of his way to follow him through the terminus. "I was afraid something would happen to him, I don't know what," Holstrom said. "I would have stayed right beside him except he seemed to resent my presence."

Holstrom's private guilt, which intensified his anxiety and doubtless accounted for his feeling that Simister resented him, was due to the fact that ten days ago, cumulatively irritated by Simister's smug prejudices and blinkered narrow-mindedness, he had anonymously mailed him three books recounting with uncompromising realism and documentation some of the least pleasant aspects of the Nazi tyranny. Now he couldn't but feel they might have helped to shake Simister up in a way he hadn't intended, and he was ashamedly glad that he had been in such a condition when he sent the package that it had been addressed in a drunken scrawl. He never discussed this matter afterwards, except occasionally to make strangely feelingful remarks about "What little things can unseat a spring in a man's clockworks!"

So, continuing Holstrom's story, he followed Simister at a distance as the latter dejectedly shuffled across the busy terminus. "Terminus?" Holstrom once interrupted his

455

story to remark. "He's a god of endings, isn't he?—and of human rights. Does that mean anything?"

When Simister was nearing an iron fence a puzzling episode occurred. He was about to pass it to the right, when someone just ahead of him lurched or stumbled. Simister almost fell himself, veering toward the fence. A nearby guard reached out and in steadying him pulled him around the fence to the left.

Then, Holstrom maintains, Simister turned for a moment and Holstrom caught a glimpse of his face. There must have been something peculiarly frightening about that backward look, something perhaps that Holstrom cannot adequately describe, for he instantly forgot any idea of surveillance at a distance and made every effort to catch up.

But the crowd from another commuters' express enveloped Holstrom. When he got outside the terminus it was some moments before he spotted Simister in the midst of a group jamming their way aboard an already crowded bus across the street. This perplexed Holstrom, for he knew Simister didn't have to take the bus and he recalled his recent complaint.

Heavy traffic kept Holstrom from crossing. He says he shouted, but Simister was making feeble efforts to get out of the crowd that was forcing him onto the bus, but, "They were all jammed together like cattle."

The best testimony to Holstrom's anxiety about Simister is that as soon as the traffic thinned a trifle he darted across the street, skipping between the cars. But by then the bus had started. He was in time only for a whiff or particularly obnoxious exhaust fumes.

As soon as he got to his office he phoned Simister. He got Simister's secretary and what she had to say relieved his worries, which is ironic in view of what happened a little later.

What happened a little later is best described by the same girl. She said, "I never saw him come in looking so cheerful, the old grouch—excuse me. But anyway he came in all smiles, like he'd just got some bad news about somebody else, and right away he started to talk and kid with everyone, so that it was awfully funny when that man called up worried about him. I guess maybe, now I think a person who's just had a narrow squeak and is very thankful to be alive.

"Well, he kept it up all morning. Then just as he was throwing his head back to laugh at one of his own jokes, he grabbed his chest, let out an awful scream, doubled up and fell on the floor. Afterwards I couldn't believe he was dead, because his lips stayed so red and there were bright spots of color on his cheeks, like rouge. Of course it was his heart, though you can't believe what a scare that stupid first doctor gave us when he came in and looked at him."

Of course, as she said, it must have been Simister's heart, one way or the other. And it is undeniable that the doctor in question was an ancient, possibly incompetent dispenser of penicillin, morphine and snap diagnoses swifter than Charcot's. They only called him because his office was in the same building. When Simister's own doctor arrived and pronounced it heart failure, which was what they'd thought all along, everyone was much relieved and inclined to be severely critical of the first doctor for having said something that sent them all scurrying to open the windows.

For when the first doctor had come in, he had taken one look at Simister and rasped, "Heart failure? Nonsense! Look at the color of his face. Cherry red. That man died of carbon monoxide poisoning."

Catch That Zeppelin!

This year on a trip to New York City to visit my son who is a social historian at a leading municipal university there, I had a very unsettling experience. At black moments, of which at my age I have quite a few, it still makes me distrust profoundly those absolute boundaries in Space and Time which are our sole protection against Chaos, and fear that my mind—no, my entire individual existence—may at any moment at all and without any warning whatsoever be blown by a sudden gust of Cosmic Wind to an entirely different spot in a Universe of Infinite Possibilities. Or, rather, into another Universe altogether. And that my mind and individuality will be changed to fit.

But at other moments, which are still in the majority, I believe that my unsettling experience was only one of those remarkably vivid waking dreams to which old people become increasingly susceptible, generally waking dreams about the past in which at some crucial point one made an entirely different and braver choice than one actually did, or in which the whole world made such a decision with a completely different future resulting. Golden glowing might-have-beens nag increasingly at the minds of some older people.

In line with this interpretation I must admit that my whole unsettling experience was structured very much like a dream. It began with startling flashes of a changed world. It continued into a longer period when I completely accepted the changed world and delighted in it and, despite fleeting quivers of uneasiness, wished I could bask in its glow forever. And it ended in horrors, or nightmares, which I hate to mention, let alone discuss, until I must.

Opposing this dream notion, there are times when I am completely convinced that what happened to me in Manhattan and in a certain famous building there was no dream at all, but absolutely real, and that I did indeed visit another Time Stream.

Finally, I must point out that what I am about to tell you I am necessarily describing in retrospect, highly aware of several transitions involved and, whether I want to or not, commenting on them and making deductions that never once occurred to me at the time.

No, at the time it happened to me—and now at this moment of writing I am convinced that it did happen and was absolutely real—one instant simply succeeded another in the most natural way possible. I questioned nothing.

As to why it all happened to me, and what particular mechanism was involved, well, I am convinced that every man or woman has rare brief moments of extreme sensitivity, or rather vulnerability, when his mind and entire being may be blown by the Change Winds to Somewhere Else. And then, by what I call the Law of the conservation of Reality, blown back again.

457

* * *

I was walking down Broadway somewhere near 34th Street. It was a chilly day, sunny despite the smog—a bracing day—and I suddenly began to stride along more briskly than is my cautious habit, throwing my feet ahead of me with a faint suggestion of the goose step. I also threw back my shoulders and took deep breaths, ignoring the fumes which tickled my nostrils. Beside me, traffic growled and snarled, rising at times to a machine-gun rata-tat-tat. While pedestrians were scuttling about with that desperate ratlike urgency characteristic of all big American cities, but which reaches its ultimate in New York, I cheerfully ignored that too. I even smiled at the sight of a ragged bum and a furcoated gray-haired society lady both independently dodging across the street through the hurtling traffic with a cool practiced skill one sees only in America's biggest metropolis.

Just then I noticed a dark, wide shadow athwart the street ahead of me. It could not be that of a cloud, for it did not move. I craned my neck sharply and looked straight up like the veriest yokel, a regular *Hans-Kopf-in-die-Luft* (Hans-Head-in-the-Air, a German figure of comedy).

My gaze had to climb up the giddy 102 stories of the tallest building in the world, the Empire State. My gaze was strangely accompanied by the vision of a gigantic, long-fanged ape making the same ascent with a beautiful girl in one paw—oh, yes, I was recollecting the charming American fantasy-film *King Kong*, or as they name it in Sweden, *Kong King*.

And then my gaze clambered higher still, up the 222-foot sturdy tower, to the top of which was moored the nose of the vast, breath-takingly beautiful, streamlined, silvery shape which was making the shadow.

Now here is a most important point. I was not at the time in the least startled by what I saw. I knew at once that it was simply the bow section of the German Zeppelin *Ostwald*, named for the great German pioneer of physical chemistry and electro-chemistry, and queen of the mighty passenger and light-freight fleet of luxury airliners working out of Berlin, Baden-Baden, and Bremerhaven. That matchless Armada of Peace, each titanic airship named for as world-famous German scientist—the *Mach*, the *Nernst*, the *Humboldt*, the *Fritz Haber*, the French-named *Antoine Henri Becquerel*, the American-named *Edison*, the Polish-named *Sklodowska*, the American-Polish *T. Sklodowska Edison*, and even the Jewish-named *Einstein!* The great humanitarian navy in which I held a not unimportant position as international sales consultant and *Fachman*—I mean expert. My chest swelled with justified pride at this *edel*—nobel—achievement of *der Vaterland*.

I knew also without any mind-searching or surprise that the length of the *Ostwald* was more than one half the 1,472-foot height of the Empire State Building plus its mooring tower, thick enough to hold an elevator. And my heart swelled again with the thought that the Berlin *Zeppelinturm* (dirigible tower) was only a few meters less high. Germany, I told myself, need not strain for mere numerical records—her sweeping scientific and technical achievements speak for themselves to the entire planet.

All this literally took little more than a second, and I never broke my snappy stride. As my gaze descended, I cheerfully hummed under my breath *Deutschland, Deutschland uber Alles.*

The Broadway I saw was utterly transformed, though at the time this seemed every bit as natural as the serene presence of the *Ostwald* high overhead, vast ellipsoid held aloft by helium. Silvery electric trucks and buses and private cars innumerable purred along far more evenly and quietly, and almost as swiftly, as had the noisy, stenchful, jerky gasoline-powered vehicles only moments before, though to me now the latter were completely forgotten. About two blocks ahead, an occasional gleaming electric car smoothly swung into the wide silver arch of a quick-battery-change station, while others emerged from under the arch to rejoin the almost dreamlike stream of traffic.

The air I gratefully inhaled was fresh and clean, without trace of smog.

The somewhat fewer pedestrians around me still moved quite swiftly, but with a dignity and courtesy largely absent before, with the numerous blackamoors among them quite as well dressed and exuding the same quiet confidence as the Caucasians.

The only slightly jarring note was struck by a tall, pale, rather emaciated man in black dress and with unmistakably Hebraic features. His somber clothing was somewhat shabby, though well kept, and his thin shoulders were hunched. I got the impression he had been looking closely at me, and then instantly glanced away as my eyes sought his. For some reason I recalled what my son had told me about the City College of New York—CCNY—being referred to surreptitiously and jokingly as Christian College Now Yiddish. I couldn't help chuckling a bit at that witticism, though I am glad to say it was a genial little guffaw rather than a malicious snicker. Germany in her well-known tolerance and noble-mindedness has completely outgrown her old, disfiguring anti-Semitism—after all, we must admit in all fairness that perhaps a third of our great men are Jews or carry Jewish genes, Haber and Einstein among them—despite what dark and, yes, wicked memories may lurk in the subconscious minds of oldsters like myself and occasionally briefly surface into awareness like submarines bent on ship murder.

My happily self-satisfied mood immediately reasserted itself, and with a smart, almost military gesture I brushed to either side with a thumbnail the short, horizontal black mustache which decorates my upper lip, and I automatically swept back into place the thick comma of black hair (I confess I dye it) which tends to fall down across my forehead.

I stole another glance up at the *Ostwald*, which made me think of the matchless amenities of that wondrous deluxe airliner: the softly purring motors that powered its propellers—electric motors, naturally, energized by banks of lightweight TSE batteries and as safe as its helium; the Grand Corridor running the length of the passenger deck from the Bow Observatory to the stern's like-windowed Games Room, which becomes the Grand Ballroom at night; the other peerless rooms letting off that corridor—the *Gesellschaftstraum der Kapitan* (Captain's Lounge) with its dark woodwork, manly cigar smoke and *Damentische* (Tables for Ladies), the Premier Dining Room with its linen napery and silver-plated aluminum dining service, the Ladies' Retiring Room always set out profusely with fresh flowers, the Schwartzwald bar, the gambling casino with its roulette, baccarat, chemmy, blackjack (*ving-et-un*), its tables for skat and bridge and dominoes and sixty-six, its chess tables presided over by the delightfully eccentric world's champion Nimzowitch, who would defeat you blindfold, but always brilliantly, simultaneously or one at a time, in charmingly baroque brief games for only two gold pieces per person per game (one gold piece to nutsy Nimzy, one to the DLG), and the supremely luxurious staterooms with costly veneers of mahogany over balsa; the hosts of attentive stewards, either as short and skinny as jockeys or else actual dwarfs, both types chosen to save weight; and the titanium elevator rising through the countless bags of helium to the two-decked Zenith Observatory, the sun deck windscreened but roofless to let in the ever-changing clouds, the mysterious fog, the rays of the stars and good old Sol, and all the heavens. Ah, where else on land or sea could you buy such high living?

459

I called to mind in detail the single cabin which was always mine when I sailed on the *Ostwald—meine Stammkabine.* I visualized the Grand Corridor thronged with wealthy passengers in evening dress, the handsome officers, the unobtrusive ever-attentive stewards, the gleam of white shirt fronts, the glow of bare shoulders, the muted dazzle of jewels, the music of conversations like string quartets, the lilting low laughter that traveled along.

Exactly on time I did a neat *"Links, marschieren!"* ("To the left, march!") and passed through the impressive portals of the Empire State and across its towering lobby to the mutedly silver-doored bank of elevators. On my way I noted the silver-glowing date: 6 May 1937 and the time of day: 1:07 P.M. Good!—since the *Ostwald* did not cast off until the tick of three P.M., I would be left plenty of time for a leisurely lunch and good talk with my son, if he had remembered to meet me—and there was actually no doubt of that, since he is the most considerate and orderly minded of sons, a real German mentality, though I say it myself.

I headed for the express bank, enjoying my passage through the clusters of high-class people who thronged the lobby without any unseemly crowding, and placed myself before the doors designated "Dirigible Departure Lounge" and in briefer German *"Zum Zeppelin."*

The elevator hostess was an attractive Japanese girl in skirt of dull silver with the DLG, Double Eagle and Dirigible insignia of the German Airship Union emblazoned in small on the left breast of her mutedly silver jacket. I noted with unvoiced approval that she appeared to have an excellent command of both German and English and was uniformly courteous to the passengers in her smiling but unemotional Nipponese fashion, which is so like our German scientific precision of speech, though without the latter's warm underlying passion. How good that our two federations, at opposite sides of the globe, have strong commercial and behavorial ties!

My fellow passengers in the lift, chiefly Americans and Germans, were of the finest type, very well dressed—except that just as the doors were about to close, there pressed in my doleful a Jew in black. He seemed ill at ease, perhaps because of his shabby clothing. I was surprised, but made a point of being particularly polite towards him, giving him a slight bow and brief but friendly smile, while flashing my eyes. Jews have as much right to the acme of luxury travel as any other people on the planet, if they have the money—and most of them do.

During our uninterrupted and infinitely smooth passage upward, I touched my outside left breast pocket to reassure myself that my ticket—first class on the *Ostwald!* —and my papers were there. But actually I got far more reassurance and even secret joy from the feel and thought of the documents in my tightly zippered inside left breast pocket: the signed preliminary agreements that would launch America herself into the manufacture of passenger zeppelins. Modern Germany is always generous in sharing her great technical achievements with responsible sister nations, supremely confident that the genius of her scientists and engineers will continue to keep her well ahead of all other lands; and after all, the genius of two Americans, father and son, had made vital though indirect contributions to the development of safe airship travel (and not forgetting the part played by the Polish-born wife of the one and mother of the other).

The obtaining of those documents had been the chief and official reason for my trip to New York city, though I had been able to combine it most pleasurably with a long overdue visit with my son, the social historian, and with his charming wife.

These happy reflections were cut short by the jarless arrival of our elevator at its lofty terminus on the 100th floor. The journey old love-smitten King Kong had made only after exhausting exertion we had accomplished effortlessly. The silvery doors spread wide. My fellow passengers hung back for a moment in awe and perhaps a little trepidation at the thought of the awesome journey ahead of them, and I—seasoned airship traveler that I am—was the first to step out, favoring with a smile and nod of approval my pert yet cool Japanese fellow employee of the lower echelons.

Hardly sparing a glance toward the great, fleckless window confronting the doors and showing a matchless view of Manhattan from an elevation of 1,250 feet minus two stories, I briskly turned, not right to the portals of the Departure Lounge and tower elevator, but left to those of the superb German restaurant *Krahenest* (Crow's Nest).

I passed between the flanking three-foot-high bronze statuettes of Thomas Edison and Marie Sklodowska Edison niched in one wall and those of Count von Zeppelin and Thomas Sklodowska Edison facing them from the other, and entered the select precincts of the finest German dining place outside the Fatherland. I paused while my eyes traveled searchingly around the room with its restful, dark wood paneling deeply carved with beautiful representations of the Black Forest and its grotesque supernatural denizens—kobolds, elves, gnomes, dryads (tastefully sexy) and the like. They interested me since I am what Americans call a Sunday painter, though almost my sole subject matter is zeppelins seen against blue sky and airy, soaring clouds.

The *Oberkellner* came hurrying toward me with menu tucked under his left elbow and saying, "Mein Herr! Charmed to see you once more! I have a perfect table-for-one with porthole looking out across the Hudson."

But just then a youthful figure rose springily from behind a table set against the far wall, and a dear and familiar voice rang out to me with "*Hier, Papa!*"

"*Nein, Herr Ober,*" I smilingly told the head waiter as I walked past him, "*heute hab ich ein Gesellshafter. Mein Sohn.*"

I confidently made my way between tables occupied by well-dressed folk, both white and black.

My son wrung my hand with fierce family affection, though we had last parted only that morning. He insisted that I take the wide, dark, leather-upholstered seat against the wall, which gave me a fine view of the entire restaurant, while he took the facing chair.

"Because during this meal I wish to look only on you, Papa." he assured me with manly tenderness. "And we have at least an hour and a half together, Papa—I have checked your luggage through, and it is likely already aboard the *Ostwald.*" Thoughtful, dependable boy!

"And now, Papa, what shall it be?" he continued after we had settled ourselves. I see that today's special is *Sauerbraten mit Spatzel* and sweet-sour red cabbage. But there is also *Paprikahuhn* and—"

"Leave the chicken to flaunt her paprika in lonely red splendor today," I interrupted him. "Sauerbraten sounds fine."

Ordered by my Herr Ober, the aged wine waiter had already approached our table. I was about to give him directions when my son took upon himself that task with an authority and a hostfulness that warmed my heart. He scanned the wine menu rapidly but thoroughly.

"The Zinfandel 1933," he ordered with decision, though glancing my way to see if I concurred with his judgment. I smiled and nodded.

"And perhaps *ein Tropfchen Schnapps* to begin with?" he suggested.

"A brandy?—yes!" I replied. "And not just a drop, either. Make it a double. It is not every day I lunch with that distinguished scholar, my son."

"Oh, Papa," he protested, dropping his eyes and almost blushing. Then firmly to the bent-backed, white-haired wine waiter, "*Schnapps also. Doppel.*" The old waiter nodded his approval and hurried off.

We gazed fondly at each other for a few blissful seconds. Then I said, "Now tell me more fully about your achievements as a social historian on an exchange professorship in the New World. I know we have spoken about this several times, but only rather briefly and generally when various of your friends were present, or at least your lovely wife. Now I would like a more leisurely man-to-man account of your great work. Incidentally, do your find the scholarly apparatus—books, *und so weiter* (et cetera)—of the Municipal Universities of New York City adequate to your needs after having enjoyed those of Baden-Baden University and the institutions of high learning in the German Federation?"

"In some respects they are lacking," he admitted. "However, for my purposes they have proved completely adequate." Then once more he dropped his eyes and almost blushed. "But, Papa, you praise my small efforts far too highly." He lowered his voice. "They do not compare with the victory for international industrial relations you yourself have won in a fortnight."

"All in a day's work for the DLG," I said self-deprecatingly, though once again lightly touching my left chest to establish contact with those important documents safely sowed in my inside left breast pocket. "But now, no more polite fencing!" I went on briskly. "Tell me all about those 'small efforts,' as you modestly refer to them."

His eyes met mine. "Well, Papa," he began in suddenly matter-of-fact fashion, "all my work these last two years has been increasingly dominated by a firm awareness of the fragility of the underpinnings of the good world-society we enjoy today. If certain historically minute key-events, or cusps, in only the past one hundred years had been decided differently—if another course had been chosen than the one that was—then the whole world might now be plunged in wars and worse horrors then we ever dream of. It is a chilling insight, but it bulks continually larger in my entire work, my every paper."

I felt the thrilling touch of inspiration. At that moment the wine waiter arrived with our double brandies in small goblets of cut glass. I wove the interruption into the fabric of my inspiration. "Let us drink then to what you name your chilling insight," I said. "*Prosit!*"

The bite and spreading warmth of the excellent *schnapps* quickened my inspiration further. "I believe I understand exactly what you're getting at . . ." I told my son. I set down my half-emptied goblet and pointed at something over my son's shoulder.

He turned his head around, and after one glance back at my pointing finger, which intentionally waggled a tiny bit from side to side, he realized that I was not indicating the entry of the *Krahenest*, but the four sizable bronze statuettes flanking it.

"For instance," I said, "if Thomas Edison and Marie Sklodowska had not married, and especially if they had not had their supergenius son, then Edison's knowledge of electricity and hers of radium and other radioactives might never have been joined. There might never have been developed the fabulous T. S. Edison battery, which is the prime mover of all today's surface and air traffic. Those pioneering electric trucks introduced by the *Saturday Evening Post* in Philadelphia might have remained an expensive freak. And the gas helium might never have been produced industrially to supplement earth's meager subterranean supply."

My son's eyes brightened with the flame of pure scholarship. "Papa," he said eagerly, "you are a genius yourself! You have precisely hit on what is perhaps the most important of those cusp-events I referred to. I am at this moment finishing the necessary research for a long paper on it. Do you know, Papa, that I have firmly established by researching Parisian records that there was in 1894 a close personal relationship between Marie Sklodowska and her fellow radium researcher Pierre Curie, and that she might well have become Madame Curie—or pehaps, Madame Becquerel, for he too was in that work—if the dashing and brilliant Edison had not most opportunely arrived in Paris in December 1894 to sweep her off her feet and carry her off to the New World to even greater achievements?

"And just think, Papa," he went on, his eyes aflame, "what might have happened if their son's battery had not been invented—the most difficult technical achievement, hedged by all sorts of seemingly scientific impossibilities, in the entire millennium-long history of industry. Why, Henry Ford might have manufactured automobiles powered by steam or by exploding natural gas or conceivably even vaporized liquid gasoline, rather than the mass-produced electric cars which have been such a boon to mankind everywhere—not our smokeless cars, but cars spouting all sorts of noxious fumes to pollute the environment."

Cars powered by the danger-fraught combustion of vaporized liquid gasoline!—it almost made me shudder and certainly it was a fantastic thought, yet not altogether beyond the bounds of possibility, I had to admit.

Just then I noticed my gloomy, black-clad Jew sitting only two tables away from us, though how he had got himself into the exclusive *Krahenest* was a wonder. Strange that I had missed his entry—probably immediately after my own, while I had eyes only for my son. His presence somehow threw a dark though only momentary shadow over my bright mood. Let him get some good German food inside him and some fine German wine, I thought generously—it will fill that empty belly of his and even put a bit of a good German smile into those sunken Yiddish cheeks! I combed my little mustache with my thumbnail and swept the errant lock of hair off my forehead.

Meanwhile my son was saying, "Also, Father, if electric transport had not been developed, and if during the last decade relations between Germany and the United States had not been so good, then we might never have gotten from the wells in Texas the supply of natural helium our Zeppelins desperately needed during the brief but vital period before we had put the artificial creation of helium onto an industrial footing. My researchers at Washington have revealed that there was a strong movement in the U.S. military to ban the sale of helium to any other nation, Germany in particular. Only the powerful influence of Edison, Ford, and a few other key Americans, instantly brought to bear, prevented that stupid injuction. Yet if it had gone through, Germany might have been forced to use hydrogen instead of hellium to float her passenger dirigibles. That was another crucial cusp."

"A hydrogen-supported Zeppelin!—ridiculous! Such an airship would be a floating bomb, ready to be touched off by the slightest spark," I protested.

"Not ridiculous, Father," my son calmly contradicted me, shaking his head. "Pardon me for trespassing in your field, but there is an inescapable imperative about certain industrial developments. If there is not a safe road of advance, then a dangerous one will invariably be taken. You must admit, Father, that the development of commercial airships was in its early stages a most perilous venture. During the 1920's there were the dreadful wrecks of the American dirigibles *Roma*, *Shenandoah*, which broke in two, *Akron*, and *Macon*, the British *R-38*, which also broke apart in the air, and *R-101*, the French *Dixmude*, which disappeared in the Mediterranean, Mussolini's *Italia*, which crashed trying to reach the North Pole, and the Russian *Maxim Gorky*, struck down by a plane, with a total loss of no fewer than 340 crew members for the nine accidents. If that had been followed by the explosions of two or three hydrogen Zeppelins, world industry might well have abandoned forever the attempt to create passenger airships and turned instead to the development of large propeller-driven, heavier-than-air craft."

Monster airplanes, in danger every moment of crash from engine failure, competing with good old unsinkable Zeppelins?—impossible, at least at first thought. I shook my head, but not with as much conviction as I might have wished. My son's suggestion was really a valid one.

Besides, he had all his facts at his fingertips and was complete master of his subject, as I also had to allow. Those nine fearfull airship disasters he mentioned had indeed occurred, as I knew well, and might have tipped the scale in favor of long-distance passenger an troop-carrying airplanes, had it not been for helium, the T.S. Edison battery, and German genius.

Fortunately I was able to dump from my mind these uncomfortable speculations and immerse myself in admiration of my son's multisided scholarship. That boy was a wonder!—a real chip off the old block, and, yes, a bit more.

"And now, Dolfy," he went on, using my nickname (I did not mind), "may I turn to an entirely different topic? Or rather to a very different example of my hypothesis of historical cusps?"

I nodded mutely. My mouth was busily full with fine *Sauerbraten* and those lovely, tiny German dumplings, while my nostrils enjoyed the unique aroma of sweet-sour red cabbage. I had been so engrossed in my son's revelations that I had not consciously noted our luncheon being served. I swallowed, took a slug of the good, red Zinfandel, and said, "Please go on."

"It's about the consequences of the American Civil War, Father," he said surprisingly. "Did you know that in the decade after that bloody conflict, there was a very real danger that the whole cause of Negro freedom and rights—for which the war was fought, whatever they say—might well have been completely smashed? The fine work of Abraham Lincoln, Thaddeus Stevens, Charles Sumner, the Freedmen's Bureau, and the Union League Clubs put to naught? And even the Ku Klux Klan underground allowed free reign rather than being sternly repressed? Yes, Father, my thoroughgoing researchings have convinced me such things might easily have happened, resulting in some sort of re-enslavement of the Blacks, with the whole war to be refought at an indefinite future date, or at any rate Reconstruction brought to a dead halt for many decades—with what disastrous effects on the American character, turning its deep simple faith in freedom to hypocrisy, it is impossible to exaggerate. I have published a sizable paper on this subject in the *Journal of Civil War Studies*."

I nodded somberly. Quite a bit of this new subject matter of his was *terra incognita* to me; yet I knew enough of American history to realize he had made a cogent point. More than ever before, I was impressed by his multifaceted learning—he was indubitably a figure in the great tradition of German scholarship, a profound thinker, broad and deep. How fortunate to be his father. Not for the first time, but perhaps with the greatest sincerity yet, I thanked God and the Laws of Nature that I had early moved my family from Braunau, Austria, where I had been born in 1889, to Baden-Baden, where he had grown up in the ambience of the great new university on the edge of the Black Forest and only 150 kilometers from Count Zeppelin's dirigible factory in Wurttemberg, at Friedrichshafen on Lake Constance.

I raised my glass of *Kirschwasser* to him in a solemn, silent toast—we had somehow got to that stage in our meal—and downed a sip of the potent, fiery, white, cherry Brandy.

He leaned toward me and said, "I might as well tell you, Dolf, that my big book, at once popular and scholarly, my *Meisterwerk*, to be titled *If Things Had Gone Wrong*, or perhaps *If Things Had Turned for the Worse*, will deal solely—though illuminated by dozens of diverse examples—with my theory of historical cusps, a highly speculative concept but firmly footed in fact." He glanced at his wristwatch, muttered, "Yes, there's still time for it. So now—" His face grew grave, his voice clear though small—"I will venture to tell you about one more cusp, the most disputable and yet most crucial of them all." He paused. "I warn you, dear Dolf, that this cusp may cause you pain."

"I doubt that," I told him indulgently. "Anyhow, go ahead."

"Very well. In November of 1918, when the British had broken the Hindenburg Line and the weary German army was defiantly dug in along the Rhine, and just before the Allies, under Marshal Foch, launched the final crushing drive which would cut a bloody swath across the heartland to Berlin—"

I understood his warning at once. Memories flamed in my mind like the sudden blinding flares of the battlefield with their deafening thunder. The company I had commanded had been among the most desperately defiant of those he mentioned, heroically nerved for a last-ditch resistance. And then Foch had delivered that last vast blow, and we had fallen back and back and back before the overwhelming numbers of our enemies with their field guns and tanks and armored cars innumerable and above all their huge aerial armadas of De Haviland and Handley-Page and other big bombers escorted by insect-buzzing fleets of Spads and other fighters shooting to bits our last Fokkers and Pfalzes and visiting on Germany a destruction greater far than our Zeps had worked on England. Back, back, back, endlessly reeling and regrouping, across the devastated German countryside, a dozen times decimated yet still defiant until the end came at last amid the ruins of Berlin, and the most bold among us had to admit we were beaten and we surrendered unconditionally—

These vivid, fiery recollections came to me almost instantaneously.

I heard my son continuing, "At that cusp moment in November, 1918, Dolf, there existed a very strong possibility—I have established this beyond question—that an immediate armistice would be offered and signed, and the war ended inconclusively. President Wilson was wavering, the French were very tired, and so on.

"And if that had happened in actuality—harken closely to me now, Dolf—then the German temper entering the decade of the 1920's would have been entirely different. She would have felt she had not been really licked, and there would inevitably have been a secret recrudescence of pan-German militarism. German scientific humanism would not have won its total victory over the Germany of the—yes!—Huns.

"As for the Allies, self-tricked out of the complete victory which lay within their grasp, they would in the long run have treated Germany far less generously than they did after their lust for revenge had been sated by that last drive to Berlin. The League of Nations would not have become the strong instrument for world peace that it is today; it might well have been repudiated by America and certainly secretly detested by Germany. Old wounds would not have healed because, paradoxically, they would not have been deep enough.

"There, I've said my say. I hope it hasn't bothered you too badly, Dolf."

I let out a gusty sigh. Then my wincing frown was replaced by a brow serene. I said very deliberately, "Not one bit, my son, though you have certainly touched my own old wounds to the quick. Yet I feel in my bones that your interpretation is completely valid. Rumors of an armistice were indeed running like wildfire through our troops in that black autumn of 1918. And I know only too well that if there had been an armistice at that time, then officers like myself would have believed that the German soldier had never really been defeated, only betrayed by his leaders and by red incendiaries, and we would have begun to conspire endlessly for a resumption of the war under happier circumstances. My son, let us drink to your amazing cusps."

Our tiny glasses touched with a delicate ting, and the last drops went down of biting, faintly bitter *Kirschwasser*. I buttered a thin slice of pumpernickel and nibbled it—always good to finish off a meal with bread. I was suddenly filled with an immeasurable content. It was a golden moment, which I would have been happy to have go on forever, while I listened to my son's wise words and fed my satisfaction in him. Yes, indeed, it was a golden nugget of pause in the terrible rush of time—the enriching conversation, the peerless food and drink, the darkly pleasant surroundings—

At that moment I chanced to look at my discordant Jew two tables away. For some weird reason he was glaring at me with naked hate, though he instantly dropped his gaze—

But even that strange and disquieting event did not disrupt my mood of golden tranquility, which I sought to prolong by saying in summation, "My dear son, this has been the most exciting though eerie lunch I have ever enjoyed. Your remarkable cusps have opened to me a fabulous world in which I can nevertheless utterly believe. A horridly fascinating world of sizzling hydrogen Zeppelins, of countless—evil-smelling gasoline cars built by Ford instead of his electrics, of re-enslaved American blackamoors, of Madame Becquerels or Curies, a world without the T.E. Edison battery and even T.S. himself, a world in which German scientists are sinister pariahs instead of tolerant, humanitarian, great-souled leaders of world thought, a world in which a mateless old Edison tinkers forever at a powerful storage battery he cannot perfect, a world in which Woodrow Wilson doesn't insist on Germany being admitted at once to the League of Nations, a world of festering hatreds reeling toward a second and worse world war. Oh, altogether an incredible world, yet one in which you have momentarily made me believe, to the extent that I do actually have the fear that time will suddenly shift gears and we will be plunged into that bad dream world, and our real world will become a dream—"

I suddenly chanced to see the face of my watch—

At the same time my son looked at his own left wrist—

"Dolf," he said, springing up in agitation, "I do hope that with my stupid chatter I haven't made you miss—"

I had sprung up too—

"No, no, my son," I heard myself say in a fluttering voice, "but it's true I have little time in which to catch the *Ostwald. Auf Wiedersehn, mein Sohn, auf Wiedersehn!*"

And with that I was hastening, indeed almost running, or else sweeping through the air like a ghost—leaving him behind to settle our reckoning—across a room that seemed to waver with my feverish agitation, alternately darkening and brightening like an electric bulb with its fine tungsten filament about to fly to powder and wink out forever—

Inside my head a voice was saying in calm yet deathknell tones, "The lights of Europe are going out. I do not think they will be rekindled in my generation—"

Suddenly the only important thing in the world for me was to catch the *Ostwald*, get aboard her before she unmoored. That and only that would reassure me that I was in my rightful world. I would touch and feel the *Ostwald*, not just talk about her—

As I dashed between the four bronze figures, they seemed to hunch down and become deformed, while their faces became those of grotesque, aged witches—four evil kobolds leering up at me with a horrid knowledge bright in their eyes—

While behind me I glimpsed in pursuit a tall, black, white-faced figure, skeletally lean—

The strangely short corridor ahead of me had a blank end—the Departure Lounge wasn't there—

I instantly jerked open the narrow door to the stairs and darted nimbly up them as if I were a young man again and not 48 years old—

On the third sharp turn I risked a glance behind and down—

Hardly a flight behind me, taking great pursuing leaps, was my dreadful Jew—

I tore open the door to the 102nd floor. There at last, only a few feet away, was the silver door I sought of the final elevator and softly glowing above it the words, "*Zum Zeppelin.*" At last I would be shot aloft to the *Ostwald* and reality.

But the sing began to blink as the *Krahenest* had, while across the door was pasted askew a white cardboard sign which read "Out of Order."

I threw myself at the door and scrabbled at it, squeezing my eyes several times to make my vision come clear. When I finally fully opened them, the cardboard sign was gone.

But the silver door was gone too, and the words above it forever. I was scrabbling at seamless pale plaster.

There was a touch on my elbow. I spun around.

"Excuse me, sir, but you seem troubled," my Jew said solicitously. "Is there anything I can do?"

I shook my head, but whether in negation or rejection or to clear it, I don't know. "I'm looking for the *Ostwald*," I gasped, only now realizing I'd winded myself on the stairs. "For the zeppelin," I explained when he looked puzzled.

I may be wrong, but it seemed to me that a look of secret glee flashed deep in his eyes, though his general sympathetic expression remained unchanged.

"Oh, the zeppelin," he said in a voice that seemed to me to have become sugary in its solicitude. "You must mean the *Hindenburg.*"

Hindenburg?—I asked myself. There was no zeppelin named *Hindenburg*. Or was there? Could it be that I was mistaken about such a simple and, one would think, immutable matter? My mind had been getting very foggy the last minute or two. Desperately I tried to assure myself that I was indeed myself and in my right world. My lips worked and I muttered to myself, *Bin Adolf Hitler, Zeppelin Fachman . . .*

"But the *Hindenburg* doesn't land here, in any case," my Jew was telling me, "though I think some vague intention once was voiced about topping the Empire State with a mooring mast for dirigibles. Perhaps you saw some news story and assumed—"

His face fell, or he made it seem to fall. The sugary solicitude in his voice became unendurable as he told me, "But apparently you can't have heard today's tragic news. Oh, I do hope you weren't seeking the *Hindenburg* so as to meet some beloved family member or close friend. Brace yourself, sir. Only hours ago, coming in for her landing at Lakehurst, New Jersey, the *Hindenburg* caught fire and burned up entirely in a matter of seconds. Thirty or forty at least of her passengers and crew were burned alive. Oh, steady yourself, sir."

"But the *Hindenburg*—I mean the *Ostwald!*—couldn't burn like that," I protested. "She's a helium zeppelin."

He shook his head. "Oh, no. I'm no scientist, but I know the *Hindenburg* was filled with hydrogen—a wholly typical bit of reckless German risk-running. At least we've never sold helium to the Nazis, thank God."

I stared at him, wavering my face from side to side in feeble denial. While he stared back at me with obviously a new thought in mind.

"Excuse me once again," he said, "but I believe I heard you start to say something about Adolf Hitler. I suppose you know that you bear a certain resemblance to that execrable dictator. If I were you, sir, I'd shave my mustache."

I felt a wave of fury at this inexplicable remark with all its baffling references, yet withal a remark delivered in the unmistakable tones of an insult. And then all my surrounding momentarily reddened and flickered and I felt a tremendous wrench in the inmost core of my being, the sort of wrench one might experience in transiting timelessly from one universe into another parallel to it. Briefly I became a man still named Adolf Hitler, same as the Nazi dictator and almost the same age, a German-American born in Chicago, who had never visited Germany or spoken German, whose friends teased him about his chance resemblance to the other Hitler, and who used stubbornly to say. "No, I won't change my name! Let that *Fuehrer* bastard across the Atlantic change his! Ever hear about the British Winston Churchill writing the American Winston Churchill, who wrote *The Crisis* and other novels, and suggesting he change his name to avoid confusion, since the Englishman had done some writing too? The American wrote back it was a good idea, but since he was three years older, he was senior and so the Britisher should change *his* name. That's exactly how I feel about that son of a bitch Hitler."

The Jew still stared at me sneeringly. I started to tell him off, but then I was lost in a second weird, wrenching transition. The first had been directly from one parallel universe to another. The second was also in time—I aged 14 or 15 years in a single infinite instant while transiting from 1937 (where I had been born in 1889 and was 48) to 1973 (where I had been born in 1910 and was 63). My name changed back to my truly own (but what is that?). And I no longer looked one bit like Adolf Hitler the Nazi dictator (or dirigible expert?), and I had a married son who was a sort of social historian in a New York City municipal university, and he had many brilliant theories, but none of historical cusps.

And the Jew—I mean the tall, thin man in black with possibly Semitic features—was gone. I looked around and around but there was no one there.

I touched my outside left breast pocket, then my hand darted tremblingly underneath. There was no zipper on the pocket inside and no precious documents, only a couple of grimy envelopes with notes I'd scribbled on them in pencil.

I don't know how I got out of the Empire State Building. Presumably by elevator. Though all my memory holds for that period is a persistent image of King Kong tumbling down from its top like a ridiculous yet poignantly pitiable giant teddy bear.

I do recollect walking in a sort of trance for what seemed hours through a Manhattan stinking with monoxide and carcinogens innumerable, half waking from time to time (usually while crossing streets that snarled, not purred) and then relapsing into trance. There were big dogs.

When I at last fully came to myself, I was walking down a twilit Hudson Street at the north end of Greenwich Village. My gaze was fixed on a distant and unremarkable pale-gray square of a building top. I guessed it must be that of the World Trade Center, 1,350 feet tall.

And then it was blotted out by the grinning face of my son, the professor.

"Justin!" I said.

"Fritz!" he said. "We'd begun to worry a bit. Where did you get off to, anyhow? Not that it's a damn bit of my business. If you had an assignation with a go-go girl, you needn't tell me."

"Thanks," I said, "I do feel tired, I must admit, and somewhat cold. But no, I was just looking at some of my old stamping grounds," I told him, "and taking longer than I realized. Manhattan's changed during my years on the West Coast, but not all that much."

"It's getting chilly," he said. "Let's stop in at that place ahead with the black front. It's the White Horse. Dylan Thomas used to drink there. He's supposed to have scribbled a poem on the wall of the can, only they painted it over. But it has the authentic sawdust."

"Good," I said, "only we'll make mine coffee, not ale. Or if I can't get coffee, then cola."

I am not really a *Prosit!*-type person.

The Glove

My most literally tangible brush with the supernatural (something I can get incredibly infatuated with yet forever distrust profoundly, like a very beautiful and adroit call girl) occurred in connection with the rape by a masked intruder of the woman who lived in the next apartment to mine during my San Francisco years. I knew Evelyn Mayne only as a neighbor and I slept through the whole incident, including the arrival and departure of the police, though there came a point in the case when the police doubted both these assertions of mine.

The phrase "victim of rape" calls up certain stereotyped images: an attractive young woman going home alone late at night, enters a dark street, is grabbed . . . or, a beautiful young suburban matron, mother of three, wakes after midnight, feels a nameless dread, is grabbed . . . The truth is apt to be less romantic. Evelyn Mayne was sixty-five long divorced, neglected, and thoroughly detested by her two daughters-in-law and only to a lesser degree by their husbands, lived on various programs of old age, medical and psychiatric assistance, was scrawny, gloomy, alcoholic, waspish, believed life was futile, and either overdosed on sleeping pills or else lightly cut her wrists three or four times a year.

Her assailant at least was somewhat more glamorous, in a sick way. The rapist was dressed all in rather close-fitting gray, hands covered by gray gloves, face obscured by a long shock of straight silver hair falling over it. And in the left hand, at first, a long knife that gleamed silver in the dimness.

And she wasn't grabbed either, at first, but only commanded in a harsh whisper coming through the hair to lie quietly or be cut up.

When she was alone again at last, she silently waited something like the ten minutes she'd been warned to, thinking that at least she hadn't been cut up, or else (who knows?) wishing she had been. Then she went next door (in the opposite direction to mine) and roused Marcia Everly, who was a buyer for a department store and about half her age. After the victim had been given a drink, they called the police and Evelyn Mayne's psychiatrist and also her social worker, who knew her current doctor's number (which she didn't), but they couldn't get hold of either of the last two. Marcia suggested waking me and Evelyn Mayne countered by suggesting they wake Mr. Helpful, who has the next room beyond Marcia's down the hall. Mr. Helpful (otherwise nicknamed Baldy, I never remembered his real name) was someone I loathed because he was always prissily dancing around being neighborly and asking if there was something he could do—and because he was six foot four tall, while I am rather under average height.

Marcia Everly is also very tall, at least for a woman, but as it happens I do not loathe her in the least. Quite the opposite in fact.

But Evelyn Mayne said I wasn't sympathetic, while Marcia (thank goodness!) loathed Mr. Helpful as much as I do—she thought him a weirdo, along with half the other tenants in the building.

So they compromised by waking neither of us, and until the police came Evelyn Mayne simply kept telling the story of her rape over and over, rather mechanically, while Marcia listened dutifully and occupied her mind as to which of our crazy fellow-tenants was the best suspect—granting it hadn't been done by an outsider, although that seemed likeliest. The three most colorful were the statuesque platinum-blond drag queen on the third floor, the long-haired old weirdo on six who wore a cape and was supposed to be into witchcraft, and the tall, silver-haired, Nazi-looking lesbian on seven (assuming she wore a dildo for the occasion as she was nuttier than a five-dollar fruit cake).

Ours really is a weird building, you see, and not just because of its occupants, who sometimes seem as if they were all referred here by mental hospitals. No, it's eerie in its own right. You see, several decades ago it was a hotel with all the rich, warm inner life that once implied: bevies of maids, who actually used the linen closets (empty now) on each floor and the round snap-capped outlets in the baseboards for a vacuum system (that hadn't been operated for a generation) and the two dumbwaiters (their doors forever shut and painted over). In the old days there had been bellboys and an elevator operator and two night porters who'd carry up drinks and midnight snacks from a restaurant that never closed.

But they're gone now, every last one of them, leaving the halls empty-feeling and very gloomy, and the stairwell an echoing void, and the lobby funereal, so that the mostly solitary tenants of today are apt to seem like ghosts, especially when you meet one coming silently around a turn in the corridor where the ceiling light's burned out.

Sometimes I think that, what with the smaller and smaller families and more and more people living alone, our whole modern world is getting like that.

The police finally arrived, two grave and solicitious young men making a good impression—especially a tall and stalwart (Marcia told me) Officer Hart. But when they first heard Evelyn Mayne's story, they were quite skeptical (Marcia could tell, or thought she could, she told me). But they searched Evelyn's room and poked around the fire escapes and listened to her story again, and then they radioed for a medical police-woman, who arrived with admirable speed and who decided after an examination that in all probability there's been recent sex, which would be confirmed by analysis of some smears she'd taken from the victim and the sheets.

Officer Hart did two great things, Marcia said. He got hold of Evelyn Mayne's social worker and told him he'd better get on over quick. And he got from him the phone number of her son who lived in the city and called him up and threw a scare into his wife and him about how they were the nearest of kin, goddamn it, and had better start taking care of the abused and neglected lady.

Meanwhile the other cop had been listening to Evelyn Mayne, who was still telling it, and he asked her innocent questions, and had got her to admit that earlier that night she'd gone alone to a bar down the street (a rather rough place) and had one drink, or maybe three. Which made him wonder (Marcia said she could tell) whether Evelyn hadn't brought the whole thing on herself, maybe by inviting some man home with her, and then inventing the rape, at least in part, when things went wrong. (Though I couldn't see her inventing the silver hair.)

Anyhow the police got her statement and got it signed and then took off, even more solemnly sympathetic than when they'd arrived, Officer Hart in particular.

THE GLOVE

Of course, I didn't know anything about all this when I knocked on Marcia's door before going to work that morning, to confirm a tentative movie date we'd made for that evening. Though I was surprised when the door opened and Mr. Helpful came out looking down at me very thoughtfully, his bald head gleaming, and saying to Marcia in the voice adults use when children are listening. "I'll keep in touch with you about the matter. If there is anything I can do, don't hesitate . . ."

Marcia, looking at him very solemnly, nodded.

And then my feeling of discomfiture was completed when Evelyn Mayne, empty glass in hand and bathrobe clutched around her, edged past me as if I were contagious, giving me a peculiarly hostile look and calling back to Marcia over my head, "I'll come back, my dear, when I've repaired my appearance, so that people can't say your're entertaining bedraggled old hags."

I was relieved when Marcia gave me a grin as soon as the door was closed and said, "Actually she's gone to get herself another drink, after finishing off my supply. But really, Jeff, she has a reason to this morning—and for hating any man she runs into." And her face grew grave and troubled (and a little frightened too) as she quickly clued me in on the night's nasty events. Mr. Helpful, she explained, had dropped by to remind them about a tenants' meeting that evening and, when he got the grisly news, to go into a song and dance about how shocked he was and how guilty at having slept through it all, and what could he do?

Once she broke of to say, almost worriedly, "What I can't understand, Jeff, is why any man would want to rape someone like Evelyn."

I shrugged. "Kinky some way, I suppose. It does happen, you know. To old women, I mean. Maybe a mother thing."

"Maybe he *hates* women," she speculated. "Wants to punish them."

I nodded.

She had finished by the time Evelyn Mayne came back, very listless now, looking like a woebegone ghost, and dropped into a chair. She hadn't got dressed or even combed her hair. In one hand she had her glass, full and dark, and in the other a large, pale gray leather glove, which she carried oddly, dangling it by one finger.

Marcia started to ask her about it, but she just began to recite once more all that had happened to her that night, in an unemotional mechanical voice that sounded as if it would go on forever.

Look, I didn't like the woman—she was a particularly useless, venemous sort of nuisance (those wearisome suicide attempts!)—but that recital got to me. I found myself hating the person who would deliberately put someone into the state she was in. I realized, perhaps for the first time, just what a vicious and sick crime rape is and how cheap are all the easy jokes about it.

Eventually the glove came into the narrative naturally: ". . . and in order to do that he had to take off his glove. He was particularly excited just then, and it must have got shoved behind the couch and forgotten, where I found it just now."

Marcia pounced on the glove at once then, saying it was important evidence they must tell the police about. So she called them and after a bit she managed to get Officer Hart himself, and he told her to tell Evelyn Mayne to hold on to the glove and he'd send someone over for it eventually.

It was more than time for me to get on to work, but I stayed until she finished her call, because I wanted to remind her about our date that evening.

She begged off, saying she'd be too tired from the sleep she'd lost and anyway she'd decided to go to the tenants' meeting tonight. She told me, "This has made me realize

473

that I've got to begin to take some responsibility for what happens around me. We may make fun of such people—the good neighbors—but they've got something solid about them."

I was pretty miffed at that, though I don't think I let it show. Oh, I didn't so much mind her turning me down—there were reasons enough—but she didn't have to make such a production of it and drag in "good neighbors." (Mr. Helpful, who else?) Besides, Evelyn Mayne came out of her sad apathy long enough to give me a big smile when Marcia said "No."

So I didn't go to the tenants' meeting that night, as I might otherwise have done. Instead I had dinner out and went to the movie—it was lousy—and then had a few drinks, so that it was late when I got back (no signs of life in the lobby or lift or corridor) and gratefully piled into bed.

I was dragged out of the depths of sleep—that first blissful plunge—by a persistent knocking. I shouted something angry but unintelligible and when there was no reply made myself get up, feeling furious.

It was Marcia. With a really remarkable effort I kept my mouth shut and even smoothed out whatever expression was contorting my face. The words one utters on being suddenly awakened, especially from that matchless first sleep that is never recaptured, can be as disastrous as speaking in drink. Our relationship had progressed to the critical stage and I sure didn't want to blow it, especially when treasures I'd hoped to win were spread out in front of my face, as it were, under a semitransparent nightgown and hastily thrown on negligee.

I looked up, a little, at her face. Her eyes were wide.

She said in a sort of frightened little-girl voice that didn't seem at all put on, "I'm awfully sorry to wake you up at three o'clock in the morning, Jeff, but would you keep this 'spooky' for me? I can't get to sleep with it in my room."

It is a testimony to the very high quality of Marcia's treasures that I didn't until then notice what she was carrying in front of her—in a fold of toilet paper: the pale gray leather glove Evelyn Mayne had found behind her couch.

"Huh?" I said, not at all brilliantly. "Didn't Officer Hart come back, or send someone over to pick it up?"

She shook her head. "Evelyn had it, of course, while I was at my job—her social worker did come over right after you left. But then at suppertime her son and daughter-in-law came (Officer Hart did scare them!) and bundled her off to the hospital, and she left the glove with me. I called the police, but Officer Hart was off duty and Officer Halstead, whom I talked to, told me they'd be over to pick it up early in the morning. Please take it, Jeff. Whenever I look at it, I think of that crazy sneaking around with the silver hair down his face and waving the knife. It keeps giving me the shivers."

I looked again at her "spooky" in its fold of tissue (so that she wouldn't have to touch it, what other reason?) and, you know, it began to give me the shivers. Just an old glove, but now it had an invisible gray aura radiating from it.

"OK," I said, closing my hand on it with an effort, and went on ungraciously, really without thinking, "Though I wondered you didn't ask Mr. Helpful first, what with all his offers and seeing him at the meeting."

"Well, I asked you," she said a little angrily. Then her features relaxed into a warm smile. "Thanks, Jeff."

Only then did it occur to me that here I was passing up in my sleep-soddenness what might be a priceless opportunity. Well, that could be corrected. But before I could invite her in, there came this sharp little cough, or clearing of the throat. We both turned and there was Mr. Helpful in front of his open door, dressed in pajamas and a belted maroon dressing gown. He came smiling and dancing toward us (he didn't really dance, but he gave that impression in spite of being six foot four) and saying, "Could I be of any assistance, Miss Everly? Did something alarm you? Is there . . . er . . .?" He hesitated, as if there might be something he should be embarrassed at.

Marcia shook her head curtly and said to me quite coolly, "No, thank you, I needn't come in, Mr. Winters. That will be fine. Good night."

I realized Baldy *had* managed to embarrass her and that she was making it clear that we weren't parting after a rendezvous, or about to have one. (But to use my last name!)

As she passed him, she gave him a formal nod. He hurried back to his own door, a highlight dancing on the back of his head. (Marcia says he shaves it; I, that he doesn't have to.)

I waited until I heard her double-lock her door and slide the bolt across. Then I looked grimly at Baldy until he'd gone inside and closed his—I had that pleasure. Then I retired myself, tossed the glove down on some sheets of paper on the table in front of the open window, threw myself into bed, and switched out the light.

I fully expected to spend considerable time being furious at my hulking, mincing officious neighbor, and maybe at Marcia too, before I could get to sleep, but somehow my mind took off on a fantasy about the building around me as it might have been a half century ago. Ghostly bellboys sped silently with little notes inviting or accepting rendezvous. Ghostly waiters wheeled noiseless carts of silver-covered suppers for two. Pert, ghostly maids whirled ghostly sheets through the dark air as they made the bed, their smiles suggesting they might substitute for nonarriving sweethearts. The soft darkness whirlpooled. Somewhere was wind.

I woke with a start as if someone or something had touched me, and I sat up in bed. And then I realized that something *was* touching me high on my neck, just below my ear. Something long, like a finger laid flat or—oh God!—a centipede. I remembered how centipedes were supposed to cling with their scores of tiny feet—and *this* was clinging. As a child I'd been terrified by a tropical centipede that had come weaving out of a stalk of newbought bananas in the kitchen, and the memory still returned full force once in a great while. Now it galvanized me into whirling my hand behind my head and striking my neck a great brushing swipe, making my jaw and ear sting. I instantly turned on the light and rapidly looked all around me without seeing anything close to me that might have brushed off my neck. I thought I'd felt something with my hand when I'd done that, but I couldn't be sure.

And then I looked at the table by the window and saw that the glove was gone.

Almost at once I got the vision of it lifting up and floating through the air at me, fingers first, or else dropping off the table and inching across the floor and up the bed. I don't know which was worse. The thing on my neck *had* felt leathery.

My immediate impulse was to check if my door was still shut. I couldn't tell from where I sat. A very tall clothes cabinet abuts the door, shutting the view off from the head of the bed. So I pushed my way down the bed, putting my feet on the floor after looking down to make sure there was nothing in the immediate vicinity.

And then a sharp gust of wind came in the window and blew the last sheet of paper off the table and deposited it on the floor near the other sheets of paper *and the glove* and the tissue now disentangled from it.

I was so relieved I almost laughed. I went over and picked up the glove, feeling a certain revulsion, but only at the thought of who had worn it and what it had been involved in. I examined it closely, which I hadn't done earlier. It was a rather thin gray kid, a fairly big glove and stretched still further as if a pretty big hand had worn it, but quite light enough to have blown off the table with the papers.

There were grimy streaks on it and a slightly stiff part where some fluid had dried and a faintly reddish streak that might have been lipstick. And it looked old—decades old.

I put it back on the table and set a heavy ashtray on top of it and got back in bed, feeling suddenly secure again.

It occurred to me how the empty finger of a gray leather glove is really very much like a centipede, some of the larger of which are the same size, flat and yellowish gray (though the one that had come out of the banana stalk had been bright red), but these thoughts were no longer frightening.

I looked a last time across the room at the glove, pinioned under the heavy ashtray, and I confidently turned off the light.

Sleep was longer in coming this time, however. I got my fantasy of hotel ghosts going again, but gloves kept coming into it. The lissome maids wore work ones as they rhythmically polished piles of ghostly silver. The bellboys' hands holding the ghostly notes were gloved in pale gray cotton. And there were opera gloves, almost armpit length, that looked like spectral white cobras, especially when they were drawn inside-out off the sinuous, snake-slender arms of wealthy guesting ladies. And other ghostly gloves, not all hotel ones, came floating and weaving into my fantasy: the black gloves of morticians, the white gloves of policemen, the bulky fur-lined ones of ploar explorers, the trim dark gauntlets of chauffeurs, the gloves of hunters with separate stalls only for thumb and trigger finger, the mittens of ice-skaters and sleigh riders, old ladies' mitts without any fingers at all, the thin, translucent elastic gloves of surgeons, wielding flashing scalpels of silver-bright steel—a veritable whirlpool of gloves that finally led me down, down, down to darkness.

Once again I woke with a start, as if I'd been touched, and shot up. Once again I felt something about four inches long clinging high on my neck, only this time under the other ear. Once again I frantically slashed at my neck and jaw, stinging them painfully, only this time I struck upward and away. I *thought* I felt something go.

I got the light on and checked the door at once. It was securely shut. Then I looked at the table by the open window. The heavy ashtray still sat in the center of it, rock firm.

But the rapist's glove that had been under it was gone.

I must have stood there a couple of minutes, telling myself this could not be. Then I went over and lifted the ashtray and carefully inspected its underside, as if the glove had somehow managed to shrink and was clinging there.

And all the while I was having this vision of the glove painfully humping itself from under the ashtray and inching to the table's edge and dropping to the floor and then crawling off . . . almost anywhere.

Believe me, I searched my place then, especially the floor. I even opened the doors to the closet and the clothes cabinet, though they had been tightly shut, and searched the floor there. And of course I searched under and behind the bed. And more than once while I searched, I'd suddenly jerk around thinking I'd seen something gray approaching my shoulder from behind.

There wasn't a sign of the glove.

It was dawn by now—had been for sometime. I made coffee and tried to think rationally about it.

It seemed to boil down to three explanations that weren't widely farfetched.

First, that I'd gone out of my mind. Could be, I suppose. But from what I'd read and seen, most people who go crazy know damn well ahead of time that something frightening is happening to their minds, except maybe paranoics. Still, it remained a possibility.

Second, that someone with a duplicate or master key had quietly taken the glove away while I was asleep. The apartment manager and janitor had such keys. I'd briefly given my duplicate to various people. Why, once before she got down on me, I'd given it to Evelyn Mayne—matter of letting someone in while I was at work. I *thought* I'd got it back from her, though I remember once having a second duplicate made—I'd forgotten why. The main difficulty about this explanation was motive. Who'd want to get the glove?—except the rapist, maybe.

Third, of course, there was the supernatural. Gloves are ghostly to start with, envelopes for hands—and if there isn't a medieval superstition about wearing the flayed skin of another's hand to work magic, there ought to be. (Of course, there was the Hand of Glory, its fingers flaming like candles, guaranteed to make people sleep while being burgled, but there the skin is still on the dried chopped-off hand.) And there are tales of spectral hands a-plenty—pointing out buried treasure or hidden graves, or at guilty murderers, or carrying candles or daggers—so why not gloves? And could there be a kind of telekinesis in which a hand controls at a distance the movements and actions of a glove it has worn? Of course that would be psionics or whatnot, but to me the parapsychological is supernatural. (And in that case what had the glove been trying to do probing at my neck?—strangle me, I'd think.) And somewhere I'd read of an aristocratic Brazilian murderess of the last century who wore gloves woven of spider silk, and of a knight blinded at a crucial moment in a tourney by a lady's silken glove worn as a favor. Yes, they were eerie envelopes, I thought, gloves were, but I was just concerned with one of them, a vanishing glove.

I started with a jerk as there came a measured *knock-knock*. I opened the door and looked up at the poker faces of two young policemen. Over their shoulders Mr. Helpful was peering down eagerly at me, his lips rapidly quirking in little smiles with what I'd call questioning pouts in between. Back and a little to one side was Marcia, looking shocked and staring intently at me through the narrow space between the second policeman and the doorjamb.

"Jeff Winters," the first policeman said to me, as if it were a fact that he was putting into place. It occurred to me that young policemen look very *blocky* around their narrow hips with all that equipment they carry snugly nested and cased in black leather.

"Officer Hart—" Marcia began anxiously.

The second policeman's eyes flickered toward her, but just then the first policeman continued, "Your neighbor Miss Everly says she handed you a glove earlier this morning," and he stepped forward into the private space (I think it's sometimes called) around my body, and I automatically stepped back.

"We want it," he went on, continuing to step forward, and I back.

I hesitated. What was I to say? That the glove had started to spook me and then disappeared? Officer Hart followed the first policeman in. Mr. Helpful followed *him* in and stopped just inside my door, Marcia still beyond him and looking frantic. Officer Hart turned, as if about to tell Mr. Helpful to get out, but just then Officer Halstead (that was the other name Marcia had mentioned) said, "Well, you've still got it, haven't you? She gave it to you, didn't she?"

I shook and then nodded my head, which must have made me look rattled. He came closer still and said harshly and with a note of eagerness, "Well, where is it, then?"

I had to look up quite sharply at him to see his face. Beyond it, just to one side of it, diagonally upward across the room, was the top of the tall clothes cabinet, and on the edge of that there balanced that damned gray glove, flat fingers dripping over.

I froze. I could have sworn I'd glanced up there more than once when I was hunting the thing, and seen nothing. Yet there it was, as if it had flown up there or else been flicked there by me the second time I'd violently brushed something from my face.

Officer Halstead must have misread my look of terror, for he ducked his head forward toward mine and rasped. "Your neighbor Mr. Angus says that it's *your* glove, that he saw you wearing gray gloves night before last! What do you say?"

But I didn't say anything, for at that moment the glove slid off its precarious perch and dropped straight down and landed on Mr. Helpful's (Angus's) shoulder close to his neck, just like the hand of an arresting cop.

Now it may have been that in ducking his head to look at it, he trapped it between his chin and collarbone, or it may have been (as it looked to me) that the glove actively clung to his neck and shoulder, resisting all his frantic efforts to peel it off, while he reiterated, his voice mounting in screams, "It's not my glove!"

He took his hands away for a moment and the glove dropped to the floor.

He looked back and forth and saw the dawning expressions on the faces of the two policemen, and then with a sort of despairing sob he whipped a long knife from under his coat.

Considerably to my surprise I started toward him, but just then Officer Hart endeared himself to us all forever by wrapping his arms around Mr. Angus like a bear, one hand closing on the wrist of the hand holding the knife.

I veered past him (I vividly recall changing the length of one of my strides so as not to step on the glove) and reached Marcia just in time to steady her as, turned quite white, she swayed, her eyelids fluttering.

I heard the knife clatter to the floor. I turned, my arms around Marcia, and we both saw Mr. Angus seem to shrink and collapse in Officer Hart's ursine embrace, his face going gray as if he were an empty glove himself.

That was it. They found the other glove and the long silver wig in a locked suitcase in his room. Marcia stayed frightened long enough, off and on, for us to become better acquainted and cement our friendship.

Officer (now Detective) Hart tells us that Mr. Angus is a model prisoner at the hospital for the criminally insane and has gone very religious, but never smiles. And he—Hart—now has the glove in a sort of Black Museum down at the station, where it has never again been seen to move under its own power. If it ever did.

One interesting thing. The gloves had belonged to Mr. Angus's father, now deceased, who had been a judge.

The Death of Princes

Ever since the discovery Hal and I made last night, or rather the amazing explanation we worked out for an accumulated multitude of curious facts, covering them all (the tentative solution to a riddle that's been a lifetime growing, you might say) I have been very much concerned and, well, yes, frightened, but also filled with the purest wonder and a gnawing curiosity about what's going to happen just ten years from now to Hal and me and to a number of our contemporaries who are close friends—to Margaret and Daffy (our wives), to Mack, Charles, and Howard, to Helen, Gertrude and Charlotte, to Betty and Elizabeth—and to the whole world too. Will there be (after ten years) a flood of tangible miracles and revelations from outer space, including the discovery of an ancient civilization compared to which Egypt and Chaldea are the merest whims or aberrations of infant intelligence, or a torrent of eldritch terrors from the black volumes between the glittering stars, or only dusty death?—especially for me and those dearly valued comrade-contemporaries of mine.

Ten years, what are they? Nothing to the universe—the merest millifraction of an eye blink, or microfraction of a yawn—or even to a young person with all his life ahead. But when they are your last ten years, or at the very best your next to last . . .

I'm also in particular concerned about what's happened to Francois Broussard (we're out of touch with him again) and to his ravishing and wise young wife and to their brilliant 15-year-old son (he would be now) and about what part that son may play in the events due ten years from this year of 1976, especially if he goes on to become a spaceman, as his father envisioned for him. For Francois Broussard is at or near the center of the riddle we think (and also fear, I must confess) we solved last night up to a point, Hal and I. In fact, he almost *is* the riddle. Let me explain.

I was born late in 1910 (a few months after Hal and before Broussard—all of us, I and my dear contemporaries, were born within a year or two of each other) too young to have been threatened in any way by World War I, yet old enough to have readily escaped the perils of military service in World War II (by early marriage, a child or two, a more or less essential job). In fact, we were all survivor types like Heinlein harps on (except my kind of survival doesn't involve fighting for my species—zoological paranoid fanaticism!—but for me and mine . . . and who *those* are, I decide) and I early began to develop the conviction that there was something special about us that made us an elite, a chosen mini-people, and that set us apart from the great mass of humanity (the canaille, Broussard had us calling those, way way back) beginning its great adventure with democracy and all democracy's wonders and Pandora ills: mass production, social

479

security, the welfare state, antibiotics and overpopulation, atomics and pollution, electronic computers and the strangling serpents of bureaucracy's red and white tape (monstrous barber pole), the breaking loose from this single planet Earth along with that other victory over the starry sky—smog. Oh, we've come a long way in sixty years or so.

But I was going to tell you about Broussard. He was our leader, but also our problem child; the mouthpiece of our ideals and secret dreams of glory, but also our mocker, severest critic, and gadfly, the devil's advocate; the one who kept dropping out of sight from time to time for years and years (we never did, we kept in touch, the rest of us) and then making a triumphant return when least expected; the socially mobile one too mysteriously hobnobbing with notorious public figures and adventuresses, with people in the news, but also with riff-raff, revolutionaries, rapscallions generally, criminals even, and low-life peasant types (we stuck mostly with our own class, we were cautious —except when he seduced us out of that); the world traveler and cosmopolite (we stayed close to the U.S.A., pretty much).

In fact, if there was one thing that stood out about Francois Broussard, first and foremost, it was that aura of the foreign and the mysterious, that air of coming from some bourne a lot farther off than Mexico or Tangier or Burma or Bangkok (places he made triumphant returns from and told us excitingly bizarre stories about, stories that glittered with wealth and high living and dissoluteness and danger; he was always most romantically attractive to our ladies then, and he's had affairs with several of them over the years, I'm fairly sure, and maybe one with Hal, it's just possible).

We never have known about his background at first hand, in the same way we do about each other's. His story, which he has never varied, is that he was a foundling brought up by an ancient and eccentric Manhattan millionaire (the romantic touch again) Pierre Broussard but also called "French Pete" and "Silver Pete," who made his pile mining in Colorado, a lifelong secret crony of Mark Twain, and educated (Francois was) by tutors and in Paris (he's named his son by his young wife Pierre, the boy he told us would become a spaceman).

In physical appearance he's a little under middle height but taller than Hal and slenderer (I'm a giant), rather dark complected with very dark brown hair, though silvered when we last saw him in 1970 six years ago. He's very quick and graceful in his movements, very fluid, even in later years. He's danced in ballet and he's never motion sick. In fact, he moves like a cat, always landing on his feet, though he once told me that gravity fields seemed unnatural to him, a distorting influence on the dance of life—he was the first person I knew to dive with aqualung, to go the Cousteau route into the silent world.

His style of dress has always accentuated his foreign air—he was also the first man I knew to wear (at different times) a cape, a beret, an ascot, and a Vandyke beard (and wear his hair long) all back in the days when it took a certain courage to do those things.

And he's always been into the occult of one sort or another, but with this difference: that he always mixes real science in with it, biofeedback with the witchcraft, Jung with the flying saucers, verified magnetism with Colonel Estobani's healing hands. For instance, when he casts a horoscope for one of his wealthy clients (we've never been his clients, any of us; for the most, we're something special) he uses the actual positions of the sun and moon and planets in the constellations rather than in the "signs"—the constellations as they were two thousand years ago and more. He's been an avid field astronomer all his life, with a real feeling for the position of the stars and all the wandering bodies at any instant. In fact, he's the only person I've even known to look at the ground and give me the feeling that he was observing the stars that shine above the antipodes—look at his knees and see the Southern Cross.

(I know I seem to be going on forever about Broussard, but really you have to know a great deal about him and about his life before you'll get the point of the explanation Hal and I discovered last night and why it hit us as hard as it did and frightened us.)

After what I've said about horoscopes and the occult, it won't surprise you to hear that our Francois made his living mostly as a fortuneteller. And in view of my remarks about mixing in science, it may not startle you all that much to learn that he was also apparently a genuine question answerer (I can't think of a less clumsy way to phrase it) especially in the field of mathematics, as if he were the greatest of lightning calculators or as if—this expresses it best—he had access to an advanced electronic computer back in the 1920's and 1930's, when such instruments were only dreams—and the memory of the failure of Cavendish's differential engine, which tried to do it all mechanically. At any rate, he had engineers and statisticians and stockbrokers among his clients, and one astronomer, for whom he calculated the orbit of an asteroid—Mack verified that story.

A queer thing about Broussard's question answering (or precision fortunetelling)—it always took him a certain minimum time to get his answers and that time varied somewhat over the years: ten hours around 1930, twelve hours around 1950, but only ten hours again in 1970. He'd tell his clients to come back in so many hours. It was very strange. (But we just mostly heard about all that. We never were his clients, as I've said, or members of his little mystic groups either—though we occasionally profited from his talent.)

A few more strange things I must tell you about Broussard while they're fresh in my memory, mostly unusual notions he had and odd things he said one time or another—a few more strange things and one vision or dream he had when he was young and that seemed to signify a lot to him.

Like Bernard Shaw and Heinlein (recalling both *Back to Methuselah* and *Children of Methuselah*) Francois Broussard has always been hipped on the idea of immortality or at least very long life. "Why do we all have to die at seventy-five or so?" he'd ask. "Maybe it's just mass suggestion on an undreamed-of scale. Why can't we live to be three hundred, at least?—and maybe there are some among us (a long-life genetic strain) who do so, secretely."

And once he said to me, "Look here, Fred, do you suppose that if a person lived well over a hundred years, he or she might betamorphose into some entirely different and vastly superior sort of being, like a caterpillar into a butterfly? Aldous Huxley suggested something of that sort in *After Many a Summer Dies the Swan*, though there the second being wasn't superior. Maybe we're all supposed to do that, but just don't live long enough for the transformation to happen. Something we lost when we lost our empire or empyry—no, I'm just being poetic."

Another pet idea of his was of people living in and coming from space—and remember, this was way before earth satellites or planetary probes . . . or flying saucers and von Daniken either. "Why can't people live in space?" he'd demand. "They wouldn't have to take along all that much of their environment. There'd be perpetual sunlight, for one thing, and freedom from the killing strain of gravity that cuts our lives short. I tell you, Fred, maybe this planet was settled from somewhere else, just like America was. Maybe we're a lost and retrogressed fragment of some great astral empire."

Speaking of the astral reminds me that there was one particular *part* of the heavens that Francois Broussard was especially interested in and somehow associated with himself—particularly in the late 1940's and early 1950's, when he was living in Arizona with its clear, starry nights that showed the Milky Way; he had some sort of occult coterie there, we learned; he'd stare and stare at it (the spot in the heavens) with and without a telescope or binoculars through the long desert nights, like a sailor on a desert island watching for a ship along a sea lane it might follow. In fact, he once spotted a new comet there, a very faint one. Not very surprising in an astrologer, what with their signs, or constellations of the zodiac, but this spot was halfway around the heavens from his natal sign, which was Pisces, or Aquarius rather by his way of figuring it. He was born February 19, 1911, though exactly how he knew the date so certainly, being a foundling, we've never learned—or at least I never have.

The spot in the heavens that fascinated or obsessed him so (*his* spot, you might say) was in Hydra, a long and straggling, quite dim constellation. Its serpent head, which lies south of zodiacal Leo, is a neat group of faint stars resembling a bishop's miter flattened down. Hydra's only bright star, located still farther south and where the serpent's heart would be, if serpents have a heart, is Alphard, often called the Lonely One, because it's the only prominent star in quite a large area. I can remember thinking how suitable that was for Francois—"the Lonely One," theatrical and Byronic.

One other thing he had odd angles on, mixing the supernatural with the scientific, or at any rate the pseudo-scientific, was ghosts. He thought they might be faintly material in some way, a dying person's last extruded ectoplasm, perhaps, or else something very ancient people transformed into, the last stage of existence, like with Heinlein's Martians. And he wondered about the ghosts of inanimate objects—or at least objects most people would think of as inanimate.

I recall him asking me around 1950, "Fred, what do you think the ghost of a computer would be like?—one of the big electric brains, so called?" (I remembered that later on when I read about Mike or Mycroft in Heinlein's *The Moon Is a Harsh Mistress*.)

But I must tell you about Francois' vision, or dream, the one that seemed to mean so much to him—almost as much as his spot in Hydra near Alphard. He's the sort of person who tells his dreams, at least his fancy cosmic or Jungian ones, and gets other people to tell theirs.

It began, he said, with him flying or rather swimming around in black and empty space—in free fall, a person might say today, but he had his dream and described it back about 1930.

He was really lost in the void, he said, exiled from earth, because the black space in which he swam was speckled with stars in every direction, whichever way he looked as he twisted and turned (he could see the full circle of the Milky Way and also the full circle of the zodiac) except there was one star far brighter than all the others, almost painfully glaring, although it was still just a point of light, like Venus to the naked eye among the planets.

And then he gradually became aware that he was not alone in the void, that swimming around with him, but rotating and revolving around him very ponderously, moving very slowly, were five huge, black, angular shapes silhouetted against the starfields. He could actually see their sides only when they happened to reflect the light of the glaring Venus-like star. Those sides were always flat, never rounded, and seemed to be made of some silvery metal that had been dulled by ages of exposure so that it looked like lead.

The flat sides were always triangles or squares or pentagons, so that he finally realized in his dream that the five shapes were the five regular, or Platonic solids, perhaps discovered by Pythagoras: the tetrahedron, the hexahedron (or cube), the octahedron, dodecahedron (twelve-sider), and icosahedron (twenty-sider). A total of fifty sides for all five bodies.

"And somehow that seemed highly significant and very frightening," Francois would say, "as though in the depths of space I'd been presented with the secret of the universe, if only I knew how to interpret it. Even Kepler thought that about the five regular solids, you know, and tried to work it out in his *Mysterium Cosmographicum.*

"But oh God, those polyhedrons were *old,*" he would go on. "As if very finely pitted by eons of meteoric dust impacting and weathered by an eternity of exposure to every variety of radiation in the electromagnetic spectrum.

"And I somehow got the feeling," he would continue, fixing you with those wild eyes of his, "that there were *things* inside those huge shapes that were older still. Things, beings, ancient objects, maybe beings frozen or mummified—I don't know—maybe material ghosts. And then it burst upon me that I was in the midst of a vast floating cemetery, the loneliest in the universe, adrift in space. Imagine the pyramids of Cheops, King and Queen's Chamber and all, weightless and lost between the stars. Well, they do make lead coffins and if the living can live in space, so can the dead—and we mightn't a very advanced civilization, an astral empire put their tombs in space?" (Harking back to his dream in the 1950's he made that "into orbit," and we all remembered his dream when at that time some nut mortician suggested orbiting globular silver urns as repositories for human ashes.)

Sometimes at that point Francois would quote those lines of Calpurnia to Caesar in Shakespeare's play "When beggars die, there are no comets seen; The heavens themselves blaze forth the death of princes." (Shakespeare was a very comet-conscious man; they had a flood of bright ones in his time.)

"And then it seemed to me," he would continue, "that all those ghosts were flooding invisibly out of those five floating mausoleums and all converging on me suffocatingly, choking me with their dust . . . and I woke up."

In 1970 he added a new thought to his vision and to his odd notions about ghosts too, his eyes still wild and bright, though wrinkle-netted: "You know how they call the neutrino the ghost particle? Well, there are some even ghostlier and still more abstract properties of existence being discovered today, or at least hypothesized, by people like Glashow, properties so weird and insubstantial that they have names, believe it or not, like strangeness and charm. Maybe ghosts are beings that have no mass or energy at all, only strangeness and charm—and maybe spin." And the bright eyes twinkled.

But now in my story of Francois Broussard (and all of us) I have to go back to about 1930, when the neutrino hadn't been dreamed of and they were, in fact, just discovering the neutron and learning how to explain isotopes. We were all students at the University of Chicago—that's how we got together in the first place. Francois was living with (sponging off?) some wealthy people there in Hyde Park who helped support the Oriental Institute and the Civic Opera and he was auditing a couple of courses we were taking—that's how we got to know him. He was wearing the cape and Vandyke then—of fine, dark brown hair, almost black, that was silky with youth.

He'd come straight from Paris on the *Bremen* in a record four-day crossing with the latest news of the Left Bank and Harry's American Bar and Gide and Gertrude Stein. His foster father, old Pierre Broussard, the crony of Mark Twain, had been dead some few years (expiring at ninety in bed—with his newest mistress) and Francois had been done out of his inheritance by conniving relatives, but that hadn't taken the gloss off the grotesque incidents and scrapes of his childhood, which made old Silver Pete sound like a crazy wizard and Francois the most comically precocious of apprentices.

What with all his art interests he seemed something of a dilettante at first, in spite of also auditing a math course in the theory of sets (then groups, *very* advanced stuff at that time) but then we got the first demonstration of his question answering. Howard was getting his master's degree in psych, except that he'd gotten conned into doing a thesis that involved doing two semester's paper work at least correlating the results of one of his thesis-professor's experiments—simple enough math, but mountains of it. Howard put off this monstrous chore until there was not a prayer of his finishing it in time. Francois learned about it, carried Howard's figures off, and came back with the answers—pages and pages of them—sixteen hours later. Howard couldn't believe it, but he checked an answer at random and it was right. He rushed the stuff to the thesis typist—and got his master's in due course.

I was there when Francois passed the stuff to Howard, saying, "Three hours to digest the figures, *ten hours to get the answers,* three hours to set them down." (There turned out to be good reason for remembering that ten-hour figure exactly.)

Oh, but he was a charmer, though, Francois was, and in many ways. (Talk about strangeness and charm, *he* had them both, all right.) I think he was having an affair with Gertrude then. His rich Hyde Park friends had set him adrift about that time and hers was the wealthiest family of any of ours, though that may have had nothing to do with it. Yes, a thoroughgoing charmer, but much more than that—a catalyst for imagination and ambition was what he was. There we were, a small bunch of rather bright and fortunate young people, thinking ourselves somehow special and exceptional, but really very naive. Avid for culture on general principles. Just finding out about Marxism and the class war, but not seriously tempted by it. Social security was not yet our concern— the stock market crash of October end, 1929, had barely begun to teach us about social insecurity. Our heroes were mostly writers and scientists—people like T.S. Eliot, Hemingway, James Joyce, Einstein, Freud, Adler, Norman Thomas, Maynard Hutchins at our own university with his Great Books and two-year bachelor's degree, yes, and Lindberg and Amelia Earhart and Greta Garbo. (What a contrast with today's comparable heroes and heroines, who seem to be mostly anti-establishment and welfare-state types: leftist social workers, drug-involved paramedics, witches and occultists, mystics and back-to-nature gurus, revolutionists, feminists, black power people, gay liberators, draft-card burners—though we did have our pacifists, come to think of it, but they were chiefly non-functional idealists. What a tremendous change all that implies.)

Anyhow, there we were with our dreams and our ideals, our feeling of being somehow different, and so you can imagine how we ate up the stuff that Francois fed us about being some sort of lost or secret aristocrats, almost as if we were members of some submerged superculture—*slans*, you might say, remembering Van Vogt's novel of a few years later; tendrilless slans! (Several of us were into science fiction. I vividly recall seeing the first issue of *Amazing* on a news stand—and grabbing it!—fifty years ago.)

I remember the exact words Francois used once. "Every mythology says that upon occasion the gods come down out of the skies and lie with chosen daughters of men. Their seed drifts down from the heavens. Well, we were all born about the same time, weren't we?"

And then, just about that time, there came what I still tend to think of as scandal and shock. Francois Broussard was in jail in a highway town west of Chicago, charged with a sex offense by a young male hitchhiker. (I've just been mentioning gay liberation, haven't I? Well, what I said about change and contrast between our times and then goes double here.) Hal and Charles went bravely off and managed to bail him out. To my lasting shame I dodged that duty of friendship, though I contributed some of the money. The upshot: almost at once, before I or any of the others saw him again, Francois jumped bail, simply disappeared, first telling Charles, who was dumbfounded by it,

"Sorry to disappoint you, but of course I'm guilty. I simply couldn't resist the creature. I thought, mistakenly, that he was one of us—an imperial page, perhaps." And that grotesque and flippant answer was the end of the whole Chicago episode, leaving us all with very mixed feelings.

But as the months and years passed, we tended to remember the glamorous things about him and forget the other—in fact, I don't think we'd have kept in touch with each other the way we did except for him, although he was the one who kept dropping out of sight. Hal married Margaret, and his editorial work and writing took him to New York City, while mine took me and Daffy, married also, to Los Angeles and the high desert near it, where I got interested in field astronomy myself. The others got their lives squared away one way or another, scattering quite a bit, but keeping in touch through class reunions and common interests, but mostly by correspondence, that dying art.

It was Elizabeth who first ran into Francois again about 1950 in Arizona, where he was living in a rambling ranch house full of Mexican curios (he'd established dual citizenship) and surrounded by his artsy-occulty, well-to-do coterie. He seemed quite well off himself, she reported, and during the next couple of years we all visited him at least once, usually while driving through east or west (U.S. 40, old 66, gets a lot of travel). I believe Elizabeth and he had something going then—she's the most beautiful, it's the consensus, of all our ladies (or should I say the feminine comrades in our group?) and has perhaps kept her youth the best (Daffy excepted!) though all of them have tended to stay slimly youthful (conceivably a shared genetic strain?—*now* I wonder about that more than ever).

The visits weren't all our doing. After he'd been rediscovered, Francois to our surprise began to write notes and sometimes long letters to all of us, and pretty soon the old magic was working again. A lot had happened—the Great Depression, fascism, World War II, Hiroshima, and now the McCarthy era of suspicion, confession, witch-hunt, and fear had started—but we'd survived it all pretty handily. I'd just begun to think of us as the Uncommitted—with the double meaning that none of us seemed to be committed to any great purpose in life, nor yet *been* committed to a mental hospital, like so many others we were beginning to know or hear of, though we had our share of severe neuroses and were getting into our middle-age crises. But with Francois exerting his magnetism once more, we began to seem like aristocrats again, even to me, but not so much secret and lost as banished or exiled, standing a little aloof from life, devoted to a mystery we didn't quite understand, yet hoped the future would make clearer. Someone once said to me, "Fred, you'd *better* live a long life."

I managed to stay with Francois three or four times myself down there in the desert. Twice Daffy was with me—she'd always liked his style, his consciously slightly comical grand manner. Once I was up to all hours stargazing with him—he had a four-inch reflector mounted equatorially. He admitted to me his peculiar interest in the Hydra area, but couldn't explain it except as a persistent compulsion to stare in that direction, especially when his mind wandered, "as if there were something invisible but very important to me lying out there," he added with a chuckle.

He did say, "Maybe that Lonely-One thing gets me about Alphard—a segregated star, a star in prison. Loneliness is a kind of prison, you know, just as real freedom is—you're there with your decisions to make and no one can help you. Slavery is much cosier."

He also had this to say about his point of interest in the heavens, that it hadn't started in Hydra but rather in the obscure constellation of Crater just to the east and south of Virgo—and now showed signs of shifting still farther west toward Canis Minor and the Little Dog Star Procyon and toward Cancer. "The mind is ultimately so whimsical," he said. "Or perhaps I mean enigmatic. Whatever walls of reason you put up, the irrational slips by."

He was still doing his question answering, making his living by it, except that now it took him twelve hours to get the answers. His slim face, clean-shaven now, was somewhat haggard, with vertical wrinkles of concentration between the eyebrows. His hair, which he wore to his shoulders, was still silky, but there were gray threads in it. He looked a little like a Hindu mystic.

And then, just as we were beginning to rely on him in some ways, he pulled up stakes and disappeared again, this time (we pieced together later) to dodge arrest for smuggling marijuana across the border. And he could hardly have run to Mexico this time, because he was wanted by their federal agents too. It appears he was one of the first to learn that they take equally stern views about such things, perhaps to impress the Colossus of the North.

Another twenty years passed, 1970 rolled or creaked around, and a remarkable number of us found ourselves living in San Francisco—or Frisco as I like to call it to the thin-lipped disapproval of the stuffier of its old inhabitants, but to the joy of its old ghosts, I'm sure, ruffians like Jack London and Sir Francis Drake. Hal and Margaret came from New York City to escape its uncollected garbage and sky blackened by all the east's industrial effluvia, Daffy (it's short for Daffodil) and I from Los Angeles to get out from under its mountainous green smog that mounds up into the stratosphere and spills over the high desert. More than half of the old crowd in all, from here and there across the country, as if summoned by an inaudible trumpet blast, or drawn by some magnetism almost as mysterious as keeps Francois' gaze fastened on the Lonely One.

We were no longer the Uncommitted, I told myself. Too many of us *had* been committed, or committed ourselves, to mental hospitals over the years—but we'd got out again. (It was beginning to be just a little remarkable that none of us had died.) I liked to think of us now (1970) as dwellers in the Crazy House, that institution in Robert Graves's *Watch the North Wind Rise* to which his new Cretans retired when they abdicated from social responsibility and the respect due age to enjoy such frivolities as pure science and purely recreational sex.

We (and Earth's whole society) were suffering the after-effects of all the earlier good advances—the pollution and overpopulation that went with nearly unlimited energy, antibiotics, and the democratic ideal. (The only spectacular new advance during the past twenty years had been spaceflight—the beginning of the probing of the planets.) And we were going downhill into the last decade or two of our lives. In that sense we had certainly become the Doomed.

And yet our mood was not so much despair as melancholy—at least I'm sure it was in my case. That's a much misunderstood word, melancholy—it doesn't just mean sadness. It is a temperament or outlook and has its happiness as well as its griefs—and especially it is associated with *the consciousness of distance*.

Do you know Dürer's wood engraving *Melencolia*? The instruments of work—carpenter's tools—are scattered about her feet, while beside her are a ladder and a strange stone polyhedron and a sphere and also a millstone on which sits a brooding cupid. On the wall behind her are a ship's bell, an hourglass, and a magic square that doesn't quite add up right. She sits there, wings folded, with a pair of compasses in one fist (to measure *distance*), elbow propped on knee and cheek on her other fist, peering with eyes that are both youthfully eager and broodingly thoughtful into the transmarine distance where are a rainbow and a bearded comet—or else the comet's "hair" may only be part of the glory of the setting sun. Just so, it seemed to me, we looked into the future and the sky, into the depths of space and time.

It was another work of high art that in a sense brought Francois Broussard back this time. I was in the great vault of Grace Cathedral atop Nob Hill, where in the clerestory they have the spaceman John Glenn and Einstein's $E = MC^2$ in stained glass. But I was looking at that one of the six Willet windows which in glorious glooms and glows both illuminates and enshrouds the words "Light after Darkness." The pavement scrutched, I turned, and there he stood beside me, smiling quizzically. I realized I was very glad to see him. His hair was grizzled, but cut very short. He looked young and nimble. He was standing on a patch of multicolored sunlight that had spilled through the glass onto the stone floor.

It turned out that he lived hardly a dozen blocks away on Russian Hill, where he had a roof (as I had and Hal too) from which to stargaze when Frisco's fogs permitted. He still made his living answering questions. "Of course, they've got computers now," he said, "but computer time is damned expensive—I charge less." (And it took him only ten hours now to get answers, I learned later—things were getting brisker. While his odd point of interest in the skies was moving from Hydra toward Cancer, just as he'd thought it would.) And he was already in touch with one of us again—Charlotte.

And he was married!—not to Charlotte, but to her daughter, who was also named Charlotte. It gave me the strangest feeling about the tricks of time to hear that, let me tell you. And not only married, but they had a son who was already ten years old—a charming youngster and very bright, he turned out to be, who wanted to be a spaceman, an ambition which his father encouraged. "He'll claim my kingdom for me in the stars," Francois once commented with a cryptic little chuckle "—or else find my grave there."

Somehow these circumstances fired us all again with youthful feelings—young Charlotte and Pierre turned out to be charmers too—and it has stayed that way with us; only yesterday I was putting together an article on the many very young female film actresses who've surfaced in the past few years, girls even by feminist definition, a sort of nymphette runnel: Linda Blair, Mackenzie Phillips, Melanie Griffith, Tatum O'Neal, Nell Potts, Mairé Rapp, Catherine Harrison, Roberta Wallach. I wonder if this accent on youth, this feeling of some imminent rebirth, has any significance . . . beyond impending second childhood in some of its observers.

At any rate, we all saw a lot of each other the next months—the Broussard trio and the rest of us—and Francois became again our leader and inspirer.

And then, most mysteriously, he disappeared again and his wife and boy with him. We've never got the straight of that except that he was mixed up with people who were vastly anti-Vietnam and (how shall I say?) prematurely all-out anti-Nixon. Even old Charlotte doesn't know (or claims so most convincingly) what's happened to young Charlotte, her daughter, and Francois and their child.

But his influence over us has stayed strong despite his absence. Like the field-astronomy thing that's so symbolic of concern with distance. Last year, in spite of Frisco's fogs, I saw the moon's roseate eclipse in May, the close conjunction of Mars and Jupiter in mid-June, and Nova Cygni 1975 crookedly deforming the Northern Cross at August's end for four nights running before it faded down so rapidly.

And then last night Hal and I were talking about it all, as we have a thousand times —in other words, we were reviewing all I've told you up to now—and then an idea struck me, an idea that gave me gooseflesh, though I didn't at first dream why. Hal had seemingly digressed to tell me about an astronomy article he'd been reading about plans to rendezvous a space probe with Halley's comet, due to return again in 1986 after its last visits in 1834 and 1910. The idea was to loop the probe around one of the big outer planets in such a way that it would come boomeranging back toward the sun and match trajectories and speeds with the comet as it came shooting in, gathering speed. It was already too late to make use of Saturn, but it could still be worked if you looped the probe around Jupiter, into its gravity well and out again.

"Hal," I heard myself asking him in an odd little voice, "where's the aphelion of Halley's comet?—you know, the point where it's farthest away from the sun. I know it's out about as far as the orbit of Pluto, but *where* in the heavens is it? *Where* would you look in the stars to see Halley's comet when it's farthest from Earth? I know you couldn't actually see it then, even with the biggest telescope. It's frozen head would be far too tiny. But *where* would you look?"

You know, it took us quite a while to find that out and we finally had to do it indirectly, although I have a fair little astronomy library. The *one* specific fact you're looking for is *never* in the books you've got at hand. (We found the aphelion *distance* almost at once—3,282,000,000 miles—but its *vector* eluded us.)

But then in Willy Ley's little 1969 McGraw-Hill book on comets we finally discovered that the perihelion of Halley's comet—its point of closest approach to the sun—was in Aquarius, which would put its aphelion at the opposite end of the zodiac—in Leo.

"But it wouldn't be in Leo," I said softly, "because Halley's comet has an inclination of almost eighteen degrees to the Ecliptic—it comes shooting in toward the sun from below (south of) the plane of the planets. Eighteen degrees south of Leo—where would that put us?"

It put us, the star chart quickly revealed, in Hydra and near Alphard, the Lonely One. And that left us silent with shock for quite a space, Hal and I, while my mind automatically worked out that even the slow movement of Francois' point of interest in the sky from south of Virgo to Alphard toward Cancer fitted with the retrograde orbit of Halley's comet. A comet follows such a long, narrow, elliptical path that it's always in one quarter of the sky with respect to earth except for the months when it whips around the sun.

But I'll be forever grateful to Ley's little book that it showed us the way, although it happens to have one whopping error in it: on page 122 it gives the radio distance of Saturn as thirteen and a half hours, when it happens to be an hour and twenty-five or so minutes—likely a decimal point got shifted one place to the right somewhere in the calculations. But the matter of radio distance has a bearing on the next point I brought up uneasily when Hal and I finally started speaking again.

"You know how it used to take Francois twelve hours to get his answers back in 1950?" I said, finding I was trembling a little. "Well, Halley's comet was in aphelion in 1948 and twelve hours is about the time it would take to get a radio answer back from the vicinity of Pluto, or of Pluto's orbit—six hours out, six hours back, at the speed of light. The ten-hour times for his answers in 1930 and 1970 would fit too."

"Or maybe telepathy also travels at the speed of light," Hal said softly. Then he shook his head as if to clear it. "But that's ridiculous," he said sharply. "Do you realize that we've been assuming that Halley's comet is some sort of spaceship, some sort of living, highly civilized, *computerized* world in space—and that perhaps the memory of it comes slowly back to man each time it reapproaches the sun?"

"Or a space cemetery," I interposed with a nervous little laugh, almost a giggle. "A group of five mausoleums forming the comet's head—although you couldn't observe them telescopically as the comet approached the sun because they'd be concealed by the coma of warmed-up gases and dust. Remember what Francois once said about the ghosts of computers? Why mightn't computers, or the effigies of computers be buried in the tombs of an astral empire?—and God knows what else. Just as the Egyptians put effigies of their servants and tools into their tombs, never dreaming that the great bearded meteor ghosting across their sweating, midnight blue Egyptian night every 76 years was another such ossuary.

"And remember Francois' cosmic dream," I continued. "That intensely bright star in it would exactly describe the sun as seen from Pluto's orbit. And out there all the dust and gases would be frozen to the surfaces of the five polyhedrons—they wouldn't make an obscuring coma."

"But you're talking about a *dream*," Hal protested. "Don't you see, Fred, that all that you're saying implies that there actually *is* some kind of elder cometary civilization and that we all are in some sense children of the comet?"

"The tail of Halley's comet brushed the earth in 1910," I said urgently. "Let's check the exact date."

That fact we found very quickly—it was May 19, 1910.

"—nine months, to a day, before Francois was born," I said shakily. "Hal, do you remember what he used to say about the seed of the gods—or of the princess of the astral empire—drifting down from the stars?"

"Just as Mark Twain (and maybe old French Pete too?) was born in 1834, the year of the previous appearance of Halley's comet, and died in 1910," Hal took up, his imagination becoming as enthralled as my own. "And think of those last two weird books of his—*The Mysterious Stranger*, about a man from elsewhere, and *Captain Stormfield's Visit to Heaven*—aboard a comet! Even that posthumous short 'My Platonic Sweetheart' about his lifelong dream-love for a fifteen-year-old girl . . . Fred, there *is* that suggestion of some weird sort of reincarnation, or mentorship . . ."

I won't set down in detail any more of the wild speculations Hal and I exchanged last night. They're all pretty obvious and maddeningly tantalizing, and wildly baroque, and only time can refute or vindicate them. Oh, I do wish I knew where Francois is, and what his son is doing, and whether a probe will be launched to loop around Jupiter.

I'm left with this: that whether he's conscious of it or not, Francois Broussard (and Hal and I, each one of us, to a lesser degree) has been mysteriously linked all his life to Halley's comet, whether diving around the sun at Venus' distance at 34 miles a second, or moving through the spaceward end of its long, narrow, elliptical orbit no faster than the moon drifts around Earth each month.

But as for all the rest . . . only ten years will tell.

A Rite of Spring

This is the story of the knight in shining armor and the princess imprisoned in a high tower, only with the roles reversed. True, young Matthew Fortree's cell was a fabulously luxurious, quaintly furnished suite in the vast cube of the most secret Coexistence Complex in the American Southwest, not terribly far from the U.S. Government's earlier most secret project, the nuclear one. And he was free to roam most of the rest of the cube whenever he wished. But there were weightier reasons which really did make him the knight in shining armor imprisoned in the high tower: His suite was on the top, or mathematicians', floor and the cube was very tall and he rarely wished to leave his private quarters except for needful meals and exercise, medical appointments, and his unonerous specified duties; his unspecified duties were more taxing. And while he did not have literal shining armor, he did have some very handsome red silk pajamas delicately embroidered with gold.

With the pajamas he wore soft red leather Turkish slippers, the toes of which actually turned up, and a red nightcap with a tassel, while over them and around his spare, short frame he belted tightly a fleece-lined long black dressing gown of heavier, ribbed silk also embroidered with gold, somewhat more floridly. If Matthew's social daring had equaled his flamboyant tastes, he would in public have worn small clothes and a powdered wig and swung a court sword at his side, for he was much enamored of the Age of Reason and yearned to quip wittily in a salon filled with appreciative young Frenchwomen in daringly low-cut gowns, or perhaps only one such girl. As it was, he regularly did wear gray kid gloves, but that was partly a notably unsuccessful effort to disguise his large powerful hands, which sorted oddly with his slight, almost girlish figure.

The crueler of Math's colleagues (he did not like to be called Matt) relished saying behind his back that he had constructed a most alluring love next, but that the unknown love bird he hoped to trap never deigned to fly by. In this they hit the mark, as cruel people so often do, for young mathematicians need romantic sexual love, and pine away without it, every bit as much as young lyric poets, to whom they are closely related. In fact, on the night this story begins, Math had so wasted away emotionally and was gripped by such a suicidally extreme Byronic sense of futility and Gothic awareness of lonliness that he had to bite his teeth together harshly and desperately compress his lips to hold back sobs as he kneeled against his mockingly wide bed with his shoulders and face pressed into its thick, downy, white coverlet, as if to shut out the mellow light streaming on him caressingly from the tall bedside lamps with pyramidal jet bases and fantastic shades built up of pentagons of almost paper-thin, translucent ivory joined with silver leading. This light was strangely augmented at irregular intervals.

For it was a Gothic night too, you see. A dry thunderstorm was terrorizing the desert outside with blinding flashes followed almost instantly by deafening crashes which reverberated very faintly in the outer rooms of the Complex despite the mighty walls and partitions, which were very thick, both to permit as nearly perfect sound-proofing as possible (so the valuable ideas of the solitary occupants might mature without disturbance, like mushrooms in a cave) and also to allow for very complicated, detectionproof bugging. In Math's bedroom, however, for a reason which will be made clear, the thunderclaps were almost as loud as outside, though he did not start at them or otherwise show he even heard them. They were, nevertheless, increasing his Gothic mood in a geometrical progression. While the lightning flashes soaked through the ceiling, a point also to be explained later. Between flashes, the ceiling and walls were very somber, almost black, yet glimmering with countless tiny random highlights like an indoor Milky Way or the restlessly shifting points of light our eyes see in absolute darkness. The thick-pile black carpet shimmered similarly.

Suddenly Matthew Fortree started up on his knees and bent his head abruptly back. His face was a grimacing mask of self-contempt as he realized the religious significance of his kneeling posture and the disgusting religiosity of what he was about to utter, for he was a devout atheist, but the forces working within him were stronger than shame.

"Great Mathematician, hear me!" he cried hoarsely aloud, secure in his privacy and clutching at Eddington's phrase to soften a little the impact on his conscience of his hateful heresy. "Return me to the realm of my early childhood, or otherwise moderate my torments and my lonliness, or else terminate this life I can no longer bear!"

As if in answer to his prayer there came a monstrous flash-and-crash dwarfing all of the storm that had gone before. The two lamps arced out, plunging the room into darkness through which swirled a weird jagged wildfire, as if all the electricity in the wall-buried circuits, augmented by that of the great flash, had escaped to lead a brief free life of its own, like ball lightning or St. Elmo's fire.

(This event was independently confirmed beyond question or doubt. As thousands in the big cube testified, all the lights in the Coexistence Complex went out for one minute and seventeen seconds. Many heard the crash, even in rooms three or four deep below the outermost layer. Several score saw the wildfire. Dozens felt tingling electric shocks. Thirteen were convinced at the time that they had been struck by lightning. Three persons died of heart failure at the instant of the big flash, as far as can be determined. There were several minor disasters in the areas of medical monitoring and continuous experiments. Although a searching investigation went on for months, and still continues on a smaller scale, no completely satisfactory explanation has ever been found, though an odd rumor continues to crop up that the final monster flash was induced by an ultrasecret electrical experiment which ran amok, or else succeeded too well, all of which resulted in a permanent increment in the perpetual nervousness of the masters of the cube.)

The monster stroke was the last one of the dry storm. Two dozen or so seconds passed. Then, against the jagged darkness and the ringing silence, Math heard his door's mechanical bell chime seven times. (He'd insisted on the bell's being installed in such a way as to replace the tiny fisheye lens customary on all the cube's cubicles. Surely the designer was from Manhattan!)

He struggled to his feet, half blinded, his vision still full of the wildfire (or after-images) so like the stuff of ocular migraine. He partly groped, partly remembered his way out of the bedroom, shutting the door behind him, and across the living room to the outer door. He paused there to reassure himself that his red nightcap was set properly on his head, the tassel falling to the right, and his black robe securely belted. Then he took a deep breath and opened the door.

Like his suite, the corridor was steeped in darkness and aswirl with jaggedy, faint blues and yellows. Then, at the level of his eyes, he saw two brighter, twinkling points of green light about two and a half inches horizontally apart. A palm's length below them was another such floating emerald. At the height of his chest flashed another pair of the green points, horizontally separated by about nine inches. At waist level was a sixth, and a hand's length directly below that, a seventh. They moved a bit with the rest of the swirling, first a little to the left, then to the right, but maintained their positions relative to each other.

Without consciousness of having done any thinking, sought any answers, it occurred to him that they were what might be called the seven crucial points of a girl: eyes, chin, nipples, umbilicus, and the center of all wonder and mystery. He blinked his eyes hard, but the twinkling points were still there. The migraine spirals seemed to have faded a little, but the seven emeralds were bright as ever and still flashed the same message in their cryptic positional Morse. He even fancied he saw the shimmer of a clinging dress, the pale triangle of an elfin face in a flow of black hair, and pale serpents of slender arms.

Behind and before him the lights blazed on, and there, surely enough, stood a slim young woman in a long dark-green grandmother's skirt and a frilly salmon blouse, sleeveless but with ruffles going up her neck to her ears. Her left hand clutched a thick envelope purse sparkling with silver sequins, her right dragged a coat of silver fox. While between smooth black cascades and from under black bangs, an elfin face squinted worriedly into his own through silver-rimmed spectacles.

Her gaze stole swiftly and apologetically up and down him, without hint of a smile, let alone giggle, at either his nightcap and its tassel, or the turned-up toes of his Turkish slippers, and then returned to confront him anxiously.

He found himself bowing with bent left knee, right foot advanced, right arm curved across his waist, left arm trailing behind, eyes still on hers (which *were* green), and he heard himself say, "Matthew Fortree, at your service, mademoiselle."

Somehow, she seemed French. Perhaps because of the raciness of the emeralds' twinkling message, though only the top two of them had turned out to be real.

Her accent confirmed this when she answered, "'Sank you. I am Severeign Saxon, sir, in search of my brother. And mooch scared. 'Scuse me."

Math felt a pang of delight. Here was a girl as girls should be, slim, soft-spoken, seeking protection, calling him "sir," and moved to laughter by his picturesque wardrobe, and favoring the fond, formal phrases he liked to use when he talked to himself. The sort of girl who, interestingly half undressed, danced through his head on lonely nights abed.

That was what he felt. What he did, quite characteristically, was frown at her severely and say, "I don't recall any Saxon among the mathematicians, madam, although it's barely possible there is a new one I haven't met."

"Oh, but my brother has not my name . . ." she began hurriedly; then her eyelashes fluttered, she swayed and caught herself. "*Pardonne*," she went on faintly, gasping a little. "Oh, do not think me forward, sir, but might I not come in and catch my breath? I am frightened by ze storm. I have searched so long, and ze halls are so lonely . . ."

Inwardly cursing his gauche severity, Math instantly resumed his courtly persona and cried softly, "*Your* pardon, madam. Come in, come in by all means and rest as long as you desire." Shaping the beginning of another bow, he took her trailing coat and wafted her past him inside. His fingertips tingled at the incredibly smooth, cool, yet electric texture of her skin.

He hung up her coat, marveling that the silky fur was not so softly smooth as his fingertips' memory of her skin, and found her surveying his spacious sanctum with its myriad shelves and spindly little wallside tables.

"Oh, sir, this room is like fairyland," she said, turning to him with a smile of delight. "Tell me, are all zoze tiny elephants and ships and lacy spheres ivory?"

"They are, madam, such as are not jet," he replied quite curtly. He had been preparing a favorable, somewhat flowery, but altogether sincere comparison of her pale complexion to the hue of his ivories (and of her hair to his jets), but something, perhaps "fairyland," had upset him. "And now will you be seated, Miss Saxon, so you may rest?"

"Oh, yes, sir . . . Mr. Fortree," she replied flusteredly, and let herself be conducted to a long couch facing a TV screen set in the opposite wall. With a bob of her head she hurriedly seated herself. He had intended to sit beside her, or at least at the other end of the couch, but a sudden gust of timidity made him stride to the farthest chair, a straight-backed one, facing the couch, where he settled himself bolt upright.

"Refreshment? Some coffee perhaps?"

She gulped and nodded without lifting her eyes. He pushed a button on the remote control in the left-hand pocket of his dressing gown and felt more in command of the situation. He fixed his eyes on his guest and, to his horror, said harshly, "What is your number, madam . . . of years?" he finished in a voice less bold.

He had intended to comment on the storm and its abrupt end, or inquire about her brother's last name, or even belatedly compare her complexion to ivory and her skin to fox fur, anything but demand her age like some police interrogator. And even then not simply, "Say, would you mind telling me how old you are?" but to phrase it so stiltedly . . . Some months back, Math had gone through an acute attack of sesquipedalianism— of being unable to find the simple word for anything, or even a circumlocution, but only a long, usually Latin one. Attending his first formal reception in the Complex, he had coughed violently while eating a cookie. The hostess, a formidably poised older lady, had instantly made solicitous inquiry. He wanted to answer, "I got a crumb in my nose," but could think of nothing but "nasal cavity," and when he tried to say that, there was another and diabolic misfire in his speech centers, and what came out was "I got a crumb in my navel."

The memory of it could still reduce him to jelly.

"Seven—" he heard her begin. Instantly his feelings did another flip-flop and he found himself thinking of how nice it would be, since he himself was only a few years into puberty, if she were younger still.

"Seventeen?" he asked eagerly.

And now it was her mood that underwent a sudden change. No longer downcast, her eyes gleamed straight at him, mischievously, and she said, "No, sir, I was about to copy your 'number of years' and say 'seven and a score.' And now I am of a mind not to answer your rude question at all." But she relented and went on with a winning smile, "No, seven and a decade, only seventeen—that's my age. But to tell the truth, sir, I thought you were asking my ruling number. And I answered you. Seven."

"Do you mean to tell me you believe in numerology?" Math demanded, his concerns doing a third instant flip-flop. Acrobatic moods are a curse of adolescence.

She shrugged prettily. "Well, sir, among the sciences—"

"Sciences, madam?" he thundered like a small Doctor Johnson. "Mathematics itself is not a science, but only a game men have invented and continue to play. The supreme game, no doubt, but still only a game. And that you should denominate as a science that . . . that farrago of puerile superstitions—! Sit still now, madam, and listen carefully while I set you straight."

She crouched a little, her eyes apprehensively on his.

"The first player of note of the game of mathematics," he launched out in lecture-hall tones, "was a Greek named Pythagoras. In fact, in a sense he probably invented the game. Yes, surely he did—twenty-five centuries ago, well before Archimedes, before Aristotle. But those were times when men's minds were still befuddled by the lies of the witch doctors and priests, and so Pythagoras (or his followers, more likely!) conceived the mystical notion"—his words dripped sarcastic contempt—"that numbers had a real existence of their own, as if—"

She interrupted rapidly. "But do they not? Like the little atoms we cannot see, but which—"

"Silence, Sovereign!"

"But, Matthew—"

"Silence, I said! —as if numbers came from another realm or world, yet had power over this one—"

"That's what the little atoms have—power, especially when they explode." She spoke with breathless rapidity.

"—and as if numbers had all kinds of individual qualities, even personalities—some lucky, some unlucky, some good, some bad, et cetera—as if they were real beings, even gods! I ask you, have you ever heard of anything more ridiculous than numbers—mere pieces in a game—being alive? Yes, of course—the idea of gods being real. But with the Pythagoreans (they became a sort of secret society) such nonsense was the rule. For instance, Pythagoras was the first man to analyze the musical scale mathematically—brilliant!—but then he (his followers!) went on to decide that some scales (the major) are stimulating and healthy and others (the minor) unhealthy and sad—"

Sovereign interjected swiftly yet spontaneously. "Yes, I've noticed that, sir. Major keys make me feel 'appy, minor keys sad—no, pleasantly melancholy . . ."

"Autosuggestion! The superstitions of the Pythagoreans became endless—the transmigration of souls, metempsychosis (a psychosis, all right!), reincarnation, immortality, you name it. They even refused to eat beans—"

"They were wrong there. Beans cassolette—"

"Exactly! In the end, Plato picked up their ideas and carried them to still sillier lengths. Wanted to outlaw music in minor scales—like repealing the law of gravity! He also asserted that not only numbers but all ideas were more real than things—"

"But excuse me, sir—I seem to recall hearing my brother talk about real numbers . . ."

"Sheer semantics, madam! Real numbers are merely the most primitive and obvious ones in the parlor game we call mathematics. Q.E.D."

And with that, he let out a deep breath and subsided, his arms folded across his chest.

She said, "You have quite overwhelmed me, sir. Henceforth I shall call seven only my favorite number . . . if I may do that?"

"Of course you may. God (excuse the word) forbid I ever try to dictate to you, madam."

With that, silence descended, but before it could become uncomfortable, Math's remote control purred discreetly in his pocket and prodded him in the thigh. He busied himself fetching the coffee on a silver tray in hemispheres of white eggshell china, whose purity of form Severeign duly admired.

They made a charming couple together, looking surprisingly alike, quite like brother and sister, the chief differences being his more prominent forehead, large strong hands, and forearms a little thick with the muscles that powered the deft fingers. All of which made him seem like a prototype of man among the animals, a slight and feeble being except for hands and brain—manipulation and thought.

He took his coffee to his distant chair. The silence returned and did become uncomfortable. But he remained tongue-tied, lost in bitter reflections. Here the girl of his dreams (why not admit it?) had turned up, and instead of charming her with courtesies and witticisms, he had merely become to a double degree his unpleasant, critical, didiactic, quarrelsome, rejecting, lonely self, perversely shrinking from all chances of warm contact. Better find out her brother's last name and send her on her way. Still, he made a last effort.

"How may I entertain you, madam?" he asked lugubriously.

"Any way you wish, sir," she answered meekly.

Which made it worse, for his mind instantly became an unbearable blank. He concentrated hopelessly on the toes of his red slippers.

"There *is* something we could do," he heard her say tentatively. "We could play a game . . . if you'd care to. Not chess or go or any sort of mathematical game—there I couldn't possibly give you enough competition—but something more suited to my scatter brain, yet which would, I trust, have enough complications to amuse you. The Word Game . . ."

Once more Math was filled with wild delight, unconscious of the wear and tear inflicted on his system by these instantaneous swoops and soarings of mood. This incredibly perfect girl had just proposed that they do the thing he loved to do more than anything else, and at which he invariably showed at his dazzling best. Play a game, any game!

"Word Game?" he asked cautiously, almost suspiciously. "What's that?"

"It's terribly simple. You pick a category, say Musicians with names beginning with B, and then you—"

"Bach, Beethoven, Brahms, Berlioz, Bartok, C.P.E. Bach (J.S.'s son)," he rattled off.

"Exactly! Oh, I can see you'll be much too good for me. When we play, however, you can only give one answer at one time and then wait for me to give another—else you'd win before I ever got started."

"Not at all, madam. I'm mostly weak on words," he assured her, lying in his teeth.

She smiled and continued, "And when one player can't give another word or name in a reasonable time, the other wins. And now, since I suggested the Game, I insist that in honor of you, and my brother, but without making it at all mathematical really, we play a subvariety called the Numbers Game."

"Numbers Game?"

She explained, "We pick a small cardinal number, say between one and twelve, inclusive, and alternately name groups of persons or things traditionally associated with it. Suppose we picked four (we won't); then the right answers would be things like the Four Gospels, or the Four Horsemen of the Apocalypse—"

"Or of Notre Dame. How about units of time and vectors? Do they count as things?"

She nodded. "The four seasons, the four major points of the compass. Yes. And now, sir, what number shall we choose?"

He smiled fondly at her. She really was lovely—a jewel, a jewel green as her eyes. He said like a courtier, "What other, madam, than your favorite?"

"Seven. So be it. Lead off, sir."

"Very well." He had been going to insist politely that she take first turn, but already gamesmanship was vying with courtesy, and the first rule of gamesmanship is, Snatch Any Advantage You Can.

He started briskly, "The seven crucial—" and instantly stopped, clamping his lips.

"Go on, sir," she prompted. "'Crucial' sounds interesting. You've got me guessing."

He pressed his lips still more tightly together, and blushed—at any rate, he felt his cheeks grow hot. Damn his treacherous, navel-fixated subconscious mind! Somehow it had at the last moment darted to the emerald gleams he'd fancied seeing in the hall, and he'd been within a hairsbreadth of uttering, "The seven crucial points of a girl."

"Yes . . .?" she encouraged.

Very gingerly he parted his lips and said, his voice involuntarily going low, "The Seven Deadly Sins: Pride, Covetousness—"

"My, that's a stern beginning," she interjected. "I wonder what the crucial sins are?"

"—envy, Sloth," he continued remorselessly.

"Those are the cold ones," she announced. "Now for the hot."

"Anger—" he began, and only then realized where he was going to end—and cursed the showoff impulse that had made him start to enumerate them. He forced himself to say, "Gluttony, and—" He shied then and was disastrously overtaken for the first time in months by his old stammer. "Lul-lul-lul-lul-lul—" he trilled like some idiot bird.

"Lust," she cooed, making the word into another sort of bird call, delicately throaty. Then she said, "The seven days of the week."

Math's mind again became a blank, through which he hurled himself like a mad rat against one featureless white wall after another, until at last he saw a single dingy star. He stammered out, "The Seven Sisters, meaning the seven antitrust laws enacted in 1913 by New Jersey while Woodrow Wilson was Governor."

"You begin, sir," she said with a delighted chuckle, "by scraping the bottom of your barrel, a remarkable feat. But I suppose that, being a mathematician, you get at the bottom of the barrel while it's still full by way of the fourth dimension."

"The fourth dimension is no hocus-pocus, madam, but only time," he reproved, irked by her wit and by her having helped him out he first stuttered. "Your seven?"

"Oh. I could repeat yours, giving another meaning, but why not the Seven Seas?"

Instantly he saw a fantastic ship with a great eye at the blow sailing on them. "The seven voyages of Sinbad."

"The Seven Hills of Rome."

"The seven colors of the spectrum," he said at once, beginning to feel less fearful of going word-blind. "Though I can't imagine why Newton saw indigo and blue as different prismatic colors. Perhaps he wanted them to come out seven for some mystical reason—he had his Pythagorean weaknesses."

"The seven tones of the scale, as discovered by Pythagoras," she answered sweetly.

"Seven-card stud," he said, somewhat gruffly.

"Seven-up, very popular before poker."

"This one will give you one automatically," he said stingily. "However, a seventh son."

"And I'm to say the seventh son of a seventh son? But I cannot accept yours, sir. I said cardinal, not ordinal numbers. No sevenths, sir, if you please."

"I'll rephrase it then. Of seven sons, the last."

"Not allowed. I fear you quibble, sir." Her eyes widened, as if at her own temerity.

"Oh, very well. The Seven Against Thebes."

"The Epigoni, their sons."

"I didn't know there were seven of *them*," he objected.

"But there should be seven, for the sake of symmetry," she said wistfully.

"Allowed," he said, proud of his superior generosity in the face of a meninine whim. "The Seven Bishops."

"Dear Sancroft, Ken, and Company," she murmured. "The Seven Dials. In London. Does that make you think of time travel?"

"No, big newspaper offices. *The Seven Keys to Baldpate,* a book."

"*The Seven Samurai,* a Kurosawa film."

"*The Seventh Seal,* a Bergman film!" He was really snapping them out now, but—

"Oh, oh. No sevenths—remember, sir?"

"A silly rule—I should have objected at the start. The seven liberal arts, being the quadrivium (arithmetic, music, geometry, and astronomy) added to the trivium (grammar, logic, and rhetoric)."

"Delightful," she said. "The seven planets—"

"No, madam! There are nine."

"I was about to say," she ventured in a small, defenseless voice, "—of the ancients. The ones out to Saturn and then the sun and moon."

"Back to Pythagoras again!" he said with a quite unreasonable nastiness, glaring over her head. "Besides, that would make eight planets."

"The ancients didn't count the Earth as one." Her voice was even tinier.

He burst out with "Earth not a planet, fourth dimension, time travel, indigo not blue, no ordinals allowed, the ancients—madam, your mind is a sink of superstitions!" When she did not deny it, he went on, "And now I'll give you the master answer: all groups of persons or things belong to the class of the largest successive prime among the odd numbers—your seven, madam!"

She did not speak. He heard a sound like a mouse with a bad cold, and looking at her, saw that she was dabbing a tiny handkerchief at her nose and cheeks. "I don't think I want to play the Game any more," she said indistinctly. "You're making it too mathematical."

How like a woman, he thought, banging his hand against his thigh. He felt the remote control and, on a savage impulse, jabbed another button. The TV came on. "Perhaps your mind needs a rest," he said unsympathetically. "See, we open the imbecile valve."

The TV channel was occupied by one of those murderous chases in a detective series (subvariety: military police procedural) where the automobiles became the real protagonists, dark passionate monsters with wills of their own to pursue and flee, or perhaps turn on their pursuer, while the drivers become grimacing puppets whose hands are dragged around by the steering wheels.

Math didn't know if his guest was watching the screen, and he told himself he didn't care—to suppress the bitter realization that instead of cultivating the lovely girl chance had tossed his way, he was browbeating her.

Then the chase entered a multistory garage, and he was lost in a topology problem on the order of: "Given three entrances, two exits, n two-way ramps, and so many stories, what is the longest journey a car can make without crossing its path?" When Math had been a small child—even before he had learned to speak—his consciousness had for long periods been solely a limitless field, or even volume filled with points of light, which he could endlessly count and manipulate. Rather like the random patterns we see in darkness, only he could marshal them endlessly in all sorts of fascinating arrays, and wink them into or out of existence at will. Later he learned that at such times he had gone into a sort of baby-trance, so long and deep that his parents had become worried and consulted psychologists. But then words had begun to replace fields and sets of points in his mind, his baby-trances had become infrequent and finally vanished altogether, so that he was no longer able to enter the mental realm where he was in direct contact with the stuff of mathematics. Thinking about topological problems, such as that of the multilevel garage, was the closest he could get to it now. He had come from that realm "trailing clouds of glory," but with the years they had faded. Yet it was there, he sometimes believed, that he had done all his really creative work in mathematics, the work that had enabled him to invent a new algebra at the age of eleven. And it was there he had earlier tonight prayed the Great Mathematician to return him when he had been in a mood of black despair—which, he realized with mild surprise, he could no longer clearly recall, at least in its intensity.

He had solved his garage problem and was setting up another when "License plates, license plates!" he heard Sovereign cry out in the tones of one who shouts, "Onionsauce, onionsauce!" at baffled rabbits.

Her elfin face, which Math had assumed to be still tearful, was radiant.

"What about license plates?" he asked gruffly.

She jabbed a finger at the TV, where in the solemn finale of the detective show, the camera had just cut to the hero's thoroughly wrecked vehicle while he looked on from under bandages, and while the soundtrack gave out with taps. "Cars have them!"

"Yes, I know, but where does that lead?"

"Almost all of them have seven digits!" she announced triumphantly. "So do phone numbers!"

"You mean, you want to go on with the Game?" Math asked with an eagerness that startled him.

Part of her radiance faded. "I don't know. The Game is really dreadful. Once started, you can't get your mind off it until you perish of exhaustion of ideas."

"But you want nevertheless to continue?"

"I'm afraid we must. Sorry I got the megrims back there. And now I've gone and wasted an answer by giving two together. The second counts for yours. Oh well, my fault."

"Not at all, madam. I will balance it out by giving two at once too. The seven fat years and the seven lean years."

"Anyone would have got the second of those once you gave the first," she observed, saucily rabbiting her nose at him. "The number of deacons chosen by the Apostles in Acts. Nicanor's my favorite. Dear Nicky," she sighed, fluttering her eyelashes.

"Empson's Seven Types of Ambiguity," Math proclaimed.

"You're not enumerating?"

He shook his head. "Might get too ambiguous."

She flashed him a smile. Then her face slowly grew blank—with thought, he thought at first, but then with eyes half closed she murmured, "Sleepy."

"You want to rest?" he asked. Then, daringly, "Why not stretch out?"

She did not seem to hear. Her head drooped down. "Dopey too," she said somewhat indistinctly.

"Should I step up the air conditioning?" he asked. A wild fear struck him. "I assure you, madam, I didn't put anything in your coffee."

"And Grumpy!" she said triumphantly, sitting up. "Snow White's seven dwarfs!"

He laughed and answered, "The Seven Hunters, which are the Flannan Islands in the Hebrides."

"The Seven Sisters, a hybrid climbing rose, related to the rambler," she said.

"The seven common spectral types of stars—B-A-F-G-K-M . . . and O," he added a touch guiltily because O wasn't really a common type, and he'd never heard of this particular Seven (or Six, for that matter). She gave him a calculating look. Must be something else she's thinking of, he assured himself. Women don't know much astronomy except maybe the ancient sort, rubbed off from astrology.

She said, "The seven rays of the spectrum: radio, high frequency, infrared, visible, ultraviolet, X, and gamma." And she looked at him so bright-eyed that he decided she'd begun to fake a little too.

"And cosmic?" he asked sweetly.

"I thought those were particles," she said innocently.

He grumphed, wishing he could take another whack at the Pythagoreans. An equally satisfying target occurred to him—and a perfectly legitimate one, so long as you realized that this was a game that could be played creatively. "The Seven Subjects of Sensational Journalism: crime, scandal, speculative science, insanity, superstitions such as numerology, monsters, and millionaires."

Fixing him with a penetrating gaze, she immediately intoned, "The Seven Sorrows of Shackleton: the crushing of the *Endurance* in the ice, the inhospitality of Elephant Island, the failure of the whaler *Southern Sky*, the failure of the Uruguayan trawler *Instituto de Pesca No. 1*, the failure on first use of the Chilean steamer *Yelcho*, the failure of the *Emma*, and the South Pole unattained!"

She continued to stare at him judicially. He realized he was starting to blush. He dropped his eyes and laughed uncomfortably. She chortled happily. He looked back at her and laughed with her. It was a very nice moment, really. He had cheated inventively and she had cheated right back at him the same way, pulling him up short without a word.

Feeling very, very good, very free, Math said, "The Seven Years' War."

"The Seven Weeks' War, between Prussia and Austria."

"The Seven Days' War, between Israel and the Arabs."

"Surely Six?"

He grinned. "Seven. For six days the Israelis labored, and on the seventh day they rested."

She laughed delightedly, whereupon Math guffawed too.

She said, "You're witty, sir—though I can't allow that answer. I must tell my brother that one of his colleagues—" She stopped, glanced at her wrist, shot up. "I didn't realize it was so late. He'll be worried. Thanks for everything, Matthew—I've got to split." She hurried toward the door.

He got up too. "I'll get dressed and take you to his room. You don't know where it is. I'll have to find out."

She was reaching down her coat. "No time for that. And now I remember where."

He caught up with her as she was slipping her coat on. "But, Severeign, visitors aren't allowed to move around the Complex unescorted—"

"Oh pish!"

It was like trying to detain a busy breeze. He said desperately, "I won't bother to change."

She paused, grinned at him with uplifted brows, as though surprised and pleased. Then, "No, Matthew," settling her coat around her and opening the door.

He conquered his inhibitions and grabbed her by her silky shoulders—gently at the last moment. He faced her to him. They were exactly the same height.

"Hey," he asked smiling, "what about the Game?"

"Oh, we'll *have* to finish that. Tomorrow night, same time? G'bye now."

He didn't release her. It made him tremble. He started to say, "But Miss Saxon, you really can't go by yourself. After midnight all sorts of invisible eyes pick up anyone in the corridors."

He got as far as the "can't" when, with a very swift movement, she planted her lips precisely on his.

He froze, as if they had been paralysis darts—and he did feel an electric tingling. Even his invariable impulse to flinch was overridden, perhaps by the audacity of the contact. A self he'd never met said from a corner of his mind in the voice of Rex Harrison, "They're Anglo body-contact taboos, but not Saxon."

And then, between his parted lips and hers still planted on them, he felt an impossible third swift touch. There was a blind time—he didn't know how long—in which the universe filled with unimagined shocking possibility: tiny ondines sent anywhere by matter transmission, a live velvet ribbon from the fourth dimension, pet miniwatersnakes, a little finger with a strange silver ring on it poking out of a young witch's mouth . . . and then another sort of shocked wonder, as he realized it could only have been her tongue.

His lips, still open, were pressing empty air. He looked both ways down the corridor. It was empty too. He quietly closed the door and turned to his ivory-lined room. He closed his lips and worked them together curiously. They still tingled, and so did a spot on his tongue. He felt very calm, not at all worried about Sovereign being spotted, or who her brother was, or whether she would really come back tomorrow night. Although he almost didn't see the forest for the trees, it occurred to him that he was happy.

Next morning he felt the same, but very eager to tell someone all about it. This presented a problem, for Math had no friends among his colleagues. Yet a problem easily solved, after a fashion. Right after breakfast he hunted up Elmo Hooper.

Elmo was classed and quartered with the mathematicians, though he couldn't have told you the difference between a root and a power. He was an idiot savant, able to do lightning calculations and possessing a perfect eidetic memory. He was occasionally teamed with a computer to supplement its powers, and it was understood, as it is understood that some people will die of cancer, that he would eventually be permanently cyborged to one. In his spare time, of which he had a vast amount, he mooned around the Complex, ignored except when he came silently up behind gossipers and gave them fits because of his remarkable physical resemblance to Warren Dean, Coexistence's security chief. Both looked like young Vermont storekeepers and were equally laconic, though for different reasons.

Math, who, though no lightning calculator, had a nearly eidetic memory himself, found Elmo the perfect confidant. He could tell him all his most private thoughts and feelings, and retrieve any of his previous remarks, knowing that Elmo would never make a critical comment.

This morning he found Elmo down one floor in Physics, and soon was pouring out in a happy daze every detail about last night's visit and lovely visitor and all his amazing reactions to her, with no more thought for Elmo than he would have had for a combined dictaphone and information-storage-and-retrieval unit.

He would have been considerably less at ease had he known that Warren Dean regularly drained Elmo of all conversations by "sensitive" persons he overheard in his moonings. Though Math wouldn't have had to feel that way, for the dour security man had long since written Math off as of absolutely no interest to security, being anything but "sensitive" and quite incapable of suspicious contacts, or any other sort. (How else could you class a man who talked of nothing but ivories, hurt vanities, and pure abstractions?) If Elmo began to parrot Math, Dean would simply turn off the human bug, while what the bugs in Math's walls heard was no longer even taped.

Math's happy session with Elmo lasted until lunchtime, and he approached the Mathematics, Astronomy and Theoretical Physics Commons with lively interest. Telling the human memory bank every last thing he knew about Sovereign had naturally transferred his attention to the things he didn't know about her, including the identity of her brother. He was still completely trustful that she would return at evening and answer his questions, but it would be nice to know a few things in advance.

The Commons was as gorgeous as Math's apartment, though less eccentrically so. It still gave him a pleasant thrill to think of all the pure intellect gathered here, busily chomping and chatting, though the presence of astronomers and especially theoretical physicists from the floor below added a sour note. Ah well, they weren't quite as bad as their metallurgical, hardware-mongering brothers. (These in turn were disgusted at having to eat with the chemists from the second floor below. The Complex, dedicated to nourishing all pure science, since that probably paid off better peacewise or warwise than applied science, arranged all the sciences by floors according to degree of purity and treated them according to the same standards, with the inhabitants of the top floor positively coddled. Actually, the Complex was devoted to the corruption of pure science, and realized that mathematics was at least fully as apt as any other discipline to turn up useful ideas. Who knew when a new geometry would not lead to a pattern of nuclear bombardment with less underkill? Or a novel topological concept point the way to the most efficient placement of offshore oil wells?)

So as Math industriously nibbled his new potatoes, fresh green peas, and roast lamb (the last a particularly tender mutation from the genetics and biology floors, which incidentally was a superb carrier of a certain newly developed sheep-vectored disease of the human nervous system), he studied the faces around him for ones bearing a resemblance to Sovereign's—a pleasantly titillating occupation merely for its own sake. Although Math's colleagues believed the opposite, he was a sensitive student of the behavior of crowds, as any uninvolved spectator is apt to be. He had already noted that there was more and livelier conversation than usual and had determined that the increase was due to talk about last night's storm and power failure, with the physicists contributing rather more than their share, both about the storm and power failure and also about some other, though related, topic which he hadn't yet identified.

While coffee was being served, Math decided on an unprecedented move: to get up and drift casually about in order to take a closer look at his candidates for Sovereign's brother (or half brother, which would account elegantly for their different last names). And as invariably happens when an uninvolved spectator abandons that role and mixes in, it was at once noticed. Thinking of himself as subtly invisible as he moved about dropping nods and words here and there, he actually became a small center of attention. Whatever was that social misfit up to? (A harsh term, especially coming from members of a group with a high percentage of social misfits.) And why had he taken off his gray kid gloves? (In his new freedom he had simply forgotten to put them on.)

He saved his prime suspect until last, a wisp of a young authority on synthetic

502

projective geometry named Angelo Spirelli, the spiral angel, whose floating hair was very black and whose face could certainly be described as girlish, though his eyes (Math noted on closer approach) were yellowish-brown, not green.

Unlike the majority, Spirelli was a rather careless, outgoing soul of somewhat racier and more voluable speech than his dreamy appearance might have led one to expect. "Hi, Fortree. Take a pew. What strange and unusual circumstance must I thank for this unexpected though pleasant encounter? The little vaudeville act Zeus and Hephaestus put on last night? One of the downstairs boys suspects collusion by the Complex."

Emboldened, Math launched into a carefully rehearsed statement. "At the big do last week, I met a female who said she was related to you. A Miss Sovereign Saxon."

Spirelli scowled at him, then his eyes enlarged happily. "Saxon, you say? Was she a squirmy little sexpot?"

Math's eyebrows lifted. "I suppose someone might describe her in that fashion." He didn't look as if he'd care much for such a someone.

"And you say you met her in El 'Bouk?"

"No, here at the fortnightly reception."

"That," Spirelli pronounced, scowling again, "does not add up."

"Well," Math said after a hiatus, "does it add down?"

Spirelli eyed him speculatively, then shrugged his shoulders with a little laugh. Leaning closer, he said, "Couple weeks ago I was into Albuquerque on a pass. At the Spurs 'n' Chaps this restless little saucer makes up to me. Says call her Saxon, don't know if it was supposed to be last name, first, or nick."

"Did she suggest you play a game?"

Spirelli grinned. "Games. I think so, but I never got around to finding out for sure. You see, she began asking me too many questions, like she was pumping me, and I remembered what Grandmother Dean teaches us at Sunday school about strange women, and I cooled her fast, feeling like a stupid, miserably well-behaved little choir-boy. But a minute later Warren himself wanders in and I'm glad I did." His eyes swung, his voice dropped. "Speak of the devil."

Math looked. Across the Commons, Elmo Hooper—no, Warren Dean—had come in. Conversation did not die, but it did become muted—in waves going out from that point.

Math asked, "Did this girl in 'Bouk have black hair?"

Grown suddenly constrained, Spirelli hesitated, then said, "No, blond as they come. Saxon was a Saxon type."

After reaching this odd dead end, Math spent the rest of the afternoon trying to cool his own feelings about Sovereign, simply because they were getting too great. He was successful except that in the mathematics library *Webster's Unabridged*, second edition, tempted him to look up the "seven" entries (there were three columns), and he was halfway through them before he realized what he was doing. He finished them and resolutely shut the big book and his mind. He didn't think of Sovereign again until he finished dressing for bed, something he regularly did on returning to his room from dinner. It was a practice begun as a child to insure he did nothing but study at night, but continued, with embellishments, when he began to think of himself as a gay young bachelor. He furiously debated changing back until he became irked at his agitation and decided to retain his "uniform of the night."

But he could no longer shut his mind on Sovereign. Here he was having an assignation (a word which simultaneously delighted him and gave him cold shivers) with a young female who had conferred on him a singular favor (another word that worked

503

both ways, while the spot on his tongue tingled reminiscently). How should he behave? How would she behave? What would she expect of him? How would she react to his costume? (He redebated changing back.) Would she even come? Did he really remember what she looked like?

In desperation he began to look up everything on seven he could, including Shakespeare and ending with the Bible. A cross-reference had led him to the Book of Revelations, which he found surprisingly rich in that digit. He was reading "And when he had opened the seventh seal, there was silence in heaven about the space of half an hour . . ." when, once again, there came the seven chimes at his door. He was there in a rush and had it open, and there was Sovereign, looking exactly like he remembered her—the three points of merry green eyes and tapered chin of flustered, triangular elf-face, silver spectacles, salmon blouse and green grandmother's skirt (with line of coral buttons going down the one, and jade ones down the other), the sense of the other four crucial points of a girl under them, slender bare arms, one clutching silver-sequined purse, the other trailing coat of silver fox—and their faces as close together again as if the electric kiss had just this instant ended.

He leaned closer still, his lips parted, and he said, "The seven metals of the ancients: iron, lead, mercury, tin, copper, silver, and gold."

She looked as startled as he felt. Then a fiendish glint came into her eyes and she said, "The seven voices of the classical Greek actor: king, queen, tyrant, hero, old man, young man, maiden—that's me."

He said, "The Island of the Seven Cities. Antilia, west of Atlantis."

She said, "The seven Portuguese bishops who escaped to that island."

He said, "The Seven Caves of Aztec legend."

She said, "The Seven Walls of Ekbatana in old Persia: white, scarlet, blue, orange, silver, and (innermost) golden."

He said, "'Seven Come Eleven,' a folk cry."

She said, "The Seven Cities of Cibola. All golden."

"But which turned out to be merely the pueblos of the Zuni," he jeered.

"Do you always have to deprecate?" she demanded. "Last night the ancients, the Pythagoreans. Now some poor aborigines."

He grinned. "Since we're on Amerinds, the Seven Council Fires, meaning the Sioux, Tetons, and so forth."

She scowled at him and said, "The Seven Tribes of the Tetons, such as the Hunk-papa."

Math said darkly, "I think you studied up on seven and then conned me into picking it. *Seven Came Through*, a book by Eddie Rickenbacker."

"The Seven Champions of Christendom. Up Saint Dennis of France! To the death! No, I didn't, but you know, I sometimes feel I know everything about sevens, past, present, or future. It's strange."

They had somehow got to the couch and were sitting a little apart but facing each other, totally engrossed in the Game.

"Hmph! Up Saint David of Wales!" he said. "The Seven Churches in Asia Minor addressed in Revelations. Thyatira, undsoweiter."

"Philadelphia too. The seven golden candlesticks, signifying the Seven Churches. Smyrna's really my favorite—I like figs." She clenched her fist with the tip of her thumb sticking out between index and middle fingers. Math wondered uncomfortably if she knew the sexual symbolism of the gesture. She asked, "Why are you blushing?"

"I'm not. The Seven Stars, meaning the Seven Angels of the Seven Churches."

"You were! And it got you so flustered you've given me one. The Seven Angels!"

"I'm not anymore," he continued unperturbed, secure in his knowledge that he'd just read part of Revelations. "The seven trumpets blown by the Seven Angels."

"The beast with seven heads, also from Revelations. He also had the mouth of a lion and the feet of a bear *and* ten horns, but he looked like a leopard."

"The seven consulships of Gaius Marius," he said.

"The seven eyes of the Lamb," she countered.

"The Seven Spirits of God, another name for the Seven Angels, I think."

"All right. The seven sacraments."

"Does that include exorcism?" he wanted to know.

"No, but it does include order, which ought to please your mathematical mind."

"Thanks. The Seven Gifts of the Holy Ghost. Say, I know tongues, prophecy, vision, and dreams, but what are the other three?"

"Those are from Acts two—an interesting notion. But try Isaiah eleven—wisdom, understanding, counsel, might, knowledge, fear of the Lord, and righteousness."

Math said, "Whew, that's quite a load."

"Yes. On with the Game! To the death! The seven steps going up to Ezekiel's gate. Zeek forty twenty-six."

"Let's change religions," he said, beginning to feel snowed under by Christendom and the Bible. "The seven Japanese gods of luck."

"Or happiness. The seven major gods of Hinduism: Brahma, Vishnu, Siva, Varuna, Indra, Agni, and Surya. Rank male chauvinism! They didn't even include Lakshmi, the goddess of luck."

Math said sweetly, "The Seven Mothers, meaning the seven wives of the Hindu gods."

"Chauvinism, I said! Wives indeed! *Seven Daughters of the Theater,* a book by Edward Wagenknecht."

"The seven ages of man," Math announced, assuming a Shakespearean attitude. "At first the infant, mewling and puking—"

"And then the whining schoolboy—"

"And then the lover," he cut in, in turn, "sighing like furnace, with a woeful ballad made to his mistress' eyebrow."

"Have you ever sighed like furnace, Matthew?"

"No, but . . ." And raising a finger for silence, he scowled in thought.

"What are you staring at?" she asked.

"Your left eyebrow. Now listen . . .

> Slimmest crescent of delight,
> Why set so dark in sky so light?
> My mistress' brow is whitest far;
> Her eyebrow—the black evening star!"

"But it's not woeful," she objected. "Besides, how can the moon be a star?"

"As easily as it can be a planet—your ancients, madam. In any case, I invoke poetic license."

"But my eyebrow bends the wrong way for setting," she persisted. "Its ends point at the earth instead of skyward."

"Not if you were standing on your head, madam," he countered.

"But then my skirt would set too, showing my stockings. Shocking. Sir, I refuse!

The Seven Sisters, meaning the Pleiades, those little stars."

Matthew's eyes lit up. He grinned excitedly. "Before I give you my next seven I want to show you yours," he told her, standing up.

"What do you mean?"

"I'll show you. Follow me," he said mysteriously and led her into his bedroom.

While she was ooh-ahing at the strangely glimmering black floor, walls, and ceiling, the huge white-fleeced bed, the scattered ivories which included the five regular solids of Pythagoras, the jet bedside lamps with their shades that were dodecahedrons of silver-joined pentagons of translucent ivory—and all the other outward signs of the U.S. Government's coddling of Matthew—he moved toward the lamps and switched them off, so the only light was that which had followed them into the bedroom.

Then he touched another switch and with the faintest whir and rustling the ceiling slowly parted like the Red Sea and moved aside, showing the desert night crusted with stars. The Coexistence Complex really catered to their mathematicians, and when Matthew had somewhat diffidently (for him) mentioned his fancy, they had seen no difficulty in removing the entire ceiling of his bedroom and the section of flat roof above and replacing them with a slightly domed plate-glass skylight, and masking it below with an opaque fabric matching the walls, which would move out of the way sidewise and gather in little folds at the urging of an electric motor.

Severeign caught her breath.

"Stars of the winter sky," Matthew said with a sweep of his arm and then began to point. "Orion. Taurus the bull with his red-eye Aldeberan. And, almost overhead, your Pleiades, madam. While there to the north is my reply. The Big Dipper, madam, also called the Seven Sisters."

Their faces were pale in the splendid starlight and the glow seeping from the room they'd left. They were standing close. Severeign did not speak at once. Instead she lifted her hand, forefinger and middle finger spread and extended, slowly toward his eyes. He involuntarily closed them. He heard her say, "The seven senses. Sight. And hearing." He felt the side of her hand lightly brush his neck. "Touch. No, keep your eyes closed." She laid the back of her hand against his lips. He inhaled with a little gasp. "Smell," came her voice. "That's myrrh, sir." His lips surprised him by opening and kissing her wrist. "And now you've added taste too, sir. Myrrh is bitter." It was true.

"But that's all the senses," he managed to say, "and you said seven. In common usage there are only five."

"Yes, that's what Aristotle said," she answered drily. She pressed her warm palm against the curve of his jaw. "But there's heat too." He grasped her wrist and brought it down. She pulled her hand to free it and he automatically gripped it more tightly for a moment before letting go.

"And kinesthesia," she said. "You felt it in your muscles then. That makes seven."

He opened his eyes. Her face was close to his. He said, "Seventh heaven. No, that's an ordinal—"

"It will do, sir," she said. She kneeled at his feet and looked up. In the desert starlight her face was solemn as a child's. "For my next seven I must remove your handsome Turkish slippers," she apologized.

He nodded, feeling lost in a dream, and lifted first one foot, then the other, as she did it.

As she rose, her hands went to his gold-worked black dressing gown. "And this too, sir," she said softly. "Close your eyes once more."

He obeyed, feeling still more dream-lost. He heard the slithering brush of his robe dropping to the floor, he felt the buttons of his handsome red silk pajama tops loosened one by one from the top down, as her little fingers worked busily, and then the draw-string of the bottoms loosened.

He felt his ears lightly touched in their centers. She breathed, "The seven natural orifices of the male body, sir." The fingers touched his nostrils, brushed his mouth. "That's five, sir." Next he was briefly touched where only he had ever touched himself before. There was an electric tingling, like last night's kiss. The universe seemed to poise around him. Finally he was touched just as briefly where he'd only been touched by his doctor. His universe grew.

He opened his eyes. Her face was still child-grave. The light shining past him from the front room was enough to show the green of her skirt, the salmon of her blouse, the ivory of her skin dancing with starlight. He felt electricity running all over his body. He swallowed with difficulty, then said harshly, "For my next seven, madam, you must undress."

There was a pause. Then, "Myself?" she asked. "*You* didn't have to." She closed her eyes and blushed, first delicately under her eyes, along her cheekbones, then richly over her whole face, down to the salmon ruffles, around her neck. His hands shook badly as they moved out toward the coral buttons, but by the time he had undone the third, his strong fingers were working with their customary deftness. The jade buttons of her skirt yielded as readily. Matthew, who knew from his long studious perusals of magazine advertisements that all girls wore pantyhose, was amazed and then intrigued that she had separate stockings and a garter belt. He noted for future reference in the Game that that made seven separate articles of clothing, if you counted shoes. With some difficulty he recalled his main purpose in all this. His hands edged under her long black curving hair until his middle fingers touched her burning ears.

He softly said, "The seven natural orifices of the *female* body, madam."

"What?" Her eyes blinked open wide and searched his face. Then a comic light flashed in them, though Matthew did not recognize it as such. Saying, "Oh, very well, sir. Go on," she closed them and renewed her blush. Matthew delicately touched her neat nostrils and her lips, then his right hand moved down while his eyes paused, marveling in admiration, at the two coral-tipped crucial points of a girl embellished on Severeign's chest.

"Seven," he finished triumphantly, amazed at his courage while lost in wonder at the newness of it all.

Her hands lightly clasped his shoulders, she leaned her head against his and whispered in his ear, "No, eight. You missed one." Her hand went down and her fingers instructed his. It was true! Matthew felt himself flushing furiously from intellectual shame. He'd known *that* about girls, of course, and yet he'd had a blind spot. There was a strange difference, he had to admit, between things read about in books of human physiology and things that were concretely there, so you could touch them. Severeign reminded him he still owed the Game a seven, and in his fluster he gave her the seven crucial points of a girl, which she was inclined to allow, though only by making an exception, for as she pointed out, they seemed very much Matthew's private thing, though possibly others had hit on them independently.

Still deeply mortified by his fundamental oversight, though continuing to be intensely interested in everything (the loose electricity lingered on him), Matthew would not accept the favor. "The Seven Wise Men of Greece—Solon, Thales, and so on," he said loudly and somewhat angrily, betting himself that those old boys had made a lot of slips in their time.

507

She nodded absently, and looking somewhat smugly down herself, said (quite fatuously, Matthew thought), "The seven seals on the Book of the Lamb."

He said more loudly, his strange anger growing, "In the Civil War, the Battle of Seven Pines, also called the Battle of Fair Oaks."

She looked at him, raised an eyebrow, and said, "The Seven Maxims of the Seven Wise Men of Greece." She looked down herself again and then down and up him. Her eyes, merry, met his. "Such as Pittacus: *Know thy opportunity.*"

Matthew said still more loudly, "The Seven Days' Battles, also Civil War, June twenty-fifth to July first inclusive, 1862—Mechanicsville, et cetera!"

She winced at the noise. "You've got to the fourth age now," she told him.

"What are you talking about?" he demanded.

"You know, Shakespeare. You gave it: the Seven Ages of Man. Fourth: 'Then a soldier, full of strange oaths and bearded like the pard, jealous in honor, sudden and quick in quarrel, seeking the bubble reputation even in the cannon's mouth.' You haven't got a beard, but you're roaring like a cannon."

"I don't care. You watch out. What's your seven?"

She continued to regard herself demurely, her eyes half closed. "Seven swans a-swimming," she said liltingly, and a dancing vibration seemed to move down her white body, like that which goes out from a swan across the still surface of a summer lake.

Matthew roared, "The Seven Sisters, meaning the Scotch cannon at the Battle of Flodden!"

She shrugged maddeningly and murmured, "Sweet Seventeen," again giving herself the once-over.

"That's Sixteen," he shouted. "And it's not a seven anyhow!"

She wrinkled her nose at him, turned her back, and said smiling over her shoulder, "Chilon: *Consider the end.*" And she jounced her little rump.

In his rage Matthew astonished himself by reaching her in a stride, picking her up like a feather, and dropping her in the middle of the bed, where she continued to smile self-infatuatedly as she bounced.

He stood glaring down at her and taking deep breaths preparatory to roaring, but then he realized his anger had disappeared.

"The Seven Hells," he said anticlimactically.

She noticed him, rolled over once, and lay facing him on her side, chin in hand. "The seven virtues," she said. "Prudence, justice, temperance, and fortitude—those are Classical—and faith, hope and charity—those are Christian."

He lay down facing her. "The seven sins—"

"We've had those," she cut him off. "You gave them last night."

He at once remembered everything about the incident except the embarrassment.

"*Seven Footprints to Satan,* a novel by Abraham Merritt," he said, eyeing her with interest and idly throwing out an arm.

"*The Seven-Year Itch,* a film with Marilyn Monroe," she countered, doing likewise. Their fingers touched.

He rolled over toward her, saying, "*Seven Conquests,* a book by Poul Anderson," and ended up with his face above hers. He kissed her. She kissed him. In the starlight her face seemed to him that of a young goddess. And in the even, tranquil, shameless voice such a supernatural being would use, she said, "The seven stages of loving intercourse. First kissing. Then foreplay." After a while, "Penetration," and with a wicked starlit smile, "Bias: *Most men are bad.* Say a seven."

"Why?" Matthew asked, almost utterly lost in what they were doing, because it was endlessly new and heretofore utterly unimaginable to him—which was a very strange concept for a mathematician.

"So I can say one, stupid."

"Oh, very well. The seven spots to kiss: ears, eyes, cheeks, mouth," he said, suiting actions to words.

"How very specialized a seven. Try eyebrow flutters too," she suggested, demonstrating. "But it will do for an answer in the Game. The seven gaits in running the course you're into. First the walk. Slowly, slowly. No, more slowly." After a while, she said, "Now the amble, not much faster. Shakespeare made it the slowest gait of Time, when he moves at all. Leisurely, stretchingly. Yes, that's right," and after a while, "Now the pace. In a horse, which is where all this comes from, that means first the hoofs on the one side, then those on the other. Right, left, right, see?—only doubled. There's a swing to it. Things are picking up." After a while she said, "Now the trot. I'll tell you who Time trots withad. Marry, he trots hard with a maid between the contract of her marriage and the day it is solemnized. A little harder. There, that's right." After a while she said, gasping slightly, "Now the canter. Just for each seventh instant we've all hoofs off the ground. Can you feel that? Yes, there it came again. Press on." After a while she said, gasping, "And now the rack. That's six gaits. Deep penetration too. Which makes five stages. Oh, press on." Matthew felt he was being tortured on a rack, but the pain was wonderful, each frightening moment an utterly new revelation. After a while she gasped, "Now, sir, the gallop!"

Matthew said, gasping too, "Is this wise, madam? Won't we come apart? Where are you taking me? Recall Cleobulus: *Avoid Excess!*"

But she cried ringingly, her face lobster-red, "No, it's not sane, it's mad! But we must run the risk. To the heights and above! To the ends of the earth and beyond! Press on, press on, the Game is all! Epimenides: *Nothing is impossible to industry!*" After a while he redded out.

After another while he heard her say, remotely, tenderly, utterly without effort, "Last scene of all, that ends this strange, eventful history, is mere oblivion. Now Time stands still withal. After the climax—sixth stage—there is afterplay. What's your seven?"

He answered quite as dreamily, "The Seven Heavens, abodes of bliss to the Mohammedans and cabalists."

She said, "That's allowable, although you gave it once before by inference. The seven syllables of the basic hymn line, as 'Hark, the herald angels sing.'"

He echoed with, "Join the triumph of the skies."

She said, "Look at the stars." He did. She said, "Look how the floor of heaven is thick inlaid with pattens of bright gold." It was.

He said, "There's not the smallest orb which thou behold'st in his motion like an angel sings. Hark." She did.

Math felt the stars were almost in his head. He felt they were the realm in which he'd lived in infancy and that with a tiny effort he could at this very moment push across the border and live there again. What was so wrong with Pythagoreanism? Weren't numbers real, if you could live among them? And wouldn't they be alive and have personalities, if they were everything there was? Something most strange was happening.

Sovereign nodded, then pointed a finger straight up. "Look, the Pleiades. I always thought they were the Little Dipper. They'd hit us in our tummies if they fell."

He said, gazing at them, "You've already used that seven."

"Of course I have," she said, still dreamily. "I was just making conversation. It's your turn, anyway."

He said, "Of course. The Philosophical Pleiad, another name for the Seven Wise Men of Greece."

She said, "The Alexandrian Pleiad—Homer the younger and six other poets."

He said, "The French Pleiad—Ronsard and his six."

She said, "The Pleiades again, meaning the seven nymphs, attendant on Diana, for whom the stars were named—Alcyone, Celaeno, Electra, Maia (she's Illusion), Taygete (she got lost), Sterope (she wed war), and Merope (she married Sisyphus). My, that got gloomy."

Matthew looked down from the stars and fondly at her, counting over her personal and private sevens.

"What's the matter?" she asked.

"Nothing," he said. Actually, he'd winced at the sudden memory of his eight-orifices error. The recollection faded back as he continued to study her.

"The Seven Children of the Days of the Week, Fair-of-Face and Full-of-Grace, and so on," he said, drawing out the syllables. "Whose are you?"

"Saturday's—"

"Then you've got far to go," he said.

She nodded, somewhat solemnly.

"And that makes another seven that belongs to you," he added. "The seventh day of the week."

"No, sixth," she said. "Sunday's the seventh day of the week."

"No, it's the first," he told her with a smile. "Look at any calendar." He felt a lazy pleasure at having caught her out, though it didn't make up for a Game error like the terrible one he'd made.

She said, "'The Seven Ravens,' a story by the Brothers Grimm. Another gloomy one."

He said, gazing at her and speaking as if they too belonged to her, "The Seven Wonders of the World. The temple of Diana at Ephesus, et cetera. Say, what's the matter?"

She said, "You said the World when we were in the Stars. It brought me down. The world's a nasty place."

"I'm sorry, Sev," he said. "You are a goddess, did you know? I saw it when the starlight freckled you. Diana coming up twice in the Game reminded me. Goddesses are supposed to be up in the stars, like in line drawings of the constellations with stars in their knees and heads."

"The world's a nasty place," she repeated. "Its number's nine."

"I thought six sixty-six," he said. "The number of the beast. Somewhere in Revelations."

"That too," she said, "but mostly nine."

"The smallest odd number that is not a prime," he said.

"The number of the Dragon. Very nasty. Here, I'll show you just how nasty."

She dipped over the edge of the bed for her purse and put in his hands something that felt small, hard, cold, and complicated. Then, kneeling upright on the bed, she reached out and switched on the lamps.

Matthew lunged past her and hit the switch for the ceiling drapes.

"Afraid someone might see us?" she asked as the drapes rustled toward each other.

He nodded mutely, catching his breath through his nose. Like her, he was now kneeling upright on the bed.

"The stars are far away," he said. "Could they see us with telescopes?"

"No, but the roof is close," he whispered back. "Though it's unlikely anyone would be up there."

Nevertheless he waited, watching the ceiling, until the drapes met and the faint whirring stopped. Then he looked at what she'd put in his hands.

He did not drop it, but he instantly shifted his fingers so that he was holding it with a minimum of contact between his skin and it, very much as a man would hold a large dark spider which for some occult reason he may not drop.

It was a figurine, in blackened bronze or else in some dense wood, of a fearfully skinny, wiry old person tautly bent over backward like a bow, knees somewhat bent, arms straining back overhead. The face was witchy, nose almost meeting pointed chin across toothlessly grinning gums pressed close together, eyes bulging with mad evil. What seemed at first some close-fitting, ragged garment was then seen to be only loath-somely diseased skin, here starting to peel, there showing pustules, open ulcers, and other tetters, all worked in the metal (or carved in even harder wood) in abominably realistic minuscule detail. Long empty dugs hanging back up the chest as far as the neck made it female, but the taut legs, somewhat spread, showed a long flaccid penis caught by the artificer in extreme swing to the left, and far back from it a long grainy scrotum holding shriveled testicles caught in similar swing to the right, and in the space between them long leprous vulva gaping.

"It's nasty, isn't it?" Sovereign said drily of the hideous hermaphrodite. "My Aunt Helmintha bought it in Crotona, that one-time Greek colony in the instep of the Italian Boot where Pythagoras was born—bought it from a crafty old dealer in antiquities, who said it came from 'Earth's darkest center' by way of Mali and North Africa. He said it was a figure of the World, a nine-thing, *Draco homo*. He said it can't be broken, must not, in fact, for if you break it, the world will disappear or else you and those with you will forever vanish—no one knows where."

Staring at the figurine, Math muttered, "The seven days and nights the Ancient Mariner saw the curse in the dead man's eye."

She echoed, "The seven days and nights his friends sat with Job."

He said, his shoulders hunched, "The Seven Words, meaning the seven utterances of Christ on the cross."

She said, "The seven gates to the land of the dead through which Istar passed."

He said, his shoulders working, "The seven golden vials full of the wrath of God that the four beasts gave to the seven angels."

She said, shivering a little, "The birds known as the Seven Whistlers and considered to be a sign of some great calamity impending." Then, "Stop it, Math!"

Still staring at the figurine, he had shifted his grip on it, so that his thick forefingers hooked under its knees and elbows while his big thumbs pressed against its arched narrow belly harder and harder. But at her command his hands relaxed, and he returned the thing to her purse.

"Fie on you, sir!" she said, "to try to run out on the Game, and on me, and on yourself. The seven letters in Matthew, and in Fortree. Remember Solon: *Know thyself.*"

He answered, "The fourteen letters in Sovereign Saxon, making two sevens, too."

"The seven syllables in Master Matthias Fortree," she said, flicking off the lamps before taking a step toward him on her knees.

"The seven syllables in Mamsel Sovereign Saxon," he responded, putting his arms around her.

And then he was murmuring, "Oh Sovereign, my sovereign," and they were both wordlessly indicating sevens they'd named earlier, beginning with the seven crucial points of a girl ("Crucial green points," he said, and "Of a green girl," said she), and the whole crucial part of the evening was repeated, only this time it extended endlessly with infinite detail, although all he remembered of the Game from it was her saying "The dance of the seven veils," and him replying "The seven figures in the Dance of Death, as depicted on a hilltop by Ingmar Bergman in his film," and her responding, "The Seven Sleepers of Ephesus," an him laboriously getting out, "In the like legend in the Koran, the seven sleepers guarded by the dog Al Rakim," and her murmuring, "Good doggie, good doggie," as he slowly, slowly, sank into bottomless slumber.

Next morning Math woke to blissful dreaminess instead of acutely stabbing misery for the first time in his life since he had lost his childhood power to live wholly in the world of numbers. Strong sunlight was seeping through the ceiling. Severeign was gone with all her things, including the purse with its disturbing figurine, but that did not bother him in the least (nor did his eight-error, the only other possible flyspeck on his paradise), for he knew with absolute certainty that he would see her again that evening. He dressed himself and went out into the corridor and wandered along it until he saw from the corner of his eye that he was strolling alongside Elmo Hooper, whereupon he poured out to that living memory bank all his joy, every detail of last night's revelations.

As he ended his long litany of love, he noticed bemusedly that Elmo had dropped back, doubtless because they were overtaking three theoretical physicists headed for the Commons. Their speech had a secretive tone, so he tuned his ears to it and was soon in possession of a brand-new top secret they did well to whisper about, and they none the wiser—a secret that just might allow him to retrieve his eight-error, he realized with a throb of superadded happiness. (In fact, he was so happy he even thought on the spur of the moment of a second string for that bow.)

So when Severeign came that night, as he'd known she would, he was ready for her. Craftily he did not show his cards at first, but when she began with "The Seven Sages, those male Scheherazades who night after night keep a king from putting his son wrongfully to death," he followed her lead with "The Seven Wise Masters, another name for the Seven Sages."

She said, "The Seven Questions of Timur the Lame—Tamurlane."

He said, "The Seven Eyes of Ningauble."

"*Pardon?*"

"Never mind. *Seven Men* (including 'Enoch Soames' and 'A.V. Laider'), a book of short stories by Max Beerbohm."

She said, "*The Seven Pillars of Wisdom*, a book by Lawrence of Arabia."

He said, "*The Seven Faces of Dr. Lao*, a fantasy film."

She said, "Just *The Seven Faces* by themselves, a film Paul Muni starred in."

He said, "The Seven Gypsy jargons mentioned by Borrow in his *Bible in Spain*."

She said, "*Seven Brides for Seven Brothers*, another film."

He said, "The dance of the seven veils—how did we miss it?"

She said, "Or miss the seven stars in the hair of the blessed damsel?"

He said, "Or the Seven Hills of San Francisco when we got Rome's?"

She said, "*Seven Keys to Baldpate*, a play by George M. Cohan."

He said, "*Seven Famous Novels*, an omnibus by H.G. Wells."

She said, "*The Seven That Were Hanged*, a novella by Andreyev."

That's my grim cue, he thought, but I'll try my second string first. "The seven elements whose official names begin with N, and their symbols," he said, and then recited rapidly, poker-faced, "N for Nitrogen, Nb for Nobelium, Nd for Neodymium,

Ne for Neon, Ni for Nickel, No for Niobrium, Np for Neptunium."

She grinned fiendishly, started to speak, then caught herself. Her eyes widened at him. Her grin changed, though not much.

"Matthew, you rat!" she said. "You wanted me to correct you, say there were eight and that you'd missed Na. But then I'd have been in the wrong, for Na is for Sodium—its old an unofficial name Natrium."

Math grinned back at her, still poker-faced, though his confidence had been shaken. Nevertheless he said, "Quit stalling. What's your seven?"

She said, "*The Seven Lamps of Architecture,* a book of essays by John Ruskin."

He said, baiting his trap, "The seven letters in the name of the radioactive element Pluton—I mean Uranium."

She said, "That's feeble, sir. All words with seven letters would last almost forever. But you've made me think of a very good one, entirely legitimate. The seven isotopes of Plutonium and Uranium, sum of their Pleiades."

"Huh! I got you, madam," he said, stabbing a finger at her.

Her face betrayal exasperation of a petty sort, but then an entirely different sort of consternation, almost panic fear.

"You're wrong, madam," he said triumphantly. "There are, as I learned only today—"

"Stop!" she cried. "Don't say it! You'll be sorry! Remember Thales: *Suretyship is the precursor of ruin.*"

He hesitated a moment. He thought, That means don't cosign checks. Could that be stretched to mean don't share dangerous secrets? No, too farfetched.

"You won't escape being shown up that easily," he said gleefully. "There are *eight* isotopes now, as I learned only this morning. Confess yourself at fault."

He stared at her eagerly, triumphantly, but only saw her face growing pale. Not ashamed, not exasperated, not contumacious even, but fearful. Dreadfully fearful.

There were three rapid, very loud knocks on the door.

They both started violently.

The knocks were repeated, followed by a bellow that penetrated all soundproofing. "Open up in there!" it boomed hollowly. "Come on out, Fortree! *And* the girl."

Matthew goggled. Sovereign suddenly dug in her purse and tossed him something. It was the figurine.

"Break it!" she commanded. "It's our only chance of escape."

He stared at it stupidly.

There was a ponderous pounding on the door, which groaned and crackled.

"Break it!" she cried. "Night before last you prayed. I brought the answer to your prayer. You have it in your hands. It takes us to your lost world that you loved. Break it, I say!"

A kind of comprehension came to Math's face. He hooked his fingers round the figure's evil ends, pressed on the arching loathsome midst.

"Who is your brother, Sovereign?" he asked.

"You are my brother, in the other realm," she said. "Press, press!—and break the thing!"

The door began visibly to give under the strokes, now thunderous. The cords in Math's neck stood out, and the veins in his forehead; his knuckles grew white.

"Break it for me," she cried. "For Sovereign!! *For Seven!*"

The sound of the door bursting open masked a lesser though sharper crack. Warren Dean and his party plunged into the room to find it empty, and no one in the bedroom or bathroom either.

513

It had been he, of course, whom Matthew, utterly bemused, had mistaken for Elmo Hooper that morning. Dean had immediately reactivated the bugs in Matthew's apartment. It is from their record that this account of Matthew and Severeign's last night is reconstructed. All the rest of the story derives from the material overheard by Dean (who quite obviously, from this narrative, has his own Achilles' heel) or retrieved from Elmo Hooper.

The case is still very open, of course. That fact alone has made the Coexistence Complex an even more uneasy place than before—something that most connoisseurs of its intrigues had deemed impossible. The theory of security is the dread one that Matthew Fortree was successfully spirited away to one of the hostiles by the diabolical spy Severeign Saxon. By what device remains unknown, although the walls of the Coexistence Complex have been systematically burrowed through in search of secret passageways more thoroughly than even termites could have achieved, without discovering anything except several lost bugging systems.

A group of daring thinkers believes that Matthew, on the basis of his satanic mathematical cunning and his knowledge of the eighth isotope of the uranium-plutonium pair, and probably with technological know-how from behind some iron curtain supplied by Severeign, devised an innocent-looking mechanism, which was in fact a matter transmitter, by means of which they escaped to the country of Severeign's employers. All sorts of random setups were made of Matthew's ivories. Their investigation became a sort of hobby in itself for some and led to several games and quasi-religious cults, and to two suicides.

Others believe Severeign's employers were extraterrestrial. But a rare few quietly entertain the thought and perhaps the hope that hers was a farther country than that even, that she came from the Pythagorean universe where Matthew spent much of his infancy and early childhood, the universe where numbers are real and one can truly fall in love with Seven, briefly incarnate as a Miss S.S.

Whatever the case, Matthew Fortree and Severeign Saxon are indeed gone, vanished without a trace or clue except for a remarkably nasty figurine showing a fresh, poisonously green surface where it was snapped in two, which is the only even number that is a prime.

The Button Molder

I don't rightly know if I can call this figure I saw for a devastating ten seconds a ghost. And *heard* for about ten seconds just before that. These durations are of course to a degree subjective judgments. At the time they seemed to be lasting forever. Ten seconds can be long or short. A man can light a cigarette. A sprinter can travel a hundred yards, sound two miles, and light two million. A rocket can launch, or burn up inside. A city can fall down. It depends on what's happening.

The word "ghost," like "shade" or "wraith" or even "phantom," suggests human personality and identity, and what this figure had was in a way the antithesis of that. Perhaps "apparition" is better, because it ties it in with astronomy, which may conceivably be the case in a farfetched way. Astronomers speak of apparitions of the planet Mercury, just as they talk of spurious stars (novas) and occultations by Venus and the moon. Astronomy talk can sound pretty eerie, even without the help of any of the witching and romantic lingo of astrology.

But I rather like "ghost," for it lets me bring in the theory of the Victorian scholar and folklorist Andrew Lang that a ghost is simply a short waking dream in the mind of the person who thinks he sees one. He tells about it in his book *Dreams and Ghosts*, published in 1897. It's a praiseworthily simple and sober notion (also a very polite one, typically English!—"I'd never suggest you were lying about that ghost, old boy. But perhaps you dreamed it, not knowing you were dreaming?" And a theory easy to believe, especially if the person who sees the ghost is fatigued and under stress and the ghost something seen in the shadows of a dark doorway or a storm-lashed window at night or in the flickering flames of a dying fire or in the glooms of a dim room with faded tapestries or obscurely patterned wallpaper. Not so easy to credit for a figure seen fully illuminated for a double handful of long seconds by someone untired and under no physical strain, yet I find it a reassuring theory in my case. In fact, there are times when it strikes me as vastly preferable to certain other possibilities.

The happening occurred rather soon after I moved from one six-story apartment building to another in downtown San Francisco. There were a remarkable number of those put up in the decades following the quake and fire of 1906. A lot of them started as small hotels, but transformed to apartments as the supply of cheap menial labor shrank. You can usually tell those by their queer second floors, which began as mezzanines. The apartment I was moving from had an obvious one of those, lobby-balcony to the front, manager's apartment and some other tiny ones to the rear.

I'd been thinking about moving for a long time, because my one-room-and-bath was really too small for me and getting crammed to the ceiling with my flies and books, yet

515

I'd shrunk from the bother involved. But then an efficient, "savvy" manager was replaced by an ineffectual one, who had little English, or so pretended to save himself work, and the place rather rapidly got much too noisy. Hi-fi's thudded and thumped unrebuked until morning. Drunken parties overflowed into the halls and took to wandering about. Early on the course of deterioration the unwritten slum rule seemed to come into effect of "If you won't call the owner (or the cops) on me, I won't call him on you." (Why did I comply with this rule? I hate rows and asserting myself.) There was a flurry of mail box thefts and of stoned folk setting off the building's fire alarm out of curiosity, and of nodding acquaintances whose names you didn't know hitting you for small loans. Pets and stray animals multiplied—and left evidence of themselves, as did the drunks. There were more than the usual quota of overdosings and attempted suicides and incidents of breaking down doors (mostly by drunks who'd lost their keys) and series of fights that were, perhaps unfortunately, mostly racket, and at least one rape. In the end the halls came to be preferred for every sort of socializing. And if the police were at last summoned, it was generally just in time to start things up again when they'd almost quieted down.

I don't mind a certain amount of stupid noise and even hubbub. After all, it's my business to observe the human condition and report on it imaginatively. But when it comes to spending my midnight hours listening to two elderly male lovers shouting horrendous threats at each other in prison argot, repeatedly slamming doors on each other and maddeningly whining for them to be reopened, and stumbling up and down stairs meanacing each other with a dull breadknife which is periodically wrested in slow-motion from hand to hand, I draw the line. More important, I am even able to summon up the energy to get myself away from the offensive scene forever.

My new apartment building, which I found much more easily than I'd expected to once I started to hunt, was an earthly paradise by comparison. The *occupants stayed out of the halls* and when forced to venture into them traveled as swiftly as was compatible with maximum quiet. The walls were thick enough so that I hadn't the faintest idea of what they did at home. The manager was a tower of resourceful efficiency, yet unobtrusive and totally uninquisitive. Instead of the clanking and groaning monster I'd been used to, the small elevator (I lived on six in both places) was a wonder of silent reliability. Twice a week the halls roared softly and briefly with a large vacuum cleaner wielded by a small man with bowed shoulders who never seemed to speak.

Here the queer second-floor feature hinting at hotel-origins took the form of three private offices (an architect's, a doctor's, and a CPA's), instead of front apartments, with stairway of their own shut off from the rest of the building, while the entire first floor except for the main entrance and its hall was occupied by a large fabrics or yards-goods store, which had in its display window an item that intrigued me mightily. It was a trim lay figure, life-size, made of ribbed white cotton material and stuffed. It had mitts instead of hands (no separate fingers or toes) and an absolutely blank face. Its position and attitude were altered rather frequently, as were the attractive materials displayed with it—it might be standing or reclining, sitting or kneeling. Sometimes it seemed to be pulling fabrics from a roller, or otherwise arranging them, things like that. I always thought of it as female, I can't say why; although there were discreet suggestions of a bosom and a pubic bump, its hips were narrow; perhaps a woman would have thought of it as male. Or perhaps my reasons for thinking of it as feminine were as simple as its small life-size (about five feet tall) or (most obvious) its lack of any external sex organ. At any rate, it rather fascinated as well as amused me, and at first I fancied it was standing for the delightfully quiet, unobstrusive folk who were my new fellow-tenants as opposed to the noisy and obstreperous quaints I had endured before. I even thought of it for a bit as the "faceless" and unindividualized protohuman being to which the Button Molder threatens to melt down Peer Gynt. (I'd just re-read that classic of Ibsen's—really, Peer stands with Faust and Hamlet and Dom Quixote and Don Juan as one of the great fundamental figures of western culture.) But then I became aware of its extreme mute expressiveness. If a face is left blank, the imagination of the viewer always supplies an expression for it—an expression which may be more intense and "living" because there are no lifeless features for it to clash with.

(If I seem to be getting off on sidetracks, please bear with me. They really have a bearing. I haven't forgotten my ghost, or apparition, or those agonizing ten seconds I want to tell you about. No indeed.)

My own apartment in the new building was almost too good to be true. Although advertised as only a studio, it contained four rooms in line, each with a window facing east. They were, in order from north to south (which would be left to right as you entered the hall: bathroom, small bedroom (its door faced you as you entered from the outside hall), large living room, and (beyond a low arched doorway) dinette-kitchen. The bathroom window was frosted; the other three had Venetian blinds. And besides two closets (one half the bedroom long) there were seventeen built-in cupboards with a total of thirty-one shelves—a treasure trove of ordered emptiness, and all, all, mine alone! To complete the pleasant picture, I had easy access to the roof—the manager assured me that a few of the tenants regularly used it for sunbathing. But I wasn't interested in the roof by day.

The time came soon enough when I eagerly supervised the transfer to my new place of my luggage, boxes, clothes, the few articles of furniture I owned (chiefly book-cases and filing cabinets), and the rather more extensive materials of my trade of fiction-writing and chief avocation of roof-top astronomy. That last is more important to me than one might guess. I like cities, but I'd hate to live in one without having easy access to a flat roof. I'd had that at my old apartment, and it was one of the features that kept me there so long—I'd anticipated difficulties getting the same privilege elsewhere.

I have the theory, you see, that in this age of mechanized hive-dwelling and of getting so much input from necessarily conformist artificial media such as TV and newspapers, it's very important for a person to keep himself more directly oriented, in daily touch with the heavens or at least the sky, the yearly march of the sun across the stars, the changing daily revolution of the stars as the world turns, the crawl of the planets, the swift phases of the moon, things like that. After all, it's one of the great healing rhythms of nature like the seas and the winds, perhaps the greatest. Stars are a pattern of points upon infinity, elegant geometric art, with almost an erotic poign-nancy, but all, all nature. Some psyhologists say that people stop dreaming if they don't look out over great distances each day, "see the horizon," as it were, and that dreams are the means by which the mind keeps its conscious and unconscious halves in balance, and I certainly agree with them. At any rate I'd deliberately built up the habit of rooftop observing, first by the unaided eye, then with the help of binoculars, and, finally, a small refracting telescope on an equatorial mounting.

Moreover—and especially in a foggy city like San Francisco!—if you get interested in the stars, you inevitably get interested in the weather if only because it so often thwarts you with its infinitely varied clouds and winds (which can make a telescope useless by setting it trembling), its freaks and whims and its own great allover rhythms. And then it gives you a new slant on the city itself. You become absorbed into the fascinating world of roofs, a secret world above the city world, one mostly uninhabited and unknown. Even the blocky, slablike highrises cease to be anonymous disfigurements, targets of protests. They become the markers whence certain stars appear or whither they trend, or which they graze with twinkling caress, and which the sun or moon touch or pass behind at certain times of the year or month, exactly like the menhirs at Stonehenge which primitive man used similarly. And through the gaps and narrow chinks between the great highrises, you can almost glimpse bits and pieces of the far horizon. And always once in a while there will be some freakish sky or sky-related event that will completely mystify you and really challenge your imagination.

Of course, roof-watching, like writing itself, is a lonely occupation, but at least it tends to move outward from self, to involve more and more of otherness. And in any case, after having felt the world and its swarming people much too much with me for the past couple of years (and in an extremely noisy, sweaty way!) I was very much looking forward to living alone by myself for a good long while in a supremely quiet environment.

In view of that last, it was highly ironic that the first thing to startle me about my new place should have been *the noise*—noise of a very special sort, the swinish grunting and chomping of the huge garbage trucks that came rooting for refuse every morning (except Sunday) at four A.M. or a little earlier. My old apartment had looked out on a rear inner court in an alleyless block, and so their chuffing, grinding sound had been one I'd been mostly spared. While the east windows of my new place looked sidewise down on the street in front and also into a rather busy alley—there wasn't a building nearly as high as mine in that direction for a third of a block. Moreover, in moving the three blocks between the two apartments, I'd moved into a more closely supervised and protected district—that of the big hotels and theaters and expensive stores—with more police protection and enforced tidiness—which meant more garbage trucks. There were the yellow municipal ones and the green and gray ones of more than one private collection company, and once at three thirty I saw a tiny white one draw up on the sidewalk beside an outdoor phone booth and the driver get out and spend ten minutes rendering it pristine with vacuum, sponge, and squeegee.

The first few nights when they waked me I'd get up and move from window to window, and even go down the outside hall to the front fire escape with its beckoning red light, the better to observe the racketty monsters and their hurrying attendants— the wide mawa into which the refuse was shaken from clattering cans, the great revolving steel drums that chewed it up, the huge beds that would groaningly tilt to empty the drums and shake down the shards. (My God, they were ponderous and cacophonous vehicles!)

But nothing could be wrong with my new place—even these sleep-shattering mechanical giant hogs fascinated me. It was an eerie and mysterious sight to see one of them draw up, say, at the big hotel across the street from me and an iron door in the sidewalk open upward without visible human agency and four great dully gleaming garbage cans slowly arise there as if from some dark hell. I found myself comparing them also (the trucks) to the Button Molder in *Peer Gynt*. Surely, I told myself, they each must have a special small compartment for discarded human souls that had failed to achieve significant individuality and were due to be melted down! Or perhaps they just mixed in the worn-out souls with all the other junk.

At one point I even thought of charting and timing the trucks' exact routes and schedules, just as I did with the planets and the moon, so that I'd be better able to keep tabs on them.

That was another reason I didn't mind being waked at four—it let me get in a little rooftop astronomy before the morning twilight began. At such times I'd usually just take my binoculars, though once I lugged up my telescope for an apparition of Mercury when he was at his greatest western elongation.

Once, peering down from the front fire escape into the dawn-dark street below, I thought I saw a coveralled attendant rudely toss my fabric-store manikin into the rear-end mouth of a dark green truck, and I almost shouted down a protesting inquiry . . . and ten minutes later felt sorry I hadn't—sorry and somehow guilty. It bothered me so much that I got dressed and went down to check out the display window. For a moment I didn't see her, and I felt a crazy grief rising, but then I spotted her peeping up at me coyly from under a pile of yardage arranged so that she appeared to have pulled the colorful materials down on herself.

And once at four A.M. in the warm morning of a holiday I was for variety awakened by the shrill, argumentative cries of four slender hookers, two black, two white, arrayed in their uniform of high heels, hotpants, and longsleeved lacy blouses, clustered beneath a streetlight on the far corner of the next intersection west and across from an all-hours nightclub named the Windjammer. They were preening and scouting about at intervals, but mostly they appeared to be discoursing, somewhat less raucously now, with the unseen drivers and passengers of a dashing red convertible and a slim white hardtop long as a yacht, which were drawn up near the curb at nonchalant angles across the corner. Their customers? Pimps more likely, from the glory of their equipages. After a bit the cars drifted away and the four lovebirds wandered off east in a loose formation, warbling together querulously.

After about ten days I stopped hearing the garbage trucks, just as the manager told me would happen, though most mornings I continued to wake early enough for a little astronomy.

My first weeks in the new apartment were very happy ones. (No, I hadn't encountered my ghost yet, or even got hints of its approach, but I think the stage was setting itself and perhaps the materials were gathering.) My writing, which had been almost stalled at the old place, began to go well, and I finished three short stories. I spent my afternoons pleasantly setting out the stuff of my life to best advantage, being particularly careful to leave most surfaces clear and not to hang too many pictures, and in expeditions to make thoughtful purchases. I acquired a dark blue celestial globe I'd long wanted and several maps to fill the space above my filing cabinets: one of the world, a chart of the stars on the same mercator projection, a big one of the moon, and two of San Francisco, the city and its downtown done in great detail. I didn't go to many shows during this time or see much of any of my friends—I didn't need them. But I got caught up on stacks of unanswered correspondence. And I remember expending considerable effort in removing the few blemishes I discovered on my new place: a couple of inconspicuous but unsightly stains, a slow drain that turned out to have been choked by a stopper-chain, a venetian blind made cranky by twisted cords, and the usual business of replacing low wattage globes with brighter ones, particularly in the case of the entry light just inside the hall door. There the ceiling had been lowered a couple of feet, which gave the rest of the apartment a charmingly spacious appearance, as did the arched dinette doorway, but it meant that any illumination there had to come down from a fixture in the true ceiling through a frosted plate in the lowered one. I put in a 200-watter, reminding myself to use it sparingly. I even remember planning to get a thick rubber mat to put under my filing cabinets so they wouldn't indent and perhaps even cut the heavy carpeting too deeply, but I never got around to that.

Perhaps those first weeks were simply too happy, perhaps I just got to spinning along too blissfully, for after finishing the third short story, I suddenly found myself tempted by the idea of writing something that would be more than fiction and also more than a communication addressed to just one person, but rather a general statement of what I thought about life and other people and history and the universe and all, the roots of it, something like Descartes began when he wrote down, "I think, therefore I am." Oh, it wouldn't be formally and certainly not stuffily philosophical, but it would contain a lot of insights just the same, the fruits of one man's lifetime experience. It would be critical yet autobiographical, honestly rooted in me. At the very least it would be a testimonial to the smooth running of my life at a new place, a way of honoring my move here.

I'm ordinarily not much of a nonfiction writer. I've done a few articles about writing and about other writers I particularly admire, a lot of short book reviews, and for a dozen or so years before I took up full-time fiction, I edited a popular science magazine. And before that I'd worked on encyclopedias and books of knowledge.

But everything was so clear to me at the new place, my sensations were so exact, my universe was spread out around me so orderly, that I knew that now was the time to write such a piece if ever, and so I decided to take a chance on the new idea, give it a whirl.

At the same time at a deeper level in my mind and feelings, I believe I was making a parallel decision running something like this: *Follow this lead. Let all the other stuff go, ease up, and see what happens.* Somewhere down there a control was being loosened.

An hour or so before dawn the next day I had a little experience that proved to be the pattern for several subsequent ones, including the final unexpected event. (You see, I haven't forgotten those ten seconds I mentioned. I'm keeping them in mind.)

I'd been on the roof in the cool predawn to observe a rather close conjunction (half a degree apart) of Mars and Jupiter in the east (they didn't rise until well after midnight), and while I was watching the reddist and golden planets without instrument (except for my glasses, of course) I twice thought I saw a shooting star out of the corner of my eye, but didn't get my head around in time to be sure. I was intrigued because I hadn't noted in the handbook any particular meteor showers due at this time and also because most shooting stars are rather faint and the city's lights tend to dim down everything in the sky. The third time it happened I managed to catch the flash and for a long instant was astounded by the sight of what appeared to be three shooting stars traveling fast in triangular formation like three fighter planes before they whisked out of sight behind a building. Then I heard a faint bird-cry and realized they had been three gulls winging quite close and fast overhead, their white underfeathers illumined by the upward streaming streetlights. It was really a remarkable illusion, of the sort that has to be seen to be fully believed. You'd think your eye wouldn't make that sort of misidentification—three sea birds for three stars—but from the corner of your eye you don't see shape or color or even brightness much, only pale movement whipping past. And then you wouldn't think three birds would keep such a tight and exact triangular formation, very much like three planes performing at an air show.

I walked quietly back to my apartment in my bathrobe and slippers. The stairway from the roof was carpeted. My mind was full of the strange triple apparition I'd just seen. I thought of how another mind with other anticipations might have seen three UFOs. I silently opened the door to my apartment, which I'd left on the latch, and stepped inside.

I should explain here that I always switch off all the lights when I leave my apartment and am careful about how I turn them on when I come back. It's partly thrift and citizenly thoughts about energy, the sort of thing you do to get gold stars at grown-ups' Sunday school. But it's also a care not to leave an outward glaring light to disturb some sleeper who perhaps must keep his window open and unshuttered for the sake of air and coolth; there's a ten-storey apartment building a quarter block away overlooking my east windows, and I've had my own sleep troubled by such unnecessary abominable beacons. On the other hand, I like to look out open windows myself; I hate to keep them wholly shaded, draped, or shuttered, but at the same time I don't want to become a target for a sniper—a simply realistic fear to many these days. As a result of all this I make it a rule never to turn on a light at night until I'm sure the windows of the room I'm in are fully obscured. I take a certain pride, I must admit, in being able to move around my place in the dark without bumping things—it's a test of courage too, going back to childhood, and also a proof that your sensory faculties haven't been dimmed by age. And I guess I just like the feeling of mysteriousness it gives me.

So when I stepped inside I did *not* turn on the 200-watt light above the lowered ceiling of the entry. My intention was to move directly forward into the bedroom, assure myself that the venetian blinds were tilted shut, and then switch on the bedside lamp. But as I started to do that, I heard the beginning of a noise to my right and I glanced toward the living room, where the street lights striking upward through the open venetian blinds made pale stripes on the ceiling and wall and slightly curving ones on the celestial globe atop a bookcase, and into the dinette beyond, and I saw a thin dark figure slip along the wall. But then, just as a feeling of surprise and fear began, almost at the same moment but actually a moment later, there came the realization that the figure was the black frame of my glasses, either moving as I turned my head or becoming more distinct as I switched my eyes that way, more likely a little of both. It was an odd mixture of sensation and thought, especially coming right on top of the star-birds (or bird-stars), as if I were getting almost simultaneously the messages *My God, it's an intruder, or ghost, or whatever* and *It isn't any of those, as you know very well from a lifetime's experience. You've just been had again by appearances.*

I'm pretty much a thoroughgoing skeptic, you see, when it comes to the paranormal, or the religious supernatural, or even such a today-commonplace as telepathy. My mental attitudes were formed in the period during and just after the first world war, when science was still a right thing, almost noble, and technology was forward-looking and labor-saving and progressive, and before folk wisdom became so big and was still pretty much equated with ignorance and superstition, no matter how picturesque. I've never seen or heard of a really convincing scrap of evidence for ancient or present-day astronauts from other worlds, for comets or moons that bumped the earth and changed history, or for the power of pyramids to prolong life or sharpen razor blades. As for immortality, it's my impression that most people do or don't do what's in them and then live out their lives in monotonous blind alleys, and what would be the point in cluttering up another world with all the worn-out junk? And as for God, it seems to me that the existence of one being who knew everything, future as well as past, would simply rob the universe of drama, excuse us all from doing anything. I'll admit that with telepathy the case is somewhat different, if only because so many sensible, well-educated, brilliant people seem to believe in some form of it. I only know I haven't experienced any as far as I can tell; it's almost made me jealous—I've sometimes thought I must be wrapped in some very special insulation against thought-waves, if there be such. I *will* allow that the mind (and also mental suggestions from outside) can affect the body, even affect it greatly—the psychosomatic thing. But that's just about all I will allow.

So much for the first little experience—no, wait, what did I mean when I wrote, "I heard the beginning of a noise"? Well, there are sounds so short and broken-off that you can't tell what they are going to be, or even for sure just how loud they were, so that you ask yourself if you imagined them. It was like that—a tick without a tock, a ding without the dong, a creak that went only halfway, never reaching that final *kuh* sound. Or like a single footstep that started rather loud and ended muted down to nothing— very much like the whole little experience itself, beginning with a gust of shock and terror and almost instantly reducing to the commonplace. Well, so much for that.

The next few days were pleasant and exciting ones, as I got together materials for my new project, assembling the favorite books I knew I'd want to quote (Shakespeare and the King James Bible, *Moby Dick,* and *Wuthering Heights,* Ibsen and Bertrand Russell, Stapledon and Heinlein), looking through the daybooks I've kept for the past five years for the entries in black ink, which I reserve for literary and what I like to call metaphysical matters, and telling my mind (programming it, really) to look for similar insights whenever they happened to turn up during the course of the day—my chores and reading, my meals and walks—and then happily noting down those new insights in turn. There was only one little fly in the ointment: I knew I'd embarked on projects somewhat like this before—autobiographical and critical things—and failed to bring them to conclusions. But then I've had the same thing happen to me on stories. With everything, one needs a bit of luck.

My next little experience began up on the roof. (They all did, for that matter.) It was a very clear evening without a moon, and I'd been memorizing the stars in Capricorn and faint Aquarius and the little constellations that lie between those and the Northern Cross: Sagitta, Delphinus, and dim Equuleus. You learn the stars rather like you learn countries and cities on a map, getting the big names first (the brightest stars and star groups) and then patiently filling in the areas between—and always on the watch for striking forms. At such times I almost forget the general dimming effect of San Francisco's lights since what I'm working on is so far above them.

And then, as I was resting my eyes from the binoculars, shut off by the roof's walls and the boxlike structure housing the elevator's motor from the city's most dazzling glares (the big, whitely fluorescent streetlights are the worst, the ones that are supposed to keep late walkers safe) I saw a beam of bright silver light strike straight upward for about a second from the roof of a small hotel three blocks away. And after about a dozen seconds more it came again, equally brief. It really looked like a sort of laser-thing: a beam of definite length (about two storys) and solid-looking. It happened twice more, not at regular intervals, but always as far as I could judge in exactly the same place (and I'd had time to spin a fantasy about a secret enclave of extra-terrestrials signaling to confederates poised just outside the stratosphere) when it occurred to me to use my binoculars on it. They solved the mystery almost at once: It wasn't a light beam at all, but a tall flagpole painted silver (no wonder it looked solid!) and at intervals washed by the roving beam of a big arc light shooting upward from the street beyond and swinging in slow circles—the sort of thing they use to signalize the opening of movie houses and new restaurants, even quite tiny ones.

What had made the incident out of the ordinary was that most flagpoles are painted dull white, not silver, and that the clearness of the night had made the arc light's wide beam almost invisible. If there'd been just a few wisps of cloud or fog in the air above, I'd have spotted it at once for what it was. It was rather strange to think of all that light streaming invisible up from the depths of the city's reticulated canyons and gorges.

I wondered why I'd never noted that flagpole before. Probably they never flew a flag on it.

It all didn't happen to make me recall my three star-birds, and so when after working over once more this night's chosen heavenly territory, including a veering aside to scan the rich starfields of Aquila and the diamond of Altair, one of Earth's closest stellar neighbors, I was completely taken by surprise again when on entering my apartment, the half a noise was repeated and the same skinny dark shape glided along the wall across the narrow flaglike bands of light and dark. Only this time the skeptical, deflating reaction came a tiny bit sooner, followed at once by the almost peevish inner remark, *Oh, yes, that again!* And then as I turned on the bedside light, I wondered, as one will, how I would have reacted if the half step had been completed and if the footsteps had gone on, getting louder as they made their swift short trip and there peered around the side of the doorway at me . . . what? It occurred to me that the nastiest and most frightening thing in the world must differ widely from person to person, and I smiled. Surely in man's inward lexicon, the phobias outnumber the philias a thousand to one!

Oh, I'll admit that when I wandered into the living room and kitchen a bit later, shutting the blinds and turning on some lights, I did inspect things in a kind of perfunctory way, but noted nothing at all out of order. I told myself that all buildings make a variety of little noises at night, waterpipes especially can get downright loquacious, and then there are refrigerator motors sighing on and off and the faint little clicks and whines that come from electric clocks, all manner of babble—that half a noise might be anything. At least I knew the identity of the black glider—the vaguely seen black form always at the corner of my eye when I had on my glasses and most certainly there now.

I went on assembling the primary materials for my new project, and a week later I was able to set down, word by mulled-over, the unembroidered, unexemplified, unproven gist of what I felt about life, or at least a first version of it. I still have it as I typed it from a penciled draft with many erasures, crossings out, and interlineations:

> There is this awareness that is I, this mind that's me, a little mortal world of space and time, which glows and aches, which purrs and darkens, haunted and quickened by the ghosts that are memory, imagination, and thought, forever changing under urgings from within and proddings from without, yet able to hold still by fits and starts (and now and then refreshed by sleep and dreams), forever seeking to extend its bounds, forever hunting for the mixture of reality and fantasy —the formula, the script, the scenario, the story to tell itself or others—which will enable it do do its work, savor its thrills, and keep on going.
>
> A baby tells itself the simplest story: that it is all that matters, it is God, commanding and constraining all the rest, all otherness. But then the script becomes more complicated. Stories take many forms: a scientific theory or a fairy tale, a world history or an anecdote, a call to action or a cry for help—all, all are stories. Sometimes they tell of our love for another, or they embody our illusioned and illusioning vision of the one we love—they are courtship. But every story must be interesting bitter, dry taste.
>
> And then there are the other mortal minds I know are there, fellow awareness, companion consciousnesses, some close, a very few almost in touching space (but never quite), most farther off in almost unimaginable multitudes, each one like mine a little world of space and time moment by moment seeking its story, the combination of

illusion and hard fact, of widest waking and of deepest dreaming, which will allow it to create, enjoy, survive. A company of loving, warring minds, a tender, rough companioning of tiny cosmoses forever telling stories to each other and themselves—that's what there is.

And I know that I must stay aware of all the others, listening to their stories, trying to understand them, their sufferings, their joys, and their imaginings, respecting the thorny facts of both their inner and their outer lives, and nourishing the needful illusions at least of those who are closest to me, if I am to make progress in my quest.

Finally there is the world, stranger than any mind or any story, the unknown universe, the shadowy scaffolding holding these minds together, the grid on which they are mysteriously arrayed, their container and their field, perhaps (but is there any question of it?) all-powerful yet quite unseen, its form unsensed, known only to the companion minds by the sensations it showers upon them and pelts them with, by its cruel and delicious proddings and graspings, by its agonizing and ecstatic messages (but never a story), and by its curt summonses and sentences, including death. Yes, that is how it is, those are the fundamentals: There is the dark, eternally silent, unknown universe; there are the friend-enemy minds shouting and whispering their tales and always seeking the three miracles—that minds should really touch, or that the silent universe should speak, tell minds a story, or (perhaps the same thing) that there should be a story that works that is all hard facts, all reality, with no illusions and no fantasy; and lastly there is lonely, story-telling, wonder-questioning, mortal me.

As I re-read that short statement after typing it out clean, I found it a little more philosophical than I'd intended and also perhaps a little more overly glamorized with words like "ecstatic" and "agonizing," "mysteriously" and "stranger." But on the whole I was satisfied with it. Now to analyze it more deeply and flesh it out with insights and examples from my own life and from my own reflections on the work of others!

But as the working days went on and became weeks (remember, I'd pretty much given up all other work for the duration of this project) I found it increasingly difficult to make any real progress. For one thing, I gradually became aware that in order to analyze that little statement much more deeply and describe my findings, I'd need to use one or more of the vocabularies of professional philosophy and psychology—which would mean months at least of reading and reviewing and of assimilating new advances, and I certainly didn't have the time for that. (The vocabularies of philosophies can be *very* special—Whitehead's, for instance, makes much use of the archaic verb "pretend," which for him means something very different from "comprehend" or "perceive.") Moreover, the whole idea had been to skim accumulated insights and wisdom (if any!) off my mind, not become a student again and start from the beginning.

And I found it was pretty much the same when I tried to say something about other writers, past and contemporary, beyond a few obvious remarks and memorable quotations. I'd need to read their works again and study their lives in a lot more detail than I had ever done, before I'd be able to shape statements of any significance, things I really believed about them.

And when I tried to write about my own life, I kept discovering that for the most part it was much too much like anyone else's. I didn't want to set down a lot of dreary dates and places, only the interesting things, but how tell about those honestly without bringing in the rest? Moreover, it began to seem to me that all the really interesting subjects, like sex and money, feelings of guilt, worries about one's courage, and concern about one's selfishness were things one wasn't supposed to write about, either because they were common to all men and women and so quite unexceptional.

This state of frustration didn't grip me all the time, of course. It came in waves and gradually accumulated. I'd generally manage to start off each day feeling excited about the project (though it began to take more and more morning time to get my head into that place, I will admit); perhaps some part of my short statement would come alive for me again, like that bit about the universe being a grid on which minds are mysteriously arrayed, but by the end of the day I would have worried all the life out of it and my mind would be as blank as the face of my manikin in the fabric shop window downstairs. I remember once or twice in the course of one of our daily encounters shaking my head ruefully at her, almost as if seeking for sympathy. She seemed to have a lot more patience and poise than I had.

I was beginning to spend more time on the roof too, not only for the sake of the stars and astronomy, but just to get away from my desk with all its problems. In fact my next little experience leading up to the ghostly one began shortly before sunset one day when I'd been working long, though fruitlessly. The sky, which was cloudless from my east windows, began to glow with an unusual violet color and I hurried up to get a wider view.

All day long a steady west wind had been streaming out the flags on the hotels and driving away east what smog there was, so that the sky was unusually clear. But the sun had sunk behind the great fog bank that generally rests on the Pacific just outside the Golden Gate. However, he had not yet set, for to the south, where there were no tall buildings to obstruct my vision, his beams were turning a few scattered clouds over San Jose (some thirty miles away) a delicate shade of lemon yellow that seemed to be the exact complement of the violet in the sky (just as orange sunset clouds tend to go with a deep blue sky).

And then as I watched, there suddenly appeared in the midst of that sunset, very close to the horizon in a cloudless stretch, a single yellow cloud like a tiny dash. It seemed to appear from nowhere, just like that. And then as I continued to watch, another cloud appeared close beside the first at the same altitude, beginning as a bright yellow point and then swiftly growing until it was as long as the first, very much as if a giant invisible hand had drawn another short dash.

During the course of the next few minutes, as I watched with a growing sense of wonder and a feeling of giant release from the day's frustrations, eight more such mini-clouds (or whatever) appeared at fairly regular intervals, until there were ten of them glowing in line there, fluorescent yellow stitches in the sky.

My mind raced, clutching at explanations. Kenneth Arnold's original flying saucers thirty years ago, which he'd glimpsed from his light plane over the American northwest, had been just such shining shapes in a row. True, his had been moving, while mine were hovering over a city, having appeared from nowhere. Could they conceivably have come from hyperspace? my fancy asked.

And then, just as the lemon sunset began to fade from the higher clouds, an explanation struck me irresistibly. What I was seeing was skywriting (which usually we see above our heads) from way off to one side, viewed edgewise. My ten mystery clouds (or giant ships!) were the nine letters—and the hyphen—of Pepsi-Cola. (Next day I confirmed this by a telephone call to San Jose; there had been just such an advertising display.)

At the time, and as the giant yellow stitches faded to gray unsewn sky-cloth, I remember feeling very exhilarated and also slightly hysterical at the comic aspect of the event. I paced about the roof chortling, telling myself that the vision I'd just witnessed outdid even that of the Goodyear blimp acrawl with colored lights in abstract patterns that had welcomed me to this new roof the first night I'd climbed up here after moving in. I spent quite a while quieting myself, so that the streetlights had just come on when I went downstairs. But somehow I hadn't thought of it being very dark yet in my apartment, so that was perhaps why it wasn't until I was actually unlocking the door that, remembering the Starbirds and the Silver Laser (and now the Mystery of the Ten Yellow Stitches!), I also remembered the events that had followed them. I had only time to think *Here we go again* as I pushed inside.

Well, it *was* dark in there and the pale horizontal bands were on the wall and the skeleton black figure slipped along them and I felt almost instantly the choked-off gust of terror riding atop the remnants of my exhilaration, all of this instantly after hearing that indefinable sound which seemed to finish almost before it began. That was one thing characteristic of all these preliminary incidents—they ended so swiftly and so abruptly that it was hard to think about them afterwards, the mind had nothing to work with.

And I know that in trying to describe them I must make them sound patterned, almost prearranged, yet at the time they just happened and somehow there was always an element of surprise.

Unfortunately the exhilaration I'd feel on the roof never carried over to the next morning's work on my new project. This time, after sweating and straining for almost a week without any progress at all, I resolutely decided to shelve it, at least for a while, and get back to stories.

But I found I couldn't do that. I'd committed myself too deeply to the new thing. Oh, I didn't find that out right away, of course. No, I spent more than a week before I came to that hateful and panic-making conclusion. I tried every trick I knew of to get myself going: long walks, fasting, starting to write immediately after waking up when my mind was hypnogogic and blurred with dream, listening to music which I'd always found suggestive, such as Holst's *The Planets*, especially the "Saturn" section, which seems to capture the essence of time—you hear the giant footsteps of time itself crashing to a halt—or William's *Sinfonia Antarctica* with its lonely windmachine finish, which does the same for space, or Berlioz's *Funeral March for the Last Scene of Hamlet*, which reaches similarly toward chaos. Nothing helped. The more I'd try to work up the notes for some story I had already three-quarters planned, the less interesting it would become to me, until it seemed (and probably was) all cliche. Some story ideas are as faint and insubstantial as ghosts. Well, all of *those* I had just got fainter as I worked on them.

I hate to write about writer's block; it's such a terribly childish, yes, frivolous seeming affliction. You'd think that anyone who was half a human being could shake it off or just slither away from it. But I couldn't. Morning after morning I'd wake with an instant pang of desperation at the thought of my predicament, so that I'd have to get up right away and pace, or rush out and walk the dawn-empty streets, or play through chess endings or count windows in big buildings to fill my mind with useless calculations—anything until I grew calm enough to read a newspaper or make a phone call and somehow get the day started. Sometimes my desk would get to jumping in the same way my mind did and I'd find myself compulsively straightening the objects on it over and over until I'd spring up from it in disgust. Now when the garbage trucks woke me at four (as they began to do again), I'd get up and follow their thunderous mechanical movements from one window or other vantage point to another, anxiously tracing the course of each can-lugging attendant—anything to occupy my mind.

Just to be doing something, I turned to my correspondence, which had begun to pile up again, but after answering three or four notes (somehow I'd pick the least important ones) I'd feel worn out. You see, I didn't want to write my friends about the block I was having. It was such a bore (whining always is) and besides, I was *ashamed*. At the same time I couldn't seem to write honestly about anything without bringing my damn block in.

I felt the same thing about calling up or visiting my friends around me in the city. I'd have nothing to show them, nothing to talk about. I didn't want to see anyone. It was a very bad time for me.

Of course I kept on going up to the roof, more than ever now, though even my binoculars were a burden to me and I couldn't bear to lug up my telescope—the weary business of setting it up and all the fussy adjustments I'd have to make made that unthinkable. I even had to *make* myself study the patterns of the lesser stars when the clear nights came, that had formerly been such a joy to me.

But then one evening just after dark I went topside and immediately noticed near Cygnus, the Northern Cross, a star that shouldn't have been there. It was a big one, third magnitude at least. It made a slightly crooked extension of the top of the cross as it points toward Cassiopeia. At first I was sure it had to be an earth satellite (I've spotted a few of those)—a big one, like the orbiting silvered balloon they called Echo. Or else it was a light on some weird sort of plane that was hovering high up. But when I held my binoculars on it, I couldn't see it move at all—as a satellite would have done, of course. Then I got really excited, enough to make me bring up my telescope (and *Norton's Star Atlas* too) and set it up.

In the much smaller and more magnified field of that instrument, it didn't move either, but glared there steadily among the lesser points of light, holding position as it inched with the other stars across the field. From the atlas I estimated and noted down its approximate co-ordinates (right ascension 21 hours and 10 minutes, north declination 48 degrees) and hurried downstairs to call up an astronomer friend of mine and tell him I'd spotted a nova.

Naturally I wasn't thinking at all about the previous ghostly (or whatever) incidents, so perhaps this time the strange thing was that, yes, it did happen again, just as though with even more brevity, and I sort of went through all the motions of reacting to it, but very unconcernedly, as if it had become a habit, part of the routine of existence, like a step in a stairway that always creaks when your foot hits it but nothing more ever comes of it. I recall saying to myself with a sort of absent-minded lightheartedness *Let's give the ghost E for effort, he keeps on trying.*

I got my astronomer friend and, yes, it was a real nova; it had been spotted in Asia and Europe hours earlier and all the astronomers were very busy, oh, my, yes.

The nova was a four-days' wonder, taking that long to fade down to naked-eye invisibility. Unfortunately my own excitement at it didn't last nearly that long. Next morning I was confronting my block again. Very much in the spirit of desperation, I decided to go back to my new project and make myself finish it off somehow, force myself to write no matter how bad the stuff seemed to be that I turned out, beginning with an expansion of my original short statement.

But the more I tried to do that, the more I re-read those two pages, the thinner and more dubious all the ideas in it seemed to me, the junkier and more hypocritical it got.

Instead of adding to it, I wanted to take and stuff away, trim it down to a nice big nothing.

To begin with, it was so much a writer's view of things, reducing everything to stories. Of course! What could be more obvious?—or more banal? A military man would explain life in terms of battles, advances and retreats, defeats and victories, and all their metaphorical analogues, presumably with strong emphasis on courage and discipline. Just as a doctor might view history as the product of great men's ailments, whether they were constipated or indigestive, had syphillis or TB—or of subtle diseases that swept nations; the fall of Rome?—lead poisoning from the pipes they used to distribute their aqueducted water! Or a salesman see everything as buying and selling, literally or by analogy. I recalled a 1920s' book about Shakespeare by a salesman. The secret of the Bard's unequalled dramatic power? He was the world's greatest salesman! No, all that stuff about stories was just a figure of speech and not a very clever one.

And then that business about illusion coming in everywhere—what were illusions and illusioning but euphemisms for lies and lying? We had to nourish the illusions of others, didn't we? That meant, in plain language, that we had to flatter them, tell them white lies, go along with all their ignorance and prejudices—very convenient rationalizations for a person who was afraid to speak the truth! Or for someone who was eager to fantasize everything. And granting all that, how had I ever hoped to write about it honestly in any detail?—strip away from myself and others, those at all close to me at least, all our pretenses and boasts, the roles we played, the ways we romanticized ourselves, the lies we agreed to agree on, the little unspoken deals we made ("You build me up, I'll build you up"), yes, strip away all that and show exactly what lay underneath: the infantile conceits, the suffocating selfishness, the utter unwillingness to look squarely at the facts of death, torture, disease, jealousy, hatred, and pain—how had I ever hoped to speak out about all that, I an illusioner?

Yes, how to speak out the truth of my real desires? that were so miserably small, so modest. No vast soul-shaking passions and heaven-daunting ambitions at all, only the little joy of watching a shadow's revealing creep along an old brick wall or the infinitely delicate diamond-prick of the first evening star in the deepening blue sky of evening, the excitement of little discoveries in big dictionaries, the small thrill of seeing and saying, "That's not the dark underside of a distant low narrow cloudbank between those two buildings, it's a TV antenna," or "That's not a nova, you wishful thinker, it's Procyon," the fondling and fondlings of slender, friendly, cool fingers, the hues and textures of an iris seen up close—how to admit to such minuscule longings and delights?

And getting still deeper into this stories business, what was it all but a justification for always *talking* about things and never *doing* anything? It's been said, "Those who can, do; those who can't, teach." Yes, and those who can't even teach, what do they do? Why, they tell stories! Yes, always talking, never acting, never being willing to dirty your fingers with the world. Why, at times you had to drive yourself to pursue even the little pleasures, were satisfied with fictional or with imagined proxies.

And while we were on that subject, what was all this business about minds never touching, never being quite able to? What was it but an indirect, mealy-mouthed way of confessing my own invariable impulse to flinch away from life, to avoid contact at any cost—the reason I lived alone with fantasies, never made a friend (though occasionally letting others, if they were forceful enough, make friends with me), preferred a typewriter to a wife, talked, talked, and never did? Yes, for minds, read bodies, and then the truth was out, the secret of the watcher from the sidelines.

I tell you, it got so I wanted to take those thumbed-over two grandiose pages of my "original short statement" and crumple them together in a ball and put that in a brown paper sack along with a lot of coffee grounds and grapefruit rinds and grease, and then repeat the process with larger and larger sacks until I had a Chinese-boxes set of them big around as a large garbage can and lug that downstairs at four o'clock in the morning and when the dark truck stopped in front personally hurl it into that truck's big ass-end mouth and *hear* it all being chewed up and ground to filthy scraps, the whole thing ten times louder than it ever sounded from the sixth floor, knowing that my "wisdom"-acorn of crumpled paper with all its idiot notions was in the very midst and getting more masticated and befouled, more thoroughly destroyed, than anything else (while my manikin watched from her window, inscrutable but, I felt sure, approving)—only in that way, I told myself, would I be able to tear myself loose from this whole damn minuscule, humiliating project, kill it inside my head.

I remember the day my mind generated that rather pitiful grotesque vision (which, incidentally, I half seriously contemplated carrying into reality the next morning). The garbage trucks had wakened me before dawn and I'd been flitting in and out most of the day, unable to get down to anything or even to sit still, and once I'd paused on the sidewalk outside my apartment building, visualizing the truck drawing up in the dark next morning and myself hurling my great brown wad at it, and I'd shot to my manikin the thought *Well, what do you think of it? Isn't it a good idea?* They had her seated cross-legged in a sort of Lotus position on a great sweep of violet sheetings that went up behind her to a high shelf holding the bolt. She seemed to receive my suggestion and brood upon it enigmatically.

Predictably, I gravitated to the roof soon after dark, but without my binoculars and not to study the stars above (although it was a clear evening) or peer with weary curiosity at the window-worlds below that so rarely held human figures, or even hold still and let the lonely roof-calm take hold of me. No, I moved about restlessly from one of my observation stations to another, rather mechanically scanning along the jagged and crenellated skyline, between the upper skyey areas and the lower building-bound ones, that passed for a horizon in the city (though there actually were a couple of narrow gaps to the east through which I could glimpse, from the right places on my roof, very short stretches of the hills behind smoky transbay Oakland). In fact, my mind was so little on what I was doing and so much on my writing troubles that I tripped over a TV-antenna cable I'd known was there and should have avoided. I didn't fall, but it took me three plunging steps to recover my balance, and I realized that if I'd been going in the opposite direction I might well have pitched over the edge, the wall being rather low at that point.

The roof world can be quite treacherous at night, you see. Older roofs especially are apt to be cluttered with little low standpipes and kitchen chimneys and ventilators, things very easy to miss and trip over. It's the worst on clear moonless nights, for then there are no clouds to reflect the city's lights back down, and as a result it's dark as pitch around your feet. (Paradoxically, it's better when it's raining or just been raining for then there's streetlight reflected by the rainclouds and the roof has a wet glisten so that obstructions stand out.) Of course, I generally carry a small flashlight and use it from time to time, but more important, I memorize down to the last detail the layout of any roof visited by night. Only this time that latter precaution failed me.

It brought me up short to think of how my encounter with the TV cable could have had fatal consequences. It made me see just how very upset I was getting from my writer's block and wonder about unconscious suicidal impulses and accidentally-on-purpose things. Certainly my stalled project was getting to the point where I'd have to do something drastic about it, like seeing a psychiatrist or getting drunk . . . or something.

But the physical fear I felt didn't last long, and soon I was prowling about again, though a little less carelessly. I didn't feel comfortable except when I was moving. When I held still, I felt choked with failure (my writing project). And yet at the same time I felt I was on the verge of an important insight, one that would solve all my problems if I could get it to come clear. It seemed to begin with 'If you could sum up all you felt about life and crystallize it in one master insight . . .' but where it went from there I didn't know. But I knew I wasn't going to get an answer sitting still.

Perhaps, I thought, this whole roof-thing with me expresses an unconscious atavistic faith in astrology, that I will somehow find the answer to any problem in the stars. How quaint of skeptical me!

On the roof at my old place, one of my favorite sights had been the Sutro TV Tower with its score or so of winking red lights. Standing almost a thousand feet high on a hill that is a thousand already, that colorful tripod tower dominates San Francisco from its geographical center and is a measuring rod for the altitude of fogs and cloud banks, their ceilings and floors. One of my small regrets about moving had been that it couldn't be seen from this new roof. But then only a couple of weeks ago I'd discovered that if you climb the short stairway to the locked door of the boxlike structure hiding the elevator's motor, you see the tops of the Tower's three radio masts poking up over and two miles beyond the top of the glassy Federal Building. Binoculars show the myriad feathery white wires guying them that look like sails—they're nylon so as not to interfere with the TV signals.

This night when I got around to checking the three masts out by their red flashes, I lingered a bit at the top of the skeleton stairs watching them, and as I lingered I saw in the black sky near them a tremorous violet star wink on and then after a long second wink off. I wouldn't have thought of it twice except for the color. Violet is an uncommon color for a light on a building or plane, and it's certainly an uncommon color of a star. All star colors are very faint tinges, for that matter. I've looked at stars that were supposed to be green and never been able to see it.

But down near the horizon where the air is thicker, anything can happen, I reminded myself. Stars that are white near the zenith begin to flash red and blue, almost any color at all, when they're setting. And suddenly grow dim, even wink out unexpectedly. Still, violet, that was a new one.

And then as I was walking away from the stars and away from Sutro Tower too, diagonally across the roof toward the other end of it, I looked toward the narrow, window-spangled slim triangle of the Trans-American Pyramid Building a half mile or so away and I saw for a moment, just grazing its pinnacle, what looked like the same mysteriously pulsing violet star. Then it went off or vanished—or went behind the pinnacle, but I couldn't walk it into view again, either way.

What got me the most, perhaps, about the violet dot was the way the light had seemed to *graze* the Pyramid, coming (it was my impression) from a great distance. It reminded me of the last time I'd looked at the planet Mercury through my telescope. I'd followed it for quite a while as it moved down the paling sky, flaring and pulsing (it was getting near the horizon) and then it had reached the top of the Hilton Tower where they have a room whose walls are almost all window, and for almost half a minute I'd continued my observation of it through the glassy corner of the Hilton Hotel. Really, it had seemed most strange to me, that rare planetary light linking me to another building that way, and being tainted by that building's glass, and in a way confounding all my ideas as to what is close and what is far, what clean and what unclean . . .

While I was musing, my feet had carried me to another observation place, where in a narrow slot between two close-by buildings I can see the gray open belfry towers of Grace Cathedral on Nob Hill five blocks off. And there, through or *in* one of the belfry's arched openings, I saw the violet star again resting or floating.

A star leaping about the sky that way?—absurd! No, this was something in my eye or eyes. But even as I squeezed my eyes shut and fluttered the lids and shook my head in short tight arcs, my neck muscles taut, to drive the illusion away, that throbbing violet star peered hungrily at me from the embrasure wherein it rested in the gray church's tower.

I've stared at many a star, but never before with the feeling that it was glaring at me.

But then (something told me) you've never seen a star that came to earth, sliding down that unimaginable distance in a trice and finding itself a niche or hiding hole in the dark world of roofs. The star went out, drew back, was doused.

Do you know that right after that I was afraid to lift my head? or look up anything? for fear of seeing that flashing violet diamond somewhere it shouldn't be? And that as I turned to move toward the door at the head of the stairs that led down from the roof, my gaze inadvertently encountered the Hilton Tower and I ducked my head so fast that I can't tell you now whether or not I saw a violet gleam in one of that building's windows?

In many ways the world of roofs is like a vast, not too irregular games board, each roof a square, and I thought of the violet light as a sort of super-chess piece making great leaps like a queen (after an initial vast one) and crookedly sidewise moves like a knight, advancing by rushings and edgings to checkmate me.

And I knew that I wanted to get off this roof before I saw a violet glow coming from behind the parapet of one of the airshafts or through the cracks around the locked door to the elevator's motor.

Yet as I moved toward the doorway of escape, the door down, I felt my face irresistibly lifted from between my hunched shoulders and against my neck's flinching opposition until I was peering through painfully winced eyeslits at the cornice of the next building east, the one that overlooked the windows of my apartment.

At first it seemed all dark, but then I caught the faintest violet glint or glimmer, as of something spying down most warily.

From that point until the moment I found myself facing the door to my apartment, I don't remember much at all except the tightness with which my hands gripped the stair-rails going down . . . and continued to grip railings tightly as I went along the sixth-storey hall, although of course there are no railings there.

I got the door unlocked, then hesitated.

But then my gaze wavered back the way I'd come, toward the stair from the roof, and something in my head began to recite in a little shrill voice, *I met a star upon the stair, A violet star that wasn't there* . . .

I'd pressed on inside and had the door shut and double locked and was in the bedroom and reaching for the bedside light before I realized that this time it *hadn't* happened, that at least I'd been spared the half sound and the fugitive dark ghost on this last disastrous night.

But then as I pressed the switch and the light came on with a tiny fizzing crackle and a momentary greenish glint and then shone more brightly and whitely than it should (as old bulbs will do when they're about to go—they arc) something else in my head said in a lower voice, *But of course when the right night came it wouldn't make its move until you were safely locked inside and unable to retreat . . .*

And then as I stared at the bright doorway and the double-locked door beyond, there came from the direction of the dinette-kitchen a great creaking sound like a giant footstep, no half-sound but something finished off completely, very controlled, very *deliberate*, neither a stamp nor a tramp, and then another and a third, coming at intervals of just about a second, each one a little closer and a little louder, inexorably advancing very much like the footsteps of time in the "Saturn" section of *The Planets*, with more instruments coming in—horns, drums, cymbals, huge gongs and bells—at each mounting repetition of the beat.

I went rigid. In fact, I'm sure my first thought was *I must hold absolutely still and watch the doorway,* with perhaps the ghost comment riding on it, *Of course! the panic reaction of any animal trapped in its hole.*

And then a fourth footsteps and a fifth and sixth, each one closer and louder, so that I'm sure my second real thought was, *The noise I'm hearing must be more than sound, else it would wake the city.* Could it be a physical vibration? Something was resounding deeply through my flesh, but the doorway wasn't shaking visibly as I watched it. Was it the reverberation of something mounting upward from the depths of earth or my subconscious mind, taking giant strides, smashing upward through the multiple thick floors that protect surface life and daytime consciousness? Or could it be the crashing around me in ruins of my world of certainties, in particular the ideas of that miserable vaunting project that had been tormenting me, all of them overset and trodden down together?

And then a seventh, eighth, ninth footstep, almost unbearably intense and daunting, followed by a great grinding pause, a monstrous hesitation. Surely something must appear now, I told myself. My every muscle was tight as terror could make it, especially those of my face and, torus-like, about my eyes (I was especially and rather fearfully conscious of their involuntary blinking). I must have been grimacing fearfully. I remember a fleeting fear of heart attack, every part of me was straining so, putting on effort.

And then there thrust silently, rather rapidly, yet gracefully into the doorway a slender, blunt-ended, sinuous leaden-gray, silver-glistening arm (or other member, I wondered briefly), followed immediately and similarly by the remainder of the figure.

I held still and observed, somehow overcoming the instant urge to flinch, to not-see. More than ever now, I told myself, my survival depended on that, my very life.

How describe the figure? If I say it looked like (and so perhaps was) the manikin in the fabrics shop, you will get completely the wrong impression; you will think of that stuffed and stitched form moving out of its window through the dark and empty store, climbing upstairs, etc., and I knew from the start that was certainly not the case. In fact, my first thought was, *It is not the manikin, although it has its general form.*

Why? How did I know that? Because I was certain from the first glimpse that it was *alive,* though not in quite the way I was alive, or any other living creatures with which I am familiar. But just the same, that leaden-gray, silver-misted integument was skin, not sewn-fabric—there *were* no sewn seams, and I knew where the seams were on the manikin.

How different *its* kind of life from mine? I can only say that heretofore such expressions as "dead-alive," "living dead," and "life in death" were horror-story cliches to me; but now no longer so. (Did the leaden hue of its skin suggest to me a drowned person? I don't think so—there was no suggestion of bloat and all its movements were very graceful.)

Or take its face. The manikin's face had been a blank, a single oval piece of cloth sewn to the sides and top of the head and to the neck. Here there was no edgestitching and the face was not altogether blank, but was crossed by two very faint, fine furrows, one vertical, the other horizontal, dividing the face rather like a mandala or the symbol of the planet Earth. And now, as I forced myself to scan the horizontal furrow, I saw that it in turn was not altogether featureless. There were two points of violet light three inches apart, very faint but growing brighter the longer I watched them and that moved from side to side a little without alternation in the distance between them, as though scanning me. *That* discovery cost me a pang not to flinch away from, let me tell you!

The vertical furrow in the face seemed otherwise featureless, as did the similar one between the legs with its mute suggestion of femininity. (I had to keep scanning the entire figure over and over, you see, because I felt that if I looked at the violet eyepoints too long at any one time they would grow bright enough to blind me, as surely as if I were looking at the midday sun; and yet to look away entirely would be equally, though not necessarily similarly disastrous.)

Or take the matter of height. The window manikin was slenderly short. Yet I was never conscious of looking down at this figure which I faced, but rather a little up.

What else did I glean as this long nightmarish moment prolonged itself almost endurably, going on and on and on, as though I were trapped in eternity?

Any other distinguishing and different feature? Yes. The sides and the top of the head sprouted thick and glistening black "hair" that went down her back in one straight fall.

(There, I have used the feminine pronoun on the figure, and I will stick with that from now on, although it is a judgment entirely from remembered feeling, or instinct, or whatever, and I can no more point to objective evidence for it that I can in the case of the manikin's imagined gender. And it is a further point of similarity between the two figures although I've said I *knew* they were different.)

What else, then, did I feel about her? That she had come to destroy me in some way, to wipe me out, erase me—I felt a calmer and colder thing than "kill," there was almost no heat to it at all. That she was weighing me in a very cool fashion, like that Egyptian god which weighs the soul, that she was, yes (And had her leaden-hued skin given me a clue here?), the Button Molder, come to reduce my individuality to its possible useful raw materials, extinguish my personality and melt me down, recycle me cosmically, one might express it.

And with that thought there came (most incidentally, you might say—a trifling detail) the answer I'd been straining for all evening. It went this way: *If you could sum up all you felt about life and crystallize it in one master insight, you would have said it all and you'd be dead.*

As tht truism(?) recited itself in my mind, she seemed to come to a decision and she lithely advanced toward me two silent steps so she was barely a foot away in the arcing light's unnatural white glare, and her slender mittenhands reached wide to embrace me, while her long black "hair" rose rustingly and arched forward over her head, in the manner of a scorpions's sting, as though to enshroud us both, and I remember thinking, *However fell or fatal, she has style.* (I also recall wondering why, if she were able to move silently, the nine footsteps had been so loud? Had those great crashes been entirely of mind-stuff, a subjective earthquake? Mind's walls and constructs falling?) In any case her figure had a look of finality about it, as though she were the final form, the ultimate model.

That was the time, if ever (when she came close, I mean), for me to have flinched away or to have shut tight my eyes, but I did not, although my eyes were blurred—they had spurted hot tears at her advance. I felt that if I touched her, or she me, it would be death, the extinguishment of memory and myself (if they be different), but I still clung to the faith (it had worked thus far) that if I didn't move away from and continued to observe her, I might survive. I tried, in fact, to tighten myself still further, to make myself into a man of brass with brazen head and eyes (the latter had cleared now) like Roger Bacon's robot. I was becoming, I thought, a frenzy of immobility and observation.

But even as I thought "immobility" and "touching is death" I found myself leaning a little closer to her (although it made her violet eye-points stingingly bright) the better to observe her lead-colored skin. I saw that it was poreless, but also that it was covered by a network of very fine pale lines, like crazed or crackled pottery, as they call it, and that it was this network that gave her skin its silvery gloss . . .

As I leaned toward her, she moved back as much, her blunt arms paused in their encirclement, and her arching "hair" spread up and back from us.

At that moment the filament of the arcing bulb fizzled again and the light went out.

Now more than ever I must hold still, I told myself.

For a while I seemed to see her form outlined in faintest ghostly yellow (violet's compliment) on the dark and hear the faint rustle of "hair," possibly falling into its original position down her back. There was a still fainter sound like teeth grating. Two ghost-yellow points twinkled a while at eye-height and then faded back through the doorway.

After a long while (the time it took my eyes to accommodate, I suppose) I realized that white fluorescent street light was flooding the ceiling through the upward-tilted slats of the blind and filling the whole room with a soft glow. And by that glow I saw I was alone. Slender evidence, perhaps, considering how treacherous my new apartment had proved itself. But during that time of waiting in the dark my feelings had worn out.

Well, I said I was going to tell you about those ten endless seconds and now I have. The whole experience had fewer consequences and less aftermath than you might expect. Most important for me, of course, my whole great nonfiction writing project was dead and buried, I had no inclination whatever to dig it up and inspect it (all my feelings about it were worn out too), and within a few days I was writing stories as if there were no such thing as writer's block. (But if, in future, I show little inclination to philosophize dogmatically, and if I busy myself with trivial and rather childish activities such as haunting game stores and amusement parks and other seedy and picturesque localities, if I write exceedingly fanciful even frivolous fiction, if I pursue all sorts of quaint and curious people restlessly, if there is at times something frantic in my desire for human closeness, and if I seem occasionally to head out toward the universe, anywhere at all in it, and dive in—well, I imagine you'll understand.)

What do I think about the figure? How do I explain it (or her)? Well, at the time of her appearance I was absolutely sure that she was real, solid, material, and I think the intentness with which I observed her up to the end (the utterly unexpected silvery skin-crackle I saw at the last instant!) argues for that. In fact, the courage to hold still and fully observe was certainly the only sort of courage I displayed during the whole incident. Throughout, I don't believe I ever quite lost my desire to *know*, to look into mystery. (But why was I so absolutely certain that my life depended on *watching* her? I don't know.)

Was she perhaps an archetype of the unconscious mind somehow made real? the

Anima or the Kore or the Hag who lays men out (if those be distinct archetypes)? Possibly, I guess.

And what about the science fiction suggestiveness about her? that she was some sort of extraterrestrial being? That would fit with her linkage with a very peculiar violet star, which (the star) I do *not* undertake to explain in any way! Your guess is as good as mine.

Was she, *vide* Lang, a waking dream?—nightmare, rather? Frankly, I find that hard to believe.

Or was she really the Button Molder? (who in Ibsen's play, incidentally, is an old man with pot, ladle, and mold for melting down and casting lead buttons). That seems just my fancy, though I take it rather seriously.

Any other explanations? Truthfully, I haven't looked very far. Perhaps I should put myself into the hands of the psychics or psychologists or even the occultists, but I don't want to. I'm inclined to be satisfied with what I got out of it. (One of my author friends says it's a small price to pay for overcoming writer's block.)

Oh, there was one little investigation that I did carry out, with a puzzling and totally unexpected result which may be suggestive to some, or merely baffling.

Well, when the light went out in my bedroom, as I've said, the figure seemed to fade back through the doorway into the small hallway with lowered ceiling I've told you about and there fade away completely. So I decided to have another look at the ceilinged-off space. I stood on a chair and pushed aside the rather large square of frosted glass and (somewhat hesitantly) thrust up through the opening my right arm and head. The space wasn't altogether empty, as it had seemed when I changed the bulb originally. Now the 200-watt glare revealed a small figure lying close behind one of the 4-by-4 beams of the false ceiling. It was a dust-filmed doll made (I later discovered) of a material called Fabrikoid and stuffed with kapok—it was, in fact, one of the Oz dolls from the 1920's; no, not the Scarecrow, which would surely be the first Oz character you'd think of as a stuffed doll, but the Patchwork Girl.

What do you make of that? I remember saying to myself, as I gazed down at it in my hand, somewhat bemused, *Is this all fantasy ever amounst to? Scraps? Rag dolls?*

Oh, and what about the lay figure in the store window? Yes, she was still there the next morning same as ever. Only they'd changed her position again. She was standing between two straight falls of sheeting, one black, one white, with her mitten hands touching them lightly to either side. And she was bowing her head a trifle, as if she were taking a curtain call.

Horrible Imaginings

Old Ramsey Ryker only commenced thinking about going to see (through one-way glass) the young women fingering their genitals *after* he started having the low-ceilinged dreams without light—the muttering dull black nightmares—but *before* he began catching glimpses of the vanishing young-old mystery girl, who wore black that twinkled, lurking in the first-floor ground-level corridors, or disappearing into the elevator, and once or twice slipping along the upstairs halls of the apartment tree (or skeleton) that is, with one exception, the sole scene of the action in this story, which does not venture farther, disturb the privacy of the apartments themselves, or take one step out into the noisy metropolitan street. Here all is hushed.

I mean by the *apartment tree* all the public or at least tenant-shared space within the thirteen-floor building where Ryker lived alone. With a small effort you can visualize that volume of connected space as a rather repetitious tree (color it red or green if it helps, as they do in "You are *here*" diagrammatic maps; I see it as pale gray myself, for that is the color of the wallpaper in the outer halls, pale gray faintly patterned with dingy silver): its roots the basement garage where some tenants with cars rented space along with a few neighborhood shopkeepers and businessmen; its trunk the central elevator shaft with open stairway beside it (the owner of the building had periodic difficulties with the fire inspectors about the latter—they wanted it walled off with heavy self-closing doors at each floor; certainly a building permit would never have been granted today—or in the last three decades, for that matter—for such a lofty structure with an open stairwell); its branches the three halls, two long, one short, radiating out from the shaft-stairwell trunk and identical at each level except for minor features; from the top floor a sort of slanted, final thick branch of stairs led, through a stout door (locked on the outside but open on the inside—another fire regulation), to the roof and the strong, floored weatherproof shed holding the elevator's motor and old-fashioned mechanical relays. But we won't stir through that door either to survey the besmogged but nonetheless impressive cityscape and hunt for the odd star or (rarer still) an interesting window.

At ground level one of the long corridors led to the street door; on the floors above, to the front fire escape. The other long ones led to the alley fire escape. The short hall was blind (the fire inspector would shake his head at that feature too, and frown).

And then of course we should mention, if only for the sake of completists, the apartment tree's micro-world, its tiniest twigs and leaflets, in a sense: all the cracks and crevices (and mouse- and rat-holes, if any) going off into the walls, ceilings, and floors, with perhaps some leading to more spacious though still cramped volumes of space.

537

But it would be discourteous of us to wander—and so frivolously—through the strange labyrinthine apartment tree with its angular one- and two-bedroom forbidden fruit, when all the time Ramsey Ryker, a lofty, gaunt old man somewhat resembling a neatly dressed scarecrow, is waiting impatiently for us with his equally strange and tortuous problems and concerns. Of these, the black nightmares were the worst by far and also in a way the cause of, or at least the prelude to, all the others.

Actually they were the worst nightmares in a restrained sort of way that Ramsey ever remembered having in the seven decades of his life and the only ones, the only dreams of any sort for that matter, without any visual element at all (hence the "black"), but only sound, touch, intramuscular feelings, and smell. And the black was really inky, midnight, moonless and starless, sooty, utter—all those words. It didn't even have any of those faint churning points of light we see, some of them tinted, when we shut our eyes in absolute darkness and when supposedly we're seeing rods and cones of our retina fire off without any photons of outside light hitting them. No, the only light in his nightmares, if any, was of the phanton sort in which *memories* are painted—a swift, sometimes extensive-seeming flash which starts to fade the instant it appears and never seems to be in the retina at all, something far more ghostly even than the nebular churnings that occur under the eyelids in the inkiest dark.

He'd been having these nightmares every two or three nights, regular almost as clockwork, for at least a month now, so that they were beginning to seriously worry and oppress him. I've said, "nightmares" up to now, but really there was only *one*, repeated with just enough changes in its details to convince him that he was experiencing new nightmares rather than just remembering the first. This made them more ominously terrifying; he'd know what was coming—up to a point—and suffer the more because of that.

Each "performance" of his frightening lightless dream, on those nights when his unconscious decided to put on a show, would begin the same way. He would gradually become aware, as though his mind were rising with difficulty from unimaginable depths of sleep, that he was lying stretched out naked on his back with his arms extended neatly down his sides, but that he was *not* in his bed—the surface beneath him was too ridged and hard for that. He was breathing shallowly and with difficulty— or rather he discovered that if he tried to investigate his breathing, speed or slow it, expand his chest more fully, he ran the danger of bringing on a strangling spasm or coughing fit. This prospect frightened him; he tried never to let it happen.

To check on this, explore the space around him, he would next in his dream try to lift up a hand and arm, stretch a leg sideways—and find out that he could *not*, that so far as any gross movement of limbs went he was paralyzed. This naturally would terrify him and push him toward panic. It was all he could do not to strain, thrash (that is, try to), gasp, or cry out.

Then as his panic slowly subsided, as he schooled himself to quietly endure this limitation on his actions, he would discover that his paralysis was not complete, that if he went about it slowly he could move a bit, wag his head about an inch from side to side, writhe a little the superficial muscles and skin under his shoulders and down his back and buttocks and legs, stir his heels and fingertips slightly. It was in this way that he discovered that the hard surface under him consisted of rough laths set close together, which were very dusty—no, *gritty*.

Next in his dream came an awareness of sound. At first it would seem the normal muttering hum of any big city, but then he'd begin to distinguish in it a faint rustling and an infinitesimal rapid clicking that was very much closer and seemed to get nearer each moment and he'd think of insects and spiders and he'd feel new terror gusting through him and there'd be another struggle to stave off hysteria. At this point in his dream he'd usually think of cockroaches, armies of them, as normal to big cities as the latter's muttering sounds, and his terror would fade though his revulsion would mount. Filthy creatures! but who could be frightened of them? True, his dear wife, now dead five years, had had a dread of stepping on one in the dark and hearing it crunch. (That reaction he found rather hard to understand. He was, well, if not exactly pleasured, then well satisfied to step on cockroaches, or mash them in the sink.)

His attention would then likely return to the muttering, growling, faintly buzzing, somehow *nasal* component of the general sound, and he'd begin to hear voices in it, though he could seldom identify the words or phrases—it was like the voices of a crowd coming out of a theater or baseball park or meeting hall and commenting and arguing droningly and wearily about what they'd just seen or heard. *Male* voices chiefly, cynical, sarcastic, deprecating, mean, sleepily savage, and ignorant, very ignorant, he'd feel sure. And never as loud or big as they ought to be; there was always a *littleness* about them. (Was his hearing impaired in his nightmares? Was he dreaming of growing deaf?) Were they the voices of depraved children? No, they were much too low—deep throat tones. Once he'd asked himself, "Midgets?" and had the thought, rich in dream wisdom, "A man lying down is not even as tall as a midget."

After sound, odor would follow, as his senses were assaulted cumulatively. First dry, stale, long-confined—somehow so natural seeming he would be unaware of the scents. But then he would smell smoke and know a special pang of fright—was he to be burned alive, unable to move? And the fire sirens when the engines came, tinied by distance and by muffling walls, no larger than those of toys?

But then he would identify it more precisely as tobacco smoke, the reeking smoke of cigars chiefly. He remembered how his dead wife had hated that, though smoking cigarettes herself.

After that, a whole host of supporting odors: toilet smells and the cheap sharp perfumes used to balance those out, stinking old flesh, the fishy reek of unwashed sex, locker rooms, beer, disinfectants, wine-laden vomit—all fitting very nicely, too, with the ignorant low growling.

After sound and odor, touch, living touch. Behind the lobe of his right ear, in his jaw's recessed angle, where a branch of the carotid pulses close to the surface, there'd come an exploring prod from the tip of something about as big as a baby's thumb, a pencil's eraserhead, snout of a mouse or of a garter snake, an embryo's fist, an unlit cigarette, a suppository, the phallus of a virile mannequin—a probing and a thrusting that did not stop and did not go away.

At that point his dream, if it hadn't already, would turn into full nightmare. He'd try to jerk his head sideways, throw himself over away from it, thrash his arms and legs, yell out unmindful of what it did to his breathing—and find that the paralysis still gripped him, its bonds growing tighter the more he struggled, his vocal cords as numb as if these were his life's last gaspings.

And then—more touches of the same puppet sort: his side, his thigh, between two fingers, up and down his body. The sounds and odors would get darker still as a general suffocating oppression closed in. He'd visualize grotesquely in imagination's lightless lightning flashes, which like those of memory are so utterly different from sight, a crowd of squatty, groping male Lilliputians, a press of dark-jowled, thickset, lowbrowed, unlovely living dolls standing or leaning in locker room attitudes, each one nursing with one hand beneath his paunch a half-erect prick with a casual lasciviousness and with the other gripping a beer can or cigar or both, while all the while they gargled out unceasingly a thick oozy stream of shitty talk about crime and sports and sex, about power and profit. He envisioned their tiny prick nubs pressing in on him everywhere, as if he were being wrapped tighter and tighter in a rubber blanket that was all miniscule elastic knobs.

At this moment he would make a supreme effort to lift his head, reckless of heart attack, fighting for each fraction of an inch of upward movement, and find himself grinding his forehead and nose into a rough gritty wooden surface that had been there, not three inches above him, all the while, like the lid of a shallow coffin.

Then, and only then, in that moment of intensest horror, he'd wake at last, stretched out tidily in his own bed, gasping just a little, and with a totally unjoyous hard-on that seemed more like the symptom of some mortal disease than any prelude to pleasure.

The reader may at this point object that by entering Ramsey's bedroom we have strayed beyond the apartment-tree limits set for the actions of this story. Not so, for we have been examining only his *memories* of his nightmares, which never have the force of the real thing. In this fashion we peered into his dream, perhaps into his bedroom, but we never turned on the light. The same applies to his thoughts about and reactions to those erections which troubled his nightmare wakings and which seemed to him so much more like tumorous morbid growths—almost, cancers—than any swellings of joy.

Now Ramsey was sufficiently sophistocated to wonder whether his nightmares were an expression, albeit an unusual and most unpleasant one, of a gathering sexual arousal in himself, which his invariable waking hard-ons would seem to indicate, and whether the discharge of that growing sexual pressure would not result in the night-mares ceasing or at least becoming fewer in number and of a lesser intensity. On the one hand, his living alone was very thoroughgoing; he had formed no new intimacies since his wife's death five years earlier and his coincidental retirement and moving here. On the other, he had a deep personal prejudice against masturbation, not on moral or religious grounds, but from the conviction that such acts demanded a living accomplice or companion to make them effectively real, no matter how distant and tenuous the relation between the two parties, an adventuring-out into the real world and some achievement there, however slight.

Undoubtedly there were guilty shadows here—his life went back far enough for him to have absorbed in childhood mistaken notions of the unhealthiness of auto-eroticism that still influenced his feelings if not his intellect. And also something of the work-ethic of Protestantism, whereby everything had its price, had to be worked and sweated and suffered for.

With perhaps—who knows?—a touch of the romantic feeling that sex wasn't worth it without the spice of danger, which also required a venturing out beyond one's private self.

Now on the last occasion—about eight months ago—when Ramsey had noted signs of growing sexual tension in himself (signs far less grotesquely inappropriate, frighten-ing, oppressive, and depressing than his current nightmares—which appeared to end with a strong hint of premature burial), he had set his imagination in a direction leading toward that tension's relief by venturing the apartment tree's street door) to a small theater called Ultrabooth, where for a modest price (in these inflated times) he could make contact with three living girls (albeit a voiceless one through heavy one-way glass), who would strip and display themselves intimately to him in a way calculated to promote arousal.

(A pause to note we've once more gone outside the apartment tree, but only by way of a remembered venturing—and memory is less real even than dream, as we have seen.)

The reason Ramsey had not at once again had recourse to these young ladies as soon as his nightmares began with their telltale terminal hard-ons, providing evidence of growing sexual pressure even if the peculiar nightmare contents did not, was that he had found their original performance, though sufficient for his purpose as it turned out, rather morally troubling and aesthetically unsatisfying in some respects and giving rise to various sad and wistful reflections in his mind as he repeated their performance in memory.

Ducking through a small, brightly lit marquee into the dim lobby of Ultrabooth, he'd laid a $10 bill on the counter before the bearded young man without looking at him, taken up the $2 returned with the considerate explanation that this was a reduction for senior citizens, and joined the half-dozen or so silent waiting men who mostly edged about restlessly yet slowly, not looking at each other.

After a moderate wait and some small augmentation of their number, there came a stirring from beyond the red velvet ropes as the previous audience was guided out a separate exit door. Ryker gravitated forward with the rest of the new audience. After a two-minute pause, a section of red rope was hooked aside, and they surged gently ahead into a shallow inner foyer from which two narrow dark doorways about fifteen feet apart led onward.

Ryker was the fourth man through the left-hand doorway. He found himself in a dim, curving corridor. On his left, wall. On his right, heavy curtains partly drawn aside from what looked like large closets, each with a gloomy window at the back. He entered the first that was unoccupied (the second), fumbled the curtains shut behind him, and clumsily seated himself facing the window on the cubicle's sole piece of furniture, a rather low barstool.

Actually his booth wasn't crampingly small. Ryker estimated its floor space as at least one half that of the apartment tree's elevator, which had a six-person capacity.

As his eyes became accommodated to the darkness of his booth and the dimness of the sizable room beyond, he saw that the latter was roughly circular and walled by rectangular mirrors, each of which, he realized, must be the window of a booth such as his own—except one window space was just a narrow curtain going to the floor. A wailing bluesy jazz from an unseen speaker gently filled his ears, very muted.

The windows were framed with rows of frosted light bulbs barely turned on—must have them on a rheostat, he thought. The floor was palely and thickly carpeted, and there were a few big pale pillows set about. From the ceiling hung four velvet-covered ropes thinner than those in the lobby. Each ended in a padded leather cuff. He also noted uneasily two velvet-covered paddles, no larger than Ping-Pong ones, lying on one of the big pillows. The dimness made everything seem grimy, as though fine soot were falling continuously from the ceiling like snow.

He sensed a stirring in the other booths, and he saw that a girl had entered the room of mirrors while he'd been intent on the paddles. At first he couldn't tell whether she was naked or not, but then as she slowly walked out, hardly glancing at the mirrors, face straight ahead like a sleepwalker's, the music began to come up and the lights too, brighter and brighter. He saw she was a blonde, age anywhere from nineteen to twenty-nine—how could you know for sure? He hoped nineteen. And she was wearing a net brassiere bordered by what looked like strips of white rabbit's fur. A tiny apron of the same kind of fur hung down over her crotch, attached to some sort of G-string, and she wore short white rabbit's fur boots.

She yawned and stretched, looked around, and then swiftly removed these items of apparel, but instead of letting them fall or laying them down on one of the pillows, she carried them over to the curtained doorway which interrupted the wall of mirrors and handed them through to someone. They were taking no chances on the fur getting dirty—how many performances a day was it the girls gave? He also realized that the right- and left-hand passages to the booths didn't join behind, as he'd imagined at first—there had to be an entry passage for the performer. Good thing he hadn't tried to go all the way around and check on the booths before picking one—and maybe lost his.

The vertical slit in the curtain widened, and the now naked blonde was joined by a naked brunette of the same undetermined youth. They embraced tenderly yet perfunctorily, as if in a dream, swaying with the music's wails, then leaned apart, brushing each other's small breasts, fingers lingering at the erecting nipples, then trailing down to touch each other's clefts. They separated then and began to work their way around the booths, facing each mirror in turn, swaying and writhing, bumping and grinding, arching back, bellying toward. The brunette was across from him, the blonde off to his left and coming closer. His mouth was dry, his breaths came faster. He was getting a hard-on, he told himself, or about to. He was jealous about the time the blonde spent at each other window and yet somehow dreaded her coming.

And then she was writhing in front of him, poker-faced, looking down toward him. Could she see him? Of course not!—he could see the windows across from him, and they just reflected his blank window. But suppose she bent down and pressed her face and flattening nose-tip against the glass, cupping her hands to either side to shut out light? Involuntarily he flinched backward, caught himself and almost as swiftly stretched his face forward to admire her breasts as she preened, trailing her fingers across them. Yes, yes, he thought desperately, dutifully, they were small, firm, not at all pendulous, big nippled with large aureoles, splendid, yes splendid, yes splendid . . .

And then he was forcing his gaze to follow her hands down her slender waist past her belly button and pale pubic hair and stretch open the lips of her cleft.

It was all so very confusing, those flaps and those ribbons of membrane, of glistening pinkish-red membrane. Really, a man's genitals were much neater, more like a good and clear diagram, a much more sensible layout. And when you were young you were always in too much of a hurry to study the female ones, too damn excited, keyed-up, overwhelmed by the importance of keeping a hard-on. That, and the stubborn old feeling that you mustn't look, that was against the rules, this was dirty. With his wife he'd always done it in the dark, or almost. And now when you were old and your eyesight wasn't so good anymore . . . One slender finger moved out from the bent stretching ones to point up, then down, to indicate clitoris and cunt. Whyn't she point out her uretha too? It was somewhere there, in between. The clitoris was hard to make out in the midst of all that red squirming . . .

And then without warning she had spun around, bent over, and was looking at him from between her spread legs, and her hand came back around her side to jab a finger twice at the shadowed sallow pucker of her anus, as if she were saying, "And here's my asshole, see? My God, how long does it take you dumb bastards to get things straight?"

Really, it was more like an anatomy lesson taught by a bored, clown-white cadaver than any sort of spicy erotic cocktail. Where was the faintest hint of the flirtatious teasing that in old times, Ryker recalled, gave such performances a point? Why, this girl had come in almost naked and divested herself of the scant remainder with all the romance of someone taking out dental plates before retiring. My God, was that how they got ready for the full act in private? Where was the slow unbuttoning, the sudden change of mind and buttoning up again? Where was the enthusiastic self-peek down her pulled-forward bodice followed by the smile and knowing wink that said, "Oh, boy, what I got down there! Don't you wish . . .?" Where was the teasing that overreached itself, the accidental exposure of a goody, pretended embarrassment, and the overhasty hiding of it, leading to further revelations, as one who covering her knees bares her rear end? Where the feigned innocence, prudish or naive? the sense of wicked play, precocious evil? Above all, where was the illusion that her body's treasures were just that? her choicest possessions and her chiefest pride, secret 'tween her and you, hoarded like miser's gold, though shared out joyously and generously at the end?

The girl, instead of graciously overhearing his racing thoughts (they must be audible!) and at least attempting to make some corrections for them in her behavior, last of all seized handholds at the corners of the window and set the soles of her feet against the sides and dangled there spread open and bent for a short while, rocking back and forth, like a poker-faced slender ape, so he could see it all at once after a fashion: asshole, cunt, and clitoris—and urethra—wherever that was.

That was the show's highpoint of excitement, or shock at any rate, for Ryker. Although a third girl appeared and the other two got her undressed and strung up by the padded straps on the velvet ropes, and did some things to her with their lips and tongues and the lightly brushing velvet paddles, that was the high point—or whatever.

Afterward he slipped out into the street feeling very conspicuous, but even more relieved. He swore he'd never visit the ignorant place again. But that night he had awakened ejaculating in a wet dream. Afterward he couldn't be quite sure whether his hand mightn't have helped and what sort of dream it had been otherwise, if any—certainly not one of his troll-haunted, buried-alive nightmares.

No, they were gone forever, or at any rate for the next five months.

And then when they did come back, against all his hopes, and when they continued on, and when he found himself balanced between the nightmares and Ultrabooth, and the days seemed dry as dust, there had come the welcome interruption of the Vanishing Lady.

The first time Ryker had seen her, so far as he could recall, they'd been at opposite ends of the long, low entry hall, a good forty feet apart. He had been fumbling for his key outside the street door, which was thick oak framing a large glass panel backed by metal tracery. She'd been standing in profile before the gray elevator door, the small window of which was lit, indicating the cage was at this floor. His gaze approved her instantly (for some men life is an unceasing beauty contest), he liked the way her dark knee-length coat was belted in trimly and the neat look of her head, either dark hair drawn in rather closely or a cloche hat. Automatically he wondered whether she was young and slender or old and skinny.

And then as he continued to look at her, key poised before the lock, she turned her head in his direction and his heart did a little fillip and ahiver. *She looked at me,* was what he felt, although the corridor was dimly lit and from this far away a face was little more than a pale oval with eye-smudges—and now her hair or hat made it a shadowed oval. It told you no more about her age than her profile had. Just the same, it was now turned toward him.

All this happened quite swiftly.

But then he had to look down at the lock in order to fit his key into it (a fussy business that seemed to take longer with each passing year) and turn it (he sometimes forgot which way) and shove the door open with his other hand, and by that time she'd moved out of sight.

She couldn't have taken the elevator up or down, he told himself as he strode the corridor a little more briskly than was his wont, for the small glass window in its door still shone brightly. She must have just drifted out of sight to the right, where the stairs were and the brass-fronted mailboxes and the window and door to the manager's office and, past those, the long and short back corridors of the ground floor.

But when he reached that foyer, it was empty and the manager's window unoccupied, though not yet dark and shuttered for the night. She must have gone up the stairs or to a back apartment on this floor, though he'd heard no receding footsteps or shutting door confirm that theory.

Just as he opened the elevator door he got the funniest hunch that he'd find her waiting for him there—that she'd entered the cage while he'd been unlocking the front door, but then not pushed a button for a floor. But the cage was as empty as the foyer. So much for hunches! He pushed the 14 button at the top of the narrow brass panel, and by the time he got there, he'd put the incident out of his mind, though a certain wistfulness clung to his general mood.

And he probably would have forgotten it altogether except that late the next afternoon, when he was returning from a rather long walk, the same thing happened to him all over again, the whole incident repeating itself with only rather minor variations. For instance, this time her eyes seemed barely to stray in his direction; there wasn't the same sense of a full look. And something flashed faintly at her chest level, as if she were wearing jewelry of some sort, a gemmed pendant—or brooch more likely, since her coat was tightly shut. He was sure it was the same person, and there was the same sense of instant approval or attraction on his part, only stronger this time (which was natural enough, he told himself later). And he went down the hall faster this time and hurried on without pausing to check the stairs and the back corridor, though his chance of hearing footsteps or a closing door was spoiled by the siren of an ambulance rushing by outside. Returning thoughtfully to the foyer, he found the cage gone, but it came down almost immediately, debarking a tenant he recognized—third or fourth floor, he thought—who said rather puzzledly in answer to a question by Ryker that he thought he'd summoned the elevator directly from One and it had been empty when it had reached his floor.

Ryker thanked him and boarded the elevator.

The cage's silvered gray paper and polished fittings made it seem quite modern. Another nice touch was the little window in its door, which matched those in the floor doors when both were shut, so that you got a slow winking glimpse of each floor as you rose past—as Ryker now glimpsed the second floor go down. But actually it was an accident vehicle smartened up, and so was the system that ran it. You had to hold down a button for an appreciable time to make the cage respond, because it worked by mechanical relays in the elevator room on the roof, not by the instant response to a touch of electronic modern systems. Also, it couldn't remember several instructions and obey them in order as the modern ones could; it obeyed one order only and then waited to be given the next one manually.

Ryker was very conscious of that difference between automatic and manual. For the past five years he had been shifting his own bodily activities from automatic to manual: running (hell, trotting was the most you could call it!—a clumping trot), going down stairs, climbing them, walking outside, even getting dressed and—almost— writing. Used to be he could switch on automatic for those and think about something else. But now he had to do more and more things a step at a time, and watching and thinking about each step too, like a baby learning (only you never did learn; it never got automatic again). And it took a lot more time, everything did. Sometimes you had to stand very still even to think.

Another floor slowly winked by. Ryker caught the number painted on the shaft side of its elevator door just below that door's little window—5. What a slow trip it was!

Ryker did a lot if his real thinking in this elevator part of the apartment tree. It wasn't full of loneliness and ambushing memories the way his apartment was, or crawling with the small dangers and hostilities that occupied most of his mind when he was in the street world outside. It was a world between those, a restful pause between two kinds of oppression, inhabited only by the mostly anonymous people with whom he shared his present half-life, his epilogue life, and quite unlike the realer folk from whom he had been rather purposefully disengaging himself ever since his wife's and his job's deaths.

They were an odd lot, truly, his present fellow-inhabitants of the apartment tree. At least half of them were as old as he, and many of them engaged in the same epilogue living as he was, so far as he could judge. Perhaps a quarter were middle-aged; Ryker liked them least of all—they carried tension with them, things he was trying to forget. While rather fewer than a quarter were young. These always hurried through the apartment tree on full automatic, as if it were a place of no interest whatever, a complete waste of time.

He himself did not find it so, but rather the only place where he could think and observe closely at the same time, a quiet realm of pause. He saw nothing strange in the notion of ghosts (if he'd believed in such) haunting the neighborhood where they'd died—most of them had spent their last few years studying that area in greatest detail, impressing their spirits into its very atoms, while that area steadily grew smaller, as if they were beetles circling a nail to which they were tethered by a thread that slowly wound up, growing shorter and shorter with every circumambulation they made.

Another floor numeral with its little window slid into and out of view—8 only. God, what snaillike, well-frog pace!

The only denizen of the apartment tree with whom Ryker had more than a recognition acquaintance (you could hardly call the one he had with the others nodding, let alone speaking) was Clancy, rough-cut manager-janitor of the building, guardian of the gates of the apartment tree and its historian, a retired fireman who managed to make himself available and helpful without becoming oppressive or officious. Mrs. Clancy was an altogether more respectable and concierge-like character who made Ryker feel uncomfortable. He preferred always to deal with her husband, and over the years a genuine though strictly limited friendship (it never got beyond "Clancy" and "Mr. Ryker") had sprung up between them.

The figure 12 appeared and disappeared in the window. He kept his eyes on the empty rectangle and gave an accustomed chuckle when the next figure was 14, with none intervening. Superstition, how mighty, how undying! (Though somehow the travel between the last two floors, Twelve and Fourteen, always seemed to take longest, by a fraction. There was food for thought there. Did elevators get tired?—perhaps because the air grew more rarified with increased altitude?)

The window above the 14 steadied. There was a clicking; the gray door slid open sideways, he pushed through the outer door, and as he did so, he uttered another chuckle that was both cheerful and sardonic. He'd just realized that after all his journeying in the apartment tree, he'd at last become interested in one of his nameless traveling companions. The elevator-tree world also held the Vanishing Lady.

It was surprising how lighthearted he felt.

As if in rebuke for this and for his springing hopes not clearly defined, he didn't see the Vanishing Lady for the next three days, although he devised one or two errands for himself that would bring him back to the apartment tree at dusk, and when he did spot her again on the fourth day, the circumstances were altered from those of their first two encounters.

Returning from another of his little twilight outings and unlocking the heavy street door, he noted that the hall and distant foyer were a little bit dimmer than usual, as if some small, normal light source were gone, with the effect of a black hole appearing suddenly in the fabric of reality.

As he started forward warily, he discerned the explanation. The doors to the elevator were wide open, but the ceiling light in the cage had been switched (or gone) off, so that where a gray door gleaming by reflection should have been, there was an ominous dark upright rectangle.

And then, as he continued to advance, he saw that the cage wasn't empty. Light angling down into it from the foyer's ceiling fixture revealed the slender figure of the Vanishing Lady leaning with her back against the cage's wall just behind the column of buttons. The light missed her head, but showed the rest of her figure well enough, her dejected posture, her motionless passivity.

As he imperceptibly quickened his stride straight toward her, the slanting light went on, picking up bits of detail here and there in the gloom, almost as if summoning them: the glossy gleam of black oxfords, the muted one of black stockings, and the in-between sheen of her sleek coat. The nearest black-gloved hand appeared to be clutching that together snugly, and from the closure there seemed to come faint diamond glimmers like the faintest ghost of a sparkler shower, so faint he couldn't be sure whether it was really there, or just his own eyes making the churning points of light there are in darkness. The farthest jetty hand held forward a small brass object which he first took for an apartment door key got out well in advance (as some nervous people will) but then saw to be a little too narrow and too long for that.

He was aware of a mounting tension and breathlessness—and sense of strangeness too. And then without warning, just as he was about to enter the cage and simultaneously switch its light on, he heard himself mutter apologetically, "Sorry, I've got to check my mailbox first," and his footsteps veered sharply but smoothly to the right with never a hesitation.

For the next few seconds his mind was so occupied with shock at this sudden rush of timidity, this flinching away from what he'd thought he wanted to do, that he actually had his keys out, was advancing the tiny flat one toward the brass-fronted narrow box he'd checked this noon as always, before he reversed his steps with a small growl of impatience and self-rebuke and hurried back past the manager's shuttered window and around the stairs.

The elevator doors were closed and the small window glowed bright. But just as he snatched at the door to open it, the bright rectangle narrowed from the bottom and winked out, the elevator growled softly as the cage ascended, and the door resisted his yank. Damn! He pressed himself against it, listening intently. Soon—after no more than five or six seconds, he thought—he heard the cage stop and its door *clump* open. Instantly he was thumbing the button. After a bit he heard the door *clump* shut and the growling recommence. Was it growing louder or softer—coming down or going away? Louder! Soon it had arrived, and he was opening the door—rather to the surprise of its emerging occupant, a plump lady in a green coat.

Her eyebrows rose at his questions, rather as had happened on the previous such occasion. She'd been on Three when she'd buzzed for the elevator, she said. No, there'd been no one in it when it arrived, no one had got off, it had been empty. Yes, the light *had* been off in the elevator when it had come up, but she hadn't missed anyone on account of that—and she'd turned it on again. And then she'd just gotten in and come down. Had he been buzzing for it? Well, she'd been pushing the button for One, too. What did it matter?

She made for the street door, glancing back at Ryker dubiously, as if she were thinking that, whatever he was up to, she didn't ever want that excited old man tracking *her* down.

Then for a while, Ryker was so busy trying to explain that to himself (Had there been time for her to emerge and shut the doors silently and hurry down the long hall or tiptoe up the stairs before the cage went up to Three? Well, just possibly, but it would have had to be done with almost incredible rapidity. Could he have *imagined* her— projected her onto the gloom inside the cage so to speak? Or had the lady in green been lying? Were she and the Vanishing Lady confederates? And so on . . .) that it was some time before he began to try to analyze the reasons for his self-betrayal.

Well, for one thing, he told himself, he'd been so gripped by his desire to see her close up that he'd neglected to ask himself what he'd do once he'd achieved that, how he'd make conversation if they were alone together in the cage—and that these questions popping up in his mind all at once had made him falter. And then there was his lifelong habit, he had to admit, of automatically shrinking from all close contact with women save his mother and wife, especially if the occasion for it came upon him suddenly. Or had he without knowing it become just a little frightened of this mysterious person who had stirred him erotically—the apartment tree was always dimly lit, there'd never been anyone else around when she'd appeared, there'd been something so woeful-melancholy about her attitude (though that was probably part of her attraction), and finally she *had* vanished three times unaccountably—so that it was no wonder he had veered aside from entering the elevator, its very lightlessness suggesting a trap. (And that made him recall another odd point. Not only had the light inside the elevator been switched off but the door, which always automatically swung shut unless someone held it open or set a fairly heavy object, such as a packed suitcase or a laden-large shopping bag, against it, had been standing open. And he couldn't recall having seen any such object or other evidence of propping or wedging. Mysterious. In fact, as mysterious as his suffocation dreams, which at least had lessened in number and intensity since the Vanishing Lady had turned up.)

Well, he told himself with another effort at being philosophical, now that he'd thought all these things through, at least he'd behave more courageously if a similar situation arose another time.

But when the Vanishing Lady next appeared to Ramsey, it was under conditions that did not fall for that sort of courage. There were others present.

He'd come in from outside and found the empty cage ready and waiting, but he could hear another party just close enough behind him that he didn't feel justified in taking off without them—though there'd been enough times, God knows, when he'd been left behind under the same circumstances. He dutifully waited, holding the door open. There had been times, too, when this politeness of his had been unavailing— when the people had been bound for a ground-floor apartment, or when it had been a lone woman and she'd found an excuse for not making her journey alone with him.

The party finally came into view—two middle-aged women and a man—and the latter insisted on holding the door himself. Ryker relinquished it without argument and went to the back of the cage, the two women following. But the man didn't come inside; he held the door for yet a third party he'd evidently heard coming behind *them*.

The third party arrived, an elderly couple, but that man insisted on holding the door in his turn for the second man and his own ancient lady. They were six, a full load, Ryker counted. But then, just as the floor door was swinging shut, someone caught it from the outside, and the one who slipped in last was the Vanishing Lady.

Ramsey mightn't have seen her if he hadn't been tall, for the cage was now almost uncomfortably crowded, although none of them were conspicuous heavyweights. He glimpsed a triangle of pale face under dark gleaming eyes, which fixed for an instant on his, and he felt a jolt of excitement, or something. Then she had whipped around and was facing front, like the rest. His heart was thudding and his throat was choked up. He knew the sheen of her black hair and coat, the dull felt of her close-fitting hat, and watched them raptly. He decided from the flash of face that she was young or very smoothly powdered.

The cage stopped at the seventh floor. She darted out without a backward glance and the elderly couple followed her. He wanted to do something but he couldn't think what, and someone pressed another button.

As soon as the cage had resumed its ascent, he realized that he too could have gotten out on Seven and at least seen where she went in, discovered her apartment number. But he hadn't acted quickly enough and some of these people probably knew he lived on Fourteen and would have wondered.

The rest got out on Twelve and so he did the last floor alone—the floor that numerically was two floors, actually only one, yet always seemed to take a bit too long, the elevator growing tired, ha-ha-ha.

Next day he eximined the names on the seventh-floor mailboxes, but that wasn't much help. Last names only, with at most an initial or two, was the rule. No indication of sex or marital status. And, as always, fully a third were marked only as OCCUPIED. It was safer that way, he remembered being told (something about anonymous phone calls or confidence games), even if it somehow always looked suspicious, vaguely criminal.

Late the next afternoon, when he was coming in from the street, he saw a man holding the elevator door open for two elderly women to enter. He hurried his stride, but the man didn't look his way before following them.

But just at that moment, the Vanishing Lady darted into view from the foyer, deftly caught the closing door, and with one pale glance over her shoulder at Ryker, let herself in on the heels of the man. Although he was too far away to see her eyes as more than twin gleams, he felt the same transfixing jolt as he had the previous day. His heart beat faster too.

And then as he hurried on, the light in the little window in the gray door winked out as the elevator rose up and away from him. A few seconds later he was standing in front of the electrically locked door with its dark little window and staring ruefully at the button and the tiny circular telltale just above it, which now glowed angry red to indicate the elevator was in use and unresponsive to any summons.

He reproached himself for not having thought to call out, "Please wait for me," but there'd hardly been time to think, and besides it would have been such a departure from his normal, habitually silent behavior. Still, another self-defeat, another self-frustration, in his pursuit of the Vanishing Lady! He wished this elevator had, like those in office buildings or hotels, a more extensive telltale beside or over its door that told which floor it was on or passing, so you could trace its course. It would be helpful to know whether it stopped at Seven again this time—it was hard to hear it stop when it got that far away. Of course you could run up the stairs, racing it, if you were young enough and in shape. He'd once observed two young men who were sixth-floor residents do just that, pitting the one's strong legs and two-or-three-steps-at-a-time against the other's slow elevator—and never learned who won. For that matter, the young tenants, who were mostly residents of the lower floors, where the turnover of apartments was brisker, quite often went charging blithely up the stairs even when the elevator was waiting and ready, as if to advertise (along with their youth) their contempt for its tedious *elderly* pace. If *he* were young again now, he asked himself, would he have raced up after a vanished girl?

The telltale went black. He jabbed the button, saw it turn red again as the cage obediently obeyed his summons.

Next afternoon found him staring rather impatiently at the red telltale on the four-teenth floor, this time while waiting to travel to the ground floor and so out. And this time it had been red for quite some while, something that happened not infrequently, since the cage's slow speed and low capacity made it barely adequate to service a building of this size. And while it stayed red it was hard to tell how many trips it was making and how long people were holding the door at one floor. He'd listened to numerous speculative conversations about "what the elevator was doing," as if it had a mind and volition of its own, which one humorist had indeed suggested. And there were supposed to be certain people (sometimes named and sometimes not) who did outrageous and forbidden things, such as jamming the floor door open while they went back to get things they'd forgotten, or picked up friends on other floor as they went down (or up), organizing an outing or party or having secret discussions and arguments before reaching the less private street. There were even said to be cases of people "pulling the elevator away" from other people who were their enemies, just to spite them.

The most colorful theory, perhaps, was that held by two elderly ladies, both old buffs of elevator travel, whom Ramsey had happened to overhear on two or three occasions. The cornerstone of their theory was that all the building's troubles were caused by its younger tenants and the teenage sons and daughters of tenants. "Mrs. Clancy told me," one of them had whispered loudly once, "that they know a way of stopping the thing between floors so they can smooch together and shoot dope and do all sorts of other nasty things—even, if you can believe, go the whole way with each other." Ryker had been amused; it gave the cage a certain erotic aura.

And every once in a while the elevator did get stuck between floors, sometimes with people in it and sometimes not, especially between the twelfth and fourteenth floors, Clancy had once told him, "like it was trying to stop at the thirteenth!"

But now the elevator's vagaries weren't all that amusing to Ramsey standing alone on the top floor, so after one more session of pettish button-pushing—the telltale had gone briefly black, but evidently someone else had beat him ot the punch—he decided to "walk down for exercise," something he'd actually done intentionally upon occasion.

As he descended the apartment tree (he thought of himself as an old squirrel sedately scampering zigzag down the barky outside of the trunk the elevator shaft made), he found himself wondering how the elevator could be so busy when all the cor-ridors were so silent and empty. (But maybe things were happening just before his footstep-heralded arrivals and after his departures—they heard him coming and hid themselves until he was by. Or maybe there was some sort of basement crisis.) The floors were all the same, or almost so: the two long corridors ending in doors of wire-reinforced glass which led to the front and alley fire escapes; these were also lit midway by frosted glass spheres like full moons hanging in space; in either wall beside these handsome globes were set two narrow full-length mirrors in which you could see yourself paced along by two companions.

The apartment tree boasted many mirrors, a luxury note like its silver-arabesqued gray wallpaper. There was a large one opposite each elevator door and there were three in the lobby.

As he ended each flight, Ramsey would look down the long alley corridor, make a U-turn, and walk back to the landing (glancing into the short corridor and the elevator landing, which were lit by a central third moon and one large window), all this while facing the long front corridor, then make another U-turn and start down the next flight.

(He did discover one difference between the floors. He counted steps going down, and while there were nineteen between the fourteenth and the twelfth floors, there were only seventeen between all the other pairs. So the cage had to travel a foot and a bit farther to make that Fourteen-Twelve journey; it didn't just *seem* to take longer, it *did*. So much for tired elevators!)

So it went for nine floors.

But when he made his U-turn onto the third floor he saw that the front corridor's full moon had been extinguished, throwing a gloom on the whole passageway, while silhouetted against the wired glass at the far end was a swayed, slender figure looking very much like that of the Vanishing Lady. He couldn't make out her pale triangle of face or gleaming eyes because there was no front light on her, she was only shaped darkness, yet he was sure it was sure it was she.

In walking the length of the landing, however, there was time to think that if he continued on beyond the stairs, it would be an undeniable declaration of his intention to meet her, he'd have to keep going, he had no other excuse; also, there'd be the unpleasant impression of him closing in ominously, relentlessly, on a lone trapped female.

As he advanced she waited at the tunnel's end, silent and unmoving, a shaped darkness.

He made his customary turn, keeping on down the stairs. He felt so wrenched by what was happening that he hardly knew what he was thinking or even feeling, except his heart was thudding and his lungs were gasping as if he'd just walked ten stories upstairs instead of down.

It wasn't until he had turned into the second floor and seen through the stairwell, cut off by ceiling, the workshoes and twill pants of Clancy, the manager, faced away from him in the lobby, that he got himself in hand. He instantly turned and retraced his steps with frantic haste. He'd flinched away again, just when he'd sworn he wouldn't! Why, there were a dozen questions he could politely ask her to justify his close approach. Could he be of assistance? Was she looking for one of the tenants? some apartment number? Etcetera.

But even as he rehearsed these phrases, he had a sinking feeling of what he was going to find on Three.

He was right. There was no longer a figure among the shadows filling the the dark front corridor.

And then, even as he was straining his eyes to make sure, with a flicker and a flash the full moon came on again and shone steadily.

Showing no one at all.

Ramsey didn't look any further but hurried back down the stairs. He wanted to be with people, anyone, just people in the street.

But Mr. Clancy was still in the lobby, communing with himself. Ramsey suddenly felt he simply had to share at least part of the story of the Vanishing Lady with someone.

So he told Clancy about the defective light bulb inside the front globe on Three, how it has started to act like a globe that's near the end of its lifetime, arcing and going off and on by itself, unreliable. Only then did he, as if idly, an afterthought, mention the woman he'd seen and then got to wondering about and gone back and not seen, adding that he thought he'd also seen her in the lobby once or twice before.

He hadn't anticipated the swift seriousness of the manager's reaction. Ramsey'd hardly more than mentioned the woman when the ex-fireman asked sharply, "Did she look like a bum? I mean, for a woman—"

Ramsey told him that no, she didn't, but he hadn't more than sketched his story when the other said, "Look, Mr. Ryker, I'd like to go up and check this out right away. You said she was all in black, didn't you? Yeah. Well, look, you stay here, would you do that? And just take notice if anybody comes down. I won't be long."

And he got in the elevator, which had been waiting there, and went up. To Four or Five, or maybe Six, Ramsey judged from the cage's noises and the medium-short time the telltale flared before winking out. He imagined that Clancy would leave it there and then hunt down the floors one by one, using the stairs.

Pretty soon Clancy did reappear by way of the stairs, looking thoughtful. "No," he said, "she's not there anymore, at least not in the bottom half of the building—and I don't see her doing a lot of climbing. Maybe she got somebody to take her in, or maybe it *was* just one of the tenants. Or . . .?" He looked a question at Ramsey, who shook his head and said, "No, nobody came down the stairs or elevator."

The manager nodded and then shook his own head slowly. "I don't know, maybe I'm getting too suspicious," he said. "I don't know how much you've noticed, Mr. Ryker, living way on top, but from time to time this building is troubled by bums—winos and street people from south of here—trying to get inside and shelter here, especially in winter, maybe go to sleep in a corner. Most of them are men, of course, but there's an occasional woman bum." He paused and chuckled reflectively. "Once we had an invasion of women bums, though they weren't that exactly."

Ramsey looked at him expectantly.

Clancy hesitated, glanced at Ramsey, and after another pause said, "That's why we turn the buzzer system off at eleven at night and keep it off until eight in the morning. If we left it on, why, any time in the night a drunken wino would start buzzing apartments until he got one who'd buzz the door open (or he might push a dozen at once, so somebody'd be sure to buzz the door), and once he was inside, he'd hunt himself up an out-of-the-way spot where he could sleep it off and be warm. And if he had cigarettes, he'd start smoking them to put him to sleep, dropping the matches anywhere, but mostly under things. There's where your biggest danger is—fire. Or he'd get an idea and start bothering tenants, ringing their bells and knocking on their doors, and then anything could happen. Even with the buzzer system off, some of them get in. They'll stand beside the street door and then follow a couple that's late getting home, or the same with the newsboy delivering the morning paper before it's light. Not following them directly, you see, but using a foot (sometimes a cane or crutch) to block the door just before it locks itself, and then coming in as soon as the coast's clear."

Ramsey nodded several times appreciatively, but then pressed the other with "But you were going to tell me something about an invasion of female bums?"

"Oh, that," Clancy said doubtfully. A look at Ramsey seemed to reassure him. "That was before your time—you came here about five years ago, didn't you? Yeah. Well, this happened . . . let's see . . . about two years before that. The Mrs. and I generally don't talk about it much to tenants, because it gives . . . gave the building a bad name. Not really any more now, though. Seven years and all's forgotten, eh?"

He broke off to greet respectfully a couple who passed by on their way upstairs. He turned back to Ramsey. "Well, anyway," he continued more comfortably, "at this time I'm talking about, the Mrs. and I had been here ourselves only a year. Just about long enough to learn the ropes, at least some of them.

"Now there's one thing about a building like this I got to explain," he interjected. "You never, or almost never, get any disappearances—you know, tenants sneaking their things out when they're behind on the rent, or just walking out one day, leaving their things, and never coming back (maybe getting mugged to death, who knows?)—like happens all the time in those fleabag hotels and rooming houses south of us. Why, half of *their* renters are on dope or heavy medication to begin with, and come from prisons or from mental hospitals. Here you get a steadier sort of tenant, or at least the Mrs. and I try to make it be like that.

"Well, back then, just about the steadiest tenant we had, though not the oldest by any means, was a tall, thin, very handsome and distinguished-looking youngish chap, name of Arthur J. Stensor, third floor front. Very polite and softspoken, never raised his voice. Dark complected, but with blonde hair which he wore in a natural—not so common then; once I heard him referred to by another tenant as 'that frizzy bleached Negro,' and I thought they were being disrespectful. A sharp dresser but never flashy— he had class. He always wore a hat. Rent paid the first of the month in cash with never a miss. Rent for the garage space too—he kept a black Lincoln Continental in the base-ment that was always polished like glass; never used the front door much but went and came in that car. And his apartment was furnished to match: oil paintings in gold frames, silver statues, hi-fi, *big*-screen TV and the stuff to record programs and films off it when that *cost*, all sorts of fancy clocks and vases, silks and velvets, more stuff like that than you'd ever believe.

"And when there was people with him, which wasn't too often, they were as classy as he and his car and his apartment, especially the women—high society and always young. I remember once being in the third-floor hall one night when one of those stunners swept by me and he let her in, and thinking, 'Well, if that filly was a call girl, she sure came from the best stable in town.' Only I remember thinking at the same time that *I* was being disrespectful, because A.J. Stensor was just a lttle too respectable for even the classiest call girl. Which was a big joke on me considering what happened next."

"Which was?" Ramsey prompted, after they'd waited for a couple more tenants to go by.

"Well, at first I didn't connect it at all with Stensor," Clancy responded, "though it's true I hadn't happened to see him for the last five or six days, which was sort of unusual, though not all that much so. Well, what happened was this invasion—no goddammit! this *epidemic*—of good-looking hookers, mostly tall and skinny, or at least skinny, through the lower halls and lobby of this building. Some of them were dressed too respectable for hookers, but most of them wore the street uniform of the day—which was high heels, skintight blue jeans, long lace blouses worn outside the pants, and lots of bangles—and when you saw them talking together palsy-walsy, the respectable-looking and the not, you knew they all had to be."

"How did it first come to you?" Ramsey asked. "Tenants complain?"

"A couple," Clancy admitted. "Those old biddies who'll report a young and good-looking woman on the principle that if she's young and good-looking she can't be up to any good purpose. But the really funny thing was that most of the reports of them came in just by way of gossip—either to me direct, or by way of the Mrs., which is how it usually works—like it was something strange and remarkable—which it was, all right! Questions too, such as what the hell they were all up to, which was a good one to ask, by the way. You see, they weren't any of them *doing* anything to complain of. It was broad day and they certainly weren't trying to pick anyone up, they weren't plying their trade at all, you might say, they weren't even smiling at anybody, especially men. No, they were just walking up and down and talking together, looking critical and angry more than anything, and very serious—like they'd picked our apartment building for a hooker's convention, complete with debates, some sort of feminist or union thing, except they hadn't bothered to inform the management. Oh, when I'd cough and ask a couple of them what they were doing, they'd throw me some excuse without looking at me—that they had a lunch date with a lady here but she didn't seem to be in and they couldn't wait, or that they were shopping for apartments but these weren't suitable—and at the same time they'd start walking toward the street door, or toward the stairs if they were on the third or second floor, still gabbing together in private voices about whatever it was they were debating, and then they'd sweep out, still not noticing me even if I held the door for them.

"And then, you know, in twenty minutes they'd be back inside! or at least I'd spot one of them that was. Some of them *must* have had front door keys, I remember thinking—and as it turned out later, some of them did."

By this time Mr. Clancy had warmed to his story and was giving out little chuckles with every other sentence, and he almost forgot to lower his voice next time a tenant passed.

"There was one man they took notice of. I forgot about that. It could have given me a clue to what was happening, but I didn't get it. We had a tenant then on one of the top floors who was tall and slim and rather good-looking—younger-looking too, although he wasn't—and always wore a hat. Well, I was in the lobby and four or five of the hookers had just come in the front door, debating of course, when this guy stepped out of the elevator and they all spotted him and made a rush for him. But when they got about a dozen feet away from him and he took off his hat—maybe to be polite, he looked a little scared, I don't know what he thought—showing his wavy black hair which he kept dyed, the hookers all lost interest in him—as if he'd looked like someone they knew, but closer up turned out not to be (which *was* the case, though I still didn't catch on then)—and they swept past him and on up the stairs as if that was where they'd been rushing in the first place.

"I tell you, that was some weird day. Hookers dressed all ways—classy-respectable, the tight-jeans and lacy-blouse uniform, mini-skirts, one in what looked like a kid's sailor suit cut for a woman, a sad one all in black looking like something special for funerals . . . you know, maybe to give first aid to a newly bereaved husband or something." He gave Ryker a quick look, continuing, "And although almost all of them were skinny, I recall there was a fat one wearing a mumu and swinging gracefully like a belly dancer.

"The Mrs. was after me to call the police, but our owner sort of discourages that, and I couldn't get him on the phone.

"In the evening the hookers tapered off and I dropped into bed, all worn out from the action, the wife still after me to call the police, but I just conked out cold, and so the only one to see the last of the business was the newsboy when he came to deliver at four-thirty about. Later on he dropped back to see me, couldn't wait to tell me about it.

"Well, he was coming up to the building, it seems, pushing his shopping cart of morning papers, when he sees this crowd of good-looking women (he wasn't wise to the hookers' convention the day before) around the doorway, most of them young and all of them carrying expensive-looking objects—paintings, vases, silver statues of naked girls, copper kitchenware, gold clocks, that sort of stuff—like they were helping a wealthy friend move. Only there is a jam-up, two or three of them are trying to maneuver an oversize dolly through the door, and on that dolly is the biggest television set the kid ever saw and also the biggest record player.

"A woman at the curb outside, who seems a leader, sort of very cool, is calling directions to them how to move it, and close beside her is another woman, like her assistant or gopher maybe. The leader's calling out directions, like I say, in a hushed voice, and the other women are watching, but they're all very quiet, like you'd expect people to be at that hour of the morning, sober people at any rate, not wanting to wake the neighbors.

"Well, the kid's looking all around, every which way, trying to take in everything—there was a lot of interesting stuff to see, I gather, and more inside—when the gopher lady comes over and hunkers down beside him—he was a runt, that newsboy was, and ugly too—and wants to buy a morning paper. He hauls it out for her and she gives him a five-dollar bill and tells him to keep the change. He's sort of embarrassed by that and drops his eyes, but she tells him not to mind, he's a handsome boy and a good hardworking one, she wished she had one like him, and he deserves everything he gets, and she puts an arm around him and draws him close and all of a sudden his downcast eyes are looking inside her blouse front and he's getting the most amazing anatomy lesson you could imagine.

"He has some idea that they're getting the dolly clear by now and that the other women are moving, but she's going on whispering in his ear, her breath's like steam, what a good boy he is and how grateful his parents must be, and *his* only worry, she'll hug him so tight he won't be able to look down her blouse.

"After a bit she ends his anatomy lesson with a kiss that almost smothers and then stands up. The women are all gone and the dolly's vanishing around the next corner. Before she hurries after it, she says, 'So long, kid. You got your bonus. Now deliver your papers.'

"Which, after he got over his daze, is what he did, he said.

"Well, of course, as soon as he mentioned the big television and player, I flashed on what I'd been missing all yesterday, though it was right in front of my eyes if I'd just looked. Why they'd been swarming on Three, why they rushed the guy from Seven and then lost interest in him when he took off his hat and they saw his hair was black dyed (instead of frizzy blonde), and why the hookers' convention wasn't still going on today. All that loot could have only come from one place—Stensor's. In spite of him being so respectable, he'd been running a string of call girls all the time, so that when he ran out on them owing them all money (I flashed on that at the same time), they'd collected the best way they knew how.

"I ran to his apartment, and you know the door wasn't even locked—one of them must have had a key to it too. Of course the place was stripped and of course no sign of Stensor.

"Then I did call the police of course but not until I'd checked the basement. His black Continental was gone, but there was no way of telling for sure whether he'd taken it or the gals had got that too.

"It surprised me how fast the police came and how many of them there were, but it showed they must have had an eye on him already, which maybe explained why he left so sudden without taking his things. They asked a lot of questions and came back more than once, were in and out for a few days. I got to know one of the detectives, he lived locally, we had a drink together once or twice, and he told me they were really after Stensor for drug dealing, he was handling cocaine back in those days when it was first getting to be the classy thing, they weren't interested in his call girls except as he might have used them as pushers. They never did turn him up though, far as I know, and there wasn't even a line in the papers about the whole business."

"So that was the end of your one-day hooker invasion?" Ryker commented, chuckling rather dutifully.

"Not quite," Clancy said, and hesitated. Then with a "What-difference-can-it-make?" shrug, he went on, "Well, yes, there was a sort of funny follow-up but it didn't amount to much. You see, the story of Stensor and the hookers eventually got around to most of the tenants in the building, as such things will, though some of them got it garbled, as you can imagine happens, that he was a patron and maybe somehow victim of call girls instead of running them. Well, anyhow, after a bit, we (the Mrs. mostly) began to get these tenant reports of a girl—a young woman—seen waiting outside the door to Stensor's apartment, or wandering around in other parts of the building, but mostly waiting at Stensor's door. And this was after there were other tenants in that apartment. A sad-looking girl."

"Like, out of all those hookers," Ryker said, "she was the only one who really loved him and waited for him. A sort of leftover."

"Yeah, or the only one who hadn't got her split of the loot," Clancy said. "Or maybe he owed her more than the others. I never saw her myself, although I went chasing after her a couple of times when tenants reported her. I wouldn't have taken any stock in her except the descriptions did seem to hang together. A college-type girl, they'd say, and mostly wearing black. And sort of sad. I told the detective I knew, but he didn't seem to make anything out of it. They never did pick up any of the women, he said, far as he knew. Well, that's all there is to the follow-up—like I said, nothing much. And after two or three months tenants stopped seeing her."

He broke off, eyeing Ryker just a little doubtfully.

"But it stuck in your mind," that one observed, "for all these years, so that when I told you about seeing a woman in black near the same door, you rushed off to check up on her, just on the chance? Though you'd never seen her yourself, even once?"

Clancy's expression became a shade unhappy. "Well, no," he admitted, glancing up and down the hall, as though hoping someone would come along and save him from answering. "There was a little more than that," he continued uneasily, "though I wouldn't want anyone making too much of it, or telling the Mrs. I told them.

"But then, Mr. Ryker, you're not the one to be gossiping or getting the wind up, are you?" he continued more easily, giving his tenant a hopeful look.

"No, of course I'm not," Ryker responded, a little more casually than he felt. "What was it?"

"Well, about four years ago we had another disappearance here, a single man living alone and getting on in years but still active. He didn't own any of the furniture, his possessions were few, nothing at all fancy like Stensor's, no friends or relations we knew of, and he came to us from a building that knew no more; in fact we didn't realize he was gone until the time for paying rent came round. And it wasn't until then that I recalled that the last time or two I spoke to him he'd mentioned something about a woman in an upstairs hall, wondering if she'd found the people or the apartment number she seemed to be looking for. Not making a complaint, you see, just mentioning, just idly wondering, so that it wasn't until he disappeared that I thought of connecting it up with Stensor's girl at all."

"He say if she was young?" Ryker asked.

"He wasn't sure. She was wearing a black outside coat and hat or scarf of something that hid her face, and she made a point of not noticing him when he looked at her and thought of asking if she needed help. He did say she was thin, though, I remember."

Ryker nodded.

Clancy continued, "And then a few years ago there was this couple on Nine that had a son living with them, a big fat lug who looked older than he was and was always being complained about whether he did anything or not. One of the old ladies in the apartment next to their bathroom used to kick to us about him running water for baths at two or three in the morning. And he had the nerve to complain to us about *them*, claiming they pulled the elevator away from him when he wanted to get it, or made it go in the opposite direction to what he wanted when he was in it. I laughed in his pimply face at that. Not that those two old biddies wouldn't have done it to him if they'd figured a way and they'd got the chance.

"His mother was a sad soul who used to fuss at him and worry about him a lot. She'd bring her troubles to the Mrs. and talk and talk—but I think really she'd have been relieved to have him off her mind.

"His father was a prize crab, an ex-army officer forever registering complaints—he had a little notebook for them. But half the time he was feuding with me and the Mrs., wouldn't give us the time of day—or of course ask it. I know *he'd* have been happy to see his loud-mouthed dumb son drop out of sight.

"Well, one day the kid comes to me here with a smart-ass grin and sayd, 'Mr. Clancy, you're the one who's so great, aren't you, on chasing winos and hookers out of here, not letting them freeload in the halls for a minute? Then how come you let—'

"'Go on,' I tell him, 'what do you know about hookers?'

"But that doesn't faze him, he just goes on (he was copying his father, I think, actually), 'Then how come you let this skinny little hooker in a black fur coat wander around the halls all the time, trying to pick guys up?'

"'You're making this up,' I tell him flat, 'or you're imagining things, or else one of our lady tenants is going to be awful sore at you if she ever hears you've been calling her a hooker.'

"'She's nobody from this building,' the kid insists, 'she's got more class. That fur coat cost money. It's hard to check out her face, though, because she never looks at you straight on and she's got this black hat she hides behind. I figure she's an old bag—maybe thirty, even—and wears the hat so you can't see her wrinkles, but that she's got a young bod, young and wiry. I bet she takes karate lessons so she can bust the balls of any guy that gets out of line, or maybe if he just doesn't satisfy her—'

"'You're pipe-dreaming, kid,' I tell him.

"'And you know what?' he goes on. 'I bet you she's got nothing on but black stockings and a garter belt under that black fur coat she keeps wrapped so tight around her, so when she's facing a guy she can give him a quick flash of her bod, to lead him on—'

"'And you got a dirty mind,' I say. 'You're making this up.'

"'I am not,' he says. 'She was just now up on Ten before I came down and leering at me sideways, giving me the come on.'

"'What were you doing up on Ten?' I ask him loud.

"'I always go up a floor before I buzz the elevator,' he answers me quick, 'so's those old dames won't know it's me and buzz it away from me.'

"All right, quiet down, kid,' I tell him. 'I'm going up to Ten right now, to check this out, and you're coming with me.'

"So we go on up to Ten and there's nobody there and right away the kid starts yammering, 'I bet you she picked up a trick in this building and they're behind one of these doors screwing, right now. Old Mr. Lucas—'

"I was really going to give him a piece of my mind then, tell him off, but on the way up I'd been remembering that girl of Stensor's who lingered behind, maybe for a long time, if there was anything to what the other guy told me. And somehow it gave me a sort of funny feeling, so all I said was something like 'Look here, kid, maybe you're making this up and maybe not. Either way, I still think you got a dirty mind. But if you did see this hooker and you ever see her again, don't you have anything to do with her—and don't go off with her if she should ask you. You just come straight to me and tell me, and if I'm not here, you find a cop and tell him. Hear me?'

"You know, that sort of shut him up. 'All right, all right!' he said and went off, taking the stairs going down.

"And did *he* disappear?" Ryker asked after a bit. He seemed vaguely to remember the youth in question, a pallid and lumbering lout who tended to brush against people and bump into doorways when he passed them.

"Well, you know, in a way that's a matter of argument," Clancy answered slowly. "It was the last time I saw him—that's a fact. And the Mrs. never saw him again either. But when she asked his mother about him, *she* just said he was off visiting friends for a while, but then a month or so later she admitted to the Mrs. that he *had* gone off without telling them a word—to join a commune, she thought, from some of the things he'd been saying, and that was all right with her, because his father just couldn't get along with him, they had such fights, only she wished he'd have the consideration to send her a card or something."

"And that was the last of it?" Ryker asked.

Clancy nodded slowly, almost absently. "That was damn all of it," he said softly. "About ten months later the parents moved. The kid hadn't turned up. There was nothing more."

"Until now," Ryker said, "when I came to you with my questions about a woman in black—and on Three at that, where this Stensor had lived. It wasn't a fur coat, of course, and I didn't think of her being a hooker—" (Was that true? he wondered) "—and it brought it all back to you, which now included what the young man had told you, and so you checked out the floors and then very kindly told me the whole story so as to give me the same warning you gave him?"

"But you're an altogether different sort of person, Mr. Ryker," Clancy protested. "I'd never think—But yes, allowing for that, that about describes it. You can't be too careful."

"No, you can't. It's a strange business," Ryker commented, shaking his head, and then added, making it sound much more casual, even comical, than he felt it, "You know, if this had happened fifty years ago, we'd be thinking maybe we had a ghost."

Clancy chuckled uneasily and said, "Yeah, I guess that's so."

Ryker said, "But the trouble with that idea would have been that there's nothing in the story about a woman disappearing, but three men—Stensor, and the man who lived alone, and the young man who lived with his parents."

"That's so," Mr. Clancy said.

Ryker stirred himself. "Well, thanks for telling me all about it," he said as they shook hands. "And if I should run into the lady again, I won't take any chances. I'll report it to you, Clancy. But not to the Mrs."

"I know you will, Mr. Ryker," Clancy affirmed.

Ryker himself wasn't nearly so sure of that. But he felt he had to get away to sort out his impressions. The dingy silvery walls were becoming oppressive.

Ryker made his walk a long one, brisk and thoughtful to begin with, dawdling and mind-wandering to finish, so that it was almost sunset by the time he reentered the apartment tree (and our story), but he had his impressions sorted. Clancy had—possibly—given the Vanishing Lady a history, funny to start with (that "hookers' convention"!) but then by stages silly, sad, sinister. Melancholy, moody, and still mysterious.

The chief retroactive effect of Clancy's story on his memories of his own encounters with the Vanishing Lady had been to intensify their sexual color, give them a sharper, coarser erotic note—an Ultrabooth note, you could say. In particular Ryker was troubled that ever since hearing Clancy narrate the loutish youth's steamy adolescent imagining that his "little hooker" had worn nothing but black stockings and a garter belt under her black fur coat, he was unable to be sure whether he himself had had similar simmering fantasy flashes during his encounters with her.

Could he be guilty, at his age, he asked himself, of such callow and lurid fantasies? The answer to that was, of course, "Of course." And then wasn't the whole romantic business of the Vanishing Lady just a retailoring of Ultrabooth to his own taste, something that made an Ultrabooth girl his alone? Somehow, he hoped not. But had he any real plan for making contact with her if she ever did stop vanishing? His unenterprising behavior when he'd had the chance to get into the elevator with her alone, and later the chance to get off the elevator at the same floor as she, and today the opportunity to meet her face to face on the third floor, indicated clearly that the answer to that question was "No." Which depressed him.

To what extent did Clancy believe in his story and in the reality of the girl who'd reportedly lingered on? He obviously had enjoyed telling it, and likely (from his glibness) had done so more than once, to suitable appreciative listeners. But did he believe she was one continuing real entity, or just a mixture of suggestion, chance, and mistaken resemblances, gossip, and outright lies? He'd never seen her himself—had this made Clancy doubt her reality, or contrariwise given him a stubborn hankering to catch sight of her himself for once at least? On the whole, Ryker thought Clancy was a believer—if only judging by his haste to search for her.

And as for the ghost idea, which you couldn't get around because it fitted her appearing and disappearing behavior so well, no matter how silly and unfashionable such a suggestion might be—Clancy's reaction to that had seemed uneasy, skepticism rather than outright "Nonsense!" rejection.

Which was very much like Ryker's own reaction to it, he realized. He knew there'd been some feelings of fear mixed in with the excitement during all his later encounters with her, before he'd heard Clancy's story. How would he feel now, after hearing it, if he should see her again, he wondered uncomfortably. More fear? Or would he now spot clues to her unreality? Would she begin to melt into mist? Would she look different simply because of what he'd heard about her?

Most likely, reality being the frustrating thing it was, he thought with an unamused inward guffaw, he'd simply never glimpse her again and never know. The stage having been set, all manifestations would cease.

But then, as he let the front door slip from his hand and swing toward its click-solemnized self-locking, he saw the Vanishing Lady forty feet away exactly as he had the first two times, real, no ghostliness anywhere (the name for the material of her coat came to his mind—velour), her shadowed face swung his way, or almost so, and modestly reaverted itself, and she moved out of sight on her black oxfords.

He reached the foyer fast as he could manage, its emptiness neither startling nor relieving him, nor the emptiness of the long back hall. He looked at the Clancys' door and the shuttered office window and shook his head and smiled. (Report this adventure? Whyever?) He started toward the stairs, but shook his head again and smiled more ruefully—he was already breathing very hard. He entered the elevator, and as he firmly pressed the Fourteen button with his thumb and heard the cage respond, he saw the dark gleaming eyes of the Vanishing Lady looking in at him anxiously, imploringly—they were open very wide—through the narrowing small window in the doors.

The next thing he was aware of, the cage was passing Three and he had just croaked out a harsh "Good evening"—the chalky aftertaste of these words was in his throat. The rest of the trip seemed interminable.

When the cage reached Fourteen, his thumb was already pressing the One button —and that trip seemed interminable too.

No sign of anyone anywhere, on One. He looked up the stairs, but he was breathing harder than even before. Finally he got back into the elevator and hovered his thumb over the 14 button. He could touch but not press it down. He brought his face close to the empty little window and waited and waited—and waited.

His thumb did not press down then, but the cage responded. The little window slipped shut. "It's out of my hands," he told himself fatalistically; "I'm being pulled somewhere." And from somewhere the thought came to him: What if a person were confined to this apartment tree forever, never leaving it, just going up and down and back and forth, and down and up and forth and back?

The cage didn't stop until Twelve, where the door was opened by a white-haired couple. Responding to their apologies with a reassuring head-shake and a signed "It's all right," Ryker pressed past them and, gasping gently and rapidly, mounted the last flight of stairs very slowly, very slowly. The two extra steps brought on a fit of swirling dizziness, but it passed and he slowly continued on toward his room. He felt frustrated, confused and very tired. He clung to the thoughts that he had reversed the elevator's course as soon as he could, despite his fright, and returned downstairs to hunt for her, and that in his last glimpse of them, her eyes had looked frightened too.

That night he had the muttering black nightmare again, all of it for the first time in weeks, and stronger, he judged afterward, than he'd ever before experienced it. The darkness seemed more impenetrable, solid, an ocean of black concrete congealing about him. The paralysis more complete, black canvas mummy wrappings drawn with numbing tightness, a spiral black cocoon tourniquet-tight. The dry and smoky odors more intense, as though he were baking and strangling in volcanic ash, while the sewer-stenches vied in disgustingness with fruity-flowery reeks meant to hide them. The sullen ghost-light of his imagination showed the micro-males grosser and more cock-roachlike in their hordes. And when finally under the goad of intensest horror he managed to stir himself and strain upward, feeling his heart and veins tearing with the effort, he encountered within a fraction of an inch his tomb's coarsely lined ceiling, which showered gritty ash into his gasping mouth and sightless eyes.

When he finally fought his way awake it was day, but his long sleep had in no way rested him. He felt tired still and good for nothing. Yesterday's story and walk had been too long, he told himself, yesterday's elevator encounter too emotionally exhausting. "Prisoners of the apartment tree," he murmured.

*　　*　　*

The Vanishing Lady was in very truth an eternal prisoner of the apartment tree, knowing no other life than there and no sleep anywhere except for lapsings that were as sudden as a drunkard's blackouts into an unconsciousness as black as Ryker's nightmares, but of which she retained no memory whatever save for a general horror and repulsion which colored all her waking thoughts.

She'd come awake walking down a hall, or on the stairs or in the moving elevator, or merely waiting somewhere in the tall and extensive apartment tree, but mostly near its roots and generally alone. Then she'd simply continue whatever she was doing for a while, sensing around her (if the episode lasted long enough, she might begin to wander independently), thinking and feeling and imagining and wondering as she moved or stood, always feeling a horror, until something would happen to swoop her back into black unconsciousness again. The something might be a sudden sound or thought, a fire siren, say, sight of a mirror or another person, encounter with a doorknob, or with the impulse to take off her gloves, the chilling sense that someone had noticed her or was about to notice her, the fear that she might inadvertently walk through a silvergray, faintly grimy wall, or slowly be absorbed into the carpet, sink through the floor. She couldn't recall those last things ever happening, and yet she dreaded them. Surely she went *somewhere*, she told herself, when she blacked out. She couldn't just collapse down on the floor, else there'd be some clue to that next time she came awake—and she was always on her feet when that happened. Besides, not often, but from time to time, she noticed she was wearing different clothes—*similar* clothes, in fact always black or some very dark shade close to it, but of a definitely different cut or material (leather, for instance, instead of cloth). And she couldn't possibly change her clothes or, worse, have them changed for her, in a semi-public place like the apartment tree—it would be unthinkable, too horribly embarrassing. Or rather—since we all know that the unthinkable and the horribly embarrassing (and the plain horrible too, for that matter) *can* happen—it would be too *grotesque*.

That was her chief trouble about everything, of course, she knew so little about her situation—in fact, knew so little about herself and the general scheme of things that held sway in this area, period. That she suffered from almost total amnesia, that much was clear to her. Usually she assumed that she lived (alone?) in one of the apartments hanging on the tree, or else was forever visiting someone who did, but then why couldn't she remember the number or somehow get inside that apartment, or come awake inside, or else get out the door into the street if she were headed that way? Why, oh why, couldn't she once ever wake in a hospital bed?—that would be pure heaven! except for the thought of what *kind* of a hospital and what things they had passing as doctors and nurses.

But just as she realized her amnesia, she knew she must have some way of taking care of herself during her unconscious times, or be the beneficiary of another's or others' system of taking care of her, for she somehow got her rest and other necessary physical reliefs, she must somehow get enough food and drink to keep her functioning, for she never felt terribly tired or seriously sick or weak and dizzy—except just before her topplings into unconsciousness, though sometimes those came without any warning at all, as sudden as the strike of pentothal.

560

She remembered knowing drunks (but not their names—her memory was utterly worthless on names) who lived hours and days of their lives in states of total blackout, safely crossing busy streets, eating meals, even driving cars, without a single blink of remembered awareness, as if they had a guardian angel guiding them, to the point of coming awake in distant cities, not having the ghost of an idea as to how they'd got there. (Well, she could hardly be a drunk; she didn't stagger and there was never a bottle in her purse, the times she came awake clutching a purse.)

But those were all deductions and surmises, unanchored and unlabeled memories that bobbed up in her mind and floated there awhile. What did she really know about herself?

Pitifully little. She didn't know her name or that of any friend or relative. Address and occupation, too, were blanks. Ditto education, race, religion, and marital status. Oh Christ! she didn't even know what city she was in or how *old* she was! and whether she was good-looking, ugly, or merely nondescript. Sometimes one of those last questions would hit her so hard that she would forget and start to look into one of the many mirrors in the apartment tree, or else begin to take off her gloves, so she could check it that way—hey! maybe find a tag with her name on it sewed inside her coat! But any of these actions would, of course, plunge her back into the black unconsciousness from which *this time* there might be no awakening.

And what about the general scheme of things that held sway in this area? What did she know about that? Precious little, too. There was this world of the apartment tree which she knew very well although she didn't permit herself to look at every part of it equally. Mirrors were taboos, unless you were so placed you couldn't see your own reflection in them; so mostly were people's faces. People meant danger. Don't look at them, they might look at you.

Then there was the outside world, a mysterious and wonderful place, a heaven of delights where there was everything desirable you could think or imagine, where there was freedom and repose. She took this on faith and on the evidence of most of her memories. (Though, sad to say, those memories' bright colors seemed to fade with time. Having lost names, they tended to lose other details, she suspected. Besides, it was hard to keep them vivid and bright when your only conscious life was a series of same-seeming, frantic, frightened little rushes and hidings and waits in the apartment tree, glued together at the ends like stretches of film—and the glue was black.)

But between those two worlds, the outside and the inside, separating them, there was a black layer (who knows how thick?) of unspeakable horrors and infinite terrors. What its outer surface was, facing the outside world, she could only guess, but its inside surface was clearly the walls, ceilings, and floors of the apartment tree. That was why she worried so much that she might become forgetful and step through them without intending to—she didn't know if she were insubstantial enough to do that (though she sometimes felt so), but she *might* be, or become so, and in any case she didn't intend to try! And why she had a dread of cracks and crevices and small holes anywhere and *things which could go through such cracks and holes,* leading logically enough to a fear of rats and mice and cockroaches and water bugs and similar vermin.

Deep down inside herself she felt quite sure, most of the time, that she spent all her unconscious life in the black layer, and that it was her experiences there, or her dreams there, that infected all her times awake with fear. But it didn't do to think of that, it was too terrible, and so she tried to occupy her mind fully with her normal worries and dreads, and with observing permitted things in the apartment tree, and with all sorts of little notions and fantasies.

One of her favorite fantasies, conceived and enjoyed in patches of clear thinking and feeling in the mostly on-guard, frantic stretches of her ragtag waking life, was that she really lived in a lovely modern hospital, occupied a whole wing of it, in fact, the favorite daughter of a billionaire no doubt, where she was cared for by stunningly handsome, sympathetic doctors and bevies of warm-hearted merry nurses who simply cosseted her to swooning with tender loving care, fed her the most delicious foods and drinks, massaged her endlessly, stole kisses sometimes (it was a rather naughty place), and the only drawback was that she was asleep throughout all these delightful operations.

Ah, but (she fantasized) you could tell just by looking at the girl—her eyes closed, to be sure, but her lips smiling—that somewhere deep within she knew all that was happening, *somewhere she enjoyed.* She was a sly one!

And then, when all the hospital was asleep, she would rise silently from her bed, put on her clothes, and still in a profound sleep sneak out of the hospital without waking a soul, hurry to this place, dive in an instant through the horror layer, and come awake!

But then, unfortunately, because of her amnesia, she would forget the snow white hospital and all her specific night-to-night memories of its delights and her wonderfully clever escapes from it.

But she could daydream of the hospital to her heart's content, almost! That alone was a matchless reward, worth everything, if only you looked at it the right way.

And then after a while, of course, she'd realize it was time to hurry back to the hospital before anyone there woke up and discovered she was gone. So she would, generally without letting on to herself what she was doing, seek or provoke an incident which would hurtle her back into unconsciousness again, transform her into her incredibly clever blacked-out other self who could travel anywhere in the universe unerringly, do almost anything—and with her eyes closed! (It wouldn't do to let the doctors and nurses ever suspect she'd been out of bed. Despite their inexhaustible loving-kindness they'd be sure to do something about it, maybe even come here and get her, and bar her from the apartment tree forever.)

So even the nicest daydreams had their dark sides.

As for the worst of her daydreams, the nastiest of her imaginings, it didn't do to think of them at all—they were pure black-layer, through and through. There was the fantasy of the eraser-worms for instance—squirmy, crawling, sleek, horny-armored things about an inch long and of the thickness and semi-rigidity of a pencil eraser or a black telephone cord; once they were loose they could go anywhere, and there were hordes of them.

She would imagine them . . . Well, wasn't it better to imagine them outright than to pretend she'd had a dream about them? for that would be admitting that she might have dreamed about them in the black layer, which would mean she might actually have *experienced* them in the black layer, wasn't that so? Well, anyway, she would start by imagining herself in utter darkness. It was strange, wasn't it, how, not often, but sometimes, you couldn't keep yourself from imagining the worst things? For a moment they became irresistible, a sort of nasty reverse delight.

Anyhow, she would imagine she was lying in utter darkness—sometimes she'd close her eyes and cup her hands over them to increase the illusion, and once, alone in the elevator, greatly daring, she had switched off the light—and then she'd feel the first worm touch her toe, then crawl inquisitively, peremptorily between her big toe and the next, as if it owned her. Soon they'd be swarming all over her, investigating every crevice and orifice they reached, finally assaulting her head and face. She'd press her lips tightly together, but then they'd block her nostrils (it took about two of them, thrusting together, to do each of those) and she'd be forced to part her lips to gasp and then they'd writhe inside. She'd squeeze her eyes tight shut, but nevertheless . . . and she had no way to guard her ears and other entries.

It was only bearable because you knew you were doing it to yourself and could stop any time you wanted. And maybe it was a sort of test to prove that, in a pinch, you *could* stand it—she wasn't sure. And although you told yourself it was nothing but imagination, it did give you ideas about the black layer.

She'd rouse from such a session shaking her head and with a little indrawn shudder, as if to say, "Who would believe the things she's capable of?" and "You're brooding, you're getting into yourself too much, child. Talk to others. Get out of yourself!" (And perhaps it was just as well there was seldom opportunity—long enough lulls—to indulge in such experimenting in the nervous, unpredictable, and sometimes breathless-paced existence of the apartment tree.)

There was any number of reasons why she couldn't follow her own advice and speak to others in the apartment tree, strike up conversations, even look at them much, do more than steal infrequent glances at their faces, but the overriding one was the deep conviction that *we had no right to be in the apartment tree* and that she'd get into serious trouble if she drew attention to herself. She might even be barred from the tree forever, sentenced to the black layer. (And if that last were the ridiculous nonsense idea it sounded like—where was the court and who would pronounce sentence?—why did it give her the cold shivers and a sick depression just to mention it to herself?)

No, she *didn't* have an apartment here, she'd tell herself, or any friend in the building. That was why she never had any keys—or any money either, or any little notebooks in which she could find out things about herself, or letters from others or even bills! No, she was a homeless waif and she had nothing. (The only thing she always or almost carried was a complete riddle to her: a brass tube slim as a soda straw about four inches long which at one end went through a smooth cork not much bigger around than an eraser-worm—don't think of those!)

At other times she'd tell herself she needn't have any fear of being spotted, caught, unmasked, shown to be an illegal intruder by the other passers-through of the apartment tree, because she was *invisible* to them, or almost all of them. The proof of this (which was so obvious, right before your eyes, that you missed it) was simply that none of them notices her, or spoke to her, or did her the little courtesies which they did each other, such as holding the elevator door for her. She had to move aside for them, not they for her!

This speculation about being invisible led to another special horror for her. Suppose, in her efforts to discover how old she was, she ever did manage to take off her gloves and found, not the moist hands of a young woman, nor yet the dry vein-crawling ones of a skinny old hag, but simply emptiness? What if she managed to open her coat and found herself, chin tucked in, staring down at lining? What if she looked into a mirror and saw nothing, except the wall behind her, or else only another mirror with reflections of reflections going back to infinity?

What if she were a ghost? Although it was long ago, or seemed long ago, she could recall, she thought, the dizzying chill *that* thought had given her the first time she'd had it. It fitted. Ghosts were supposed to haunt one place and to appear and disappear by fits and starts, and even then to be visible only to the sensitive few. None of the ghost stories she knew told it from the ghosts' side—what they thought and felt, how much they understood, and whether they ever knew what they were (ghosts) and what they were doing (haunting).

(And there even had been the "sensitive few" who had seemed to see her—and she looked back at them flirtatiously—though she didn't like to remember those episodes because they frightened her and made her feel foolish—whyever had she flirted? taken that risk?—and in the end made her mind go blurry. There'd been that big fat boy—whatever had she seen in him?—and before him a gentle old man, and before *him*—no, she certainly didn't have to push her memory back that far, no one could make her!)

But now that thought—that she might be a ghost—had become only one more of her familiar fancies, coming back into her mind every once in a while as regular as clockwork and with a little but not much of the original shock the idea had once given her. "Part of my repertoire," she told herself drolly. (God knows how she'd manage to stand her existence if things didn't seem funny to her once in a while.)

But most times weren't so funny. She kept coming back and coming back to what seemed after all the chief question: How *long* had her conscious life, *this* conscious life, lasted? And the only final answer she could get to this, in moments of unpanic, was that she couldn't tell.

It might be months or years. Long enough so that although not looking at their faces, she'd gotten to know the tenants of the apartment tree by their clothes and movements, the little things they said to each other, their gaits and favorite expressions. Gotten to know them well enough so that she could recognize them when they'd changed their clothes, put on new shoes, slowed down their gait, begun to use a cane. Sometimes completely new ones would appear and then slowly become old familiars—new tenants moving in. And then these old familiars might in their turn disappear—moved away, or died. My God, had she been here for decades? She remembered a horror story in which a beautiful young woman woke from a coma to find herself dying of old age. Would it be like that for her when she at last faced the mirror?

And if she *were* a ghost, would not the greatest horror for such a being be to die as a ghost?—to feel you had one tiny corner of existence securely yours, from which you could from time to time glimpse the passing show, and then be mercilessly swept out of that?

Or it might, on the other hand, be only minutes, hours, days at most—of strangely clear-headed fever dreaming, or of eternity-seeming withdrawal from a drug. Memory's fallible. Mind's capable of endless tricks. How could you be sure?

Well, whatever the truth was about the "How long?" business, she needn't worry about it for a while. The last few days (and weeks, or hours and minutes, who cared?) she'd been having a brand-new adventure. Yes, you could call it a flirtation if you wanted, but whatever you called it and in spite of the fact that it had its bad and scary parts, it had made her feel happier, gayer, braver, even more devil-may-care than she had in ages. Why, already it had revealed to her what she'd seen in the big fat boy and in the old man before him. My goodness, she'd simply *seen* them, felt interest in them, felt concern for them, yes, loved them. For that was the way it was now.

But that was then and this was now.

From the first time she'd happened to see Ryker (she didn't know his name then, of course) gazing so admiringly and wonderstruck at her from the front door, she'd known he couldn't possibly mean her harm, be one of the dangerous ones who'd send her back to the hospital or the black layer, or whatever. What had surprised her was the extent of her own inward reaction. She had a friend!—someone who thought she amounted to something, who *cared*. It made her dizzy, delirious. She managed to walk only a few steps, breasting the emotional tide, before she collapsed happily into the arms of darkness.

The second time it happened almost exactly the same way, only this time she was anticipating and needed only the barest glimpse—a flicker of her eyes his way—to assure herself that there hadn't been any mistake the first time, that he did feel that way about her, that he loved her.

By the time of their third meeting, she'd worked herself up into a really daring mood—she'd prepared a surprise for him and was waiting for him in the elevator. She'd even mischievously switched off the light (when she had the strength to do things like that, she knew she was in fine fettle), and was managing somehow to hold the door open (that surprised even her) so that she'd gradually be revealed to him as he came down the hall—a sort of hide-and-seek game. As to what happened after that, she'd take her chances!

Then when he'd walked past her, making a feeble excuse about his mailbox—that was one of the bad parts. What was the matter with him? Was he, a tenant, actually scared of her, a trespasser, a waif? And if so, how was he scared of her?—as a woman or as a possible criminal who'd try to rob or rape him, or maybe as a ghost? Was he shy, or had his smiles and admiration meant nothing, been just politeness? She almost lost her hold on the door then, but she managed not to. "Hurry up, hurry up, you old scaredy cat!" she muttered perkily under her breath. "I can't hold this door forever!"

And then someone on an upper floor buzzed the elevator, startling her, and she did lose her hold on the doors and they closed and the cage moved upward. She felt a sudden surge of hopelessness at being thwarted by mere chance, and she blacked out.

But next time she came awake her spirits were soon soaring again. In fact, that was the time when on sheerest impulse, she'd darted into a crowded elevator after him, which was something she never did—too much chance of being forced against someone and revealing your presence that way even if invisible.

Well, *that* didn't happen, but only because she kept herself pressed as flat against the door as possible and had some luck. At the first stop she hopped out thankfully, and changing her plans simply flew up the stairs, outdistancing the creaking cage, and when he didn't get out at Twelve, went on to Fourteen, and changing her plans again (she had the feeling it was almost time to black out), she simply followed him as he plodded to his room and noted its number before she lost consciousness. That was how she learned his name—by going to the mailboxes next time and checking his number, which said: R. RYKER. Oh, she might be a stupid little orphan of the apartment tree, but she had her tricks!

That time his arrival down on the ground floor front hall caught her unawares. Another man was holding the elevator door for two other ladies and with an encouraging glance at Ryker (he smiled back!) she darted in after them (she didn't mind a *few* fellow passengers, she could dodge them), thinking the man would go on holding the door open for Ryker. But he didn't, and she hesitated to hold it open from where she was standing (it would have looked too much like magic to the others) and so that chance of a shared ride and meeting was botched.

But that one failure didn't break her general mood of self-confidence and being on top of the situation. In fact, her mind seemed to be getting sharper and her memories to be opening. She got a hunch that something had once happened on the third floor in the front hall that was important to her, and it was while brooding there about it that she had her second unexpected encounter with Ryker. He came walking down the stairs and saw her and for a moment she thought he was going to march straight up to her, but once again his courage or whatever seemed to fail him and he kept on down and in her disappointment she blacked out.

These unanticipated meetings wouldn't do, she told herself, they didn't work, so the next time Ryker arrived by the front door she was waiting for him in the lobby. Then, just as things appeared to be working out, *her* courage failed, she got a sudden terrible fit of stage fright and fled up the stairs, though managing to turn at the top of the first flight and watch. She saw him pass the elevator after a hurried inspection of it and move toward the mailboxes and back hall. But he returned from there almost at once and entered the elevator. She realized that he'd gone to the back hall to look for her and, her courage restored, she flew down the stairs, but there was only time to peer once through the little elevator window at him (and he peered back) before the cage's ascent blocked the window. She waited dejectedly by the shaft, heart faintly the elevator stop at the top—and then immediately start down again. Was he coming back on her account? she asked herself, feeling dizzy, her mind wavering on the edge of blackness. She managed to hold onto her consciousness just long enough for it to tell her that, indeed, he was!—and looking anxious and expectant as he came out of the elevator—before it blacked out entirely.

*   *   *

Ramsey Ryker did not reenter the apartment tree from his own apartment until the next evening. Any attentive and thoughtful observer, had there been one to accompany him down in the elevator and match his measured footsteps to the front door, would have deduced two things about him.

First, from cologne-whiff overlying a faintly soapy fragrance and from gleaming jowl, spotless white collar, faintly pink scalp between strands of combed white hair, and small even tie-knot, that he had recently bathed, shaved very closely, and arrayed himself with equal care, so that except for his age you might have been sure he was going out on a romantic date.

Second, from his almost corpselike pallor, his abstracted expression, and "slow march" ritualistic movements, that the evening's business was a not altogether pleasurable or at least a very serious one.

And if the observer had in addition been an *imaginative* or perhaps merely suggestible person, he might have added these two impressions together and got the sinister total of "If ever a man could be said to have dressed himself for his own funeral . . ."

And if that same hypothetical observer had been on hand twenty minutes later to witness Ryker's return to the apartment tree, he would have got an additional funereal shudder from the circumstance that Ryker's lapel now sported a white carnation while his left hand carefully held a small floral spray, the chief feature of which was a white orchid.

But even this observer would have been surprised at the expression of excited delight that suffused and faintly colored Ryker's pale forward-straining countenance as he entered the hall. Of course sometimes merely getting cleaned up and dressed and venturing outdoors will cheer an elderly person amazingly, but this mood change seemed to and indeed did have a more specific outside stimulus.

For Ryker saw that the circumstances of his third encounter with the Vanishing Lady had been reproduced. There was that same expression of additional gloom, a black hole opening, swiftly seen to be due to the elevator doors standing open and the cage dark, and the dim-gleaming slender figure of the Vanishing Lady in profile just inside and just beyond the column of control buttons.

But this time her posture did not seem dejected but relaxedly alive: her head was bent, it's true, but it also seemed turned a little in his direction, as if she were scanning his approach coquettishly, there was more if anything of an elusive shimmering dim sparkle about her shoulders and her front, she held again (left hand this time, the nearer one) that mysterious little brass object he'd mistaken for a key, the total effect being surprisingly erotic, as if it were a black-and-silver drawing, "Assignation in the Shadows"; while all the while he hurried on eagerly, faster and faster, fiercely arming himself against any last-minute cringings aside, determined to let only a premature closing of its doors bar him from that elevator tonight.

Without the slightest hesitation he strode into the dark cage, bowing slightly to her as he did so, reaching his right hand toward the top of the buttons column, where the light switch was, to turn it on, and said in a low and respectful voice, "Good evening." This last came out deeper and more resonant than he'd intended, so that it had a rather sepulchral sound. And his third movement was not completed, for just as he entered, she raised her head and simultaneously reached her black-gloved right hand and that arm across her body and the lower half of her face, apparently anticipating his intention to switch on the light, so that his own hand drew back.

He turned facing her as he stepped past her and settled his back against that of the elevator. Her outstretched arm concealed her lips, so he couldn't tell if she smiled or not, but her gleaming eyes followed him as he moved across the cage, and at least they didn't frown. The effect was provocative, alluring.

But her outreached hand did not turn on the light. Instead its black forefinger seemed to lay itself against the flat brass between the 12 and 14 buttons. But she must have pressed one or the other of those in so doing, for the doors growled shut and the cage moved upward.

That plunged the cage in gloom, but not quite as deeply as he would have expected, for the strange pale glimmering around her neck and her black coat's closure seemed to strengthen a little, almost sparkle (real or imagined? her body's aura, could it be? or only his old eyes dazzling?) and a twinkle of other light came in by the little window as they passed the second floor. In his state of heightened awareness he dimly yet distinctly saw her right hand drop away into its sleeve and then in one swift backward motion strip the glove from her right hand, which then uncurled gracefully toward him palm upward through the dark between them like a slender white sash ending in five slim white ribbons of unequal length. Advancing a step and bowing his head toward it, he gently received its cool weightless length upon his own fingers, touched his lips to the smooth slim palm, and withdrawing laid across it the white orchid he'd been carrying. Another little window winked by.

She pressed the slender spray against her throat and with her yet-gloved hand touched his as if in thanks. *She* wondered why she had pressed *between* the buttons and why the cage had responded, why she had not blacked out while drawing off her glove. Dark memories threatened opening, not without fear. She tugged a little at Ryker's hand in drawing her own away.

Emboldened, he advanced another step, bringing him almost against her. Her cat-triangular small face tilted up toward his, half of it pale, the other half dark mouth, gray gleaming eyes, their shadowed orbits under slim black brows. His left hand brushed her side and slid behind her, pressed her slim back. His right sought out the fingers at her throat holding his orchid and caressed them, playing with them gently. He felt her suede-soft gloved fingers creeping at the back of his neck.

She slid the orchid with its insubstantial spray inside her coat and her ungloved moist hand stroked his dry cheek. His hand felt out two large round buttons at her neck, tilted them through their thread-bordered slits, and the collar of her coat fell open. The diamond sparkling that had long puzzled him intensified, gushed up and poured out fountainlike, as if he had uncovered her aura's nest—or was his old heart blowing up a diamond hurricane? or his old eyes jaggedly spinning out a diamond migraine pattern? He gazed down through this ghostly scintillation, these microscopic stars, at a landscape pearly gray and cool as the moon's, the smooth valley where the orchid lodged between her small jutting breasts with their dark silver nipples, a scene that was not lost, though it swung and narrowed a little, when her small hands drew his head down to hers and their lips met in a leisurely kiss that dizzied him unalarmingly.

It occurred to him whimsically that although the pearly landscape he continued to admire might seem to stretch on and on, it had an exceedingly low black sky, an extremely low ceiling, air people would say. Now why should that fantasy carry overtones which were more sinister than amusing? he wondered idly.

It was at that moment that he became aware that he was smelling cigar smoke. The discovery did not particularly startle or alarm him, but it did awaken his other senses a little from their present great dreamy preoccupation, though not entirely. Indeed, in one sense that preoccupation deepened, for at that moment the tip of her tongue drew a very narrow line into their kiss. But at the same time, as he noted that the elevator had come to rest, that its creaking groan had been replaced by a growling mutter which he liked still less, while a wavering ruddy glow, a shadowed reddish flickering, was mounting the walls of the cage from some unknown source below, and that the thin reek of cigar smoke was becoming more acrid.

Unwillingly, wearily (he was anything but tired, yet this cost an effort), he lifted his gaze without breaking their kiss, without thinking of breaking it, and continuing to fondle her back and neck, until he was looking across her shoulder.

He saw, by the red glow, that the door of the cage had opened without his having noticed it and that the elevator was at the fourteenth floor.

But not *quite* at the fourteenth floor, for the outer door was closed tight and the little window in it that had the numeral 14 painted under it stood about eighteen inches higher than it should.

So the floor of the cage must be the same distance below the floor of Fourteen.

Still unalarmed, grudging each effort, he advanced his head across her shoulder until he could look down over it. As he did so, she leaned her head back and turned it a little sideways, accommodating, so that their kiss was still unbroken, meanwhile hugging him more tightly and making muffled and inarticulate crooning sounds as if to say "It is all right."

The space between the two floors (which was also the space between the ceiling of Twelve and the floor of Fourteen) was wide open, a doorway five feet wide and scarcely one foot high in the raw wall of the shaft, and through that doorway there was pouring into the bottom of the cage from the very low-ceilinged thirteenth floor a pulsing crimson glow which nevertheless seemed more steady in hue, more regular in its variations of intensity than that of any fire.

This furnace-light revealed, clustered around their ankles but spreading out more scatteredly to fill the elevator's carpeted floor, a horde of dark squat forms, a milling host of what appeared to be (allowing for the extreme foreshortening) stocky Lilliputian human beings, some lifting their white faces to peer up, others bent entirely to the business at hand. For instance, two pairs of them struggled with dull metal hooks almost as large as they were and to which stout cords were attached, others carried long prybars, one jauntily balanced on his shoulder what looked like a white paper packet about as big (relative to him) as an unfolded Sunday newspaper, while more than half of them held between two fingers tiny black cylinders from one end of which interweaving tiny tendrils of smoke arose, forming a thin cloud, and which when they applied the other ends to their tiny mugs, glowed winkingly red in the red light, as if they were a swarm of hellish lightless fireflies.

It may seem most implausible to assert that Ramsey Ryker did not feel terror and panic at this extremely grotesque sight (for he realized also that he had somehow penetrated the realm of his nightmares) and highly unlikely to record that his kiss and the Vanishing Lady's continued unbroken (save for the hurried puffings and inhalations normal in such a contact), yet both were so. True, as he wormed his head back across her shoulder to its first vantage point, his heart pounded alarmingly, there was a roaring in his ears, and waves of blackness threatened to overwhelm his vision and forced their way up into his skull, while the simple shifting movement he intended proved unexpectedly difficult to execute (his head felt heavy, not so much looking over her shoulder as slumped on it)—but these were physical reactions with many causes. His chief mental reactions to the beings he'd seen clustered around their feet were that they would have been interesting at another time and that they presumably had their own place, business, and concerns in the great scheme of things, and that just now he had his own great business and concerns he must return to, as hopefully they to theirs. Also, the Vanishing Lady's caresses and murmurings of reassurance and encouragement had their helpful and soothing effects.

But when he was once more gazing down into what we may call without any sarcasm his steep and narrow valley of delights, he could no longer tell whether the ghostly silver sparks that fountained from it were inside or outside his eyes and skull, the exquisite outlines wavered and were lost in mists, his fingers fondling her neck and her low back grew numb and powerless, all power save that of vision drained from his every part, he grew lax, and with her hands solicitously supporting and guiding him, he sank by degrees, his heavy head brushing her black coat entirely open and resting successively against her naked breasts, belly, and thighs, until he was laid out upon his back corner-to-corner in the small cage, head to the front of it, feet to the back, level with the hitherto unsuspected thirteenth floor, while the Vanishing Lady in assisting him had stooped until she now sat upon her heels, her upper body erect, her chin high, having never once looked down.

With a slow effortless movement she regained her full stature, her hands trailing limply down, one of them still gripping the brass tube. The jaunty homunculus lifted his white paper packed to the other, and she clipped it securely between thumb and forefinger, still without the slightest downward glance, raised it until it was before her eyes, and eagerly but carefully unfolded it.

Ryker watched her attentively from the floor. His entire consciousness, almost, had focused in on her until he saw only her face and shoulders, her busy hands and matchless breasts. They looked very clear but very far away, like something seen through the wrong end of a telescope. He was only most dimly aware of the movements closer to him, of the way the two large dull hooks were being effortfully fitted under his shoulders and beneath his armpits. He watched with great interest but no comprehension, aware only of the beauty of the sight, as she fitted the cork-protected end of the brass tube into one nostril, delicately applied the other end to the flat unfolded square of white paper, and slowly but deeply inhaled. He did not hear the distant windlass creaking nor feel the hooks tighten against his armpits as he was dragged out of the elevator into the thirteenth floor and his consciousness irised in toward nothingness.

Nor did the Vanishing Lady honor either his disappearance or his captors' with even one last glance as she impatiently shifted the brass tube to her other nostril and applied it to an edge of the diminished pile of crystals outspread on the white packet paper, the sight of which had instantly recalled to her mind the use of that tube and much more besides, not all of which she was tickled to relearn: the sullen waitings for Artie Stensor, her own entrapment by the thirteenth floor, the finding of Artie there in his new and degenerate imprisoned form, the sessions that reduced her also to such a form, her deal with the reigning homunculi, the three services (or was it four?) she'd promised them, the luring and entrapment of the other two tenants. She put all that out of her mind as she inhaled slowly, very evenly, and deeply, the mouth of the brass tube like that of some tiny reaping machine eating its way up and down the edge of the coke or "snow" or whatever else you might call the sovereign diamond sparkling dream drug, until the paper was empty.

She felt the atoms of her body loosening their hold on each other and those of her awareness and memory tightening theirs as with a fantastic feeling of liberation she slowly floated up through the ceiling of the cage into the stale air of the dark and cavernous shaft and then rose more and more swiftly along the black central cables until she shot through the shaft's ceiling, winked through the small lightless room in which were the elevator's black motor and relays, and burst out of the apartment tree into the huge dizzying night.

South shone the green coronet of the Hilton, west the winking red light that outlined the tripod TV tower atop Sutro Crest, northeast the topaz-sparkling upward-pointing arrow of the Transamerican Pyramid. Farther east, north, and west, all lapped in low fog, were the two great bridges, Bay and Golden Gate, and the unlimited Pacific Ocean. She felt she could see, go anywhere.

She spared one last look and sorrow pang for the souls entombed—or, more precisely, *immured*—in San Francisco and then, awareness sharpening and consciousness expanding, sped on up and out, straight toward that misty, nebulaswathed multiple star in Orion called the Trapezium.

The Curse of the Smalls
and the Stars

Late one nippy afternoon of early Rime Isle spring, Fafhrd and the Gray Mouser slumped pleasantly in a small booth in Salthaven's Sea Wrack Tavern. Although they'd been on the Isle for only a year, and patronizing this tavern for an eight-month, the booth was recognized as *theirs* when either was in the place. Both men had been mildly fatigued, the former from supervising bottom-repairs to *Seahawk* at the new moon's low tide—and then squeezing in a late round of archery practice, the latter from bossing the carpentering of their new warehouse-and-barracks—and doing some inventorying besides. But their second tankards of bitter ale had about taken care of that and their thoughts were beginning to float free.

Around them the livening talk of other recuperating laborers. At the bar they could see three of their lieutenants grousing together—Fafhrd-tall Skor, and the somewhat reformed small thieves Pshawri and Mikkidu. Behind it the keeper lit two thick wicks as the light dimmed as the sun set outside.

"Lankhmar," Fafhrd mused, drawing a wet circle with the firmly socketed iron hook that had become his left hand after the day's bow bending, "I've heard somewhere of such a city, I do believe. 'Tis strange how oftentimes our thoughts do chime together, as if we were sundered halves of some past being, but whether hero or demon, wastrel or philosopher, harder to say."

"Demon, I'd say," the Mouser answered instantly, "a demon warrior. We've guessed at him before. Remember? We decided he always growled in battle. Perhaps a were-bear."

After a small chuckle at that, Fafhrd went on, "But then (that night twelve moons gone and five in Lankhmar) we'd had twelve tankards each of bitter instead of two, I ween, yes, and lacing them too with brandy, you can bet—hardly to be accounted best judges twixt phantasm and the veritable. Yes, and didn't two heroines from this fabled isle next moment stride into the Eel, as real as boots?"

Almost as if the Northerner hadn't answered, the small gray-smocked, gray-stockinged man continued in the same thoughtful reminiscent tones as he'd first used, "And you, liquored to the gills—agreed on that!—were ranting dolefully about how you dearly wanted work, land, office, sons, other responsibilities, and e'en a wife!"

"Yes, and didn't I get one?" Fafhrd demanded. "You too, you equally then-drunken destiny-ungrateful lout!" His eyes grew thoughtful also. He added, "Though perhaps comrade or co-mate were the better word—or even those plus partner."

"Much better all three," the Mouser agreed shortly. "As for those other goods your

571

drunken heart was set upon—no disagreement there!—we've got enough of those to stuff a hog!—except, of course, far as I know, for sons. Unless, that is, you count our men as our grown-up unweaned babes, which sometimes I'm inclined to."

Fafhrd, who'd been leaning his head out of the booth to look toward the darkening doorway during the latter part of the Mouser's plaints, now stood up, saying, "Speaking of them, shall we join the ladies? Cif and Afreyt's booth 'pears to be larger than ours."

"To be sure. What else?" the Mouser replied, rising springily. Then, in a lower voice, "Tell me, did the two of them just now come in? Or did we blunder blindly by them when we entered, sightless of all save thirst-quench?"

Fafhrd shrugged, displaying his palm. "Who knows? Who cares?"

"*They* might," the other answered.

✳   ✳   ✳

Many Lankhmar leagues east and south, and so in darkest moonless night, the archmagus Ningauble conferred with the sorceress Sheelba at the edge of the Great Salt Marsh. The seven luminous eyes of the former wove many greenish patterns within his gaping hood as he leaned his quaking bulk perilously downward from the howdah on the broad back of the forward-kneeling elephant which had borne him from his desert cave across the Sinking Land through all adverse influences to this appointed spot. While the latter's eyeless face strained upwards likewise as she stood tall in the doorway of her small hut, which had traveled from the Marsh's noxious center to the same dismal verge on its three long rickety (but now rigid) chicken-legs. The two wizards strove mightily to outshout (outbellow or outscreech) the nameless cosmic din (inaudible to human ears) which had hitherto hindered and foiled all their earlier efforts to communicate over greater distances. And now, at last, they strove successfully!

Ningauble wheezed, "I have discovered by certain infallible signs that the present tumult in realms magical, botching my spells, is due to the vanishment from Lankhmar of my servitor and sometimes student, Fafhrd the barbarian. All magics dim without his credulous and kindly audience, while high quests fail lacking his romantical and custard-headed idealism."

Sheelba shot back through the murk, "While I have ascertained that my illspells suffer equally because the Mouser's gone with him, my protégé and surly errand boy. They will not work without the juice of his brooding and overbearing malignity. He must be summoned from that ridiculous rimplace of Rime Isle, and Fafhrd with him!"

"But how to do that when our spells won't carry? What servitor to trust with such a mission to go and fetch 'em? I know of a young demoness might undertake it, but she's in thrall to Khakht, wizard of power in that frosty area—and he's inimical to both of us. Or should the two of us search out in noisy spirit realm to be our messenger that putative warlike ascendant of theirs and whilom forebear known as the Growler? A dismal task! Where'er I look I see naught but uncertainties and obstacles—"

"I shall send word of their whereabouts to Mog the spider god, the Gray One's tulelary deity!—this din won't hinder prayers," Sheelba interrupted in a harsh, clipped voice. The presence of the vacillating and loquacious over-sighted wizard, who saw seven sides to every question, always roused her to her best efforts. "Send you like advisos to Fafhrd's gods, stoneage brute Kos and the fastidious cripple Issek. Soon as they know where their lapsed worshippers are, they'll put such curses and damnations on them as shall bring them back squealing to us to have those taken off."

"Now why didn't *I* think of that?" Ningauble protested, who was indeed sometimes called the Gossiper of the Gods. "To work! To work!"

*   *   *

In paradisiacal Godsland, which lies at the antipodes of Nehwon's death pole and Shadowland, in the southernmost reach of that world's southernmost continent, distanced and guarded from the tumultuous northern lands by the Great eastward-rushing Equatorial Current (where some say swim the stars), sub-equatorial deserts, and the Rampart Mountains, the gods Kos, Issek, and Mog sat somewhat apart from the mass of more couth and civilized Nehwonian deities, who objected to Kos' lice, fleas, and crabs, and a little to Issek's effeminacy—though Mog had contacts among these, as he sarcastically called 'em, "higher beings."

Sunk in divine, somnolent broodings, not to say almost deathlike trances, for prayers, petitions, and even blasphemous name-takings had been scanty of late, the three mismatched godlings reacted at once and enthusiastically to the instantaneously-transmitted wizard missives.

"Those two ungodly swording rogues!" Mog hissed softly, his long thin lips stretched slantwise in a half spider grin. "The very thing! Here's work for all of us, my heavenly peers. A chance to curse again and to bedevil."

"A glad inspiro that, indeed, indeed!" Issek chimed, waving his limp-wristed hands excitedly. "I should have thought of that!—our chiefest lapsed worshippers, hidden away in frosty and forgotten far Rime Isle, farther away than Shadowland itself, *almost* beyond our hearing and our might. Such infant cunning! Oh but we'll make them pay!"

"The ingrate dogs!" Kos grated through his thick and populous black beard. "Not only casting us off, their natural heavenly fathers and rightful da's, but forsaking *all* - decent Nehwonian deities and running with atheist men and gone a-whoring after stranger gods beyond the pall! Yes, by my lights and spleen, we'll make 'em suffer! Where's my spiked mace?"

(On occasion Mog and Issek had been known to have to hold Kos down to keep him from rushing ill-advised out of Godsland to seek to visit personal dooms upon his more disobedient and farther strayed worshippers.)

"What say we set their women against them, as we did last time?" Issek urged twitteringly. "Women have power over men almost as great as gods do."

Mog shook his humanoid cephalothorax. "Our boys are too coarse-tasted. Did we estrange from them Afreyt and Cif, they'd doubtless fall back on amorous arrangements with the Salthaven harlots Rill and Hilsa—and so on and so on." Now that his attention had been called to Rime Isle, he had easy knowledge of all overt things there—a divine prerogative. "No, not the women this time, I ween."

"A pox on all such subleties!" Kos roared. "I want tortures for 'em! Let's visit on 'em the strangling cough, the prick-rot, and the Bloddy Melts!"

"Nor can we risk wiping them out entirely," Mog answered swiftly. "We haven't worshippers to spare for that, you fire-eater, as you well know. Thrift, thrift! Moreover, as you should also know, a threat is always more dreadful than its execution. I propose we subject them to some of the moods and preoccupations of old age and of old age's bosom comrade, inseparable though invisible-seeming—Death himself! Or is that too mild a fear and torment, thinkest thou?"

"I'll say not," Kos agreed, suddenly sober. "I know that it scares *me*. What if the gods should die? A hellish thought."

"That infant bugaboo!" Issek told him peevishly. Then turning to Mog with quickening interest, "So, if I read you right, old Arach, let's narrow your silky Mouser's interests in and in from the adventure-beckoning horizon to the things closest around him: the bed table, the dinner board, the privy, and the kitchen sink. Not the far-leaping highway, but the gutter. Not the ocean, but the puddle. Not the grand view outside, but the bleared windowpane. Not the thunder-blast, but the knuckle-crack—or ear-pop."

Mog narrowed his eight eyes happily. "And for your Fafhrd, I would suggest a different cld-age curse, to drive a wedge between them, so they can't understand or help each other: that we put a geas upon him to count the stars. His interests in all else will fade and fail; he'll have mind only for those tiny lights in the sky."

"So that, with his head in the clouds," Issek pictured, catching on quick, "he'll stumble and bruise himself again and again, and miss all opportunities of earthly delights."

"Yes, and make him memorize their names and all their patterns!" Kos put in. "There's busy-work for an eternity. I never could abide the things myself. There's such a senseless mess of stars, like flies or fleas. An insult to the gods to say that we created them!"

"And then, when those two have sufficiently humbled themselves to us and done suitable penance," Issek purred, "we will consider taking off or ameliorating their curses."

"I say, leave 'em on always," Kos argued. "No leniency. Eternal damnation!—that's the stuff!"

"That question can be decided when it arises," Mog opined. "Come, gentlemen, to work! We've some damnations to devise in detail and deliver."

* * *

Back at the Sea Wrack Tavern, Fafhrd and the Gray Mouser had, despite the latter's apprehensions, been invited to join with and buy a round of bitter ale for their lady-friends Afreyt and Cif, leading and sometimes office-holding citizens of Rime Isle, spinster-matriarchs of otherwise scionless dwindling old families in that strange republic, and Fafhrd's and the Mouser's partners and co-adventurers of a good year's standing in questing, business, and (this last more recently) bed. The questing part had consisted of the almost bloodless routing from the Isle of an invading naval force of maniacal Sea-Mingolds, with the help of twelve tall berserks and twelve small warrior-thieves the two heroes had brought with them, and the dubious assistance of the two universes-wandering hobo gods Odin and Loki, and (minor quest) a small expedition to recover certain civic treasures of the Isle, a set of gold artifacts called the Ikons of Reason. And they had been *hired* to do these things by Cif and Afreyt, so business had been mixed with questing in their relationship from the very start. Other business had been a merchant venture of the Mouser (Captain Mouser for this purpose) in Fafhrd's galley *Seahawk* with a mixed crew of berserks and thieves, and goods supplied by the ladies, to the oft-frozen port of Noombrulsk on Nehwonmainland—that and various odd jobs done by their men and by the women and girls employed by and owing fealty to Cif and Afreyt.

As for the bed part, both couples, though not yet middle-aged at least in looks, were veterans of amorous goings-on, wary and courteous in all such doings, entering upon any new relationships, including these, with a minimum of commitment and a maximum of reservations. Ever since the tragic deaths of their first loves, Fafhrd's and the Mouser's erotic solacing had mostly come from a very odd lot of hard-bitten if beauteous slave-girls, vagabond hoydens, and demonic princesses, folk easily come by if at all and even more easily lost, accidents rather than goals of their weird adventurings; both sensed that anything with the Rime Isle ladies would have to be a little more serious at least. While Afreyt's and Cif's love-adventures had been equally transient, either with unromantic and hardheaded Rime Islanders, who are atheistical realists even in youth, or with sea-wanderers of one sort or another, come like the rain—or thunder-squall, and as swiftly gone.

All this being considered, things did seem to be working out quite well for the two couples in the bed area.

And, truth to tell, this was a greater satisfaction and relief to the Mouser and Fafhrd than either would admit even to himself. For each was indeed beginning to find extended questing a mite tiring, especially ones like this last which, rather than being one of their usual lone-wolf forays, involved the recruitment and command of other men and the taking on of larger and divided responsibilities. It was natural for them, after such exertions, to feel that a little rest and quiet enjoyment was now owed them, a little surcease from the batterings of fate and chance and new desire. And, truth to tell, the ladies Cif and Afreyt were on the verge of admitting in their secretest hearts something of the same feelings.

So all four of them found it pleasant during this particular Rime Isle twilight to take a little bitter ale together and chat of this day's doings and tomorrow's plans and reminisce about their turning of the Mingols and ask each other other gentle questions about the times before they'd all four met—and each flirt privily and cautiously with the notion that each now had two or three persons on whom they might always rely fully, rather than one like-sexed comrade only.

During the course of this gossiping Fafhrd mentioned again his and the Mouser's fantasy that they were halves—or perhaps lesser fractions, fragments only—of some noted or notorious past being, explaining why their thoughts so often chimed together.

"That's odd," Cif interjected, "for Afreyt and I have had like notion and for like reason: that she and I were spirit-halves of the great Rimish witch-queen Skeldir, who held off the Simorgyans again and again in ancient times when that island boasted an empire and was above the waves instead of under them. What was your hero's name—or mighty rogue's?—if that likes you better."

"I know not, lady, perhaps he lived in times too primitive for names, when man and beast were closer. He was identified by his battle-growling—a leonine cough deep in the throat when'er he entered an encounter."

"Another like point!" Cif noted. "Queen Skeldir announced her presence by a short dry laugh—her invariable utterance when facing dangers, especially those of a sort to astound and confound the bravest."

"Gusorio's my name for our beastish forebear," the Mouser threw in. "I know not what Fafhrd thinks. Great Gurorio. Gusorio the Growler."

"Now he begins to sound like an animal," Afreyt broke in. "Tell me, have you ever been granted vision or dream of this Gusorio, or heard perhaps in darkest night his battle growl?"

But the Mouser was studying the dinted table top. He bent his head and his gaze traveled across it.

"No, milady," Fafhrd answered for his abstracted comrade. "At least not I. It's something we heard of a witch or fortuneteller, figment, not fact. Have you ever heard Queen Skeldir's short dry laugh, or had sight of that fabled warrior sorceress?"

"Neither I nor Cif," Afreyt admitted, "though she is in the Isle's history parchments."

But even as she answered him, Fafhrd's questioning gaze strayed past her. She looked behind and saw the Sea Wrack's open doorway and the gathering night.

Cif stood up. "So it's agreed we dine at Afreyt's in a half hour's time?"

The two men nodded somewhat abstractedly. Fafhrd leaned his head to the right as he continued to stare past Afreyt, who with a smile obligingly shifted hers in the opposite direction.

The Mouser leaned back and bent his head a little more as his gaze trailed down from the table top to its leg.

Fafhrd observed, "Astarion sets soon after the sun these nights. There's little time to observe her."

"God forbid I should stand in the evening star's way," Afreyt murmured humorously as she too arose. "Come, cousin."

The Mouser left off watching the cockroach as it reached the floor. It had limped interestingly, lacking a mild leg. He and Fafhrd drank off their bitters, then slowly followed their ladies out and down the narrow street, the one's eyes thoughtfully delving in the gutter, as if there might be treasure there, the other's roving the sky as the stars winked on, naming those he knew and numbering, by altitude and direction, those he didn't.

*   *   *

Their work well launched, Sheelba retired to Marsh center and Ningauble toward his cavern, the understorm abating, a good omen. While the three gods smiled, invigorated by their cursing. The slum corner of Heaven they occupied now seemed less chilly to Issek and less sweatily enervating to Kos, while Mog's devious mind spider stepped down more pleasant channels.

Yes, the seed was well planted and left to germinate in silence might have developed as intended, but some gods, and some sorcerers too, cannot resist boasting and gossiping, and so by way of talkative priests and midwives and vagabonds, word of what was intended came to the ears of the mighty, including two who considered themselves well rid of Fafhrd and the Mouser and did not want them back in Lankhmar at all. And the mighty are great worriers and spend much time preventing anything that troubles their peace of mind.

And so it was that Pulgh Arthonax, penurious and perverse overlord of Lankhmar, who hated heroes of all description, but especially fair-complected big ones like Fafhrd, and Hamomel, thrifty and ruthless grand master of the Thieves Guild there, who detested the Mouser generally as a freelance competitor and particularly as one who had lured twelve promising apprentices away from the guild to be his henchmen— these two took counsel together and commissioned the Assassins Order, an elite within the Slayers' Brotherhood, to dispatch the Twain in Rime Isle before they should point toe toward Lankhmar. And because Arth-Pulgh and Hamomel were both most miserly magnates and insatiably greedy withal, they beat down the Order's price as far as they could and made it a condition of the commission that three fourths of any portable booty found on or near the doomed Twain be returned to them as their lawful share.

So the Order drew up death warrants, chose by lot two of its currently unoccupied fellows, and in solemn secret ceremony attended only by the Master and the Recorder divested these of their identities and rechristened them the Death of Fafhrd and the Death of the Gray Mouser, by which names only they should henceforth be known to each other and within the profession until the death warrants were served and their commissions fulfilled.

*   *   *

Next day repairs to *Seahawk* continued, the low tide repeating, Witches Moon being only one day old. During a late morning break Fafhrd moved apart from his men a little and scanned the high bright sky toward north and east, his gaze ranging. Skor ventured to follow him across the wet sand and copy his peerings. He saw nothing in the gray-blue heavens, but experience had taught him his captain had exceptionally keen eyesight.

"Sea eagles?" he asked softly.

Fafhrd looked at him thoughtfully, then smiled, shaking his head, and confided, "I was imagining which stars would be there, were it now night."

Skor's forehead wrinkled puzzledly. "Stars by day?"

Fafhrd nodded. "Yes. Where think *you* the stars are by day?"

"Gone," Skor answered, his forehead clearing. "They go away at dawn and return at evening. Their lights are extinguished—like winter campfires! for surely it must be cold where the stars are, higher than mountaintops. Until the sun comes out to warm up things, of course."

Fafhrd shook his head. "The stars march west across the sky each night in the same formations which we recognize year after year, dozen years after dozen, and I would guess gross after gross. They do not skitter for the horizon when day breaks or seek out lairs and earth holes, but go on marching with the sun's glare hiding their lights—under cover of day, one might express it."

"Stars shining by day?" Skor questioned, doing a fair job of hiding his surprise and bafflement. Then he caught Fafhrd's drift, or thought he did, and a certain wonder appeared in his eyes. He knew his captain was a good general who made a fetish of keeping track of the enemy's position especially in terrain affording concealment, as forest on land or fog at sea. So by his very nature his captain had applied the same rule to the stars and studied 'em as closely as he'd traced the movements of the Mingol scouts fleeing across Rime Isle.

Though it was strange thinking of the stars as enemies. His captain was a deep one! Perhaps he did have foes among the stars. Skor had heard rumor that he'd bedded a queen of the air.

*   *   *

That night as the Gray Mouser and Cif leisurely prepared for bed in her low-eaved house tinted a sooty red on the northwestern edge of Salthaven City, and whilst that lady busied herself at her mirrored dressing table, the Mouser himself sitting on bed's edge set his pouch upon a low bedside table and withdrew from it a curious lot of commonplace—and arranged them in a line on the table's dark surface.

Cif, made curious by the slow regularity of his movements she saw reflected cloudily in the sheets of silver she faced, took up a small flat black box and came over and sat herself beside him.

The objects included a toothed small wooden wheel as big almost as a Sarheenmar dollar with two of the teeth missing, a finch's feather, three look-alike gray round pebbles, a scrap of blue wool cloth stiff with dirt, a bent wrought iron nail, a hazelnut, and a dinted small black round that might have been a Lankhmar *tik* or Eastern half-penny.

Cif ran her eye along them, then looked at him questioningly.

He said, "Coming here from the barracks at first eve, a strange mood seized me. Low in the sunset glow the new moon's faintest and daintiest silver crescent had just materialized like the ghost of a young girl—and just in the direction of this house, at that, as though to signal your presence here—but somehow I had eyes for the gutter and the pathside. Which is where I found those. And a remarkable lot they are for a small northern seaport. You'd think Ilthmar at least . . ." He shook his head.

"But why collect 'em?" she queried. *Like an old ragpicker,* she thought.

He shrugged. "I don't know. I think I thought I might find a use for them," he added doubtfully.

She said, "They do look like oddments that might be involved in casting a spell."

He shrugged again, but added, "They're not all what they seem. *That,* for in-stance—" He pointed at one of three gray spherelets, "—is not a pebble like the other two, but a lead slingshot, perhaps one of my own."

Struck by his thrusting finger, *that* rolled off the table and hit the terrazzo floor with a little dull yet clinky thud, as if to prove his observation.

As he recovered it, he paused with his eyes close to the floor to study first the crushed black marble of the terrazzo flecked with dark red and gold, and second Cif's near foot, which he then drew up onto his lap and studied still more minutely.

"A strangely symmetric pentapod coral outcrop from sea's bottom," he observed and planted a slow kiss upon the base of her big toe, insinuated the tip of his tongue between it and the next.

"There's an eel nosed around in my reef," she murmured.

Laying his cheek upon her ankle, he sighted up her leg. She was wearing a singlet of fine brown linen that tied between her legs. He said, "Your hair has exactly the same tints as are in the flooring."

She said, "You think I didn't select the marble for crushing with that in mind? Or add in the gold flakes? Here's a present of sorts for you." And she pushed the small flat black box down her leg toward him from her groin to her knee.

He sat up to inspect it though keeping her foot in his lap.

On the black fabric lining it, there lay like a delicate mist cloud the slender translu-cent bladder of a fish.

Cif said, "I am minded to experience your love fully tonight. Yet not as fully, mind you, as to wish that we fashion a daughter together."

The Mouser said, "I've seen the like of this made of thinnest leather well oiled."

She said, "Not as effectual, I believe."

He said, "To be sure, here, it would be something from a fish, this being Rime Isle. Tell me, did harbor master Groniger fashion this, as thrifty with the Isle's sperm as with its coins?" Then he nodded.

He reached over and drew her other foot up on his lap also. After saluting it similarly he rested the side of his face on both her ankles, and sighted up the narrow trough between her legs. "I am minded," he said dreamily but with a little growl in his voice, "to embark on another slow and intensely watchful journey, mindful of every step, such as that by which I arrived at this house this eve."

She nodded, wondering idly if the growl were Gusorio's, but it seemed too faint for that.

* * *

In the bow of a laden grainship sailing north from Lankhmar across the Inner Sea to the land of the Eight Cities, the Death of Fafhrd, who was tall and lank, dire as a steel scarecrow, said to his fellow passenger, "This incarnation likes me and likes me not. 'Tis a balmy journey now but it'll be long and by all accounts cold as witchcunt at the end, albeit summer. Arth-Pulgh's a mean employer, and unlucky. Hand me a medlar from the sack."

The Death of the Gray Mouser, lithe as a weasel and forever smiling, replied, "No meaner nor no curtser than Hamomel. Working for whom, however, is the pits. I've not yet shaken down to this persona, know not its likings. Reach your own apples."

* * *

A week later, the evening being unseasonably balmy and Witches Moon at first quarter near the top of the sky, a hemispherical silver goblet brimful of stars and scattering them dimmed by moonwine all over the sky as it descended toward the lips of the west, drawn down by the same goddess who had lifted it, Afreyt and Fafhrd after supping alone at her violet tinted pale house on Salthaven's northern edge were minded to wander across the great meadow in the direction of Elvenhold, a northward slanting slim rock spire two bowshots high, chimneyed and narrowly terraced, that thrust from the rolling fields almost a league away to the west.

"See how her tilt," Fafhrd observed of that slender mountainlet, "directs her at the dark boss of the Targe—" (naming the northernmost constellation in the Lankhmar heavens) "—as if she were granite arrow aimed at skytop by the gods of the underworld."

"Tonight the earth is full of the heat of these gods' forges, pressing summer scents from spring flowers and grasses. Let's rest a while," Afreyt answered, and truly although it was not yet May Eve, the heavy air was more like Midsummer's. She touched his shoulder and sank to the herby sward.

After a stare around the horizon for any sky wanderer on verge of rise or set, Fafhrd seated himself by her right side. A low lurhorn sounded faintly from the town behind them or the sea beyond that.

"Night fishers summoning the finny ones," he hazarded.

"I dreamed last night," she said, "that a beast thing came out of the sea and followed me dripping salt drops as I wandered through a dark wood. I could see its silver scales between the dark boles in the gloom. But I was not afeared, and it in turn seemed to respond to this cue, for the longer it followed me the less it became like a beast and the more like a seaperson, and come not to work a hurt on me but to warn me."

"Of what?" and when she was silent, "It's sex?"

"Why, female—" she answered at once, but then becoming doubtful "—I think. Had it sex? I wonder why I did not wait for it to catch up, or perhaps turn sudden and walk toward it? I think I felt, did I so, and although I feared it not, it would turn to a beast again, a deep-voiced beast."

"I too dreamed strangely last night, and my dream strangely chimed with yours, or was it by day I dreamed? For I have begun to do that," Fafhrd announced, dropping himself back at full length on the springy sward, the better to observe the seven spiraled stars of the Targe. "I dreamt I was pent in the greatest of castles with a million dark rooms in it, and that I searched for Gusorio (for that old legend between the Mouser and me is sometimes more than a joke) because I'd been solemnly told, perchance in a dream within the dream, that he had a message for me."

She turned and leaned over him, her eyes staring deep into him as she listened. Her palely golden hair fell forward in two sweeping smooth cascades over her shoulders. He readjusted his position slightly so that five of the stars of Targe rose in a semicircle from her forehead (his eyes straying now and again toward her shadowed throat and the silver cord lacing together the sides of her violet bodice) and he continued, "In the twelve times twelve times twelfth room there stood at the far door a figure clad all in silver scale mail (there's our dreams chiming) but its back was toward me and the longer I looked at it, the taller and skinnier it seemed than Gusorio should be. Nevertheless I cried out to it aloud and in the very instant of my calling knew that I'd made an irreparable mistake and that my voice would work a hideous change in it and to my harm. See, our dreams clink again? But then, as it started to turn, I awoke. Dearest princess, did you know that the Targe crowns you?" And his right hand moved toward the silver bow drooping below her throat as she bent down to kiss him.

But as he enjoyed those pleasures and their continuations and proliferations while the moon sank, which pleasures were greatly enhanced by their starry background, the far ecstacies complementing the near, he marveled how these nights he seemed to be walking at once toward brightest life and darkest death, while through it all Elvenhold loomed in the low distance.

*　　*　　*

"No question on it, Captain Mouser's changed," Pshawri said with certainty, yet also amazedly and apprehensively, to his fellow lieutenant Mikkidu as they tippled together two evenings later in a small booth of the Sea Wrack. "Here's yet another example if't be needed. You know the care he has for our grub, to see that cookie doesn't poison us. Normally he'll taste a spoon of stew, say what it lacks or not, even order it dumped (that happened once, remember?) and go dancing off. Yet this very afternoon I spied him standing before the roiling soup kettle and staring into it for as long as it takes to stow *Flotsam's* mainsail and then rig it again, watching it bubble and seethe with greatest interest, the beans and fish flakes bobbing and the turnips and carrots turning over, as though he were reading there auguries and prognostics on the fate of the world!"

Mikkidu nodded, "Or else he's trotting about bent over like Mother Grum, seeing things even an ant ignores. He had me stooping about after him over a route that could have been the plan of a maze, pointing out in turn a tangle of hair combings, a penny, a pebble, a parchment scrap scribbled with runic, mouse droppings, and a dead cockroach."

"Did he make you eat it?" asked Pshawri.

Mikkidu shook his head wonderingly. "No chewings . . . and no chewings out either.

He only said at the end, when my legs had started to cramp, 'I want you to keep these matters in mind in the future.'"

"And meantime Captain Fafhrd—"

The two semi-rehabilitated thieves looked up. Skor from the next booth had thrust over his balding head, worry-wrinkled, which now loomed above them. "—is so busy keeping watch on the stars by night—and by day too, somehow—that it's a wonder he can navigate Salthaven without breaking his neck. Think you some evil wight has put a spell on both?"

Normally the Mouser's and Fafhrd's men were mutually rivalrous, suspicious, and disparaging of each other. It was a measure of their present concern for their captains that they pooled their knowledge and took frank counsel together.

Pshawri shrugged as hugely as one so small was able. "Who knows? 'Tis such footling matters, and yet . . ."

"Chill ills abound here," Mikkidu intoned. "Khahkht the Wizard of Ice, Stardock's ghost fliers, sunken Simorgya . . ."

*　　*　　*

At the same moment Cif and Afreyt in the former's sauna chatted together with even greater but more playful freedom. Afreyt confided with mock grandeur, "I'll have you know that Fafhrd compared my niplets to stars."

Cif chortled midst the steam and answered coarsely with mock pride, "The Mouser likened my arse hole to one. *And* to the stem dimple of a pome. And his own intrusive member to a stiletto! Whate'er ails them doesn't show in bed."

"Or does it?" Afreyt questioned laughingly. "In my case, stars. In yours, fruits and cutlery too."

*　　*　　*

As the Deaths of Fafhrd and the Mouser jounced on donkeyback at the tail of a small merchant troop to which they'd attached themselves traveling through the forested land of the Eight Cities from Kvarch Nar to Illik Ving, Witches Moon being full, the former observed, "The trouble with these long incarnations as the death of another is that one begins to forget one's own proper persona and best interests, especially if one be a dedicated actor."

"Not so, necessarily," the other responded. "Rather, it gives one a clear head (What head clearer than Death's?) to observe oneself dispassionately and examine without bias the terms of the contract under which one operates."

"That's true enough," Fafhrd's Death said, stroking his lean jaw while his donkey stepped along evenly for a change. "Why think you this one talks so much of booty we may find?"

"Why else but that Arth-Pulgh and Hamomel expect there will be treasure on our intendeds or about them? There's a thought to warm the cold nights coming!"

"Yes, and raises a nice question in our order's law, whether we're being hired principally as assassins or robbers."

"No matter that," Death of the Mouser summed up. "We know at least we must not hit the Twain until they've shown us where their treasure is."

581

"Or treasurers are, more like," the other amended, "if they distrust each other, as all sane men do."

*　　*　　*

Coming in opposite directions around a corner behind Salthaven's coucil hall after a sharp rainshower, the Mouser and Fafhrd bumped into each other because the one was bending down to inspect a new puddle while the other studied the clouds retreating from arrows of sunshine. After grappling together briefly with sharp growls that turned to sudden laughter, Fafhrd was shaken enough from his current preoccupations by this small surprise to note the look of puzzled and wondrous brooding that instantly replaced the sharp friendly grin on the Mouser's face—a look that was undersurfaced by a pervasive sadness.

His heart was touched and he asked, "Where've you been keeping yourself, comrade? I never seem to see you to talk to these past days."

"'Tis true," the Mouser replied with a sharp grimace, "we do seem to be operating on different *levels*, you and I, in our movings around Salthaven this last moon-wax."

"Yes, but where are your *feelings* keeping?" Fafhrd prompted.

Heart-touched in turn and momentarily impelled to seek to share deepest and least definable difficulties, the Mouser drew Fafhrd to the lane side and launched out, "If you said I were homesick for Lankhmar, I'd call you liar! Our jolly comrades and grand almost-friends there, yes, even those good not to be trusted female troopers in memory revered, and all their perfumed and painted blazonry of ruby (or mayhap emerald?) lips, delectable tits, exquisite genitalia, they draw me not a whit! Not even Sheelba with her deep diggings into my psyche, nor your spicedly garrulous Ning. Nor all the gorgeous palaces, piers, pyramids, and fanes, all that marble and cloud-capped biggery! But oh . . ." and the underlook of sadness and wonder became *keen* in his face as he drew Fafhrd closer, dropping his voice, ". . . the *small things*—those, I tell you honest, *do* make me homesick, aye yearningly so. The little street braziers, the lovely litter, as though each scraps were sequined and bore hieroglyphs. The hennaed and the diamond dusted footprints. I knew those things, yet I never looked at them closely enough, savored the *details*. Oh, the thought of going back and counting the cobblestones in the Street of the Gods and fixing forever in my memory the shape of each and tracing the course of the rivulets of rainy trickle between them! I'd want to be rat size again to do it properly, yes even ant size, oh there is no end to this fascination, the universe written in a pebble!"

And he stared desperately deep into Fafhrd's eyes to ascertain if that one had caught at least some shred of his meaning, but the big man whose questions had stirred him to speak from his inmost being had apparently lost the track himself somewhere, for his long face had gone blank again, blank with a faint tone of melancholia and eyes wandering doubtfully upward.

"Homesick for Lankhmar?" the big man was saying. "Well, I do miss her stars, I must confess, her southern stars we cannot see from here. But oh . . ." And now *his* face and eyes fired for the brief span it took him to say the following words, ". . . the thought of the still more southern stars we've never seen! The untraveled southern continent below the Middle Sea. Godsland and Nehwon's life pole and over 'em the stars a world of men have died and never seen. Yes, I am homesick for those lands indeed!"

The Mouser saw the flare in him dim and die. The Northerner shook his head. "My

582

mind wanders," he said. "There are a many of good enough stars here. Why carry worries afar? Their sorting is sufficient."

"Yes, there are good pickings now here along Hurricane street and Salt, and leave the gods to worry over themselves," the Mouser heard himself say as his gaze dropped to the nearest puddle. He felt *his* flare die—if it had ever been. "Things will shake down, get done, sort themselves out, and feelings too."

Fafhrd nodded and they went their separate ways.

* * *

And so time passed on Rime Isle. Witches Moon grew full and wanted and gave way to Ghostsmoon, which lived its wraith-short life in turn, and Midsummer Moon was born, sometimes called Murderers Moon because its full runs low and is the latest to rise and earliest to set of all full moons, not high and long like the full moons of winter.

And with the passage of time things did shake down and some of them got done and sorted out after a fashion, meaning mostly that the out of the way became the commonplace with repetition, as it has a way of doing.

Seahawk got fully repaired, even refitted, but Fafhrd's and Afreyt's plan to sail her to Ool Plerns and fell timber there for wood-poor Rime Isle got pushed into the future. No one said, "Next summer," but the thought was there.

And the barracks and warehouse got built, including a fine drainage system and a cesspool of which the Mouser was inordinately proud, but repairs to *Flotsam*, though hardly languishing, went slow, and Cif's and his plan to cruise her east and trade with the Ice Gnomes north of No-Ombrulsk even more visionary.

Mog, Kos, and Issek's peculiar curses continued to shape much of the Twain's behavior (to the coarse-grained amusement of those small-time gods), but not so extremely as to interfere seriously with their ability to boss their men effectively or be sufficiently amusing, gallant, and intelligent with their female co-mates. Most of their men soon catalogued it under the heading "captains' eccentricities," to be griped at or boasted of equally but no further thought of. Skor, Pshawri, and Mikkidu did not accept it quite so easily and continued to worry and wonder now and then and entertain dark suspicions as befitted lieutenants, men who are supposedly learning to be as imaginatively responsible as captains. While on the other hand the Rime Islers, including the crusty and measuredly friendly Groniger, found it a good thing, indicative that these wild allies and would-be neighbors, questional protégés of those headstrong freewomen Cif and Afreyt, were settling down nicely into law-abiding and hard-headed island ways. The Gray Mouser's concern with small material details particularly impressed them, according with their proverb: rock, wood, and flesh; all else a lie, or, more simply still: Mineral, Vegetable, Animal.

Afreyt and Cif knew there had been a change in the two men, all right, and so did our two heroes too, for that matter. But they were inclined to put it down to the weather or some deep upheaval of mood as had once turned Fafhrd religous and the Mouser calculatedly avaricious. Or else—who knows?—these might be the sort of things that happened to anyone who settled down. Oddly, neither considered the possibility of a curse, whether by god or sorcerer or witch. Curses were violent things that led men to cast themselves off mountaintops or dash their children's brains out against rocks, and women to castrate their bed partners and set fire to their own hair if there wasn't a handy volcano to dive into. The triviality and low intensity of the curses misled them.

When all four were together they talked once or twice of supernatural influences on human lives, speaking on the whole more lightly than each felt at heart.

"Why don't you ask augury of Great Gusorio?" Cif suggested. "Since you are shards of him, he should know all about both of you."

"He's more a joke than a true presence one might address a prayer to," the Mouser parried and then riposted, "why don't you or Afreyt appeal for enlightenment to that witch—or warrior-queen of yours, Skeldir, she of the silver scale-mail and the short dry laugh?"

"We're not on such intimate terms as that with her, though claiming her as ancestor," Cif answered, looking down diffidently. "I'd hardly know how to go about it."

Yet that dialogue led Afreyt and Fafhrd to recount the dreams they'd previously shared only with each other. Whereupon all four indulged in inconclusive speculations and guesses. The Mouser and Fafhrd promptly forgot these, but Cif and Afreyt stored them away in memory.

And although the curses on the Twain were of low intensity, the divine vituperations worked steadily and consumingly. Ensamples: Fafhrd became much interested in a dim hairy star low in the west that seemed to be slowly growing in brightness and luxuriance of mane and to be moving east against the current, and he made a point observing it early each eve. While it was noticed that the busily peering Captain Mouser had a favorite route for checking things out that led from the Sea Wrack, where he'd have a morning nip, to the low point in the lane outside, to the windy corner behind the council hall where he'd collided with Fafhrd, to his men's barracks and by way of the dormitory's closet, which he'd open and check for mouseholes, to his own room and shelfed closet and to the kitchen and pantry, and so to the cesspool behind them of which he was so proud.

So life went on tranquilly, busily, unenterprisingly in and around Salthaven as spring gave way to Rime Isle's short sharp summer. Their existence was rather like that of industrious lotus eaters, the others taking their cues from the bemused and somewhat absentminded Twain. The only exception to this most regular existence promised to be the day of Midsummer eve, a traditional Isle holiday, when at the two women's suggestion they planned a feast for all hands (and special Isle friends and associates) in the Great Meadow at Elvenhold's foot, a sort of picnic with dancing and games and athletic competitions.

*   *   *

If anyone could be said to have spent an unpleasant or unsatisfactory time during this period, it was the wizards Sheelba and Ningauble. The cosmic din had quieted down sufficiently for them to be able to communicate pretty well between the one's swamp hut and the other's cave and get some confused inkling of what Fafhrd and the Mouser and their gods were up to, but none of that inkling sounded very logical to them or favorable to their plot. The stupid provincial gods had put some unintelligible sort of curse on their two pet errand boys, and it was working after a fashion, but Mouser and Fafhrd hadn't left Rime Isle, nothing was working out according to the two wizards' wishes, while a disquieting adverse influence they could not identify was moving northwest across the Cold Waste north of the Land of the Eight Cities and the Trollstep Mountains. All very baffling and unsatisfactory.

*   *   *

At Illik Ving the Death of the Twain joined a caravan bound for No-Ombrulsk, changing their mounts for shaggy Mingol ponies inured to frost, and spent all of Ghostsmoon on that long traverse. Although early summer, there was sufficient chill in the Trollsteps and the foothills of the Bones of the Old Ones and in the plateau of the Cold Waste that lies between these ranges, for them to refer frequently to the seed bags of brazen apes and the tits of witches, and hug the cookfire while it lasted, and warm their sleep with dreams of the treasures their intendeds had laid up.

"I see this Fafhrd as a gold-guarding dragon in a mountain cave," his Death averred. "I'm into his character fully now, I feel. And onto it too."

"While I dream the Mouser as a fat gray spider," the other echoed, "with silver, amber, and leviathan ivory cached in a score of nooks, crannies, and corners he scuttles between. Yes, I can play him now. And play with him too. Odd, isn't it, how like we get to our intendeds at the end?"

Arriving at last at the stone-towered seaport, they took lodgings at an inn where badges of the Slayers' Brotherhood were recognized, and they slept for two nights and a day, recuperating. Then Mouser's Death went for a stroll down by the docks and when he returned, announced, "I've taken passage for us in an Ool Kroot trader. Sails with the tide day after tomorrow."

"Murderers Moon begins well," his wraith-thin comrade observed from where he still lay abed.

"At first the captain pretended not to know of Rime Isle, called it a legend, but when I showed him the badge and other things, he gave up that shipmasters' conspiracy of keeping Salthaven and western ports beyond a trade secret. By the by, our ship's called the *Good News*."

"An auspicious name," the other, smiling, responded. "Oh Mouser, and oh Fafhrd, dear, your twin brothers are hastening toward you."

*   *   *

After the long morning twilight that ended Midsummer Eve's short night, Midsummer Day dawned chill and misty in Salthaven. Nevertheless there was an early bustling around the kitchen of the barracks, where the Mouser and Fafhrd had taken their repose, and likewise at Afreyt's house, where Cif and their nieces May, Mara, and Gale had stayed overnight.

Soon the fiery sun, shooting his rays from the northeast as he began his longest loop south around the sky, had burnt the milky mist off all Rime Isle and showed her clear from the low roofs of Salthaven to the central hills with the leaning tower of Elvenhold in the near middle distance and the Great Meadow rising gently toward it.

And soon after that an irregular procession set out from the barracks. It wandered crookedly and leisurely through town to pick up the men's women, chiefly by trade, at least in their spare time, sailorwives, and other island guests. The men took turns dragging a cart piled with hampers of barley cakes, sweetbreads, cheese, roast mutton and kid, fruit conserves and other Island delicacies, while at its bottom packed in snow were casks of the Isle's dark bitter ale. A few men blew woodflutes and strummed small harps.

At the docks Groniger, festive in holiday black, joined them with the news. "The *Northern Star* out of Ool Plerns came in last even to No-Ombrulsk. I spoke with her master and he said the *Good News* out of Ool Kroot was at last report sailing for Rime Isle one or two mornings after him."

At this point Ourph the Mingol begged off from the party, protesting that the walk to Elvenhold would be too much for his old bones and a new crick in his left ankle, he'd rest them in the sun here, and they left him squatting his skinny frame on the warming stone and peering steadily out to sea past where *Seahawk, Flotsam, Northern Star,* and other ships rode at anchor among the Island fishing sloops.

Fafhrd said to Groniger, "I've been here a year and more and it still wonders me that Salthaven is such a busy port while the rest of Nehwon goes on thinking Rime Isle a legend. I know *I* did for a half lifetime."

"Legends travel on rainbow wings and sport gaudy colors," the harbormaster answered him, "while truth plods on in sober garb."

"Like yourself?"

"Aye," Groniger grunted happily.

"And 'tis not a legend to the captains, guild masters, and kings who profit by it," the Mouser put in. "Such do most to keep legends alive." The little man (though not little at all among his corps of thieves) was in a merry mood, moving from group to group and cracking wise and gay to all and sundry.

Skullick, Skor's sub-lieutenant, struck up a berserk battle chant and Fafhrd found himself singing an Ilthmar sea chanty to it. At their next pick-up point tankards of ale were passed out to them. Things grew jollier.

A little ways out into the Great Meadow, where the thoroughfare led between fields of early ripening Island barley, they were joined by the feminine procession from Afreyt's. These had packed their contribution of toothsome edibles and tastesome potables in two small red carts drawn by stocky white bearhounds big as small men but gentle as lambs. And they had been augmented by the sailorwives and fisherwomen Hilsa and Rill, whose gift to the feast was jars of sweet-pickled fish. Also by the witch-woman Mother Grum, as old as Ourph but hobbling along stalwartly, never known to have missed a feast in her life's long history.

They were greeted with cries and new singings, while the three girls ran to play with the children the larger procession had inevitably accumulated on its way through town.

Fafhrd went back for a bit to quizzing Groniger about the ships that called at Salthaven port, flourishing the hook that was in his left hand, for emphasis. "I've heard it said, and seen some evidence for it too, myself, that some of them hail from ports that are nowhere on Nehwon seas I know of."

"Ah, you're becoming a convert to the legends," the black-clad man told him. Then, mischeivously, "Why don't you try casting the ships' horoscopes with all you've learned of stars of late, naked and hairy ones?" He frowned. "Though there was a black cutter with a white line that watered here three days ago whose home port I wish I could be surer of. Her master put me off from going below, and her sails didn't look enough for her hull. He said she hailed from Sayend, but that's a seaport we've had reliable word that the Sea-Mingols burned to ash less than two years agone. He knew of that, he claimed. Said it was much exaggerated. But I couldn't place his accent."

"You see?" Fafhrd told him. "As for horoscopes, I have neither skill or belief in astrology. My sole concern is with the stars themselves and the patterns they make. The hairy star's most interesting! He grows each night. At first I thought him a rover, but he keeps his place. I'll point him out to you come dark."

"Or some other evening when there's less drinking," the other allowed grudgingly. "A wise man is suspicious of his interests other than the most necessary. They breed illusions."

The groupings kept changing as they walked, sang, and danced—and played—their way up through the rustling grass. Cif took advantage of this mixing to seek out Pshawri and Mikkidu. The Mouser's two lieutenants had at first been suspicious of her interest in and influence over their captain—a touch of jealousy, no doubt—but honest dealing and speaking, the evident genuineness of her concern, and some furtherance of Pshawri's suit to an Island woman had won them over, so that the three thought of themselves in a limited way as confederates.

"How's Captain Mouser these days?" she asked them lightly. "Still running his little morning check-up route?"

"He didn't today," Mikkidu told her.

"While yesterday he ran it in the afternoon," Pshawri amplified. "And the day before that he missed."

Mikkidu nodded.

"I don't fret about him o'er much," she smiled at them, "knowing he's under watchful and sympathetic eyes."

And so with mutual buttering up and with singing and dancing the augmented holiday band arrived at the spot just south of Elvenhold that they'd selected for their picnic. A portion of the food was laid out on white-sheeted trestles, the drink was broached, and the competitions and games that comprised an important part of the day's program were begun. These were chiefly trials of strength and skill, not of endurance, and one trial only, so that a reasonable or even somewhat unreasonable amount of eating and drinking didn't tend to interfere with performance too much.

Between the contests were somewhat less impromptu dancings than had been footed earlier: Island stamps and flings, old-fashioned Lankhmar sways, and kicking and bouncing dances copied from the Mingols.

Knife-throwing came early—"so none will be mad drunk as yet, a sensible precaution," Groniger approved.

The target was a yard section of mainland tree-truck almost two yards thick, lugged up the previous day. The distance was fifteen long paces, which meant two revolutions of the knife the way most contestants threw. The Mouser waited until last and then threw underhand as a sort of handicap, or at least seeming handicap, against himself, and his knife embedded deeply in or near the center, clearly a better shot than any of the earlier successful ones, whose points of impact were marked with red chalk.

A flurry of applause started, but then it was announced that Cif had still to throw; she'd entered at the last possible minute. There was no surprise at a woman entering; that sort of equality was accepted on the Isle.

"You didn't tell me beforehand you were going to," the Mouser said to her.

She shook her head at him, concentrating on her aim. "No, leave his dagger in," she called to the judges. "It won't distract me."

She threw overhand and her knife impacted itself so close to his that there was a *klir* of metal against metal along with the woody *thud.* Groniger measured the distances carefully with his beechwood ruler and proclaimed Cif the winner.

"And the measures on this ruler are copied from those on the golden Rule of Prudence in the Island treasury," he added impressively, but later qualified this by saying, "actually my ruler's more accurate than that ikon; doesn't expand with heat and contract with cold as metals do. But some people don't like to keep hearing me say that."

"Do you think her besting the captain is good for discipline and all?" Mikkidu asked Pshawri in an undertone, his new trust in Cif wavering.

"Yes, I do!" that one whispered back. "Do the Captain good to be shook up a little, what with all this old-man scurrying and worrying and prying and pointing out he's going in for." *There,* he thought, *I've spoken it out to someone at last and I'm glad I did!*

Cif smiled at the Mouser. "No, I didn't tell you ahead of time," she said sweetly, "but I've been practicing—privately. Would it have made a difference?"

"No," he said slowly, "though I might have had second thoughts about throwing underhand. Are you planning to enter the slinging contest too?"

"No, never a thought of it," she answered. "Whatever made you think I might?"

Later the Mouser won that one, both for distance and accuracy, making the latter cast so powerful that it not only holed the center of the bull's-eye into the padded target box but went through the heavier back of the latter as well. Cif begged for the battered slug as a souvenir, and he presented it to her with elaborate flourishes.

"'Twould have pierced the cuirass of Mingsward!" Mikkidu fervently averred.

The archery contests were beginning, and Fafhrd was fitting the iron tang in the middle of his bow into the hardwood heading of the leather stall that covered half his left forearm, when he noted Afreyt approaching. She'd doffed her jacket, for the sun was beating down hotly, and was wearing a short-sleeved violet blouse, blue trousers wide-belted with a gold buckle, and purple-dyed short holiday boots. A violet handkerchief confined a little her pale gold hair. A worn green quiver with one arrow in it hung from her shoulder, and she was carrying a big longbow.

Fafhrd's eyes narrowed a bit at those, recalling Cif and the knife throwing. But "You look like a pirate queen," he greeted her and then only inquired, "you're entering one of the contests?"

"I don't know," she said with a shrug. "I'll watch along through the first."

"That bow," he said casually, "looks to me to have a very heavy pull and tall as you are, to be a touch long for you."

"Right on both counts," she agreed, nodding. "It belonged to my father. You'd be truly startled, I think, to see how I managed to draw it as a stripling girl. My father would doubtless have spanked me soundly if he'd ever caught me at it, or rather lived long enough to do that."

Fafhrd lifted his eyebrows inquiringly, but the pirate queen vouchsafed no more. He won the distance shot handily but lost the target shot (through which Afreyt also watched) by a fingersbreadth to Skor's other sub-lieutenant Mannimark.

Then came the high shot, which was something special to Midsummer Day on Rime Isle and generally involved the loss of the contestant's arrow, for the target was a grassy, nearly vertical stretch on the upper half of the south face of Elvenhold. The north face of the slanting rock tower actually overhung the ground a little and was utterly barren, but the south face, though very steep, sloped enough to hold soil to support herbage, rather miraculously. The contest honored the sun, which reached this day his highest point in the heavens, while the contesting arrows, identified by colored rags of thinnest silk attached to their necks, emulated him in their efforts.

Then Afreyt stepped forward, kicked off her purple boots, and rolled up her blue trousers above her knees. She plucked her arrow, which bore a violet silk, from her quiver and threw that aside. "Now I'll reveal to you the secret of my girlish technique," she said to Fafhrd.

Quite rapidly she sat down facing the dizzy slope, set the bow to her bare feet, laying the arrow between her big toes and holding it and the string with both hands, rolled back onto her shoulders, straightened her legs smoothly, and loosed her shot.

It was seen to strike the slope near Fafhrd's yellow, skid a few yards higher, and then lie there, a violet taunt.

Afreyt, bending her legs again, removed the bow from her feet, and rolling sharply forward, stood up in the same motion.

"You practiced that," Fafhrd said, hardly accusingly, as he finished screwing the hook back in the stall on his left arm.

She nodded. "Yes, but only for half a lifetime."

"The lady Afreyt's arrow didn't stick in," Skullick pointed out. "Is that fair? A breath of wind might dislodge it."

"Yes, but there is no wind and it somehow got highest," Groniger pointed out to him. "Actually it's accounted lucky in the high shot if your arrow doesn't embed itself. Those that don't sometimes are blown down. Those that do stay up there are never recovered."

"Doesn't someone go up and collect the arrows?" Skullick asked.

"Scale Elvenhold? Have you wings?"

Skullick eyed the rock tower and shook his head sheepishly. Fafhrd overheard Groniger's remarks and gave the harbormaster an odd look but made no other comment at the time.

Afreyt invited both of them over to the red dogcarts and produced a jug of Ilthmar brandy, and they toasted her and Fafhrd's victories—the Mouser's too and Cif's, who happened along.

"This'll put feathers in your wings!" Fafhrd told Groniger, who eyed him thoughtfully.

The children were playing with the white bearhounds. Gale had won the girls' archery contest and May the short race.

Some of the younger children were becoming fretful, however, and shadows were lengthening. The games and contests were all over now, and partly as a conquence of that the drinking was heavying up as the last scraps of food were being eaten. Among the whole picnic group there seemed to be a feeling of weariness but also (for those no longer very young but not yet old) new jollity, as though one party were ending and another beginning. Cif's and Afreyt's eyes were especially bright. Everyone seemed ready to go home, though whether to their own places or the Sea Wrack was a matter of age and temperament. There was a chill breath in the air.

Gazing east and down a little toward Salthaven and the harbor beyond, the Mouser opined that he could already see low mist gathering around the bare masts there, and Groniger confirmed that. But what was the small lone dark figure trudging up-meadow toward them in the face of the last low sunlight?

"Ourph, I'll be bound," said Fafhrd. "What's led him to make the hike after all?"

But it was hard to be sure the big northerner was right; the figure was still far off. Yet the signal for leaving had been given, things were gathered, the carts repacked, and all set out, most staying near the carts, from which drinks continued to be forthcoming. And perhaps these were responsible for a resumption of the morning's impromptu singing and dancing, though now it was not Fafhrd and the Mouser but others who took the lead in this. The Twain, after a whole day of behaving like old times, were slipping back under the curses they knew not of, the one's eyes forever on the ground, with the effect of old age unsure of its footing, the other's on the sky, indicative of old age's absent-mindness.

Fafhrd turned out to be right about the up-meadow trudger, but it was few words they got from Ourph as to why he'd made the hike he'd earlier begged off from.

The old Mingol said only to them, and to Groniger, who happed to be by, "The *Good News* is in." Then, eyeing the Twain more particularly, "Tonight stay away from the Sea Wrack."

But he would answer nothing more to their puzzled queries save, "I know what I know and I've told it," and two cups of brandy did not loosen his Mingol tongue one whit.

The encounter put them behind the main party, but they did not try to catch up. The sun had set some time back, and now their feet and legs were lapped by the ground mist that already covered Salthaven and into which the picnic party was vanishing, its singing and strumming already sounding tiny and far off.

"You see," Groniger said to Fafhrd and eyeing the twilt but yet starless sky while the mist lapped higher around them, "you won't be able to show me your bearded star tonight in any case."

Fafhrd nodded vaguely but made no other answer save to pass the brandy jug as they footed it along: four men walking deeper and deeper, as it were, into a white silence.

*   *   *

Cif and Afreyt, very much caught up in the gayety of evening party and bright-eyed drunk besides, were among the first to enter the Sea Wrack and encounter arresting silence of another sort, and almost instantly come under the strange, hushing spell of the scene there.

Fafhrd and the Mouser sat at their pet table in the low-walled booth playing backgammon, and the whole tavern frightenedly watched them while pretending not to. Fear was in the air.

That was the first impression. Then, almost at once, Cif and Afreyt saw that Fafhrd couldn't be Fafhrd, he was much too thin; nor the Mouser the Mouser, much too plump (though every bit as agile and supple-looking, paradoxically).

Nor were the faces and clothing and accouterments of the two strangers anything really like the Twain's. It was more their expressions and mannerisms, postures and general manner, self-confident manner, those and the fact of *being at that table*. The sublime impression the two of them made that they were who they were and that they were in their rightful place.

And the fear that radiated from them with the small sounds of their gaming; the muted rattle of shaken bone dice in one or the other's palm-closed leather cup, the muted clatter as the dice were spilled into one or other of the two low-walled felt-lined compartments of the backgammon box, the sharp little clicks of the bone counters as they were shifted by ones and twos from point to point. The fear that riveted the attention of everyone else in the place no matter how much they pretended to be understanding the conversations they made, or tasting the drinks they swallowed, or busying themselves with little tavern chores. The fear that seized upon and recruited each picnic newcomer. Oh yes, this night something deadly was coiling here at the Sea Wrack, make no mistake about it.

So paralyzing was the fear that it cost Cif and Afreyt a great effort to sidle slowly from the doorway to the bar, their eyes never leaving that one little table that was for

590

now the world's hub, until they were as close as they could get to the Sea Wrack's owner, who with downcast and averted eye was polishing the same mug over and over.

"Keeper, what gives?" Cif whispered to him softly but most distinctly. "Nay, sull not up. Speak, I charge you!"

Eagerly that one, as though grateful Cif's whiplash command had given him opportunity to discharge some of the weight of dread crushing him, whispered them back his tale in short, almost breathless bursts, though without raising an eye or ceasing to circle his rag.

"I was alone here when they came in, minutes after the *Good News* docked. They spoke no word, but as though the fat one were the lean one's hunting ferret, they *scented out* our two captains' table, sat themselves down at it as though they owned it, then spoke at last to call for drink.

"I took it them, and as they got out their box and dice cups and set up their game, they plied me with harmless seeming and friendly questions mostly about the Twain, as if they knew them well. Such as: How fared they in Rime Isle? Enjoyed they good health? Seemed they happy? How often came they in? Their tastes in drink and food and the fair sex? What other interests had they? What did they like to talk of? As though the two of them were courtiers of some great foreign empire come hither our captains to please and to solicit about some affair of state.

"And yet, you know, so *dire* somehow were the tones in which those innocent questions were asked that I doubt I could have refused them if they'd asked me for the Twain's hearts-blood or my own.

"This too: The more questions they asked about the Twain and the more I answered them as best I might, the more they came to look like . . . to resemble our . . . you know what I'm trying to say?"

"Yes, yes!" Afreyt hissed. "Go on."

"In short, I felt I was their salve. So too, I think, have felt all those who came into the Sea Wrack after them, save for old Mingol Ourph, who shortly stayed, somehow then parted.

"At last they sucked me dry, bent to their game, asked for more drink. I sent the girl with that. Since then it's been as you see now."

There was a stir at the doorway through which mist was curling. Four men stood there, for a moment bemused. Then Fafhrd and the Mouser strode toward their table, while old Ourph settled down on his hams, his gaze unwavering, and Groniger almost totteringly sidled toward the bar, like a man surprised at midday by a sleepwalking fit and thoroughly astounded at it.

Fafhrd and the Mouser leaned over and looked down at the table and open backgammon box over which the two strangers were bent, surveying their positions. After a bit Fafhrd said rather loudly, "A good rilk against two silver smerduke on the lean one! His stones are poised to fleet swiftly home."

"You're on!" the Mouser cried back. "You've underestimated the fat one's back game."

Turning his chill blue eyes and flat-nosed skull-like face straight up at Fafhrd with an almost impossible twist of his neck, the skinny one said, "Did the stars tell you to wager at such odds on my success?"

Fafhrd's whole manner changed. "You're interested in the stars?" he asked with an incredulous hopefulness.

"Mightily so," the other answered him, nodding emphatically.

"Then you must come with me," Fafhrd informed him, almost lifting him from his stool with one fell swoop of his good hand and arm that at once assisted and guided, while his hook indicated the mist-filled doorway. "Leave off this footling game. Abandon it. We've much to talk of, you and I." By now he had a brotherly arm—the hooked one, this time—around the thin one's shoulders and was leading him back along the path he'd entered by. "Oh, there are wonders and treasures undreamed amongst the stars, are there not?"

"Tresures?" the other asked cooly, pricking an ear but holding back a little.

"Aye, indeed! There's one in particular under the silvery asterism of the Black Panther that I lust to show you," Fafhrd replied with great enthusiasm, at which the other went more willingly.

All watched astonishedly, but the only one who managed to speak out was Groniger, who asked, "Where are you going, Fafhrd?" in rather outraged tones.

The big man paused for a moment, winked at Groniger, and smiling said, "Flying."

Then with a "Come, comrade astronomer," said another great arm-sweep, he wafted the skinny one with him into the bulging white mist, where both men shortly vanished.

Back at the table the plump stranger said in loud but winning tones, "Gentle sir! Would you care to take over my friend's game, continue it with me?" Then in tones less formal, "And have you noticed that these mug dints on your table together with the platter burn make up the figure of a giant sloth?"

"Oh, so you've already seen that, have you?" the Mouser answered the second question, returning his gaze from the door. Then, to the second, "Why, yes, I will, sir, and double the bet!—it being my die cast. Although your friend did not stay long enough even to arrange a chouette."

"*Your* friend was most insistent," the other replied. "Sir, I take your bet."

Whereupon the Mouser sat down and proceeded to shake a masterly sequence of double fours and double threes so that the skinny man's stones, now his own, fleeted more swiftly to victory than ever Fafhrd had predicted. The Mouser grinned fiendishly, and as they set up the stones for another game, he pointed out to his more thinly smiling adversary in the table top's dints and stains the figure of a leopard stalking the giant sloth.

All eyes were now back on the table again save those of Afreyt. And of Fafhrd's lieutenant Skor. Those four orbs were still fixed on the mist-bulging doorway through which Fafhrd had vanished with his strangely unlike doublegoer. Since babyhood Afreyt had heard of those doleful nightwalkers whose appearance, like the banshee's, generally betokened death or near mortal injury to the one whose shape they mocked.

Now while she agonized over what to do, invoking the witch queen Skeldir and lesser of her own and (in her extremity) others' private deities, there was a strange growling in her ears—perhaps her rushing blood. Fafhrd's last word to Groniger kindled in her memory the recollection of an exchange of words between those two earlier today, which in turn gave her a bright inkling of Fafhrd's present destination in the viewless fog. This in turn inspired her to break the grip upon her of fear's and indecision's paralysis. Her first two or three steps were short and effortful ones but by the time she went through the doorway she was taking swift giant strides.

Her example broke the dread-duty deadlock in Skor and the lean, red-haired, balding giant followed her in a rush.

But few in the Sea Wrack except Ourph and perhaps Groniger noted either departure, for all gazes were fixed again on the one small table where now Captain Mouser in person contested with his dread were-brother, battling the Islanders' and his men's fears for them as it were. And whether by smashing attack, tortuous back game, or swift running one like the first, the Mouser kept winning again and again and again.

And still the games went on, as though the series might well outlast the night. The stranger's smile kept thinnning. That was all, or almost all.

The only fly in this ointment of unending success was a nagging doubt, perhaps deriving from a growing languor on the Mouser's part, a lessening of his taunting joy at each new win, that destinies in the larger world would jump with those worked out in the little world of the backgammon box.

*   *   *

"We have reached the point in this night's little journey I'm taking you on where we must abandon the horizontal and embrace the vertical," Fafhrd informed his comrade astronomer, clasping him familiarly about the shoulders with his left hand and arm, and wagging the forefinger of his right before the latter's cadaver face, while the white mist hugged them both.

The Death of Fafhrd fought down the impulse to squirm away with a hawking growl of disgust close to vomiting. He abominated being touched except by outstandingly beautiful females under circumstances entirely of his own commanding. And now for a full half-hour he had been following his drunken and crazy victim (sometimes much too closely for comfort, but that wasn't his own choosing, Aarth forbid) through a blind fog, and mostly trusting the same madman to keep them from breaking their necks in holes and pits and bogs, and putting up with being touched and arm-gripped and back-slapped (often by that doubly disgusting hook that felt so like a weapon), and listening to a farrago of wild talk about long-haired asterisms and bearded stars and barley fields and sheep's grazing ground and hills and masts and trees and the mysterious southern continent until Aarth himself couldn't have held it, so that it was only the madman's occasional remention of a treasure or treasures he was leading his Death to that kept the latter tagging along without plunging exasperated knife into his victim's vitals.

And at least the loathsome cleavings and enwrappings expressive of brotherly affection that he had made himself submit to had allowed him to ascertain in turn that his intended wore no undergarment of chain mail or plate or scale to interfere with the proper course of things when knife time came. So the Death of Fafhrd consoled himself as he broke away from the taller and heavier man under the legitimate and friendly excuse of more closely inspecting the rock wall they now faced at a distance of no more than four or five yards. Farther off the fog would have hid it.

"You say we're to climb this to view your treasure?" He couldn't quite keep his incredulity out of his voice.

"Aye," Fafhrd told him.

"How high?" his Death asked him.

Fafhrd shrugged. "Just high enough to get there. A short distance, truly." He waved an arm a little sideways, as though dispensing with a trifle.

"There's not much light to climb by," his Death said somewhat tentatively.

Fafhrd replied, "What think you makes the mist whitely luminous an hour after sunset? There's enough light to climb by, never fear, and it'll get brighter as we go aloft. You're a climber, aren't you?"

"Oh, yes," the other admitted diffidently, not saying that his experience had been gained chiefly in scaling impregnable towers and cyclopean poisoned walls behind which the wealthier and more powerful assassin's targets tended to hide themselves—difficult climbs, some of them, truly, but rather artificial ones, and all of them done in the line of business.

Touching the rough rock and seeing it inches in front of his somewhat blunted nose, the Death of Fafhrd felt a measurable repugnance to setting foot or serious hand on it. For a moment he was mightily minded to whip out dagger and end it instanter here with the swift upward jerk under the breastbone, or the shrewd thrust from behind at the base of the skull, or the well-known slash under the ear in the angle of the jaw. He'd never have his victim more lulled, that was certain.

Two things prevented him. One, he'd never had the feeling of having an audience so completely under his control as he'd had this afternoon and evening at the Sea Wrack. Or a victim so completely eating out of his hand, so walking to his own destruction, as they said in the trade. It gave him a feeling of being intoxicated while utterly sober, it put him into an "I can do anything, I am God" mood, and he wanted to prolong that wonderful thrill as far as possible.

Two, Fafhrd's talk perpetually returning to treasure, and the way the invitation now to climb some small cliff to view it so fitted with his Cold Waste dreams of Fafhrd as a dragon guarding gold in a mountain cavern—combined to persuade him that the Fates were taking a hand in tonight's happening, the youngest of them drawing aside veil and baring her ruby lips to him and soon the more private jewelry of her person.

"You don't have to worry about the rock, it's sound enough, just follow in my footsteps and my handholds," Fafhrd told him impatiently as he advanced to the cliff's face and mounted past him, the hook making harsh metallic clashes.

His Death doffed the short cloak and hood he wore, took a deep breath and, thinking in a small corner of his mind, "Well, at least he won't be able to fondle me more while we're climbing—I hope!" went up after him like a giant spider.

It was as well for Fafhrd that his Death (and the Mouser's too) had neglected to make close survey of the landscape and geography of Rime Isle during this afternoon's sail in. (They'd been down in their cabin mostly, getting into their parts.) Otherwise he might have known that he was now climbing Elvenhold.

*   *   *

Back in the Sea Wrack the Mouser threw a double six, the only cast that would allow him to bear off his last four stones and leave his opponent's sole remaining man stranded one point from home. He threw up the back of a hand to mask a mighty yawn and over it politely raised an inquiring eyebrow at his adversary.

The Death of the Mouser nodded amiably enough, though his smile had grown very thin-lipped indeed, and said, "Yes, it's as well we write finished to my strivings. Was it eight games, or seven? No matter. I'll seek my revenge some other time. Fate is your girl tonight, cunt and arse hole, that much is proven."

A collective sigh of relief from the onlookers ended the general silence. They felt the relaxation of tension as much as the two players and to most of them it seemed that the Mouser in vanquishing the stranger had also dispersed all the strange fears that had been loose in the tavern earlier and running along their nerves.

"A drink to toast your victory, salve my defeat?" the Mouser's Death asked smoothly. "Hot Gahveh perhaps? With brandy in't?"

"Nay, sir," the Mouser said with a bright smile, collecting together his several small stacks of gold and silver pieces and funneling them into his pouch, "I must take these bright fellows home and introduce 'em to their cell mates. Coins prosper best in prison, as my friend Groniger tells me. But sir, would you not accompany me on that journey, help me escort 'em? We can drink there." A brightness came into his eyes that had nothing whatever in common with a miser's glee. He continued, "Friend who discerned the tree sloth and saw the black panther, we both know that there are mysterious treasures and matters of interest compared to which these clinking counters are no more than that. I yearn to show you some. You'll be intrigued."

At the mention of "treasure," his Death pricked up his ears much as his fellow assassin had at Fafhrd's speaking the word. Mouser's would-be nemesis had had his Cold Waste dreams too, his appetites whetted by the privations of long drear journeying, and by the infuriating losses he'd had to put up with tonight as well. And he too had the conviction that the fates must be on his side tonight by now, though for the opposite reason. A man who'd been so incredibly lucky at backgammon was bound to be hit by a great bolt of unluck at whatever feat he next attempted.

"I'll come with you gladly," he said softly, rising with the Mouser and moving with him toward the door.

"You'll not collect your dice and stones?" the one queried. "'Tis a most handsome box."

"Let the tavern have it as a memorial of your masterly victory," his Death replied negligently, with a sort of muted grandiloquence. He tossed aside an imaginary blossom.

Ordinarily *that* would have been too much to the Mouser, arousing all his worst suspicions. Only rogues pretended to be *that* carelessly munificent. But the madness with which Mog had cursed him was fully upon him again, and he forgot the matter with a smile and a shrug.

"Trifles both," he agreed.

In fact the manner of the two of them was so lightly casual for the moment, not to say la-di-da, that they might well have gotten out of the Sea Wrack and lost in the fog without anyone noticing, except of course for old Ourph, whose head turned slowly to watch the Mouser out the door, shook itself sadly, and then resumed its mediations or cogitations or whatever.

Fortunately there were those in the tavern deeply and intelligently concerned for the Mouser, and not bound by Mingolly fatalisms. Cif had no impulse to rush up to the Mouser upon his win. She'd had too strong a sense of something more than backgammon being at stake tonight, too lingering a conviction of something positively unholy about his were-adversary, and doubtless others in the tavern had shared those feelings. Unlike most of those, however, any relief she felt did not take her attention away from the Mouser for an instant. As he and his unwholesome doublegoer exited the doorway she hurried to it.

Pshawri and Mikkidu were at her heels.

They say the two ahead of them as dim blobs, shadows in the white mist, as it were, and followed only swiftly enough to keep them barely in sight. The shadows moved across and down the lane a bit, paused briefly, then went on until they were traveling along back of the building made of gray timbers from wrecked ships that was the council hall.

Their pursuers encountered no other fog venturers. The silence was profound, broken only by the occasional *drip-drip* of condensing mist and a few very brief murmurs of conversation from ahead, too soft and fleeting to make out. It was eerie.

"He's following his regular morning route," Mikkidu whispered softly.

Cif nodded, but Pshawri gripped Mik's arm in warning, setting a finger to his lips.

But true enough to the second lieutenant's guess, they followed their quarry to the new-built barracks and saw the Mouser bow his doublegoer in. Pshawri and Mikkidu waited a bit, then took off their boots and entered in stocking feet most cautiously.

Cif had another idea. She stole along the side of the building, heading for the kitchen door.

Inside, the Mouser, who had uttered hardly a dozen words since leaving the Sea Wrack, pointed out various items to his guess and watched for his reactions.

Which threw his Death into a state of great puzzlement. His intended victim had spoken some words about a treasure or treasures, then taken him outside and with a mysterious look pointed out to him a low point in a lane. What could that mean? True, sunken ground sometimes indicated something buried there—a murdered body, generally. But who'd bury a treasure in the lane of a dinky northern seaport, or a corpse, for that matter? It didn't make sense.

Next the gray-clad baffler had gone through the same rigmarole at a corner behind a building built of strangely weathered, heavy-looking wood. That had for a moment seemed to lead somewhere, for there'd been an opalescent something lodged in one of the big beams, its hue speaking of pearls and treasure. But when he'd stooped to study it, it had turned out to be only a worthless seashell, worked into the gray wood Aarth knew how!

And now the riddlesome fellow, holding a lamp he'd lit, was standing in a bunkroom beside a closet he'd just opened. There didn't seem to be much of anything in it.

"Treasure?" the Mouser's Death breathed doubtfully, leaning forward to look more closely.

The Mouser smiled and shook his head. "No. Miceholes," he breathed back.

The other recoiled incredulously. Had the brains of the masterly backgammon player turned to mush? Had something in the fog stolen away his wits? Just what *was* happening here? Maybe he'd best out knife and slay at once, before the situation became too confusing.

But the Mouser, still smiling gleefully, as if in anticipation of wonders to behold, was beckoning him on with his free hand into a short hall and then a smaller room with two bunks only, while the lamp he held beside his head made shadows crawl around them and slip along the walls.

Facing his Death, he threw open the door of a wider closet, stretched himself to his fullest height and thrust his lamp aloft, as if to say, "Lo!"

The closet contained at least a dozen shallow shelves smoothly surfaced with black cloth, and on them were very neatly arrayed somewhere between a thousand and a myriad tiny objects, as if they were so many rare coins and precious gems. As if, yes . . . but as to what these objects really were . . . recall the nine oddments the Mouser had laid out on Cif's bed table three months past . . . imagine them multiplied by ten hundred . . .the booty of three months of ground peering . . . the loot of ninety days of floor delving . . . you'd have a picture of the strange collection the Mouser was displaying to his Death.

And as his Death leaned closer, running his gaze incredulously back and forth along the shelves, the triumphant smile faded from the Mouser's face and was replaced by the same look of desperate wondering he'd had on it when he told Fafhrd of his yearning for the small things of Lankhmar.

* * *

"We've reached our picnic ground," Afreyt told Skor as they strode through the mist. "See how the sward is trampled. Now cast we about for Elvenhold."

"'Tis done, lady," he replied as she moved off to the left, he to the right, "but why are you so sure Captain Fafhrd went there?"

"Because he told Groniger he was going flying," she called to him. "Earlie Groniger had said that none could climb Elvenhold without wings."

"But the Captain could," Skor, taking her meaning, called back, "for he's scaled Stardock," thinking, though not saying aloud, *But that was before he lost a hand.*

Moments later he sighted vertical solidity, and was calling out that he'd found what they were seeking. When Afreyt caught up with him by the rock wall, he added, "I've also found proof that Fafhrd and the stranger did indeed come this way, as you deduced they would."

And he held up to her the hooded cloak of Fafhrd's Death.

*　　*　　*

Fafhrd, followed closely by his Death, climbed out of the fog into a world of bone-white clarity. He faced away from the rock to survey it.

The top of the mist was a flat white floor stretching east and south to the horizon, unbroken by treetop, chimney or spire of Salthaven, or mast top in the harbor beyond. Overhead the night shone with stars somewhat dimmed by the light of the round moon, which seemed to rest on the mist in the southeast.

"The full of Murderers Moon," he remarked oratorically, "the shortest and the lowest running full of the year, and come pat on Midsummer's Day Night. I told you there'd be light enough to climb by."

His Death below him savored the appropriateness of the lunar situation but didn't care much for the light. He'd felt securer climbing in the fog with the height all hid. He was still enjoying himself, but now he wanted to get the killing done as soon as Fafhrd revealed where the cave or other treasure spot was.

Fafhrd faced around to the tower again. Soon they were edging up past the grassy stretch. He noted his white flagged arrow and left it where it was, but when he came to Afreyt's he reached over precariously, snagged it with his hook, and tucked it in his belt.

"How much further?" his Death called up.

"Just to the end of the grass," Fafhrd called down. "Then we traverse to the opposite edge of Elvenhold, where there's a shallow cave will give our feet good support as we view the treasure. Ah, but I'm glad you came with me tonight! I only hope the moon doesn't dim it too much."

"How's that?" the other asked, a little puzzled, though considerably enheartened by the mention of a cave.

"Some jewels shine best by their own light alone," Fafhrd replied somewhat cryptically. Clashing into the next hold, his hook struck a shower of white sparks. "Must be flint in the rock hereabouts," he observed. "See, friend, minerals have many ways of making light. On Stardock the Mouser and I found diamonds of so clear a water they revealed their shape only in the dark. And there are beasts that shine, in particular glowwasps, diamondflies, firebeetles, and nightbees. I know, I've been stung by them. While in the jungles of Klesh I have encountered luminous flying spiders. Ah, we arrive at the traverse." And he began to move sideways, taking long steps.

His Death copied him, hastening after. Footholds and handholds both seemed surer here, while back at the grass he'd twice almost missed a hold. Beyond Fafhrd he could see what he took to be the dark cave mouth at the end of this face of the rock pylon they'd mounted. Things seemed to be happening more quickly while simultaneously time stretched out for him—sure sign of climax approaching. He wanted no more talk—in particular, lectures on natural history! He loosened his long knife in its scabbard. Soon! Soon!

Fafhrd was preparing to take the step that would put him squarely in front of the shallow depression that looked at first sight like a cave mouth. He was aware that his comrade astronomer was crowding him. At that moment, although the two of them were clearly alone on the face, he heard a short dry laugh, not in the voice of either of them, that nevertheless sounded as if it came from somewhere very close by. And somehow that laugh inspired or stung him into taking, instead of the step he'd planned, a much longer one that took him just past the seeming cave mouth and put his left foot on the end of the ledge, while his right hand reached for a hold beyond the shallow depression so that his whole body would swing out past the end of this face, and he would hopefully see the bearded star which was currently his dearest treasure and which until this moment tonight Elvenhold itself had hid from him.

At the same moment his Death struck, who had perfectly anticipated his victim's every movement except the last inspired one. His dagger, instead of burying itself in Fafhrd's back, struck rock in the shallow depression and its blade snapped. Staggered by that and vastly surprised, he fought for balance.

Fafhrd, glancing back, perceived the treacherous attack and rather casually booted his threatener in the thigh with a free foot. By the bone-white light of Murderers Moon, the Death of Fafhrd fell off Elvenhold and, glancingly striking the very steep grassy slope once or twice, was silhouetted momentarily, long limbs writhing, against the floor of white fog before the latter swallowed him up and the scream he'd started. There was a distant *thud* that nevertheless had a satisfying finality to it.

Fafhrd swung out again around the end of the cliff. Yes, his bearded star, though dimmed by the moonlight, was definitely discernable. He enjoyed it. The pleasure was, somewhat remotely, akin to that of watching a beautiful girl undress in almost dark.

"Fafhrd!" Then again, "Fafhrd!"

Skor's shout, by Kos, he told himself. And Afreyt's! He pulled himself back on the ledge and, securely footed there, called, "Ahoy! Ahoy below!"

*   *   *

Back at the barracks things were moving fast and very nervously, notably on the part of the Mouser's Death. He almost dirked the vaunting idiot on sheer impulse in overpowering disgust at being shown that incredible mouse's museum of trash as though it were a treasure of some sort. Almost, but then he heard a faint shuffling noise that seemed to originate in the building they were in, and it never did to slay when witnesses might be nigh, were there another course to take.

He watched the Mouser, who looked somewhat disappointed now (had the idiot expected to be praised for his junk display?), shut the closet door and beckon him back into the short hall and through a third door. He followed, listening intently for any repetition of the shuffling noise or other sound. The moving shadows the lamp cast were a little unnerving now; they suggested lurkers, hidden observers. Well, at least the idiot hadn't deposited in his trash closet the gold and silver coins he'd won this night, so presumably there was still hope of seeing their "cell mates" and some real treasure.

Now the Mouser was pointing out, but in a somewhat perfunctory way, the features of what appeared to be a rather well-appointed kitchen: fireplaces, ovens, and so forth. He rapped a couple of large iron kettles, but without any great enthusiasm, sounding their dull, sepulchral tones.

His manner quickened a little, however, and the ghost at least of a gleeful smile returned to his lips, as he opened the back door and went out into the mist, signing for his Death to follow him. That one did so, outwardly seeming relaxed, inwardly alert as a drawn knife, poised for any action.

Almost immediately the Mouser stooped, grasped a ring, and heaved up a small circular trapdoor, meanwhile holding his lamp aloft, its beams reflecting whitely from the fog but not helping vision much. The Mouser's Death bent forward to look in.

Thereafter things happened very rapidly indeed. There was a scuffling sound and a thud from the kitchen. (That was Mikkidu tripping himself by stepping on the toe of his own stocking.) The Mouser's death, his nerves tortured beyond endurance, whipped out his dirk, and next fell dead across the cesspool mouth with Cif's dagger in his ear, thrown from where she stood against the wall hardly a dozen feet away.

And somewhere, along with these actions, there were a brief growl and a short dry laugh. But those were things Cif and the Mouser claimed afterwards to have heard. At the present moment there was only the Mouser still holding his lamp and peering down at the corpse and saying as Cif and Pshawri and Mikkidu rushed up to him, "Well, he'll never get his revenge for tonight's gaming, that's for certain. Or do ghosts ever play backgammon, I wonder? I've heard of them contesting parties at chess with living mortals, by Mog."

*　　*　　*

Next day at the Council Hall Groniger presided over a brief but well-attended inquest into the demise of the two passengers on the *Good News*. Badges and other insignia about their persons suggested they were members not only of the Lankhmar Slayers Brotherhood, but also of the even more cosmopolitan Assassins Order. Under close questioning, the captain of the *Good News* admitted knowing of this circumstance and was fined for not reporting it to the Rime Isle harbormaster immediately on making port. A bit later Groniger found that they were murderous rogues, doubtless hired by foreign parties unknown, and that they had been rightly slain on their first attempts to practice their nefarious trade on Rime Isle.

But afterwards he told Cif, "It's as well that you slew him, and with his dagger in his hand. That way, none can say it was a feuding of newcomers to the Isle with foreigners their presence attracted here. And that you, Afreyt, were close witness to the other's death."

"I'll say I was!" that lady averred. "He came down not a yard from us, eh Skor? almost braining us. And with his hand death-gripping his broken dagger. Fafhrd, in future you should be more careful of how you dispose of your corpses."

When questioned about the cryptic warning he'd brought the Mouser and Fafhrd, old Ourph vouched, "The moment I heard the name *Good News* I knew it was an ill-omened ship, bearing watching. And when the two strangers came off and went into the Sea Wrack, I perceived them as dressed up, slightly luminous skeletons only, with bony hands and eyeless sockets."

"Did you see their corpses at the inquest so?" Groniger asked him.

"No, then they were but dead meat, such as all living become."

*   *   *

In Godsland the three concerned deities, somewhat shocked by the final turn of events and horrified to see how close they'd come to losing their chief remaining worshippers, lifted their curses from them as rapidly as they were able. Other concerned parties were slower to get the news and to believe it. The Assassins Order posted the two Deaths as "delayed" rather than "missing," but prepared to make what compensation might be unavoidable to Aarth Pulgh and Hamomel. While Sheelba and Ningauble, considerably irked, set about devising new strategems to procure the return of their favorite errand boys and living touchstones.

*   *   *

The instant the gods lifted their curses, the Mouser's and Fafhrd's strage obsessions vanished. It happened while they were together with Afreyt and Cif, the four of them lunching al fresco at Cif's. The only outward sign was that the Twain's eyes widened incredulously as they stared and then smiled at nothing.

"What deliciously outrageous idea has occurred to you two?" Afreyt demanded, while Cif echoed, "You're right! And it had to be something like that. We know you two of yore!"

"Is it that obvious?" the Mouser inquired, while Fafhrd fumbled out, "No, it's nothing like that. It's . . . No, you've all got to hear this. You know that thing about stars I've been having? Well, it's gone!" He lifted his eyes. "By Issek, I can look at the blue sky now without having it covered with the black flyspecks of the stars that would be there now if it were dark!"

"By Mog!" the Mouser exploded. "I had no idea, Fafhrd, that your little madness was so like mine in the tightness of its grip. For I no longer feel the compulsion to try to peer closely at every tiny object within fifty yards of me. It's like being a slave who's set free."

"No more ragpicking, eh?" Cif said. "No more bent-over inspection tours?"

"No, by Mog," the Mouser asserted, then qualified that with a "Though of course little things can be quite as interesting as big things; in fact, there's a whole tiny world of . . ."

"Uh-uh, you better watch out," Cif interrupted, holding up a finger.

"And the stars too are of considerable interest, my unnatural infatuation with 'em aside," Fafhrd said stubbornly.

Afreyt asked, "What do you think it was, though? Do you think some wizard cast a spell on you? Perchance that Ningauble you told me of, Fafhrd?"

Cif said, "Yes, or that Sheelba you talk of in your sleep, Mouser, and tell me isn't an old lover?"

The two men had to admit that those explanations were distant possibilities.

"Or other mysterious or even otherworldly beings may have had a hand in it," Afreyt proposed. "We know Queen Skeldir's involved, bless her, from the warning laughter you heard. And, for all you make light of him, Gusorio. Cif and I did hear those growlings."

Cif said, the look in her eyes half wicked, half serious, "And has it occurred to any of you that, since Skeldir's warnings went to you two men, that *you* may be transmigrations of her? and we—Skeldir help us!—of Great Gusorio? Or does that shock you?"

"By no means," Fafhrd answered. "Since transmigration would be such a wonder, able to send the spirit of woman or man into animal, or vice versa, a mere change of sex should not surprise us at all."

*   *   *

The backgammon box of the two Deaths was kept at the Sea Wrack as a curiosity of sorts, but it was noted that few used it to play with, or got good games when they did.